READER'S DIGEST
SELECT EDITIONS

READER'S DIGEST
SELECT EDITIONS

www.readersdigest.co.uk

The Reader's Digest Association Limited
11 Westferry Circus Canary Wharf London E14 4HE

For information as to ownership of copyright in the material of this book, and acknowledgments, see last page.

Printed in Germany
ISBN 978 0 276 44289 6

SELECTED AND CONDENSED
BY READER'S DIGEST

THE READER'S DIGEST ASSOCIATION LIMITED, LONDON

CONTENTS

This fast-paced debut novel, inspired by the work of the brilliant Albert Einstein, comes from a writer who's spent years studying physics and making its most complex yet fascinating aspects easier to understand. In *Final Theory*, Alpert imagines a scenario in which Einstein's elusive 'theory of everything' falls into the wrong hands, unleashing a terrible new force for destruction. Pitting his hero, David Swift, against some very powerful people, he builds his story to a truly scintillating climax.

The wonderful, subtle aroma of coffee wafts from the pages of this entrancing novel. It's 1895, and Robert Wallis, poet and dandy, thinks his money worries are over when he's employed by a merchant, Samuel Pinker, to describe the various flavours of coffee, alongside Pinker's spirited daughter. But the young man has much to learn and, in the course of an expedition to the heart of Africa, discovers how to distinguish love from the selfish pursuit of sensual pleasure.

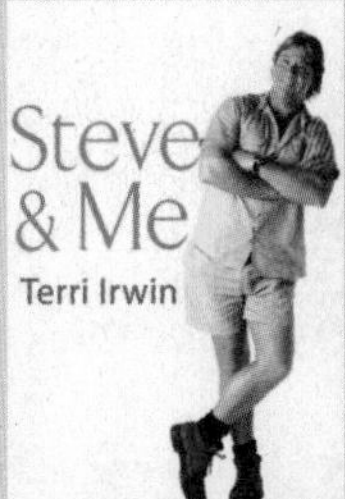

STEVE & ME

TERRI IRWIN

341

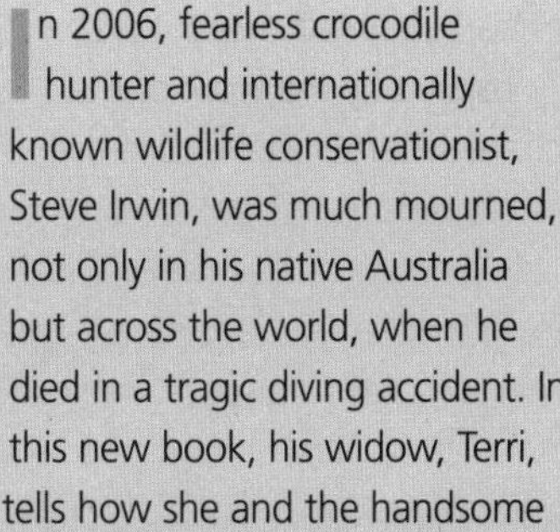

In 2006, fearless crocodile hunter and internationally known wildlife conservationist, Steve Irwin, was much mourned, not only in his native Australia but across the world, when he died in a tragic diving accident. In this new book, his widow, Terri, tells how she and the handsome Australian met, fell in love and married in fairy-tale style, embarking on a family life enriched by their shared passion for wildlife. It's a deeply enjoyable biography, packed with entertaining incident, warmth and humour.

Author Tess Gerritsen used to work as a doctor, so it's no surprise that she is able to bring the world of 19th-century medicine so vividly to life. Starring the real-life physician, Dr Oliver Wendell Holmes, who worked in Boston in the 19th century, *The Bone Garden* is told in flashback, prompted by the discovery of a woman's skeleton, dating from the early 1800s, in a Boston garden. Forensic evidence indicates foul play, and her story puts her right at the heart of a crime novel steeped in historical fact and atmosphere.

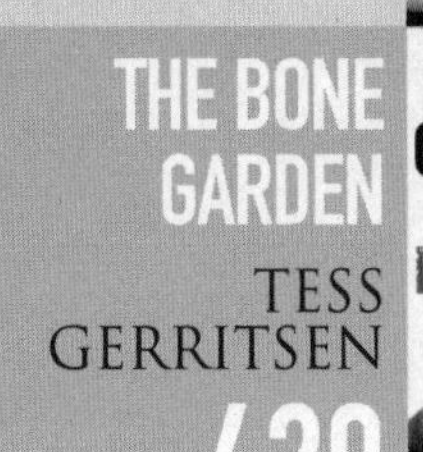

THE BONE GARDEN

TESS GERRITSEN

429

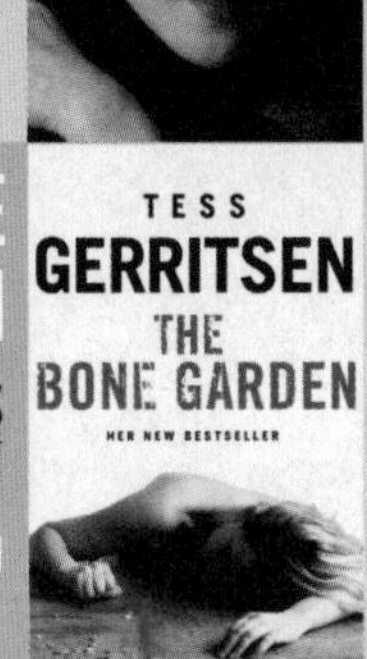

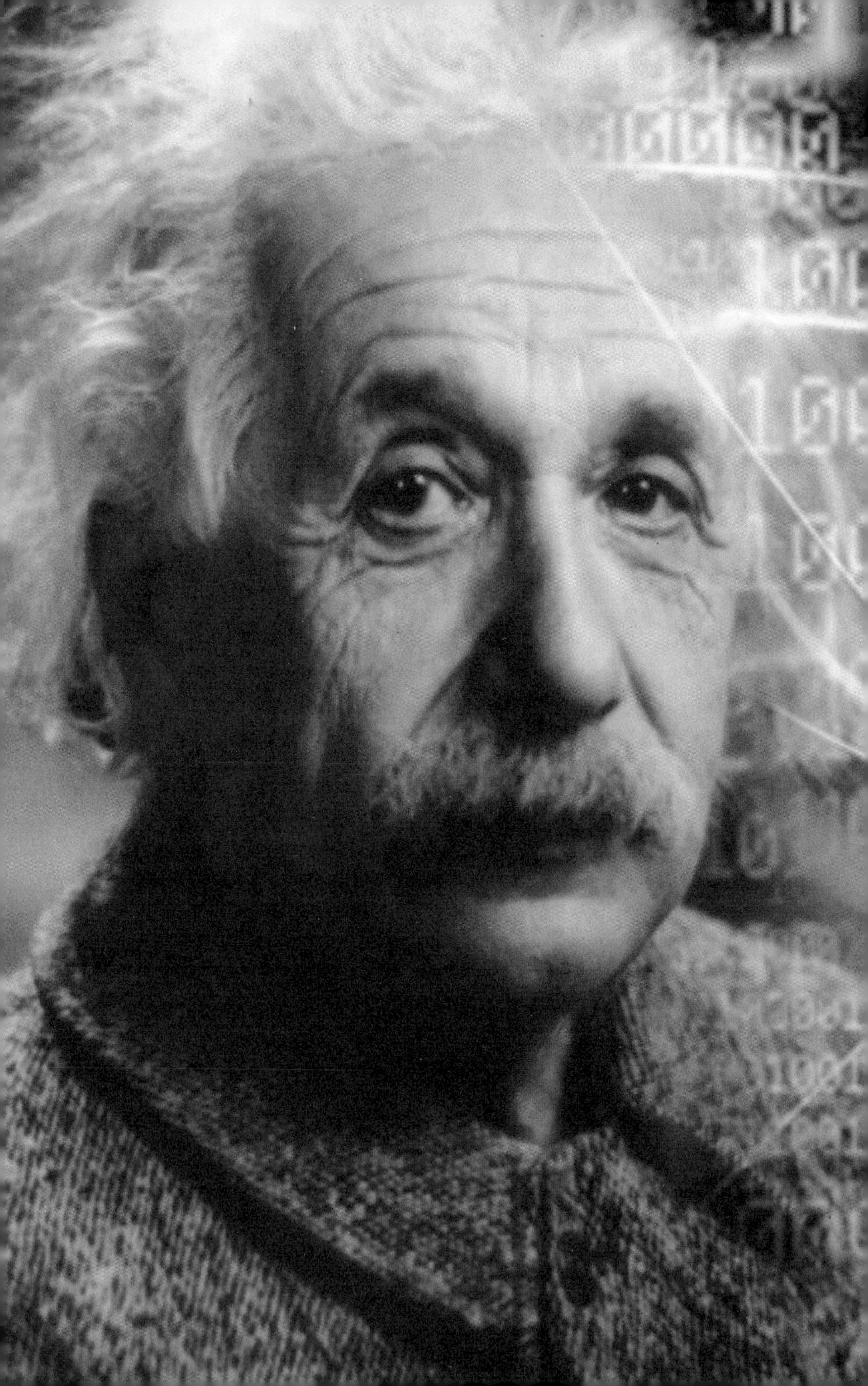

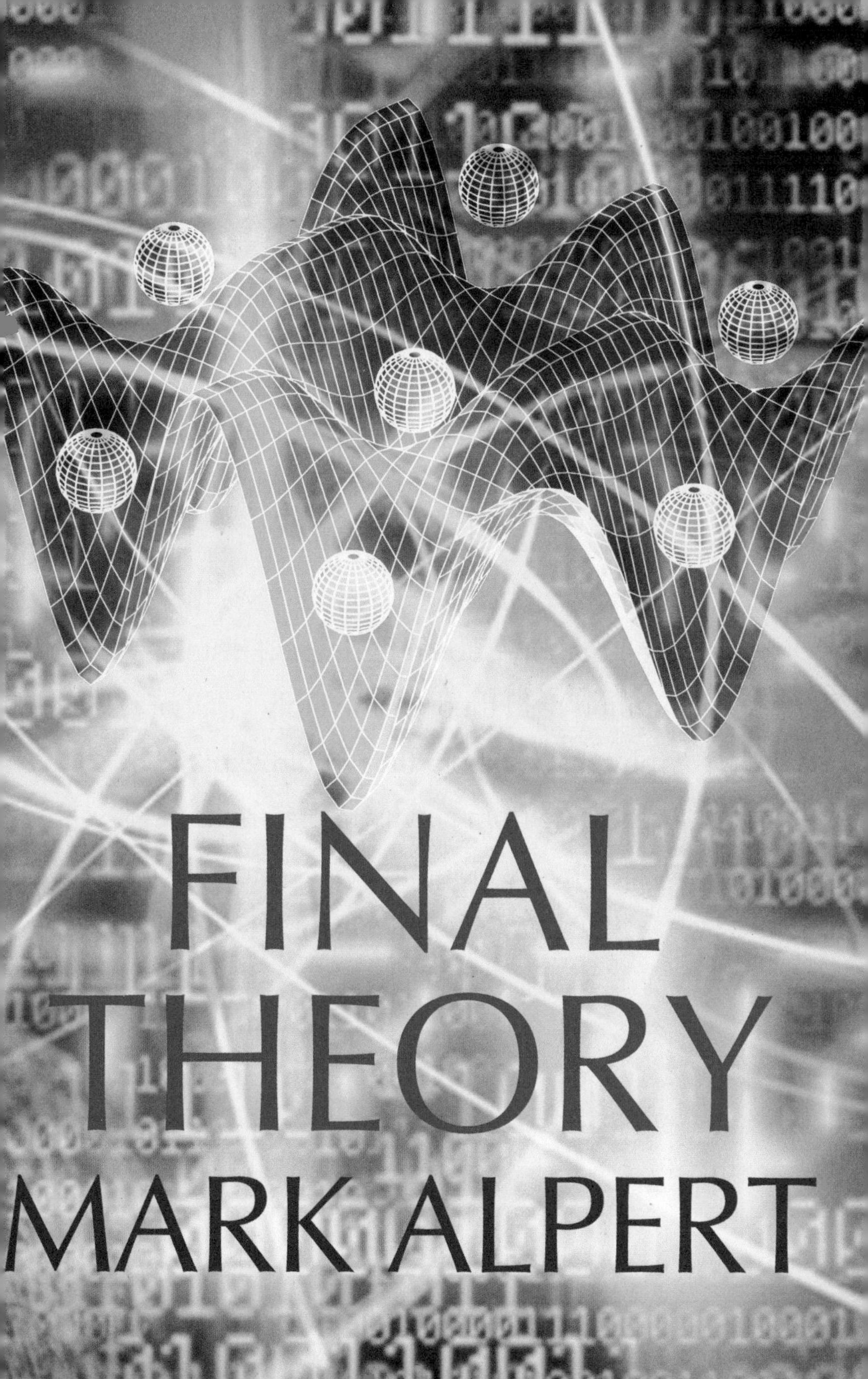
FINAL
THEORY
MARK ALPERT

Two words in German—*'Einheitliche Feldtheorie'*—are the last that David Swift hears his mentor and friend, Dr Kleinman, utter before he dies.

David, a physics lecturer, knows that Kleinman must be referring to Einstein's unified field theory—the Holy Grail of physics. A theory that would explain everything from gravity to electricity . . . But why was Kleinman so concerned about it on his deathbed?

CHAPTER ONE

Hans Walther Kleinman, one of the great theoretical physicists of our time, was drowning in his bathtub. A stranger with long, sinewy arms had pinned Hans's shoulders to the porcelain bottom.

Although the water was only thirty centimetres deep, the pinioning arms kept Hans from raising his face to the surface. He clawed at the stranger's hands, trying to loosen their grip, but the man was a *shtarker*, a young vicious brute, and Hans was a seventy-nine-year-old with arthritis and a weak heart. Flailing about, he kicked the sides of the tub, and the lukewarm water sloshed all around him. He couldn't get a good look at his attacker—the man's face was a shifting, watery blur. The *shtarker* must have slipped into the apartment through the open window by the fire escape, then rushed into the bathroom when he realised that Hans was inside.

As Hans struggled, he felt the pressure building in his chest. It started under his sternum, and quickly filled his whole rib cage. A negative pressure, pushing inwards from all sides, constricting his lungs. Within seconds it rose to his neck, a hot, choking tightness, and Hans opened his mouth, gagging. Water rushed down his throat. Hans devolved into a creature of pure panic, a primitive animal going into its final convulsions. *No, no, no!* Then he lay still.

But it wasn't the end, not yet. When Hans regained consciousness, he was lying face down on the tiled floor, coughing up bath water. His eyes ached and his stomach lurched and each breath was an excruciating gasp. Then he felt a sharp blow between his shoulder blades and heard someone say in a jaunty voice, 'Time to wake up!'

The stranger grabbed him by the elbows and rolled him over. Still breathing hard, Hans looked up at his attacker. A huge man, a hundred kilograms at the least. Shoulder muscles bulging under his black T-shirt, camouflage pants tucked into black boots. Small bald head, black stubble on his cheeks and a scar on his jaw. Most likely a junkie, Hans guessed. After he kills me, and tears the place apart, he'll realise I don't have a cent.

The *shtarker* stretched his thin lips into a smile. 'Now we'll have a little talk, yes? You can call me Simon, if you like.'

The man had an unusual accent. His eyes were small and brown, his nose was crooked, and his skin was the colour of a weathered brick—he could be Spanish, Russian, Turkish, almost anything. Hans tried to say, 'What do you want?' but he only retched again.

Simon looked amused. 'Yes, yes, I'm so sorry about that. But I needed to show you I'm that serious, eh?'

Oddly enough, Hans wasn't afraid now—he was furious. He propped himself up on his elbows. 'You made a mistake this time, you *ganef*. I have no money. I don't even have a bank card.'

'I don't want money, Dr Kleinman. I'm interested in physics, not money. You're familiar with the subject, I assume?'

Hans's rage subsided as disturbing questions occurred to him: how had this man found out his name? How did he know he was a physicist?

Simon seemed to guess what he was thinking. 'Don't be so surprised, Professor. I'm not as ignorant as I look.'

'Who are you? What are you doing here?'

'Think of it as a research project. On a very challenging and esoteric topic.' Simon's smile broadened. 'I admit some of the equations weren't easy to understand. But some clients of mine explained it, you see, and hired me to get information from you.'

'What are you talking about? Are you some kind of spy?'

Simon chuckled. 'No, no. I'm an independent contractor.'

Hans's mind was racing. The *shtarker* was a terrorist, maybe. But why target him? Like most nuclear physicists of his generation, Hans had done some classified work for the Defense Department in the fifties and sixties, but he'd spent most of his life doing strictly non-military theoretical research.

'I have some bad news for your clients, whoever they are,' Hans said. 'They picked the wrong physicist. My field is particle physics. All my research papers are on the Internet!'

The stranger shrugged. 'You've jumped to the wrong conclusion. I don't care about your papers. I'm interested in someone else's work, not yours.'

'Why are you in my apartment, then? Did you get the wrong address?'

Simon's face hardened. He pushed Hans down on his back and placed one hand flat on his rib cage, leaning forward. 'This person is someone you knew. Your professor at Princeton fifty-five years ago? The wandering Jew from Bavaria? The man who wrote *Zur Elektrodynamik bewegter Körper*?'

Hans struggled to breathe. The man's hand felt impossibly heavy.

Simon leaned over some more. 'He admired you, Dr Kleinman. He thought you were one of his most promising assistants. You worked together quite closely in his last few years, didn't you?'

Hans couldn't have replied even if he'd wanted to. He could feel his vertebrae grinding against the tiles.

'Yes, he admired you. But more than that, he trusted you. He conferred with you about everything. Including his *Einheitliche Feldtheorie*.'

At just that moment one of Hans's ribs snapped. The pain knifed through his chest and he opened his mouth to scream, but he couldn't draw enough breath. He was terrified. He saw what this stranger wanted from him, and he knew that in the end he'd be unable to resist.

Simon finally removed his hand from Hans's chest. As Hans took a deep breath he felt the knife of pain again on his left side. His pleural membrane was torn, which meant that his left lung would soon collapse.

Simon stood over him. 'So do we understand each other?'

Hans nodded, then closed his eyes. I'm sorry, *Herr Doktor*, he thought. I'm going to betray you. In his mind's eye he saw the professor again. But not like the pictures everyone knew, the unkempt genius with the wild white hair. What Hans remembered was the professor in the last months of his life. The drawn cheeks, the sunken eyes, the defeated grimace. The man who'd glimpsed the truth but, for the sake of the world, couldn't speak it out loud.

Hans felt a kick in his side, just below his broken rib. Pain ripped through his torso, and his eyes sprang open.

'No time for sleeping,' Simon said. 'We have work to do. I'm going to get some paper from your desk.' He walked out of the bathroom. 'If there's something I don't understand, you'll explain it to me. Like a seminar, yes?'

With the stranger out of sight, some of Hans's fear lifted and he was able to think again. And what he thought about were the *shtarker*'s black stormtrooper boots. Hans felt a wave of disgust. The man was trying to look like a Nazi. In essence, that's what he was, a Nazi, no different from the thugs marching down the streets of Frankfurt when Hans was seven years old.

Simon returned with a ball-point pen and a legal pad. 'All right, from the beginning,' he said, offering Hans the pen and pad.

'Go to hell,' Hans rasped.

Simon gave him a mildly scolding look. 'You know what I think, Dr Kleinman? I think you need another bath.'

In one swift motion he picked Hans up and plunged him into the water again. If anything, the second time was more terrifying than the first, because now Hans knew what lay ahead—the tightening agony, the frantic twisting, the mindless descent into blackness.

This time it took a tremendous effort to emerge from the abyss. When Hans opened his eyes, his vision was fuzzy round the edges, his breathing shallow.

'Are you there, Dr Kleinman? Can you hear me?' asked a muffled voice.

When Hans looked up he saw the silhouette of the *shtarker*, but his body seemed to be surrounded by a penumbra of vibrating particles.

'If you look at the situation logically, you'll realise that all this subterfuge is absurd. You can't hide something like this for ever.'

Hans looked at the penumbra surrounding the man and saw that the particles weren't actually vibrating; they were popping in and out of existence, pairs of particles and antiparticles appearing like magic from the quantum vacuum. This is amazing, Hans thought. If only I had a camera.

'Your professor had other confidants, who have been most helpful. One way or another we'll get what we need. So why make this hard on yourself?'

The evanescent particles seemed to grow larger as Hans stared at them. Soon it became clear that they weren't particles at all but infinitely thin strings stretching from one curtain of space to another. The strings shivered between the undulating curtains, which curled into tubes and cones. The elaborate dance was proceeding exactly as *Herr Doktor* had described!

'I'm sorry, Dr Kleinman, but my patience is wearing thin. I don't enjoy doing this, but you leave me no choice.'

The man kicked him three times in the left side of his chest, but Hans didn't even feel it. The diaphanous curtains of space had folded round him. Hans could see them so clearly, like curving sheets of blown glass.

The other man obviously couldn't see them. He let out a sigh. 'I guess this will require more vigorous persuasion.' He retreated to the hallway closet. 'Let's see what we have here.' After a moment he returned carrying a plastic bottle of rubbing alcohol and a steam iron.

Hans forgot about the man. He saw nothing but the lacy folds of the universe, curving round him like an infinitely soft blanket.

DAVID SWIFT was in an unusually good mood. He and Jonah, his seven-year-old son, had just spent a marvellous afternoon in Central Park. To cap off the day, David had bought ice-cream cones from a pushcart at 72nd Street, and now father and son were strolling through the sultry June twilight towards David's ex-wife's apartment. Jonah was in a good mood, too, because in his right hand—his left hand held the ice-cream cone—he brandished a brand-new triple-shot Super Soaker. He idly pointed the high-tech water gun at windows, mailboxes, pigeons, but David wasn't concerned. He'd emptied its reservoir before they'd left the park.

'So why does the water come out so fast?' Jonah asked.

David had explained the process twice, but he loved having this kind of conversation with his son. 'When you move the red pump handle, that pushes the water from the big reservoir to the smaller one, which has some air in it, and the air molecules get squeezed and start pushing on the water.'

'I don't get it. Why do they push the water?'

'Because air molecules are always bouncing around, see? And when you squeeze them together, they bounce against the water more.'

'Can I bring the gun to school for show-and-tell?'

'Uh . . . I don't know. I don't think they allow water guns in school. But there's definitely science in this thing. The guy who invented it was a scientist. A nuclear engineer who worked for NASA.'

A bus lunged down Columbus Avenue and Jonah tracked it with his water gun. 'Why didn't *you* become a scientist, Dad?'

David thought for a second before answering. 'Well, not everyone can be a scientist. But I write books about the history of science, and I get to teach courses about people like Isaac Newton and Albert Einstein. A long time ago, in graduate school, I did some real science. And it was all about space.'

'You mean spaceships that can go a billion miles per second?'

'No, it was about the shape of space. What space would look like if there were only two dimensions instead of three.'

'I don't get it. What's a dimension?'

'A universe with two dimensions has length and width, but no depth. Like a giant sheet.' David spread his hands, palms down, as if he were smoothing a sheet. 'I had this teacher, Professor Kleinman, one of the smartest scientists in the world. We wrote a paper together about two-dimensional universes.'

Jonah turned back to watch the traffic, he was so bored. 'I'm gonna ask Mom if I can take the Super Soaker to show-and-tell.'

A minute later they walked into the apartment building where Jonah and his mother lived. David had lived there, too, until two years ago, when he and Karen had separated. Now he had a small apartment closer to his job at Columbia University. Every weekday he picked up Jonah from school at three o'clock and delivered him to his mother four hours later. But David's heart always sank as he walked through the old lobby. He felt like an exile.

When the elevator reached the fourteenth floor, David saw Karen standing in the apartment's doorway. She wore a grey business suit, the standard uniform of a corporate lawyer. Her arms folded across her chest; she scrutinised her ex-husband, glancing with evident disapproval at the stubble on his face and his mud-caked jeans. Then her eyes fixed on the Super Soaker. Jonah handed the gun to David and slipped past his mother into the apartment.

Karen shook her head. She whisked a stray lock of blonde hair to the side. 'What the hell were you thinking?'

'Look, I already told Jonah the rules. No shooting at people. We went to the park and shot at the rocks and trees. It was fun.'

'You think a machine gun is appropriate for a seven-year-old?'

'It's not a machine gun. And the box said seven and up.'

Karen narrowed her eyes and pursed her lips. 'You know what kids do with those Super Soakers? There was a story on the news. In Staten Island a bunch of kids put gasoline in the gun instead of water so they could turn it into a flamethrower. They nearly burnt down their whole neighbourhood.'

David took a deep breath. He didn't want to fight. 'OK, OK, calm down. Just tell me what you want me to do.'

'Take the gun home. I don't want that thing in my house.'

Before David could respond, the telephone rang inside. Then Jonah called out, 'I'll get it!' David wondered if it was Karen's new boyfriend, a hearty grey-haired lawyer with two former wives and a lot of money.

Jonah came to the door with the cordless phone. 'It's for you, Dad.' He shrugged. 'The man says he's with the police.'

DAVID SAT in the back seat of a taxi speeding north towards St Luke's Hospital. It was getting dark now, and as they hurtled through the traffic on Amsterdam Avenue, the lurid orange letters of neon signs flashed by.

Attacked, the police detective said. Professor Kleinman had been attacked in his apartment on 127th Street. Now he was in critical condition at the emergency room of St Luke's. And he'd asked for David Swift. Whispered a phone number to the paramedics. You better hurry, the detective had said.

David squirmed with guilt. He hadn't seen Professor Kleinman in over three years. The old man had become a recluse since he'd retired from Columbia. Lived in a tiny apartment in West Harlem, gave all his money to Israel. No wife, no kids. His whole life had been physics.

Twenty years earlier, when David was a grad student, Kleinman had been his adviser. David had liked him from the start. Neither aloof nor severe, he sprinkled Yiddish into his discourses on quantum theory. Once a week David went to Kleinman's office to hear him elucidate the mysteries of wave functions and virtual particles. After two years of frustration, David had to admit he was in over his head. He simply wasn't smart enough to be a physicist. So he switched to the next best thing: a PhD in the history of science.

Kleinman was disappointed but understanding. They stayed in touch; when David began research for his book—a study of Albert Einstein's collaborations with his various assistants—Kleinman offered his recollections of the man he called *Herr Doktor*. The book, *On the Shoulders of Giants*, made David's reputation, and he was now a full professor at Columbia's history of science programme.

The taxi screeched to a halt in front of the St Luke's emergency room. After paying the driver, David rushed through the automatic glass doors and immediately spied a trio of New York City police officers next to the intake desk. Two of them were in uniform, and the third was a plain-clothes detective, a handsome Latino in a neatly pressed suit. That's the man who called me, David thought. He remembered the detective's name: Rodriguez.

His heart pounding, David approached him. 'Excuse me? I'm David Swift. Are you Detective Rodriguez?'

The detective nodded soberly, but the two patrolmen seemed amused.

The paunchy sergeant smiled at David. 'Hey, you got a permit for that thing?' He pointed at the Super Soaker. David was so distracted he'd forgotten he was still holding Jonah's water gun.

Rodriguez placed a hand on his shoulder. 'Please come with us, Mr Swift. Mr Kleinman insists on talking to you.' The detective led David down a corridor while the two patrolmen walked behind.

'What happened?' David asked. 'You said he was attacked.'

'We got a report of a burglary in progress. Someone across the street saw a man enter from the fire escape. When the officers arrived, they found Mr Kleinman in the bathroom, critically injured.'

'What do you mean, critically injured?'

'Mr Kleinman has third-degree burns, a collapsed lung and damage to his other organs. The doctors say his heart is failing. I'm sorry, Mr Swift.'

They came to a room marked TRAUMA CENTER. Through the doorway David saw two nurses standing beside a bed surrounded by medical equipment—a cardiac monitor, a crash cart, a defibrillator and an IV pole.

Detective Rodriguez grabbed his arm. 'Mr Swift, I want you to ask Mr Kleinman if he remembers anything from the attack. The paramedics said that while he was in the ambulance he kept repeating a couple of names, Einhard Liggin and Feld Terry. Do you know either of those people?'

David repeated the names silently: Einhard Liggin, Feld Terry. They were unusual, even for German names. And then it hit him.

'They're not names,' he said. 'It's two words in German. *Einheitliche Feldtheorie.* Unified field theory.'

Rodriguez stared at him. 'And what the hell is that?'

David gave the same explanation he would have given Jonah. 'It's a theory that would explain all the forces of nature. Everything from gravity to electricity to the nuclear forces. Researchers have been working on the problem for decades, but no one's come up with the theory yet.'

Rodriguez frowned. 'Just ask Mr Kleinman what he remembers.'

David said, 'All right, I'll try,' but he was perplexed now. Why would Kleinman repeat those particular words? Unified field theory was a somewhat old-fashioned term. String theory, M-theory and quantum gravity were the names of the more recent approaches to the problem, although Kleinman hadn't been enthusiastic about any of them.

Rodriguez took the Super Soaker. 'You better go in now.'

David nodded. He stepped in the room and approached the bed.

What he noticed first were the bandages, the thick gauze pad taped to the right side of Kleinman's face and the blood-soaked wrappings across his chest. David could see dried blood under the old man's white hair and purple bruises on his shoulders. But the worst thing was the blue tinge to his skin, which meant his heart could no longer pump the oxygenated blood from his lungs to the rest of his body. The doctors had strapped an oxygen mask to his face and put him in a sitting position to drain his lungs.

Kleinman opened his eyes and slowly raised his left hand to his face. With curled fingers he tapped the plastic mask covering his mouth and nose.

David leaned over the bed. 'Dr Kleinman? It's me, David.'

Watery, dull eyes locked on David. Kleinman tapped his mask again. The moist rattle in his chest was the fluid backing up into his lungs.

'Professor, someone attacked you in your apartment. The police want to know if you remember anything.'

The old man coughed, spraying pinkish spittle on the inside of his mask. 'He was right. *Mein Gott*, he was right!'

'Professor, please listen. This is important.'

'Everyone thought he failed . . . but he succeeded. He succeeded! But he couldn't . . . publish it. *Herr Doktor* saw . . . the danger. Much worse . . . than a bomb. Destroyer . . . of worlds.'

David stared at the old man. *Herr Doktor?* Destroyer of worlds? He clasped Kleinman's hand. 'Tell me about the man who hurt you.'

'That's why the *shtarker* came. That's why . . . he tortured me.'

'Tortured?' David felt a sickening jolt.

'He wanted me . . . to write it down. But I didn't. I didn't!'

'Write what down? What did he want?'

Kleinman smiled behind the mask. '*Einheitliche Feldtheorie*,' he whispered. '*Herr Doktor*'s . . . last gift.'

David was bewildered. The easiest explanation was that the trauma of the attack had dredged up memories from half a century ago. David had written in his book about the endless stream of calculations on the blackboard in Einstein's office, the long futile search for a field equation that would encompass both gravity and electromagnetism. It was not unreasonable that Kleinman, in his final delirium, would think back to those days.

'I'm sorry I never . . . told you. *Herr Doktor* couldn't . . .' Kleinman coughed again. 'He couldn't burn his notebooks. The theory was . . . too beautiful.' He let out another violent cough and doubled over.

One of the nurses rushed to the bed. She propped the professor back up to a sitting position. His oxygen mask was filled with pink froth.

The nurse removed the mask and cleaned it, but when she tried to put it back on, Kleinman batted it away. 'No!' he croaked. 'Enough!'

The nurse turned to her partner, who was staring at the cardiac monitor. 'Get the resident,' she ordered. 'We need to intubate.'

Kleinman leaned against David, who put his arm round the old man. The gurgling in his chest seemed louder now and his eyes darted wildly. 'I'm dying,' he rasped. 'There's not . . . much time.'

David's eyes began to sting. 'It's all right, Professor. You're going to be—'

Kleinman raised his hand and gripped David's collar. 'You were very close . . . to the truth. Once I'm gone . . . they might come after you.'

David felt a prickle in his stomach. 'Who are you talking about?'

Kleinman tightened his grip. 'I have . . . a key. *Herr Doktor* gave me this gift. And now I give it . . . to you. Keep it safe. Don't let . . . them get it!'

With surprising strength, he pulled David close. 'Remember the numbers. Four, zero . . . two, six . . . three, six . . . seven, nine . . . five, six . . . four, four . . . seven, eight, zero, zero.'

As soon as he spoke the last digit, the professor let go of David's collar and slumped against his chest. 'Now repeat . . . the sequence.'

Despite his confusion, David put his lips near Kleinman's ear and repeated the sequence. Although he had never been able to master the equations of quantum physics, David had an aptitude for memorising strings of numbers.

'Good boy,' the old man murmured. 'Good boy.' Then his eyes closed and his chest stopped gurgling.

THE EMERGENCY-ROOM RESIDENT kicked David out of the Trauma Center and half a dozen doctors and nurses tried to resuscitate the professor. But David knew it was hopeless. Kleinman was gone.

Rodriguez and the two patrolmen intercepted him in the corridor. The detective handed back the Super Soaker. 'Did he tell you anything, Mr Swift?'

'He was going in and out. It didn't make a lot of sense.' David shook his head. 'He said he was tortured.'

'Tortured? Why?'

Before David could answer, someone shouted, 'Hey! Hold it right there!'

It was a tall, ruddy, thick-necked man wearing a crew cut and a grey suit. He was flanked by two more ex-linebackers who looked much the same. The three of them marched down the corridor at a brisk clip. When they reached the cops, the guy took out his ID and flashed the badge.

'Agent Hawley, FBI. Are you working the Kleinman case?'

'Yeah, that's our case,' Rodriguez replied.

Agent Hawley gave a hand signal to one of his companions, who headed for the Trauma Center. Then Hawley passed a folded letter to Rodriguez. 'We're taking over. Here's the authorisation.'

Rodriguez scowled as he read it. 'You don't have jurisdiction here.'

'If you have a complaint, take it up with the US attorney.'

David wondered why the FBI was so interested in the murder of a retired physicist. He felt the prickle in his stomach again.

Hawley pointed at him. 'Who's this guy?' he asked Rodriguez.

The detective shrugged. 'Kleinman asked for him. His name's David Swift. They just finished talking and he—'

'Son of a bitch! You let this guy talk to Kleinman?' Hawley narrowed his eyes. 'Are you a physicist, Mr Swift?'

David frowned. 'No, I'm a historian. And it's Dr Smith, if you don't mind.'

The agent returned from the Trauma Center and whispered something in Hawley's ear. Hawley's face turned blank and hard. 'Kleinman's dead, Mr Swift. That means you're coming with us.'

The third agent yanked back David's arms, and snapped handcuffs on his wrists. The Super Soaker clattered to the floor.

'What the hell are you doing?' David yelled. 'Am I under arrest?'

Hawley didn't bother to reply. He grabbed David's arm and the agent who'd handcuffed him picked up the Super Soaker. Then all three FBI men escorted David to the emergency exit.

CHAPTER TWO

Simon was playing Tetris in the driver's seat of his Mercedes, keeping one eye on the electronic game and the other on St Luke's Hospital. Jabbing his cellphone buttons, he could easily manoeuvre the Tetris blocks into place while cars pulled up to the emergency room. Relaxed yet watchful, he started looking at the vehicles on Amsterdam Avenue as if they were oversized Tetris blocks—squares and T-bars and zigzags and L-shapes—cruising down the darkening street.

It's all about flexibility, Simon thought. Whatever game you're playing, you have to be willing to adjust your strategy. Just look at what happened with Hans Kleinman tonight. Kleinman's mind had gone soft before Simon could get anything useful out of him. Then a pair of patrol cars pulled up in front of the professor's apartment building. Simon didn't panic—he simply adjusted his strategy. First he evaded the police by climbing the fire escape to the roof and jumping to the warehouse next door. Then he got into his Mercedes and followed the ambulance taking Kleinman to St Luke's. He had a new plan: wait until the police officers leave the hospital, then take another crack at getting the *Einheitliche Feldtheorie*.

The Tetris blocks piled up at the bottom of the cellphone's screen, leaving a deep hole at the far left. Then a straight I-bar began to descend. Simon whipped it to the left and four rows of blocks vanished with a software-generated sigh. Very satisfying. Like slipping the knife in.

A moment later, Simon saw a black Suburban come down Amsterdam

Avenue. The car slowed, then parked by the hospital's loading dock. Three large men in grey suits jumped out and marched in formation to the service entrance. From their gait, Simon recognised them as ex-Marines, most likely with the FBI. The men flashed their badges as they entered the hospital. US intelligence was apparently interested in Professor Kleinman, too. Simon wasn't perturbed. American agents had good training, good discipline, but he knew he could eliminate them. Because he worked on his own, his instincts were keener. That was one of the two great advantages of a freelance career. The other was money. Since he'd left the Spetsnaz, Simon could earn more in one day than a platoon of Russian paratroopers could earn in a year.

Before he expected it to happen, the three agents emerged from one of the hospital's emergency exits. They had a prisoner in tow, his hands cuffed behind his back. He was a bit shorter than the FBI men but trim and athletic, dressed in sneakers, jeans and a T-shirt. The third agent was carrying a brightly coloured toy gun. For a moment Simon wondered whether the prisoner was some eccentric New Yorker who'd threatened the doctors with his Super Soaker. But just before the agents shoved him into the car, they slipped a black hood over his head. OK, Simon thought. The prisoner isn't a random madman. He's someone the agents want to interrogate.

The driver of the Suburban switched on his headlights and pulled away from the kerb. Simon would let them get a couple of blocks ahead before following. There was no point in sticking around the hospital—the fact that the agents had left was a strong indication Kleinman was dead. Luckily, though, he appeared to have shared some secrets with a younger colleague.

Simon pressed the off button on his cellphone, ending the Tetris game. But before the device shut down, it flashed a photograph on the screen, a photo that was programmed to appear whenever he turned it on or off. It was stupid, saving a personal photo on a business phone, yet he did it anyway. He didn't want to forget their faces. Sergei with his corn-silk hair and blue eyes. Larissa in her blonde curls, just weeks shy of her fourth birthday.

The screen went black. Simon shifted the Mercedes into gear.

IT WAS A WOMAN'S VOICE with a thick southern accent. 'All right, Hawley, you can take it off now.'

David gasped for air as the hood came off. He felt nauseous from breathing for so long through the black cloth, which was damp with his own sweat. He squinted at first, his eyes painfully adjusting to the fluorescent light.

He was seated at a grey table in a bare, windowless room. Agent Hawley was rolling up the hood, and his two partners were inspecting the Super Soaker. Across the table was a broad, big-bosomed, sixtyish woman with an impressive helmet of platinum-blonde hair.

'You all right, Mr Swift?' she asked. 'You look a little ragged.'

David was not all right. He was scared, disorientated and thoroughly confused. This woman didn't look like an FBI agent. In her bright red jacket and white blouse, she looked like a grandmother dressed up for a bingo game.

'Who are you?' he asked.

'I'm Lucille Parker, honey.' She reached for a pitcher of water and a couple of Dixie cups. 'Hawley, take them cuffs off.'

Agent Hawley grudgingly unlocked the handcuffs. David rubbed his sore wrists and studied Lucille. Her lipstick was the same colour as her jacket. Her face was pleasantly creased, and she had a pair of reading glasses hanging from a chain round her neck. But she also had a coiled wire running behind her left ear, the same radio headset all government agents used.

'Am I under arrest?' David asked. 'If I am, I want to speak to a lawyer.'

She smiled. 'No, sorry if we gave you that impression.'

'Impression? Your agents handcuffed me and put a bag over my head.'

'It's standard procedure, honey. This building is a secure facility. We can't divulge the location, so we have to use the hood.'

David stood up. 'Well, if I'm not under arrest, I'm free to leave.'

Agent Hawley gripped his shoulder. Still smiling, Lucille shook her head. 'I'm afraid it's a little more complicated than that.' She slid a Dixie cup towards him. 'Sit down, Mr Swift. Have a drink of water.'

The hand on David's shoulder grew heavier. He took the hint and sat down. 'It's Dr Swift,' he said. 'And I'm not thirsty.'

'You want something stronger, maybe?' She winked at him, then reached into her jacket pocket and pulled out a silver flask. 'This here is genuine Texas white lightning, a hundred and eighty proof. Care for a snort?'

'No, thank you.'

'That's right, I forgot.' She put the flask back in her jacket. 'You never touch the stuff, do you? Because of your daddy, right?'

David stiffened in his chair. 'What's going on?' he demanded.

'Calm down, honey. It's in your file.' She reached into a bag and pulled out two folders. She put on her reading glasses and opened the thin one. 'Let's see, father's name, John Swift. Hired as bus driver for the Metropolitan Transit Authority, 1975. Terminated after arrest for driving while intoxicated, 1979. Sentenced to three years after conviction for assault,

1981.' She looked David in the eye. 'I'm sorry. It must have been awful.'

'You have quite a research department here,' David observed. 'Did you dig this up in the past half-hour?'

'No, we started a few days ago.' She opened the thick folder. 'This is the file for the late professor. Let me tell you, some of this physics is rough going. I mean, what the hell is the Kleinman–Gupta effect anyway?'

'It's a phenomenon that happens when certain unstable atoms decay. Dr Kleinman discovered it with Amil Gupta in 1965. I'd be happy to tell you all about it in my office.'

Lucille took off her glasses. 'I can see you're getting impatient, Mr Swift, but you'll have to bear with me. You see, Professor Kleinman had access to classified information, and we suspect there may have been a breach.'

David looked askance. 'What are you talking about? It's been forty years since he worked for the government. He persuaded every physicist at Columbia to sign a statement against nuclear weapons.'

'I never said he was working on weapons. He approached the Defense Department after 9/11. He offered to help the counterterrorism effort.'

David considered the possibility. 'What was he working on?'

'I'm not at liberty to say. But I can show you something.' She riffled through Kleinman's folder and pulled out a reprint of an old research paper. 'It's one of the few things in his file that ain't classified.'

The paper, published in *Physical Review* in 1975, was titled 'Measurements of the Flux of Rho Mesons'. It was loaded with complex equations.

'This is why we brought you here, Mr Swift. The first priority of a counterterrorism operation is to ensure the terrorists don't know our defences. We have to find out what Kleinman might have told them about our work.'

David scrutinised the article, trying his best to understand. Kleinman had apparently discovered that focusing a beam of radiation on uranium atoms could generate intense showers of particles called rho mesons. Presumably this could be used to detect the enriched uranium in a nuclear warhead.

'Was he working on an active scanning system?' David asked. 'Something that could detect a warhead hidden in a truck or a shipping container?'

'I can neither confirm nor deny,' Lucille answered. 'But I think you see now why we're taking this so seriously.'

David was just about to look up from the paper when something on the last page caught his eye. There was a table comparing the properties of the rho meson with those of its close cousins, the omega and phi mesons. The last column of the table listed the lifetimes of the particles.

'So what did Kleinman tell you, Mr Swift?' Lucille asked.

David was still staring at the numbers in the table. After several seconds he looked up. 'You're lying,' he said. 'Dr Kleinman wasn't working on a detector. He wasn't working for the government at all.'

She put on a hurt, uncomprehending look. 'What? Are you—?'

David tapped his finger on the last page of Kleinman's paper. 'The lifetime of a rho meson is less than 10^{-23} second.'

'So? What does that mean?'

'It means your research department screwed up when they concocted this cover story. Even if a rho meson were moving at the speed of light, it would go less than a trillionth of an inch before it decayed. You couldn't detect those particles coming from a nuclear warhead, so it would be impossible to build a scanning system based on this paper.'

Lucille pressed her lips together. The lines round her eyes deepened, but these weren't laughter lines.

'Why don't you tell me the real reason why you're so interested in Dr Kleinman,' said David. 'It's some kind of weapon, isn't it?'

Lucille didn't reply. Instead she took off her jacket and draped it over her chair. A shoulder holster rode against the side of her blouse. She turned to the agents with the Super Soaker. 'You boys finished with that thing yet?'

One of the agents placed the water gun on the table. 'It's clean, ma'am.'

'What a relief. Now contact logistics and tell 'em we're gonna need transportation to the airport in ten minutes.'

The agent retreated to the far end of the room and muttered into the microphone in his sleeve. Lucille reached into her jacket and pulled out a pack of Marlboros and a Zippo lighter emblazoned with the Lone Star of Texas. She glared at David as she shook a cigarette out of the pack. 'You're a real pain in the ass, you know that?' With a flick of her wrist she lit her cigarette. 'Remember the nurse who was in Kleinman's hospital room?' She closed the Zippo and put it back in her jacket. 'Well, one of our agents talked to her. She said the professor whispered some numbers in your ear.'

Shit, David thought.

'A long string of numbers, she said. She don't remember them, of course. But I bet you do.'

He did. He saw the sequence of numbers in his mind's eye, almost as if they were floating in the air. That was the way David's memory worked.

'You're gonna tell us those numbers now.' Lucille rolled up her sleeve, exposing an antique silver watch. 'I'm gonna give you thirty seconds.'

While Lucille leaned back, Agent Hawley removed the hood from his pocket. David's throat tightened, and he gripped the table to steady himself. He realised that even if he revealed the numbers, they wouldn't let him go. As long as the digits remained in his head, he was a security risk.

'I need some idea why you want the numbers,' he said. 'If you can't tell me the reason, take me to someone who can.'

Lucille let out a long sigh. She drowned her cigarette in one of the Dixie cups, then stood up. 'All right, Mr Swift, under the authorisation of the Patriot Act, I'm declaring you an enemy combatant.' She turned to Hawley. 'Put the cuffs back. We'll do the shackles in the car.'

Hawley grabbed his arm and shouted, 'Get up!' but David remained frozen in his seat, his heart pumping fast and his legs quivering.

One of the other agents tapped Hawley on the shoulder. 'Uh, sir? I can't raise logistics. There's nothing but static on every channel.'

Lucille reached for the microphone clipped to the collar of her blouse and pressed a button. 'Black One to logistics. Logistics, do you read?'

Before she could get an answer, a deep percussive boom shook the walls.

AS SIMON WALKED towards the garage where the black Suburban was parked, it occurred to him that if he ever wanted to switch careers he could always find work as a security consultant. He could certainly give the FBI a few tips. Inside the guardhouse booth at the entrance to the garage there was only one agent, a stocky young grunt in an orange windbreaker and a New York Yankees cap, an unconvincing attempt to look like a parking attendant. Stationing only one agent was a mistake, Simon thought. You should never cut corners on perimeter defence.

Simon had changed into a business suit and carried a leather briefcase now. When he knocked on the booth's bulletproof glass, the agent looked him over, then opened the door a crack. 'What is it?'

'Sorry to bother you. I was wondering about monthly parking rates.'

'We don't—'

Simon wrenched the door open and slammed his shoulder into the agent's gut, knocking him down. There was only one surveillance camera in the booth, pointed so high it couldn't view the floor. Another mistake. Lying on top of the agent, Simon thrust his combat knife into the man's heart.

When Simon stood up, he was wearing the windbreaker and the Yankees cap. He'd also removed the Uzi and the field munitions from his briefcase. Hiding the submachine gun under the windbreaker, he exited the booth.

There were plenty of video cameras trained on him as he walked down the long ramp to the garage, so he kept his head down. He saw half a dozen Suburbans parked near an unmarked steel door. When he was about ten metres away, the door opened and an agitated man in a grey suit peered out.

'Anderson!' the man shouted. 'What the hell are you—?'

Simon fired his Uzi. Conveniently, the agent fell face down and his body kept the door from closing. Simon raced to the doorway, arriving just in time to cut down a third agent who'd rushed to his partner's aid. They're making it too easy, Simon thought.

Just past the doorway was the command-and-control room where the agents had been stationed. Simon first disabled the radio transceiver, then scanned the bank of video monitors. He found his target on the screen marked SUB-3A. which showed one of the interrogation rooms on the sub-basement level. Simon was already familiar with the layout of the complex; over the years he had acquired several sources in US intelligence who had revealed, for a small fee, a great deal about the workings of their agencies.

One more barrier remained, a second steel door at the far end of the room. This door had an alphanumeric keypad controlling the lock, but, luckily for Simon, the FBI had committed yet another foolish error, installing a single dead bolt instead of a stronger locking mechanism.

Simon removed half a kilogram of C-4 from his munitions bag. It took him eighty-three seconds to mould the explosive round the bolt, insert the blasting caps, and run the detonator cord across the control room. Crouched behind a pillar, Simon muttered, '*Na zdorovye!*' then detonated the charge.

AS SOON AS THEY HEARD the blast, Lucille and Hawley and the two other agents pulled out their Glocks.

'Son of a bitch,' Hawley cried. 'What the hell was that?'

Lucille seemed calmer. She gave her agents a hand signal, holding up her index and middle fingers. The three men slowly approached the door. Then Hawley flung it open, and his two partners dashed into the corridor. After an anxious second they yelled, 'Clear!'

Lucille breathed a whoosh of relief. 'All right, Hawley stays here to secure our detainee. The others come with me to identify the threat.' She gathered her folders and turned to David. 'Agent Hawley's gonna be just outside that door, Mr Swift. If you make so much as a peep, he's gonna shoot. Understand?' Without waiting for an answer, she barrelled into the corridor.

'Ma'am?' Hawley asked. 'What if I can't hold the position?'

'You're authorised to take the necessary steps.'

Hawley went into the corridor and closed the door behind him. The room became so quiet David could hear the hum of the lights.

Necessary steps. The meaning was clear. David had information so valuable that the Bureau would destroy him before letting anyone else get it.

Terrified, David jumped to his feet. He had to get out. He looked around wildly for some escape route, maybe a ceiling panel he could prise loose, an air duct he could crawl through. But the ceiling and walls were solid concrete. There was nothing in the room except the chairs and the table holding the pitcher, the cups and the Super Soaker.

Then he noticed something else. In her haste, Lucille had left her bright red jacket on the back of her chair. Tucked in its pockets were a Zippo lighter and a flask of alcohol. And David remembered what his ex-wife had said about the dangers of Super Soakers.

SIMON HAD ONE GOOD THING to say about the security at the FBI complex: they hadn't put the circuit breakers in an obvious place. He had to follow the twists and turns of the exposed cables before he found the utility closet. But his opinion of the agency plummeted once again when he saw that the closet was unlocked. He shook his head as he entered the small room and located the electrical panel. If I were a taxpayer, he thought, I'd be outraged.

With the flip of a switch, the complex went dark. Simon reached into his pocket and took out a pair of thermal infrared goggles. He turned on the device and adjusted the head strap so the binocular scope fitted snugly over his eyes. He could find his way to the staircase by following the residual heat in the fluorescent lights.

He descended two flights before he heard footsteps. Very quietly, he backtracked to the landing. After a few seconds he saw three flashlight beams lancing down the corridor. On the infrared display he saw a warm hand gripping a bright cylinder and a ghastly face that looked like it had been dipped in glow paint. Simon fired two rounds into the shining head.

A gruff voice yelled, 'Cut the lights!' and the two other flashlight beams disappeared. Silently, Simon came down the stairs, stepped over the body of the dead agent, and peered round the corner. Two figures crouched in the corridor, the closer one in a shooting stance, sweeping his pistol back and forth with both hands. Simon picked him off with one shot to the forehead, but before he could take out the third agent, a bullet whizzed by his ear.

Simon ducked round the corner as another bullet streaked past. The third agent was firing blindly in his direction. Not bad, he thought. At least this one has some spirit. When he peered down the corridor again, the agent had turned sideways to present a smaller target, and on the infrared screen Simon saw a thick figure with massive breasts. He hesitated before raising his Uzi—the agent was a babushka! She could be Simon's grandmother. And in that moment of hesitation she fired three more shots at him.

He flattened himself against the wall. Jesus, that was close! He prepared to return fire, but the babushka turned tail and vanished round a corner.

As Simon started to go after her, he heard a muffled shout behind him. He stopped in his tracks. A distant but loud male voice shouted, 'You heard me, Hawley! Open the goddamn door!'

THE LIGHTS WENT OUT just as David slipped his hand into Lucille's jacket. He froze for a second, then took a deep breath and pulled out the silver flask. He set it gently on the table, memorising its position; then he removed Lucille's Zippo and reached carefully for the Super Soaker.

Luckily, he'd filled and refilled the gun's reservoir at least a dozen times and could easily take off the lid by touch. He grabbed the silver flask and unscrewed the cap. It held maybe eight ounces of liquor, and as Lucille had promised it was nearly pure alcohol—the fumes stung his eyes as he poured it in. But he needed a pint to generate the shooting pressure. Shit!

Even though the room was pitch-black, he closed his eyes so he could think. Water. There were two Dixie cups of water on that table. You could dilute alcohol up to fifty per cent and it would still burn. After some careful groping, he found one cup, fished out the dead cigarette and poured about three ounces of water into the tank. Then he located the other cup and poured in three more ounces. He hoped to hell it was enough.

David closed the tank and quietly pumped the handle. Just as he reached for the Zippo, gunfire echoed down the corridors of the complex. Startled, he knocked the lighter off the table and it skittered into the darkness.

David got down on his hands and knees and groped for the lighter. More gunshots echoed down the corridor, closer this time. David banged his head against a chair, and as he reached under the table he felt the Zippo.

Trembling, he opened the lighter and spun the flint wheel. The flame arose like a small miracle. David leapt to his feet, grabbed the Super Soaker and pointed it at the door. He heard a third burst of gunfire as he positioned the flame in front of the nozzle, but he didn't flinch this time.

'Hawley!' he shouted. 'Open the door! You gotta let me out!'

'Shut up!' a low voice hissed on the other side of the door. Hawley obviously didn't want to draw the attention of whoever was shooting.

'You heard me, Hawley!' David bellowed. 'Open the goddamn door!'

Several seconds passed. He's preparing himself, David thought. To take necessary steps. His only option is to kill me.

Then the door opened and David pulled the trigger.

SIMON SAW ANOTHER AGENT on the infrared screen. This one stood in front of a door, holding a flashlight and a pistol. Simon crept a little closer, keeping his Uzi trained on the man. Then the agent opened the door wide and all at once a brilliant white plume erupted.

Simon was blinded. The scorching plume expanded until it turned his display into a blank white rectangle. He tore off the goggles and ducked into a crouch. The fireball dissipated after a couple of seconds, leaving the FBI agent rolling on the floor, trying to extinguish the fire on his jacket.

Then Simon heard a series of rubbery squeaks. The noise was moving past him by the time he realised what it was: the sneakers of the prisoner. Simon got to his feet and chased him down the pitch-black corridor. He was just a few strides from tackling the man when something clattered to the floor. In the next instant he stepped on something plastic and hollow and tumbled backwards, smacking his skull against a door frame.

He lay there, stunned. The still-smouldering FBI agent ran right past him after the prisoner. A true American idiot, Simon thought. Dedicated but oblivious. He stood up, put the goggles back on and picked up his Uzi.

WITHOUT SLOWING DOWN, David lit the Zippo again, and the flame illuminated a circle around him. He saw nothing but blank walls on either side. He could hear Agent Hawley's footfalls echoing behind.

David made a left and raced down a different corridor, desperately searching for an exit. He was running as fast as he could when he tripped over something that felt like a sack of laundry. David relit the Zippo and saw that he was sprawled on top of a corpse. It was one of Hawley's grey-suited partners, a pair of bloody holes in his forehead. Choking with horror, David leapt to his feet. Then he noticed that the body lay at the foot of a staircase. A moment later Hawley rounded the corner, so David doused the Zippo and dashed madly up the steps.

After ascending three flights, he spied a faint yellow glow through a jagged doorway. He ran through a room full of smashed video monitors, then hurtled over two more corpses without a second thought. He was in a parking garage now and he could smell the New York air. He bolted up the ramp towards the glorious streetlight.

But it was a hundred feet to the top of the ramp and there was nowhere to take cover. He looked over his shoulder and saw Hawley. The agent slowly raised his Glock. Then a shot rang out and Hawley crumpled to the ground.

David was too confused to feel any relief. He ran up the ramp, and within seconds he stood on a deserted street of office buildings. He read the sign on the corner: Liberty and Nassau streets. He was in Lower Manhattan, three blocks north of the Stock Exchange.

By the time Simon finished off the charred FBI agent and reached the top of the ramp, half a dozen patrol cars were coming down Liberty Street. The babushka must have radioed the NYPD for back-up, he thought. Cursing in frustration, he ducked behind a newsstand as the cars screeched to a halt.

But his fury lasted only a moment. It's all about flexibility, he reminded himself as he walked back to his Mercedes. The first step was to identify the prisoner and determine his connection to Kleinman. Then it was just a matter of tracking down his contacts. Sooner or later this fellow in sneakers would lead him to the *Einheitliche Feldtheorie.*

Simon felt a grim satisfaction as he looked up at the skyscrapers on Broadway. Very soon, he thought, all this will be gone.

CHAPTER THREE

'Goddamn it, Lucy! What the hell happened?'

Lucille sat in a conference room at the FBI's office on Federal Plaza, speaking on a secure phone line with the Bureau's director. She'd evacuated the complex on Liberty Street and set up a temporary command post at the New York regional headquarters, and all off-duty agents had been rousted from their beds. Now, at fifteen minutes after midnight, Lucille handled the difficult task of delivering bad news to her boss.

'They surprised us,' she admitted. 'They eliminated logistics and disabled our comms; then they cut off the power. We lost six agents.' Lucille was amazed she could report this so calmly. 'I take full responsibility, sir.'

'Who the hell did this? Did you get any video?'

'No, sir, unfortunately the surveillance systems were destroyed. But we know they carried Uzis and used C-4. Probably had infrared scopes, too.'

'Are you thinking Al-Qaeda?'

'No, it was too sophisticated for them. It was a pretty slick operation.'

'What about the detainee? You think he's in league with them?'

Lucille hesitated. 'At first I would have said no. I mean, the guy's a history professor. No criminal record, no unusual travel or international phone calls. But Kleinman gave him a numeric key, probably an encryption code for a computer file. Maybe they were trying to sell the information.'

'What are the chances of getting him back? The secretary of defence is going nuts over this. He's calling me every half-hour for an update.'

'Tell him it's under control. We got the NYPD running checkpoints at bridges and tunnels, and agents at all train and bus stations. We got a driver's licence photo and a photo from some book he wrote, and we'll have flyers distributed in the next hour or so. Don't worry, he ain't going nowhere.'

DAVID RAN UPTOWN along the Hudson River. His overriding impulse was to get as far as possible from Liberty Street. But he was too worried about being pulled over by a cop to hail a cab or hop on a subway. So he ran up the river bike path, blending in with the late-night exercise fanatics.

He made it all the way to 34th Street before he slowed to a halt. Breathing hard, he leaned against a lamppost. 'Christ,' he whispered, 'this can't be happening.' He'd spent five minutes listening to the dying words of a physics professor and now he was running for his life.

One thing was clear: the FBI agents weren't the only ones who wanted Kleinman's secret. Someone else had tortured the professor, and attacked the Liberty Street complex. And David had no idea who they were.

He had to make a plan. He knew it would be unwise to go to his or Karen's apartment; the FBI probably had both places under surveillance. For the same reason, he couldn't risk going to friends or colleagues. No, he needed to get out of New York, maybe figure out a way to cross the Canadian border. He couldn't rent a car—the federal agents would see the credit-card transaction—but maybe he could get on a train or a bus.

David found an ATM and withdrew as much cash as he could. The FBI would discover these transactions too, but there was no avoiding it. Then he made a beeline for Penn Station.

As soon as he walked through the station's Eighth Avenue entrance, though, he knew he was too late. The ticket hall was swarming with police. At the entrances to the tracks the cops were asking every passenger for identification. David headed for the Seventh Avenue exit, but a fresh wave of police officers poured into the concourse and formed a solid line blocking the stairways and escalators. They began asking for driver's licences.

Trying his best to look casual, David turned round and retraced his steps, but there were cops at the Eighth Avenue exits now, too. Exposed and panicky, he looked for a newsstand or fast-food joint where he could gather his wits, but most of the shops on the concourse were closed for the night. The only place open was a dismal little bar called the Station Break. David hadn't seen the inside of a bar in years, and just the thought of entering the Station Break made his gorge rise. But this was no time to be picky.

Inside the bar, a dozen beefy guys in their twenties were cavorting around a table loaded with Budweiser cans. All wore identical custom-made T-shirts with the words PETE'S BACHELOR PARTY printed on them. They were noisy as hell, and had apparently driven everyone else out of the place, except for the bartender, who stood behind the cash register with a disgusted frown.

David took a seat at the bar. 'I'll have a Coke, please.'

Without a word, the bartender reached for a cloudy glass and filled it with ice. There was a television on the wall, but the sound was turned off; a young blonde anchorwoman stared soberly into the camera next to the words TERROR ALERT.

'Hey, she's hot!' one of the bachelor partiers yelled. 'Oh, yeah! Read me the news, baby! Come on, read it to Larry!'

While his friends laughed uproariously, Larry approached the bar. He had a gut the size of a beach ball hanging over his belt, and his eyes were bloodshot. 'Hey!' he yelled. 'How much is a shot of Jägermeister?'

The bartender's frown deepened. 'Ten dollars.'

'Jesus H. Christ!' Larry thumped a fat fist on the bar. 'That's why I never come into the city any more!'

Ignoring him, the bartender gave David his Coke. 'That's six dollars.'

Larry turned to David. 'See what I mean? It's a fucking rip-off! It's three times more expensive than in Jersey!'

David said nothing. He didn't want to encourage the guy. He had enough to worry about already. He handed the bartender a twenty.

'Hey, what's your name, pal?' Larry stuck out his right hand.

David gritted his teeth. 'It's Phil. Listen, I'm a little—'

'Good to meetya, Phil! I'm Larry Nelson.' He found David's hand and pumped it vigorously. Then he pointed at his friends. 'These are my buddies from Metuchen. Pete over there's getting married Sunday.'

The bridegroom was slumped over the table, his head nearly hidden by Budweiser cans. His eyes were closed, and his face was pressed against the tabletop. David grimaced. That was me twenty years ago, he thought.

'We were gonna take the twelve thirty back to Jersey,' Larry added, 'but the cops started checking ID and the line stretched all the way across the station, so we missed the train. Now we gotta wait an hour for the next one.'

'Won't they let you on the train if you don't have any ID?' David asked.

'Nah, not tonight. We saw one guy who said he left his wallet at home. The cops took him away. It's one of those terror alerts.'

David's stomach twisted. Jesus, he thought. I'll never make it out of here.

'The one good thing,' Larry added, 'is I got the evening shift this week, so I don't have to show up at the police station till four.'

David stared at him for a moment. 'You're a cop?'

He nodded proudly. 'A dispatcher for the Metuchen PD.'

Amazing, David thought. He'd found the one cop in the tristate area who wasn't searching for him. He tried to remember what little he knew about New Jersey. 'I live pretty close to Metuchen, you know. New Brunswick.'

'No shit!' Larry turned to his friends. 'Hey, dudes, listen up! This guy's from New Brunswick!'

Several of them halfheartedly raised their beer in salute. Their spirits are running down, David thought. They need a pick-me-up.

'Look, Larry, I'd like to do something for Pete. In honour of his wedding and all. How about I buy everyone a shot of Jägermeister?'

Larry's eyes widened. 'Hey, that would be great!'

David got off his stool and held up his hands. 'Jäger shots for everybody!'

Suddenly revived, the bachelor partiers let out a whoop. When David turned to the bartender, though, the man didn't look too pleased.

'Let's see the money first,' he said. 'It's gonna be a hundred thirty.'

David pulled a thick roll of twenties out of his pocket and laid it on the bar. 'Just keep 'em coming.'

KAREN LAY IN BED next to Amory van Cleve, the managing partner of Morton McIntyre & van Cleve. The lawyer slept on his back, his manicured hands clasped over his chest. With his full head of grey hair, his patrician nose and chin, he looked pretty damn good for a sixty-year-old, she decided. And he was dignified, mannerly and cheerful. Best of all, he knew what mattered to Karen, something David had never seemed to grasp.

A siren moaned down Columbus Avenue. There seemed to be a lot of them tonight. Probably heading for a fire somewhere, or maybe a water-main break. She'd check the papers in the morning.

Of course, she couldn't blame it all on David. Karen herself hadn't realised what she wanted until halfway through their marriage. When they'd met, she was a naive twenty-three-year-old student, and David was five years older and already a successful professor at Columbia. But within a decade she was a senior associate at Morton McIntyre & van Cleve, and earning more than twice as much as her husband. Moreover, she knew exactly what she wanted now: a comfortable home, a private school for her son and a more prominent place in the city's social circles.

Karen could forgive David for not sharing these interests. What she couldn't forgive was his complete disregard for her desires. He seemed to take a perverse pleasure in looking as dishevelled as possible, and he wouldn't even consider moving to a bigger apartment. The breaking point came when he refused an offer to become chairman of his department—and an extra $30,000 a year—because it would 'interfere with his research'.

Oh, stop thinking about David, she told herself. What was the point? She had Amory now. They'd already talked about buying an apartment. A place on the East Side would be a nice change. Park Avenue, maybe.

Karen was so busy envisioning the perfect apartment that she didn't hear the doorbell ring. She heard the pounding on the door, though. 'Mrs Swift?' an urgent bass voice called. 'Are you there, Mrs Swift?'

She sat up in bed, her heart racing. Who would knock at her door at this hour? And why were they using the name she'd given up two years ago?

'Open up, Mrs Swift. This is the FBI. We need to speak to you.'

The FBI? What was this, a practical joke? Then she remembered the phone call from the police detective asking for David. She gave Amory a shake. 'There's some men at the door. They say they're with the FBI.'

He opened his eyes. 'What?' he croaked. 'What time is it?'

'Just get up and see who it is.'

Amory sighed, then reached for his glasses and got out of bed. He put a maroon bathrobe over his yellow pyjamas. Karen threw on an old T-shirt and sweatpants. She followed him out of the bedroom but hung back while he went to the foyer and peered through the peephole.

'I'm sorry, gentlemen, but I need to see your badges before I let you in,' he said, through the door. After a few seconds, he looked back over his shoulder at Karen. 'They're FBI, all right,' he said. 'I'll see what they want.'

Karen started to shout, 'Wait, don't—' but she was too late. Amory unlocked the dead bolt and turned the knob. The next instant, two enormous men in grey suits threw him down on his back. Two more agents rushed into the apartment pointing guns.

'Don't move!' one of them shouted, a tall, broad-shouldered blond man. He gave his partner a hand signal. 'Go check the bedrooms.'

Karen took a step back. She felt the door of Jonah's bedroom against her spine. 'Please, don't! I have a child! He's—'

'*Don't move!*' The gun shook in the blond man's hand.

Through the bedroom door Karen heard footsteps, then a weak, frightened 'Mommy?' But both agents were moving towards her now, guns raised.

In one motion she pushed the door open and threw herself on top of her son. 'No!' she screamed. 'Don't hurt him!'

The agents stood over her, their guns pointing straight down. She could feel Jonah shaking in fear and confusion, but he was safe.

While the blond agent stood guard, the other one opened the bedroom closet, then inspected the other rooms. In the background, Karen could hear Amory's outraged voice: 'You can't search the place without a warrant!'

After a few seconds, the agent returned. 'No one else is here.'

The blond agent stepped away to confer with his partners. Karen sat up, clutching Jonah and shuddering with relief.

Amory lay on his stomach a few feet away, his hands tied behind his back. 'You're going to be sorry! I'm on close terms with the US attorney!'

The blond agent scowled at him. 'Shut up, Grandpa.' He turned to Karen. 'Where's your ex-husband, Mrs Swift?'

'Is that why you burst in here? To look for David?'

'Just answer the—'

'You bastard! You pulled a gun on a seven-year-old boy!'

While Karen glared at the FBI man, Jonah tugged the front of her T-shirt. His face was damp. 'Where's Daddy?' he cried. 'I want Daddy!'

For a moment the agent seemed to falter, but soon his features hardened again. 'David Swift is wanted for murder. We took necessary precautions.'

No, Karen thought. It's impossible. David had plenty of faults, but violence wasn't one of them. 'That's a lie!' she said.

He narrowed his eyes. 'I knew some of the men he killed, Mrs Swift.' Then he spoke into the microphone hidden in the sleeve of his jacket. 'This is Agent Brock. We got three to bring in.'

'HERE'S TO PHIL! You the man, Phil! You the fucking MAN!'

Round the table at the Station Break, the members of Pete's bachelor party raised their glasses of Jägermeister to toast David's alter ego, the generous Phil from New Brunswick. This was the third round of drinks he'd bought, and even Pete, the drunken bridegroom, raised his head from the table to mutter, 'You the man!' David threw his arm round him. 'No, YOU the man!' But though he bellowed with the rest of them, he surreptitiously slid his shot glasses towards Larry, who was only too happy to empty them.

Larry opened a plastic bag that lay on the table and took out a neatly folded PETE'S BACHELOR PARTY T-shirt. 'Look!' he boomed. 'I got this extra T-shirt. You know what I'm gonna do? I'm gonna make Phil an official member of Pete's party!'

David stood up and slipped on the T-shirt. Everyone cheered. Then someone yelled, 'Hey, it's almost one thirty—we're gonna miss the train again!'

'Let's go!' Larry ordered. 'Someone help Pete.'

While two of the partiers grabbed Pete, David shouted, 'Wait for me!' in a slurred voice and toppled to the floor.

Larry bent over him. 'Hey, Phil, you all right?'

'I'm a little . . . fucked up,' David slurred. 'Could you . . . gimme a hand?'

'Sure, buddy, no problem.' Larry grasped David's arm, picked him up, and steered him out of the bar.

The station's concourse was nearly empty of commuters now but still teemed with police officers. Half a dozen cops stood in front of the entrance to Track 10. Larry pumped his fist in the air as they approached.

'All right, NYPD!' he boomed. 'Go get those terrorists!'

A gaunt police sergeant held out his hands as if stopping traffic. 'OK, fellas, settle down. Just take out your driver's licences.'

As the others pulled out their wallets, David made a show of patting his pockets. 'Shit!' he yelled. 'Oh shit!' He fell to his hands and knees and began a drunken search of the floor.

Larry bent over him again. 'What's wrong, Phil?'

'My wallet,' David gasped, clutching Larry's shoulder. 'Can't find it . . .'

'Did you leave it in the bar?'

David shook his head. 'Don't know . . . It could be anywhere.'

The police sergeant came over. 'What's the matter?'

'Phil lost his wallet,' Larry told him.

With his mouth hanging open, David looked up at the sergeant. 'I don't understand . . . It was . . . right here.'

The cop furrowed his brow. 'You don't have any ID on you?'

'He's Phil,' Larry explained, 'from New Brunswick.' He pointed at the PETE'S BACHELOR PARTY T-shirt. 'He's with us.'

The sergeant frowned. 'You need ID to get on the train.'

As if on cue, an automated voice announced, 'Attention. Last call for the Northeast Corridor train boarding on Track 10, with service to Newark, Elizabeth, Rahway, Metuchen, New Brunswick and Princeton Junction.'

'We gotta get on that train!' Larry shouted. He pulled out his own wallet. 'Look, I'm with the Metuchen PD. My badge is right here. I'm telling you, Phil's my bud.'

The sergeant looked at the badge, still frowning. Oh, no, David thought. They're going to arrest me. A wave of nausea surged through him.

'Watch out!' Larry warned. 'Phil's gonna hurl!'

The police sergeant stepped back, shoving David towards Larry. 'Get this guy out of here. Go on, get him on the train.'

SIMON SAT at an antique desk in one of the overpriced suites at the Waldorf-Astoria. The hotel charged $2,000 a night for a stuffy parlour and a bedroom decorated like a tsarist bordello. Out of principle, Simon had refused to pay it; instead he'd filched a credit-card number from one of the Internet's leaky conduits—an unsuspecting Oregonian named Neil Davison was paying for Simon's stay, as well as the rack of lamb and half-litre of Stolichnaya he'd ordered from room service.

As Simon knocked back another glass of vodka he stared at his laptop's screen, which displayed the web page of Columbia's physics department. The list of faculty members included photographs. Simon scrolled down the page, but he didn't see the man in sneakers. He checked the faculty listings of twenty other universities. After an hour he slammed the laptop shut and tossed the empty Stoli bottle in the trash. It was infuriating.

To calm himself, he went to the window and stared at the lights of Park Avenue. Even at two in the morning, taxis were streaming down the street. As he watched the cabs, Simon wondered whether he'd missed something crucial. He went to his duffle bag, and removed the book he'd used to track down Kleinman. Packed with useful information about all the physicists who'd assisted Einstein, it was called *On the Shoulders of Giants*.

As Simon opened the book he caught a glimpse of something familiar. He turned to the inside flap of the back cover and smiled.

'Hello, David Swift,' he said. 'It's a pleasure to meet you.'

CHAPTER FOUR

Despite the pleading of Larry, Pete and the other bachelor partiers, David declined to get off the train at Metuchen. The whole drunken crew gave him high fives as they exited the train, and chanted, 'Phil! Phil! Phil!' as they stood on the platform. David acknowledged their cheers with a thumbs-up, then slumped back in his seat, exhausted.

As the train pulled away from the station, David began to shiver. He rubbed his arms, but he couldn't stop trembling. He realised that it was his body's delayed response to all the terrifying events of the past four hours. It's all right, he told himself. You're speeding away from New York now.

By the time the train pulled into New Brunswick he'd stopped shivering. He decided to stay on until Trenton, then get a Greyhound bus for Toronto. But as the train continued westward, David began to see the flaws in this plan. What if they were checking ID at the bus stations, too? He couldn't count on finding another bachelor party. And by the time the bus reached the border, the police would probably be looking for him there as well.

Soon the conductor announced, 'Arriving at Princeton Junction. Service here to Princeton via the Princeton Branch Line.' It was the three *Princeton*s in a row that did it. David immediately thought of someone who could help him. He hadn't seen her in twenty years but he knew she still lived in Princeton. Best of all, she was one of the pioneers of string theory, and he suspected only a physicist could make sense of the story he had to tell.

BACK IN 1989, while David was still a graduate student in physics, he attended a conference at Princeton on string theory—a new idea that promised to resolve a long-standing problem. Although Einstein's theory of relativity explained gravity to perfection, and quantum mechanics could account for every nuance of the subatomic world, the two theories were mathematically incompatible. For thirty years Einstein had tried to unify the two sets of physical laws, with the aim of creating a single overarching theory that could explain all the forces in nature. But all of Einstein's published solutions turned out to be flawed, and after his death many physicists concluded that his quest had been misguided. The universe, they said, was just too complex to be described by a single set of equations.

In the seventies, some physicists revived the idea of a unified theory by hypothesising that all the fundamental particles were minuscule strings of energy. By the eighties, string theorists claimed that the strings vibrated in ten dimensions, six of which were curled into manifolds too small to see. The theory was incomplete and unwieldy, yet fired the imaginations of researchers all over the world. One of them was Monique Reynolds, a twenty-four-year-old grad student at Princeton.

David saw her for the first time at the closing session of the conference. Monique delivered a presentation on multidimensional manifolds. She was tall and beautiful, her face like an ancient portrait of a Greek goddess, but with a helmet of intricately woven corn rows, and skin the colour of a Kahlúa and cream. In her long yellow dress and her gold bracelets, against the drabness of the auditorium she blazed like a particle shower.

Women physicists were uncommon enough in the eighties, but a black female string theorist was a rare phenomenon indeed. When she began her presentation, though, the scientists at the conference accepted her as one of their own because she spoke their language, the abstruse tongue of mathematics. Moving to the blackboard, she scribbled a long sequence of equations representing the fundamental parameters of the universe: the speed of light, the gravitational constant, the mass of the electron, the strength of the nuclear force. Then she manipulated them until they condensed into a single, elegant equation describing the space around a vibrating string.

After she finished her presentation, David jumped out of his seat and made his way to the stage so he could introduce himself.

Monique raised her eyebrows when David mentioned his name. A look of pleasure crossed her face. 'Sure, I know you!' she exclaimed. 'I read the paper you did with Hans Kleinman. Relativity in a two-dimensional space-time. That was a nice piece of work.'

David was amazed that she'd actually read his paper. Their conversation continued for several hours, moving first to the faculty lounge, where he met some other Princeton grad students, then to a local restaurant. After a few drinks, David asked Monique how she got interested in physics, and she told him it was all because of her father, a man who never got past ninth grade but was always devising theories about the world. By midnight, David and Monique were the last customers left in the restaurant, and by 1 a.m. they were groping each other on the couch in her tiny apartment.

For David, this sequence of events was fairly typical. He was in the middle of the six-month drinking binge that clouded his second year in graduate school, and when he was drinking with a woman he usually tried to go to bed with her. So everything was progressing along the usual lines, but something went unaccountably wrong. All at once, David started crying.

He got to his feet, humiliated. Monique asked him what was wrong, but he couldn't tell her. He knew why he was crying. Compared with Monique Reynolds, he was worthless. 'I'm sorry,' he said. 'I have to go.'

He kept crying as he walked away from her apartment across the darkened Princeton campus. 'You idiot,' he muttered. 'It's all the booze. You can't think straight.' The week before, he'd failed his exams. No more drinking, he told himself. But it wasn't until two months later, after he'd been kicked out of Columbia's physics programme, that he quit drinking for ever.

In the following years, David straightened out his life and pursued his doctorate in history. In 2001, he came across an article about Monique in *Scientific American.* She was still at Princeton pursuing string theory, but David was less interested in the physics than in the biographical details revealed in the last few paragraphs of the article. She'd grown up in a poor neighbourhood in DC, where her mother had been a heroin addict and her father had been shot dead in a robbery when she was two months old. David felt an ache in his chest. She'd told him that her father had inspired her to become a physicist, but she'd never actually known the man.

David thought about Monique after his marriage fell apart, and a few times he came close to calling her. But each time he Googled her instead. He learned that she was now a full professor of physics, and a photograph in the online *Princeton Packet* showed her standing in front of a modest two-storey house with a large front porch, which David recognised as 112 Mercer Street, the house where Albert Einstein had lived for the last twenty years of his life. It was now a private residence for professors associated with Princeton's Institute for Advanced Study.

That's where David headed as he got off the train.

LUCILLE WAS ON THE PHONE with her agents in Trenton when the secretary of defence barged into the conference room. She nearly dropped the receiver. She'd met him once, at a White House ceremony, and they'd exchanged pleasantries. But now the man loomed in front of her, his square head cocked, his small eyes squinting disapproval behind rimless glasses. Although it was three o'clock in the morning, his thin grey hair was neatly combed and his tie hung straight. A two-star air-force general carried his briefcase.

Lucille hung up and dutifully rose to her feet. 'Mr Secre—'

'Sit down, Lucy.' He waved her back to her seat. 'No need for formalities. I just wanted to see how the operation was going. The air force was kind enough to fly me to New York.'

Great, Lucille thought. It would have been nice if someone had warned me. 'Well, sir, we think we have a fix on the detainee. We have information that he's in New Jersey now and we're—'

'What? I thought you had the guy pinned down in Manhattan.'

Lucille shifted in her seat. 'There was a delay getting Swift's photo to the police. Once we'd distributed the flyers, an officer assigned to Penn Station recognised the suspect. He said Swift boarded a New Jersey Transit train with a bunch of drunk yahoos. In the confusion, he failed to check for ID.'

The secretary frowned. 'That's inexcusable. If this were a real army, that officer would be shot.'

Lucille decided to ignore the bizarre comment. 'Our agents in New Jersey boarded the train at Trenton but didn't find the suspect. We're looking into the possibility that Swift got off with the drunk guys in Metuchen.'

'That doesn't sound promising. What other leads do you have?'

'We've positioned surveillance teams at the residences of Swift's colleagues at Columbia. And we brought in his ex-wife for questioning. She's downstairs with her son and her boyfriend, a man named Amory van Cleve.'

'Jesus!' The secretary raised his hand to his forehead. 'Don't you know who that is? Van Cleve raised twenty million in the last election campaign!'

Lucille stiffened. 'Sir, I'm just following orders. The Bureau's director told me to pursue this case with due vigour.'

'Believe me, Lucy, this project is one of the Pentagon's top priorities. But you can't use standard interrogation techniques on Amory van Cleve. When the president was up here last spring, they played golf together.'

'Well, what do you suggest, sir?'

He looked over his shoulder at the air-force general. The man opened the briefcase and pulled out a folder. The secretary leafed through its contents. 'OK, it says here this guy Swift has a history of substance abuse.'

'He had a drinking problem when he was in his twenties.'

'Once a drunk, always a drunk. We can say the guy moved on to cocaine, and he's been dealing the stuff to rich brats at Columbia. The Bureau was about to arrest him, but he and his friends managed to surprise the agents and kill half a dozen of them. How's that for a cover story?'

Lucille tried to think of a diplomatic answer. 'There are a few problems. First of all, the Bureau wouldn't ordinarily—'

'I don't need details. Just fix up the story and give it to van Cleve and the ex-wife. Maybe they'll lose enough sympathy for Swift that they'll tell us where he might be hiding. And give the same story to the press. That way, we can get a nationwide manhunt going.'

Lucille shook her head. 'We should tell the Bureau director—'

'Don't worry, the director will go along with it.' He handed the folder to the air-force general, then headed for the door. 'No time for second-guessing, Lucy. You go to war with the army you have.'

DAVID HAD VISITED Einstein's home on Mercer Street once before, when he was writing *On the Shoulders of Giants.* The Institute for Advanced Study had granted him a half-hour visit. He spent most of his allotted time in the study on the first floor. David had felt a strange giddiness as he gazed at the desk by the window. He imagined Einstein scratching away with his fountain pen, filling page after page with spacetime metrics and Ricci tensors.

David approached the house in darkness now. He walked up the porch steps, pressed the doorbell and waited. To his dismay, no lights came on. After half a minute, he rang the bell again. He noticed that the door frame had recently been rebuilt. The new jambs were still unpainted, and a new lock had been installed in the door, its brass keyhole gleaming.

He was about to press the bell a third time when he heard someone yell, 'What the hell are you doing?' just a few feet behind him.

He spun round and saw a barefoot, bare-chested young man come up the porch steps. Dressed only in a pair of jeans, he had long blond hair and impressive pectoral muscles. He also had a baseball bat in his hands.

David stepped away from the door, holding his hands out to show they were empty. 'I'm sorry to bother you so late. I'm—'

'Sorry? You're gonna be a hell of a lot sorrier in a minute.' As soon as the man reached the top step, he swung the bat at David.

David's instincts took over. He rushed forward and slammed a forearm into the guy's chest, knocking him over. His bare back hit the porch with a resounding slap, and David wrenched the bat out of his hands.

'Drop the bat and step away from him!'

David looked up and saw Monique in the doorway, wearing a bright yellow nightshirt and holding a snub-nosed revolver in both hands.

He let the bat clatter to the porch and took three steps back. 'Monique,' he said. 'It's me, David. I'm—'

'Shut up!' She kept the gun pointed at his head. 'Keith, are you all right?'

The bare-chested man propped himself up on his elbows. 'Yeah, I'm OK.'

'Monique, it's me,' David repeated. 'David Swift. We met at Strings '89, when you delivered your paper on Calabi-Yau manifolds.'

Her brow furrowed. Then her mouth opened in recognition. She lowered the revolver and flipped the safety switch. 'What the hell's going on? Why did you come here in the middle of the night? I almost blasted your head off.'

'You know this guy, Mo?' Keith asked, getting to his feet.

She nodded. 'I knew him in graduate school. Barely.'

David gave her a beseeching look. 'Listen, I need your help. I wouldn't have bothered you if it wasn't important. Can we go inside and talk?'

After a few seconds, Monique let out a sigh. 'Ah hell. Come in. I won't be able to get back to sleep anyway.' She held the door open for him.

Keith picked up the bat. 'Hey, man, I'm sorry,' he said. 'I thought you were one of those Nazis.'

'Nazis? What are you talking about?'

'You'll see when we get inside.'

David stepped into the living room he remembered from his previous visit. But now it looked like it had been vandalised. A dozen bricks had been dug out from the fireplace, the walls were pocked with gaping holes that must have been made with a sledgehammer, and the floorboards had been ripped up. Worst of all, swastikas were spray-painted everywhere, and on the ceiling were the words NIGGA GO HOME.

'Oh, no,' David whispered. He turned to Monique.

'Skinhead punks, probably high-school kids,' she said. 'I see them hanging out at the bus-stop, in their leather jackets and Doc Martens.'

'When did this happen?'

'Last weekend, when I was visiting friends in Boston. They hit almost every part of the house. Luckily, they left the kitchen, and didn't do much to the furniture.' She pointed at a black leather sofa and a red Barcelona chair.

Keith stepped over one of the holes in the floor, his thumbs hooked in his jeans. 'When we heard the bell, we thought it was the punks, checking if the house was empty. I went out the back door to surprise 'em.'

Monique slipped her arm round his waist. 'Keith's a sweetheart,' she said. 'He's stayed with me every night this week.'

Keith kissed the top of her head. 'What else could I do? You're my best customer.' He turned to David, a big smile on his face. 'See, I work on Mo's Corvette. At the Princeton Auto Shop.'

David stared at them for a moment, confused. Monique, a renowned string theorist, was dating her car mechanic? It seemed so unlikely. But he had bigger things to worry about. 'Monique, could we sit down somewhere? I know this is a bad time, but I'm in a lot of trouble.'

She raised an eyebrow. 'We can go in the kitchen,' she said.

The kitchen was huge, a modern addition to the house. A marble-topped counter ran under a bank of cabinets, and a round table sat in a breakfast nook. Monique led David to the table. As they sat down, she turned to Keith.

'Baby, could you make some coffee? I'm dying for a cup.'

'Sure thing. Colombian Supremo, right?'

She nodded. Once he had walked across the room to the coffee machine she leaned across to David. 'All right. What's the problem?'

SIMON WAS STARING at his laptop in the overpriced suite at the Waldorf-Astoria. He assumed that David Swift had the sense to steer clear of his apartment and his office at Columbia and any other place where the FBI might be waiting. So, with the help of the Internet, Simon was investigating the history professor's secret desires.

By 3 a.m., he'd managed to hack into Columbia's internal network, and he soon made a fortunate discovery: the network administrator was monitoring the Internet activity of faculty members. Simon was able to download the URLs of every website David Swift had visited in the past nine months. A long list of them ran down the laptop's screen, 4,755 in all. Of those, 1,126 were Google searches. What you search for reveals what you desire, Simon thought. And he had a program that could identify the Christian names in any sample of text. It showed that David Swift had typed a name in 147 of his searches. Only one name appeared more than once.

When Simon did the search himself, he quickly saw why.

He called the hotel's front desk and told the concierge to have his Mercedes ready in five minutes. He was going to New Jersey.

DAVID TOOK a deep breath. 'Hans Kleinman's dead,' he began. 'He was murdered tonight.'

Monique jerked in her chair. 'Murdered? How? Who did it?'

'I don't know. The police said it was a burglary gone bad, but I think it was something else.' He paused. 'I talked to Kleinman in the hospital before he died. That's how this nightmare started.'

She stared blankly at the polished surface of the kitchen table. 'Lord,' she whispered. 'This is awful. First Bouchet and now Kleinman.'

The first name gave David a jolt. 'Bouchet?'

'Yeah, Jacques Bouchet. You know him, don't you?'

David knew him well. Bouchet was one of the grand old men of French physics, a brilliant scientist who'd helped design Europe's most powerful particle accelerators. He was also one of Einstein's assistants in the fifties.

'What happened?'

'His wife called the director of the institute today. She said he died last week and she wanted to set up an endowment in his honour. Apparently he slit his wrists in the bathtub.'

David had interviewed Bouchet for *On the Shoulders of Giants.* They'd shared a magnificent dinner at the physicist's country home in Provence and played cards until 3 a.m. Bouchet was a wise, funny, carefree man.

'Was he sick? Is that why he did it?'

'The director didn't say. But he did mention that the wife sounded like she still couldn't believe it was suicide.'

David's mind began to race. Of course, Einstein's assistants were all quite old now. One would expect them to start dying off. But not this way.

'Do you have a computer I can borrow?' he asked.

Monique pointed at a black laptop on the kitchen counter.

David moved the laptop to the table, turned it on and called up Google's home page. 'Amil Gupta,' he said as he typed the name into the search engine. 'He also worked with Einstein in the fifties.'

In a second the search results appeared. Most were about Gupta's work as director of the Robotics Institute at Carnegie Mellon University. In the eighties, he'd left physics and started a software company. Within a decade he was worth several hundred million dollars. When David had interviewed Gupta, it had been a struggle. All Gupta wanted to talk about was robots.

David satisfied himself that there was no terrible news yet about Gupta. Keith came to the table holding a mug of coffee in each hand.

'Here you go,' he said to David. 'You want milk or sugar?'

David took the mug gratefully. 'No, no, black is fine.'

Keith handed the other mug to Monique. 'Listen, Mo, I'll head upstairs. I gotta be at the shop at eight.' He leaned close. 'You gonna be all right?'

She kissed his cheek. 'Yeah, baby. Go get some rest.'

David gulped down his coffee. Easy to see she was fond of the hunk. And at that moment she seemed just as young. Her face had hardly changed since the last time David saw her. He turned back to the laptop. There was one more name to check. He typed 'Alastair MacDonald' into the search engine.

MacDonald was the unluckiest of Einstein's assistants. In 1958, he suffered a nervous breakdown and went home to Scotland, but he never recovered; a few years later, his family had him committed to an asylum. When David visited him there in 1995, he just sat and stared straight ahead.

A long list of results came up on the screen, but they turned out to be different Alastair MacDonalds. David typed 'Holyrood Mental Institution' into the search engine next to the name.

Only one result came up, a news item in the *Glasgow Herald*, dated June 3, just nine days ago, and headed INQUIRY AT HOLYROOD.

> The Scottish Executive Health Department announced today that it would conduct an inquiry into a fatal accident at the Holyrood Mental Institution. Alastair MacDonald, 81, was found dead in the facility's hydrotherapy pool Monday morning. Officials said that MacDonald drowned sometime during the night. The department is seeking to determine if lapses in staff supervision contributed to the accident.

David shivered as he stared at the screen. MacDonald drowned in a therapy pool, Bouchet slit his wrists in a bathtub. And Detective Rodriguez had said the police found Kleinman in his bathroom. The three old physicists were linked not only by their history with Einstein, but by a horrible modus operandi. But what was the motive? The only clues were Kleinman's last words: *Einheitliche Feldtheorie.* Destroyer of worlds.

Monique read the item over his shoulder. 'Very strange,' she whispered.

David turned and looked her in the eye. It was time to present his hypothesis. 'What do you know about Einstein's papers on unified field theory?'

'Einstein's papers?' She shrugged. 'He was trying to come up with a classical theory with strict cause and effect and no quantum uncertainties. And none of his solutions held up. His last papers were nonsense.'

David shook his head. 'Einstein discovered a working solution. He just didn't publish it.'

She cocked her head and gave him a quizzical look. 'Oh, really? Did someone send you a long-lost manuscript?'

'No, that's what Kleinman told me before he died. He said, "*Herr Doktor* succeeded"—those were his exact words. And that's why he was killed tonight, why all of them were killed.'

Monique's face turned serious. 'Look, David, I understand you're upset, but there's no way Einstein could have formulated a unified theory. All he knew about were gravity and electromagnetism. Physicists didn't understand the weak nuclear force until the sixties and they didn't figure out the strong force until ten years later. So how could Einstein come up with a theory of everything if he didn't understand two of the four fundamental forces? It's like building a jigsaw puzzle with half the pieces.'

'But he wouldn't have to know all the details to construct a general theory. It's more like a crossword puzzle than a jigsaw. As long as you have enough clues, you can figure out the pattern.'

'Well, if he came up with a valid theory, why didn't he publish it?'

'All this was happening just a few years after Hiroshima. Einstein knew his equations had made the atom bomb possible. It was agonising for him. I think he foresaw that a unified theory could be used for military purposes. Maybe something even worse than a nuclear bomb.'

'What do you mean? What could be worse?'

'I don't know. Something so terrible that he couldn't publish the theory. But he couldn't just erase it. So he entrusted it to his assistants. He probably gave each of them one little piece of it. He actually thought that in a few years the Americans and Russians would lay down their arms and form a world government, and his assistants just had to wait until that day before revealing the theory.' David's eyes began to sting. 'They waited their whole lives.'

Monique gave him a sympathetic look, but she clearly didn't believe a word of what he was saying. 'David, it's an extraordinary hypothesis. And extraordinary claims require extraordinary proof.'

David steeled himself. 'Kleinman told me a series of numbers tonight, a key he said Einstein had given him. The proof is what happened afterwards.'

Then he told her about his FBI interrogation and the massacre that followed. At first she just stared, incredulous, but by the time he finished, Monique seemed just as shell-shocked as he had been.

She grabbed his shoulder. 'Who attacked the place? Terrorists?'

'I don't know; I never saw them. But I bet they killed Kleinman and Bouchet and MacDonald. Maybe one of them let something slip. So the terrorists went after them, tortured them for information. But after they started turning up dead, the American intelligence agencies must have figured out something was going on. That's why the FBI agents showed up so quickly at the hospital. They probably had Kleinman under surveillance.'

Monique let go of his shoulder. 'Maybe you're right about the killings; maybe the terrorists went after Kleinman and the others because of some secret project they were all working on. But I can't believe the project was Einstein's unified field theory. It's too implausible.'

David turned away from Monique, wondering how to convince her. As he stared at the kitchen walls, a thought occurred to him.

'Look around,' he said, pointing at the walls and cabinets. 'Look at this kitchen. There's no damage here, no graffiti. Why would a bunch of New Jersey skinheads trash every room in this house except the kitchen?'

'What does this have to do with—?'

'There weren't any skinheads, Monique. Somebody tore this place apart to look for Einstein's notebooks. They searched under the floorboards and poked through the plaster to check the spaces between the walls. And they put swastikas everywhere to make it look like vandalism. They didn't touch the kitchen because it was added to the house long after Einstein died.'

Monique raised her long slender fingers to her mouth.

'I'd guess the FBI did the search,' David continued. 'I'd also guess they didn't find any notebooks.'

Monique's eyes narrowed and a deep crease appeared between her eyebrows. She was clearly livid. Neo-Nazi skinheads were bad enough, but federal agents spray-painting swastikas? That was another class of evil entirely.

She lowered her hand. 'What were Kleinman's numbers?'

David wrote the numbers in pencil on a sheet of notebook paper.

4 0   2 6   3 6   7 9   5 6   4 4   7 8 0 0

He passed the paper to Monique and she scrutinised the numbers.

'The distribution looks nonrandom,' she noted. 'Three zeroes, three fours and three sixes, but only a single pair of sevens. In a sequence of this size, it's improbable to have more triplets than pairs.'

'Could it be a key for decrypting a computer file?'

'The size is right. Sixteen digits, and each can be transformed to four bits of digital code. That would make sixty-four bits, the standard length for an encryption cipher. But with a nonrandom sequence, you could break the code too easily.' Monique brought the paper a little closer to her face. 'You wrote this in an odd way. The numbers are paired up except at the end.'

He took the paper from her. 'Huh,' he grunted. 'Kleinman's lungs were failing, so the numbers came out in gasps, and that's the way I see the sequence in my memory. Two-digit numbers and four digits at the end.'

'But is it possible Kleinman wanted the numbers that way?' Monique took the paper and drew lines between the blocks. 'Five of the two-digit numbers are between twenty-five and sixty; that's a fairly tight grouping.'

The numbers still looked pretty random to David. But then he saw it, clear as day. 'Minutes and seconds,' he said. 'That's why they're below sixty.'

'What? You're saying this is some kind of time measurement?'

'No, not time. These are spatial dimensions. Geographic coordinates, latitude and longitude. The first two-digit number is angular degrees, the second is arc minutes, and the third is arc seconds.'

Monique stared at him for a moment; then her face broke into a smile. 'All right, Dr Swift,' she said. 'It's worth a shot.'

She went to her laptop, found Google Earth and typed in the numbers. 'I'm assuming the latitude is forty degrees north, otherwise you'd be in the Pacific Ocean. For longitude, I'm assuming seventy-nine degrees west.'

David stood beside her so he could see the screen. The first image that came up was a grainy satellite photo. At the top was a large building shaped like an H. Below was a row of smaller buildings next to a long rectangular yard crisscrossed by walkways. A college campus, David thought.

'Where is this place?'

'Hold on, I'll call up the street map.' Monique clicked on an icon that put labels on each of the buildings and streets. 'It's in Pittsburgh. The coordinates are centred on 5000 Forbes Avenue. Newell-Simon Hall.'

David recognised the name. He'd visited the building once before. 'That's the Robotics Institute at Carnegie Mellon. Where Amil Gupta is.'

Monique found the institute's website and clicked on the list of faculty members. 'Gupta's the director, right? The extension for the director's office is 7800.' She beamed in triumph. 'The last four digits in the sequence!'

David stared at the screen. 'This can't be the right message.'

'What are you talking about? Kleinman was telling you to go to Gupta to safeguard the theory. It's obvious!'

'That's the problem. It's too obvious. Everyone knows that Gupta worked with Einstein. There's a whole chapter about it in my book. So why go to all this trouble of devising this complicated code if that's the only thing he wanted to say? There's got to be something else hidden in the numbers.'

'Well, there's only one way to find out. Talk to Gupta.'

'We can't call him. I'm sure the feds have tapped his phone.'

Monique turned off her laptop and closed it. 'Then we go to Pittsburgh.'

'Are you crazy? We can't just show up at Gupta's house. The FBI probably has the place under surveillance.'

She zipped the laptop into a carrying case and headed out of the kitchen. 'We're two smart people, David. We'll figure out a way.'

He followed her into the living room. 'Wait a second. The police are already hunting for me. It was a miracle I even got out of New York.'

She picked up the revolver from where she had left it on the mantelpiece. 'No, I'm gonna get to the bottom of this. Those guys broke into my house—*my house!*—and sprayed swastikas on my walls.'

David sighed. 'That gun won't do you any good. They've got hundreds of agents and thousands of cops. You can't just shoot your way through.'

'Don't worry, I'm not planning to start any gunfights. We're going to be sneaky, not stupid. The FBI won't be looking for my car, so just keep your face hidden and we'll be all right. Now I'm going to get some clothes. You want me to get you a razor from Keith's shaving kit?'

He nodded. He couldn't argue with her any more. She was like an unstoppable force of nature. 'What are you going to tell Keith?'

'I'll leave him a note, tell him we had to go to a conference or something.' She went to the foyer and started climbing the staircase. 'He's got three other girlfriends he can spend time with. The boy's got stamina.'

He nodded again. So her relationship with Keith wasn't that serious. David found, to his surprise, that he was quite pleased by this fact.

CHAPTER FIVE

Karen paced inside an interrogation room at the FBI offices in Federal Plaza. First she walked past the locked steel door. Then she passed a mirror that ran almost the whole length of the wall. Chairs surrounded a metal table in the centre of the room, but Karen was too agitated to sit. Instead she circled the room, dizzy with fear and outrage and fatigue. The agents had taken Jonah away from her.

At 5 a.m. she heard footsteps in the corridor. A key turned in the lock, and the agent who'd arrested her stepped into the room. Karen remembered his name: Agent Brock. Tall, blond and muscle-bound, he still wore that ugly grey jacket with the shoulder holster bulging underneath.

'Where's my son?' Karen demanded. 'I want to see my son!'

Brock had cold blue eyes. 'Whoa, slow down! Your son's all right. He's asleep in one of the rooms down the hall.'

Karen didn't believe it. 'Take me there. I need to see him right now.' She tried to move round him to get to the door.

He sidestepped in front of her. 'I need to ask you a few questions first.'

'Look, I'm a lawyer. I may not practise criminal law, but I know this is illegal. You can't hold us here without charges.'

Brock grimaced. 'We can file charges if that's what you want. How about criminal child neglect? Does that sound legal enough for you?'

'What are you talking about?'

'I'm talking about your ex-husband's drug habit. And how he financed it by selling cocaine to his students at Columbia. He did most of his dealing in Central Park after he picked up your son from school.'

Karen stared at him. 'That's insane! The worst thing they do in the park is play with Super Soakers.'

'We have surveillance videos showing the transactions. The Family Court will want to find out whether you were involved too. They may decide to take custody of your son until they've investigated the matter.'

Karen was sure he was bluffing. 'OK, prove it.'

'You'll see it on the news tonight. Your ex-husband started working with the Latin Kings, the gang that controls the drug trade in Upper Manhattan. Last night they shot three agents who were doing an undercover buy from Swift and another three on the surveillance team.'

Karen let out a disgusted snort. The story was absurd. Anyone who knew David would recognise that immediately. But why had the FBI concocted it? She sat down in one of the chairs. 'All right, Agent Brock, for the moment I'll take your word for it. What do you want from me?'

He pulled a notebook out of his jacket. 'We need information on your ex-husband's contacts in New Jersey. Swift is a fugitive now and looking for a friend to help him out. A very close friend, if you know what I mean. Does he have any friends like that in New Jersey?'

How pathetic, she thought, trying to play on her jealousy. 'I have no idea.'

'Come on. You don't know anything about his love life?'

'Why should I care? We're not married any more.'

Brock stood in front of Karen's chair and leaned over, bringing his face within inches of hers. 'You're not being very cooperative. If we don't give the Family Court a favourable report, they may assign your son to foster care.'

Karen got to her feet, brushed past Brock and headed straight for the mirror. She tried to peer through the glass but all she could see was her own reflection. 'OK,' she said to the mirror. 'Amory van Cleve. Does the name ring a bell? He knows half the lawyers in the Justice Department, and he's not going to be pleased when I tell him what you've been doing to me.'

Brock was coming towards her. 'No one's there, Karen.'

'Get this idiot out of my sight!' Karen shouted. 'Amory's gonna talk to his friends at Justice and make sure all of you go to jail!'

For about five seconds the room was silent. Then the door opened and an older woman in a white blouse and reading glasses stepped in. 'Are you all right, honey?' she drawled. 'I heard some shouting and I thought—'

Karen spun round. 'Don't even start!' she yelled. 'Take me to my son!'

DAVID AWOKE in the low-slung passenger seat of Monique's Corvette. Groggy and disorientated, he gazed out of the windshield. The car was travelling on an interstate through a lush, hilly landscape. He felt a dull ache in his lower back, no doubt caused by all his running the night before, and remembered why he was speeding across the country.

He shifted in the uncomfortable seat. Monique had one hand on the wheel and the other was rummaging inside a box of cookies. Before she'd left she'd changed into a white blouse and khaki shorts. David watched her from the corner of his eye, staring at her gorgeous neck and long thighs. After a while, though, he began to feel like a voyeur, so he yawned to get her attention.

Monique turned to him. 'Finally!' she said. 'You've been out for three hours.' She offered him the box. 'Want breakfast?'

'Sure, thanks.' David stuffed a cookie into his mouth. 'Where are we?'

'Western Pennsylvania. Less than an hour from Pittsburgh.'

He saw the read-out on the dashboard clock: 8.47. 'You're making good time.' He pulled two more cookies out of the box, then looked at Monique again. 'Hey, you must be exhausted. You want me to drive for a while?'

'No, I'm fine,' she said quickly. 'I'm not tired.' She clearly didn't like the idea of him driving her Corvette.

'Are you sure?' he asked.

'Yeah, I like long drives. I do some of my best thinking when I'm on the road. I came up with the idea for my latest paper driving down to DC.'

That's where she's from, he remembered. Where her father was murdered and her mother became a heroin addict. David wanted to ask whether she still had family there, but he didn't. 'So what were you thinking about just now?' he asked instead. 'Before I woke up, I mean.'

'Hidden variables. Something you're probably familiar with.'

David put down the cookie box. Hidden variables were an important part of Einstein's quest for a unified theory. In the thirties, he became convinced that there was an underlying order to the strange quantum behaviour of subatomic particles. The microscopic world looked chaotic only because no one could see the hidden variables, the detailed blueprints of the universe.

Monique frowned. 'I can't picture it. Quantum theory just won't fit into a classical framework. It's like trying to shove a square peg into a round hole.'

'Well, Einstein always compared quantum mechanics to a game of dice.' David remembered a paragraph from *On the Shoulders of Giants*. 'When you throw a pair of dice, the numbers look random, but they aren't. If you had perfect control over all the hidden variables—how hard you throw the dice, the angle of their trajectory, the air pressure in the room—you could throw sevens every time. And Einstein thought the same was true of elementary particles. You could understand them perfectly if you found the hidden variables connecting quantum mechanics to a classical theory.'

Monique shook her head. 'It sounds good in principle, but believe me, it's not so simple.' She stared at the road ahead. David could tell she was still thinking over the problem. It occurred to him that she might have more than one reason for going to Pittsburgh. He'd assumed that her chief motivation was anger towards the FBI agents who'd invaded her home, but now he began to suspect that something else was driving her. She wanted to know the theory of everything. Even if she couldn't tell another living soul.

And David wanted to know it too. A memory from the night before came back to him. 'Professor Kleinman mentioned something else last night. The paper I did in graduate school, on relativity in two-dimensional spacetime.'

'The one you cowrote with Kleinman?'

'Yeah. He said I'd come close to the truth. We were looking at Flatland—the hypothetical universe with just two spatial dimensions—and we found that two-dimensional masses do not exert a gravitational pull on each other, but they do change the shape of the space around themselves. We also formulated a model for a two-dimensional black hole.'

She gave him a puzzled look. 'How did you manage that?'

'We created a scenario where two particles collided to form the hole. I don't remember all the details. But there's a copy of the paper on the web.'

Monique thought about it, tapping her fingers on the steering wheel. 'Interesting. Classical theory is normally so beautiful and smooth, but black holes are the big exception. Their physics is funky as hell.'

She lapsed into silence as they barrelled down the Pennsylvania Turnpike. David saw a road sign, PITTSBURGH, 37 MILES, and felt a spike of anxiety. Instead of pondering the possible outlines of Einstein's unified theory, they should be figuring out a way to reach Amil Gupta. And even if they did, what could they do next? The task was too enormous to contemplate.

After a while, Monique turned to him. David thought she was going to ask another question about his paper, but instead she said, in a determinedly matter-of-fact tone, 'So you're married now, right?'

'What gave you that idea?'

'I read your book. I saw it was dedicated to someone named Karen.'

'Karen and I got divorced two years ago.'

'Does she know what happened to you last night?'

'No. I can't call her because the FBI will trace it.' His anxiety spiked again. 'I hope those agents don't start harassing them.'

'Them?'

'We have a seven-year-old son. His name is Jonah.'

Monique smiled. 'That's wonderful. What's he like?'

'Well, he loves science. He also loves baseball and Pokémon, and you should have seen him in the park yesterday with that Super—'

Then she glanced at him and her smile died. 'What's wrong?'

He took a breath. 'How the hell are we gonna get through this?'

She reached over to pat his knee. 'Let's take it one step at a time. First we talk to Gupta.' She pointed at another road sign: NEW STANTON SERVICE AREA, 2 MILES AHEAD. 'We better stop; we're almost out of gas.'

David kept an eye out for state troopers as they coasted into the service area. No patrol cars in front of the Shell station, thank God. Monique filled the Corvette's tank. Then she drove to the parking lot, past a concrete building containing a Burger King and a Starbucks.

'I hate to be difficult, but I need to pee,' she said. 'What about you?'

'I'll stay in the car,' he said. A trooper might be stationed inside.

She parked in a vacant corner of the lot, and he handed her a couple of twenty-dollar bills. 'Could you pick up a few things while you're in there? Some sandwiches, some water, maybe some chips?'

'You mean you're getting tired of cookies?' She smiled as she opened the door, and headed for the rest rooms.

Once she was gone, David realised that he did need to urinate pretty badly. He stepped out of the car and walked to a stand of trees about fifty feet away. The only person in sight was an old man walking his dachshund. David stepped behind the biggest tree, and unzipped his fly. But as he headed back to the Corvette, the dog walker shouted, 'Hey, you!' David froze.

The man came close, and thrust a rolled-up newspaper at David's chest. 'I saw what you did!' he scolded. 'Don't you know they have bathrooms here?'

Amused, David said, 'Look, I'm sorry. It was an emergency.'

'It's disgusting! You should be—' The old man stopped abruptly and stared at David, then glanced at the newspaper in his hand. Some of the colour drained out of his face. Then he spun round and started running away.

At that same moment David heard Monique yell, 'Get back here!' As he jogged towards the Corvette, she started the engine. 'Come on, get in!'

As soon as David slipped into the passenger seat, the Corvette took off. Within seconds they were on the entrance ramp to the turnpike. 'Why'd you have to talk to that geezer?' she yelled.

David was shaking. The old man had recognised him.

The speedometer rose to ninety. 'The next exit better be close,' Monique said. 'We have to get off before that guy calls the cops.'

She reached into the bulky plastic bag that sat between them and pulled out the *Pittsburgh Post-Gazette.* 'I saw this in the newsstand next to Starbucks.' She handed him the paper.

The front-page headline read SIX AGENTS KILLED IN NEW YORK DRUG RAID, and below that, 'Police Seeking Columbia Professor'. Above the headline was the photograph from the back flap of *On the Shoulders of Giants.*

SIMON GAZED at the tranquil Delaware River from Washington Crossing State Park in New Jersey. He stood in a deserted parking lot, leaning against the side of a bright yellow Ferrari.

He'd taken the car—a 575 Maranello coupé—from the Princeton Auto Shop. Keith, the car mechanic he'd found at Monique Reynolds's house, had told him where to find the keys. This was helpful, considering Simon had been forced to abandon his Mercedes after the Princeton police failed to catch him for speeding. It would have been even more helpful if Keith had revealed where Swift and Reynolds had gone, but he insisted he didn't know, even after Simon cut off three of his fingers and sliced his bowels open.

Simon shook his head. All he had to go on now was a note that Monique had left on the kitchen counter. He pulled the folded sheet of paper out of his pocket and studied it again, but it offered no clues.

Keith: I'm so sorry about this, but David and I had to rush off. He has some important results we need to evaluate. I'll call you when I get back.

Simon put the note back into his pocket and checked his watch: 9.25. Nearly time for his daily chat with his client. Every morning, at exactly 9.30, Henry Cobb called him to get an update on the mission. 'Henry Cobb' was almost certainly an alias. Simon had never met the man, but, judging from his accent, his real name was more likely Abdul or Muhammad. But one thing was clear: whatever the nationality of Henry's organisation, they had significant resources. To prepare Simon for the mission, Henry had sent him a whole crate of textbooks on particle physics and general relativity. More important, he'd wired $200,000 to cover expenses and promised a million when the job was finished.

The ironic thing was that Simon would have gladly done the work for free if he'd known what it was all about. He hadn't perceived the full extent of Henry's ambitions until a week ago, when he'd visited the Provençal home of Jacques Bouchet and confronted the French physicist while he was in the bathtub. After a brief, watery struggle the old man started talking. Unfortunately, he knew only a few pieces of the *Einheitliche Feldtheorie*, but told Simon quite a lot about the possible consequences of misusing the equations, obviously expecting him to be horrified, but instead Simon was exultant. Feeling a surge of triumph, he slit the physicist's wrists and watched the clouds of blood billow in the bath water.

At precisely 9.30, Simon's cellphone rang. Simon raised the device to his ear. 'Hello, this is George Osmond,' he said. His own alias.

'Good morning, George. Tell me, how was the game last night?' The slow, careful voice with the Middle Eastern accent.

'A little disappointing,' Simon said. 'Scoreless, actually.'

A long pause. 'What about the pitcher?'

'Out for the season, I'm afraid. Interference from the Yankees. They tried to turn it into another drug scandal. You can read about it in today's papers.'

This time the silence stretched for nearly half a minute. 'I'm not happy about this,' Henry finally said. 'How will we win without the pitcher?'

'Don't worry, I have another prospect. A younger man, a college player, very promising. He worked closely with the pitcher. I came close to contacting him last night but he left town suddenly.'

Henry let out a dissatisfied grunt. 'This is unacceptable,' he said. 'I'm paying you a good salary and I expect better results than this.'

Simon felt a twinge of irritation. 'Calm down. You'll get your money's worth. I know someone with the Yankees who can help me find this player.'

'With the Yankees?' his client muttered. 'You have a friend there?'

'Strictly a business relationship. As soon as the Yankees know where he is, this guy will pass the information to me.'

'For a fee, I assume?'

'Naturally. And I'm going to need a budget increase to cover it.'

'Money isn't a problem. But are you sure you can trust this man?'

'I've scheduled a meeting to assess his intentions. I'll keep you informed.'

Simon closed the phone and put it back in his pocket. He hated dealing with clients. It was by far the most disagreeable part of his job. But he wouldn't have to do it much longer. If everything went according to plan, this mission would be his last.

As he turned back to the Delaware River, Simon heard the whine of an SUV. He looked over his shoulder and saw a black Suburban turn in to the parking lot. It parked at the other end of the lot, and a man in a grey suit stepped out and started walking across the asphalt.

The agent stopped a few metres from the Ferrari. 'Nice ride,' he said. 'Must have cost you a bundle.'

Simon shrugged. 'Just a tool of the trade.'

'I wouldn't mind getting a tool like that for myself.'

'That may be possible. My offer still stands. Thirty thousand now, another thirty if your information leads to capture.'

'Well, I guess this is my lucky day. I just got a transmission from headquarters while I was driving down here.' He folded his arms across his chest. 'You got the money on you?'

Keeping his eyes on the agent, Simon reached one hand into the Ferrari to pick up the briefcase that had been resting on the passenger seat. 'The first payment's in here. In twenty-dollar bills.'

The agent eyed the briefcase greedily. 'We got a report that a citizen spotted Swift an hour ago. At a rest stop on the Pennsylvania Turnpike.'

Simon glanced at the Pennsylvania side of the river. 'Which rest stop?'

'New Stanton Service Area, thirty miles east of Pittsburgh. The state police put up roadblocks but they haven't found him yet.'

Simon handed over the briefcase. 'I'll be in touch about the second payment. Expect a call within twelve hours, Mr Brock.'

FROM HIS VANTAGE POINT a hundred yards away, David gazed at Newell-Simon Hall, trying to remember the location of Amil Gupta's office. He and Monique were in the neighbouring arts centre, crouched inside an empty classroom apparently used for a course in theatre set design; scattered among the desks were wooden boards painted to look like trees, houses, cars and storefronts. A panel showing the front of a barber shop, with the words SWEENEY TODD running across the top, stood next to the window.

It was almost noon. They'd spent more than an hour navigating the backstreets of the Pittsburgh suburbs to get to Carnegie Mellon. Monique parked in the university's main lot, and they made their way across campus to the arts centre, which sat on a rise above Newell-Simon Hall, and offered an excellent view of the parking lot between the two buildings.

The first thing David noticed was the Highlander robotic vehicle, a custom-designed Hummer with a big silver orb mounted on its roof. He'd read about it in *Scientific American*. One of Gupta's pet projects, the Highlander could travel hundreds of miles without a driver. A couple of students from the Robotics Institute were testing the vehicle, watching it autonomously navigate the parking lot. The orb on the car's roof contained a laser scanner that detected obstacles in its path. One of the students held a radio control box that could shut off the engine if the robot car went haywire.

The second thing David noticed was the black Suburbans. Two were parked near the entrance to Newell-Simon, and another two were at the back of the lot. He pointed them out to Monique. 'Those are government cars.' Next he pointed at a pair of men in T-shirts and shorts. 'Check out those guys with the football. Why play catch in a parking lot?'

'They look a little too old to be students,' Monique noted.

'Exactly. And the bare-chested guy lying on the grass has to be the palest sunbather I've ever seen.'

'There are two more on the other side of the building.'

David shook his head. 'It's my own fault. They beefed up surveillance once they found out we were on the turnpike.' He slumped against the wall.

Monique leaned next to him. 'Well, the next step is obvious. You stay here and I'll go in. They're not looking for me.'

'What? What if the guy at the rest stop saw your licence plate?'

'That geezer? He was running for his life. He didn't see a thing.'

David frowned. 'It's too risky. Those agents are eyeballing everyone who comes near that building. They've already been to your house, remember?'

'I know it's risky. You have a better idea?'

He looked around the room for inspiration. 'There are probably some costumes around here. What if you—?'

Before David could finish, he heard a rumbling in the hallway outside the classroom. He grabbed Monique and pulled her behind the Sweeney Todd panel. They heard the jangling of keys. David was certain that FBI agents would storm into the classroom. But when the door opened he saw only a cleaning lady, a woman in a blue smock pushing a large canvas waste cart.

Peeking round the edge of the scenery, David watched the cleaning woman pick up a trash can and pour its contents into the cart. She was a tall, young black woman and David realised that she and Monique looked very much alike. They had the same long legs, the same defiant tilt of the head. Just as she reached the door, he came out of hiding.

'Excuse me?' he said to the cleaning woman's back.

She whirled round. 'What the . . . ?'

'Sorry to startle you. My colleague and I were putting the final touches on the set for tonight's show.' He nudged Monique forward. 'This is Professor Gladwell, and I'm Professor Hodges. Of the drama department.'

The woman regarded them angrily. 'You scared the hell out of me! I thought this room was empty till one o'clock.'

David smiled. 'Usually it is, but we're doing some last-minute work.'

'Well, what do you want? You got something to throw out?'

'Actually, I was wondering about that smock you're wearing. Is there any chance we can borrow it for a few hours?'

'This thing?' She glanced down at her smock. 'What do you want it for?'

'One of the characters in our show is a cleaning lady, but I'm not happy with the costume. I just need to copy your uniform.'

The woman narrowed her eyes. 'Look, I gotta wear this while I'm working. It's a long walk back to janitorial supplies to get another one.'

'I'm willing to compensate you for the inconvenience.' David reached into his pocket and peeled off ten twenties.

She stared at the $200 in his hand. Warily, she began to take off the smock. 'Just don't tell anyone in Building Services, all right?'

'I won't say a word. And we're going to need your cart.'

She gave the smock to David. 'I don't care about the cart. There's one in the basement.' She whisked the $200 out of his hand and left the room.

David locked the door and turned to Monique. She stared grimly at the uniform. 'A cleaning woman. How original. Black women clean offices, so those agents won't give me a second look, right?'

'Hey, I'm sorry. I just thought—'

'No, you're right. That's the sad thing about it.' She grabbed the smock from David and started putting it on. 'It doesn't matter how many degrees you earn or papers you publish. In their eyes I'm just a cleaning woman.' Monique bit her lip. 'Now get in there.' She pointed at the load of trash inside the canvas cart. 'You can lie on the bottom and I'll pile the garbage on top of you. Then both of us can get inside the building to see Gupta.'

LUCILLE PARKER sat in one of the passenger seats of the C-21, the air force's version of the Learjet, as it streaked over western Pennsylvania. She looked out of the window and saw the city of Pittsburgh up ahead, a grey block straddling the Monongahela River.

The call from the Bureau director came as the plane began its descent. Lucille picked up the radio handset. 'Black One here.'

'Hello, Lucy,' the director said. 'What's going on?'

'I'm about ten minutes from Pittsburgh International. We have ten agents surrounding Gupta's building and another ten inside. Video cameras in all the entrances, and listening devices on all the floors.'

'Maybe we should just grab Gupta now and see what he knows.'

'No, if we detain Gupta now, Swift won't come near the place. But if we keep our heads low, we can nab both of them.'

'All right, I'm counting on you, Lucy. I'm getting tired of fielding calls from the secretary of defence. Is there anything else you need?'

Lucille hesitated. This was going to be tricky. 'I need personnel files for every agent in the New York region.'

'Why?'

'The more I think about what happened at Liberty Street, the more I'm convinced there's been a breach. The attackers knew too much about our operations. I think they had help from inside.'

The director sighed again. 'Jesus. Just what we need.'

IT WAS DARK and uncomfortable, and smelt worse than David had expected. Someone had thrown the remains of a breakfast burrito into the garbage piled on top of him. And the edge of a wooden board dug into his shoulder blades as Monique pushed the cart out of the Purnell Arts Center down the path towards Newell-Simon Hall.

After his eyes adjusted to the dark, David noticed a small tear in the canvas lining. He wriggled forward and peered through the opening. They were in the parking lot now; in a few more seconds they'd be inside the building. David held his breath until they passed through Newell-Simon's service entrance. Monique steered to the freight elevator and pushed the cart inside.

They arrived on the fourth floor, rolled down a corridor and came to the reception area for Amil Gupta's office, which David recognised from his last visit to the Robotics Institute. A sleek black desk crowded with computer monitors stood in the centre of the room, but the receptionist was no longer a tall blonde, but a very young man, eighteen years old at the most.

The kid was staring at a computer screen and madly manipulating a joystick. He was most likely a computer geek working his way through college. He had a pudgy face, with olive skin and thick black eyebrows.

'Excuse me?' Monique said. 'I'm here to clean Dr Gupta's office.'

The boy's eyes stayed on whatever game he was playing.

'Excuse me? I'm going into his office, all right?'

Still no response. The boy's mouth hung open as he stared at the screen. There was no emotion on his face, just a steady concentration. It occurred to David that there might be something wrong with him.

Monique gave up and headed for the door behind the desk. She grasped the knob but it didn't turn. She turned back. 'You gotta unlock the door.'

The boy didn't answer, but David heard a loud whirring start up. Monique looked bewildered as a boxy silver machine, about the size of a suitcase, rolled towards her on caterpillar treads. It stopped at her feet, extended a robotic arm and pointed a bulb-shaped sensor at her.

The machine looked a bit like a tortoise with a very long neck. A synthesised voice came out of its speakers: 'Good morning! I'm the AR-21 Autonomous Receptionist. Can I help you?'

Monique glanced at the teenager, wondering if he was playing a joke.

The machine reorientated its sensor so that it tracked her face. 'Please tell me what you want and I will attempt to help you.'

With obvious reluctance, she looked into its bulbous sensor. 'I'm the cleaning woman. Unlock the door.'

'I'm sorry,' the AR-21 replied. 'I didn't understand. Did you say, "Curriculum brochure"? Please answer yes or no.'

For a moment David thought she was going to kick the thing. 'I need . . . to get into . . . Dr Gupta's . . . office.'

'Professor Amil Gupta is the director of the Robotics Institute. Would you like to schedule an appointment? Answer yes or no.'

Raising her hands in surrender, Monique stomped back to the cart and pushed it out of the room. They moved rapidly down the corridor to a supply room and she manoeuvred it inside.

As soon as the door closed, she swept aside the crumpled papers and dirty rags that covered David's head and shoulders. He looked up at her exasperated face; then he cautiously raised his head and surveyed the room.

The walls were lined with metal shelves holding janitorial and office supplies. In the corner was a large stainless-steel sink. No sign of surveillance cameras. Listening devices were a different matter, though, and without a word he clambered out of the cart, went to the sink, and turned on the water. He pulled Monique close and whispered in her ear, 'You have to go back to the reception room and get the kid's attention.'

'It's not gonna work. He looks like he's handicapped or something. Is there another way into Gupta's office?'

'I don't know. I haven't been here in years. I can't remember what—'

Something suddenly bumped into the back of David's heel. He looked down and saw a blue disc, about the size of a Frisbee. It was moving slowly across the supply room, leaving a wet, zigzagging trail on the linoleum.

Monique saw it too, and let out a startled cry. David clapped his hand over her mouth. 'It's just a floor-cleaning robot,' he whispered.

'Someone should put that thing out of its misery.'

David stared at the device as it crawled away. It looked like an oversized insect, with a spindly black antenna rising from its rim. Gupta fitted all his robots with radio transmitters because he was obsessed with monitoring their progress. When David interviewed him ten years ago, the old man had proudly shown him a computer screen detailing the locations of all the autonomous machines wandering the corridors. The memory gave David an idea.

'If we can't get to Gupta, we'll get him to come to us,' he said, stepping towards the robot. He grasped the machine's antenna, and snapped it off.

The robot immediately let out a deafening, high-pitched alarm. 'What did you do?' Monique cried. 'Shut it off!'

David picked up the device and turned it over, frantically looking for a power switch, but there was nothing on the underside but dripping holes and spinning brushes. Giving up, he ran to the sink, and smashed the robot hard against the stainless-steel edge. The plastic shell broke in two, spilling cleaning fluid and circuit boards. The noise abruptly cut off.

Breathing hard, David turned to Monique and saw a queasy look on her face. It was clear what she was thinking. The FBI agents must have heard the alarm. One of them would come soon to investigate. For several seconds she just stood there, her eyes fixed on the door. David felt helpless. Their plan had collapsed. They couldn't save themselves, much less the world.

Then the door opened and Amil Gupta stepped inside.

'OK, TALK TO ME. What's our status?'

Lucille stood in a mobile command post that the Bureau had towed to the Carnegie Mellon campus that morning. From the outside it looked like an ordinary office trailer, but inside it held more electronics than a nuclear sub.

At one end was a bank of video screens displaying live images of the various offices, laboratories, elevators and corridors in Newell-Simon Hall. A pair of technicians sat facing the screens and wore headphones to monitor the listening devices. At the other end, two more technicians examined the digital traffic on the Robotics Institute's Internet connections. In the middle, Lucille was grilling Agent Crawford, her dutiful second-in-command.

'Gupta's been in his office since ten o'clock,' Crawford reported, reading off his BlackBerry screen. 'At eleven-oh-five, he went to the break room for coffee, returned at eleven-oh-nine. You see him now on screen number one.'

The screen showed Gupta at his desk, leaning back in his swivel chair and staring at his computer monitor. The man was small but spry, a five-foot-tall seventy-six-year-old with grey hair and a doll-like brown face. He wore a beautiful olive-green Italian suit no government employee could afford.

'What's on his computer?' Lucille asked.

'Software code, mostly,' Crawford replied. 'He downloaded a monster-size program as soon as he got into the office—in all likelihood, one of his artificial-intelligence programs. He's been making small changes to it for the past two hours. He's also gotten a dozen emails, but nothing unusual.'

'Any visitors come to his office?'

Agent Crawford glanced at his BlackBerry again. 'One of his students came into reception and made an appointment to see him next week. No other visitors except a Fed-Ex deliveryman and a cleaning woman.'

'Did you run them through the biometric data base?'

'We didn't see the need. None of the visitors fit the profile.'

Lucille frowned. 'I don't care if it's a ninety-nine-year-old biddy in a wheelchair. Get their images off the video and run 'em through the system.'

He nodded rapidly. 'Yes, ma'am, right away. I'm sorry if—'

Before he could finish, one of the technicians let out a yelp and tore off his headphones. 'Some kind of alarm went off on the fourth floor.'

Lucille's scalp began to tingle. She turned to screen number one. 'Look, the old man's heading out of the office!'

Crawford leaned over the technician's shoulder. 'Switch to the camera in the reception room. Let's see where he's going.'

The technician pushed a button. Screen number one showed a homely teenage boy and a strange mechanical contraption.

'Where did he go?' Lucille asked. 'Is there another way out?'

Crawford started blinking wildly. 'Uh, I have to check the floor plan.'

'There's no time for that. Get some agents up there right now!'

David grabbed Professor Gupta and covered his mouth while Monique locked the door behind him. The old man was surprisingly light, hardly more than a hundred pounds, so it was easy to carry him to the corner of the supply room. He was nearly twice David's age and yet his delicate frame and unlined face gave him a childlike appearance.

'Dr Gupta?' David whispered. 'Do you remember me? I'm David Swift. I interviewed you once about your work with Dr Einstein, remember?'

The professor's eyes, jittery white marbles with dark brown centres, regarded David uncertainly for a second, then widened in recognition. His lips moved under David's hand. 'What are you—?'

'Please!' David hissed. 'Don't speak above a whisper.'

'Your offices are under surveillance,' Monique added, bending over David's shoulder. 'There may be listening devices in this room.'

Gupta was obviously terrified, but he nodded, acquiescing, and David removed his hand. 'Listening devices?' he whispered. 'Who's listening?'

'The FBI, for certain,' David replied. 'Maybe others. Some very dangerous people are looking for you, Professor. We have to get you out of here.'

Gupta shook his head, bewildered. Unruly grey hair fell across his forehead. 'Is this some kind of joke? David, I haven't seen you in years, and now you come in here with . . .' He pointed at Monique's uniform. 'Who are you?'

'Monique Reynolds, of the Institute for Advanced Study.'

He looked at her. 'The string theorist?' When she nodded, he gave a weak smile. 'I'm familiar with your work. But why are you dressed like that?'

David was getting impatient. 'We have to get going. Professor, I'm going to help you into the waste cart and then—'

'The waste cart?'

'Please just come with us. There's no time to explain.'

David gripped Gupta's arm but the old man jerked out of his grasp. 'I'm not going anywhere until you tell me what's going on.'

David gazed at the ceiling for a moment, trying to tamp his fears and clear his head. Then he looked Gupta in the eye. '*Einheitliche Feldtheorie*,' he whispered. 'That's what they want.'

The German words had a delayed effect on Gupta. At first he simply lifted his eyebrows in mild surprise, but after a few seconds his face went slack. He fell back against the wall and stared blankly at the shelves.

David leaned over the old man and continued whispering. 'Someone's trying to piece the theory together. Maybe they're terrorists, maybe spies. First they went after MacDonald, then Bouchet and Kleinman.' He paused.

'I'm sorry, Professor. All three of them are dead. You're the only one left.'

Gupta looked up at him. 'Kleinman? He's dead?'

David nodded. 'I saw him in the hospital. He'd been tortured.'

'No, no, no . . .' Gupta clutched his stomach and groaned.

Monique put her arm round him. 'Shhh-shhh,' she whispered.

David imagined agents racing up the stairways. He pressed on. 'The government figured out what was going on. That's why the FBI put you under surveillance and why they've been chasing me for sixteen hours.'

Gupta's face was shiny with sweat. 'How do you know this?'

'Before Kleinman died, he gave me a sequence of numbers. It turned out to be the geographic coordinates of your office. I think he wanted me to safeguard the theory somehow.'

The professor stared at the floor. 'His worst nightmare,' he muttered. 'This was *Herr Doktor*'s worst nightmare.'

'What was he afraid of? Was it a weapon?'

Gupta shook his head. 'He never told me. He told the others, but not me.'

'What? What do you mean?'

The old man took a deep breath. 'Einstein was a man of conscience, David. In 1954 my wife was pregnant with our first child. The last thing *Herr Doktor* wanted to do was put me in danger, so he parcelled out the equations to the others. None of them was married, you see.'

David leaned closer. 'Wait a second,' he whispered. 'You're saying you don't know the unified theory? Not even part of it?'

'I don't know any of the equations or underlying principles. My colleagues swore they wouldn't tell a soul, and they kept their oath.'

'This doesn't make any sense,' David sputtered, feeling dizzy with dismay. 'Kleinman's code pointed to you. Why did he—?'

David stopped. He'd heard a quick metallic rattle, quiet but unmistakable, coming from the door. Someone was trying the knob.

AGENT CRAWFORD HOVERED OVER the video console, murmuring instructions through his radio headset. Lucille stood behind him. On the monitor she saw Agents Walsh and Miller march into Gupta's reception room. The teenage boy was still sitting at the desk.

Walsh approached the teenager. 'You have to get Professor Gupta!' he shouted. 'There's a fire in the computer lab!'

The boy didn't look up. He just stared at the large flat-panel screen on his desk. Lucille got a glimpse of some kind of computer game.

Agent Walsh leaned across the desk and got in the boy's face. 'Are you deaf? This is an emergency! Where's Professor Gupta?'

The teenager simply tilted his head and continued playing his game. Meanwhile, Agent Miller went to the door to Gupta's office. 'It's locked,' he said. 'See if there's a buzzer on the desk.'

As Walsh shoved the boy's chair aside to examine the desktop, his hand hit the keyboard and the screen went blank. The teenager leapt out of his chair and began to scream, flapping his hands as if they were burning.

Lucille stared at the monitor. She'd seen this kind of behaviour before. The boy's autistic, she thought. She grabbed the radio headset from Crawford. 'Forget the boy,' she yelled into the microphone. 'Just get the door open!'

Walsh and Miller opened their backpacks and removed the breaching equipment. Walsh positioned the forked end of a Halligan bar between the door and the jamb, and Miller swung a sledgehammer against the tool. After just three swings, they prised the door open and rushed into Gupta's office. Lucille saw them on another monitor, striding past the professor's desk.

'He's not here,' Walsh reported over the radio. 'But there's another door behind the bookshelves. Should we proceed in that direction?'

'Hell, yes!' Lucille bellowed.

Beside her, Crawford flipped through floor maps of Newell-Simon Hall. 'That door isn't in the plans. It must be a recent renovation.'

Lucille looked at him with disgust. 'I want six more agents on the fourth floor, you hear? Every room has to be searched!'

While Crawford fumbled for his radio, one of the technicians came up with a print-out in his hand. 'Uh, Agent Parker?' he said.

'What now?'

'I did the data-base search you asked for, running the surveillance images through the face-recognition system. I think I found something.'

'HEY, ANYONE IN THERE?'

All three of them froze. David, Monique and Professor Gupta held their breath at the same time, and the only sound in the supply room came from the water still running in the sink.

Then there was an urgent pounding on the door, so violent it made the walls shiver. 'This is the fire department! Open up!'

Gupta pointed at the door and gave a questioning look. David shook his head. It definitely wasn't the fire department.

Now a clanking noise came from the corridor. Something heavy scraped against the door frame. Then a thunderous slam shook the room. In the narrow gap between the door and the jamb, a forked metal bar poked through.

Monique pulled her revolver from her shorts, and David didn't stop her, even though he knew they didn't have a chance in hell.

Luckily, Professor Gupta took control. He grasped Monique's arm, forcing her to lower the gun. 'You don't need that,' he whispered. 'I have a better idea.'

He reached into his jacket, pulled out a gadget that looked a bit like a BlackBerry and began stabbing the keyboard with his little thumbs. On the miniature screen was a layout of Newell-Simon Hall with flashing icons.

Another tremendous slam pummelled the door, but Gupta stayed bent over his tiny screen, his thumbs working furiously. The third slam was accompanied by a deep metallic groan, the sound of the steel buckling.

Then David heard a familiar whirring in the corridor, and the synthesised voice of the AR-21 Autonomous Receptionist: 'WARNING! Hazardous levels of radiation have been detected. Evacuate the area immediately.'

An alarm sounded from the public-address speakers and strobe lights on the ceiling began to flash. Gupta had obviously rewired the building's electrical systems so he could control them with his handheld device. Beneath the noise, David heard the FBI agents yelling, then a clatter as they dropped their breaching tools and the sound of footsteps racing for the exit.

Monique squeezed Gupta's shoulder. The old man smiled sheepishly. 'The warning was already in the program,' he explained. 'We originally developed this class of robots for the Defense Department. Reconnaissance in battlefield environments. The military version is called the Dragon Runner.'

'We better get going,' David said. 'The agents will be back in a few minutes with their Geiger counters.' He led the professor to the waste cart. 'It's not the most comfortable ride, but just lie still until we get past the surveillance cameras, OK? Then we'll just have to take our chances with the—'

'Those surveillance cameras?' Gupta interjected. 'They transmit their signals wirelessly, correct?'

'Uh, yeah, I suppose,' David answered.

Gupta smiled again. 'Then we can do something about it. Take me to room 407. The jamming equipment is in there. After that, my students will help us. But first we have to get Michael.'

'Michael?'

'He sits at my reception desk. He likes to play computer games there.'

David frowned. 'I'm sorry, Professor, but why do you—?'

'We can't leave him behind. He's my grandson.'

LUCILLE STUDIED the print-out. On the left was a camera image of a cleaning woman pushing a canvas cart into Amil Gupta's reception room. On the right was a page from the FBI's dossier on Monique Reynolds, professor of physics at Princeton's Institute for Advanced Study. The Bureau had assembled the dossier in advance of the undercover operation at her home on 112 Mercer Street. They had concluded that Professor Reynolds was an innocent bystander, but now it seemed that this conclusion had been premature.

Lucille's thoughts were interrupted by a commotion at the other end of the command post. Agent Crawford was shouting into his headset. 'Affirmative, retreat to the ground floor and hold positions.'

Lucille put down the print-out. 'What's going on?'

'We got a report of radiation on the fourth floor. I'm withdrawing everyone until we can get the hazmat team up there.'

Lucille tensed. 'Radiation? Who reported it?'

Crawford shouted the question into his headset, then got an answer. 'An alarm went off from a surveillance drone, from a Dragon Runner.'

'What? We haven't deployed any surveillance drones!'

'But Agent Walsh said he was certain it was a Dragon Runner.'

'Look, I don't care . . .' Lucille remembered the odd contraption in Gupta's reception room. 'That's one of Gupta's robots! It's a trick!' She ripped Crawford's headset off and spoke into the microphone. 'Everyone return to their previous positions. There's no radiation danger in the—'

'Agent Parker!' a technician called out. 'Check screen number five!'

Lucille looked at the screen just in time to see Monique Reynolds pushing her cart down a corridor. Jogging beside her was the autistic teenager.

Then every screen in the bank of video monitors went black.

AFTER DRIVING the Ferrari as fast as he dared for four hours, Simon reached Carnegie Mellon and headed straight for the Robotics Institute. He found a dozen burly men in shorts and T-shirts guarding the entrance, their semiautomatics resting in barely concealed holsters.

Simon parked quickly and hid behind a neighbouring building. His intuition had been correct. Swift and Reynolds had travelled west to rendezvous with Amil Gupta. Henry Cobb had told Simon that Gupta had no knowledge of the unified theory. But the FBI had clearly assumed otherwise.

Simon pulled out a pair of tactical binoculars. Outside the service entrance, a tall agent holding an M-16 stood next to a line of handcuffed women in blue smocks. A few yards away, two more agents were rooting through a canvas waste cart, tossing garbage into the air. Then a heavyset woman in a white blouse and a red skirt trotted over to the agents and began shouting. Simon felt a shock of recognition: it was the babushka who'd nearly killed him the night before. From the look on her face, something had gone wrong.

Then he spotted another swarm of agents surrounding a peculiar-looking vehicle. Its passenger compartment had been replaced by a massive block of machinery topped by a large silver orb. Simon had seen this vehicle before, in a magazine article about robotic cars. He remembered that the orb contained a rotating laser scanner designed to detect obstacles in the vehicle's path. One FBI agent interrogated the two students who were testing the car, while the others shone their flashlights into every nook and cranny. Finally, the agents allowed the test to continue, and the students walked behind the robotic car as it navigated its way out of the parking lot.

But as it turned right onto Forbes Avenue, Simon noticed that the silver orb didn't rotate. The laser scanner wasn't functioning, yet the car made a flawless turn. This could mean only one thing: it had a hidden driver.

Grinning, Simon rushed back to his Ferrari.

IN A DARK COMPARTMENT within the Highlander, Amil Gupta hunched over the drive-by-wire panel. Four people were crammed inside the narrow space: David squeezed between Gupta and Monique, while Michael crouched at the other end, playing with a Game Boy—Gupta had warned that his grandson would scream if touched. David could see FBI agents on the panel screen, which showed a live video feed from one of the car's cameras.

Using the black hand grips to the left and right of the screen, Gupta manoeuvred the Highlander onto Forbes Avenue, driving at a snail's pace so his students could keep up on foot.

'Where are we going?' David asked.

'No particular direction,' Gupta replied. 'I'm just trying to put some distance between us and those gentlemen from the FBI.'

'Head for the East Campus lot,' Monique said. 'That's where my car's parked. I can't stay cooped up like this much longer.'

Gupta nodded. 'All right, but it's going to take a few minutes.'

David shifted his leg, being careful not to brush against Michael. The teenager's fingers were dancing over the Game Boy but the rest of his body was locked in a foetal curl. David watched the screen as a cartoon soldier fired his rifle at a yellow building; then he leaned towards Gupta. 'Your grandson seems calmer now,' he whispered. 'The game has quite an effect on him.'

'That's a symptom of autism,' Gupta said. 'A preoccupation with certain activities to the exclusion of all else. It's his way of shutting out the world.'

'Is that the game that was on your reception-room computer?'

'Yes, it's a program the army uses for combat training. I've tried to interest him in *Major League Baseball*, but all he wants to play is *Warfighter*.'

'Where are his parents?'

The professor shook his head. 'My daughter is a drug addict. She's never told me who Michael's father is. The boy's lived with me for the past five years.' Gupta's hands seemed to tighten round the hand grips.

The drive-by-wire screen showed the vast East Campus parking lot. Gupta guided the Highlander through the entrance, then pressed a button for a panoramic view. 'Dr Reynolds, could you locate your car?'

Monique craned her neck. She pointed at a red Corvette about a hundred yards away. 'That's it.'

Gupta touched the screen at that spot. A white X flashed over the Corvette. Then he pressed another button. 'I've switched to autonomous operation.'

Without his touching the controls, the vehicle took the shortest navigable path towards the Corvette, expertly weaving between the parked cars.

'Remarkable, isn't it?' Gupta said. 'Autonomous navigation is an extremely complex decision-making process, and decision-making is the key to intelligence and consciousness.' He turned to David and Monique. 'This was why I switched from physics to robotics. I recognised that *Herr Doktor*'s dream of universal peace would never become a reality until there was a fundamental change in human consciousness. I thought if we could teach machines how to think, we might learn something about ourselves.' He bowed his head and sighed. 'But we've run out of time. Our machines have the intelligence of a termite. Enough to navigate a parking lot, but no more.'

The Highlander arrived at its programmed destination. David turned to Gupta, but the old man was still staring at the floor.

'Such a waste,' he muttered. 'Poor Alastair, the secret drove him mad. Jacques and Hans were stronger, but the theory tormented them, too. You know what Hans told me the last time I saw him? He said it might be better for everyone if they all let the unified theory die with them. And Hans loved the theory more than anyone.'

'When was the last time you saw Kleinman?' David asked.

'About four years ago. Hans had just retired from Columbia and he seemed a bit depressed, so I invited him to Carnegie's Retreat for two weeks.'

'Carnegie's Retreat? What's that?'

'The name makes it sound grander than it really is. It's just an old hunting cabin in West Virginia owned by Carnegie Mellon and available to faculty members, but hardly anyone goes there. It's too remote.'

'Are there computers in this cabin?'

'Yes, we installed a computer so Michael could play his games.'.

Monique looked at David. 'What are you thinking? That Kleinman hid the equations there?'

He nodded. 'It's a possibility. The cabin would be a good hiding place. Nobody except for Amil knows that Kleinman was ever there.'

Gupta seemed unconvinced. 'I never saw Hans at the computer in Carnegie's Retreat. And if he hid the theory there, why didn't he tell me?'

'Maybe he was afraid that someone would interrogate you.'

Before Gupta could respond, Monique pointed at the screen. 'Something's happening!' The two students who'd followed the vehicle to the lot were waving at the camera, looks of concern on their faces.

Gupta pushed another button. The concealed hatch at the very top of the Highlander opened with a hiss and they all scrambled out. As soon as David's sneakers touched the asphalt, he heard the whine of the sirens. Half a dozen black-and-white patrol cars raced down Forbes Avenue, towards Newell-Simon Hall. The FBI had called in reinforcements.

Monique rushed to the Corvette and unlocked its doors. 'Quick! Get in the car. Before they close the street.'

David stopped her. 'Wait a minute. The FBI is probably reviewing its surveillance videos right now. Once they figure out who you are, every cop in Pennsylvania will be looking for a red Corvette.'

One of the students timidly raised his hand. 'Uh, Professor Gupta? You can borrow my car.' He pointed at a beat-up grey Hyundai Accent.

Monique stared at the thing, her mouth open.

Gupta patted the young man on the back. 'That's very generous, Jeremy. We'll return it as soon as we can. In the meantime, I think you and Gary should leave town for a few days. Take a bus to the Finger Lakes, do some hiking in the gorges. All right, boys?'

The students nodded, delighted to do a favour for their adored professor. Jeremy gave his car keys to Gupta, who passed them to David.

Monique still stood by the Corvette's open door. 'It took me seven years to save up for this car,' she said. 'Seven years!'

He dropped the keys into her palm. 'Come on, give the Accent a spin,' he said. 'I hear it's got a nifty little engine.'

CHAPTER SIX

Karen had assumed that Jonah was still asleep. She'd put him to bed as soon as they came home, and when she went into his room a few hours later, he was still under his Spider-Man blanket, his face pressed into the pillow. But as she turned to leave he rolled over.

'Where's Daddy?' he asked.

She sat on the edge of his bed and brushed the blond hair out of his eyes. 'Hey, sweetie-pie,' she murmured. 'Feel better?'

Jonah batted her hand away and sat up. 'Why are the police looking for him? Did Daddy do something bad?'

'What did the agents tell you last night?'

'They said Daddy was in trouble. And they asked me if he had any girlfriends. Are they angry at Daddy? Because he has girlfriends now?'

'No, honey, no one's angry. What happened last night was a mistake, all right? Those agents came to the wrong apartment.'

'They had guns. I saw them.' Jonah's eyes widened at the memory. 'Are they gonna shoot Daddy when they find him?'

She wrapped her arms round her son and held him tight. He started crying then, his chest heaving, and in a moment Karen was crying, too.

After a minute or two, she wiped the tears from her face and looked Jonah in the eye. 'OK, I want you to get dressed as quickly as you can.'

He gave her a confused look, his cheeks flushed. 'Where are we going?'

'We're going to see a friend of mine. She can help us fix this mistake, so Daddy won't be in trouble. Just get dressed. We'll talk about it on the way.'

As she headed for her own bedroom, the doorbell rang. She froze. Then, cautiously, she approached the door and squinted through the peephole.

Amory stood on the doormat looking anxious, a gauze pad on his forehead. He was holding a cellphone to his ear and nodding.

Karen opened the door. Amory closed the phone, then stepped inside.

'You have to come downtown with me, Karen. The US attorney wants to speak with you immediately.'

She scowled. 'Are you crazy? I'm not going back there!'

'It's not the FBI, it's the US attorney. He wants to apologise for the conduct of the agents last night.'

'Apologise?' Karen shook her head, dumbfounded. 'If he wants to apologise, he should come here and beg my son for forgiveness.'

'He has some information about your ex-husband's drug case. They've identified a co-conspirator, a professor named Monique Reynolds. Her mother's a junkie and her sister's a prostitute.'

Karen waved her hand. 'They're making up stories again.'

'They've seen this woman with him, Karen. Are you sure David never mentioned her?' Amory stared at her intently, studying her eyes.

Karen grew suspicious. 'What's going on? Are you interrogating me?'

He chuckled, but it sounded forced. 'No, no, I just want to establish—'

'I thought you were on my side!'

Amory stepped towards her. 'Of course I'm on your side. I'm just trying to make things a little easier for you.' He stroked Karen's arm.

The caress made her skin crawl. The old bastard was working with the FBI. She shrugged off his hand. 'I can take care of this myself.'

His smile disappeared. 'Karen, listen. Some powerful people are involved in this case. Don't do anything rash. It won't be good for you or your son.'

She opened the door. 'Get out of here, Amory.'

She was planning to do something very rash indeed.

SITTING AT HIS DESK in his West Wing office, the vice-president poked unhappily at his dinner, a small, dry piece of chicken breast surrounded by steamed carrots. Ever since his fourth heart attack, the White House chefs had been serving him meals like this. He yearned for a Porterhouse steak.

There was a knock on the door. 'Yes?' he said.

His chief of staff stepped into the office, but before he could speak the secretary of defence charged past him. 'We need to talk,' he declared.

The vice-president signalled his chief of staff to leave and close the door. 'What is it this time?' he asked the secretary of defence.

'We have a problem with Operation Shortcut.'

The vice-president felt a twinge in the centre of his chest. 'I thought you said everything was under control.'

'It's the FBI's fault.' The secretary jabbed the air with his glasses. 'First they lost a detainee because they brought him to a poorly defended installation; then they botched the surveillance and let another target slip away.'

'Who are these targets?'

'They're professors, probably ultraliberal Looney Tunes. I wouldn't be surprised if they're working with Al-Qaeda. Or maybe the Iranians. Of course, the Bureau doesn't have a clue. The director put a woman in charge of the operation. Lucille Parker. All I know about her is that she's from Texas.'

The vice-president took a sip from his glass of water. Operation Shortcut had started about two weeks ago, after the National Security Agency picked up an email full of cryptic language and strange equations, traced to a computer at a mental institution in Glasgow, Scotland. It turned out that its author was a former physicist who'd worked with Albert Einstein. The equations were just a fragment of a larger theory, but the word from the experts was that this theory could give the United States a powerful new weapon in the war on terrorism. By the time the NSA task force got its act together, however, three of its four intelligence targets were dead. Some foreign government or terrorist group was also pursuing the theory.

'So what's your plan?' the vice-president asked.

'I need an executive order deploying the Delta Force. It's time for the Pentagon to take over.'

AT EXACTLY 6 P.M., while they were driving down Route 19 through the hills of West Virginia, Michael's Game Boy emitted a *ping* and a synthesised voice announced, 'It's time for dinner.'

'It's time for dinner, Grandpa,' the boy said.

These were the first words David had heard Michael say. His voice was as crisp and emotionless as the Game Boy's.

Gupta leaned forward from the back seat. 'Excuse me, David,' he said. 'You don't happen to have any food in the car, do you?'

David nodded. 'We bought some stuff this morning. Let me see what's left.' He rummaged through the plastic bag of supplies Monique had purchased and found a packaged turkey sandwich. 'Does Michael like turkey?'

'No, I'm afraid not. Do you have anything else?'

'Just a bag of potato chips and a few cookies.'

'Oh, he likes potato chips. But only with ketchup.'

David found a few ketchup packets that Monique had luckily thrown into the bag. He passed them to Gupta, along with the chips.

Monique glanced at the rearview mirror, her lips pressed into a thin line. 'Do you and Michael live alone, Professor?' she asked.

Gupta squeezed ketchup onto a chip. 'Yes, it's just the two of us. My wife died twenty-six years ago. But he isn't much trouble.'

David felt a pang of sympathy for the old man. During his interview for *On the Shoulders of Giants*, Gupta had told David about his long string of personal tragedies. His first child, a son, died of leukemia when he was twelve. His daughter was badly injured in a car accident. And in 1982 a stroke killed his wife at the age of forty-nine. Amil had shown David her picture—a dark-haired Eastern European beauty, slender and unsmiling.

Gupta had mentioned something else about his wife during that interview, but David couldn't recall the details. He twisted round in his seat. 'Your wife, she was also a student at Princeton, wasn't she?'

'No, not exactly. Hannah attended some graduate seminars in physics but she never actually enrolled. The war interrupted her education, so she lacked the proper academic credentials to enroll.'

Now David remembered. Hannah Gupta was a Holocaust survivor, one of the many Jewish refugees that Einstein had helped after the Second World War, by sponsoring their immigration and finding them jobs at Princeton's laboratories. This was what had brought Amil and Hannah together.

'Yes, I have fond memories of those seminars,' Gupta continued. 'Hannah sat in the back and there was quite a competition to get her attention. Both Jacques and Hans were interested too, sneaking looks at her.'

'Really?' David was intrigued. 'How heated did it get?'

'Oh, not very. I was engaged to Hannah before Jacques or Hans could get up the nerve to speak to her.' The professor smiled. 'We all remained friends, thank goodness. Hans became the godfather to both my children.'

Fascinating, David thought. He wished he'd known about this story earlier, so he could have included it in his book. As soon as the thought occurred to him, though, he realised how foolish it was. Einstein's discovery of the unified field theory was a much more glaring omission.

After a few more miles they turned west at County Highway 33, a one-lane road that snaked through the hills. Occasionally they passed a weathered trailer home, but the road was empty now except for a yellow sports car about a quarter of a mile behind them.

'Where's your daughter now, Professor?' Monique asked.

He grimaced. 'In Columbus, Georgia. It's a good town for addicts. Plenty of methamphetamine for the soldiers at Fort Benning.'

'Have you tried sending her to a treatment programme?'

'Many times. Elizabeth is very stubborn. She ran away at fifteen and she's been living in squalor ever since. I won't tell you what she does for a living. Even if Michael weren't autistic, I would have taken custody of him.'

A vertical crease appeared between Monique's eyebrows. 'Your daughter won't go into treatment if you're the one suggesting it,' she said. 'There's too much bitterness between you. You need someone else to do the intervention.'

Gupta leaned forward and narrowed his eyes. 'I tried that,' he said. 'I asked Hans to go down to Georgia and talk some sense into her. He threw away all her drugs and got her enrolled in an outpatient treatment centre. He even found a decent job for her, doing secretarial work for one of the generals at Fort Benning. Two and a half months later she went on a binge. That's when Michael came to live with me for good.'

The old man slumped back in his seat, breathing hard. Suddenly, the yellow sports car they had seen a minute ago zoomed ahead of them, racing at least eighty miles an hour down the curving road.

'What the hell was that?' David yelled, startled.

Monique leaned forward to get a better look. 'It's not a patrol car. Not unless the cops in West Virginia drive Ferraris now.'

'A Ferrari?'

She nodded. 'A 575 Maranello coupé. There are only fifty of them in the whole country. The dean of the engineering school at Princeton has one. I see him all the time at Keith's shop. It breaks down pretty regularly.'

Instead of racing ahead, the Ferrari began to slow. Within a few seconds it was creeping along at thirty miles an hour just a dozen yards ahead of them.

'What's with this guy?' David said. 'Now he's sightseeing.'

Monique's cheek twitched. 'It's got New Jersey plates,' she whispered.

At the bottom of the hill the Ferrari raced ahead; then it stopped in front of a single-lane bridge over a stream, blocking their way.

David saw a big, bald man in a black T-shirt and camouflage pants jump out of the car and crouch behind it. A cold wash of terror flooded David's chest as he realised that the man was gazing down the barrel of a stubby black machine gun. Its muzzle was pointed at the Hyundai's tyres.

Monique saw the man, too. 'I'm turning round!' she yelled.

David grabbed Monique's knee. 'Don't slow down! He's gonna shoot the tyres! Head over there.' He pointed at a gap in the trees on the left side of the road, an overgrown path leading down to the stream.

'Are you crazy? We can't—'

Three loud metallic clanks shook the Hyundai as a burst from the machine gun hit the front fender. Without any more argument, Monique stepped on the gas and jerked the car towards the side of the road. As the Hyundai careened down the path, she clung to the steering wheel and they all bounced in their seats. Much too fast, they thudded over the rocky stream bed. Then they were on the opposite bank and Monique floored it. The engine roared in protest, but the car climbed up the bank like a billy goat and found the path to the highway. As their tyres hit the asphalt, David looked in the side mirror and saw the bald man rushing back to the Ferrari.

'Better gun it!' David shouted. 'He's coming after us!'

Monique stomped on the accelerator. But soon they started to climb a high mountain ridge, and the Hyundai struggled to reach seventy miles an hour.

David looked over his shoulder through the rear window. No sign yet of the Ferrari, but in the back seat Professor Gupta was thoroughly alarmed.

'What's going on?' he gasped, his eyes unnaturally wide.

'It's all right, Professor,' David lied. 'We're going to be all right.'

He shook his head fiercely. 'I have to get out! Let me out of the car!'

He unbuckled his seat belt and reached for the door handle. Luckily the door was locked, and before Gupta could unlock it, David scrambled into the back seat and grabbed the old man's wrists. He looked out of the rear window again and saw the yellow Ferrari about fifty yards behind them.

David quickly faced forward to warn Monique, but she'd already seen it.

'That's the dean's car!' she hissed.

'He's gaining,' David said. 'Can't you go any faster?'

'No, I can't! I'm driving a Hyundai!' She shook her head. 'He must have gone looking for us, but he found Keith instead. That's how he got the car.'

As they approached the top of the ridge, the bald man rolled down the window of the Ferrari and pointed his Uzi. David shoved Michael and Professor Gupta to the floor. The teenager let out an ear-piercing scream.

'He's gonna shoot!' David shouted at Monique.

The first blast shattered the rear window, showering glass on their backs. The second punched holes in the windshield. David clambered back into the front. He found Monique unharmed but weeping.

'Keith's dead, isn't he?' she cried.

They both knew the answer. David put his hand on her shoulder.

The Hyundai crested the ridge and started to pick up speed as they barrelled downhill. The bald man fired his Uzi again but the bullets missed the car as they rounded a sharp curve. Monique stared at the road ahead in ferocious concentration, her whole body a tense arc of nerves and muscle.

The road straightened out, becoming a steep chute that sliced through the woods. The Hyundai was going over a hundred miles an hour, but the Ferrari was still close behind. Trees whipped past in an unbroken blur; then David saw a break, about a hundred yards ahead. A narrow strip of asphalt branched off to the left. He glanced at Monique; she was looking at it, too.

Turning round, David stared at the Ferrari. The bald man was taking careful aim now. Not yet, David silently pleaded. One more second.

Monique swerved violently to the left. The Hyundai tilted on its right wheels, on the verge of rolling over, then bounced back onto the asphalt, and sped down the narrow road. Surprised, the bald man looked up from his gun sight and turned his wheel too far, sending the Ferrari into a vicious counterclockwise spin. It glided across the road like a bright yellow pinwheel, and smacked into the trees with a sickening crunch.

LUCILLE SAT BEHIND the desk in Amil Gupta's office, speaking on her cellphone. Her team had messed up big time, but Lucille felt sure that with a little legwork they would locate the suspects. That's why she got so furious when the director of the Bureau informed her the Pentagon was taking over.

'What the hell are they thinking?' she shouted into the phone. 'It's illegal for the army to participate in a domestic operation!'

'I know,' the director replied. 'But they have an executive order. And the Delta Force has experience with manhunts.'

'But where are they gonna go? The suspects could be anywhere by now.'

'According to the deployment plan, the troops are flying into Andrews Air Force Base and they'll spread out from there, using helicopters.'

Lucille shook her head. 'Sir, just give me more time.'

'It's too late, Lucy. The troops are already loading into their C-17s. You have control of the operation until midnight. Then we'll do the handover.'

She said nothing. A silent protest.

The director said, 'I've got to go to a meeting now,' and hung up.

She stared at her cellphone. The screen said CALL ENDED 19:29, then displayed the FBI seal. But she wasn't really looking at the screen; she was looking at the end of her career in the Bureau. For thirty-four years she'd struggled through the ranks. A month ago, the director had promised to make her head of the Dallas office, but that wasn't going to happen now.

Agent Crawford edged towards her warily, like a whipped dog. 'Uh, Agent Parker? We've finished the analysis of Gupta's computer system.'

Lucille turned to him. She was in charge for four more hours, so she might as well make the best of it. 'Did you find any physics documents?'

'No, it's all robotics. Software code and hardware designs. We also found the program that allows him to communicate with his robots. That's how he got the Dragon Runner to sound the radiation alert.'

She needed to see the source of her undoing. 'Show me the program.'

Crawford leaned over the desk and used the mouse to click on a triangular icon on the computer screen. 'This layout shows the location and status of each robot. Gupta sent them commands using a wireless device.'

'Wireless?' She felt a flutter of hope in her chest. Wireless devices periodically sent signals to their networks. 'Can we track it down?'

'No, Gupta's device uses short-range radio only. To control robots at other locations he sends commands by land line via a local transmitting node.'

'What other locations? Where else does he have robots?'

'There are some in the computer science department and the engineering hall. Also a few at Gupta's house.'

'Anywhere outside Pittsburgh?'

With a click of the mouse, a map of the United States unfolded across the screen. There were four flashing dots in California, one in Tennessee, one in West Virginia, two in Georgia and half a dozen near Washington, DC.

'What about this location?' Lucille pointed at the flashing dot in West Virginia. It was the closest one to Pittsburgh.

Crawford clicked on the dot and a label appeared beside it. 'Carnegie's Retreat, Jolo. I haven't seen the name in any of Gupta's records.'

'Do we have any agents operating in that part of West Virginia?'

'Agents Brock and Santullo are on I-77, helping the state police run a roadblock. They're about fifty miles from Jolo.'

'Tell them to head over there as fast as they can.'

IT WAS FULLY DARK by the time they reached Carnegie's Retreat, but in the glare of the Hyundai's headlights David could see enough of the place to know that Andrew Carnegie would never have spent a night there. It was a one-storey shack constructed from railroad ties in a small clearing in the woods. Carnegie Mellon University had let the place fall into disrepair.

They got out of the car, leaving the lights on so they could see. When they reached the front door, Gupta found the key under a flowerpot.

As David grabbed the key, a muffled boom echoed against the hills.

'What was that?' he hissed.

Gupta chuckled. 'Don't worry. The locals like to ramble through the woods with shotguns in the evenings and hunt down their supper.'

'I'm beginning to see why none of the professors come here.'

'Oh, it's not so bad. The people in this area are quite interesting. They have a church where they do snake handling. They hardly ever get bitten.'

David inserted the key in the lock, and after a couple of tries the door opened. He ran his hand along the wall until he found the light switch.

Inside, the cabin looked more inviting. There was a stone fireplace and a brown shag rug. A massive oak table held a computer and a monitor.

Gupta went straight to the computer system, but as he hunted for the power strip he saw something else. 'Look, Michael! I forgot we left this thing here. And the batteries are still charged.'

Kneeling on the floor, he flipped a few switches and a four-legged robot emerged from under the table. About two feet high and three feet long, it looked like a miniature brontosaurus. Its body was made of shiny black plastic, and its neck and tail were segmented, allowing them to undulate in a creepily realistic way. On its head were two red LEDs that looked like eyes, and on its back was an antenna. The creature turned its head from side to side. 'Would you like to play ball, Michael?' asked a synthesised voice.

The teenager stopped playing *Warfighter*. For the first time David saw him smile, and at that moment his joyful face looked a lot like Jonah's. Michael ran to the shag rug, picked up a bright pink ball and rolled it. The dinosaur robot turned its head, then lumbered after it.

'It's programmed to go after anything pink,' Gupta explained.

Monique glanced impatiently at the computer on the oak table.

'Uh, Professor,' David said. 'Could we look through the files now?'

'Yes, yes, of course!' The old man pulled up a chair and turned on the computer. David and Monique looked over his shoulder.

Gupta opened the computer's file inventory and scrolled down it to a folder labelled MICHAEL'S BOX. To open it he typed in a password—REDPIRATE79. 'These are the documents we made four years ago,' he said.

The seven Microsoft Word files were arranged in order of when they were last modified, from July 27, 2004 to August 9, 2004. The first file was labelled VISUAL. The names of the next six were 322, 512, 845, 641, 870 and 733.

Gupta opened Visual. 'I remember this one,' he said. 'On our first night here, I downloaded a research paper one of my students had written about visual-recognition programs. Maybe Hans inserted something into it.'

The paper was a typical grad-student effort: long, plodding, impenetrable. As Gupta scrolled through the pages, David kept expecting to see a sudden orderly sequence of equations that had nothing to do with visual recognition. But instead the paper slogged on and on.

'That's one down,' Gupta said when he reached the end. 'Six more to go.'

He clicked on the file labelled 322. The document was very large and took some time to open. After five or six seconds a long alphabetical list of names appeared on the screen, each accompanied by a telephone number. Gupta scrolled down the seemingly endless parade of entries.

Monique shook her head. 'Why download a phone directory?'

'Michael did it. He went through a phase when he was obsessed with phone numbers. Each file is a directory for an area code.'

David stared at the digital blur rising from the bottom of the screen; then Professor Gupta abruptly stopped scrolling. 'I have an idea,' he said. 'Any equation has an equals sign, so I'll just search for that symbol.'

David nodded. It was worth a shot.

THE ARGUN GORGE is one of the most battle-scarred places in Chechnya, but in Simon's dreams the canyon was always pristine. He glided like a hawk above the narrow Argun River, which was flanked by the granite slopes of the Caucasus Mountains. The road along its eastern bank was built to transport Russian tanks, but now he could see just a single vehicle and it wasn't military. Swooping down, Simon recognised his own car, a grey Lada sedan. In the driver's seat was his wife, Olenka, and in the back were Sergei and Larissa. They were coming to visit Simon, who was stationed twenty kilometres south. The highway was safe—all the Chechen rebels had been killed or driven deeper into the mountains—but in his dreams Simon protectively followed the car anyway. And then the Lada rounded a bend and he saw the black helicopter loaded with Hellfire missiles.

In reality, Simon didn't hear about the attack until an hour afterwards, when his commander informed him that the American special forces had crossed again into Chechnya. After 9/11, the Delta Force had started hunting down Al-Qaeda fighters who'd retreated with the Chechens, but their Apache helicopters had a bad habit of firing at noncombatants. As Simon drove his troop carrier to the site of the reported American attack, he fully expected to see another peasant massacre. Instead he saw the blackened shell of his Lada, with his wife's charred skeleton behind the wheel. The explosion had blown Sergei and Larissa into a muddy ditch.

Simon never discovered how a team of trained commandos could have mistaken his family for a band of terrorists. Because the Delta Force operation was classified, the American and Russian generals covered up the incident. When Simon filed a protest, his commander gave him a canvas bag filled with hundred-dollar bills. Simon hurled the bag at his commander and came to America, hoping to locate the pilot and gunner of the Apache.

It was an impossible task. Simon didn't even know the men's names. In his dreams, though, he saw their faces. He saw the pilot holding the controls steady while the gunner launched the Hellfire. He saw the flames spurt from the back of the rocket. Then Simon was suddenly in the Lada with his children. He felt a tug on the collar of his shirt, the tug of a small hand.

Simon opened his eyes. It was dark. He was lodged between the driver's seat of the Ferrari and the inflated air bag. The car had struck a tree on the passenger side, leaving the left half unscathed. A wizened old hillbilly was tugging at his collar. The man's pick-up truck idled alongside.

Wrenching his left hand free of the air bag, Simon grasped the hillbilly by the wrist. 'Yer alive!' the man yelped.

Simon kept his grip. 'Help me out of here,' he ordered.

The door wouldn't open, so the hillbilly pulled him through the window. Simon winced as his right foot touched the ground—the ankle was sprained.

The old man helped him to the pick-up. 'I thought you were dead for sure,' he marvelled. 'We gotta git you to the hospital.'

Simon grabbed the hillbilly and threw him against the truck. He clasped both hands round his neck. 'Did you see a grey Hyundai?' he demanded.

The man shook his head in a quick, spastic jitter.

'Then you're useless.' Simon tightened his hold, felt the larynx crumple.

He let the dead man drop to the dirt, then limped back to the Ferrari and retrieved his Uzi and sidearms. He took out his cellphone and dialled a number. The line began to ring and a voice answered, 'Brock here.'

WHILE PROFESSOR GUPTA searched the voluminous files on his computer, David wandered over to a window at the back of the cabin, too agitated to watch the screen, and looked out at the night sky. When he felt a tap on his shoulder, he spun round, expecting to see Gupta.

It was Monique. 'I have another question about the Flatland paper.'

Her request seemed to come out of nowhere, but after a moment David understood. She wanted to take one last guess at the theory of everything before Gupta unveiled the equations. 'What do you want to know?'

'Your model of a two-dimensional black hole—did it contain CTCs?'

A CTC was a closed timelike curve. Essentially, it was a path that allowed a particle to travel back and forth in time, arriving at the exact same point where it started. 'Yeah, but Flatland has all kinds of weird things you wouldn't necessarily see in a three-dimensional universe.'

'And did the spacetime have a wormhole?'

David nodded. 'Yeah, that's right.' A wormhole was a tunnel through the hills and valleys of spacetime. In Flatland, particles diving into the black hole emerged in a separate universe on the other side.

'While we driving down, I started thinking about why Kleinman said your paper was close to the truth,' Monique said. 'There might be a connection with geons. Gravitational electromagnetic entities. The premise is that elementary particles aren't objects sitting in spacetime; they're knots in the fabric of spacetime itself. Like tiny wormholes.'

'But I got the impression physicists abandoned that effort.'

'That's because no one could formulate a stable geon. But a few years ago, researchers resurrected the idea as a possible unification theory. They came up with a particle that looks like a microscopic wormhole with CTCs. It's a classical field theory, with the potential to explain the uncertainties of quantum mechanics. The CTCs are the key. On the smallest scales of spacetime, causation becomes skewed. The particle is influenced by the future as well as the past. But an outside observer can't measure events that haven't happened, so the best he can do is calculate probabilities.'

David tried to picture it, a particle that somehow knew its own future. 'So the future events are Einstein's hidden variables?'

She nodded. 'A complete description of the universe exists, but it's unreachable at any one moment in—'

She was interrupted by the sound of Gupta's hand smacking the table. The professor shouted, 'Damn!' and glared at the computer screen.

Monique rushed over. 'What is it? What did you find?'

'First I searched the files for the equals sign, then I tried the integral sign. No results. Then it occurred to me that Hans inserted the information into the computer's operating system. But I just ran a line-by-line comparison, and found no alterations to the software.' He turned to David, his eyes glassy with fatigue. 'I'm afraid we've come all this way for nothing.'

'Maybe it's hidden somewhere else in the cabin,' David suggested.

Gupta sighed. 'Why are you so convinced Hans hid the theory here?'

'He wouldn't have hidden anything in your office or home. The theory would have fallen right into the government's hands if they came—'

'Please, we have to re-examine each step in your argument. Let's start with the numbers Hans gave you. Twelve were the latitude and longitude coordinates of the Robotics Institute?'

'Yes.' David closed his eyes for a moment and saw the numbers floating across the backs of his eyelids. 'And the last four were your phone extension.'

Gupta leaned back in his chair, stroking his chin. But the sixteen numbers were still floating across David's field of view, gliding past the computer screen before him. And on that screen, David saw another sequence of numbers in a neat column: 322, 512, 845, 641, 870 and 733.

He pointed at the screen. 'Are these file names supposed to be area codes? One for each of the phone directories?'

The professor looked annoyed. 'Yes, yes. I told you.'

David tapped his finger on the file name at the top of the column, the number 322. 'This can't be an area code.' He tapped 733. 'Neither can this.'

Gupta turned in his chair. 'What are you talking about?'

'My son asked me the other day how many area codes there were. I found out there couldn't be more than 720. An area code can't start with a zero or a one, and the last two digits can't be the same. Telephone companies reserve those numbers for special uses.'

Gupta squinted at the screen. 'I probably mistyped them.'

'But Kleinman could have changed the file names in seconds. That would explain why the numbers don't make sense. It's another key.'

Monique came forward. 'But there are eighteen digits, not sixteen.'

'Let's concentrate on the first twelve,' David replied. 'Can you get on the website that maps latitude and longitude?'

Monique grasped the mouse, clicked on Internet Explorer and found the site. 'OK, read the numbers to me.'

David had already memorised the sequence. 'Three, two, two, five, one, two, eight, four, five, six, four, one.'

A map appeared on the screen, with the Chattahoochee River on the left. 'The address closest to the location is 3617 Victory Drive,' Monique reported. 'In Columbus, Georgia.'

Gupta elbowed David and Monique aside. He gazed angrily at the screen. 'That's Elizabeth's address,' he shouted. 'My daughter! That little—'

But before he could finish the sentence, the cabin's front door burst open.

LUCILLE WAS in the passenger seat of one of the Bureau's SUVs, racing down Route 52, blue lights flashing. While Agent Crawford steered round traffic, she spoke by satellite phone with Agents Brock and Santullo, who were crouched in the woods outside a cabin in Jolo. The connection was poor.

'Brock, this is Parker,' Lucille shouted into the phone. 'I didn't copy your last transmission. Say again. Over.'

'Roger, we've sighted Gupta, Swift, Reynolds and the unidentified teenage male in the house. We're moving to a new position to get a better view inside.

There's a window on the other . . .' A surge of static buried his last words.

'Roger, I copied most of that. Stay behind cover until back-up gets there. Don't confront the suspects unless they attempt to leave. You hear me, Brock?'

'Affirmative. We'll hold at the new position. Over and out.'

Lucille felt a twinge of misgiving. But she was only half an hour from Jolo, and three State Police patrol cars were even closer.

Brock's voice erupted from the satellite phone. 'Mayday, mayday! Request permission to move in immediately.'

She pressed the phone to her ear. 'What is it? Are they trying to leave?'

'They're crowded round the computer! Request permission to move in before they delete mission-critical information!'

She took a deep breath. Her primary task was to secure information vital to national security, but Bureau computer experts had retrieved deleted data from a hundred hard drives. 'Permission denied. Back-up is twenty minutes away. Hold your position until they get there.'

'Roger, we're moving in!'

Lucille thought he'd misheard her. 'No! Do *not* move in!'

'Roger, we're going radio dark until we capture the suspects. Over and out.'

THERE WERE TWO of them. Two muscle-bound bruisers in dark blue jumpsuits with gold FBI letters. One was a tall and blond, and the other was a swarthy Mediterranean type. Both held 9mm Glocks that they levelled at Amil, David and Monique.

Professor Gupta instinctively stepped in front of Michael, who was kneeling next to his toy brontosaurus.

'*Move again and I'll blow your brains out!*' the blond agent yelled. '*Get your hands in the air!*'

The old man slowly raised his hands. 'Please . . . please stand up, Michael.' His voice was shaky. 'And hold up your hands like this.'

The blond agent pivoted, pointing his gun at David now. The man's nose was misshapen, probably broken many times, and his cheeks were webbed with fine, red lines. He looked more like a bar brawler than an FBI agent.

As David raised his hands he glanced at Monique. He knew there was a revolver tucked in the back of her shorts. He also knew if she reached for it, they were as good as dead. He shook his head ever so slightly: *Don't do it*. After a second of uncertainty, she raised her hands, too.

The blond agent turned to his partner. 'Cover 'em, Santullo.'

The man patted David down roughly, then moved on to the professor.

Gupta looked at his grandson. 'Michael, this man is going to touch you in a minute. But don't worry, it won't hurt at all.'

The agent leered. 'What's wrong with the kid? He retarded?'

The old man kept his eyes on Michael. 'Don't scream. It'll soon be over.'

His reassurances seemed to work: when Michael was searched, he whined but didn't scream.

Then the agent turned to Monique. He quickly discovered her revolver. 'Well, look at this,' he crowed, checking the cylinder and holstering his own gun. 'This is a lucky break. I just found the murder weapon.'

Monique glared at him. 'What the hell are you talking about?'

He returned to his partner's side. 'I'm talking about this.' He pointed the gun at Santullo's head and fired.

It happened so fast that Santullo's eyes were still focused on Amil, David and Monique as the bullet sped through his skull. The impact knocked him to the floor, and his Glock fell out of his hand. The blond agent picked it up.

Michael started screaming as soon as he heard the gunshot. He dropped to the shag rug and clamped his hands over his ears. Stunned, David stared at the blood fountaining from the dead man's temple.

The blond agent flipped the safety on the Glock and trained the revolver on his captives. 'All right,' he said. 'Before the troopers show up, we're gonna take a little walk through the woods and meet a friend of mine.' He grabbed Michael by the collar of his shirt and pressed the revolver to his head. 'You're all gonna walk in single file. If anyone runs, the kid's dead.'

Monique was now on the agent's left side and David was on his right. She gave David an urgent look and he understood: the man was vulnerable. He couldn't see both of them at once. Now was the time to make a move.

Gupta's face was contorted into a fierce grimace. 'Stop this right now, you imbecile!' he shouted. 'Get your hands off my grandson!'

David had noticed that the robot brontosaurus was waving its segmented tail just a few feet away from Monique. His eyes fixed on the machine's spindly antenna; he mouthed the word *antenna* to Monique and pointed at the thing. At first Monique just looked confused. Then David clenched his right hand into a fist and twisted it. That did the trick. Monique bent over the machine and snapped off its antenna.

The alarm was even louder than David remembered. The agent automatically let go of Michael and pointed the revolver at the noise.

David rushed over and slammed his shoulder into the agent's back. The man toppled forward, his chest smacking the floor. The revolver stayed in his hand, though, and he squeezed off a shot that exploded the dinosaur and silenced the alarm. David fell on top of him and pinned the agent's shooting arm. He fired again, wildly, and David pounded the man's face into the floor. Yet two more shots rang out, and David heard Monique scream.

SIMON PARKED the old man's pick-up at the rendezvous point, a bend in a dirt road a kilometre south of the cabin. He doused the headlights, then looked at the glowing hands of his watch: 9.21. Brock was due in nine minutes. Simon had promised him $250,000 for delivering all four targets alive.

He rolled down the window, listening for the sound of five people stumbling through leaf litter. But all he heard was the whine of cicadas, the wind rustling in the trees. Then he heard a high-pitched shriek and four gunshots.

It's just Agent Brock executing his partner, he told himself. But why four shots? One bullet to the head was usually sufficient. All his instincts were telling Simon something had gone wrong.

DAVID DIDN'T PAUSE for a second. Enraged, he brought his knee down on the agent's forearm. The gun slipped out of the man's hand, but David kept on swinging his fists into the man's face until he felt someone behind him, pulling his arms back. 'Enough, enough! He's unconscious!'

He turned round and saw Monique. She appeared to be unhurt. She reached into the agent's shoulder holster and removed his semiautomatic, then retrieved Santullo's gun. 'Here, take this,' she said, handing David the Glock. 'Cover him in case he wakes up. I'll take care of Amil.'

'Amil?' David looked over his shoulder and saw Michael crouched on the rug with his hands still pressed to his ears. Beside him, Professor Gupta lay in a puddle of blood. It was gushing from a hole in his left thigh.

'Quick, take off your T-shirt,' she told David. Then she rushed over to Gupta and ripped off his left trouser leg. She folded David's shirt into a pad, and placed it over Gupta's wound, pressing it firmly to stanch the bleeding. 'Take deep breaths, Professor,' she told him. 'You need to slow your heartbeat.' She turned to David. 'We have to get him to a hospital.'

'No!' Gupta cried. 'You have to get to Georgia. The man said the troopers were coming. If they catch you, they'll get the *Einheitliche Feldtheorie.*'

'We can't leave you,' Monique said. 'You'll bleed to death.'

'As soon as the authorities get here, they'll rush me to the hospital. Believe me, they won't let me die. I'm too important to them.'

She shook her head. Gupta touched her cheek, then pointed at his grandson.

'Take Michael with you,' he said. 'If the police find him, they'll put him in an institution. Don't let that happen. Please, I'm begging you.'

She kept her hand on the bandage, but she nodded. Then Gupta turned to David, pointing at the computer. 'Before you go, you need to destroy the hard drive, so the FBI doesn't see the code.'

Without a word, David lifted the computer and hurled it to the floor. The plastic case cracked open and he wrenched out the hard drive, which looked like a miniature turntable with a stack of silver discs. He pounded the glass platters with the handle of the Glock, smashing them into tiny slivers.

Just as he finished, he heard a siren. It was the wail of a state-trooper car speeding up the gravel road. Two more sirens sounded farther off. Then David heard the rapid fire of a machine gun. 'Come on!' he yelled. 'We gotta go!'

SIMON DEALT WITH the state troopers first. Leaning against one of the trees next to the road, he strafed the windshield of the leading patrol car, killing both officers inside. The car slid off the gravel and smashed into a boulder. The driver of the second vehicle didn't see the wreck until he came round the curve. He managed to stop, but Simon picked him off before he could throw the car into reverse. The third driver wisely stayed out of range. The task was done: now the troopers would cower behind rocks and tree trunks for the next half-hour, allowing Simon to focus his attention elsewhere.

He hobbled up the road to the cabin. The first sign of trouble was the open door. The second was the trio of bodies lying on the floor inside. Only one of them was dead—Brock's partner, obviously. A diminutive Indian man, the esteemed Professor Gupta, lay unconscious in a pool of blood. Someone had field-dressed his leg wound, but the bandage was soaked. And last but not least, Agent Brock writhed on his belly, groaning in pain.

Simon stood there, deciding what to do. Swift and Reynolds, his primary targets, were probably not far away, running blindly through the woods with their teenage companion. Under ordinary circumstances, Simon would have pursued them, but his ankle was growing inflamed and it wouldn't support his weight much longer. He'd have to be content with interrogating Gupta.

Brock staggered to his feet. His face was a bloody mess but he was otherwise serviceable. Working together, they could probably carry Gupta through the woods to the pick-up.

Simon grabbed the back of Brock's neck and shoved him towards the professor. 'I have a new job for you, Mr Brock,' he said. 'And if you want to stay alive, I suggest you take it.'

CHAPTER SEVEN

Lucille knelt beside the body of Tony Santullo and forced herself to look at the gaping hole in his temple. She pushed all guilt and anger from her mind, and concentrated on reconstructing what had transpired in the cabin. She examined the position of Santullo's corpse and the pattern of the blood splatter. She noted the presence of two other pools of blood at the other end of the room, suggesting additional casualties.

Agent Crawford stood behind her, holding a radio to his ear. 'Brock, come in,' he shouted. 'Respond at once, over.'

Lucille shook her head. For twenty-four hours she'd suspected that there was a traitor on the task force. Now she knew who it was.

'Come in, Brock,' Crawford repeated. 'Come in, come—'

He abruptly lowered the radio and cocked his head, listening. Lucille heard it, too: the beating of helicopter rotors. She rose and followed Crawford out of the cabin. They saw three Blackhawks skimming over the hills, their spotlights illuminating the treetops. It was the advance guard of the Delta Force.

NAKED TO THE WAIST, David ran headlong into the darkness, trying to follow Monique as she crashed through the undergrowth. With his left hand he groped at tree trunks and branches, and with his right he dragged Michael along. The teenager screamed at first, but soon became too winded to protest. They tore through the black forest, propelled by sheer terror.

They came to a clearing and Monique stopped short. David almost ploughed into her. 'What are you doing?' he hissed. 'Let's go, let's go!'

'Where are we going? How do you know we're not running in circles?'

He looked up at the stars. The Little Dipper was to their right, which meant they were travelling west. He took Monique's hand and pointed it to the left. 'We should go this way, start heading south. Then we—'

'Oh, no, what's that?'

Three points of light rose above the treetops behind them. As David stared, he heard helicopter rotors in the distance. He grabbed Michael's elbow and pushed Monique forward. 'Go! Under the trees!'

They dived into the woods again and scrambled up a rocky slope. The going was tougher here, more rugged. Monique tripped over something and landed with a cry. As David rushed to her side, he heard a slow deep voice say, 'Stop right there.' Then he heard the sound of two rifles being cocked into firing position.

David froze. A flashlight came on and the beam ran over them.

'What y'all doin' out here? This ain't no place for a picnic.'

David squinted into the glare and saw a hefty man in overalls and a flannel shirt, pointing a shotgun at them. To his left was another man with a shotgun, an old toothless fellow in a baseball cap, and to his right was a short, stocky boy, maybe eight or nine years old. The boy carried a homemade slingshot and had an oddly flattened face.

'You hear me?' the fat man said. He had a thick brown beard and a dirty bandage taped over his left eye. 'I asked you a question.'

David nodded. These were the backwoods hunters that Professor Gupta had mentioned, a grandfather, father and son, no doubt. West Virginia mountain men—not inclined to sympathise with a black physicist and a bare-chested history professor, but probably not fond of the government either.

'We're in trouble,' David admitted. 'They're coming to arrest us.'

The fat man fixed his good eye on him. 'Who's coming?'

'The FBI. And the state troopers. They're working together.'

The man snorted. 'What'd you do, rob a bank?'

'We didn't do anything wrong. It's an illegal government operation.'

'What the hell do you mean by—?'

He was interrupted by his son, who suddenly let out a high-pitched squawk, like the call of a tropical bird. The boy's face broke into a distorted smile and he swayed from side to side. With a jolt, David realised what was wrong with him. The boy had Down syndrome.

All right, he thought. They had something in common. David pointed at Michael, who was crouched on the ground. 'They're after our son. They're trying to take him away from us.'

Monique stared at him, aghast. But the hunters seemed to accept that the dusky-skinned teenager was their son. The hefty one lowered his gun a few degrees. 'Your boy, is he sick?' he asked.

'The doctors want to put him in a mental hospital. They followed us here from Pittsburgh, and now they're bringing in helicopters.'

The boy with Down syndrome gazed at the sky. The old fellow in the cap exchanged looks with the fat man. Then both of them lowered their weapons. The fat one turned off his flashlight.

'Follow me,' he ordered. 'The trail's this way.'

SIMON RECOGNISED the helicopters by their silhouettes. Blackhawks flying low, just a few metres above the treetops. That was a Delta Force tactic, flying below radar coverage. Simon's pulse raced—his enemies were near.

He and Brock soon reached the pick-up truck and heaved Professor Gupta into the bench seat behind the cab. Then Brock collapsed in the passenger seat and Simon got behind the wheel. He knew the Blackhawk pilots would spot the truck's headlights, so he put on his infrared goggles. He drove fast, because they didn't have much time. The professor was going into shock.

They were about twenty kilometres south of the cabin, across the Virginia state line, when Simon saw a house at a bend in the road. The name on the mailbox caught his attention. It was spelt in plastic letters that stood out clearly against the cold metal: DR MILO JENKINS. Simon skidded to a halt, and turned into Dr Jenkins's driveway.

THE HUNTERS moved like ghosts through the forest, following a twisting trail up the slope of a narrow mountain valley. Although they walked so fast that David, Monique and Michael could barely keep up, they made no sound. David was guided by the moonlight glinting off the barrels of their guns.

For about half an hour they marched up a steep ridge. When they reached the crest, David turned round to see the spotlights of all three helicopters prowling the hills and hollows far below.

The hunters continued along the ridge line for a mile or so, then descended into a neighbouring valley. After several minutes, David saw a light on the hillside. Soon they came upon a decrepit plywood shack resting on cinder blocks. A pair of mangy dogs yowled, but quieted as the men approached.

The fat man turned to David. 'This is our home,' he said, offering his hand. 'My name's Caleb. That's my pa and my boy, Joshua.'

David shook his hand. 'I'm David. This is my wife, Monique.' The lie was effortless. 'And this is my son, Michael.'

Caleb opened the door. 'Come set down. Y'all could use a rest, I bet.'

The shack was just one long room. There were no windows; the only light came from a naked bulb suspended from the ceiling. Some plastic bowls and a hot plate sat on a table. A grey army blanket lay on the floor behind a couple of kitchen chairs. At the very back was a pile of cardboard boxes and crumpled clothing. Without a word, Caleb's father took off his cap, turned on the hot plate and opened a can of Dinty Moore stew.

Caleb tousled his son's black hair, which looked like it hadn't been washed in some time. 'Joshua's my special gift from the Lord,' he said.

'Mingo County Social Services has been trying to take him away ever since his ma died. That's why I built this place up here. Usually the sheriff's department leaves us alone.' He walked over to the heap of old clothes draped over the boxes, picked out a T-shirt and handed it to David. 'Here, put this on. You folks are welcome to spend the night.'

David was still worried about the helicopters. 'Thanks for the offer, Caleb, but I think we should keep moving.'

'Where are you headed, brother? If you don't mind my asking.'

'Columbus, Georgia. My wife's got family down there.'

'How you gonna get there?'

'We left our car behind when the cops started chasing us. But we'll get to Columbus somehow. We'll walk if we have to.'

Caleb shook his head. 'I think I can help y'all. A man in our church named Graddick is supposed to drive to Florida tomorrow. He's gonna come here around midnight to pick up the serpents. I'm sure he'll give y'all a ride.'

'Serpents?' David thought he'd misheard.

'I caught a few timber rattlers. Graddick's gonna take 'em to a Holiness church in Tallahassee. It's a serpent-handling church, just like ours.' Caleb opened one of the cardboard boxes and removed a small wooden crate. It had a Plexiglas lid with small circular holes. 'We try to help our Florida brothers, but it ain't exactly legal. That's why we move the serpents at night.'

David peered through the Plexiglas. A rust-coloured snake, about as thick as a man's forearm, was coiled inside the crate.

Caleb set the crate on the floor, removed two more from the box and stacked them on top, then picked them all up. 'I'm gonna take these out and clean 'em. There's beef jerky in the cupboard if you're hungry.'

Joshua followed Caleb out of the shack. Caleb's father was still at the table, eating stew out of the can, and Michael was crouched on the floor with his Game Boy. Monique sank onto the army blanket, her face exhausted.

David sat beside her. 'You all right?' he asked, his voice low.

She stared at Michael and shook her head. 'Look at him,' she whispered. 'Now he has nobody. Not even his grandfather.'

'Don't worry, OK? The FBI will get Amil to a hospital.'

'It's my fault. All I cared about was the theory.' She clutched her forehead. 'Mama was right. I'm a cold-hearted bitch.'

'Listen, it's not your fault. It's the—'

'And you're no better!' She raised her head and gave him a challenging look. 'Have you thought about what you're gonna do once you find it?'

David hadn't. The vague instructions Dr Kleinman had given him were his only guidance. 'We'll have to entrust it to some neutral party, I guess. Maybe some international organisation. Einstein was a strong supporter of the UN.'

'Oh, screw Einstein! He should have destroyed the theory as soon as he realised the danger. But the equations were too damn important to him. He was a cold-hearted bastard, too.' She lay down on the blanket. 'Ah, the hell with it,' she said. 'Wake me when the snake man gets here.'

David grasped the edge of the blanket and folded it over her. Then he sat beside Michael, the other member of his new family.

The teenager was engrossed in *Warfighter*, so David watched the action on the Game Boy's screen. A soldier in a khaki uniform was racing down a dark hallway. Another soldier appeared at the end of the hall but Michael's soldier shot him down, then rushed into a small room, where he sprayed his M-16 at half a dozen figures. Soon they all lay on the floor. Then Michael's soldier opened a door at the other end of the room, the screen went black, and a message flashed: CONGRATULATIONS! YOU'VE REACHED LEVEL SVIA/4!

David guessed this must be an incredibly high expertise level, but Michael didn't show even a hint of satisfaction. David bent close and pointed at the screen. 'What happens now?'

'It goes back to Level A1.' Michael's voice was monotone.

David smiled. 'So you won the game, huh? That's great.'

'No, I didn't win. It goes back to Level A1.'

David nodded. OK, whatever. 'But it's a fun game anyway, right?'

Michael's attention had returned to *Warfighter*. After ten minutes, he had advanced to Level B3. Caleb's father fell asleep in his chair. Then David heard agitated voices outside. Alarmed, he rushed to the door and opened it an inch. Caleb was talking with another fat man with a brown beard and a shotgun. That must be Graddick, David thought. He stepped outside.

Caleb spun round. 'Go get your wife and your boy! You gotta leave now!'

'What is it? What's wrong?'

Graddick stepped forward. His deep-set eyes were an unearthly shade of blue. 'Satan's army is on the move. There's a convoy of Humvees coming down Route 83. And the black helicopters are landing on the ridge.'

PROFESSOR GUPTA lay on a mahogany table in Dr Milo Jenkins's dining room, with cushions under his legs to elevate them. Simon had been lucky indeed to find Jenkins; he was an old-fashioned country doctor who worked out of his home and had some experience treating the gunshot injuries of his hillbilly neighbours. He'd jammed a surgical clamp into the wound to stop the bleeding, and cleverly fashioned an intravenous line, which he hung from the chandelier. But Jenkins shook his head as he leaned over the blood-slicked table. Simon, who was pointing his Uzi at the doctor, sensed that something had gone awry.

Jenkins turned round to face him. 'It's like I told you,' he drawled. 'If you want to save his life, you gotta get him to a hospital.'

Simon frowned. 'I don't care about saving his life. I just need him to regain consciousness long enough for us to have a little talk.'

'Well, that ain't gonna happen either. He don't have enough blood to deliver oxygen to his organs.'

'So do a transfusion.'

'You think I got a blood bank in my refrigerator?'

Keeping the Uzi trained on Jenkins, Simon rolled up his right sleeve. 'My blood type is O negative. Universal donor.'

AT 5 A.M., just as the sun was rising over Washington, DC, the vice-president stepped through the side entrance to the West Wing.

The secretary of defence was sitting in a wingback chair in the lobby, a copy of the *New York Times* in his lap. He'd scribbled some notes in the front-page margins. The man never sleeps, the vice-president thought. He spends the whole night roaming the corridors of the White House.

The secretary jumped to his feet and shook the *Times* angrily. 'We got a problem,' he barked. 'Here, read it yourself.'

FBI ALLEGATIONS QUESTIONED

by Gloria Mitchell

A New York City police detective has challenged the Federal Bureau of Investigation's claim that a Columbia University professor was involved in the brutal slaying of six FBI agents on Thursday evening.

The FBI has launched a nationwide search for David Swift in the aftermath of the murders, which allegedly occurred during an undercover drug-buying operation in West Harlem. The Bureau claims that Swift, a history professor, was the leader of the cocaine-selling ring and ordered the killing of the undercover agents once their identities were revealed.

However, a detective in the Manhattan North homicide task force stated yesterday, on condition of anonymity, that FBI agents arrested Swift at St Luke's Hospital three hours before the killings allegedly took place.

The vice-president was too incensed to read any further. 'How the hell did this happen?'

The defence secretary swivelled his head. 'Typical cop stupidity. The detective gets his revenge on the feds for taking the Kleinman case from him.'

'Can we shut him up?'

'Oh, we took care of that already. The bigger problem is Swift's ex-wife. She prodded the *Times* into doing the story, and she and her son are staying with the reporter who wrote it. But we have half a dozen agents staking out the apartment. As soon as the reporter leaves for work, we'll move in.'

The vice-president nodded. 'And how's West Virginia progressing?'

'No worries there. One Delta Force squadron is in place, and two more are en route. They may have captured the fugitives already. I'll call today from Georgia. I'm going to Fort Benning to give a speech to the infantrymen.'

DAVID AWOKE in the back of Graddick's station wagon and found Monique sleeping snuggled against his chest. He was a bit startled; they'd dozed off several hours earlier at opposite ends of the cargo area. Perhaps Monique had instinctively backed away from the rattlesnake crates, concealed under a tarp below the rear window. Whatever the reason, she lay in his arms, her ribs gently rising with each breath, and David was struck by an almost painful feeling of tenderness for her.

Trying his best not to wake her, he raised his head and looked out of the window. It was early morning, and they were travelling down a highway bordered on both sides by southern pines. Graddick was whistling to a gospel tune on the car radio, and Michael was fast asleep on the back seat. After a while, David saw a sign: I-185 SOUTH, COLUMBUS. They were in Georgia.

Monique began to stir. She twisted round and opened her eyes. Surprisingly, she didn't pull away from his embrace. 'What time is it?'

David looked at his watch. 'Almost seven. You sleep all right?'

'Yeah, I'm better now.' She rolled onto her back and clasped her hands under her head. 'Sorry about last night. I got a little testy, I guess.'

'Being chased by the US Army could make anyone irritable.'

She smiled. 'You're not upset about the nasty things I said about Einstein?'

He shook his head, smiling back at her. 'No, not at all. In fact, you were right in some ways.'

'You mean Einstein really was a cold-hearted bastard?'

'I wouldn't go that far. But he could be pretty callous. He deserted his children after his first marriage fell apart. He left Mileva and their two sons in Switzerland while he went to Berlin to work on relativity. And he never acknowledged the daughter he and Mileva had before they were married.'

'Whoa, hold the phone. Einstein had an illegitimate daughter?'

'Yeah, her name was Lieserl. She was born in 1902, when Einstein was still a penniless tutor in Bern. Because it was a scandal, their families hushed it up; Mileva went back to her home in Serbia to have the baby. And then Lieserl either died or was put up for adoption. No one knows for sure.'

'What? How come nobody knows?'

'Einstein stopped mentioning her in his letters. Then Mileva returned to Switzerland and they got married. Neither of them talked about Lieserl again.'

Monique abruptly turned away from him, and stared at the floor.

'Hey, what's wrong?' David asked.

She shook her head. 'Nothing. I'm fine.'

Emboldened by their closeness, he cupped her chin and turned her face. 'Come on. No secrets between colleagues.'

She hesitated, then turned away again. 'When I was seven, my mother got pregnant. The father was probably one of the guys she bought heroin from. She gave the baby away, and never told me anything except that it was a girl.'

A tear pooled in the corner of her eye, then trickled down her cheek. Unable to stop himself, David leaned over and kissed it, tasting the salt on his lips. Then Monique closed her eyes and he kissed her mouth.

They kissed for at least a minute. Monique wrapped her arms round his waist and pulled him closer. The station wagon began to slow, obviously approaching the Columbus exit, but David kept on kissing her as the car cruised down the exit ramp. Finally he pulled back and looked at her. They gazed at each other for several seconds, neither saying a word. Then the station wagon made a sharp right turn and came to a stop.

They quickly disentangled themselves and looked out of the window. The car was parked in front of a run-down strip mall. David could tell they were near Fort Benning because the names of the stores shared a military theme: Ranger Rags, Combat Zone Chicken, a tattoo parlour called Ike's Inks. A few yards further down was a cinder-block building with a neon sign on its roof in the shape of a buxom woman reclining over the words THE NIGHT MANEUVERS LOUNGE. At least two dozen cars were parked in front of the bar and a seedy-looking bouncer guarded the entrance.

Graddick heaved himself out of the driver's seat and lumbered round the station wagon to open the rear door.

David scanned the street. 'Where are we?' he asked.

Graddick pointed at the Night Maneuvers Lounge. 'See the number over the door? That's the address you gave me—3617 Victory Drive.'

'No, this can't be right.' It was supposed to be Elizabeth Gupta's address.

'I know this place,' Graddick drawled. 'Before I was saved, I was a soldier in Satan's army. I was stationed here at Benning and we used to go to Victory Drive every time we got a weekend pass.' Scowling fiercely, he spat on the asphalt. 'VD Drive, we called it. It's a cesspool of harlotry.'

David remembered what the professor had said about his drug-addict daughter. 'The woman we need to see, I think she works in that bar.'

Graddick narrowed his eyes. 'This woman is kin to your wife?'

David nodded. 'That's right, they're cousins.'

'Harlotry and fornication,' Graddick muttered, frowning at the building. It looked like he wanted to tear the thing down with his bare hands.

It occurred to David this mountain man might prove useful. 'Yeah,' he said. 'We've got to try to help Elizabeth somehow.'

Graddick cocked his head. 'You mean you want to save her?'

'Absolutely. Otherwise she's going straight to hell.'

Graddick glanced at the rattlesnake crates. 'Well, I don't have to be in Tallahassee till five o'clock.' He smiled, and threw his arm round David's shoulders. 'All right, let's go into that den of iniquity and do the Lord's work!'

'No, no, I'll go into the bar alone, OK? Wait until we come out the back door. If she starts making a fuss, you can help me carry her to the car.'

'Good idea, brother!'

David squeezed Monique's arm, then slid out of the station wagon and headed for the lounge. He took a deep breath as he stepped through the door, and smiled as he handed the ten-dollar cover charge to the bouncer.

Inside, the room was blue with cigarette smoke. The old ZZ Top song 'She's Got Legs' blared from the speakers. On a stage, two topless dancers twined round a silver pole in front of an audience of hopelessly drunk GIs. The sight of all the uniforms made David nervous, but he edged closer to the stage and focused on the dancers. Neither the freckled redhead nor the lily-white blonde looked like she could be related to Professor Gupta.

David wandered to the bar and surveyed the three women doing lap dances for the soldiers on the bar stools. Two more blondes and another redhead. He began to worry that Elizabeth had gone home already. Or maybe she'd started dancing at a different club.

Just as he was giving up hope, David noticed someone in an olive-green army jacket slumped over a table in the far corner. At first he thought it was a GI who'd passed out, but as he moved closer he saw a lustrous fan of black hair. It was a woman sleeping. Under the army jacket, she was wearing nothing but a bright red bikini bottom and a pair of knee-high white boots.

David approached, sat in the chair opposite hers and gently rapped his knuckles on the table. 'Uh, excuse me?'

No response. David rapped a little harder. 'Excuse me?'

The woman slowly lifted her head. 'What the hell do you want?'

A smear of crimson lipstick ran from the corner of her mouth to the centre of her left cheek, and one of her false eyelashes had become partially detached, but her skin was the exact same shade as Michael's, and her tiny, doll-like nose looked just like Professor Gupta's.

Breathing fast, David leaned across the table. 'Elizabeth?'

'Don't call me that! My name's Beth.' She curled her upper lip. Her teeth had a brown stain near the gum line. Meth mouth, the addicts called it.

'OK, Beth. Listen, I was hoping we could just talk for a minute.'

She suddenly stood up, and her army jacket flapped open, giving a glimpse of a gold locket swinging on a chain between her breasts. 'It's twenty in the parking lot, fifty at the motel.'

He rose to his feet. 'All right, let's go to the parking lot.'

'You gotta pay first.'

David handed over a twenty and she headed for the emergency exit. Walking behind her, he noticed that she had a limp, which was the final confirmation of her identity. Elizabeth Gupta had been hit by a car as a young girl, breaking her left leg in three places.

She walked outside to a grimy alcove between the club's wall and a pair of Dumpsters. David spotted Graddick stepping out of the station wagon.

'Actually, Beth, I'm a friend of your father. I want to help you.'

She gazed at him blankly for a moment, then clenched her rotting teeth. 'My father? What are you talking about?'

'Professor Gupta told me where I could find you. We're trying to—'

'That fuck!' She rushed at him, aiming long nails at his eyes.

David braced himself, hoping to catch her by the wrists, but before she could get close enough, Graddick grabbed her from behind.

'Mother of abominations!' he shouted. 'Repent before judgment falls!'

Elizabeth lifted her right knee and smashed her heel down on Graddick's toes. He let go of her, howling in pain, and she sprang towards David.

He managed to deflect her right hand, but the nails of her left raked his neck. It was like battling a wild animal, and David was beginning to think he'd have to knock her out. But then Elizabeth saw something out of the corner of her eye. She stopped in her tracks. Then she raced across the parking lot towards Monique and Michael, who stood in front of Graddick's car.

'Michael!' she cried, flinging her arms round her son.

THE DELTA FORCE had set up its field headquarters in a Pentecostal church in Jolo. Lucille stared at the simple wood-frame building and shook her head. The special forces obviously had no patience for local sensitivities.

Lucille and Agent Crawford stepped into the church and started looking for Colonel Tarkington, the squadron commander. His men had organised a command post beside the pulpit. Two soldiers worked the radio, another pair bent over a map, and two more pointed their M-16s at a group of sullen hillbillies. Lucille shook her head again; then she spotted Tarkington at the back of the church, shouting orders into a field radio. She waited until he ended the transmission before approaching him.

'Colonel, I'm Special Agent Lucille Parker, your FBI liaison. I want to talk about the evidence seized at Carnegie's Retreat last night.'

The colonel eyed her for several seconds. 'What about it?'

'You need to send the damaged computer to the Bureau's lab in Quantico. We may be able to extract some of the data from the shattered hard drive.'

'Don't worry about it, darling. We sent all that stuff to the DIA.'

Lucille bristled. 'With all due respect, sir, our equipment at Quantico is far superior to anything the Defense Intelligence Agency has.'

'I told you, the DIA got it. Besides, we ain't gonna need that information. We're gonna find those fugitives before lunchtime. I got an operation to run here.' He marched over to the pulpit to confer with his men.

Lucille stood there for a moment, fuming. To hell with him, she thought. She stormed out of the church and back to her SUV.

Agent Crawford hurried to keep up. 'Where are we going now?' he asked.

She was about to say, 'DC,' but then an idea occurred to her. 'That computer in Carnegie's Retreat had a connection to the Internet, right?'

Crawford nodded. 'Yes, a cable connection, I think.'

'Phone their service provider. Find out if there was any activity last night.'

ELIZABETH GUPTA lay in a bathrobe on her bed in room 201 of the Army Mule Motel, across the street from the Night Maneuvers Lounge. Monique sat on the edge of the bed, stroking her hair and murmuring softly, as if she were a five-year-old with the flu. Michael sat in one of the chairs, playing with his Game Boy, while David peeked through the curtains, checking for unusual activity on Victory Drive. They'd sent Graddick out to get coffee.

Monique unwrapped a Nutri-Grain bar she'd bought from the motel's vending machine. 'Here, have some of this.'

'Nah, ain't hungry,' Elizabeth rasped. Since her screaming fit in the parking lot, she hadn't spoken more than a dozen words.

Monique held the Nutri-Grain bar right under her nose. 'Come on, take a bite. You need to eat something.' Her voice was gentle but firm.

Surrendering, Elizabeth nibbled at the bar; then she sat up so she could sip some water from a Styrofoam cup that Monique pressed to her lips. Within seconds she was jamming the bar into her mouth and picking up the crumbs, staring fixedly at Michael the whole time.

When she'd finished eating, she pointed at her son. 'I can't believe he's grown so much. The last time I saw him, he barely came up to my shoulders.'

'So your father never brought him down here for visits?' Monique asked.

Elizabeth scowled. 'He never even sent me pictures. I used to call collect on Michael's birthday, but he wouldn't accept my calls.'

'I'm so sorry.' Monique bit her lip. 'I didn't—'

'So is he dead? He told me I'd never see Michael again while he was alive.'

David stepped away from the window. 'Your father's in the hospital. He told us to bring Michael here because he didn't want him to go to an institution.'

Elizabeth gave him a suspicious look. 'That doesn't sound like my father. And why is he in the hospital?'

'Let's start from the beginning, OK? I used to be a student of your father's friend, Hans Kleinman. You remember him?'

Her face relaxed a bit. 'Sure, I know Hans. He's my godfather. He's also the only person in the world that my father hates more than me.'

'Your father didn't hate him. They were close colleagues.'

Elizabeth shook her head. 'My father hates him because Hans is smarter than he is. And Hans was in love with my mother. I saw him at her funeral and he was bawling like a baby.'

David tried to picture it, his old teacher weeping at Hannah Gupta's grave. It seemed so unlikely. But there was no time for this. He had to get to the point. 'Your father told us Hans came to Columbus to help you get straight.'

She looked down. 'Yeah, he got me a job, and he found an apartment for me, too. I even got Michael back for a few months. But I fucked it up.'

'Beth, Dr Kleinman died a couple of days ago, but he left—'

'Hans is dead?' She sat bolt upright. 'What happened?'

'I can't go into all the details right now, but he left a message—'

'Jesus Christ!' She raised her hand to her forehead. There had obviously been a strong connection between her and the old physicist.

David sat on the bed. 'Beth, I'm going to be honest with you. We're in a lot of trouble. Dr Kleinman had a scientific secret plenty of people would love to get their hands on. Did he leave you a computer when he came?'

'Nah. He got me a television, but I had to pawn it after I lost my job at the base.' Elizabeth folded her arms across her stomach. 'Hans called me then. He said he was gonna get me into another treatment programme.' She shut her eyes. 'I was high, so I told him to fuck off. That was the last time we ever talked.' She bent forward, and her body began to shake with sobs.

Monique went over to Michael and gently brought the teenager to his mother's side. Elizabeth automatically embraced him. He seemed to have a natural tolerance for her touch, though he didn't look at her. He turned a bit to the side so he could go on playing *Warfighter*.

After a while, Elizabeth pulled back and wiped the tears from her eyes. 'Still playing that war game,' she sighed. 'I'd have thought he'd be sick of it by now. He started when I was working at Fort Benning. Hans fixed one of the computers in my office so Michael could play the game.' She ran her hand through the boy's hair. 'On the days when the school for autistic kids was closed, I'd take him to work, and he'd sit there playing for hours.'

David's mind was racing. 'Wait a second. Dr Kleinman worked on one of the computers in your office at Benning?'

'Yeah, on my first day. He and my boss were old friends, so Hans had free run of the place. The VCS office—Virtual Combat Simulation—had crap they didn't even use, so they let Michael play with it.'

David exchanged a look with Monique, then focused on the Game Boy in Michael's hands. The screen showed the same dark hallway that David had seen the night before. Once again, an animated soldier burst into a room and fired his M-16. And again a message flashed: CONGRATULATIONS! YOU'VE REACHED LEVEL SVIA/4!

David bent over until his face was right in front of the teenager's. 'Michael, what's on Level SVIA/4?'

The boy tucked in his chin. 'I can't get to that level,' he said in his toneless voice. 'It goes back to Level A1.'

'I know, you told me that. But why can't you go to Level SVIA/4?'

'The Game Boy doesn't have that level. It's only on the program that runs on the server. That's how Hans set it up.'

'And why did he set it up that way?'

Michael opened his mouth wide, as if he were about to start screaming. Instead, for the first time, he looked David in the eye. 'He told me it would be safe! It was a safe place!'

DR MILO JENKINS lay face down on his living-room carpet with a bullet hole in his head. Simon had finished him off at 9 a.m., shortly after the hillbilly doctor announced that Professor Gupta was out of danger. The shots woke up Agent Brock, who was sprawled on the doctor's living-room sofa, but after a few seconds he rolled over and went back to sleep.

Simon would have loved some sleep himself. He'd had precious little of it, and the blood transfusion had weakened him. But his client, the enigmatic Henry Cobb, was due to make his daily phone call at 9.30, and Simon felt obliged to give him some favourable news.

He stepped into the dining room and approached the table where Gupta lay. The tiny professor slept fitfully on his back. Whatever painkillers Dr Jenkins had given him had surely worn off, which was what Simon wanted.

He pounded his fist on the sutured hole in Gupta's thigh. The old man convulsed, emitting a long, ragged moan.

Simon bent over the table. 'Wake up, Professor. Time for class.'

Gupta opened his eyes. 'What? Who are you?'

'That's not important. The important thing is finding your friends, David Swift and Monique Reynolds. You were with them last night.'

Gupta furrowed his brow—a sign that his memory was coming back.

Simon tightened his grip. 'You remember. And I think you also remember where they were headed.'

The old man narrowed his eyes. 'Who are you?' he repeated.

'I told you, that's not important. Where are Swift and Reynolds?'

Gupta's eyes darted to the left and for the first time he took in his surroundings. 'You're not FBI,' he whispered.

'No, I'm not.' Simon tore the gauze dressing off the professor's wound.

Gupta let out a scream. But when Simon studied the man's face he didn't see the usual frozen look of terror. The professor bared his teeth instead. 'Imbecile!' he hissed. 'You're just as stupid as that agent!'

Irritated, Simon dug two fingers into the wound. 'If you don't tell me where Swift and Reynolds are, I'll unpeel the skin of your leg, strip by strip.'

The professor lurched forward and glared at him with maniacal eyes. 'You brainless Russian pig! I'm Henry Cobb!'

CHAPTER EIGHT

'This is crazy,' Monique said. 'We're wasting our time.'

They were in the station wagon again, but now they were arguing instead of kissing. The car was parked at a gas station on Victory Drive, about a quarter of a mile south of the Night Maneuvers Lounge, and Elizabeth Gupta was making a call at a payphone. Graddick stood guard nearby, holding a cup of Dunkin' Donuts coffee.

'It's not crazy,' David insisted. 'It makes perfect sense.'

Monique shook her head. 'If Kleinman wanted to keep the theory away from the government, why would he put it on a US army computer?'

'Military computers are the most secure systems in the world. And he hid the equations in a piece of war-gaming software no one uses any more. And even if you reached *Warfighter*'s highest expertise level and found them, you wouldn't understand what they meant unless you were a physicist.'

Before Monique could reply, Elizabeth came striding back to the station wagon. She wore spandex leggings and a T-shirt now, but she still looked very much like a hooker. 'There's no answer,' she told David through the car window. 'Sheila probably went away for the weekend.'

David frowned. He'd hoped Sheila—a friend of Elizabeth's who still worked in the Virtual Combat Simulation office—could help them get into Fort Benning. 'Do you know anyone else who still works there?'

'Nah, nobody. Most of the guys in that office were computer geeks. The whole time I was there, they never once said hello.'

Another idea occurred to David. 'Beth, do you have any steady customers who work at the base?' he asked.

Her voice turned defensive. 'I got some once-a-week guys. Plenty of 'em.'

'Are any of them military police?'

'Yeah, I know a sergeant in the MPs. I've known him for years.'

'Do you know his phone number?'

Instead of answering, she reached into the back and snapped her fingers. Michael's head shot up from his Game Boy.

'Columbus directory,' she said sternly. 'Mannheimer, Richard.'

'706 544 1329,' Michael recited, then returned to his game.

Elizabeth smiled. 'Ain't that something? He memorised the Columbus phone book when he lived with me. The Macon phone book too.'

David wrote the number on a scrap of paper. He wasn't particularly surprised by Michael's memory feat; he knew that many autistic children had amazing powers of recall. What unsettled him was how Elizabeth used her son's skill. It must have been a convenient way to keep track of her johns.

He handed her the scrap of paper. 'Call the sergeant. Tell him you've got some friends in town who need passes to get on the base. Tell him we want to go visit our little brother, but we left our IDs at home by mistake.'

'Mannheimer ain't gonna do this for nothing, you know.'

David took out his wallet and removed five twenties. 'I'll cover it.'

Elizabeth stared at the twenty-dollar bills and licked her lips. She snatched the money out of his hand and headed back to the payphone.

David looked at Monique, but she turned away from him. He stretched his arm across the seat and touched her shoulder. 'Hey, what's wrong?'

'What do you think she's gonna do with that money? She's gonna spend it all on meth and then it's back to the strip club.'

'Look, we need her help. If you have a better idea, why don't you—?'

'Something's wrong,' Monique said. She pointed at the payphone.

Graddick stood beside Elizabeth, shouting at her. She ignored him and kept talking into the receiver. He grabbed her by the waist and started dragging her towards the station wagon. David was confused until he looked down Victory Drive and saw half a dozen black SUVs parked in front of the Night Maneuvers Lounge. A swarm of men in suits were leaping out of the vehicles and surrounding the strip club.

Graddick opened the wagon's rear door and pushed Elizabeth inside. 'Start the engine, brother! Satan's on our tail!'

IF THIS HAD BEEN an ordinary job, Simon would have shot his client by now. Professor Amil Gupta, a.k.a. Henry Cobb, was the most arrogant, infuriating man he'd ever worked for. As soon as the professor had revealed his identity he started excoriating Simon in the most unpleasant terms, and he continued to insult him as Simon re-bandaged the professor's bullet wound, Then, once Gupta was able to walk, he began shouting orders: he and Simon would take the pick-up to Georgia to follow the targets, while Agent Brock drove Dr Jenkins's Dodge van to New York. When Simon asked why Brock was going to New York, Gupta told him to shut up and find the keys.

Because Jenkins's house was outside the cordon the American forces had set up, Simon encountered no resistance on the back roads of southwestern

Virginia. By 11 a.m. they had reached I-81 and were heading south. The professor reclined in the passenger seat with his injured leg propped on the dashboard, checking his watch every five minutes and fulminating about the depths of human stupidity.

After they crossed into Tennessee, he abruptly pointed at a sign saying EXIT 69 BLOUNTVILLE. 'Get off the highway,' he ordered. 'Because of your incompetence, Swift and Reynolds have probably made contact with my daughter already. I've done some work with a Blountville defence contractor, and they're hooked into my surveillance network. If I'm right about where Swift and Reynolds are going, we may be able to observe them.'

Simon travelled about two kilometres down Route 394 to the sprawling one-storey building where Mid-South Robotics was located. Because it was Saturday morning, there was only one car in the lot. Simon pulled up next to it; then he and Professor Gupta headed for the security guard's booth.

SERGEANT MANNHEIMER was balding, beak-nosed and loudmouthed. He sat in the back seat of the station wagon with his arm round Elizabeth's waist, casting lascivious glances at Monique, who sat with Michael in the cargo area. Graddick grumbled as he drove towards Fort Benning; he obviously wasn't happy about visiting the army base. But David had insisted that it was necessary for Elizabeth's salvation.

As they approached the security gate, David noticed a long line of cars. It seemed a lot of traffic for a Saturday morning. Pointing at the gate, he turned to Mannheimer. 'What's going on?'

The sergeant was toying with the gold locket round Elizabeth's neck. 'Everyone's coming to see Darth Vader. He's giving a speech today.'

'Darth Vader?'

'Yeah, the secretary of defence.'

David saw half a dozen MPs inspecting the cars at the front of the line, opening trunks and looking under chassis. 'Shit. They've beefed up security.'

'Chill out, dude,' Mannheimer said. 'Those are my boys.'

David grew ever more nervous as the car inched to the front of the line. When they reached the gate, a young corporal with an M-9 pistol in his holster stuck his face in the driver's-side window.

'Licence and registration,' he ordered. 'And ID for all passengers.'

Mannheimer leaned forward. 'Hey, Murph,' he called cheerily. 'These guys are with me. We're just going to the PX to do a little shopping.'

Murph saluted halfheartedly and waved them through the gate.

As soon as Lucille saw the records of Gupta's Internet activity—in particular, the web page showing the location of 3617 Victory Drive—she issued new orders for the Bureau's Learjet. Two hours later, she and Agent Crawford strode into the Night Maneuvers Lounge, which had been secured by agents from the Atlanta office. The bartender, who was also the club's manager, had recognised David Swift from the photograph the agents showed him, and said he'd seen the suspect leave the club with a dancer who, it turned out, was Beth Gupta, the professor's daughter. The Atlanta agents failed to find her in her temporary residence at a motel across the street. The manager had told them he had no idea where Beth could be.

Lucille went straight to the bar. A short, fat, bearded man was standing behind it. 'So you're in charge of this lovely establishment?' she asked.

He nodded. 'Like I said before, I don't know where Beth is.'

'Does she have any friends here in town?'

He pointed at the dancers lined up at the bar, shivering in their G-strings. 'Sure, the girls are all friends. Talk to Amber or Britney.'

'Any other friends?'

'There's a girl named Sheila, a real stuck-up bitch. She came in once to give me hell. She and Beth used to work together on the base.'

This was news. 'Beth had a civilian job at Fort Benning?'

'Yeah, before she came here. Working with computers, she said.'

Lucille thought of the wrecked computer she saw in the cabin in West Virginia. The suspects were following a digital trail and she could make a good guess as to their next destination.

The first things David saw were the jump towers, three tall spires looming over the barracks and administrative buildings of Fort Benning. Paratroopers were leaping from the arms of the spires and floating to the ground like seedpods from an enormous steel flower.

Sergeant Mannheimer instructed Graddick to park behind a yellow building called Infantry Hall. The Virtual Combat Simulation office was in its west wing. David had concocted a story explaining why they needed to go there, but Mannheimer seemed to care only about Elizabeth. He pulled her out of the car and led her towards the building's rear entrance.

Graddick looked at David with concern. 'What's going on, brother?'

David squeezed his shoulder reassuringly. 'Just stay here till we get out, all right? It'll be a few minutes. Then we'll get to work on Elizabeth's soul.'

Graddick nodded. Monique and David rushed Michael through the entrance and up the stairs, catching up with Elizabeth and the sergeant at an unmarked door on the third floor. Mannheimer rummaged through his pockets and found a skeleton key. But before he could slip it into the lock, David heard an oddly familiar noise coming down the hall. He turned round and saw a Dragon Runner, the boxy, silver surveillance robot that Gupta had developed. The machine pointed its bulblike sensor at them.

David froze. 'Shit! They found us!'

Mannheimer chuckled and the robot rolled past. 'Those things ain't operational yet. They're still working out the bugs.' He opened the door.

They stepped into the room. It was a big space, maybe forty feet long. At one end, racks of servers hummed and blinked on their steel shelves. Opposite them was a desktop PC with an extra-large flat-panel screen, and in the centre of the room were two hollow, transparent spheres at least nine feet high and resting on platforms studded with metal rollers.

Monique stood in the doorway and stared at the spheres, just as befuddled as David. But Michael headed straight for a cabinet. While his mother and the sergeant disappeared into an adjoining office, he removed a bulky black device that David recognised as a pair of virtual-reality goggles. Beaming with joy, Michael strapped them on and adjusted them; then he dashed to the computer and began tapping its keyboard.

David and Monique looked over his shoulder. After a few seconds, the screen showed an image of a soldier standing in a wide green field. The soldier wore a khaki uniform and a helmet emblazoned with a big red number 1.

'He's loading *Warfighter*,' David whispered.

The words READY TO START? appeared on the screen. Michael returned to the cabinet and pulled out a plastic mock-up of an M-16. Then he opened a side hatch in one of the spheres, and wriggled into the giant transparent ball.

'What's he doing in there?' Monique said.

Michael closed the hatch and donned the VR goggles. Holding the plastic rifle like a real infantryman, he started walking forward, but the sphere just spun round him, rotating in place. After a while, Michael quickened his pace and the sphere rotated faster. Pretty soon he was galloping like a hamster in an exercise wheel. When David looked at the computer screen, he saw the khaki-clad soldier running across the field.

'This is fantastic,' David said. 'Michael can see the whole simulation on his goggles. He's running inside a virtual world.'

'That's great,' Monique replied. 'But what's going to happen when he reaches Level SVIA/4?'

'I don't know. There may be a way to download the theory from the server. But I bet you have to use the VR interface to access it.'

David studied the icons at the bottom of the screen until he found the one he wanted: TWO-PLAYER GAME. He clicked on it, then went to the cabinet and found another pair of VR goggles and another plastic rifle.

'I'm going in,' he said, stepping towards the second sphere.

SIMON STOOD GUARD in the testing lab at Mid-South Robotics while Professor Gupta studied surveillance videos on the lab's computer. The screen was divided into a dozen squares, each showing a live feed from one of the Dragon Runners deployed at Fort Benning. Just before noon, the computer let out a *ping*—the face-recognition program had found a match. Simon moved closer and saw a tall, ugly soldier with his arm round a woman. Then he saw Swift, Reynolds and Gupta's grandson.

'Interesting,' the professor said. 'They're at the VCS office.' He paused, deep in thought. 'That's where Elizabeth worked. The job Hans got her.'

On the screen, the targets entered a room and closed the door behind them, cutting off the surveillance. Gupta quickly exited the program.

'Kleinman!' he shouted. 'That old fool thought he was being clever. Hiding the thing right under my nose!'

'You mean the *Einheitliche Feldtheorie*?'

A new window popped up on the screen and Gupta typed in a password. 'Luckily, all VCS programs are designed for remote access.' The screen showed a list of military servers and activity reports. 'Just as I thought,' he said. 'They're running *Warfighter*.'

'Can they download the theory? Can they delete it?'

Gupta clicked on one of the servers, then turned and glared at Simon. 'Go into the supply room. There might be a joystick.'

DAVID STOOD in a wide field bordered by southern pines. Turning to the right, he saw forested hills. When he turned left, the virtual-reality display showed a break in the trees and a cluster of low buildings. The graphics were amazingly realistic. He even heard birdcalls through the headset. After a couple of seconds, he realised that the simulated landscape had been designed to look like the wooded training grounds of Fort Benning. He could see the jump towers above the tops of the trees.

'What are you waiting for?'

David raised his rifle when he heard the voice through the headphones.

He could see the barrel of his M-16 on the display, but there were no figures in the field or the woods. 'Hey!' he called. 'Who's there?'

'It's me, dummy.' Monique's voice. 'I'm at the terminal. You look just like Michael's soldier, but you got a big red 2 on your helmet.'

'How did you . . . ?'

'You seemed a little lost, so I found a microphone at the terminal to tell you which way to go. Michael's in the village.'

He pointed his rifle at the buildings. 'You mean over there?'

'Yeah, and he's already reached Level B2. From what I can tell, you have to get close to him before he reaches SVIA/4.'

Very gingerly, David took a step forward. The sphere turned effortlessly under his feet. He stepped left and the sphere turned sideways. He began to walk towards the break in the trees. 'This feels almost normal,' he said.

'Try running. You've got a long way to go.'

He broke into a trot. The VR display showed the landscape advancing: the buildings loomed larger and David started to see dark figures face down in the grass. They were the black-clad enemy soldiers that David had seen on the Game Boy. 'It looks like Michael took care of these guys.'

'Keep your eyes open. He didn't get all of them.'

'What if they shoot me? How many lives do you get?'

'Let me check the instruction file.' There was a pause. 'OK, if you get shot in the body, you can't move but you can still fire your gun. If you get shot in the head, you go back to the start. Michael just made it to Level B3.'

David picked up the pace, zigzagging round the dead soldiers. After a few seconds, he reached the village. On one side of the main street was a row of two-storey buildings; on the other was a church. The street was empty except for fallen soldiers. David ran down the middle until he came to a yellow warehouse. Half a dozen corpses lay outside the entrance. Struggling to keep his balance inside the spinning sphere, he slowed and peered through the doorway. It was dark but he could make out bodies on the floor.

He was just about to take a step inside when he heard gunshots. They seemed to be coming from behind, so he wheeled round. An enemy soldier was racing down the street, firing an AK-47. David aimed the plastic rifle and pulled the trigger. The enemy soldier dropped to his knees. He was grimacing in pain, but still clutched his rifle.

'Shoot him in the head!' Monique yelled. 'Quick, in the head!'

David fired at the soldier's skull. The figure sank to the ground.

'Go inside the building! Michael's on the second floor.'

He turned back and stepped inside. The display darkened as he went down a long, narrow corridor. He was beginning to feel queasy.

'Go left. *Left!* There's a stairway!'

He turned left, stumbling like a drunk. Gunshots echoed down the corridor but he saw only white flashes. 'I gotta stop. Something's behind me.'

'No, keep going. Michael's at Level C3. He's almost finished.'

David found the stairway, and the display brightened. At the top, he went down another corridor, passing bare rooms with corpses on the floor.

'Turn right when you get to the end of the hall. Then you—'

A soldier bolted out of one of the rooms, a few feet ahead. Startled, David dropped his M-16. He instinctively raised his hands, braced for virtual death. But the soldier merely continued down the hall. David belatedly noticed he wore a khaki uniform and had a red 1 on his helmet. It was Michael.

Elated, David picked up his rifle. At the end of the corridor, Michael's soldier turned right, and David heard a barrage of gunfire. By the time he caught up to the boy, all six enemies lay face down on the floor.

'That's it!' Monique cried. 'You're at the final level!'

Michael's soldier approached a doorway at the other end of the room. David held his breath, expecting to see *Herr Doktor*'s equations at last. But instead they entered a room lined with dozens of grey metal lockers. Michael's soldier touched the nearest locker with his M-16. A new rifle materialised in his hands, this one equipped with a grenade launcher.

David's heart sank. 'Damn it! How long does this go on?'

'Wait a second. Look at the letters on the lockers.'

Each locker was marked with a set of initials: the first had PVT for private, the second CPL for corporal and so on. David recognised the first dozen military ranks, then the abbreviations became obscure: WO/1, CMSAF, MGYSGT.

'Check out the far wall,' Monique said. 'The second to last locker.'

David spotted SVIA/4. 'The letters on the Game Boy!'

He rushed to the locker and tapped it with his M-16. On the VR display, David saw the virtual grenade launcher materialise on his rifle. At the same time the initials on the door abruptly rearranged themselves, the VI rotating ninety degrees. The result was an equation: $S \leq A/4$.

David didn't recognise it. But he wasn't the physicist. 'Monique, do you see that?' he called into the microphone. 'Do you—?'

'*Look out!*'

He heard gunfire again. He turned round to see Michael's soldier fall to the floor. Then the VR display turned red, as if splashed with blood.

IT WAS A POOR SUBSTITUTE for war, Simon thought as he looked over Gupta's shoulder at the computer screen. The program was absurdly unrealistic. When the two soldiers were shot, they didn't writhe on the ground or scream for their mothers. They simply collapsed.

After Gupta dispatched his opponents, he advanced towards the locker with the odd symbols on its door. Toggling the joystick, he extended his soldier's rifle so that it touched the locker. A grenade launcher appeared on the rifle, then a message flashed: READY TO DOWNLOAD? YES OR NO?

Gupta clicked on YES. The message changed to DOWNLOAD COMPLETE IN 46 SECONDS. 'I'm sorry, *Herr Doktor*,' the professor whispered as the numbers ticked down. 'But you shouldn't have kept me waiting.'

'DAVID? WHERE ARE YOU? My screen's going haywire!'

He could hear Monique's voice but couldn't see anything. The VR display showed only a thick red mist. The last thing he remembered was Michael's soldier falling, and as he pictured this image he recalled that another soldier had stood behind Michael's. A soldier with the number 3 on his helmet.

David tore off the goggles. Outside the transparent sphere, Monique was bent over the terminal, frantically working the keyboard. 'Someone's accessing the server,' she yelled. 'There's a download in progress!'

In the sphere to his left, Michael raised his rifle and began running again. He was starting another game.

'We have to go back to the start,' David said.

'You don't have time! There's only twenty seconds left!'

Unable to think of another option, David strapped on his goggles. The red mist was fading now, and he expected to find himself back in the field outside the village. But once the last red wisps vanished, he saw a row of lockers with stencilled initials on their doors. He was on his hands and knees, still in the locker room. He'd been shot in the body, not the head.

He couldn't move forward but he could point his weapon. The soldier with the 3 on his helmet stood in front of the locker, which now showed a countdown on its door. As the read-out reached 0:09, David pulled the trigger.

SIMON NOTICED some movement on the computer screen. Something small and round bounced against the row of lockers and passed out of sight. 'What was that?' he asked. 'Something moved across the screen to the left!'

Frowning, the professor flicked his joystick left. A green egg-shaped object lay on the floor. Simon recognised it at once. It was a US Army M406 grenade.

DAVID'S LEGS nearly buckled when he stepped out of the sphere. 'What happened?' he asked as he staggered towards Monique. 'Did we stop it?'

She stayed bent over the terminal. 'Why did you use the grenade? All you had to do was shoot the bastard to break his connection.'

'But we stopped the download, right? He didn't get the theory, did he?'

'Oh, yeah, you stopped the download. You also crashed *Warfighter* and deleted all the program files.'

He gripped the edge of the desk. 'The file containing the theory?'

'It's gone. Crashing *Warfighter* permanently corrupted it.'

His stomach lurched. It was like stepping into the sphere again, but now the whole universe was spinning. The blueprints of the cosmos, the hidden design of reality—all gone in an instant because of his error.

Monique finally lifted her gaze from the screen. She was smiling. 'Luckily, Dr Kleinman took precautions. He built an escape hatch for the file. Just before the program was deleted, it saved the data on a flash drive.'

'What?'

In her palm she held a silver cylinder about three inches long and an inch wide. 'The theory's in here, I hope. I better grab a laptop to make sure.'

David went limp. He stared at the flash drive. Until that moment he hadn't realised how important the theory was to him.

While Monique searched for a laptop, Michael emerged from his sphere. He put his VR goggles and rifle back, then picked up his Game Boy, his face as expressionless as ever.

A moment later his mother came out of the adjoining office.

'Where's Mannheimer?' David asked Elizabeth.

'Asleep on the director's couch.'

'Listen, we have to leave before anyone gets suspicious.' He went to the window and noticed two disturbing developments. First, Graddick's station wagon was no longer parked by the rear entrance. And second, a squadron of MPs was running towards the building.

David pulled Michael down the corridor, heading for the front of the building. Elizabeth clattered behind with Monique, who was carrying a sleek silver laptop she'd found. When David reached the stairway above the front entrance, he heard voices below, then laughter and a burst of cheering.

They barrelled downstairs and emerged in an entry hall crowded with soldiers and civilians. It was some kind of reception. David threaded through the crowd, terrified that someone would raise the alarm, but in half a minute they were outside in a stream of people heading for the parking lots.

After about ten minutes the crowd had thinned out, but the four of them continued walking, following signs that said WEST GATE, EDDY BRIDGE. Soon they saw a river up ahead, spanned by a two-lane bridge. On the near side was a security gate. The barrier was down and several cars were backed up behind it, waiting to leave the base, but the two MPs at the gate stood there like statues. Shit, David thought, they've locked the place down. He considered doing an about-face, but the MPs had already spotted them.

They strolled up to the gate like an eccentric family on a hike. 'Hey, soldiers!' David called. 'Is this the way to the campground?'

'You mean the Uchee Creek Campground, sir?' one MP replied.

'Yeah, yeah, that's the one.'

'It's over the bridge and two miles south. But you can't cross the bridge now, sir. There's a security alert. We're awaiting further orders.'

'The alert is only for cars. Pedestrians can go through, right?'

The MP thought about it for a moment. 'Just wait here, sir.'

While David and Monique exchanged nervous looks, a Humvee sped up to the gate. The driver jumped out and ran to the MPs with a couple of flyers. The MPs turned their backs, so David quietly led Michael, Monique and Elizabeth round the barrier. The bridge was a hundred feet away.

'Halt!' One of the MPs had turned round. 'Where d'ya think you're going?'

David didn't stop. 'Sorry, we're in a rush!'

The other MP pointed his pistol. '*Stop right there!*'

Within seconds all the soldiers had drawn their M-9s. No one saw the rattlesnake until it landed at their feet. It bounced on the asphalt, and sank its fangs into the first moving thing it saw, which happened to be the calf of an MP's leg. The soldier screamed; then a second snake came flying through the air. David looked ahead and saw Graddick crouched by the riverbank.

With a great heave, Graddick tossed his third rattler, then waved at David. 'Come on, you sinners!' he shouted. 'Get in the car!'

KAREN AND JONAH were in Brownsville, one of the poorest neighbourhoods in Brooklyn, having spent the entire day with her friend Gloria Mitchell, the *New York Times* reporter in whose apartment they were staying. Slow-moving black SUVs had been trailing them wherever they went.

As they hurried through a deserted playground, a tall, thick-necked man stepped out of the shadows. It was 9 p.m., and the light was so dim that Karen saw only a silhouette. She couldn't make out his face, but she could tell he was wearing a suit, and she noticed a coiled wire snaking behind his left ear. She stopped in her tracks and squeezed Jonah's hand.

Gloria marched up to the agent. 'Hey, buddy, are you lost?' she asked. 'The Bureau's office is in Federal Plaza, in case you were wondering.'

'What makes you think I'm with the Bureau?' he answered.

'Your cheap suit, for one thing. And the fact that your pals have been following me all day long.'

'I'm not interested in you. Just your friend.'

'Well, forget about it. If you arrest her, it's gonna be all over the front page of the *New York Times* tomorrow morning.'

The agent reached into his jacket and pulled out a gun. 'I read the *Post*,' he said. Then he aimed at Gloria's head and fired.

Karen grabbed Jonah and pressed his face into her belly so he wouldn't see. Her legs trembled as the agent stepped forward and a wedge of streetlight illuminated his face. His nose was swollen, and bruises mottled his forehead, but she recognised him nonetheless. It was Agent Brock.

CHAPTER NINE

Simon knocked back another glass of Stoli. He sat in the living room of a modest house in Knoxville belonging to Richard Chan and Scott Krinsky, two of Professor Gupta's former students. While Gupta used the telephone in their kitchen, Richard poured vodka into Simon's glass. He and Scott worked at Oak Ridge National Laboratory, where they built equipment for generating high-intensity proton beams. Pale, gangly and boyish, they treated Professor Gupta with an almost fanatical reverence. And they weren't surprised when Simon and Gupta showed up at their doorstep. The young physicists were clearly co-conspirators, recruited by Gupta long ago.

As soon as Simon set his empty glass on the coffee table, Richard filled it again. Simon leaned back in his chair. 'So you gentlemen work with beam lines, correct? Guiding the protons as they go round in the accelerator?'

Both of them nodded, but neither said a word. They obviously weren't too comfortable chatting with a Russian mercenary.

'It must be a complicated job,' Simon continued. 'Making sure all the particles are targeted properly. Determining ideal conditions for impact. Some strange things can happen when the protons smash together, eh?'

Richard and Scott exchanged glances. They were probably wondering how this hired killer had learned about particle physics.

'And if you had a unified theory that specified exactly how to set up the particle collisions, you could produce some interesting effects, no?'

Their eyes showed alarm now. 'I'm . . . I'm sorry,' Richard stammered. 'I don't know what you're talking—'

'Don't worry.' Simon chuckled. 'Your professor told me all about the *Einheitliche Feldtheorie.* Otherwise, I wouldn't have known what information to extract from *Herr Doktor*'s colleagues.'

At that moment, Gupta stepped into the room. He gave Richard and Scott a kindly smile, then pointed at Simon. 'Come. We have something to discuss.'

Simon followed him into the kitchen. 'Was that Brock on the phone?'

The professor nodded. 'He's got Swift's ex-wife and son. Now he's driving south as fast as he can. This could be a useful bargaining chip.'

'Assuming Swift has the theory. We don't know for certain.'

'Of course he has the theory. Don't be stupid.'

'He deleted everything from the server. Maybe that was his intention all along, to erase the theory. Maybe that's what Kleinman told him to do.'

'It's the last thing Kleinman would have wanted.' Gupta seemed unconcerned. 'Trust me, Swift has it. And the next step in humanity's ascent is inevitable. Nothing can stop us from staging our demonstration.'

'We still have to find him before the American soldiers do.'

'That's also inevitable. My daughter is a methamphetamine addict.' The old man grinned. 'And by now I'm sure she's getting a little desperate.'

IN A REMOTE CLEARING in the Cherokee National Forest, Graddick gathered dead leaves and branches for a campfire. After the escape from Fort Benning, David had wanted to head for Mexico or Canada, but Graddick argued that too many of Satan's minions stood between them and the border. Instead he drove into northern Alabama, up the sinuous roads of Sand Mountain. By nightfall they'd crossed into Tennessee and reached the Great Smokies.

Graddick seemed to know every hill and hollow. At a crossroads called Coker Creek he went down a dirt path, parked the station wagon behind a thicket and began collecting kindling. David marvelled at the mountain man's generosity. They'd met him just the night before, and now he was risking his life for them. Although David hadn't told him about the unified field theory, Graddick clearly understood that something enormous was at stake.

The crescent moon gave a pale glow to the pleated hills around them.

David sat in the clearing with Michael, who'd propped his Game Boy on a tree stump. His mother was asleep in the station wagon; she'd grown agitated during the long drive, cursing and shivering, but quieted down eventually. Monique had spent half her time comforting her and the other half studying the laptop she'd purloined from the VCS lab.

The good news was that the flash drive did indeed hold a scientific paper written by Albert Einstein more than fifty years ago. The bad news was that it was in German. The title was '*Neue Untersuchung über die Einheitliche Feldtheorie*', which David could sort of translate—a new understanding of the unified field theory, most likely. But that was as far as he could go.

Monique now sat alone on a grassy patch in the clearing, still staring at the laptop's screen, examining the paper's dozens of pages of equations.

After stuffing a few wads of newspaper into the woodpile, Graddick set it alight with a match. He went to the station wagon and returned with five cans of Dinty Moore beef stew, which he opened and placed near the fire. Then he sat down next to David and pointed at the eastern horizon.

'We're gonna head up to Haw Knob tomorrow,' he said. 'We'll drive along the Smithfield Road until it ends, then hike up the mountain.'

'Why there?' David asked.

'It's a good place to hide. They got limestone caverns, and a spring. And you can see for miles around. I'll keep you supplied and you can hole up till the end of the summer. By then the heathens will give up the hunt.'

David tried to picture it, spending the summer in a limestone cavern. The plan was worse than impractical—it was hopeless. The army and the FBI wouldn't stop looking for them. Even if, by some miracle, they made it across the border, sooner or later the Pentagon would track them down.

After a few minutes, Graddick stood up and went to the fire. With his hand wrapped in a grey handkerchief, he retrieved the heated Dinty Moore cans, and distributed them with some plastic spoons. Before David could take a bite of stew, he looked up and saw Monique looming over him.

'I got something,' she said. 'But you're not going to like it.'

David rose to his feet and led her to the edge of the clearing. 'Is it there?' he asked. 'The unified theory?'

'I didn't think so at first. But the more I looked at the equations, the more they reminded me of the formulae you see in topology. You know, the mathematics of surfaces and shapes and knots. That made me think of the geons we talked about, the knots in spacetime. Here, let me show you.'

Monique sat next to him and opened the laptop. She pointed at the top of the screen. 'This is the unified field equation, expressed in the language of differential topology. It's similar to the classical equations of relativity, but it encompasses particle physics. Einstein found that all particles are geons. Each particle is a different kind of twist in spacetime, and the forces are ripples in the fabric.' She pulled David closer and pointed lower down the page. 'This is one of the solutions. It describes a fundamental particle with a negative charge. It's a geon, a minuscule wormhole with closed timelike curves. The solution even specifies the mass of the particle. Do you recognise it?'

Just beneath her fingernail was: $M = 0.511\ MeV/c^2$.

'The mass of an electron,' David whispered.

'And he's got at least twenty more solutions for particles with different charges and spins. Most of these particles weren't discovered until long after Einstein died. He predicted the existence of quarks and the tau lepton. And he's got solutions for particles that haven't even been found yet.'

Monique scrolled through the file, revealing page after page of topological equations. David stared at the screen with a burgeoning sense of joy. It was the ultimate triumph of physics, a single set of equations that could describe everything from the inner workings of a proton to the structure of the galaxy.

He smiled at Monique. 'This isn't too different from string theory, except the particles are loops of spacetime instead of strings of energy.'

'There's another similarity. Take a look at this.' She scrolled down to an equation that stood out from the others: $S \leq A/4$.

'That's the equation I saw in *Warfighter*!'

Monique nodded. 'It's called the holographic principle. The *S* stands for the maximum amount of information that can be jammed into a region of space, and the *A* stands for the surface area of that region. Basically, all the information in any three-dimensional space—the position of every particle, the strength of every force—can be contained in the two-dimensional surface area of the space. So you can think of the universe as a hologram.'

'Wait a second, I think I've heard of this.'

'String theorists have been talking about the principle for years, but Einstein used it half a century ago to map out the history of the universe. It's in the second section of the paper, right here.'

She pointed at another equation. Beside it was a sequence of computer graphics apparently reproducing Einstein's sketches. The first image showed a pair of flat sheets moving towards each other. In the second image the sheets bent and rippled as they collided, and in the third they pulled away from each other, now pockmarked with newly born galaxies:

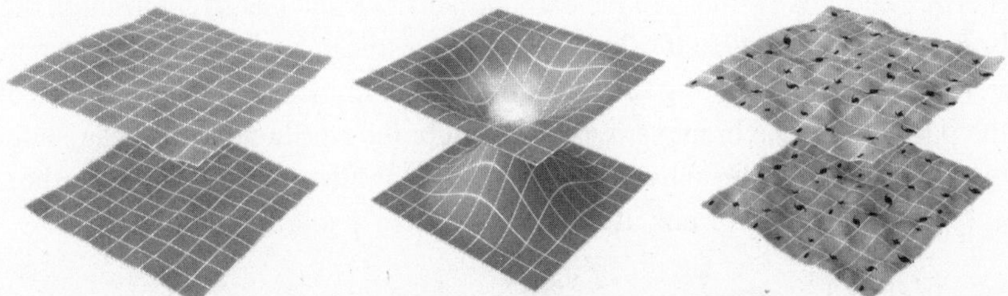

'What are those things?' David asked. 'They look like sheets of tinfoil.'

'In string theory, those are called branes,' Monique said. 'They look two-dimensional in the diagrams, but each actually represents a three-dimensional universe. Every galaxy and star and planet in our universe is contained in one of the branes. The other brane is a separate universe, and they're both moving through a larger space called the bulk, which has ten dimensions.'

'Why are they colliding?'

'One of the few things that can leave the brane and travel through the bulk is gravity. One brane can gravitationally attract another, and when they collide they twist and generate energy. I've worked on the idea, but nothing I've done comes close to this. Einstein worked out equations for our brane and how it evolved. His unified theory explains how everything got started.'

'You mean the Big Bang?'

'That's what these diagrams are showing. Two empty branes collide and the energy from the crash fills our universe, eventually turning into atoms and stars and galaxies, all hurtling outwards in a gigantic wave.' She looked him in the eye. 'This is it, David. The answer to the mystery of Creation.'

He studied the drawings, bewildered. 'But where's the proof?'

'The proof is here!' Monique stabbed at the formulae below the diagrams. 'Einstein predicted all the observations astronomers have made for fifty years. The expansion rate of the universe, the breakdown of matter and energy, it's all right here!'

'So why did you say I wasn't going to like it?' David asked.

She took a deep breath and scrolled down to another page. 'There's something else that can travel out of the brane and into the extra dimensions of the bulk. You remember what a neutrino is, right?'

'Sure. It's like the electron's kid brother. A particle with no charge and very little mass.'

'Well, some physicists have speculated that there's a particle called a sterile neutrino that doesn't usually interact with other particles in our universe.

Sterile neutrinos fly through the extra dimensions and pass right through our brane like water molecules through a sieve. Einstein's equation for this particle predicts that twisting the spacetime of our brane can generate bursts of the particles. If the brane is twisted enough, the sterile neutrinos can shoot out of one part of our universe and travel to another part by taking a short cut through the bulk. Look at this.' She pointed at another diagram:

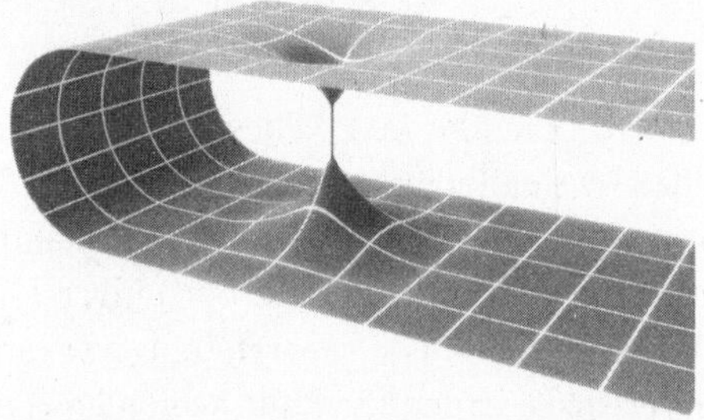

David recognised the picture. 'That's a wormhole, right? A bridge that connects distant regions of spacetime?'

'Yeah, but only sterile neutrinos can take this short cut. And the particles can gain energy as they move through the extra dimensions. A hell of a lot of energy if the beam of neutrinos is orientated the right way.'

David frowned. 'And when the energised particles return to our universe?'

Monique closed the laptop. 'The returning particles can trigger a violent warping of the local spacetime. The amount of energy released depends on how you set up the experiment. Under the right conditions, you could use this process to generate heat or electricity. But you could also use it as a weapon.'

A breeze rustled the needles of the pine tree beside them. Though the air was still warm, David felt a chill. 'So you can choose the point where the particles re-enter our universe? Launch the beam from Washington and ricochet it through the extra dimensions so that it hits a bunker in Tehran?'

She nodded. 'You'd have fine-tune control over the coordinates of the target and the size of the blast. A single burst of sterile particles could take out a nuclear lab in North Korea, even if it's buried a mile underground.'

Now David knew why the FBI had chased them halfway across the country. A weapon like this would be perfect for the war on terror. The Pentagon could eliminate its enemies without deploying commandos or cruise missiles. Because the particle beam would travel through the extra dimensions, it would evade radar, antiaircraft fire and all other defences.

'How much energy can the beam deliver? What's the upper limit?'

'There's no limit. You could use this technology to blow up an entire continent.' She swallowed. 'But here's the worst part: it's a lot easier to build this kind of weapon than to manufacture a nuke. All you need are the equations and a team of engineers. Al-Qaeda could do it without much trouble.'

David turned away from her and stared at the campfire. 'Shit!' he muttered. 'No wonder Einstein didn't want to publish it.'

'In the last part of the paper he gave the formulae for generating the beams. You'd have to warp a tiny piece of spacetime in a perfectly spherical pattern. You could probably set it up by smashing protons together in a collider.'

David's heart started pounding. 'You mean someone could build this weapon using a particle accelerator?'

'The accelerators at the national laboratories are already designed to maximise the number of particle collisions. You know the Tevatron, the collider at Fermilab? The physicists there can cram trillions of protons into a beam narrower than a human hair. You'd have to adjust the collider in exactly the right way to warp the spacetime and generate the sterile neutrinos, but Einstein's equations would allow you to calculate the necessary adjustments.'

Her last words rang across the clearing. David nervously looked over his shoulder and saw Graddick toss an empty Dinty Moore can into the fire. Then the mountain man picked up a full one and headed for his station wagon.

David turned back to Monique. 'OK, we have two choices. We can smuggle the flash drive across the border and make contact with the UN, or maybe we can find a better place than—'

'No, we can't hide it.' Monique removed the flash drive from the USB port of the laptop. 'We have to destroy it.'

David tensed. 'Are you nuts! This is the theory of everything. We can't throw it away. Kleinman told me to keep it safe. Those were his last words.'

Monique wrapped her fingers round the silver cylinder. 'It's too risky, David. Believe me, I don't want to do this. But we have to think of everyone's safety. The terrorists want this theory as much as the government does, and they've already come close to getting it. Remember the soldier in *Warfighter*, with the number three on his helmet?'

'It's too late. We've seen the theory. It's in our heads now.'

'I didn't show you all the equations. And my memory isn't as good as yours. After we destroy the flash drive, we should turn ourselves in to the FBI. I'd rather deal with them than the terrorists.'

David grimaced. 'It won't be so easy. Look, why don't we—?'

A distant shout interrupted him. Graddick came running back, sweaty and wild-eyed. 'She's not in the car!' he yelled. 'Elizabeth's gone!'

BETH STUMBLED down the dirt road until she saw a light blinking through the leaves ahead. She sprinted towards it and came to Route 68, an empty one-lane highway glowing faintly in the moonlight. Her teeth chattering, she began walking, hoping to find a gas station.

She was just about to collapse when she rounded a bend and saw a long, low building. It was a small strip of stores, all closed, with a deserted parking lot beside it. She clutched her stomach, suddenly nauseous. Then she saw it, in front of a post office: a BellSouth payphone. For a moment Beth stood there, paralysed. Then she went to the phone. With trembling fingers she dialled the operator and placed a collect call to the only number she knew from memory. After a brief wait, the bastard came on the line.

'Hello, Elizabeth dear. What a pleasant surprise.'

LUCILLE SLAMMED HER FIST on one of the huge transparent spheres in the Virtual Combat Simulation lab. After spending sixteen hours dissecting the lab's servers and terminals, a team of Defense Department computer experts had just concluded that the data stored in the war-gaming software had been irretrievably lost. The army had botched the search for the suspects; after letting them slip off the base, the post commander had waited two hours before alerting the state police in Georgia and Alabama. The Delta Force had set up checkpoints on highways out of Columbus, but they didn't have enough troops to guard all the roads.

In fury, Lucille turned away from the spheres and slumped into a chair behind the terminal. She dug into her pocket and found a pack of Marlboros. Luckily, there were two cigarettes left. As she searched for her Zippo with the Lone Star on it, Agent Crawford marched in.

'Ma'am, I have something from Washington.'

'What now? They're reassigning the case to the Marine Corps?'

Crawford held up a palm-size digital recorder. 'Someone left a message on your voicemail at headquarters. I think you'll recognise the voice.' Grinning, he pressed a button on the recorder, and it began to play.

'*Hello, Lucy. This is David Swift. I see from the newspapers that you're looking for me. I suppose you want to continue the conversation we started back in New York. I've been a little busy the past couple of days, but I think I can make some time for you this morning. I've turned on my cellphone so you can find me. I have just one request: don't bring any soldiers with you. If I see even one helicopter or Humvee, I'm gonna pulverise the package I picked up at Fort Benning. Are we clear?*'

THEY CALLED THIS MOUNTAIN RANGE the Great Smokies because of all the water vapour rising from its tree-covered slopes. Mixing with the hydrocarbons exuded by the pine forest, the vapour usually thickens into a smoky blue haze. But this morning a stiff breeze had dispelled the mist and David could see mile after mile of sunlit hills and valleys.

He stood at the top of Haw Knob, looking down at a road twisting some 600 feet below. No black SUVs had come down the road yet, but it was still early. The FBI needed time to retrieve his cellphone's GPS coordinates, which had been transmitted to the nearest tower when he'd turned it on. From the summit, David had an excellent view of the trail the agents would use.

Graddick had left his station wagon on a dirt road a few miles to the west. He'd led them to Haw Knob and planned to retreat to his car before the agents pounced, but now he seemed reluctant to leave. He stood in front of Michael with his hands covering the boy's head and murmured an unintelligible blessing. The batteries in Michael's Game Boy had died, but the teenager had accepted this with equanimity, and seemed unbothered by the fact that his mother was no longer with them. Meanwhile, Monique glanced anxiously at David, waiting for him to give the word. They'd thrown the shattered laptop in the Tellico River, but she still held the flash drive in her fist.

David stepped to a jagged, grey, semicircular outcrop that jutted from the summit like a giant tiara. Reaching across the rock shelf, he picked up a loose chunk of quartzite. He turned to Monique. 'All right, I'm ready.'

She came to his side and placed the flash drive on the shelf. As David raised the heavy rock, he gazed at the dazzling green mountains all around them, folded in myriad shapes like the wrinkles of spacetime. Then he swung the rock down as hard as he could against the silver cylinder.

The plastic case shattered and the circuit board inside cracked into a dozen pieces. David aimed his second blow at the memory chip and the silicon disintegrated into hundreds of black shards. He pounded the chip to dust, then scooped the debris into his palm and threw it over the lip of Haw Knob's eastern slope. The wind scattered it across the pine forest.

Monique forced a smile. 'Well, that's that. Back to the drawing board.'

David hurled the rock down the slope, then grasped her hand. All at once he was overcome with a blend of sadness and sympathy and gratitude and relief. Impulsively he raised her hand to his lips and kissed the brown skin between her knuckles. She gave him a curious look, surprised but not displeased. Then she spotted something over his shoulder and her face tensed. He turned and saw a convoy of black SUVs snaking down the highway.

He stepped back from the cliff and pulled Monique behind the outcrop. 'Get over here!' he yelled at Graddick, who immediately dragged Michael into the shadow of the rock shelf.

The cars reached the trailhead, and parked on the shoulder of the road. One by one the car doors opened and the men in grey suits poured out.

David turned to Graddick. 'It's time for you to go.'

Graddick's fists clenched, but after a moment he clapped his hand on David's shoulder. 'I'll go, but not far. If there's any trouble, I'll come back.' He raised his hand in blessing, then spun round and scuttled down Haw Knob's western slope.

The federal agents were marching single file up the trail. David ducked behind the outcrop and checked on Michael, though he was more concerned about Monique, because the agents would question her the hardest.

He took her hand and squeezed it. 'They'll split us up for interrogations.'

She leaned against him and pressed her finger to his lips. 'Stop worrying, all right? I've already forgotten the equations.'

He didn't believe it. 'Come on. Last night you—'

'It's true. I've always been good at forgetting things. I don't even remember the title of the paper. Untersoochick-something?'

Michael turned to Monique. '"*Neue Untersuchung über die Einheitliche Feldtheorie*,"' he said in flawless German.

David stared at the boy. 'What? Where did you see those words?'

The boy heard the fear in David's voice. His eyes strained to the left.

'Please, Michael. Did you read the file when you played *Warfighter*?'

Michael's cheeks turned pink, but he didn't answer.

David grasped the boy's shoulders. 'Did you ever download the file from the server? Maybe a long time ago, when you lived with your mother?'

He shook his head in quick jerks. 'It was a safe place!'

'How much of it did you read? How much, Michael?'

'I didn't read it!' he screamed. 'I wrote it! I wrote it all down and put it on the server! Hans told me it was a safe place!'

'What? I thought Kleinman put the theory there.'

'No, he made me memorise it. Now let me go!' The boy struggled.

David held tight. 'What do you mean? You memorised the whole theory?'

'Leave me alone! I don't have to tell you anything unless you have the key!' With a terrific wrench, he freed his arm from David's grasp and punched him in the stomach.

It was a solid punch. David lost his balance and landed on his back. And as he lay in the dirt, a string of numbers passed before his eyes. They were the sixteen digits Dr Kleinman, on his deathbed, had called 'the key'. The first twelve were the coordinates of the Robotics Institute at Carnegie Mellon; the last four were the phone extension of Professor Gupta's office—not Gupta's direct line, but the number for the reception area, where Michael sat.

Monique bent over him. 'Hey? Are you all right?'

He nodded. Fighting off dizziness, he crawled back to the rock shelf and peeked over the top. The agents were charging up the final stretch of trail.

The teenager was hunched against the outcrop. David didn't touch him. Instead, he employed Elizabeth's technique. He snapped his fingers under Michael's nose, then recited the numbers: 'Four, zero . . . two, six . . . three, six . . . seven, nine . . . five, six . . . four, four . . . seven, eight, zero, zero.'

Michael looked up. '"*Neue Untersuchung über die Einheitliche Feldtheorie.*" *Die allgemeine Relativitätstheorie war eine rationelle Theorie der Gravitation und der metrischen Eigenschaften des Raumes* . . .'

It was the text of Einstein's paper, spoken with a German accent exactly like Kleinman's. The old physicist had found a marvellously clever hiding place. Michael would never be tempted to share the formulae, because he didn't understand a single word. And under normal circumstances, no one would dream of looking for them inside the mind of an autistic teenager.

David grabbed Monique's arm. 'Do you hear this? He knows the whole theory! If the FBI gets us, they're gonna interrogate him, and find out he's hiding something.' He removed his cellphone from his pocket and tossed it to the ground. 'Come on. Let's get out of here!'

LUCILLE BOUNDED UP the last stretch of the path and came to a big, grey outcrop in the middle of a grassy clearing. A dozen agents fanned out to the left and right, pointing their Glocks in all directions. Holding her own semi-automatic, Lucille sidled to the edge of the rock shelf. No one was hiding behind it. Then she scanned the western slope of the mountain and caught a glimpse of three figures running under the pine trees.

She turned to her agents. 'Go, go, go! They're straight ahead!'

The men hurtled down the slope, moving twice as fast as Lucille could. But as they reached the forest, Agent Jaworsky suddenly let out a cry and tumbled to the ground. The other men stopped in their tracks, bewildered. A moment later, a fist-size rock struck Agent Keller in the forehead.

'Look out!' she yelled. 'Someone's in the trees!'

The agents crouched in the grass and started firing wildly. The gunshots echoed against the mountainside. The barrage went on for almost a minute.

Finally a large object landed with a thud on the forest floor. The agents rushed towards a heavy, bearded man, whose chest had been ripped open by the bullets. Lucille had no idea who the dead man was.

MONIQUE LOST SIGHT of David and Michael soon after the gunfire started. She ran blindly down the slope, leaping over roots and rock piles, ducking under the pine branches and skidding through heaps of dead needles.

After what seemed like an eternity the gunfire stopped. That was when Monique saw she was alone. The forest was empty on all sides. She jogged up the next ridge, moving in the direction where she thought she'd find David and Michael, but all she saw was a dirt road up ahead. As she stumbled downhill again, she heard a distant but familiar shrieking. It was Michael.

Monique sprinted towards his echoing screams, hoping to hell he wasn't hurt. Then, without any warning, she felt a sharp blow to the back of her head. Her vision blurred and she dropped to the ground.

Just before she blacked out she saw two men looming over her. One was a big bald man carrying an Uzi. The other was Professor Gupta.

SIMON DRAGGED Reynolds's inert body to the pick-up truck, Gupta limping alongside. Brock was several hundred yards to the north, pursuing Swift and the teenager. Simon bound Reynolds's wrists and ankles, and dumped her beside Elizabeth, who lay bound and gagged on the back seat of the truck.

When Gupta received the phone call from his daughter the night before, Simon and the professor had immediately driven to the Great Smokies and picked her up. In return for a small vial of methamphetamine, she showed them where Swift and Reynolds had stopped for the night. The camp was abandoned, but Simon suspected that the fugitives were still nearby. When he rendezvoused with Agent Brock, he ordered him to monitor the emergency frequency on his FBI radio. They heard the transmissions about the planned assault on Haw Knob, and had just parked their vehicles on a dirt road and were racing towards the summit when Gupta heard his grandson screaming.

Now Elizabeth started to struggle as Simon dumped Reynolds beside her, and her thrashing woke up the dazed physicist. Reynolds opened her eyes and then she began thrashing, too.

'Fuck!' she yelled. 'Get me out of here!'

Simon frowned. There was no time to tie a gag on her; he had to drive north quickly to help Brock intercept the others. He climbed into the driver's seat, started the engine and headed down the rutted road.

From the passenger seat, Gupta looked over his shoulder at the two squirming women. 'I'm sorry about the cramped quarters, Dr Reynolds.'

Reynolds gaped at him. 'I thought the agents got you!'

'No, my associate reached me first.' He pointed at Simon.

'But he's one of the terrorists! He drove the yellow Ferrari.'

Gupta shook his head. 'Simon isn't a terrorist; he's my employee. He's assigned to do what you were doing, Dr Reynolds—finding the *Einheitliche Feldtheorie.* Now that we have the crucial equations, we can unwrap *Herr Doktor*'s gift and let it transform the world.'

'But we don't have the theory any more. We destroyed the only copy.'

'No, we have it. We had it all along, but I was too foolish to see. Michael memorised the equations, didn't he?'

Reynolds kept her mouth shut but her face gave her away.

Gupta smiled. 'Years ago I asked Hans what he would do with the theory when he died. He said, "Don't worry, Amil, it'll stay in the family." At the time I assumed he meant the family of physicists, the scientific community. I didn't realise the truth until yesterday, when I saw that a copy of the theory was in *Warfighter*.' He propped his injured leg on the dashboard. 'Hans was a pacifist. Putting *Herr Doktor*'s theory in a war game would have been anathema to him. But Michael loves *Warfighter*, and he loves to make copies of everything he memorises. What's more, he's a member of the family. Both my family and *Herr Doktor*'s.'

Simon turned away from the road for a moment and stared at the professor. 'What are you saying? Was the old Jew your father?'

Gupta chuckled. 'No, the relation was on my wife's side.'

Simon had no time to enquire further. In the next instant he rounded a bend in the road and saw Brock's vehicle up ahead, the old Dodge van that had formerly belonged to Dr Milo Jenkins. The driver's seat was empty. When Simon rolled down his window he could hear the teenager's shrieks quite clearly, coming from a ravine just east of the road.

DAVID COULDN'T STOP Michael from screaming. He'd started when the FBI agents opened fire, and he'd continued as they ran through the forest, taking a frantic gulp of air after every shriek. The boy tore through the undergrowth in a straight path, and David struggled to catch up. After the gunfire ceased Michael slackened his pace, but the screams kept erupting from his throat.

David had lost sight of Monique but he couldn't stop. He was worried that

Michael's screams would make it easy for the FBI to find them. In a desperate burst of speed, he caught up to the boy.

'Michael,' he panted. 'Stop screaming .. Everyone . . . can hear you.'

The teenager let out another shriek. David clapped his hand over Michael's mouth, but the boy pushed him away. He descended into a narrow ravine with rocky cliffs that made his screams even louder. At the limits of his endurance, David flung himself down the slope and grabbed Michael from behind. But the boy jammed an elbow into his ribs. David stumbled back, landing at the edge of a brook. And as he looked downstream he saw a man in a grey suit.

David's skin went cold. It was the renegade agent who'd tried to abduct them two days ago. Now he carried an Uzi instead of a Glock.

David snatched Michael's hand and began running in the opposite direction. At first Michael resisted, but when they heard a burst from the Uzi he sprinted ahead. After a while, David realised he'd made a mistake. As they moved north, the cliffs on either side grew higher, and after a few hundred yards the ravine dead-ended in another fractured cliff, too steep to climb.

In a frenzy, David scanned the wall of rock. Low down, he saw a dark horizontal fissure that seemed to go deep into the cliff. One of Graddick's limestone caverns, he thought. David clambered up to it, then pulled Michael up. While the boy scurried to the back, still screaming, David lay on his stomach and looked out of the opening. He reached into the back of his jeans for the pistol he'd taken from the agent who was hunting them.

After a minute the agent approached the cliff, trying to figure out where the screams were coming from. David steadied the Glock on the lip of the fissure, aiming at the ground in front of the agent. Then he fired.

The man whirled round and ran to a thicket. He started firing his Uzi at the cliff, but the bullets whanged harmlessly against the rock. David was inside a natural bunker. He could hold off this guy for hours. When the real FBI agents came near, David would surrender to them. It was a grim prospect, but better than surrendering to the terrorists.

After a while, Michael's screams began to ebb. David peered over the lip and saw the agent still crouching in the thicket. And then he spotted another man, a bald man, in the middle of the ravine. He wore camouflage pants and a black T-shirt. With his right hand he wielded a Bowie knife and with his left he clutched a squirming boy by the scruff of his neck. The tableau was so strange that it took David several seconds to recognise the youngster. When he did, the pain in his chest was so sharp he dropped his pistol.

'Dr Swift?' the bald man shouted. 'Your son wants to see you.'

CHAPTER TEN

The van came to a stop. Because Karen's hands were tied behind her back, she couldn't look at her watch, but she guessed that it had been about six hours since they'd left the pine forest. Shivering, she squirmed closer to Jonah. 'Please don't let them take him away again,' she whispered. When they took her son before, Karen had nearly gone out of her mind, and although Brock had brought Jonah back to the van only twenty minutes later, the boy cried for hours afterwards.

Brock stepped out of the driver's seat and walked round the van. When he opened the rear doors, Karen got a whiff of dank air and saw a large, dark warehouse with broken windows and crumbling walls. Three white delivery trucks were parked nearby, and a dozen young men stood next to the vehicles. They had the unmistakable look of graduate students: skinny, pale and poorly dressed. Their eyes widened as they stared at Jonah and Karen and the two other women prisoners, all of them bound and gagged and lying on the van's floor. Then Brock yelled, 'What are you waiting for?' and the students leapt forward.

Jonah contorted wildly as a pair of them climbed into the van and picked him up. Karen screamed, 'No!' behind her gag and another pair of students came for her. She jerked her body but they held on tight, carrying her out of the van and across the warehouse.

They approached one of the delivery trucks. The words FERMI NATIONAL ACCELERATOR LABORATORY had been stencilled on the side panel. A lanky, dishevelled student rolled up the door to the truck's cargo hold. Karen sobbed in relief as she was set down beside her son.

From the floor of the cargo hold she saw their two fellow prisoners, the calm black woman and her jittery companion, being transferred to another truck. Karen looked for clues that might reveal where on earth they were, but saw none. Then she noticed a commotion at the other end of the warehouse. Two students were struggling to carry yet another bound prisoner from a pick-up truck. Karen's throat tightened—it was David. He was bucking so violently that the students dropped him to the floor. Karen screamed behind her gag again. Then a third student joined the others and together they lifted David and bore him towards the last delivery truck.

It was late, well past midnight. The trucks were moving down a winding road. Monique could feel the turns in her stomach.

To her left, Professor Gupta and his students stood round a computer that had been set up in the far corner of the cargo hold. Just a few feet away, Michael sat on the floor, playing *Warfighter* on his newly recharged Game Boy. Gupta had been huddled with his grandson for hours, asking whispered questions about the *Einheitliche Feldtheorie* while his students entered Michael's answers into the computer, but now the professor had apparently got everything he needed. He grinned in triumph at the screen, then came over to where Monique lay.

'For a physicist, this is a dream come true, Dr Reynolds,' he said. 'We've developed a program that simulates the creation of the extra-dimensional neutrino beam. Thanks to the information we got from Jacques Bouchet and Alastair MacDonald, we already knew we could use the Tevatron collider at Fermilab to generate the beam. Once Michael told us the field equations, we calculated the necessary adjustments to the collider. Now we can do trial runs on the computer, so we'll know precisely how to configure our experiment at the Tevatron. The beam will be aimed so that it returns to our universe about five thousand kilometres above North America. Everyone on the continent will be able to see the burst. The particles will accelerate as they plough through the extra dimensions; then they'll re-enter the spacetime sheet. The re-entry should release several thousand terajoules of energy—the equivalent of a one-megaton nuclear blast. Because the beam will be targeted so far above the atmosphere, it won't cause damage on the ground. But it'll be spectacular. For several minutes it'll blaze like a new sun!'

Why is Gupta doing this? Monique thought. Unable to pose the question aloud, she stared at the professor and narrowed her eyes.

He read her look and nodded. 'We need to make a public demonstration, Dr Reynolds. If we simply tried to publish the unified theory, the authorities would suppress the information. The government wants the theory for itself, so it can build its weapons in secret. But the *Einheitliche Feldtheorie* doesn't belong to any government. And it's much more than a blueprint for making weapons. By exploiting it, we could produce limitless electricity. No more coal-burning generators or nuclear reactors. We could apply the technology to medicine, precisely targeting the neutrino beams to kill cancer cells. We could use the beams to launch rockets and propel them across the solar system. When humankind wakes up tomorrow morning, Dr Reynolds, they'll see the full splendour of the unified theory.'

Monique didn't doubt the truth of what Gupta was saying. The unified theory was so all-encompassing, it could certainly lead to wonderful inventions. But there was a terrible price. She stared at Gupta and shook her head.

The professor raised an eyebrow. 'What is it? Are you afraid?'

She nodded vigorously.

Gupta moved a step closer and rested his hand on her shoulder. 'We need to overcome our fears before we can step into the new age. And that's what I've done, Dr Reynolds. I'm not afraid of anything any more.'

DAVID SAT with his back against the wall of the cargo hold. The truck had stopped fifteen minutes ago and the students had loaded a dozen wooden crates inside, then moved to a different truck in the convoy. Now David was alone in the truck with the bald maniac, who was alternately cleaning his Uzi and swigging from a bottle of Stolichnaya.

For the thousandth time, David tried to loosen the cord that bound his hands behind his back. His fingers were numb, and sweat dripped down his cheeks and soaked into his gag. As he struggled, he fixed his gaze on the man who'd held a knife to Jonah's throat. His fury put new strength into his sinews, but after a while he closed his eyes. It was his own damn fault.

When David opened his eyes, the bald man was standing over him. He held out the bottle of vodka. 'Comrade, take a break from your valiant efforts. You look like you need a drink.'

David shook his head. 'Fuck you!' he shouted through the gag, but it came out as a desperate gurgle.

The mercenary shrugged. 'All right, then.' Grinning, he took a long pull. 'My name's Simon, by the way. I want to offer my compliments, Dr Swift. The book you wrote was very helpful.'

David controlled his rage and focused his attention on the killer. Although he had a thick Russian accent, his English was excellent. Contrary to appearances, this was no brainless hit man.

Simon took another swig of vodka. 'The past few hours have been a little dull for me. Before the last stop I was in the professor's truck, but he was busy interrogating his grandson. To pass the time, I had a chat with Gupta's daughter, and I found something that might be of interest to you.'

He pulled a circular object out of the pocket of his camouflage pants and cupped it in his palm. David recognised Elizabeth Gupta's gold locket. Simon opened it and stared at the picture inside. 'I suppose you'd consider this a late addition to your historical research, eh? It certainly explains a few things.'

He turned the locket round so David could see the picture. It was a sepia-toned photograph of a mother and daughter. The mother was a beauty with long dark hair; the girl was about six years old.

'Elizabeth said this was taken in Belgrade before the war.' Simon pointed to the daughter. 'This is Hannah, Elizabeth's mother. She came to America after the war and married Gupta.' His finger shifted to the dark-haired mother. 'And this is Elizabeth's grandmother. She died in the concentration camps. She was half Jewish, you see. Here, I'll show you.'

He prised the picture out of the locket. On the reverse side someone had scribbled *Hannah and Lieserl.*

Simon grinned. 'You recognise that name, don't you? Elizabeth told me the whole story. Her grandmother was *Herr Doktor*'s bastard daughter.'

Under any other circumstances, David would have been bowled over. For an Einstein historian, this was the equivalent of discovering a new planet. Like most researchers, David had assumed that Lieserl died in infancy. Now he knew that she'd not only survived, she had living descendants. But in his present state he could feel no joy in the revelation.

Simon put the photograph back into the locket. 'After the war, *Herr Doktor* learned what had happened to his daughter. He sent for Hannah, who'd been hiding with a Serbian family, but he never acknowledged his relationship with the girl.' He slipped the locket back into his pocket. 'Hannah told Gupta about it, though. And Kleinman, too. That's why they fought over her. Both of them wanted to marry *Herr Doktor*'s granddaughter.'

He took another gulp of vodka. He'd drunk half the bottle by now and was starting to slur his words. 'You should know the history behind this operation, because you're a historian. After Gupta married Hannah, he became *Herr Doktor*'s protégé, his closest assistant. And when *Herr Doktor* confided that he'd discovered the *Einheitliche Feldtheorie*, Gupta assumed the old Jew would share the secret with him. But *Herr Doktor* must have sensed there was something wrong with Gupta even back then, and passed the theory to Kleinman and the others. And that drove Gupta mad.'

The mercenary stared at the walls of the hold for half a minute or so; then he turned back to David. 'For years he's been planning this demonstration, building up his little army of students. He's convinced them that they're going to save the world, that people will start dancing in the streets once they see the flash in the sky from the neutrino beam.' He made a disgusted face. 'He's a madman, you see. And madmen can be very persuasive.'

Simon took one more swallow of Stoli, then thrust the bottle at David again. 'Look, you have to drink. I won't take no for an answer. We're going to toast Gupta's new age of enlightenment.'

He began to fumble at the knot that tied the gag over David's mouth. The vodka had made his fingers clumsy, but he managed to loosen the cloth.

When the gag came off, David took a gulp of fresh air and looked Simon in the eye. 'And how much is Gupta paying for your services?'

Simon frowned. 'That's an impolite question, Dr Swift. I didn't ask how much you earned from your book, did I?'

'This is different. You know what's going to happen after everyone sees the burst. The Pentagon will start its own research and—'

'Yes, yes, I know. Every army in the world will try to develop this weapon. But no one's going to be doing any research in the Pentagon. Or anywhere else near Washington, DC.'

David stared at the mercenary. 'What do you mean?'

Simon's eyes held a glint of satisfaction. 'Gupta's demonstration will be even more impressive than he expects. I'm going to change the orientation of the neutrino beam so that it re-enters our universe inside the Jefferson Memorial.' He pointed the Stoli bottle and closed one eye as if aiming down its neck. 'The Pentagon, the White House and Congress will all be incinerated, along with everything else in a ten-kilometre-wide circle.'

David's mouth went dry. 'Who's paying you to do this? Al-Qaeda?'

Simon shook his head. 'No, this is for myself. For my family, actually.'

'Your family?'

Simon put down the bottle and reached into his pocket again. This time he took out a cellphone. 'Yes, I had a family. Not so different from yours, Dr Swift.' He turned on the phone and held it so that David could see the picture on the screen. 'Those are my children. Sergei and Larissa. They died in the Argun Gorge, in southern Chechnya. You've heard of the place, I assume?'

'Yes, but—'

'My boy Sergei, he was six years old. Larissa was just four. They were killed with their mother in a rocket attack. A Hellfire rocket launched from a US Delta Force helicopter, in another botched counterterrorism operation.' Simon spat on the floor. 'I'm going to eliminate everyone involved in commanding and deploying that unit. That's why I've targeted the Pentagon and the civilian leaders as well. The president, the vice-president, the secretary of defence.' He snapped the phone shut. 'I have only one opportunity to strike, so I need a wide blast zone.'

David felt sick. This was the very thing Einstein had feared. And it was going to happen in a few hours. 'But it was an accident. How can you—?'

'I don't care!' He picked up the bottle of Stoli by its neck and waved it like a club. 'It's intolerable! It's unforgivable!'

'But you're going to kill millions of—'

Something hard smashed into David's cheek. Simon had struck him with the bottle. David fell sideways and his forehead slammed against the truck bed. Before he could pass out, Simon grabbed his collar and pulled him up.

'Yes, they're going to die!' he screamed. 'Why should they live when my children are dead? I'm going to kill them all!' He let go of the collar.

David sank to the floor and let darkness overtake him.

LUCILLE ARRIVED AT THE FBI headquarters very early Monday morning so she wouldn't run into any of her colleagues, but when she got to her office she discovered that the goons from the Defense Intelligence Agency had already cleaned out her desk. Her files on Kleinman, Swift, Reynolds and Gupta were gone. The only things left were her certificates of commendation and a glass paperweight in the shape of a Texas six-shooter.

Well, she thought. Now it won't take so long to pack.

Lucille had taken full responsibility for her team's failure to apprehend the suspects. After the vice-president himself had informed her that the mission no longer required the FBI's assistance, she had offered her resignation, and it had been accepted.

Now she found a cardboard box and loaded everything inside. For thirty-four years she'd poured her heart and soul into the Bureau, but there seemed precious little to show for it. She gazed with resentment at the antiquated computer on her desk, the cheap plastic tray of her in-box.

And then she saw the folder on the tray. One of the agents on the overnight shift must have delivered it after the goons came through. Lucille stared at the thing, telling herself to leave it alone. In the end her curiosity got the better of her. She picked it up.

It was a list of Professor Gupta's recent cellphone calls. She'd requested the information from his cellular carrier three days ago, but the idiots had taken their time. The records were pretty sparse, but she noticed something unusual. Every day for the past two weeks, Gupta had placed a call to the same number at precisely 9.30 a.m. Never a minute earlier or later.

Lucille reminded herself that she was no longer assigned to the case. In fact, she'd already filled out her retirement forms.

But she hadn't submitted them yet.

SIMON WAS DRIVING the truck at the head of the convoy as they sped towards the lab's East Gate. It was five o'clock in the morning, just a few minutes after dawn, and he was still a bit wobbly from last night's binge. To wake himself up, he reached into his windbreaker and clasped the stock of his Uzi.

The truck jounced over a railroad crossing and the suburban landscape changed to wide green fields, a stretch of virgin Illinois prairie. They were on federal property now, the eastern edge of the laboratory's grounds. Up ahead inside a small guardhouse sat a fat woman in a blue uniform.

Simon slowed his truck to a halt, and handed over a thick sheaf of forged invoices and requisition letters. 'Here you go, sweetheart,' he said, trying to sound like an American truck driver. 'We're making an early delivery today.'

The woman carefully examined the papers, comparing them with a list on her clipboard. 'It's not on the schedule.'

'No, but we have all the approvals.'

She lifted her head. 'All right, step out of the truck and open the back doors. And tell the drivers behind you to do the same.'

Simon frowned. 'It's been approved. Didn't you see the letters?'

'Yeah, but I gotta inspect everything that comes in. Just turn—'

He cut her off by pumping two bullets into her skull. Then he went to the next truck and knocked three times on the rear door. 'Open up, Professor,' he shouted. 'We need to take on another load.'

Within half a minute the students had stowed the corpse in the cargo hold and mopped up the blood from the asphalt. Simon returned to his truck. Gupta got in on the passenger side, and shot him a stern look.

'No more killing, please,' he said. 'I used to work here.'

Simon shifted the truck into gear. The convoy began moving again. 'Tell me about the control room,' he growled. 'How many people will be there?'

'Don't worry, there won't be more than a skeleton crew. Five or six operators at the most.' He waved his hand dismissively. 'It's because of all the budget cuts. The government doesn't pay for physics any more. National laboratories need private donations to keep their accelerators running.'

The road veered left and Simon saw a strangely shaped building on the horizon. It looked like a pair of giant mattresses leaning against each other. Close to it, a low embankment swept across the grassland in a great circle.

Gupta pointed at the unusual building. 'That's Wilson Hall, the lab headquarters. I used to have an office on the sixteenth floor.' He lowered his arm slightly. 'Under that ridge is the Tevatron's beam tunnel, a four-mile ring with a thousand superconducting magnets to guide the beams. Protons go clockwise, antiprotons counterclockwise.' Then he pointed at a windowless structure directly above the tunnel. 'And that's Collision Hall. Where the protons and antiprotons smash into each other. Where we'll launch the neutrinos into the extra dimensions.'

Simon drove past a row of cylindrical tanks, each bearing the words DANGER COMPRESSED HELIUM. Then he came to a long reflecting pool in front of Wilson Hall, which mirrored its odd silhouette.

'Turn here and go behind the building,' Gupta instructed. 'The control room is next to the Proton Booster.'

The convoy coasted down a driveway to a parking lot in front of a low, U-shaped structure. There were fewer than half a dozen cars in the lot.

Simon parked the truck and began issuing orders. One team of students unloaded the crates of electronic equipment, while another transferred all the hostages to the truck that Brock was driving. 'Take them to a secure location,' Simon ordered the former FBI man. 'There are some unoccupied structures about a kilometre west. Find one and sit tight for a couple of hours.'

Brock shrugged. 'Why are we keeping them alive? We'll have to shoot them eventually. All of them except the professor's daughter, I mean.'

Simon lowered his voice. 'It amuses the professor to keep them alive, but I don't care. Once you're out of sight, do whatever you want.'

THE STUDENTS HAD DUMPED David next to Monique and Elizabeth, but as soon as the truck started moving he squirmed towards Karen and Jonah. As he struggled across the floor, his son's eyes widened and his ex-wife began to cry. Someone had retied David's gag, so he couldn't say a word; he simply huddled close to his family. He was still aching from the beating Simon had given him, but his chest swelled with relief.

After a couple of minutes, the truck stopped once more. Brock opened the rear door and David saw a dome-shaped, grass-covered mound. It was about twenty feet high and a hundred feet across, and sat atop some kind of large bunker. The truck was parked in front of an entrance in the side of the mound. Over a roll-up door that Brock had wrenched open, a sign said FERMI NATIONAL ACCELERATOR LABORATORY, BOOSTER NEUTRINO EXPERIMENT.

Brock climbed into the cargo hold and cut the cords binding David's ankles, then did the same for Jonah and Karen and Monique. He ignored Elizabeth, who had passed out in the corner. Keeping one hand on his Uzi, which hung from a shoulder strap, he hoisted the others to their feet.

'Get off the truck,' he ordered. 'We're going into that shed.'

David's heart thumped; the agent was obviously leading them to a hidden spot where he could kill them. But Brock was right behind Jonah, pointing his Uzi at the boy's head, and David didn't dare to step out of line.

They entered a dark room lit only by flickering LEDs. Brock closed the door and told them to keep moving. They descended a spiral stairway. Then Brock flipped a light switch, and they found themselves on a platform overlooking an enormous spherical tank resting in a concrete pit. The platform was level with the flattened top of the steel sphere, which was crowned with a circular panel, like a giant manhole cover. David realised that he'd read about the tank in *Scientific American*. It was part of an experiment for studying neutrinos. To detect them, researchers needed a huge apparatus, and a transparent carbon-containing liquid. The tank was filled with mineral oil. When the neutrinos hit the carbon atoms in the oil, they emitted flashes of light.

'Sit down!' Brock yelled. 'Against the wall!'

This is it, David thought as they cowered on the floor. This is when the bastard starts shooting. Brock came closer, carefully aiming his machine gun. Monique leaned against David, while Karen closed her eyes and bent over Jonah. But instead of firing, Brock tore off David's gag.

'Go ahead, Swift, start screaming,' he said. 'We're way underground.'

Brock turned away and gazed at the giant spherical tank. He strolled to the top of the tank and stomped his foot on the steel panel. The clang echoed against the walls. 'What's in here?'

'Mineral oil,' David said. 'A quarter-million gallons of it.'

Brock fiddled with the clamps round the panel till he figured out how to release them. Then he pressed a red button and an electric motor began to hum. The panel opened like a clamshell, revealing a pool of clear liquid.

'Well, look at that.' Kneeling at the side of the pool, Brock dipped one of his hands into the mineral oil. Then he stood up and held the glistening hand in the air. 'Swift,' he said, staring at David, 'we got a score to settle.'

David swallowed hard. 'Go ahead,' he said. 'Just don't hurt the others.'

Brock stared at Karen, then at Monique. 'No, I'm gonna hurt them, too.'

THE TAKEOVER of the Tevatron's control room was effortless. As soon as Simon stepped through the door with his Uzi, the gaunt-faced operators at their consoles raised their hands above their heads. While Professor Gupta's students took their places, Simon locked the Fermilab employees inside a nearby storage closet. He assigned four students to sentry duty, handing each a radio and an Uzi. Two of them took up positions in the parking lot while the other pair patrolled the entrances to the collider's beam tunnel.

The professor directed his students like an orchestra conductor. His eyes swept across the screens, surveying all the readings. After a while one of the students called out, 'Initiating proton injection.'

Gupta replied, 'Excellent,' and smiled at his idiot grandson, who sat in the corner with his Game Boy.

Simon approached. 'Are we getting close?'

Gupta nodded. 'Yes, very close. Our timing was lucky. The operators were already preparing a new store of particles when we arrived. Now we've made the necessary adjustments and we're transferring the protons to the Tevatron ring. That will take ten minutes or so. To inject the antiprotons may take a little longer. We have to be careful that we don't cause a quench.'

'A quench? What's that?'

'Something to be avoided at all costs. The magnets that steer the particles are superconducting, which means they work only if they're cooled to four hundred and fifty degrees below zero. The Tevatron's cryogenic system keeps the magnets cold by pumping liquid helium round the coils.'

Simon remembered the tanks of compressed helium he'd seen while driving past the beam tunnel. 'So what can go wrong?'

'Each particle beam carries ten million joules of energy. If we aim it the wrong way, it'll tear the beam pipe. Even if we make a very small error, the particles can spray one of the magnets and heat the liquid helium inside. If it heats too much, the helium becomes a gas and bursts out. Then the magnet ceases to be superconducting and electrical resistance melts the coils.'

Simon frowned. 'Could you fix it?'

'Possibly. But it would take a few hours. And a few more hours to recalibrate the beam line. But I told you, we're going to be careful.'

'And what about the targeting of the neutrinos?' Simon asked. 'When will you input the coordinates for the burst?'

'We'll do that when we inject the antiproton bunches. The trajectory of the neutrinos will depend on the exact timing of the—' He stopped and stared blankly into space; then he smiled. 'Do you hear that?' he whispered.

Simon listened. He heard a low, quick beeping.

'The protons are circulating in the beam pipe!' Gupta shouted. 'The signal starts low and rises in pitch as the beam grows more intense.' Tears leaked from the professor's eyes. 'What a glorious sound!'

Simon nodded. It sounded like an unusually rapid heartbeat. A slab of muscle pounding frantically just before the end.

THE ELECTRICAL CORD sliced into David's wrists. He made a final attempt to yank his hands free as Brock stepped towards Karen and Jonah. All the hours of struggling in the truck's cargo hold had loosened the cord a few millimetres, but it wasn't enough. He screamed in frustration as the agent approached Karen, who was hunched round Jonah. As Brock gripped the back of her neck, David stood up and hurtled towards them.

His only hope was momentum. He lowered his right shoulder and charged like a battering ram, but Brock saw him coming. At the last moment he stepped to the side and extended his foot into David's path to trip him. David landed on his face, his forehead cracking against the concrete. Blood streamed from his nostrils into his mouth.

Brock laughed. 'Nice move.' He went back to the tank of mineral oil. This time he dipped both hands into the pool. 'Come on, Swift!' he yelled. 'Don't you have any fight left in you?'

David clenched his teeth. Get up, he told himself, get up! He clambered to his feet and lurched forward, but he seemed to be moving in slow motion.

Brock sidestepped again and grabbed the cord binding his wrists, then spun him round and forced him to his knees. 'I'm gonna take off your wife's gag,' he whispered, 'so you can hear her scream.' He threw David to the floor.

David's head hit the concrete a second time and pain knifed into his skull. But he didn't black out. He bit his lower lip until it bled, putting all his will into remaining conscious.

Woozy and terrified, he saw Brock pull Karen from Jonah and drag her towards the steel tank. He watched him tear off her gag and heard her make a barely audible whimper more heart-rending than any scream. He thrashed on the floor, trying to rise to his feet. As he struggled, his right hand slipped out of the cord, which Brock had inadvertently smeared with mineral oil.

David was so surprised that he stayed on the floor for a few seconds, keeping both hands behind his back. All at once he could think clearly. He knew he was too weak to fight. But suddenly he saw how he could incapacitate Brock. He reached into his back pocket and gripped the cigarette lighter he'd taken from Agent Parker, the Zippo embossed with the Lone Star of Texas. Pretending his hands were still tied, he stumbled to his feet.

Brock let go of Karen. 'That's more like it!' he crowed, squaring off. 'Bring it on, big guy. See what you can do.'

David staggered forward until he stood right in front of the agent.

Brock shook his head, disappointed. 'You don't look so good—'

David spun the Zippo's flint wheel and thrust the lighter into Brock's face. The agent raised his arms reflexively, and both his oily hands caught fire. With all his remaining strength, David grabbed Brock by the waist and pushed him backwards. Then he shoved him into the tank of mineral oil.

The flames spread across the pool as soon as Brock's hands hit the surface. But even without the fire, the agent would have been doomed. The human body is mostly water, and it's impossible to swim in a fluid that's less dense, such as mineral oil. Brock sank like a stone.

THE SIGNAL in the control room no longer sounded like a heartbeat. The pitch had steadily risen until each beep was like a shrill, inhuman cry.

Professor Gupta turned to Simon with a smile of ecstasy on his face. 'The beam is strong,' he declared. 'All the protons are in the ring.'

'So are we ready to input the target coordinates?' Simon asked.

'Yes. Then we'll load the antiprotons into the collider.'

The professor moved towards the console manned by Richard Chan and Scott Krinsky, the young physicists from Oak Ridge National Laboratory. But before he could issue any instructions, Simon grasped his arm.

'Wait!' he said, aiming his Uzi at Gupta's forehead. 'We need to make a small adjustment. I have a new set of coordinates.'

Gupta gaped at him. 'What are you doing? Get your hands off me!'

Richard and Scott turned their heads. Several students rose from their seats, but Simon wasn't worried. None of them was armed.

'If you value your professor's life,' he said calmly, 'I suggest you sit down.'

'WHY ARE YOU calling me? You don't work for me any more.'

Lucille hardly recognised the Bureau director's voice. It snarled out of the earpiece of her telephone. 'Sir,' she started again, 'I have new—'

'I don't want to hear it. You're retired now. Hand in your gun and badge and get out of the building.'

'Please, sir! Listen! I've identified a cellphone number that may—'

'No, *you* listen. I just lost my job because of you. The vice-president has already chosen my replacement and leaked his name to Fox News.'

She took a deep breath. The only way to make him listen was to get it out fast. 'This suspect could be working with Amil Gupta. His phone is registered to an alias, a Mr George Osmond. For two weeks he's turned on his phone once a day to receive a call from Gupta, then immediately turned it off. But I think he just made a mistake. He turned it on at one o'clock this morning and it's been tracking his position ever since.'

'You know what, Lucy? It's not my problem any more.'

'I got the tracking data from the cellular carrier. It looks like the suspect travelled along secondary roads to the Fermi National—'

'Look, why are you telling me this? You should be talking to Defense.'

'I tried, sir, but those DIA idiots keep saying they don't need assistance!'

'Let them hang, then! Let them all go to hell! I'm through.'

DAVID LED KAREN, Jonah and Monique back to the truck as the underground lab's sprinkler system extinguished the fire in the tank. Once they were outside, he untied the cords on their wrists. Karen and Jonah fell into his arms, weeping. But Monique ran back to the lab.

'Wait a second,' David called. 'Where are you going?'

'We gotta find a phone! They took our cellphones.'

David gently disentangled himself from his ex-wife and son and returned to the lab's doorway. Monique was searching the long banks of computers.

'We gotta call for help,' she cried. 'Gupta's made the preparations for the spacetime rupture. If they're targeting Washington, they're— Whoa, what's this?' She pointed at a metal panel not too far from the door.

It was an intercom, with a row of labelled buttons below the grille of a loudspeaker. 'Don't press CONTROL ROOM,' David warned. 'That's probably where Gupta is.'

'Maybe we can find one of the Tevatron's engineers, convince him to turn off the power for the collider.' She pressed the button labelled TEVATRON. 'Hello? Hello?'

No one answered. But David heard a rapid, high-pitched beeping.

'Shit!' Monique whispered. 'I know that signal.' She grasped his arm to steady herself. 'The beams are almost ready.'

'What? What do—?'

'No time, no time!' She headed for the doorway, pulling him along. 'We got fifteen minutes at the most.'

She raced for the truck and grasped the handle of the driver's door. It was locked. The keys were probably still in Brock's trousers. 'Damn,' she yelled. 'We're gonna have to run. The beam tunnel's this way.'

While Monique dashed towards the Tevatron ring, David rushed over to Karen, who was kneeling beside Jonah. Leaving them alone scared the hell out of him, but what was happening in the collider was even more frightening.

'We have to split up,' he said. 'You and Jonah should get away from here as fast as you can.' He pointed at a strip of asphalt 200 yards north. 'Go to that road and make a left. If you see security guards, tell them there's a fire in the beam tunnel and they need to shut off the power. Got that?'

Karen nodded. David was amazed at how calm she was. She squeezed his hand. 'Go, David,' she said. 'Before it's too late.'

SIMON WAS IN A QUANDARY. He'd tried calling Brock on the radio, but there was no response. He tried three more times and heard nothing but static.

Simon was still holding Professor Gupta at gunpoint, and the students were obediently adjusting the proton and antiproton beams so that they conformed to the new target coordinates. In about ten minutes they would be ready, and after another two minutes of acceleration the collisions would begin. But what if Swift and Reynolds had somehow escaped from Brock?

After several seconds of thought, Simon shoved Gupta forward. Holding him by the scruff of his neck, he addressed the students. 'Professor Gupta and I are going to observe the experiment at another location. I expect you to follow the orders I've given. If the demonstration fails, I plan to kill your professor. And then I'll come back and kill each one of you.'

The students nodded fearfully and turned back to their screens. Simon opened the cabinet that held the keys to the tunnel access points. The professor's idiot grandson stared at them for a moment, then returned his attention to the Game Boy as Simon dragged Gupta out of the door.

IT WAS HALF A MILE to the Tevatron. David and Monique ran down a road, then dashed across a muddy field. Soon they could see the grass-covered ridge and a low cinder-block structure with a chain-link gate at its entrance.

Monique pointed at the structure. 'That's the F-Two access point to the tunnel. The gate will be locked, but I remember seeing fire axes at every access point the last time I worked on an experiment here.'

With a final sprint they arrived at the building and located the fire-safety cabinet. Monique removed the axe and rushed to the building's entrance. Through the gate, David saw a stairway going down to the tunnel.

'Where are the control panels for shutting down the beams?' he asked.

'There are manual shutdown switches inside the tunnel, but Gupta probably disabled them. I bet that was one of the first things he did.'

'How can you shut down the accelerator if the switches are disabled?'

Monique hefted the axe. 'With this thing. One clean cut through the beam pipe should do the trick.'

'But you're gonna get showered with radiation!'

She nodded grimly. 'That's why you're gonna stay and guard the entrance.'

He gripped her elbow. 'Let me do it. I'll go down instead.'

She looked at him as if he'd just said something asinine. 'That's ridiculous. You have a kid, a family. I don't have anyone. It's a simple calculation.' She jerked her arm out of his grasp and raised the axe.

She was just about to bring it down on the gate's lock when the bullet tore through her. David saw the blood spurt out of her side, just above her waist. He grabbed her shoulders as she collapsed and swiftly pulled her round the corner. 'Monique!' he screamed.

Her face contorted in pain as he laid her on the ground and pulled up her shirt. There was an entry wound on the left side of her abdomen and an exit wound on the right. 'What happened?' she gasped.

He peered round the corner, and spotted a pair of Gupta's students about fifty yards away. Both of them carried Uzis. One was speaking into a radio.

David turned back. Kneeling, he slipped one arm under Monique's back and the other under her knees. 'I'm getting you out of here,' he said. But she screamed as he tried to lift her, and blood gushed from her wounds.

'Put me down,' she groaned. 'There's another access point a half-mile south of here. Just take the axe and go!'

Simon locked Professor Gupta inside a storage closet in Collision Hall. He could have easily killed the old man, but he decided it would be more fitting if the professor lived to see the results of his experiment.

Just as Simon was leaving the hall, he received a radio transmission from the pair of students he'd assigned to patrol the beam tunnel. Three minutes later he arrived at the F-Two tunnel entrance. The students were nervously training their guns at Reynolds, who lay in a pool of blood, barely alive.

'Was she alone?' Simon asked. 'Did you see anyone else?'

One of the students pushed his glasses up the bridge of his nose. 'After Gary shot her, I'm pretty sure someone pulled her round the corner. But I didn't get a good look at him.'

Simon stepped towards the myopic dunce. 'Which way did he go?'

'I don't know. I was busy calling you on the radio, and by the time we—'

With a pull of the trigger, Simon silenced the fool. Then he turned and executed the other one, too. These students were useless. Now Swift was running to another entrance, and Simon had no idea which one.

Then the wounded woman let out a broken moan. Perhaps, Simon thought, she knew where Swift was. He removed his combat knife from its sheath.

DAVID RAN THROUGH a stand of oak trees, which gave him some cover as he followed the curving ridge above the beam tunnel. He refused to look back to where he'd left Monique. He had to push everything out of his mind except the beam line.

Carrying the fire axe, he sprinted towards the E-Zero entrance, a structure identical to the one he'd just left. A yellow electric cart was parked next to the building; it was probably used to ferry maintenance workers or tow equipment from one access point to another, but no one was on the job yet. All he heard was a low hum from the stairway leading down to the tunnel.

He examined the gate. It was secured with a chain and a lock, but the chain was thin. David smashed through it with his axe, opened the gate and dashed down the steps. But he had to stop at another locked gate. Through its bars he could see the beam pipe, long and curving and silver-grey, running about a foot above the tunnel floor. This was another thing he'd read about in *Scientific American.* The superconducting magnets sandwiched most of the pipe; they were strung along its length like beads on a giant necklace, except that each magnet was about twenty feet long and shaped like a coffin. The magnets kept the protons and antiprotons in line, travelling in tight beams inside the steel pipe. With the flip of a switch, the same magnets would draw the beams together and ignite the apocalypse.

The second gate was tougher than the first. It was locked with two dead bolts that extended from the jamb. When he took a swing at them, the blade didn't even make a dent. He swung again and the head of the axe broke off.

Lacking a better idea, David ran back up the stairway and looked around wildly for some kind of deliverance. Then his eyes fixed on the electric cart.

Luckily, the cart's motor started with the push of a button. David got into the driver's seat and steered towards the entrance, which looked just wide enough. Flooring the pedal, he accelerated to about twenty miles per hour, then leapt out of the cart and watched it careen down the stairway.

The crash was tremendously loud. He rushed down the steps and saw the cart balanced on a heap of crumpled fencing. The back wheels were spinning madly in the air—the accelerator pedal had evidently got stuck—but David managed to squeeze past and clamber through the breach.

He slid to the tunnel's concrete floor, which was littered with glass from the cart's headlights. A few feet away, David found a control panel on the wall. He opened the panel and threw the shutdown switch. But nothing happened. The long line of superconducting magnets kept on humming. Gupta had disabled the switches, as Monique had predicted.

David picked up a heavy steel bar that had been torn from the gate. He couldn't see any other option. All the power lines for the collider ran along the arched ceiling, out of reach. No, the only way to shut down the Tevatron was to smash the beam pipe and disrupt the stream of particles, which would then spray into his body like a trillion tiny darts. David's eyes began to sting. Well, he thought, at least it'll be quick.

But as he stepped towards a section of the beam pipe that ran between two of the magnets, he noticed another pipe just above, with HE printed on it in black letters. It was the pipe that delivered ultracold liquid helium to the magnets. The helium was what made the magnets superconducting—it lowered the temperature of their titanium coils to the point where they could conduct electricity without any resistance. As David stared at the thing, he realised there was another way to stop the particle beams.

Gripping the bar, he took aim at the helium pipe. All he needed to do was make a puncture. Once exposed to the air, the liquid helium would turn into a gas and escape; then the magnets would overheat and the Tevatron would shut down automatically. David struck the pipe as hard as he could. The blow made an inch-wide dent. He struck again in the same spot, making the dent deeper. One more time should bust it, he thought. Then someone grabbed the bar out of his hands.

'NO, MA'AM, there's nothing going on. Just another beautiful day at the lab. Seventy-five degrees and not a cloud in the sky.' Adam Ronca, Fermilab's chief of security, had a cheery Chicago accent.

'What about your incident reports?' Lucille asked him. 'Any signs of unusual activity in the past few hours?'

'Well, let's see.' She could hear him rustling some papers on the other end of the phone. 'At four twelve a.m., the guard at the West Gate saw some movement in the woods. Turned out to be a fox. And at six twenty-eight the fire department responded to an alarm at the Neutrino Detector.'

'An alarm?'

'They've been having trouble with the sprinkler—' A burst of static interrupted him. 'Excuse me, Agent Parker. The fire chief is calling on the radio.'

Lucille shouted, 'Wait!' but he'd already put her on hold.

After nearly a minute, Ronca came back on the line. 'Sorry about that, ma'am. The fire chief spotted a couple of trespassers. Some woman and her kid. It happens more than you'd think.'

Lucille squeezed the telephone receiver. She thought of Swift's ex-wife and son, who had disappeared two days before. 'Is the woman in her mid-thirties, blonde, about five eight? With a seven-year-old boy?'

'Hey, how did you know—?'

'Lock down the lab. A terrorist attack may be in progress.'

'Whoa, hold on. I can't—'

'Look, I know the director of the Bureau's Chicago office. He'll send over some agents. Just make sure no one leaves the facility!'

PROFESSOR GUPTA knew exactly where he was. The closet he was locked inside wasn't far from the Collider Detector, Fermilab's crown jewel. He could hear its low hum. The detector was like a giant wheel, more than ten metres high, with the beam pipe where an axle would be. The protons and antiprotons would collide at the centre of the wheel, a point surrounded by instruments that normally tracked the trajectories of the quarks, mesons and photons ejected from the high-energy collisions. But today, no particles would fly out from the centre of the wheel. Instead the collisions would tear a hole in our universe, allowing the sterile neutrinos to escape into the extra dimensions beyond, and no instrument on the planet would detect their presence until they came screaming back to our spacetime. Gupta had overheard the new target coordinates that Simon had given to his students. He guessed that the re-entry point was somewhere along the Eastern Seaboard.

The professor lowered his head and stared at the floor. It wasn't his fault. He couldn't be blamed if his orders weren't properly carried out. The problem was simple human perversity.

As Gupta sat there in the darkness he heard a new noise, a distant thrumming. It was the sound of the RF system, which was now generating an oscillating radio-frequency field to accelerate the protons and antiprotons. Every time the particles went round the ring, fifty thousand times a second, the RF field gave them another boost. In less than two minutes the proton and antiproton swarms would reach their top energies and the superconducting magnets would point the beams at each other. He would know soon enough whether the experiment had worked.

DAVID LAY FACE UP on the floor of the tunnel. Simon loomed over him, stepping on his chest. Dizzy and gasping, David grabbed the man's leather boot and tried to lift it off his rib cage, but the mercenary just pressed down harder, and pointed his Uzi at David's forehead. The hum of the superconducting magnets grew louder and the floor of the tunnel began to vibrate.

'Hear that?' Simon's sweaty face broke into a grin.

David twisted and kicked and beat his fists against Simon's leg, but after a while his strength began to ebb. His head throbbed and he was crying in pain and despair. It was his own fault, the whole damn thing. He'd thought he could glimpse the theory of everything without suffering consequences, and now he was being punished for this sin of pride.

Simon chuckled. 'It hurts, doesn't it? You felt it for only a few seconds. Imagine what it's like to live with it for five years. But I'm happy now. I've done what my children wanted me to do.'

David shook his head. 'You're crazy!' he gasped.

'Maybe so, maybe so. But I've done it anyway.' Simon clenched his free hand into a fist. 'No one's going to laugh over my grave,' he muttered. He blinked, and pinched the bridge of his nose.

David stared intently at the mercenary's face. The man looked drowsy. His jaw was slack and his eyelids were drooping. Then David looked at the liquid-helium pipe. It was slightly bent at a junction, like there might be a small leak in the fitting—not enough to overheat the magnets, but enough to displace oxygen. And because helium was the second-lightest element, it would expand more rapidly in the upper part of the tunnel.

Simon blinked a few more times. 'What are you staring at?' He lowered the Uzi to within a foot of David's brow. 'I should shoot you right now!'

The mercenary was breathing fast, one of the symptoms of oxygen deprivation. Another was loss of muscle coordination. David held up his hands. Maybe he still had a chance. 'No, don't shoot!' he yelled.

Simon curled his lip. 'You pitiful worm! You . . .'

David waited until Simon blinked again. Then he swung his right arm and batted the Uzi out of Simon's hands. As the submachine gun skittered across the concrete, Simon shifted his weight off the foot that was crushing David's chest. Gripping the boot with both hands, David wrenched it like a corkscrew and Simon crashed to the floor.

David rose to his feet but stayed low. It took him a second to spot the Uzi, which had slid twenty feet down the tunnel. Before he could go three steps, Simon caught up to him and grabbed his waist. The mercenary threw him against the wall and sprinted towards the gun.

For a moment David just stared in horror. Then he turned and raced back to the tunnel entrance. He was running on instinct, thinking only of escape, but there was no escape now unless he shut down the collider. While Simon reached for his Uzi, David searched frantically for something heavy to fling at the beam pipe. Then he saw the electric cart still balanced precariously on the crumpled gate, its motor still turning the rear wheels in midair.

He heard footsteps behind him. Simon was charging down the tunnel. Clutching the front of the yellow cart, David pulled with all his might. But it didn't budge. The cart was at least 400 pounds, and it rested on a heap of twisted metal. David pulled again, but the thing was stuck.

Simon raised his Uzi and took aim. David let out an animal yell, a scream of defiance. The mercenary fired, but David crouched to make one last pull and the bullets whizzed over his head. And in the same instant the cart finally yielded to his will and slid into the tunnel.

The vehicle bucked like a bull as soon as its wheels touched the floor. Simon lowered his gun and hurtled forward. He dived towards the cart, reaching for the steering wheel, but his boots slipped on broken glass. He fell into the path of the cart as it barrelled towards the beam pipe.

David leapt over the broken gate and rolled to the side, behind a concrete wall. Then there was a flash of white light and a deafening bang.

PROFESSOR GUPTA HEARD a distant pop. A moment later, the hum of the superconducting magnets subsided. Within a few seconds, Collision Hall was silent. The Tevatron had shut down.

Crouched in the corner of the storage closet, his heart thumping, Gupta heard the shrill cries of his students. They were fairly close, shouting 'Professor! Professor!' in anguished voices. Gupta crawled to the front of the closet and pounded his fist on the door.

The voices came closer. 'Professor? Is that you?'

Someone found the key. Richard and Scott rushed in. The others followed right behind, crowding into the small space.

'What happened?' Gupta rasped as Richard helped him up.

Scott came forward, an Uzi hanging from his shoulder. 'Seconds before impact there was an explosion in the E-Zero sector of the beam tunnel.'

'So the collisions never started? There was no spacetime rupture?'

'No, the explosion disrupted the beam line and the Tevatron went down.'

Gupta felt a warm rush of relief. Thank heaven.

'We started looking for you after the shutdown,' Scott added. 'We were afraid Simon would kill you like he said.' He bit his lower lip. 'He killed Gary and Jeremy. We found their bodies. I took one of their Uzis.'

Gupta stared at the ugly black gun. 'Where's Michael?' He searched for his grandson's face. 'Didn't he come with you?'

'Uh, no,' Scott replied. 'I haven't seen him since we left the control room.'

The professor shook his head. 'Give me that gun,' he ordered.

Without hesitation, Scott handed over the Uzi.

Gupta cradled it at his hip as he stepped out of the closet. 'We're heading back to the control room. Let's find Michael and restart the experiment.'

Richard stared at him in dismay. 'But there's major damage to the beam line. The readings showed that half a dozen of the magnets are down.'

Gupta waved his hand dismissively. 'We can repair the damage. We have all the necessary equipment.' He marched through Collision Hall towards the exit, his students straggling in his wake.

As they stepped outside, Scott caught up to him. 'There's another problem, Professor,' he said. 'The security guards know we're here. We saw three of them heading for the control room right after we left, and more are coming.'

Gupta kept going. 'It doesn't matter. We're going to fulfil our destiny. The *Einheitliche Feldtheorie* can't stay hidden any longer.'

'Professor, please listen! We have to get out before they arrest us!'

Gupta raised the Uzi, pointing the barrel at the fool's chest. The other students stopped in their tracks. 'I'll shoot anyone who tries to stop me!' he yelled. 'Nothing in the world can stop me now!'

He turned and headed for Wilson Hall. As he reached the ridge, a black SUV pulled off the road and three men in grey suits jumped out. They crouched behind the vehicle, pointing their pistols at him and shouting.

Gupta pivoted towards the men and raised his Uzi, but before he could pull the trigger he saw a yellow muzzle flash from one of their pistols. A 9mm bullet sped through the air, moving as straight as a high-energy proton, though not nearly as fast. The collision splintered Gupta's skull.

AN AMBULANCE and a fire truck idled beside the F-Two tunnel entrance. David quickened his pace, hobbling as fast as he could towards the cinder-block building. He'd blacked out after the explosion in the beam tunnel, so he had no idea how much time had passed since he'd left Monique. Twenty minutes? Thirty? He remembered the terrible wounds to her stomach, and hoped to God the paramedics had got to her in time.

When he was about twenty yards away he saw a body on the ground with a sheet covering it. Two firefighters in full gear stood nearby. David stumbled to a halt. His chest tightened as he spotted a second sheet-covered corpse a few feet to the left. Then, further to the left, he saw two paramedics in blue jumpsuits heaving a stretcher into the back of the ambulance. He caught a glimpse of a brown face with an oxygen mask over the mouth. 'Monique!' he cried, bounding towards the stretcher. She was alive!

A third paramedic, a tall kid with a black moustache, intercepted him. 'Hey, slow down, buddy. What happened to you?'

David pointed at the stretcher. 'How is she? Is she going to be all right?'

'Don't worry, we stabilised her. She's lost a lot of blood, but she'll be OK.' He stared with evident concern at the gashes on David's forehead. 'It looks like you could use some help, too.'

Tensing, David stepped back. He'd been so concerned about Monique, he'd forgotten what he'd just gone through himself. Although he'd rolled behind a concrete wall before the beam pipe shattered, he knew that high-energy protons could generate nasty secondary particles. 'Don't touch me,' he warned. 'I was in the beam tunnel, so I might be hot.'

The kid's moustache twitched. He backed away and turned to one of the firefighters. 'Alex! I need a radiation reading, quick!'

Alex rushed over with a Geiger counter. David held his breath as the firefighter waved the thick metal tube in front of him, tracing a convoluted pattern from his head to his feet.

The man finally looked up. 'Nothing detectable,' he said. 'You're clean.'

David whistled in relief. 'You should send a unit to the E-Zero entrance. There's another fatality down there.'

Alex shook his head. 'What the hell's going on? We got people shooting Uzis, we got a wacko teenager on a rampage, and you're saying—'

'Hold on. A teenager?'

'Yeah, some nut job screaming in the lot by the control room and bashing all the equipment in the trucks . . . Hey, where do you think you're going?'

David started running. As the firefighter reached for his radio, he dashed past the building. He was exhausted to the point of collapse, but he had just enough strength left to scramble along the curving ridge until he reached the sprawling complex that housed the Tevatron's control room.

He charged into the lot where Gupta's trucks were parked. First he noticed the black Suburbans positioned at both exits to prevent anyone leaving. Then, to his delight, he saw Karen and Jonah, sitting on the hood of one of the SUVs. Two FBI agents stood nearby, offering Jonah a breakfast bar and Karen a cup of water. Neither of them pulled out his gun as David jogged towards them. One even smiled as Jonah slid off the hood into David's arms.

After waiting for father and son to finish hugging, the agents took David aside and patted him down. Then their grey-haired commander came over.

'I'm Agent Cowley,' he announced as he shook David's hand. 'Are you all right, Dr Swift?'

David eyed him warily. Why was he being so nice? 'Yeah, I'm fine.'

'Your ex-wife's told us about the ordeal you've been through. You're a very lucky man.' Turning serious, the agent lowered his voice. 'Professor Gupta is dead, I'm afraid.'

'So you know about Gupta? What he was trying to do?'

'I got a run-down from Agent Parker on the way over. We'd greatly appreciate it, though, if you could come back to our office and fill in the blanks. After we get you bandaged up, I mean.' The agent smiled in a grandfatherly way and squeezed David's shoulder.

This false politeness didn't fool David, of course, but he smiled back. 'All right, I can do that,' he said. 'But I'd like to see Michael first.'

'Michael? You mean Professor Gupta's grandson?'

'Yeah, I want to see if he's OK. He's autistic, you know.'

Agent Cowley thought it over. 'Sure, you can see him. The boy was screaming his head off when we found him, but now he won't say a word.'

The agent led David to one of Gupta's trucks. As they came close, David saw a heap of broken computer equipment that looked like it had been tossed from the back of the truck. The agents had roped off the area with yellow crime-scene tape, but it seemed unlikely that they'd recover anything. All Gupta's computers had been prised open and the hard drives removed. Shiny splinters of the glass memory disks were scattered across the parking lot.

Michael stood just outside the crime-scene tape, flanked by two more agents. His hands were cuffed behind his back, but he was grinning at the pile of shattered equipment as if it were a birthday present.

Cowley gave a signal and the agents stepped back. 'Here he is, Dr Swift. He made quite a mess, but he's settled down.'

David gazed in wonder at the damaged circuits, chips and disks that had held, for a brief time, the unified field theory. He realised now that he'd seriously underestimated Michael. Although the boy had fallen prey to his grandfather's wiles, David felt certain that he would never reveal the theory to the FBI, however much they interrogated him. He was, after all, Einstein's great-great-grandson. Just as Hans Kleinman had kept the vow he'd made to *Herr Doktor*, Michael would keep the promise he'd made to Hans.

David smiled and pointed at the debris. 'Michael, did you do this?'

The teenager leaned forward, bringing his lips close to David's ear. 'I had to,' he whispered. 'It wasn't a safe place.'

EPILOGUE

On a warm Saturday afternoon in October, it was hard to imagine a better place to be than the school yard on West 77th Street. Two dozen kids were tossing footballs, dribbling basketballs and waving lacrosse sticks. Their parents mostly sat on the benches eating barbecue chicken from the take-out place across the street. But David stood in the middle of the action, playing catch with Jonah and Michael. The boys had been practising baseball every weekend since August, and it showed.

Karen sat on one of the benches with Ricardo, her new boyfriend. Ricardo was a bassist in a jazz combo. The guy never wore socks, and was practically penniless, but she was crazy about him.

Monique sat on a neighbouring bench, reading the *New York Times.* She and Michael had been coming into the city regularly since she gained custody of the teenager. Monique had bonded with the boy during the two weeks she was recovering from her wounds at the University of Chicago Medical Center. The FBI had let David and Michael visit her every day; at that point, the agents were still playing nice, still hoping to wheedle some information out of them. When the Bureau finally gave up, the agents tried to release Michael to his mother, but Beth Gupta wouldn't take him. So the head of the FBI task force—Lucille Parker, the same woman who'd interrogated David—surprised everybody by recommending that the boy live with Monique.

David tossed the ball to Jonah. The more he thought about it, the more he realised how lucky they were. Agent Parker could have kept them in detention for months, wearing them down with interrogations, but instead she went easy on them. From the evidence at Fermilab, she had probably come to the conclusion Einstein had reached half a century earlier: the theory of everything was dangerous and had to stay hidden.

As the baseball went round again, David saw that Karen and Ricardo were leaving. They were going to one of Ricardo's gigs; Jonah would spend the night at David's apartment. Karen waved goodbye, blowing kisses at Jonah. And then she bent over to kiss Monique. For David, the most surprising thing of all was that his ex-wife and his new girlfriend had become close friends. The horrible episode at Fermilab had drawn them together. The universe was indeed a strange and wondrous place.

'Hey, Dad!' Jonah yelled. 'Throw the ball already!'

David lobbed the baseball and took off his mitt. 'Play with Michael for a while, OK? I gotta take a break.'

He went to Monique's bench. She was reading something in the paper's International section, her eyebrows curled in concentration. David sat down next to her and she pointed at a story near the bottom of the page. The headline was: PHYSICISTS DISCOVER NEW PARTICLE.

'I know these researchers,' she explained. 'They're at the Large Hadron Collider in Geneva. They found a boson with a rest mass of two hundred and thirty-six billion electron volts.'

'And what does that mean, exactly?'

'According to the standard theories, this new particle shouldn't exist. But the unified field theory predicted it.' Her forehead creased with worry. 'It's a clue, David. And when physicists see clues, they start theorising. After a few more discoveries, they'll piece it together.'

'You mean the unified theory? Someone's going to rediscover it?'

She nodded. 'For all we know, some grad student at Princeton or Harvard could be working on the equations right now.'

David took her hand. There was nothing else to do. For the moment *Herr Doktor*'s secret was safe in Michael's head, but all their precautions could be for naught if another physicist discovered the theory and published it. David shivered as he stared at the school yard full of frenetic children. It's all so fragile, he thought. It could be gone in an instant.

Then he moved his hand to Monique's belly, splaying his fingers over the soft cotton of her blouse.

She turned and smiled. 'She won't start kicking till the fourth month.'

David smiled back. 'How come you keep saying "she"?'

Monique shrugged. 'I just have a feeling. I had a dream the other night that we were taking her home from the hospital. I was putting her in the car, strapping her into the infant seat, and all of a sudden she started talking. She actually introduced herself to me. She said her name was Lieserl.'

'Whoa. Pretty strange.' He rubbed her belly just above the navel. 'So is that what you want to call her? Lieserl? Or maybe Albert if it's a boy?'

She made a face. 'Are you crazy? The last thing the world needs is another Einstein.'

David laughed, and although he knew it was strictly impossible, he could have sworn he felt something move under his palm.

MARK ALPERT

Home: Manhattan, USA
Profession: journalist
Website: www.markalpert.com

It's perhaps no surprise to learn that the author of *Final Theory*, which centres on Albert Einstein's lifelong quest for a 'theory of everything', is a self-confessed 'science geek' who majored in astrophysics at Princeton University. Alpert was an above-average student who wrote a fine thesis on the subject of relativity, which was well received by the scientific community and highly praised by his professor. 'I got the greatest compliment you can get from a physicist,' Alpert recalls. 'He said excitedly, "This solution is non-trivial!"'

Soon after he graduated, Mark Alpert was attracted to creative writing and enrolled in a special programme at Columbia University. However, two years later, like many aspiring authors, he realised it was not going to be easy to make ends meet as a writer, and so he decided to become a journalist. He worked for newspapers in Pennsylvania, New Hampshire and Alabama, before returning to his home town of New York to write for various magazines and for the Cable News Network channel. Eventually, in 1998, he returned to his scientific roots and became an editor at *Scientific American*, where he still works today. 'The purpose of my job is to simplify bewildering ideas such as string theory, extra dimensions and parallel universes,' he explains.

Alpert's fascination with Einstein began when he was at college, but it was while he was working on a special edition about the legendary scientist for *Scientific American* that he was inspired to write *Final Theory*. 'Over the years I've written and edited many stories that described Einstein's long, futile search for a unified theory, which has been called the Holy Grail of physics: a single set of equations that would incorporate both relativity and quantum mechanics, combining the physics of the galaxies and stars with the laws of the subatomic realm. And I've often wondered: What would have happened if Einstein had succeeded in this quest? The discovery of a unified theory would be the greatest achievement in the history of science, but it could also have unintended consequences. Einstein knew all too well that his Special theory of relativity had laid the groundwork for the atomic bomb. Would he have published the unified theory if he knew it would have paved the way for weapons that were even more terrible? Or would he have kept it a secret?'

In the novel, Alpert enjoyed including many recent inventions, such as driverless cars, surveillance robots and virtual-reality combat. As part of his research, he also made a trip to Fermilab, a cutting-edge accelerator laboratory established by the US Atomic Energy Commission in 1967 and located about forty-five miles west of Chicago, Illinois. Anyone can tour the facility and Alpert did so. 'I knew I wanted the climax of the novel to take place there and, luckily, I was able to get a private tour of the Tevatron, the four-mile-long circular tunnel where protons and antiprotons are accelerated to nearly the speed of light and then smashed together. The best part was the requisite safety briefing, during which the officials explained the various hazards we might encounter in the tunnel, such as radioactivity left over from stray proton collisions, or the possibility of asphyxiation from helium escaping from the superconducting magnets. As I took notes, I thought: Great material! This book is going to write itself. And that's what happened, more or less.'

SCIENCE—THE FINAL FRONTIER?

As far as we know, Albert Einstein did not realise his dream of completing a unified field theory (or 'theory of everything' as it's more colloquially known) before his death in 1955. Its existence in *Final Theory* is pure fiction. Interestingly, however, the publication of Alpert's novel coincides with an exciting time for physicists, as 2008 sees the start-up of the Large Hadron Collider at the Geneva-based CERN laboratory of the Organisation for Nuclear Research (right). Physicists will be descending on the lab for the unveiling of the world's largest particle accelerator, which they hope will produce a breakthrough in the ongoing search for the elusive theory of everything. To date, the development of string theory is the closest that anyone has come to finding an answer to tantalising questions about the very nature of our universe.

The Various Flavours of Coffee

ANTHONY CAPELLA

Coffee. Sometimes its aroma is reminiscent of the smoky scent of a bonfire; sometimes it brings to mind the fresh pages of a newly opened book or the lemony tang of a citrus fruit. Its flavours are as numerous and diverse as the many facets of a woman's love.

And turning such sublime scents into words, while constantly tempted by the proximity of his employer's daughter, is Robert Wallis's new challenge . . .

One

Who is he, this young man who strolls towards us down Regent Street, a carnation in his collar and a cane in his hand? We may deduce that he is well off, since he is dressed in the most fashionable clothes—but we would be wrong. We may deduce that he likes fine things, since he stops to look in the window of Liberty, the new department store devoted to the latest styles—or is that simply his own reflection he is admiring, the curling locks that brush his shoulders? We may deduce that he is hungry, since his footsteps speed up as they take him towards the Café Royal, that labyrinth of gossip and dining rooms off Piccadilly, and that he is a regular here, from the way he greets the waiter by name, and takes a *Pall Mall Gazette* from the rack as he moves towards a table. Perhaps we may even conclude that he is a writer, from the way he pauses to jot something down in that calfskin pocket book he carries.

Come along; I am going to introduce you to this ludicrous young man. Perhaps after an hour or two in his company you will consider you know him a little too well. I doubt that you will like him very much; I do not like him very much myself. He is—well, you will see what he is. But perhaps you may be able to look past that and imagine what he will become. Just as coffee does not reveal its true flavour until it has been picked, husked, roasted and brewed, so this particular specimen has one or two virtues to go along with his vices . . . Despite his faults, you see, I retain a sort of exasperated affection for the fellow.

The year is 1896. His name is Robert Wallis. He is twenty-two years old. He is me, my younger self, many years ago.

In 1895 I had been sent down from Oxford, having failed my Preliminary Examinations. My expulsion surprised no one but myself: I had done little work, and had chosen as my associates young men notable for their idleness and dissolution. I learned very little, and spent my afternoons writing poetry, and my father's allowance on silk waistcoats, fine wines, slim volumes of verse bound in yellow vellum and other *objets* essential to the artistic life, all available on ready credit. Since my talent for poetry, like my allowance, was rather more meagre than I cared to acknowledge, it was inevitable that this state of affairs would eventually come to a sorry end. By the time I was sent down I had exhausted both my funds and my father's patience, and I was faced with the necessity of finding a source of income.

London, at that time, was a great seething cesspit of humanity, yet even in that dung-heap lilies grew. Out of nowhere, it seemed, there had come upon the capital an outpouring of frivolity. The Queen, in mourning, had retired from public life. Released from her attention, the Prince had begun to enjoy himself, and, where he led, the rest of us followed. Courtiers mingled with courtesans, dandies moved among the demi-monde, aristocrats dined with aesthetes. Our emblem was the green carnation; our style was what came to be known as Nouveau, and our mode of speech was the epigram—the more paradoxical the better, preferably tossed into the conversation with a practised, weary melancholy. We celebrated the artificial above the natural, the artistic above the practical, and laid claim to extravagant vices that few had any intention of indulging in. It was a glorious time to be young and in London, and I was to miss most of it—curse it!—all because of a chance remark I happened to make in the hearing of a man named Pinker.

I was having breakfast in the Café Royal—a plate of oysters and a dish of thickly sliced ham with green sauce—when the waiter brought my coffee. Without looking up from my newspaper I drank some, frowned, and said, 'Damn it, Marsden, this coffee tastes rusty.'

'It's ver same as all ver other customers is drinking,' the waiter said haughtily. 'None of vem, as I'm aware, have seen the necessity for complaint.'

'Are you saying I'm pernickety, Marsden?'

'Will there be anyfink else, sir?'

'As a waiter, Marsden, you have mastered every skill except waiting. As a wit, you have mastered every requirement except humour.'

'Fank you, sir.'

'And, yes, I am pernickety. For a well-made cup of coffee is the proper beginning to an idle day. Its aroma is beguiling, its taste is sweet, yet it leaves behind only bitterness and regret. In that it resembles, surely, the pleasures of love.' Rather pleased with this, I again sipped the coffee that Marsden had brought. 'Although in this case,' I added, 'it seems to taste of nothing much except mud. With, perhaps, a faint aftertaste of rotten apricots.'

'My pleasure, sir.'

'I don't doubt it.' I turned my attention back to the *Gazette*.

'Will the young gentleman be paying for his breakfast this morning?' the waiter enquired, with just a trace of fashionably weary melancholy.

'On my account, please, Marsden. There's a good fellow.'

AFTER A WHILE I became aware that someone had sat at my table. Glancing over my newspaper, I saw that my companion was a small, gnome-like gentleman, whose sturdy frock coat marked him out from the usual dandies who frequented that place. I was expecting to be joined by my friends Morgan and Hunt, but since the room was mostly unoccupied it would be no great inconvenience to move to another table when they arrived. The same surfeit of tables made it all the more surprising that the stranger should sit at mine.

'Samuel Pinker, sir, at your service,' the gnome-like gentleman said, with a slight inclination of his head.

'Robert Wallis.'

'I could not help overhearing your remark to that waiter. May I?' He reached for my cup, raised it to his nostrils, and sniffed it delicately.

I watched him, unsure whether to be wary or amused.

Eyes half closed, Samuel Pinker inhaled the aroma of the coffee twice more, very deliberately. He put it to his lips and sipped it. Then he made a curious sucking sound, and seemed to swill the liquid around his mouth. 'Neilgherry,' he said regretfully. 'Over-brewed, not to mention over-roasted. You are quite right, though. Part of the batch was spoilt. The taste of rotting fruit is faint but detectable. May I ask whether you are in the trade?'

'Which trade?'

'Why, the coffee trade.'

I think I laughed out loud. 'Good heavens, no.'

'Then may I ask, sir,' he persisted, 'what trade you *are* in?'

'I am in no trade at all.'

'Forgive me—I should have said, what is your profession?'

'I do not profess anything very much. I am neither a doctor nor a lawyer, nor anything useful.'

'How do you support yourself, sir?' he asked impatiently.

In truth I did not support myself just then, my father having recently advanced me a further small sum, with strict injunctions that there would be no more. However, it seemed absurd to quibble. 'I am a poet,' I confessed.

'A famous one? A great one?' Pinker asked eagerly.

'Alas, no. Fame has not yet clasped me to her fickle breast.'

'Good,' he muttered. 'But you can write? You can use words well?'

'As a writer I consider myself the master of everything except language—'

'Confound these epigrams!' Pinker cried. 'I mean, can you describe? Well, of course you can. You described this coffee. You called it "rusty". Yes—and "rusty" it is. I should never have thought of it, but "rusty" is the . . . the . . .'

'The *mot juste*?'

'Exactly.' Pinker gave me a look that combined doubt with a certain steely determination. 'Enough talk. I am going to give you my card.'

'I shall certainly accept it,' I said, mystified, 'although I believe I am unlikely to have need of your services.'

He was scribbling something briskly on the back of his business card. 'You misunderstand me, sir. It is *I* who have need of *you*.'

'You mean, as some kind of secretary? I'm afraid I—'

Pinker shook his head. 'No, no. I have three extremely proficient secretaries already. You would make a very poor addition to their number.'

'What, then?' I asked, somewhat piqued.

'My need,' Pinker said, looking me in the eye, 'is for a writer. When I have found this gifted individual, he will join me in an enterprise that will make fantastically wealthy men of us both.' He handed me the card. 'Call on me at this address tomorrow afternoon.'

IT WAS MY FRIEND George Hunt's opinion that the mysterious Mr Pinker intended to start a literary magazine. He believed I should take up the coffee merchant's offer and call.

'He hardly seemed a literary type,' I said, turning the card over. On the back was written in pencil, *Admit to my office, please. S.P.*

The third member of our group, Percival Morgan, laughed suddenly. 'I know what your Mr Pinker wants.' He tapped the back page of the *Gazette*. '"Branah's patented invigorating powders,"' he read aloud. '"Guaranteed to restore rosy health to the convalescent. Enjoy the effervescent vigour of the alpine rest cure in a single efficacious spoonful." It's obvious, isn't it? The man wants you to write his advertising.'

I had to admit that this sounded much more likely. Doubtless Pinker simply had a new coffee he wished to puff. I felt a sudden disappointment. For a moment I had hoped—well, that it might be something more exciting.

'Advertising,' Hunt said thoughtfully, 'is the unspeakable expression of an unspeakable age.'

'On the contrary,' Morgan said, 'I adore advertising. It is the only form of modern art to concern itself, however remotely, with the truth.'

They looked at me expectantly. But for some reason I was no longer in the mood for epigrams.

THE FOLLOWING AFTERNOON saw me sitting at my desk, working on a translation of a poem by Baudelaire. At my side, a goblet of yellow Venetian glass was filled with pale Rhenish wine; I was writing with a silver pencil on mauve paper infused with oil of bergamot, and I was smoking innumerable cigarettes of Turkish tobacco, all in the approved manner, but even so it was utterly tedious work. Were it not for the three pounds the publisher had promised me, I would have jacked it in hours ago. My rooms were off St John's Wood High Street, close to the Regent's Park, and on a sunny spring day such as this I could hear the distant cries of the ice-cream sellers as they paced back and forth by the gates. It made staying inside rather difficult.

'Hang it,' I said aloud, putting down my pencil.

I picked up Pinker's card and looked at it again. There was an address in Narrow Street, Limehouse. The thought of getting out of my rooms, if only for an hour or two, tugged at me like a dog pulling at its master's leash.

On the other side of the desk was a pile of bills. Of course, it was inevitable that a poet should have debts. You could scarcely call yourself an artist if you did not. But just for a moment I grew dispirited at the thought of having to find the means to pay them off. If I agreed to do Mr Pinker's advertisements, and he could be prevailed upon to pay me a retainer . . .

I made a decision. Pausing only to pick up Pinker's card, and to pull on a paisley-pattern coat, I hastened to the door.

AS THE HANSOM CAB clattered down Drury Lane, it exuded a rich smell of leather and sweating horse, which mingled with the odour of the river that crept up the side streets. Despite Bazalgette's new sewers, the putrid cesspits of the tenements still leaked into London's underground streams. Other smells came from the industries clustered along the waterfront. Roasting hops from the breweries—that was pleasant enough, as was the scent of exotic botanicals from the gin distilleries. But then came a reek of boiling horse bones from the glue factories, and fish guts from Billingsgate.

Approaching the Port of London, we passed beneath great towering warehouses. From one came the rich smell of tobacco leaves, from the next a sugary waft of molasses. The river was full of vessels: sloops and schooners, eel boats and tea clippers, gleaming mahogany-decked steamers and grimy working barges, all nosing higgledy-piggledy through the chaos.

As the cab turned towards Limehouse I felt a stirring of excitement at the boundless, busy energy of it all; at the industry and endeavour that pours out from this great city all over the globe.

THE YOUNG MAN about my own age who opened the door to the house in Narrow Street was clearly one of the proficient secretaries Pinker had spoken of. He was impeccably dressed, his white collar was neatly starched, and his hair, gleaming with Macassar oil, was short—much shorter than my own curling locks. 'Can I help you?' he said, giving me a cool glance.

I handed him Pinker's card. 'Would you tell your employer that Robert Wallis, the poet, is here?'

The young man examined the card. 'You're to be admitted. Follow me.'

The building was, I now saw, a kind of warehouse. Bargemen were unloading burlap sacks from a jetty, and storemen were hurrying to various parts of the store, a sack on each shoulder. The smell of roasting coffee hit me, a bitter, beguiling perfume that caught at the back of the throat, filling the nostrils and the brain. A man could become addicted to it.

The secretary led me up some stairs and showed me into an office. One window looked onto the street; another, much larger, gave onto the warehouse, and Samuel Pinker was standing there, watching the bustle below. Next to him, under a glass bell jar, a small brass instrument clattered quietly, unreeling onto the polished floor thin loops of white paper printed with symbols. Another secretary was sitting at a desk, writing.

Pinker turned and saw me. 'I will take four tons of the Brazilian and one of the Ceylon,' he said sternly.

'I beg your pardon?' I said, nonplussed.

'Payment will be freight on board, with the proviso that none spoils during the voyage.'

I realised he was dictating. 'Oh, of course. Do carry on.'

He frowned at my impertinence. 'Ten per cent will be held back against future samples. I remain, et cetera, et cetera. Take a seat.'

This last comment clearly being addressed to me, I sat.

'Coffee, Jenks, if you please,' Pinker said to the secretary. 'The four and the nine, with the eighteen to follow.' He turned his gaze back to me. 'You told me you were a writer, Mr Wallis,' he said sourly. 'Yet my secretaries have been unable to find a single work by you in any Charing Cross bookshop. Mr W. H. Smith's subscription library has never heard of you. Even the literary editor of *Blackwood's Magazine* is unfamiliar with your work.'

'I am a poet,' I said, somewhat taken aback by the diligence of Pinker's researches. 'But not a published one. I thought I had made that clear.'

'You said you were not yet famous. Now I discover you are not yet even heard of.' He sat down heavily on the other side of the table.

'I apologise if I gave the wrong impression. But—'

'Hang the impression, Mr Wallis. All I ask from you is *precision*.'

In the Café Royal, Pinker had seemed diffident, even unsure of himself. Here in his own offices, his manner was authoritative. 'Take me, for example. Would I still be a merchant if I had never sold a single sack of coffee?'

'It's an interesting question—'

'It is not. A merchant is someone who trades. Ergo, if I do not trade, I am not a merchant.'

'But a writer, by the same token, must therefore be someone who *writes*,' I pointed out. 'It is not strictly necessary to be read as well. Only desirable.'

'Hmm.' Pinker seemed to weigh this. 'Very well.' I had the feeling I had passed some kind of test.

The secretary returned with a tray on which were four thimble-sized cups and two steaming jugs, which he placed in front of us.

'So,' his employer said, gesturing to me. 'Tell me what you make of these.'

The coffee was evidently freshly brewed—the smell was deep and pleasant. I tried some, while Pinker watched expectantly.

'It's excellent,' I said.

'And? You are a writer, are you not? Words are your stock in trade?'

'Ah.' I realised now what he wanted. 'It is . . . invigorating. Like a . . . seaside rest cure. I can think of no better, balmier, more bracing pick-me-up than Pinker's breakfast blend. It will aid the digestion, restore the concentration and elevate the constitution, all at once.'

'*What?*' The merchant was staring at me.

'Of course, it needs a little work,' I said modestly. 'But I think—'

'Try the other one,' he said impatiently.

I started to pour from the second jug. 'Not in the same cup!' he hissed.

'Sorry.' I filled a second thimble-sized cup and sipped from it. 'It's different,' I said, surprised. Here were two coffees, both palpably excellent, whose excellence varied from each other as chalk from cheese. 'This one,' I said slowly, 'has an almost . . . smoky flavour.'

Pinker nodded. 'It does indeed.'

'Whereas this one,' I pointed at the first cup, 'is more . . . flowery.'

'Flowery!' Pinker seemed impressed. 'Let me make a . . .' He pulled the secretary's pad towards him and jotted down the word *flowery*. 'Go on.'

'This second cup has . . . a sort of tang. More like pencil shavings.'

'Pencil shavings.' Pinker wrote this down too. 'Exactly.'

'While the other—chestnuts, perhaps?' I said.

'Perhaps,' Pinker said, making a note. 'What else?'

'This one,' I indicated the second cup, 'tastes of spice.'

'Which spice?'

'I'm not sure,' I confessed.

'Never mind,' Pinker said. 'Ah, there you are. Capital. Pour it, will you?'

I turned. A young woman had entered with another jug of coffee. She was, I noted, rather attractive. She wore the Rational style of dress: a tailored jacket, buttoned to the neck, worn above a long skirt without a bustle. It revealed little of the slight figure underneath. Her features, though, were alert and lively, and her hair, carefully pinned, was elegant and golden.

She filled one of the cups and handed it to me. 'My thanks,' I said, catching her eye with a smile as I took it. If she noticed my interest, she did not reveal it; her face was a mask of professional detachment.

'Perhaps you would take notes, Emily,' Pinker said, pushing his pad towards her. 'Mr Wallis was just trying to decide which spice our finest Brazilian reminded him of, but inspiration has temporarily deserted him.'

The secretary seated herself at the table and raised her pen. For a moment I could have sworn I discerned a hint of amusement in her grey eyes.

I drank some of the new coffee. It was very ordinary. In fact, the taste was familiar. 'This is what they serve at the Café Royal!'

'Very like it, yes.' Pinker was smiling. 'Is it—ha!—is it rusty?'

'A little.' I tried some more. 'And dull. Very dull. With a faint aftertaste of . . . wet towels.' I glanced at the stenographer. She was busy writing it all down—or rather, I now saw, making a series of curious squiggles on her pad. This must be the Pitman's Phonographic Method I had read of.

'Wet towels,' Pinker repeated with a chuckle. 'Very good, though I'm afraid I have never actually tasted a towel, wet or dry.'

'And it smells like . . . old carpet,' I said. Immediately, my words were translated into more dashes and strokes.

'Carpet!' Pinker nodded. 'Anything else?'

'A whiff of burnt toast.' More squiggles.

'Burnt toast. Well. That will do, I think, for the moment.'

'So which one of these is yours?' I asked Pinker, gesturing at the jugs.

'What?' He seemed surprised by the question. 'Oh, all of them.'

'And which do you want to advertise?'

'Advertise?'

'Of this one,' I said, pointing to the first jug, 'you might say . . . "A choice concoction, the cream of the colonies, with an ambrosial chestnut taste."' Was it my imagination or did the secretary give a faint snort of laughter?

'My dear Wallis,' Pinker said, 'you would make a terrible advertising man. People want their coffee to taste of coffee, not chestnuts. The essence of advertising is to conceal the truth, by revealing only those parts that coincide with what the public wants to hear. The essence of a code, on the other hand, is to fix the truth precisely for the benefit of the few.'

'That's very good,' I said, impressed. 'That's almost an epigram. Er . . . what's this about a code?'

'I am going to make you a proposal, Mr Wallis,' Pinker said, looking at me intently. 'We live in an Age of Improvement.' He pulled a watch from his fob pocket. 'Take this timepiece. It is more accurate than any watch produced in previous decades, and less costly. Next year, it will be cheaper and more accurate still. More accurate timepieces mean more accurate railways, which mean more trade, which means cheaper, more accurate timepieces.'

He reached into his fob pocket again and dug something out with his thumb and forefinger. 'Look at this.' He was staring at a tiny nut-and-bolt. 'What a remarkable thing this is, Wallis. The bolt was made in Belfast, the nut in Liverpool. Yet they fit together exactly. The threads, you see, have been standardised. A few years ago, every workshop and machine room in the country produced their own design of thread. It was chaos. It was impractical. Now, thanks to the impetus of Improvement, there is only one. Are you a believer in the theories of Mr Darwin?'

I said that, on balance, I probably was.

Pinker nodded approvingly. 'Darwin shows us that Improvement is inevitable. For species, of course, but also for countries, for individuals, even for nuts and bolts. Now, let us consider how Mr Darwin's ideas may benefit the coffee trade. First, how may the brewing process be Improved? I will tell you, Mr Wallis. By steam. If every café and hotel had its own steam engine for making coffee, we would see consistency. Consistency!'

'Wouldn't it make the cafés rather . . . well, rather hot?'

'The engine I am describing is a miniature one. Jenks! Foster!' he called. 'Bring in the apparatus, will you?'

After a pause and a certain amount of banging, the two male secretaries wheeled in a trolley on which sat a curious mechanism. It seemed to consist of a copper boiler and a quantity of brass pipes, levers, dials and tubing.

'Signor Toselli's steam-powered coffee-machine,' Pinker said proudly. 'As demonstrated at the Paris Exhibition. The steam is forced through the grounds one cup at a time, giving a much superior taste.'

'How is it heated?'

'By gas, although we anticipate an electric model eventually.' He paused. 'I've ordered eighty.'

'Eighty! Where will they all go?'

'To Pinker's Temperance Taverns.' Pinker jumped to his feet and started pacing. Behind him, Jenks was lighting the boiler. 'Oh, you are about to point out that there exists, at this time, not a single Pinker's Temperance Tavern in the land. But they will come, Wallis. Look at London. A public house on every corner! Gin palaces, most of 'em, where the working man is fleeced of his hard-earned wages. Intoxication makes him a wife beater, incapacitates him, ruins him for employment the next day. Coffee offers no such drawbacks. It does not dull the senses but sharpens them. Why should we not have a coffee house on every street instead? It would be an Improvement, would it not? Yes? Then it *will* happen. And I will be the one to make it happen.' He sat down, dabbing at his forehead with his sleeve.

'You mentioned a code,' I said. 'I still don't quite see—'

'Yes. Demand and supply, Mr Wallis. Demand and supply.'

He paused and I waited, and the secretary's hand paused on her pad. She had exceptionally long, elegant fingers.

'The difficulty with my plans,' Pinker explained, 'is cost. Coffee is much more expensive than beer, say, or gin. It comes from further away, of course. You order it through an agent, who gets it from another agent . . . It's a wonder it reaches us at all.' He looked at me. 'So we ask ourselves—what?'

'We ask ourselves,' I suggested, 'how the supply could be Improved?'

Pinker snapped his fingers. 'Exactly! We've made a start with this Exchange. You've heard of the Exchange, I take it?'

I had not.

He placed his hand on the bell jar in which the printing machine still clattered quietly to itself. 'The London Coffee Exchange will revolutionise the way we do business. It's linked by submarine cable to New York and Amsterdam. Prices will standardise—all across the world. The price will fall—it's bound to.' He shot me a crafty look. 'Can you spot the difficulty?'

I thought. 'You don't know what you're getting. You're buying on cost alone. You want to find the good stuff, and let other people get the dross.'

Pinker sat back and smiled. 'You've got it, sir. You've got it.'

The apparatus suddenly gave out a kind of wheezing, bubbling screech. Jenks pulled some levers, and an unpleasant gargling sound issued from its several throats as liquid and steam hissed into a miniature cup.

I said, 'If you have a code—no, code's not quite the word—if you have a trading *vocabulary*, a way of describing the coffee that you and your agents have fixed in advance, then even though you're in different countries—'

'Exactly!'

Jenks placed two tiny cups in front of Pinker and me. I picked up mine. It contained thick black liquid topped with hazelnut-brown froth. I rotated the cup: the contents were dense and sluggish, like oil. I raised it to my lips—

It was as if the very essence of coffee had been concentrated into that morsel of liquid. Burnt embers and wood smoke danced across my tongue and caught at the back of my throat. The texture was like molasses, and a faint, chocolatey sweetness lingered. I finished the tiny cup in two gulps, but the taste seemed to grow and deepen in my mouth afterwards.

Pinker, watching me, nodded. 'You have a palate, Mr Wallis, albeit rough and somewhat untutored. More importantly, you have the gift of using words. Find me the words that can capture the elusive taste of coffee, so that two people in different parts of the world can telegraph a description to each other and each know exactly what it means. Make it authoritative, evocative, but above all precise. That is your task. We shall call it . . . ' He paused. 'We shall call it the Pinker–Wallis Method Concerning the Clarification and Classification of the Various Flavours of Coffee. What do you say?'

'It sounds fascinating,' I said politely. 'But I could not possibly do what you suggest. I am a writer—an artist—not some manufacturer of phrases.'

'Ah. Emily anticipated that this might be your response.' Pinker nodded towards the secretary, whose head was still bent over her notebook. 'At her suggestion, I took the liberty of establishing your father's address and sending him a telegram about this offer of employment. You may be interested to see the Reverend Wallis's reply.' Pinker pushed a telegram across the table;

it started with the word *Hallelujah!* 'He seems quite keen to be relieved of the burden of supporting you,' Pinker said drily. '"Tell him allowance terminated stop. Grateful opportunity stop. God bless you sir stop."'

'Ah,' I said. My throat had gone dry. 'You mentioned fantastic wealth.'

'Did I?'

'Yesterday, at the Café Royal. You said that if I entered into your . . . scheme, we would both become fantastically wealthy men.'

'Ah, yes.' Pinker considered. 'That was a figure of speech. I was employing . . .' He glanced at the secretary. 'What was I employing?'

'Hyperbole,' she said. It was the first time she had spoken. Her voice was low, but again I thought I discerned a faint note of amusement. I glanced at her, but her head was still lowered demurely over the notepad.

'Exactly. I was employing hyperbole. As a literary person, I'm sure you appreciate that.' Pinker's eyes glinted. 'Of course, at the time I was not fully apprised of your own somewhat straitened circumstances.'

'What remuneration—exactly—are you suggesting?'

'Emily here informs me that Mrs Humphrey Ward was paid ten thousand pounds for her last novel. I propose to pay you at the same rate.'

'Ten thousand pounds?' I repeated, amazed.

'I said the same *rate*, sir, not the same *amount*.' He smiled. 'Mrs Ward's opus is approximately two hundred thousand words long—so that is six shillings and thruppence a word. I will pay you six and thruppence for every descriptor adopted for our code. And a bonus of twenty pounds when it is complete. That is fair, is it not?'

I passed my hand across my face. My head was spinning. 'It must be called the Wallis–Pinker Method. Not the other way round.'

Pinker frowned. 'As a Pinker is the originator, surely Pinker's must be the greater share of the credit.'

'As the writer, the bulk of the work will fall to me.'

'Hmm.' Pinker considered. 'Very well,' he conceded abruptly. 'The Wallis–Pinker Method.'

'And, as this is a literary work, I will need an advance. Thirty pounds.'

'That is a very considerable amount.'

'It is customary,' I insisted.

To my surprise, Pinker shrugged. 'Thirty pounds it is, then. Do we have an agreement, Mr Wallis?'

I hesitated. I had been going to say that I would have to think about it. But—I could not help it—I glanced at the girl. Her eyes were shining, and she gave me . . . not a smile exactly, but a tiny signal, the eyes widening with the briefest nod of encouragement. In that moment I was lost.

'Yes,' I said.

'Good,' the merchant said, standing up and offering me his hand. 'We start in this office tomorrow morning, sir, sharp at ten o'clock. Emily, will you be so good as to show Mr Wallis out?'

AS WE REACHED the bottom of the stairs I stopped her. 'Would it be possible to look round the warehouse? I am curious to know more about the business to which Mr Pinker has decided I am to be apprenticed.'

'Of course,' she said simply, and led me into the vast storeroom I had glimpsed earlier.

It was a curious place—devilish hot, from the line of roasting drums that stood to one side, the flames of their burners bright in the gloom. The boat had been unloaded now, and the big doors onto the jetty were closed, with only a fat blade of sunlight pushing through the gap between them. The air was full of a peculiar mistiness, caused, I now saw, by a thick dust of cotton-like fibres. I reached into it and the air eddied around my hand.

'Coffee parchment,' she explained. 'Some of the beans we receive have not yet been milled.'

Her words meant little to me. 'And all this coffee belongs to Pinker?'

'*Mr* Pinker,' she said, 'owns four warehouses, of which the two largest are in bond. This is merely the clearing house.' She pointed. 'The coffee comes in by boat. Then it is sampled, weighed, milled, roasted and stored according to its country of origin. Over there is Brazil; over here is Ceylon; Indonesia is behind us—there is not so much of that: the Dutch take most of the crop. The pure arabicas we keep over here, for safety.'

'Why must pure arabicas be kept safer than the rest?'

'Because they are the most valuable.' She took a step towards a stack of plump jute sacks. One was already open. 'Look,' she said.

I looked. The sack was filled with beans—iron-coloured, gleaming. She scooped up a handful to show me. They were small, each one notched like a peanut, and as they fell back through her fingers they hissed like rain.

'Mocca,' she said reverently. 'Every one a jewel.' She pushed her arm in up to the elbow, swirling it round and releasing a great waft of that dark, charred aroma. 'A whole sack like this is like a sack full of treasure.'

'May I?' I slid my arm in beside hers. The beans closed around my wrist, as liquid might, but they were light, as insubstantial as chaff. The rich, bitter smell filled my nostrils. I pushed deeper and, among the oiled smoothness of the beans, I thought I felt, for an instant, the soft, dry touch of her fingers.

'Your Mr Pinker is quite a character,' I said.

'He is a genius,' she said calmly.

'An impresario of coffee?' As if by accident, I slid my thumb gently over her wrist. She stiffened and withdrew her arm, but otherwise she did not react. This was a woman who did not simper and shriek for the sake of it.

'A genius,' she repeated. 'He means to change the world.'

'With his Temperance Taverns?'

'That is part of it, yes.' She looked at me coolly. 'You think him ridiculous.'

I shook my head. 'I think him misguided. The working man is never going to prefer arabicas to gin.'

She gave a dismissive shrug. 'Perhaps.'

'You disagree?'

She dipped her hand into the sack again and watched the dark beans drip between her fingers. 'These are not just beans, Mr Wallis,' she said. 'They are the seeds of a new civilisation.' She glanced up. I followed her gaze, towards the window that looked down from Pinker's office. The coffee merchant was standing at the glass, watching us.

'He is a great man,' she said simply. 'He is also my father.' She withdrew her hand, wiping it on a handkerchief as she stepped towards the burners.

'Miss Pinker,' I said, catching her up. 'I had no inkling. I must apologise if I have offended. And I also apologise for . . .' I hesitated, 'for my behaviour towards you, which was inappropriate to someone in your position.'

'What behaviour was that?' she asked innocently.

Overcome with confusion, I did not reply.

'I hope, Mr Wallis,' she said, 'you will treat me no differently from any of my father's other employees.'

A rebuke, or an invitation? If so, it was a heavily coded one.

She held my gaze for a moment. 'We are both here to work, are we not? Any personal feelings must be put on one side.'

I LEFT THE WAREHOUSE exhilarated at having blundered into gainful employment, and confused by my flirtation with the lovely Emily Pinker.

I took a boat to the Embankment, then crossed the Strand to Wellington Street. Here there were several cheap and cheerful establishments I had frequented before, all of a reliably high standard. Tonight was a night for celebration: I had the promise of my thirty pounds advance.

Pausing only to eat a meat pudding at the Savoy Tavern window, I entered the grandest of the bagnios at Number 18. On the first floor, behind heavy curtains, was a receiving room lined with red damask where half a dozen of the prettiest girls in London reclined in their negligées on upholstered divans.

I chose the one whose long, elegant fingers reminded me of Miss Pinker.

Two

Pinker looks up as his daughter comes into his office and begins to clear the various cups and jugs that litter the desk. 'Well?' he says mildly. 'What do you think of our aesthete, Emily?'

She takes a cloth and wipes some spilt grounds from the polished mahogany before she replies. 'He is certainly not quite what I expected.'

'In what way?'

'Younger, for one thing. And somewhat full of himself.'

'Yes,' Pinker agrees. 'But an older man might be more fixed in his opinions. This one, I hope, will be less inclined to run away with your idea.'

'It is hardly my idea,' she murmurs.

'Do not be modest, Emily. Of course it is your idea, and must remain so.' Pinker watches her as she places crockery on the tray. 'Will you tell Mr Wallis? That the Guide originated with you, I mean?'

She stacks up the cups. 'No,' she says after a moment. 'At this stage, the less he knows the better. Anything we say might somehow get back to our competitors—even, perhaps, to Howell.'

'As ever, you are very wise, Emily.' Her father turns his head, watching the stock ticker as it stutters and pecks at its endless flow of tape. 'Let us hope, then, that he is up to the job.'

THE NEXT MORNING it was the turn of Jenks, the senior secretary, to show me around. It soon became clear that the warehouse was a vast but very simple mechanism for the accumulation of profits. 'The material', as Jenks called the coffee, came in on the high tide, was swept from point to point around the great warehouse, hulled, milled and roasted, before being swept out again on another tide, its worth quadrupled.

He showed me ledgers recording the movement of each bag. Most of the coffees that came to this store were destined for just four blends: Pinker's Mocca Mix, Pinker's Old Government Java, Pinker's Ceylon and Pinker's Fancy. Jenks explained that the Ceylon blend had originally been sourced from Pinker's own plantations in that country; now, blight having all but wiped out the crop, the name was more of a description of the style than an indicator of origin, with cheaper Brazilian coffee making up most of the mix.

I must have looked surprised, because he said sternly, 'It is a standard business practice—there is nothing sharp about it. Other merchants commonly adulterate their blends with foreign substances. Chicory, oats, maize, sorghum, flavoured with wood ash and molasses. Pinker's never does that.'

'I see.' To change the subject I said, 'The failure of your estates in Ceylon must have been a blow.'

'Not really. The land was cheap, the labour easily redirected to other crops. There was a small book loss, which we have written off against our assets.'

I nodded. These terms—book loss, written off—meant nothing to me.

In the office, Jenks showed me how a merchant samples, or 'cups', as he called it. An exact amount of ground beans was placed in a standard-sized cup. After water was added, one waited precisely two minutes before pushing the grounds to the bottom with a spoon and tasting the result.

'Like this,' Jenks said. He dipped his spoon into the cup with a practised, dainty flick, then raised it to his mouth and slurped noisily, deliberately sucking in air with the liquid—much as Pinker had done at the Café Royal.

'How does it taste?' I asked.

He shrugged. 'I don't know. I have little palate. My concern is with the business side of things.' There was a note of disdain in his voice.

'But a poor business it would be if the coffee did not taste of anything.'

'Then it is fortunate for us all that you're here,' he said with a sniff.

At that moment the merchant himself joined us and we began work. A burner was brought in and connected to the gas. We were supplied with cups and kettles of water, as well as a rough fellow called South, whose job was to fetch samples of coffee. There were also two steel buckets.

'For the coffee,' Pinker explained. 'If you actually drink it all, you'll jump out of your skin.'

We were also supplied with Emily, who took up her position at the side of the table with her notepad. I smiled at her, and she nodded back.

'I suggest we start with the various categories of odour,' Pinker said.

I gave it a moment's thought. 'No. We must deal first with appearance, and only then proceed to smell, taste, aftertaste and so on.'

Pinker considered. 'Very well.'

I sent South off to get a handful of coffee from every sack in the warehouse. Eventually the beans were arranged in little heaps on the table.

'Hmm.' I considered. 'We will have to decide on words for several different shades of black, beginning with the blackest form of black there is.'

A silence fell upon us. It was, in fact, quite hard to think of a word to describe the blackness of the darkest beans. 'The pure black of a cow's nose,' I said at last. Pinker made a face. 'Or the glistening black of a slug at dawn—'

'Too fanciful. And, if I may so, hardly appetising.'

'The black of a moonless night.'

Pinker tutted.

'Too poetic for you? What about charcoal, then?'

'But charcoal is not quite black. It is a kind of grey, somewhere between the grey of Cornish slate and the grey of a mouse's fur.' This was from Emily. I glanced at her. 'My apologies,' she added, 'you probably don't require another opinion, when your own is already so pronounced.'

'No—you make a good objection,' I said. 'What about sable?'

'Crow,' Pinker countered.

'Anthracite.'

'Tar.'

'Jet,' I said.

Pinker nodded. No one could argue that jet was not very black indeed.

'We have our first word,' Emily said, writing it down. 'But you should perhaps bear in mind that these beans are only black because we have roasted them. In their natural state they are actually light brown.'

'Of course,' I said. 'I was aware of that.' Needless to say, I had forgotten. 'Naturally, we must consider the roast. In the meantime we ask ourselves—if those are jet, then what are these?' I poked at some more beans.

'Those are . . . iron,' Emily said.

'Indeed,' I agreed. 'Iron they certainly are.'

'This is getting easier,' she commented as she wrote it down.

'And these?' Pinker said, pointing at a third pile.

I picked up one of the beans and scrutinised it closely. 'Pewter.'

'I agree,' Emily said, writing it down.

'And so we come to brown.' I glanced at the beans. 'Shades of wood. Some of these might be called mahogany, some ash, some oak.'

Abruptly, Pinker stood up. 'I have other affairs to attend to. You two carry on.' He strode to the door and pulled it open. 'Jenks, where are you?'

Then he was gone. I looked at Emily. She kept her eyes on her pad.

'I have been trying,' I said softly, 'to fix in my mind a word that would describe the precise colour of your eyes.'

She stiffened, and I saw a little colour rise in her cheeks.

'They too are a kind of grey,' I suggested. 'But brighter, I think, than charcoal or Cornish slate.'

There was a moment's silence. Then she said, 'We should continue.'

'Of course. In any case, it is not a question that should be hurried. I shall need to give the matter much further thought.'

'There is no need to put yourself to the trouble,' she said, a hint of ice in her voice. 'Let us return our thoughts to the colour of these beans.'

'You are a hard taskmaster, Miss Pinker.'

'I am merely aware that the task before us is a considerable one.'

'Considerable, perhaps, but not irksome,' I said gallantly. 'No labour could be tedious in such company.'

'But I fear I am becoming a distraction to you,' she said. The hint of ice had become positively arctic. 'Perhaps I should see if Mr Jenks or Mr Simmons is free to take my place—'

'No need,' I said hastily. 'I will attend to my duties all the more conscientiously because you have commanded it.'

We stared at the heaps of grey-green raw beans. Neither of us, I am sure, was thinking about coffee. I stole another glance at her.

'Whereas the colour of your cheeks,' I said, 'reminds me of a ripe—'

'Mr Wallis.' She slammed her pad forcefully on the table. 'If my cheeks have colour in them, it is because I am angry at you for teasing me like this.'

'Then I apologise. I meant no harm. Quite the reverse, in fact.'

'But you must see,' she said in a low, urgent voice, 'you are putting me in an impossible position. If I leave the room, my father will want to know why; then he will dismiss you and the Guide will not get written. Yet if I stay, I suspect you will take advantage of the situation to tease me even more.'

'I swear on my honour that I shall do no such thing.'

'You must promise to disregard my sex entirely.'

'I had thought you too modern to shrink like a violet from a perfectly natural attraction on my part,' I said. 'However, if you prefer it I shall in future try to think of you as if you were a boy.'

She gave me a suspicious look, but lifted her pencil over her pad.

'These beans . . .' I picked up a handful and closed my fist around them, shaking them. 'We might compare their colour to leaves.'

'In what way?'

'New leaf is pale green. Summer leaf, of course, is darker. Autumn leaf is more like the paler, more yellow beans.'

'Very well.' She wrote it down.

'And so we come to aroma. For that, we must prepare some samples.'

'I will light the burner.'

She busied herself boiling water, and I watched her. I had been wrong when I considered that those Rational garments of hers did not flatter her. Rather, the absence of a corset allowed one to appreciate what her natural shape would be—in other words, her naked figure . . .

Just then Pinker came back and found me looking at his daughter. He must have been able to guess what was going through my mind.

'Is Mr Wallis proving industrious, Emily?' he said sharply.

She gazed at me coolly. 'Mr Wallis is progressing quite well, Father. Though not as rapidly, I believe, as he would like. I fear my girlish chatter has been a distraction.'

'On the contrary, Miss Pinker has been an inspiration,' I said smoothly.

Pinker's eyes narrowed. 'Very well. Perhaps, Wallis, I might help you cup your first sample.'

'There is no need,' I said. 'Jenks has already explained the principles.'

'I shall observe, then.'

He watched me, arms folded, as I measured the beans, ground them in a handmill and added the hot water. I waited exactly two minutes by my watch, then pushed the foaming crust of grounds to the bottom with the spoon. When I lifted the spoon, however, the liquid was still thick with coffee grains. I put it to my lips anyway and tried to slurp it. The inevitable and immediate result was that I choked, spluttering coffee all over the table.

'My dear Wallis,' Pinker cried, 'you were meant to taste it, not spray it.'

'A catch in the throat,' I croaked, when speech was possible. 'My apologies. I will try again.' Embarrassed, I tried again to slurp the coffee; this time I managed to keep the liquid in my mouth, but it was a close thing.

'Emily, my dear, I fear your new colleague will be unable to speak for the rest of the afternoon,' Pinker chortled.

'That will be no great hardship,' Emily said. Her mouth twitched. 'At least, for everyone but Mr Wallis.'

'Perhaps . . .' Pinker wiped his eyes with his finger. 'Perhaps his waistcoat will speak for him!'

Now it was the turn of Emily Pinker to splutter and choke. I stared at the two of them. It was true that my waistcoat that day was a vivid yellow hue, but even a Limehouse coffee merchant could surely see that it was *à la mode*.

Pinker wiped his eyes again. 'Forgive us, my dear Wallis. Here, let me show you. There is a knack.' He spooned a little coffee into his mouth, slurped it noisily with a kind of gargling motion. 'The trick is to aspirate the liquid with the lips and tongue. Aspirate, aerate and ultimately expectorate.'

I followed his lead, and this time the reaction of my audience was more restrained. I was then called upon to master the art of spitting the tasted coffee into the bucket. Pinker demonstrated, efficiently ejecting a thin stream with a pinging sound as it hit the metal.

'Imagine that you are whistling,' he explained. 'And be decisive.'

I glanced at Emily. 'Perhaps your daughter would prefer not to be present at what might, I fear, prove a somewhat indelicate display,' I suggested.

Pinker turned to his daughter, who said, 'Oh, come, Mr Wallis. Let us be thoroughly modern and not shrink like violets from what is only natural.'

'Yes, of course.' I turned reluctantly back to the table.

'Together?' Pinker said. He spooned some coffee into his mouth. I followed suit. We aspirated and aerated, and then he pinged a thin stream of brown liquid accurately into the bucket.

I leaned towards the bowl and expectorated as delicately as I could. My delicacy was counterproductive; it simply meant that I squirted coffee in the general area of the receptacle. Some missed the target altogether.

'I do apologise,' I said, my face as red as beetroot. Neither Pinker heard me. The father's shoulders were shaking. His eyes were closed, and from under the lashes tears squeezed. Emily had jammed her hands under her armpits, and was rocking herself backwards and forwards on her chair, her bowed head nodding vigorously with the effort of containing her laughter.

'I see this is amusing for you,' I said stiffly.

'If you ever fail as a poet,' Pinker gasped, 'you have a certain future in the music halls. It is the preparatory pose, sir—the pose is wonderful. And the solemn expression! As if you were about to declaim, rather than dribble.'

'I don't believe I dribbled.' I was still rather red in the face.

'My dear young fellow,' he said, suddenly serious, 'we have baited you enough. Forgive us. I will let you resume your duties.'

He went to the door. When he had gone there was a silence.

I said bitterly, 'I suppose you think me ridiculous.'

Emily said quietly, 'No, Robert. But perhaps you now think yourself ridiculous, and that, I think, is what my father intended.'

'I see.'

'If we are to work together we must be comfortable with one another. And we cannot do that if either of us is attempting to get the upper hand.'

'Yes. I understand.'

'I will promise not to laugh at you if you promise not to flirt with me.'

'Very well. You have my word.' I sat down heavily.

'Believe me,' she added, her mouth twitching, 'I lose more by the deal.'

PERHAPS PINKER remained suspicious of my intentions. At any rate, we were soon joined by a dark-haired young woman, a couple of years younger than Emily. She placed a large pile of books on the table with a thump.

'My sister Ada,' Emily explained. 'Ada, this is Robert Wallis.'

Ada's terse 'Pleased to meet you' suggested that she probably wasn't.

I picked up one of the books and glanced at the spine. '*Water Analysis for Sanitary Purposes*. Good heavens.'

She removed the book from my hand. 'Professor Frankland's work is the standard text on the valency of compounds.'

'Ada hopes to go up to Oxford,' Emily said. 'That's where you were, Robert, wasn't it?'

That got Ada's attention. 'Oh? Which college?'

'Christ Church.'

'Are the laboratories any good?'

'I have absolutely no idea.'

'What about the Clarendon? Is that an asset?'

She questioned me for ten minutes, but I was a disappointment. I could describe walking across the college deer park at dawn, arm in arm with a couple of drunken fellows, or punting to Wytham for a lunch of grilled trout, but of the lecture halls and academics she named I knew almost nothing.

However, her presence was useful. The object of our glossary was, after all, to communicate, and we were able to test our progress on Ada.

At around twelve o'clock, Emily stretched. 'Perhaps it is a consequence of this unaccustomed scrutiny I am giving to my own perceptions,' she said, 'but I find I am actually quite ravenous.'

'I am rather hungry too. Where is good round here?'

'There's a place in Narrow Street that does excellent eel pies. In fact, I have been thinking of little else these last twenty minutes. They serve them with mashed potatoes, and a little of the eel liquor as a sauce—'

'I have to go to Hoxton, to buy some chemicals,' Ada interjected.

'Then it looks as if it will just be you and I,' I said to Emily.

'Emily, may I have a word?' Ada said quickly.

They conferred on the landing in low voices. I went to the door to listen.

'. . . promised Father nothing objectionable would take place.'

'Don't be such a nincompoop, Ada. There is about as much chance of me succumbing to Mr Wallis's purple compliments over a harmless lunch as there is of that river freezing over. If you're really so concerned, come with us.'

'You know I can't. You'll have to take the Frog.'

I heard Emily sigh. 'We can't possibly talk with the Frog there.'

'Robert does nothing *but* talk as far as I can see. But very well—if you can bear to go with him, then go.'

I WOULD NEVER have believed such a delicate creature could put away so much food. I watched open-mouthed as Emily finished off an eel pie with mash, a dozen oysters, a slice of trout pie and a plate of whelks with parsley butter, all washed down with half a pint of hock-and-seltzer.

'I told you I had an appetite,' she said, wiping her lips with a napkin. 'Are you going to finish those oysters, or shall we order some more?'

'I had not realised,' I said as she reached for my plate, 'that lunch with you was going to turn into a competition.'

Over the course of that meal I learned more about her family. The girls' mother having died many years before; Pinker had been left with a prosperous business inherited from her father, and three daughters, of whom Emily was the eldest. These girls he resolved to bring up in the most advanced way possible. The tutors all came from the various societies—the Society for the Advancement of Knowledge, the Royal Scientific Societies and so on. The children had been encouraged to read books and attend public lectures.

'It's why he is amenable to the idea of us working,' she explained. 'Having invested so much in our education, he wants to see us give something back.'

'That's a somewhat . . . prosaic attitude to take to his own flesh and blood.'

'Oh, no—quite the opposite. He believes in business, believes in its principles, I mean, its power to do good.'

'And you? Is that how you see it?'

She nodded. 'Working is the expression of my moral beliefs. It is only by showing that women can be worth as much as men in the workplace that we will prove we are worthy of the same political and legal rights.'

'Good Lord.' Suddenly, working to pay off my wine merchant seemed rather ignoble by comparison.

TOWARDS THE END of the meal I pulled out my cigarette case. 'Mind if I smoke?' I said automatically.

'I do, rather,' Emily said, surprising me. 'We will not be able to taste my father's coffees accurately after breathing a fug of tobacco.'

'These make no fug.' I was a little offended. My fine Turkish cigarettes, from Benson's in Old Bond Street, filled a room with a drowsy, perfumed mist. 'Besides, smoking is one of the very few things I am good at.'

She sighed. 'Very well, then. Let us have one each before we go back.'

'Excellent,' I said, though this was even more surprising. I offered her the case, and struck a lucifer.

It is a sensual pleasure to light a woman's cigarette: her eyes are on the kiss of flame against the tip; yours are on the downward sweep of her lashes, the delicate shape of her pursed upper lip. 'Thank you,' she said, blowing a little trumpet of smoke from the side of her mouth. I lit my own.

She looked at the cigarette in her hand. 'If my father notices the smell on us,' she said, 'you must say that it was only you, not me, who was smoking.'

'A woman is entitled to her secrets.'

'I've always hated that expression—it makes it sound as if we're entitled to nothing else. You'll be saying we're the weaker sex next.'

'You don't think so?'

'Oh, Robert. You really are quite hopelessly old-fashioned, aren't you?'

'On the contrary. I am every inch *à la mode*.'

'One can be fashionable and still be old-fashioned—underneath your fine clothes. I'm sorry, am I making you blush?'

I said quietly, 'I didn't think you cared for what is under my clothes.'

She gazed at me for a moment. 'I was referring to your thoughts.'

'Oh, I try not to have any of those. They get in the way of my fine feelings.'

'What does that *mean*, exactly?' she asked with a frown.

'I have absolutely no idea. It is much too clever for me. I find that at least three-quarters of what I say goes completely over my own head.'

'Then you must be too clever by three-quarters.'

'Do you know, if I had said that it would have been quite amusing.'

'But a woman, of course, cannot be witty.'

'Not when she is as beautiful as you are.'

She breathed smoke into the air. 'You are flirting with me again, Robert.'

'No, I am flattering you, which is not the same thing at all. Women are an ornamental gender. It is the secret of their success.'

She sighed. 'I doubt if I will ever be as ornamental as you. And, unlike an ornament, I do not intend to sit on a mantelpiece gathering dust. Now, shall we put these out and get back to work?'

It was a great shame, I reflected, that Emily Pinker was a respectable middle-class bourgeois and not a whore. There was something combative, even challenging, about her manner that I was finding quite irresistible.

WHAT I LEARNED, in those first weeks at Pinker's offices, was the absolute treachery of words. Take a word like *medicinal.* To one person, it might mean the sharp tang of iodine; to another, the sickly-sweet smell of chloroform; to a third, the rich, spicy warmth of a cough mixture. It became clear that the code would work only if two people meant exactly the same taste or smell when they used a certain word. If we were to make the Guide truly practical, we would need a sample case: a small, stout travelling box containing a selection of the key scents, to which the taster could refer.

It was Ada who grasped the practical aspects of this—as a scientist, she understood the techniques by which an aroma could be distilled, and I think she was pleased to have found a role for herself. A perfumier, Mr Clee, was found and briefed. From then on Ada dealt with the technical issues of fixing various scents in a way that would withstand the heat of the tropics.

I, meanwhile, was becoming more confident in my judgments, more precise in my terms. It became a kind of obsession. I was walking along the Strand one evening when I smelt the odour of hot nuts, their shells scorched by burning coals. I turned: an urchin was standing by a brazier, shovelling walnuts into a paper cone. It was exactly the aroma of a Java as the water first hits the beans. On another occasion I was in a bookshop in Cecil Court, examining a volume of verse, when I realised that the smell of beeswax on well-preserved leather is almost identical to the aftertaste of a Yemen mocca. And then nothing would satisfy me but a cup of the same brew.

I had taken samples back to my rooms by now, so that I could indulge my addiction the moment I woke up, and clear my head as well. For my head, most mornings, was generally very thick. I spent my days with Emily and Ada; I continued to spends my evenings, and my advance, with the girls of Wellington Street and Mayfair.

ONE AFTERNOON I was striding up and down the office, twirling my cane and talking volubly—despite the presence of the bucket I tended to ingest more coffee than I should, and consequently became quite excitable—when I glanced down and saw a leg under the table.

I looked up. Emily was sitting at one end, taking notes; Ada was at the other, deep in a science book. I glanced down again. The leg must have realised that it was visible: it shifted surreptitiously.

'I smell . . .' I sniffed the air ostentatiously. 'I smell an intruder.'

Emily looked at me curiously.

'There is a whiff,' I explained, 'of . . .' I sniffed again . . . 'of disobedient puppy dogs and wickedness. *Fe fi fo fum*.'

Emily clearly thought I had taken leave of my senses.

'It is the smell,' I announced, 'of little children who are hiding where they should not.' With my cane I solemnly rapped the table. 'Who's there?'

A small, frightened voice issued from beneath the wood. 'Me.'

'It's only the Frog,' Emily said.

'Go away,' Ada muttered. 'Begone, troublesome amphibian.'

A small child hopped out from under the table. She squatted on the floor like a frog and croaked.

'Why aren't you in the schoolroom, Frog?' Ada said sternly.

'Mrs Walsh is ill.'

'The governess,' Emily explained to me. 'She suffers from neuralgia.'

'Anyway, I'd rather be in here with all of you,' the child said, springing up. She was about eleven years of age: her legs seemed much too long for her body, and her eyes had a slightly pouched quality that did indeed make her look very like a frog. 'Can't I stay? I shan't be trouble, and I can help guard Emily from Robert's poetic licences as well as anyone.'

'He's Mr Wallis to you,' Ada said. She looked a little embarrassed. 'And there is no question of guarding Emily from anything.'

The girl frowned. 'But why must I always be left out? I'll be good. Father said I could stay if I asked you.'

'You can stay on condition you don't say a word,' Emily said firmly.

The girl turned her big eyes on me. 'I'm Philomena,' she said. 'When she was little Ada couldn't say Philomena, so she called me Frog instead. But actually I quite like being a frog.' She hopped up onto a chair. 'Don't mind me. You had just got to where you were saying it was like lemons.'

Thereafter, there was often quite a crowd in our little cupping room. Ada ignored me whenever possible, but the porter, South, and the child, Frog, both stared at me open-mouthed while I tasted, as if I were a creature from some exotic country—a gallery, I'm ashamed to say, to which I occasionally played, coming up with fanciful descriptions and word plays that elicited from the Frog gasps of admiration, and from Emily the faintest of sighs.

'DO YOU MEAN to ravish Emily?' the Frog demanded.

Emily and I had just returned from one of our lunches; Emily had gone to hang up her coat, so I was alone with the child.

'I'm not sure that's altogether a polite question.'

'Ada thinks you do. I heard her ask Emily if she'd been ravished by Lord Byron yet. That's what Ada calls you.' She paused. 'If you do ravish Emily, you'll have to marry her. That's the rule. Then I can be a bridesmaid.'

'I think your father might have an opinion on that subject.'

'Shall I ask *him* if I can be a bridesmaid?' the Frog said hopefully.

'I meant an opinion on who she marries. It's rather up to him, you see.'

'Oh, he's very keen to marry her off,' she assured me. 'I'm sure you'll do. Are you rich?'

'Not in the least.'

'You *look* rich.'

'That's because I'm a spendthrift.'

'What's a spendthrift?'

'Someone who doesn't earn as much as they ought to. And who keeps buying nice things even when they oughtn't.'

'Like wedding rings?'

I laughed. 'Not wedding rings. Weddings rings aren't nice things.'

'I HAVE SOMETHING to show you,' Pinker announced one day, bounding into the office. 'Put on your coats—it cannot wait.'

Outside, his carriage was waiting, and we set off at a smart trot. I sat next to Emily, facing backwards. The carriage was a narrow one, and I could feel the warmth of her thigh against mine as we rounded corners.

We drew up not far from Tower Bridge, in Castle Street. On the corner was what had once been a public house. Workmen were putting the finishing touches to a smart new door; there were clear windows where once there would have been frosted glass, and above it all was a black and gold sign proclaiming that this was a Pinker's Temperance Tavern.

We dismounted. Bursting with pride, Pinker took us on a tour at breakneck speed. Inside, everything was black and gold. 'It is our livery,' he said. 'The colours will be replicated in every establishment. The waiters will have black uniforms, with a gold motif. And white aprons, as they wear in France.'

I looked around. The place was extraordinary. Every inch of wood was painted black, and gold was the only other colour. It was more like the inside of a hearse than a tavern. At the rear, behind what had once been the bar, was the contraption Pinker had demonstrated at our first meeting, chugging quietly to itself. Jenks was kneeling next to it, adjusting the dials.

'Are we operational?' Pinker called.

'Almost, sir.' As Jenks spoke, a gust of steam hissed out of a valve.

'Well?' Pinker turned to us, rubbing his hands. 'What do you think?'

'It's wonderful, Father.'

'Robert?'

'Remarkable,' I said. 'Most impressive. There is just one thing . . .'

'Yes?'

'Do you think people—ordinary people—will want to go and drink coffee somewhere that is actually called a Temperance Tavern? One might as well advertise a foodless restaurant or a grape-free wine.'

Pinker frowned. 'Then what would you call it?'

'Well, anything. You could call it . . .' I looked around. My eye fell on the sign that said: CASTLE STREET. 'You could call it Castle Coffee.'

'Castle.' Pinker considered. 'Hmm. Castle. Castle Coffee. Yes—it has a ring. It sounds dependable. Emily? What do you say?'

'I think Robert has a point. Castle would, perhaps, be better.'

Pinker nodded. 'Castle it is, then. I'll have the workmen change the sign.'

So was born one of the most famous trademarks in the history of coffee. But something else was conceived that day, amid that bustle of industry. As Pinker stalked outside to find the foreman, his daughter turned to me.

'Yes, thank you, Robert. That was tactfully done. And Castle is undoubtedly the better name.'

I shrugged. 'It's hardly a big matter.'

She smiled at me—a smile that lingered a fraction longer than it might have done. Then, suddenly bashful, she dropped her gaze.

'Come along!' Pinker called from outside.

In the carriage back to Limehouse, it seemed to me that the pressure of her thigh against mine was withdrawn just a little less than it had been before.

MANY OF MY LUNCHTIME conversations with Emily were about the subject of Reform. For her, modernity was synonymous with a social conscience, and she took it for granted that I was as keen to change the world as she.

When she first raised the matter of Social Evil, I replied that I had no interest in politics, adding, 'In this, surely, I am like most politicians.'

She did not respond, although her face bore a pained expression.

I said airily, 'Wealth, of course, would be quite wasted on the poor. One only has to look at the hideous things the lower classes spend their money on to be thankful that no one has given them any more of it.'

She sighed deeply.

'And I cannot think why any woman would want the vote, when one sees what ghastly people already have it. One would approve so much more of democracy were it not so frightfully common.'

'Robert,' she said, 'do you ever speak seriously?'

'Only when I care absolutely nothing for the subject under discussion.'

'I don't believe you do so even then,' she muttered.

'I shall take that as a compliment, dear Emily. How I should hate to get an undeserved reputation for sincerity.'

'Robert, shut *up*.'

I fell silent.

'These epigrams. Not only are they deeply unoriginal, they are barely even amusing. I cannot help feeling that they are nothing but a verbal tic or habit, with no more sense to them than that croaking noise the Frog makes.'

I opened my mouth. 'Wait,' she said, holding up her hand. 'You are about to say that sense is greatly overrated: what is needed in the world is more nonsense; or that all epigrams are meaningless, that is why they are so profound; or that showing off is the basis of all art, in that lies its genius; or—or—some other silly construction.'

I wanted her good opinion, and so I learned not to epigrammatise, and to speak seriously on serious matters. But of course, the speaking seriously was a pose—the epigrams, for all their shallowness, were closer to my real nature. Still, who would not want to wax lyrical about Reform, when those sparkling grey eyes were drinking in your every word? Who would not pretend to care about the poor, when your reward was such a smile? Before long, Miss Pinker had me attending Meetings.

Oh, how she loved a Meeting! There were Meetings of the Society for the Promotion of International Civilisation, Meetings of the Fabians, Meetings of the Theosophists. There were even Temperance Dinners, at which we discussed the need to raise the tax on gin while cradling glasses of fine claret.

At some of these Meetings there was much earnest discussion about what a Rational Marriage might look like. I noticed that the men and women tended to take it different ways—the women wanted equality and independence, by which they meant equal status with their husbands, while the men wanted equality and independence, by which they meant something less like a marriage and more like the freedom of being a bachelor.

As we were walking back to the office after one of these Meetings, I made a flippant remark about one of the speakers and Emily turned to me and said crossly, 'Do you actually believe that, Robert, or is it just another pose?'

'It is one of my most strongly held opinions, and I shall certainly have discarded it by tea time.'

'The question,' she said, ignoring me, 'is whether men and women should have the same political rights.'

I recalled that we were talking about that old chestnut Votes for Women, and I prepared to be serious. 'But men and women have separate spheres—'

'Oh, yes,' she interrupted. 'The woman has the drawing room, and the man has politics and business and the whole of the rest of the world. That isn't equality; it's like saying the prisoner has the freedom of her cell.'

'But any woman has to accept the authority of her husband—'

'Why?'

I must have looked confused, because she added, 'Oh, it's never talked about, of course. We're meant to say that suffrage can't possibly undermine a man's right to be the master of his own home. It's just that no one can give me a good reason why men have to be the masters in the first place.'

'But look at men's achievements—'

'That's a circular argument. Men have had the opportunities.'

'But your argument is circular too, my dear Emily. You're saying that women would have achieved more if they had been given the opportunity. But men had the opportunities in the first place because they took them.'

This incensed her even more. 'So it all boils down to brute force and rape?'

'Rape? Where does rape come into it?'

'Because by *your* definition marriage and rape are one and the same. Whereas I happen to believe that men and women can only love each other fully when they are equals.'

'But men and women are different,' I pointed out. 'The fact that we're having this extraordinary argument proves it.'

She stopped and stamped her foot on the pavement. 'And if we were married, you would be able to tell me that as my husband you were right, and that would be an end of it?'

'I can tell you I'm right now. I don't see you agreeing.'

'Because you haven't proved your point.' She was flushed and angry. 'And I suppose you think I shouldn't have a job?'

'Emily, how did we get onto jobs? I thought we were talking about votes. And then somehow we got onto marriage—'

'Don't you see—it's all the same?' And then she would not talk to me, and walked on in a furious silence.

I lit a cigarette and caught up with her. 'I'd offer you one,' I said, 'but . . .'

'But a woman shouldn't smoke in the street?'

'I was going to say, but you're already fuming.'

LATER, WHEN SHE had calmed down, I said, 'I'm sorry we quarrelled.'

She looked surprised. 'We didn't quarrel, Robert. We argued.'

'Is there a difference?'

'Arguing is a pleasure and quarrelling isn't.' She sighed. 'The limitations of a woman's rights in marriage is a subject on which I tend to become heated. It is a long-standing disagreement I am having with my father. He is completely modern in every way but that. I think it may have something to do with not having a wife—he feels that choosing, or at least approving, our husbands is his last responsibility towards us.'

'What sort of husband does he intend for you?'

'That's the problem. In his head he wants someone modern—someone like himself, a man of industry. But in his heart he wants someone with connections and social standing.'

'It's a rare combination.' I glanced at her. 'And you? What sort of man will capture your heart?'

She rolled her eyes. 'Robert! You sound like something from a novel. No one's going to capture any bit of me, thank you very much. My hand, and my affection, will be bestowed on someone . . .' she thought for a moment '. . . someone I can admire. Someone who has achieved something in the world, and intends to go on achieving great things. Someone who can see what's wrong, but who knows how to put it right; someone with such passion that he can make other people see things his way simply by speaking. I always imagine him with an Irish accent, actually, but that may be because I know he will have determined views on Home Rule. I intend to be his helpmeet, you see, and, although no one else will ever know it, privately he will always acknowledge that he couldn't have done any of it without me.'

'Ah,' I said. It is always disconcerting to realise that someone else finds admirable exactly the sort of person one would least like to be. 'And what if you can't find that man?'

'Then I shall just have to settle for someone who captures my heart,' she said, linking her arm in mine.

'Sure, and dat's a very foine way of tinking.'

Three

Emily stands in her father's office, looking down on Robert as he leaves Pinker's for the evening. She continues to watch until he is out of sight, leaning closer to the window so that she can follow him down Narrow Street. When he has gone she finds that her breath has left a coffee-scented blossom on the glass. Without thinking, she touches the tip of her finger to the cool, hard glass and traces four petals, then a stalk.

Something is happening to her. She is not sure whether to be intrigued or alarmed, whether to approve or disapprove of this physical awakening that is slowly taking hold of her, warming her like an apricot in a glasshouse.

She turns back to the desk, picks up her notes. Apricot—that is one of the flavours they discovered today, in some of the moccas and the better South Americans: the concentrated golden aroma of an apricot preserve. It will take its place on the chart of flavours, between blackberry and apple.

Straw, the aroma of barley stalks just before harvest. Liquorice, dark and soft and sweet. Leather, rich and polished, like her father's old armchair. Lemon, so astringent it puckers the lips . . . As her eyes scan her notes she finds she can recall them all, the tastes bursting across her palate like exotic flowers, each one coaxing open the closed bud of her senses a little more.

She has not told anyone what working on the Guide is doing to her—not her sisters, and certainly not her father. He has already had cause to suspect her of dangerous passions; he must suspect nothing now.

It is because she is a female that she feels this ridiculous sensuality. And that is why she must fight it. No man, she is sure, will ever allow women to work alongside him if he believes them to be as weak and foolish as she is.

She picks up one of the cups in which they have been cupping today's samples. It contains, still, a tiny morsel of Colombian Excelsos, long since cold. As she sniffs it she fancies that she can just discern, caught in the cup, the soft aroma of Robert's breath.

She inhales it, closing her eyes, allowing brief delicious fantasies to flit through her mind. *His breath and mine, mingling together, like a kiss . . .*

She turns back to the window and breathes it back onto the glass, over her rubbed-out flower. Like something written in invisible ink, the flower slowly reappears, just for a moment, before fading once again from view.

EMILY AND I did not only taste her father's coffees; we also ranked them. Initially I had been reluctant to do this, pointing out to my employer that good and bad are moral judgments, and as such have no place in Art.

Pinker sighed. 'But in Commerce, Robert, one makes such decisions every day. Of course one cannot directly compare a heavy, resinous Java with a delicate Jamaican. But it is the same coin that pays for them, and so one must ask oneself where that coin is best spent.'

It was true that some coffees seemed to be consistently of higher quality than others. We noticed that when we particularly liked a coffee, it was often labelled 'mocca'—and yet that word seemed to cover a multitude of styles: some heavy, some light, some with an intriguing floral aroma.

'The coffees of mocca,' Pinker said when I asked him about it, 'are not as other coffees.' He went to the shelf and pulled out a great atlas. 'Now, then,' he said, flipping through the pages. 'Yes. There. What do you see?'

I looked at where his finger was pointing. Where Persia and Africa met, separated by a crack of water, there was a fly-spot. I looked harder. The fly-spot was labelled 'Al-Makka'.

'Mocca,' he said. 'Or as the Arabs call it, Makka. Source of the greatest coffees in the world.' He tapped it. 'This is the cradle not just of coffee—of everything. Mathematics. Philosophy. Storytelling. Architecture.'

'Why are their coffees so particularly fine?'

'Good question, Robert. Damned if I know the answer.' He paused. 'Some merchants swear that moccas have a faint chocolate taste. Some even adulterate other beans with cocoa powder to replicate it. What do you think?'

I searched my memory. 'Some have a note of chocolate, certainly. But not the very finest—those seem to me to have an extraordinary fragrant quality, more in the range of honeysuckle or vanilla.'

'My feelings exactly. Which would tell us what?'

'That mocca is not one coffee but several?'

'Precisely.' His finger made a circle round the Red Sea. 'The Arabs used to have a monopoly on growing coffee. Then the Dutch stole some seedlings and took the bush to Indonesia, and the French stole from them and took it to the Caribbean, and the Portuguese stole from *them* and took it to Brazil. So let us assume the Arabs stole it too. Have you met Richard Burton?'

I shook my head.

'I was introduced to him at a reception,' Pinker said. 'Burton was a great man—fêted for his explorations of the Islamic world. He had not long returned from one of his Arabian jaunts, and he told me of an extraordinary walled city he had found, in a part of East Africa that was lush and temperate. He claimed the coffee bushes grew wild there, propagating themselves wherever the surplus fruits fell to the ground. Coffee traders, he said, were considered so important to the economy that they were forbidden to leave the city on pain of death. It was a place of great wealth, apparently; Burton talked of ivory, precious stones, gold . . . and what he called darker transactions. Slavery, one presumes. But the coffee, he said, was the best he had tasted in all his years of wandering. And—this is what sticks in my mind—he said it smelt fragrant, like honeysuckle blossom.'

'Like that mocca?'

'Exactly. And something else that interested me—the town is called Harar, but the name of that region in the local tongue is Kaffa. Burton thought the word "coffee" must surely have the same root.'

I thought a moment. 'So the coffee beans that grow wild in Kaffa—'

'Are sold, perhaps, by the merchants of Harar to traders, who bring them, eventually, to Al-Makka. From where they are shipped to the rest of the world. If you were a trader in, say, Venice or Constantinople, you might well label the coffees you purchased by their port of origin; you might not even be told which country a particular lot had been grown in. So you would call everything that passed through Al-Makka "mocca".'

'Intriguing. And where did Burton say this walled town of Harar was?'

Pinker ran his fingers over the map. He had the latest atlas, yet there was still a small part of Africa that had not been tinted with one of the colours of the empires that had named and claimed all the other territories. It was a space the size of a man's hand in the mid-part of the continent.

He tapped it thoughtfully. 'Here,' he said. 'Burton places it here.'

We both stared at the map.

'What an extraordinary thing coffee is, Robert,' he said at last. 'To be able to do good at both ends—temperance in England, civilisation elsewhere.'

'Remarkable,' I said. 'And even more so when one considers the profit generated in the middle.'

'Exactly. Remember Darwin—it is the profit that makes all else possible. It is not Charity that will change the world, but Commerce.'

MONEY WAS STILL flowing through my own hands like water, and very soon my advance was gone. I had somehow got through thirty pounds in about the same number of days.

The pawnshop on Edgware Road was a foul place. Ike, the old Russian who ran it, would take anything from jewellery to rag-and-bone, and as you walked in you were hit by a sour, fungal smell not unlike wet, rotting fur.

Behind the counter Ike rubbed his hands. 'Good morning, young man,' he said with a quick smile. 'What have yer got?'

I showed him—a vellum-bound edition of Coventry Patmore three silk waistcoats I no longer wore, two beaver-skin top hats, a carved ivory cane.

'These are fine,' he said, running his hands over the goods. 'Very fine.'

'How much?'

He scratched his head with a pencil stub. 'Three guineas,' he said at last.

'I was hoping for six.'

He shrugged. 'I'll have to sell them on.'

'Perhaps this is the wrong place. I can easily take them to the West End.'

'They're specialist, sir. You won't find a better price.' He brightened. 'Of course, if you was wanting more cash, I could always advance you a sum.'

'I didn't know you offered such a . . . service.'

'Not in the usual way, sir, oh, no. But for someone like yourself, someone with prospects. My fees are very reasonable.'

'You'd charge interest?'

Another shrug. 'A small percentage, payable weekly.'

'How much could I borrow?'

He smiled. 'Step into my office and we can look through the paperwork.'

EMILY HAD DECIDED she wanted to be taken out for dinner. There was a masked ball at Covent Garden, and she was greatly desirous of seeing, as she put it, my former bohemian haunts, not to mention some of the beautiful actresses of whom she had read in the newspapers.

'Your father would never forgive me if I took you somewhere unsuitable,' I told her.

'I think I can stand an actress or two, Robert. Unless the urge to go on the stage has somehow become contagious, I shall be quite safe.'

'Very well,' I said. 'If it is actresses you want, then it is to Kettners' we must go. It will be handy for the ball, too.'

The following day I went to see Henri, the French maître d'hôtel who administered the warren of dining rooms off Church Street. We settled on the menu and wines, and I selected a table in a curtained alcove. It gave the option of privacy, but had a view along the largest of the upstairs dining rooms when the curtains were open.

That left the question of what to wear. We had opted to take our costumes to the restaurant and change for the ball after the meal but, even so, evening dress would look as if one were hardly making an effort.

Barely had I left Kettners' when my eye fell on a jacket of dark blue otterskin in a window in Great Marlborough Street. It would look magnificent with the cravat of French lace I had spied a few days before in Jermyn Street. I walked into the shop and enquired the jacket's price. Three guineas—a reasonable sum, the tailor pointed out, for so unique a garment.

'AH, MR WALLIS,' Ike greeted me. 'And only a day late, too.'

'Late?'

'With your interest. Two pounds, although next time there will have to be a small additional charge to cover the delay.' He shrugged. 'You are a man of business yourself now. You know how it is.'

'A man of business? In what way?'

'You have become, like me, a trader, I hear. In the world of coffee?'

'Oh—yes. Yes, I suppose I have.'

'I am sure your enterprise fares rather better than my own little operation.'

'It does fare tolerably well—but I have need of a little more cash.'

'More?' Ike raised his eyebrows.

'Shall we say another fifteen pounds?' I prompted.

'Certainly. Although,' he said thoughtfully, 'if it were twenty, the rate of interest would be rather less. A discount for the larger sum, you see.'

'Oh. Very generous. Twenty it is, then.'

I signed the paperwork and handed him two pounds back. 'Your interest.'

He bowed. 'A pleasure doing business with you, Mr Wallis.'

I ARRIVED AT KETTNERS' early and chose Emily's buttonhole from the flower stall at the door. The clientele did not disappoint; there were more pretty thespians on hand than in many a Drury Lane theatre.

Then Emily arrived, and my heart stood still. I had never before seen her out of her office clothes. Tonight she was wearing a simple, low-cut dress of black velvet embroidered with tiny sequins, and a cloak of red cloth trimmed with grey fur. When she greeted me, she allowed the cloak to slip off her bare shoulders; as I took it I caught a tantalising whiff of Guerlain's Jicky, and inhaled the perfect mixture of warm fragrance and warm female skin.

'You may say something, Robert,' she said with a hint of—entirely fetching—awkwardness as she sat down in the chair the waiter was holding for her.

I recovered myself. 'You look absolutely beautiful.'

'Though I feel woefully underdressed beside you,' she commented, taking up her napkin. 'Thank goodness. Now, where are my actresses?'

I pointed out various personalities. Emily exclaimed over every morsel of gossip. 'You should do tours,' she said, when I had finished. 'But tell me, Robert, is this place not rather tame compared to the Café Royal?'

'Oh! No one goes there any more,' I assured her. 'It is far too crowded.'

'Ah. I suppose I must expect epigrams here.' Emily looked around the room. 'Dear Robert,' she said fondly, 'who would ever have thought, six weeks ago, that you and I would be sitting here like this?'

Our hors d'oeuvres arrived, and I enjoyed watching the gusto with which she tipped the oyster shells up to her mouth: the tightening of her neck, and the delicate convulsions of her throat.

'Robert?' Emily was frowning at me. 'You seem unusually quiet.'

'I am struck dumb by how beautiful you look.'

'Now you're just being silly. I don't believe you have ever been struck dumb in your life.'

The soup, a silky velouté of artichokes, was excellent, and the trout magnificent. Henri came by, and Emily told him that she had decided to become an actress immediately, if this was how they got treated. 'Oh!' that stalwart replied, 'but you are far prettier than any of the actresses here tonight.' He glanced at me, and I thought I detected the merest quiver of his left eyelid.

The conversation flowed this way and that—I can barely remember what we spoke about; I had learned that the way to amuse Emily Pinker best was to be serious occasionally, so I expect we talked a little of important things. Eventually our meal staggered to a close. I signed the bill while Emily went to change into her costume. From the activity around the dining room, it was clear that many of the other patrons were also going on to the ball.

Emily returned in the costume of a harlequin, with a Pierrot cap and a half-mask of white silk. For my part, I had a simple eye-mask of black feathers that went rather well with my new jacket.

As we left the restaurant she stumbled and grabbed my arm. 'I am a little tipsy,' she murmured in my ear. 'You have to promise not to take advantage.'

'We should arrange a time and place to meet. That way, if we are separated, we can find each other again.'

'Good! Where shall it be?'

'Shall we say, under the opera clock, at two?'

For reply she squeezed my arm, which she kept hold of as we headed to the street. Shaftesbury Avenue was full of carriages heading to the ball, and people in carnival thronged the pavements. Suddenly I heard a shout. 'Wallis! Wait up!' I turned. A Pantaloon and a Punchinello were hailing me as they descended from a cab accompanied by two female marionettes. Despite the greasepaint they wore, I recognised Hunt and Morgan.

'Where have you been?' Punchinello cried.

'In Kettners'.'

'No—where have you *been*? Hunt is published at last—a villanelle in the *Yellow Book*! And you nowhere to be found for weeks!'

'I have been busy—'

Pantaloon snapped his fingers. 'We knew inspiration must have struck.'

'Not with poetry. I have had employment.'

'Employment?' Punch shrank back in mock horror. 'The last time we saw you, you had been asked by that funny little gnome—'

'May I introduce Miss Emily Pinker?' I said quickly.

Morgan made an exaggerated 'Ah!' with his made-up lips. 'Charmed. And this is . . . this is . . . um, Miss Daisy. And Miss Deborah.'

The marionettes giggled. They were, I realised with a sinking heart, *demi-mondaines*. And I was responsible for Emily's welfare that night. If there was any suggestion of impropriety, Pinker would blame me.

'I've met you before,' Daisy said to me under her breath.

I stiffened. 'I'm afraid I don't remember you. You're an actress?'

'You could call it that,' Daisy said. 'A performer, anyway.' Her friend shrieked with laughter.

By now we were all surging into the Opera colonnade, and it was possible to contrive to be separated from our companions. Inwardly I cursed Hunt and Morgan. What had they been thinking of, bringing such women here? Fortunately, Emily seemed not to have noticed anything amiss.

'Isn't this extraordinary?' she said, gazing at the crowd.

There must have been over a thousand people, all disguised. An orchestra was tuning up in the pit, though it was much too crowded to dance. Waiters in elaborate costumes pushed through the crowd with trays of wine; stilt-walkers, jugglers and dancers jostled us as we moved through the throng. I lost sight of Emily for a second, then found her again. I guided her to a quiet corner on the balcony where we could watch the antics below.

'This would have been unthinkable even a few years ago,' I said.

By way of reply she reached for my hand. Then, to my astonishment, her hands reached round my head and she brought our lips together. Our masks collided. Laughing eyes met mine—laughing eyes that were dark, not grey.

I stiffened as I realised it was not Emily in my arms, and the young woman spun away from me with a laugh. It must have happened when we were separated on the stairs.

I hurried back—but everywhere I looked there were harlequins. I found Hunt in the ballroom. 'Have you seen Emily?' I shouted. 'I've lost her.'

'How perfect,' he said vaguely. He peered around the room with studied insouciance, pulling out a cigarette holder. 'I really should find Bosie. I promised him I would look out for him. He does so hate a crowd.'

'Bosie!' I exclaimed. 'Not Lord Alfred Douglas?'

He nodded. 'Oscar has written him a love letter from prison. Had you heard? He is still completely infatuated.'

Bosie! Oscar Wilde's lover—the original wonderful boy—and Hunt had been socialising with him! 'Will you introduce me?' I said eagerly.

'Oh, very well. If I'm not mistaken, that's him over there.'

I followed the direction of his gaze—and immediately glimpsed a possible Emily stepping through the crowd. 'Blast!' I said. 'I'll be right back.'

I followed the elusive figure, but lost her again. I thought, If I cannot find her, perhaps she can find me. So I walked slowly through the crowd, back and forth, trying to make myself visible. After a few minutes I glanced up at the balcony. A harlequin with a Pierrot cap like Emily's was being passionately embraced by a masked male figure in a dark otterskin suit. Then more figures came between us, and when I looked again they were gone.

AT A QUARTER TO TWO I went outside. She was under the clock, waiting. I hurried forward. 'Are you all right?'

'Of course.' She sounded surprised. 'Were you worried?'

'A little.'

She slipped her arm through mine. 'Did you think I had taken offence?'

'At what?'

She leaned in close. 'I know it was you, so don't pretend it wasn't.'

'I don't know what you're referring to.'

Her only answer was a laugh.

'WHERE ARE WE going now?' she asked as we walked down Drury Lane.

'I'd rather thought of putting you in a cab.'

She hesitated, then nodded. 'It is probably time to go home now.'

I spied a cab coming round the corner and whistled to it. 'Limehouse,' I told the cabman, handing Emily up.

'Good night, Robert,' she said, smiling at me. 'I've had a wonderful time.'

'And I too.'

She leaned down and kissed me quickly on the cheek then the cabman flicked his whip.

The night had passed off without any major disasters, thank God. I retraced my steps through the crowds to Wellington Street, and entered the relative calm of the brothel at Number 18 with a sigh of relief.

I WAS IN a foul mood the next day. It was not hard to pinpoint the cause of my temper: Hunt was published. I should have been pleased for him, but all I could feel was a dull throb of envy. While I had been flirting and drinking coffee, my friend had been forging a reputation.

Over the days that followed I made a concerted effort to do some writing. My feelings for Emily—the kind of thing in which poets had found inspiration for centuries—provoked only some flat, insipid sonnets.

'What are you doing, Robert?' the Frog demanded one lunchtime.

'I am writing poetry,' I said with a sigh.

'I like poems. Robert, will you write me a poem about a crocodile?'

'Oh, very well. If you absolutely promise to go away afterwards.'

Within two minutes I had dashed something off.

The hunger of the crocodile
Is awesome to behold:
For breakfast he eats fifty eggs,
Scrambled, then served cold.

And then he has a plate of ham,
Served with English mustard,
A dozen kippers, smoked of course,
On which he pours hot custard.

But what he likes to eat the most
Is quite another question:
His favourite dish is little girls,
Which gives him indigestion.

She stared at me, open-mouthed. 'That's brilliant! You really are a poet!'

I sighed. 'If only real poetry were that easy.'

'Now can I have one about a caterpillar?' she said hopefully.

'I thought you had promised to go away.'

'I promise to go away for three times as long if you write me one more poem. That's a very advantageous proposition—three aways for two poems.'

'Ah, the famous Pinker gift for negotiation. Let's see, then . . .'

'This is a curious business,'
The missionary said.
'I seem to have a caterpillar
Living in my head.

'He must have been inside those pears
The cook served up for tea,
And since I ate his old abode
His new address is me.

'I hear him singing in my ear;
My mouth is his front door;
And when he has too much to drink
I hear the beggar snore.'

The Frog clapped. Emily, who had come into the room as I was extemporising this nonsense, said, 'That is really very sweet, Robert. You should send it to a children's publisher.'

'I am a poet,' I said shortly. 'Heir to a glorious tradition of rebels and decadents. Not a composer of nursery rhymes and doggerel.'

DETERMINED TO FIND the time to write, I tried doing without sleep, keeping myself up with the help of vast quantities of Pinker's product. The first time I did this, I was elated to find that I had completed twenty lines of lyric ode. But the next night, caffeine and fatigue battled each other to a stalemate, producing a dull headache and some duller couplets. The next day at work I was so fatigued that I was short with Emily. We had a silly argument over the wording of a paragraph, and to my astonishment she burst into tears.

'I'm sorry,' she said, drying her eyes on a handkerchief. 'I'm a little tired.'

'So am I,' I said with feeling.

'Why is that, Robert?' she asked, looking at me a little oddly, it seemed.

'I have been trying to write.'

'I see—and that is the only reason you have been so . . . off recently?'

'I suppose it must be.'

Again she seemed to look at me oddly. 'I thought you were tired of *me*.'

'What on earth do you mean?'

'At the ball—Robert, when you kissed me—I thought perhaps . . . But of course, you are a bohemian: a kiss means rather less to you—'

'Emily,' I sighed, 'I did not—' I stopped. I had been about to say, 'I did not kiss you,' but something made me pause. I thought, I *would* have kissed her, if I had known she would not have rejected my advances, or gone running to her father. And now, it seemed, she had been kissed by a stranger she thought was me. And had not minded. Had rather liked it, in fact.

I had a choice. I could tell her the truth, which would heartily embarrass her, or I could accept the greater truth of what had happened that evening.

I said slowly, 'If I have been short with you, darling Emily, it is because I could not be sure whether I had overstepped the mark.'

'Did I give that impression—in any way?' she said quietly.

I had no idea. 'You did not.' I took a step towards her. I hoped my stand-in had been a good kisser. Though not so good that I could not live up to his example. 'But we had both had much to drink that night. I was not certain . . .'

'If you overstep,' she said, 'I will be sure to tell you.'

She tasted of cream, of meringues and vanilla and milky coffee. I pressed my hand into the small of her back, gently drawing her in to me, and in the midst of that wonderful kiss she gasped with pleasure.

Footsteps! We drew apart just as the door opened. It was Jenks. Emily turned away in confusion. The secretary threw us a suspicious glance.

'I am getting honeysuckle, floral aromas, very bright and smooth,' I said quickly. 'Perhaps a little citrus. But the mouthfeel is excellent.'

The secretary's eyes raked the room. He saw, I am sure, that there was no coffee on the table, but he said nothing.

'Emily?' I said.

'Yes?' She turned back towards me.

'What did you think?'

'It was . . . it was very pleasant, Robert. Though perhaps a little strong. Excuse me—I have left something . . . something downstairs.'

MUCH LATER she returned, carrying a thick folder of papers, which she placed on the table and ostentatiously began to go over.

'Every minute you were not with me was an age—' I began.

'Not now,' she interrupted. 'We both have work to do.'

I was baffled. 'Before, you seemed to prefer my attentions to work.'

'That was before Jenks surprised us. It has brought me to my senses.'

'Jenks? What does he matter? What does anyone matter?'

'We are both my father's employees. We should not—we must not—do anything unprofessional. We cannot betray his trust.'

'Now you're being inconsistent.'

'There must be no more kissing,' she said firmly. 'Promise me that.'

'Very well. I will try not to think of kissing you more than—what? Once every . . . six or seven seconds?'

'Robert!'

'I cannot help the way I feel, Emily. And no more, I think, can you. But if you wish it, I will refrain from kissing you again.'

WE KISSED beside the river, we kissed behind her sisters' backs, we kissed with the *crema* of a freshly made coffee moustachioing our lips. Sometimes she would murmur, 'Robert—we mustn't,' but she kissed me anyway. Once she said, 'I wish I did not like it so much, then I might find it easier to stop.'

'But why should we stop?'

'Because it is wrong.'

'But how can it be wrong? We must seize the moment, for joy is fleeting, and besides, I think I hear Ada clumping up the stairs.'

'WHERE SHALL WE EAT?' I asked Emily later.

'Unfortunately, I shall not be able to have lunch with you today, Robert. I have promised the Suffrage Society to go out selling their leaflets.'

'You mean, in public?'

'Yes. Don't look so surprised. Someone has to do it.'

'Then I will come with you. We can have lunch afterwards.'

She frowned. 'I suppose you could stand next to me and look helpful. But you will have to promise not to pass any of your flippant remarks.'

We took up position next to the entrance to the Underground station on King William Street in the City. Emily held up one of her leaflets, and in a querulous small voice called, 'Votes for Women! The truth for a penny!'

A couple of people glanced at us curiously, but no one stopped. 'Oh dear,' she said anxiously. 'They don't seem terribly keen. Votes for Women!'

'How long do we have to do this for?' I asked.

'Until the leaflets are gone, I suppose.'

I held out my hand. 'You had better give me half, or we shall never get lunch. In any case, you are doing it wrong. There is an art to selling things.'

'I am doing it exactly as the Society instructed.'

'Then we shall see who is more successful.' I crossed the road and stopped an elderly lady. 'Excuse me, madam, may I sell you this pamphlet? It contains everything you need to know about the Suffrage Movement.'

'Oh.' She smiled and examined the leaflet. 'How much is it?'

'One penny, though you can give more if you like.'

'Here's sixpence—I shan't want change.' She pushed a coin into my hand.

'Thank you,' I said, pocketing the money. 'Have a pleasant day.'

'Votes for Women,' Emily called on the other side of the road, waving her pamphlet aloft. There was a frown of irritation on her face. I laughed.

Two young women walked past me. 'Excuse me,' I said, catching them up. 'You look as if you ought to read about Votes for Women.' I pushed two pamphlets into their hands. 'That'll be tuppence, please.'

Smiling back at me, the younger one found me the money. 'What is it all—' she began, but I had no time to chat.

Turning to a young clerk, I said, 'Chum, want to find out what women really think?' I had my next sale.

I glanced across the street. Emily had stopped shouting and had adopted my method of accosting people.

A middle-aged man was heading towards me. 'This leaflet,' I said, walking alongside him and showing him the cover, 'contains all the filthy arguments of the suffragists. Sexual equality, free love—it's all in there.'

'I'll take two,' he said, eyeing the leaflet anxiously.

'Good man. That'll be a shilling.' As he walked away I saw Emily giving me a furious look. 'The one who sells least buys lunch!' I called. She scowled.

'Good afternoon, ladies,' I said to a group of shopgirls. 'Sensational stuff, this—everyone's reading it.' I made four sales, and when I had finished I strolled back to Emily. 'All gone,' I said smugly.

'People are only buying them from you because you're a man,' Emily said crossly. 'It's the same old problem all over again.'

'ROBERT, WILL YOU tell me a poem?' the Frog asked hopefully.

I was still in an indulgent mood after lunch. 'What sort of poem?'

'The one you told me last time, about the caterpillar. You didn't finish it,' she said anxiously. 'You left the man with a caterpillar inside him and I have been hardly able to concentrate on arithmetic ever since.'

'You see, Robert,' Emily murmured behind me. 'The artist has moral responsibilities after all. Though since the Frog never concentrates on her arithmetic anyway, you must not feel too guilty.'

'I should not want to be held liable for poor sums,' I assured the Frog. 'Let me see . . .' A moment's thought, a little jotting on a scrap of paper . . .

'I am timing you,' Emily said. 'You have to do it in less than a minute.'

'That is hardly fair. I need a little longer—'

'I should stop protesting, if I were you, and concentrate on writing.'

'Oh, very well . . .'

'Too late!'

'I have it!' I jumped up.

> 'This really is most vexing,'
> The missionary said,
> 'That dratted caterpillar is
> Still living in my head.
>
> 'I did not offer him free board,
> Or ask him here to stay,
> But now he is so comfortable
> He will not go away.'
>
> —So said this mournful cleric;
> He gave a heavy sigh;
> And as he did so, from his mouth
> There flew a butterfly.

It was nonsense, of course, but the Frog applauded and Emily smiled fondly, and just for a moment I felt a sense of triumph greater than any that the publication of a sonnet in the *Yellow Book* could have given me.

HER HEART IS SINGING. Her head is troubled. Not by the small white lie she told Robert—Emily knows perfectly well that it was not he who tried to kiss her at the ball, but it had amused her to tease him a little, especially when she saw how envious it made him. What is perplexing her is that this relationship, according to the codes of her class, does not exist. Those who court may fall in love; those who fall in love may marry. But what of those who do not officially court, who are thrown together by fate, or by work?

She doubts her father will let her marry him; she is not even sure, yet, if that is what she wants herself. So she does what she can—gently singing his praises, but not so much that her father suspects her of losing her head.

She tells him that Robert—'although a silly young man, and quite the most annoying aesthete'—is working not only hard but well; that he would be an asset to the company when he has grown up a little. She points out that, as an artist, he sees things in a way that might be useful to them.

Her father listens, and nods, and does not suspect.

One person who *does* suspect is Jenks. For some time now she has been aware that her father's senior secretary harbours a certain fondness for her, but she did not think he would embarrass himself by saying anything.

One afternoon, however, as she is transcribing her shorthand notes, the secretary enters the room and carefully shuts the door behind him. 'Miss Pinker,' he begins. 'I must speak with you.'

Immediately she knows what he is going to say. But he surprises her.

'I would not dream of telling you what you should or should not do,' he says fiercely. 'And I would never criticise a fellow employee, let alone one who has acquired your good opinion. But I have to tell you that, on at least two occasions, Wallis has been seen frequenting a certain street in Central London, the nature of which leads me to question his character.'

'I see,' she says calmly. 'And which street is this?'

He hesitates. 'A part of Covent Garden well known for its . . . associations. I have a friend who is performing at the Lyceum Theatre. I was waiting at the stage door one evening—it backs onto the street I am referring to. Wallis was entering one of the buildings, a . . . notorious place.'

'Are you quite sure that it was him you saw?'

He nods. 'I would have said nothing if I had not been sure. But how could I stay silent, knowing what I know? Imagine if there had been some . . . some beastliness on his part towards you and I had done nothing.'

'Yes,' she says. 'Yes, I do see that. I must thank you for speaking out.'

'I will talk to your father and have him dismissed.'

'No,' she hears herself saying, 'I will mention this to my father myself, when the moment is right. It is a delicate matter.'

He frowns. 'Surely it would be better coming from a man—'

'I do not want my father to feel pressed into acting precipitately. The Guide is essential to Pinker's. Robert should finish it before any discussion is had.'

'So you are going to say nothing?' he says, suddenly suspicious.

'You have spoken to me. That must have been difficult, and I appreciate it, but now it is done, you have discharged your responsibilities. It is me, after all, not my father, who would be at risk—'

'If you will not speak to him, I must.'

'Please, Simon,' she says. 'Let us leave it. Please? For my sake.'

She can tell that he is suddenly seeing her in a different light.

'Well, I have said my piece,' he says abruptly, turning to the door.

As he goes she says, 'When was this? That you last saw him, I mean.'

'The last time was on Friday evening.'

She thinks, Earlier that afternoon, we had kissed.

A MIXTURE OF EMOTIONS kick their way across her heart. Anger and disgust, principally. But she is a modern woman—she tries to think rationally.

Perhaps it is partly her own fault. Perhaps she is inflaming his passions with her kisses and he must find release in . . . she cannot bear to think what.

For a week she cannot bring herself to touch him. Then they discover that muscat grapes and coriander seeds share some floral characteristics; that hazelnuts and freshly churned butter have a similar creamy fragrance. As they join the various parts of the Guide together, so they find hidden connections between different tastes and aromas—a palette of the senses. And, somehow, when Robert takes her in his arms, everything that happens in that other world where men keep their secret desires seems not to matter.

And when she does think about those other women, the faceless, nameless ones who lie with him, she is surprised to discover that what she feels for them is not so much pity or even disgust, but a sudden jolt of envy.

Four

At last the Guide was complete. The perfumer had made up a dozen stout mahogany boxes, which opened to reveal a series of shelves holding thirty-six small glass-stoppered bottles of aromas. Meanwhile, a printer was running off the pamphlet that explained how the scents should be used. I insisted that it be bound in calfskin vellum, ostensibly so that it would withstand the rigours of the field, but actually because I wanted my first printed work to look as much as possible like a volume of verse.

The conclusion of the Guide left me with a quandary. Since I was being paid by the word, there was no obvious reason for me to remain at Pinker's. But, equally, I was not wasting their money by staying. To Emily I muttered something about wanting to refine my phrasing when the first reports came in from Pinker's agents, but we both knew my motives were quite different.

Pinker never commented on my presence, but he frequently found me small tasks to keep me busy. One day he placed before Emily and me half a dozen squat tins with roughly printed labels. One bore an elaborate picture of an angel, another a picture of a lion.

'What are these?' Emily asked.

Her father's eyes twinkled. 'Shall we taste them and find out?'

We had boiling water brought up and cupped the first tin's contents.

'Well?' Pinker demanded.

'Very ordinary,' I said.

'And the next?'

I proceeded to the second tin. 'If I am not mistaken, this has been glazed with sugar water to lend an artificial sweetness.'

The others, too, were either bland, tainted or flavoured with additions.

'Can you tell us where these excrescences came from?' I asked.

'Certainly.' Pinker tapped one of the tins. 'This is Arbuckle's. When you ask for coffee anywhere from New York to Kansas City, this is what you get.' He pointed to the second tin. 'This is Chase and Sanborn's. They have from Boston to Montreal.' The finger moved along the row. 'This is Lion coffee . . . This is Seal . . . This is Folger's, of San Francisco and the gold-rush lands. And this is Maxwell House, which hails from Nashville and the South. In all, just six makes—brands, as they call them there—share out the coffee consumption of the most vigorous nation on earth. Six!'

'How can they control an entire industry?'

'Their proprietors have made a private arrangement with the Brazilian Government. They have effectively bypassed the Exchange; as they say over there, they have cornered the market. If the price of coffee is too low, they buy up stocks to create a shortage, and release them only when prices are better. If the price is high, they refuse to sell, and sit back and wait for it to fall to a level that suits them. And all because the public trust their name.'

'It is the standardisation you spoke of when you interviewed me.'

'Yes.' Pinker pursed his lips. 'It is the future,' he said. 'And we must beat it or be left behind.'

'But they are in America. England is something else entirely, surely.'

Pinker shook his head. 'We are all one market now, Robert. And what persuades a housewife in Sacramento or Washington to part with her money will also work in Birmingham or Bristol.'

'You don't intend to sell a coffee as poor as these, though, surely?'

Pinker hesitated. 'I shall reduce the number of my blends to two,' he said. 'Castle Premium will be supplied to the Temperance Taverns, Castle Superior to the shops. Thus customers will have the reassurance of knowing they are buying the same trusted name for home use that they enjoy when they go out.'

'The same name, yes, but not the same coffee,' I pointed out.

'I suspect that distinction will pass most people by. It is for the greater good, Robert; our success will mean the success of the Temperance Taverns, and a sober, more efficient economy will benefit the whole nation. We must look to America and the new methods that have been proven to work.'

'But you do not control the market, as the Americans do.'

'No. That is something that must be factored in.'

'In what way?'

'All in good time, Robert. All in good time. In the meantime, will you give some thought to how my blends might be constructed?'

I TOOK UP the conversation again with Emily when we were alone.

'Your father seems very keen on these blends of his,' I commented.

'It is nothing new.' She picked up some of the beans we were examining. 'This Java, for example, has an excellent body but is a little bland in taste. Mocca is more likely to be the opposite—full of flavour but thin in the mouth. Combining them makes for a coffee that is easy to enjoy.'

I glanced at her. 'It is a kind of marriage of flavours.'

'It is, but . . .' She sighed. 'I think it is like mixing paint on a palette. It is easy to produce brown by combining the other colours, but just because it is easy does not mean you should.'

'Quite. The colours are much better appreciated on their own.'

She was silent for a moment. It was not often that she criticised her father. 'Of course, he has commercial considerations to think of. He has such great plans. If you only knew the half of them.'

'I should like to.'

Another sigh. 'He has to be careful whom he tells, and when.'

'Of course. And you are family, and I am not. Although I hope that one day I may be considered closer than I am now.'

At that, she blushed.

'And now, let us perform a marriage of our own.' I held out my hand.

'What *do* you mean?'

'I mean, between these two coffees,' I said, pointing to the mocca and the Java on the table in front of us. 'Their flavours have been flirting for such a long time now. Let us bless their union and assist them in consummating it.'

'Robert!'

I ground the beans together, then spooned the grounds into the cups and added the water. The mix, in fact, was not bad. 'A happy union after all,' I said, smiling at her until she pretended to hit me.

And so, through flirtations and false constructions, we danced our way in mutual ignorance towards the greatest misunderstanding of all.

'HOW DO WE DO?' Pinker demanded for the twentieth time, stepping into the room. 'Are my blends concluded?'

'Very nearly,' I admitted. I was alone there except for the Frog, Emily having taken the afternoon off to go shopping.

Pinker stopped dead. 'What on earth are you wearing, Robert?'

'It is a jacket made in the Indian style.'

'Perhaps it would seem less brilliant under the glare of an oriental sun.'

'It cost eight pounds,' the Frog said eagerly from the floor, where she was squatting. 'It's the only one of its kind in all London.'

'I am not surprised.' Pinker looked at me and sighed. 'Leave us, would you, dear Philomena? Mr Wallis and I have some matters to discuss.'

Obligingly the Frog hopped away, croaking.

'I have no idea why she insists on making that extraordinary noise,' Pinker muttered. 'I suppose she'll grow out of it.' He glanced at me. 'My daughters are each in their own way unconventional, Robert.'

'They are a great credit to you,' I said politely.

'They are a great worry. Doubtless all parents fret about their children. But when there is only one parent the sum of worry is doubled.'

'I can imagine.'

'Can you?' He glanced at me again. 'You must think it strange I employ my own daughters.'

'I had not considered it,' I said carefully.

'Emily needs to be occupied. She needs a sense of purpose—to know that what she is about is creating some good in the world. She would never be happy, for example, running some minor aristocrat's household.'

I began to see where this might be going now, and I could hardly believe my good fortune. 'Of course,' I agreed. 'She is a modern woman. She must not on any account be thrown back into the past.'

'Exactly!' Pinker gripped my arm. 'Thrown back into the past—that is exactly what she fears. You put it well—you have the gift of words.'

'I do my best,' I said modestly. 'But if I am able to express the sentiment, it is because I feel it—I too wish to look forward.'

'Yes.' He released my arm. 'You must come to dinner, Robert. We have much to talk about.'

'I would like that very much.'

'Good. Saturday at six. Jenks will give you the address.'

He was thinking that I might marry his daughter. It was extraordinary—with a fortune such as he must have, he could have bought his daughter into the upper classes, or cemented an alliance with another wealthy tradesman. I was an artist, and I was penniless. True, I was educated, and—I liked to think—not without talent or charm, but in the normal way of things there was no way I would have been considered a suitable match. To have won him over was a great coup. I would never have to take employment again.

I CONSIDERED CAREFULLY what to wear for dinner at the merchant's house. I wanted Pinker to think of me as a suitable future son-in-law. I should wear something impressive, I decided: something that declared that I was somebody of distinction within my own sphere. After some searching I found the very thing: a jacket of green Jacquard silk, inlaid with gems, which seemed to shimmer with the iridescence of a mallard's neck. It was on display in Liberty, along with a magnificent blue turban, fastened with a garnet brooch. The ensemble cost six pounds, however, a sum I could no longer afford.

I went to Ike and explained that I was in need of a little more cash.

Ike raised his eyebrows. 'More? But if you do not mind me pointing it out, Mr Wallis, you are a little behind with the loans you already have.'

'This is for an . . . investment. I am hoping to make a proposal of marriage,' I explained.

'*Ahh.* And is this a union which we might expect to have good prospects—financially, that is?'

'Indeed. But in the meantime I shall inevitably have some further expenses. Shall we say another forty pounds?' I suggested.

Once again I signed some papers, and once again, when he handed me the money, I handed him two pounds back. 'Your interest.'

He bowed. 'And may I be the first to wish you, and your enterprise, every success.' He laughed. 'Though I should perhaps point out that the loan will be repayable even if you are unsuccessful in your suit.'

PINKER LIVED a short distance from his warehouse, in a fine square of black-stoned Georgian houses. The door was opened by a liveried footman, with a maid standing at his side to take my coat and cane.

'They are in the drawing room, sir,' the footman murmured.

I stepped through the door he indicated. The drawing room was lit by electric lamps, which cast a flattering glow across the faces of the three Pinker daughters, who were all dressed up for the occasion. Even Ada did not look quite so plain as usual, while the Frog—uncomfortable in a frock—was scowling, but at least looked for once like a girl. Pinker, seated in a high-backed chair, was talking to a thickset man in a sober black coat. Emily, next to them, looked ravishing in a gown of green velvet.

'Robert, there you are,' Pinker said. 'May I introduce Hector Crannach?'

'Wheel,' the thickset man said in a heavy Scottish accent, looking me up and down as he crushed my hand, 'they'd warned me that ye were a pote, Wallish, but they'd no' warned me that ye might forget your clothes.'

'I beg your pardon?' I said, frowning.

'Ye've turned up to dinner in your dreshing gown, man.'

Pinker chuckled. 'Hector, you must curb your famous plain-speaking tonight. And, Robert, you will have to forgive Crannach if he is not quite *au fait* with the latest fashions. He has just returned from Brazil.'

'Hector is Father's general manager,' Emily added, offering me her hand. 'Hello, Robert. Are you in fact a Mughal or a Mikado tonight?'

'Tonight,' I said, kissing her fingers, 'I am a triumph of style over style. Although, if you are referring to my jacket, I think the design is Persian.'

'Ay've travelled exstensively in Pusha,' Crannach announced. 'And ay've never sheen a jacket quite like tha'. Though I did once shee a carrrpet like it, in Morocca,' he added, turning to Ada and the Frog.

I laughed along with them, but I was forming a strong dislike for this Scot.

'Father has been explaining your Guide, Robert,' Emily said quickly. I saw now that one of the mahogany sample boxes had been placed on the table and opened, revealing the tiers of bottles. 'Hector's most impressed.'

'Oh, aye,' Hector said dismissively. 'I dinnae deny tha' such a shkeem may be of shome yuice.'

'But?' That was Pinker. 'You have a reservation, Hector?'

'Out there in the feelt,' Hector said portentously, 'and in particular the truppics, I fear yon Guide'll nae last six month.'

'And why not?' I asked.

'Terramites,' he said brusquely. 'Truppical terramites as big as ma fist. They'll do fae the box. And the heat, man—the terrabull heat—that'll boil those fine pear-fumes of yoursh away to nothin'.'

'I am not as intimate as you evidently are with termites,' I said, 'but the principles should remain sound whatever the conditions. And the pamphlet should withstand even the terrabull heat o' the truppics, I imagine.'

I felt a sharp pain in my ankle. I looked down. Emily's pointed shoe was just withdrawing back under her gown.

'In any case,' I said smoothly, 'you are wrong to call it my Guide. It is as much the work of the eldest Miss Pinker, who has been my indefatigable assistant these past few weeks.' I kissed her hand again. Hector glowered.

'Ha' ye ever been tae the truppics, Robert?' he asked sourly.

It was then that I made the first of many mistakes that evening.

'Not yet. I intend to, to get some writing done,' I said casually. 'It seems to be the last place where one can avoid being bothered by one's friends.'

THE EVENING proceeded well enough. Hector bored us all with an account of his travels around Malaya, Ceylon and the Caribbean—or, as he put it, 'M'lair, Shillon and the Carrybeena'. I can no longer be bothered to record his conversation phonetically; you will have to use your imagination.

You will have to use your imagination, too, to picture Emily's beauty at the dinner table that night—in the soft glow cast by Pinker's electric lights, the globes of her milky bosom, accentuated by the cut of her gown, were quite mesmerising. I noticed Hector glancing surreptitiously at them too.

It transpired that Hector's job was to go from one equatorial country to another, starting up plantations for Pinker and checking on his existing ones. At one point the sour Scot launched into a long explanation of the difficulties of growing coffee in the mountains of Jamaica.

'You tell us that coffee is now the most cultivated crop in the world—more plentiful even than cotton or rubber,' I interjected. 'Yet you wish us to believe that it is fiendishly difficult to grow. Surely it cannot be both.'

'Robert,' Emily murmured reprovingly.

'No, he makes a good point,' Hector said equably. 'But I'm afraid, Robert, you reveal your ignorance of conditions in the field. Aye, coffee's easy enough to grow. But that disnae mean it's easy to make a profit. It's four years from clearing the forest to picking your first crop—four years of planting, weeding, irrigating, before you see a penny. Coffee is grown in mountainous regions. It has to be dried, then transported—and the biggest cost is not the last two thousand miles by ship, but the hundred miles getting it to the sea.'

'Which is why, increasingly, we are looking to establish plantations in areas that already have good trading routes,' Pinker added.

'And why we must ensure that—' Hector began.

Pinker interrupted him. 'Hector, we have talked business long enough. My daughters are getting bored.'

'I'm not bored,' the Frog said. 'I like hearing about all the different countries. But I should like to know if you met any cannibals.'

Hector, it seemed, had not only met cannibals, but had been received into the highest echelons of cannibal society. After ten minutes I stifled a yawn.

'What adventures you have had, my dear Crannach. And you relate them so thrillingly. You shot them all, you say? How I do envy you. I myself have never shot anything more exciting than my cuffs.'

The Frog giggled. Hector glared. Emily only sighed.

THE FOOD WAS EXCELLENT, the bill of fare extensive. What with one thing and another, it was several hours before the ladies excused themselves. The footman placed a box of cigars on the table and withdrew. Crannach took his leave—I think he had probably had rather too much to drink; if so, it was fortuitous, as I needed to speak to Pinker man to man.

My employer poured himself a tumbler of port. 'Tell me, Robert,' he said thoughtfully, 'where do you see yourself, say, five years from now?'

I took a deep breath. 'Well . . . married, I suppose.'

Pinker nodded. 'That's good. Marriage gives a man purpose.'

'I'm glad you approve.'

'Of course, a man with the expense of a household needs money.'

'He certainly does,' I agreed, pouring myself some more port.

'And tell me something else,' he said. 'I have noticed that, while the specific task for which I engaged your services is now completed, you are still coming to my office almost every day. Is there, perhaps, a reason for this?'

'There is,' I agreed with a faint smile.

'I thought as much.' He clipped the end off a cigar, puffed at a candle to get the cigar going, then chuckled. 'I was the same at your age.'

'Really?'

'Yes. I was burning with ambition. I had met Susannah—the girls' mother—and I only had one thought in my head.'

This was an unexpected stroke of luck. If Pinker had once been in the shoes of an impoverished suitor himself, my job would be that much easier.

'So.' He puffed contentedly. 'Pinker's is a family business. More than that: our business is our family. It's something we pride ourselves on. And you'—he pointed with the cigar—'fit into that family very well.'

'Thank you,' I said. This was going better than I could have hoped.

'When I first met you I wondered, to be frank, if you were man enough for the job. But you are an amusing young fellow, Robert, and I have become fond of you. I want you to become a permanent part of the Pinker family.'

I could hardly believe what I was hearing. It seemed there was no need for me to convince Pinker of my suitability as a husband.

He puffed on his cigar. 'Perhaps you are wondering if you are up to it.'

'No, I am confident—'

He chuckled. 'Of course you are. And why not? You have the energy of youth.' He leaned forward. 'Energy. It's the critical ingredient. Never forget it. Every morning you have to wake up and say to yourself, I am ready. I am equal to this challenge. I am man enough. Every morning!'

'Quite,' I said, slightly taken aback by Pinker's attitude to matrimony.

'What you are considering is an adventure—a challenge. There will be times when it is difficult. And you will think, Why am I doing this?'

I laughed along with him.

'Of course,' he said, suddenly serious again, 'your lack of experience will make it harder. You have none whatsoever, I suppose?'

'Well, I've, er, actually there has been the odd occasion—'

'Believe me, it will still be a shock. But we were all inexperienced once—and what I wouldn't give to be in your shoes, a young man again, setting out on this great journey! Now, then. Let's talk money.'

'Very well.' I took a deep breath. 'I really don't have very much.'

To my surprise, Pinker grinned. 'I thought as much. Everything I've paid you so far has been spent, hasn't it?'

'I'm afraid it has, yes.'

'Do you have debts?'

'A few.'

Emboldened by his indulgent smile, I explained about Ike and his loans.

'So you've been borrowing more principal to pay the interest?' Pinker winced. 'Oh, that's very bad. But it's a detail; it can be taken care of when you have an income. Shall we say three hundred a year? With another three hundred for your expenses? And a year's money in advance?'

It was less than I had hoped, but it seemed ignoble to haggle. 'Very well.'

'There'll be a bonus if the enterprise is as fruitful as we both expect.'

I stared at him. The coffee merchant was actually proposing to give me a bonus for getting his beautiful daughter pregnant! 'I accept with pleasure.'

'Excellent.'

'I just hope Emily does,' I joked. 'I'd better go and ask her, hadn't I?'

Pinker frowned. 'Ask her what?'

'If she'll marry me.'

The frown deepened. 'You will do no such thing.'

'But—now you and I have agreed these terms—what is left to delay us?'

'Oh my God.' Pinker passed his hand over his brow. 'You prize fool—you surely didn't imagine . . . What do you think I am offering you?'

'Well . . . your daughter's, er, hand—'

'I was offering you a career,' he snapped. 'You said you wanted to go abroad—said you were ambitious—that you needed employment in order to become marriageable. You can't marry Emily. It's unthinkable.' He stared at me, aghast. 'What does she know of this?'

'Um—'

'If you have so much as touched her,' he hissed, 'I'll have you whipped from here to Threadneedle Street.' He put his hand to his forehead. 'Oh Lord—we must avoid another scandal.' He picked up the tumbler of port, looked at it, then put it down on the table again. 'I need to speak to Emily. I will see you in my office, sir, at nine tomorrow morning. Good night.'

Misunderstandings, cross-purposes, mixed messages. Yes, yes, I know—how appropriate that the first consequence of producing the Guide should be a muddle on such an epic scale.

I WALKED AS FAR as the City. It was raining, and the Jacquard jacket and turban were soon drenched. Eventually I found a cab that would take me to Marylebone. I trudged back to my rooms through the drizzle, wondering how the evening could have gone quite so wrong.

As I neared my front door I noticed two men lurking in a doorway. I ignored them, but as I pushed the key into the lock I heard footsteps. Something small, hard and heavy, like a billiard ball in a sock, smashed against my neck. As I spun round I was felled by another crack across the side of my head. My first thought, as I hit the ground, was that Pinker had sent thugs to warn me off, but even in my semi-concussed state I knew it was unlikely.

One of the men bent over me. In his hand was a tiny blackjack. 'Don' even *fink* of leaving the cun'ry wiffat payin' your debts,' he hissed.

In a big house like Pinker's, anyone could bribe a servant to send word when something important occurred. News of my falling-out with Pinker had probably spread by now to every interested party in London.

'Are you from Ike? Tell him I'll pay.' I realised I could not pay. 'I'll borrow some more from him tomorrow.'

'Don't be fick,' the man spat. 'Why would Ike want ter lend you more?'

'So that I can pay his interest.'

'I don't fuckin' fink so.' He raised the blackjack. It was no longer than a pair of gloves, and he glanced over me casually, selecting where to use it. He tapped my stomach and I was seized by an excruciating pain.

'Ike's calling in the debt,' he said. 'All of it. Yer've got a week ter pay.'

THE FOLLOWING MORNING I had an equally difficult interview with Pinker. No cudgels were involved, but only because there was no need for them.

To my surprise, when I was shown into his office Emily was there too. She was standing in front of the desk at which her father was sitting, so after a moment's hesitation I went to stand next to her. She said nothing, although her eyes widened when she saw the bruise on my forehead.

'Emily and I have spent much of the night talking,' Pinker said. 'There are certain things I think you need to be made aware of.' He addressed his daughter. 'Emily, are you in love with Mr Wallis?'

'No, Father.'

The words were like a hammer, smashing all my hopes like glass beads.

'Have you ever suggested to him that you might be in love with him?'

'No, Father.'

'Do you wish to be married to Mr Wallis?'

'Perhaps, Father.'

I looked at her, perplexed. This was making no sense.

'Explain, if you will, the circumstances in which you would consent to take him as your husband.'

She hesitated. 'I am not in love with Robert, but we are friends—good friends. I believe he has the makings of a kind, able man. I believe that he wants to do good in the world. I should like to be able to help him.'

There was more—much more; it came out of her beautiful lips like a speech. She had not found anyone else in her life to love and be loved by. She must marry someone. The question was, What marriage would most advance the causes and interests dearest to her heart? She and I liked each other; we were believers in the Rational Marriage, in the greatness of Humanity; more than this, she knew that the thought of our eventual union would sustain me through the long, difficult years ahead, and thus she felt it was her duty to make this small contribution to the cause of Civilisation.

I listened, stunned, to this noble nonsense. She appeared to be saying that she wanted to sacrifice her virginity on the altar of my Improvement.

'Very well,' Pinker said. 'Emily, please leave Robert and me alone now. And if I may say so, your words do you, and this family, great credit.' He pulled a handkerchief from his sleeve as she left and blew his nose.

'You have heard Emily,' he said when he could speak again. 'If you loved her before, I am sure you love her even more now that you fully understand the fineness of her feelings. You are a very lucky young man.' He paused. 'I am prepared to give my permission for the two of you to be married.'

'Thank you,' I said, astonished.

'But you will have to be in a position to settle a thousand pounds on her.'

'But how can I possibly do that? I have no money whatsoever.'

'Africa, of course. You must go and make your fortune.'

He laid it all before me. The plan had clearly been formulating in his mind for some time; my wanting to marry his daughter was simply an obstacle that had now been turned to advantage.

His plantations in Ceylon had failed, and would have to be replanted with tea. His plantations in India were becoming too expensive—the sepoys had turned rebellious; there was talk of independence. Africa was the coming place. In the Protectorate, in Uganda, in countries as yet unnamed, men of vision and energy were establishing vast coffee gardens that one day would rival those of Sumatra and Brazil. It was a rush, of course, to get the best places, but Pinker had stolen a march. Thanks to our Guide, and Burton's inside knowledge, he had established that the best coffee-growing conditions were in that part of Abyssinia known as Kaffa, southwest of Harar. It was land no one else wanted, and he had bought it—all fifty thousand acres.

He waved his hand airily. 'Of course, you don't have to plant it all. I am simply protecting us from competition in the future.'

I stared at him. 'It is the size of London,' I said.

'Exactly.' He jumped up, rubbing his hands. 'And you are its regent. You will go down in history, Robert—the man who brought Civilisation to Kaffa.'

For there was more, of course. I was not being sent to Africa simply to grow coffee beans. 'The most precious seeds you plant will be invisible. When they see what you achieve with your modern methods of cultivation; when they see how you govern them properly through the principles of free trade and fair dealing; when they see the wonders that prosperity can bestow, then, Robert, it is my belief they will turn to God. Give a heathen charity and he remains a heathen, and the charity is soon gone; give him a contract of employment and you have pointed him on the road to eternal life.'

'How do I get there?' I asked, my mind now on roads.

He sighed. 'By camel, I believe. There is a trade route from the coast.'

'And what shall I do while I am waiting for the coffee to grow? It takes four or five years to get a crop, I understand.' Four years, I thought as I said it. My God—I was being sent away for four years.

'You will trade as well, as Pinker's buying agent in that part of Africa. After all, no one knows the Guide better than you. I am arranging for you to operate under the auspices of a local merchant—you may have seen his mark on some of our moccas.' Pinker pulled a piece of paper from the shelves behind him and laid it on the table. At the top was an Arabic sign, one that I had seen on sacks of Harar coffee.

'His name is Ibrahim Bey,' Pinker continued. 'His family have been merchants for generations. Hector will accompany you, and assist you in picking out the right spot for the farm, employing a headman and so on, before he goes on to India. If you are a success, as I am sure you will be, you will have both my daughter's hand and my blessing.' He frowned. 'Until that time, of course, nothing is official. It is a private understanding between us—a probation, as it were: a chance to show what you are made of.' His mood abruptly lightened again. 'All this expertise at your disposal, Robert. A fortune to be made, a fair lady to be won and history to be written. How I envy you.'

Five

SS Battula, *8th June, 1897*

My darling Emily,

I write this to you as we progress along the northern shore of Egypt. Five days ago we put in to Genoa to take on stores—what a pleasure it was to stand on dry land after so long at sea! My plan to go overland, see Venice, then rejoin Hector at Suez has, as you predicted, proved impossible. It seems we are in a race against the coming of the rainy season and Hector is impatient to get the plantation up and running.

We dine each night at the captain's table, where we are sixteen, including the captain and first officer. Hector is very thick with the nautical fraternity and spends many hours discussing nor'westers, spinnakers, bilges and other manly concerns with the gravest of faces. Then we have a brace of missionaries, destined for the Sudan, and no fewer than six ladies who are off to India, visiting relatives.

As the only one among us with experience of the regions for which we are destined, Hector is in great demand. He settles many an argument with a definitive utterance on subjects as diverse as the correct headgear for a visit to a mosque and whether one need carry a pistol in the jungle. Dearest Emily, I have not forgotten the promise you extracted from me before I left, but sometimes I am sorely tempted to mock him just a little.

I think you would like the missionaries. One of them asked me if I intended to build a church on my plantation! It was not a question that had occurred to me before, but I suppose I probably shall, in good time.

In good time . . . As I write these words I realise how very long I shall be away. Being apart from you for almost five years is going to be very hard. Of course, it will all be worth it to marry you at the end. It is wonderful to be able to think of you as my partner in this great project of saving Africa, and as you say, being physically together in the same place is not as important as this togetherness of mind and purpose.

I had better go now as it is time to dress for dinner. The captain is a stickler for protocol. I came down on the first evening in my green waistcoat and was taken aside for a 'word of advice' about 'the need to keep up appearances'. I tried to explain that a white-tie dinner suit is considered a little old-fashioned now in polite circles, but in vain.

With much love from your future husband,

Robert

SS Battula, *the North Pole, 12th June, 1897*

Dear Frog,

Here I am at the North Pole. Admittedly, it is a funny sort of Pole, surrounded by warm blue sea, with the coast of Egypt visible to the south and the occasional palm tree poking up on the skyline, but Hector has got me practising with my sextant and theodolite and, since the North Pole is where the sextant informs me we are, at the North Pole we must be.

Why, you may ask, is it necessary to know precisely where one is? A good question, and one I put to Hector myself. It seems that we are soon going to be living in the Bush, and that this Bush, moreover, is not a nice English laburnum, or a well-pruned magnolia, but a larger and more fearsome species of Bush, in which it is possible to get quite lost. And when we come to plant our Coffee, Hector informs me, it is important to plant it in Straight Lines, so that everyone can see how neat and well regulated a White Man's Plantation is, and for this we will need to know how to Survey. I had thought myself quite able to Survey already—I am surveying a large whisky-and-soda at this very moment—but apparently I am a Flippant Egypt, or possibly a Flipping Eejit, I forget which.

Dearest Frog, will you look up 'Hectoring' in your dictionary, and tell your sister what it says? Don't tell her I put you up to it, though.

Regards,

Robert

Hotel Pension Collos, Alexandria, 20th June, 1897

My dear Hunt,

Landed at last! The voyage was tedious beyond belief, made worse for being entirely without female company—or rather, without female company of the necessary kind, for there was in fact a large consignment of twittering women on board, who were clearly being sent to India for the sole purpose of finding a husband. One of them even tried to flirt with Hector, which shows you how desperate she must have been. He told me brusquely later that he'd once considered marriage, but had decided it was 'incompatible with a life of adventure and travel'. I forbore from pointing out that if it wasn't for marriage, I would be tucked up in the Café Royal as we spoke.

If you want to write to me, the best place is via Aden. I'll be there in a fortnight—we have to wait here for a Suez boat, a delay which is bothering my travelling companion greatly, and me somewhat less so.

Best,
Wallis

Hotel Pension Collos, Alexandria, 27th June, 1897

Dear Frog,

Greetings—I write to you these quickly scribbled lines
Composed in what are sometimes called 'Alexandrines'.

Actually I don't do anything of the sort—an Alexandrine is much too difficult and tedious for a letter. And it is far too hot today for rhymes. Instead, I shall tell you about Alexandria. We landed here early on Friday morning, just as the muezzin *were calling the faithful to prayer.*

All the passengers were on deck. First, beyond the inky blue-black of the sea, a few lights twinkled on the horizon. The sky lightening . . . the salmon-coloured mist of an African dawn . . . an impression of towers and minarets . . . then, instantly, the sky brilliantly alight as the sun hoisted itself like a huge sail over our heads, while, before us, the great white city of the East slipped serenely past our bow.

As we edged into harbour, a host of tiny black children dived for the sixpences we tossed into the water. The gangplank was quickly surrounded by dozens of rubbery-lipped camels, gargling and spitting and being beaten about the head by yelling Arab gentlemen in long white shirts. Most of the women here go about veiled, but that is as far as their modesty extends: it is considered no more shocking here to show your breasts than it would be for us to go bare-headed.

Today I saw a man who had stuck iron spikes through his chest; on the end of each spike he had placed an orange, though whether this was to prevent anyone else from accidentally piercing themselves or because it was a convenient place to keep his lunch, I could not say.

With best regards,

Your future brother-in-law, Robert

SS Rutalin*, 30th June, 1897*

My dearest, dearest Emily,

Your letter reached me just before we left Alexandria. Your exhortations are unnecessary: I am being charming to Hector. Only last night at dinner I amused him by reciting nursery rhymes in a Scottish accent.

And, yes, I am sorry about that letter to the Frog. I promise not to mention ladies' bare chests to her again. I suppose it was indelicate, but if you saw the lack of concern with which people display themselves here, you would understand why I did not think anything of it.

We are now back on board ship, passing through Suez. And I have been watching some splendid dawns. Every morning the sky is streaked with the colours of an English hedgerow: primrose pink and daffodil yellow. With the first glimpse of the sun all colour is instantly burnt out, except for the dazzling green of the water and the dazzling silver-blue of the sky. The glare is so bright that one's eyes hurt. Hector has taken to wearing an eyeshade, which makes him look a bit like a sickly parrot.

I only wish that you were here, but the thought of you is more than enough. My love for you will sustain me during the long years ahead.

Your ever-loving Robert

Grand Hotel de l'Univers, Aden, 2nd July, 1897

Dear Mr Pinker,

I have made contact with the coffee wholesalers here in Aden, as you suggested. The Bienenfeld brothers had some extremely good lots: the one that impressed most was a light mocca, small-beaned, mahogany-brown after roasting, with notes of blueberry and lime and a very low acidity. I purchased all they had and ordered it shipped as soon as possible.

I am keen to meet Ibrahim Bey, though there are rumours that his business is in trouble. At present he is on a trading trip in the interior: we may catch up with him when we cross to Zeilah, on the African side.

With best wishes,

Wallis

Grand Hôtel de l' Univers, Aden, 2nd July, 1897

Dear Hunt,

The Grand Hotel de l'Univers is a cockroach-infested shack, and Aden is hell—an expanse of volcanic rock, lying at sea level, sheltered from every breeze but utterly exposed to the pitiless glare of the sun. This is not even the hottest part of the year and the mercury reaches 130 degrees every day. There isn't a blade of grass, or a palm tree, in the whole place.

The British are only here because it's the midpoint between Africa, India, Australia and home—a sort of military-cum-mercantile staging camp for British Empire Incorporated. No one actually lives here, and though some people have been 'stationed' here for a few years, most are passing through. The quicker I get out of this oven, the happier I'll be.

The fact is, I am at a bit of a low ebb. I seem to have all the responsibilities and disadvantages of marriage and employment, without benefiting from the domestic comforts and financial rewards that should accompany them! How I am to become an artist while stuck in a fetid, stinking jungle I have no idea. It is enough to make one weep . . .

Yours in adversity,
Robert

SS Carlotta, *Zeilah Creek, Africa! 7th July, 1897*

Dear Morgan,

Thank you for your letter, which reached me in Aden. We have now left that hellhole, thank God, in a steamer barely bigger than a biscuit tin. It was quite a squeeze to get our luggage on board. We have accumulated enough for over thirty porters. As well as the crates of farming and building tools, fish-hooks and beads for dish-dash, there is a sturdy cash chest, with padlock, containing 800 Austro-Hungarian dollars, which for some reason have become the universal currency hereabouts, possibly because each one is the size of a small silver dinner plate. Among the British, rupees are also in use, although the natives sometimes grumble about taking them, since they have no value anywhere except India.

My wardrobe includes two alpaca bush-suits from Simpson's, a great quantity of flannel trousers, long and short, and my red velvet smoking jacket. My library consists of a volume entitled Coffee: Its Cultivation and Profit, *by Lester Arnold, which Hector assures me contains everything there is to know about that fine crop; an actor's stage script of* The Importance of Being Earnest, *six blank pocketbooks, the* Yellow Book *for April 1897, and Francis Galton's* Hints to Travellers. *We also have a medicine chest, which has been stocked as per Galton's instructions.*

Kuma, our cook, is a fine fellow. He comes with a letter of recommendation from one Captain Thompson of Bengal, who says, 'He is not the bravest of boys, but he cannot be faulted in his ability to get hot food ready after a day's march. Leave him in Aden when you have finished with him, as I hope to return for another safari in a year or so's time.'

Hector becomes visibly more cheerful the nearer he gets to the Equator. He has been striding about manfully organising everything, shouting at the natives and making lists. It makes me tired just to look at him.

Sometimes I think I am going to wake up and find this is all some terrible dream. The only consolation are the sunsets, the most beautiful I have ever seen. When the sun sinks down, touches the water and bursts, flushes of gold, amethyst, carmine and violet colour the sky, then fade into the darkness, leaving only the dazzling frost of the moonlight and the utter blackness of the swamp . . . Oh, and a million small flying creatures that come and bite your skin with all the ferocity of piranhas.

Regards,

Robert

Dear Frog,

You will notice that this letter bears no return address: that is because we are now Nowhere. Nowhere is a topsy-turvy sort of place: trees grow in the water, as casually as if they were on dry land; the fish, meanwhile, skip about on top of the mudflats, possibly to escape the crocodiles, who spend more time in the water than the fish do.

Our little boat measures no more than twenty feet from brass bow to mahogany stern. We eat outside, under a kind of awning, and are chugging against the current, a wide, mocca-brown, silt-filled creek that appears not to move at all but which occasionally shoots a sunken log past us at great speed towards the sea. Occasionally we pass a village, and then the natives come out onto the bank and stare. The children all have big tummies, as if they had been blown up with a pump.

As for me, I am looking quite the Arab these days—before leaving Aden I had my hair cut by a local barber. Now I am completely shorn except for a single lock at the occiput, by which Muhammad lifts you up on Judgement Day. Hector sighs when he looks at me and calls me a 'fullish pup'. Which, no doubt, I am.

Yours fullishly,

Abu Wally (as Kuma calls me! It is Arab, I think, for 'Master Wallis')

Zeilah, July

Dearest Emily,

I cannot tell you how much I am missing you. When I think back to those innocent days cupping coffees in your father's office, they already feel like another lifetime. Will you still remember me in half a decade? Will we still be able to laugh with each other? I am sorry to sound despondent—it is just that being out here, everything back in London feels like a dim, distant dream. Sometimes I even wonder if I am ever going to come back at all . . . I know you told me to think optimistically, but really it is almost impossible not to wallow sometimes.

Today I opened the sample bottles in the Guide and smelt some of the scents that most remind me of home—apples, and gingerbread, and tea roses, and hazelnuts . . . Then I tried to mix up a scent that reminded me of you—that Jicky you sometimes wore: a mixture of jasmine, cedar and citrus. It made me feel quite emotional. I cried like a child.

Dearest Emily, please don't mind me missing you. I will buck up tomorrow, I expect.

Your loving, Robert

EMILY SITS at the office table, copying figures from a pile of receipts into a ledger. She can see that the Guide has already proved its worth. Pinker's is buying more high-quality coffees than ever before. Many coffees previously thought to be the finest have turned out to have quite low scores—the Monsooned Malabar so prized by many connoisseurs is surprisingly rank. But other regions have thrown up gems: notably Antigua and Guatemala. She frowns. Along with the fine coffees, there seems to be a large amount of inferior stuff, particularly the cheapest coffee of all—African liberica, dense and flavourless. It can be picked up for almost nothing: indeed, there is a glut of it. No reputable merchant would be stockpiling it, unless . . .

Her father is showing a visitor round the warehouse, a well-dressed man with quick eyes and a lively smile.

'Ah, Emily, there you are. Brewer, may I introduce my daughter?'

The man steps forward and shakes her hand. 'I am very pleased to make your acquaintance, Miss Pinker.'

'Mr Brewer is the Member of Parliament for Ealing,' Pinker explains. 'He has a particular interest, as I do, in Free Trade.'

She looks at the visitor with interest. 'You're a Liberal?'

'Indeed. And although we currently find ourselves out of government, I have no doubt that, with the aid of forward-thinking men like your father, we will soon command the popular vote again. Our watchword will be Freedom—freedom of thought, freedom to spend your wages as you wish, freedom to do business without government interference.'

'And is your party also in favour of freedom for women?' she asks.

He nods. 'As you know, there has been a Suffrage Bill every year for the past five years, and every year it has been talked out by the Tories. That is the kind of abuse of procedure we are determined to stamp out.'

'But first things first, eh?' Pinker says. 'Free Trade, then social issues.'

Brewer turns his kindly eyes to Emily. For a moment a gentle glint of amusement seems to pass between them. 'First we need to be in government,' he agrees, but he is speaking more to her now than her father. 'And for that we need the support of business. So, yes, Free Trade first.'

They have stopped by the front door. Brewer's tour is clearly at an end, and her father impatient to get on, but both she and the MP are lingering.

'Perhaps we might discuss this again,' he says.

'I should like that,' she agrees. 'Very much.' She looks at her father.

'What? Oh, yes—you must come to dinner, Arthur.'

'So YOU ARE GOING to support the Liberals financially?' she says to her father, when the MP has left.

'I am. It seems to be the only way to get any influence. And they need funds if they are to oust the Tories.' He shoots her a glance. 'Do you approve?'

'I think it's an excellent idea. But why do we need influence?'

He makes a sour face. 'It is as we suspected—William Howell has joined his plantations to the syndicate. He is part of the corner now. Even with the Guide, it makes it impossible to compete.'

'And your Mr Brewer can help?'

'A Liberal Government will no more want the market run by a few rich men and foreign governments than we do. They will stop it by regulation, if necessary. But in the short term . . .' He looks at her intently. 'Mr Brewer believes they can help us break the cartels. It is just the cause they have been looking for. They are already working their way onto the key committees.'

She sighs. 'It seems a very long way from making a good cup of coffee.'

'Yes,' he agrees. 'But it is the way of all business, I suspect, to move from small issues to larger ones.'

She remembers now what it was she came to ask him. 'Does this have anything to do with the cheap liberica we have been purchasing?'

'Ah.' He nods. 'Yes. You'd better come into the office.'

Half an hour later they are still sitting at the big table where she used to work with Robert. The Guide is open on the table, and in front of them half a dozen used cups show where they have been tasting various samples.

'So you see,' Pinker is saying, 'the Guide has turned out to have a double function. The work Robert did for me, on blending, in those last weeks, was crucial.' He points to a cup. 'Take a cheap, coarse coffee like this, categorise its deficits, then add just enough of those coffees that you see, from the Guide, will compensate for them.' He gestures to three or four other cups. 'And then you have a coffee that has no discernable faults.'

'But a coffee that also has no particular virtues, surely,' she points out.

'Yes—but you know, Emily, people don't always agree on what flavours they like in a coffee. By blending a coffee according to the principles of the Guide, we can eradicate all the attributes that might otherwise stop people from buying Castle. We end up with a coffee no one dislikes. A coffee whose taste is consistent. And all for a fraction of the cost.'

'Robert would be somewhat unhappy to hear you say that, I imagine.'

'Robert is not a businessman.' He looks at her carefully. 'There was a reason why I sent him away, you know, and it was not only to do with money.'

'Yes,' she says. 'I know.' Two spots of pink appear in her cheeks.

He says quietly, 'Perhaps once distance has cooled your affection, you will decide that he is not the man for you after all. If that happens . . . you have no obligation to him. In matters of the heart, as in business, we must do what is best. Not necessarily what we had planned.'

'I understand,' she says. 'And I promise I will make no hasty decision.'

Zeilah, 31st July

Dear Hunt,

We have been waiting in this godforsaken hole for three long weeks. Only now do I realise what a haven Aden was—it might have been a dump, but it was a well-stocked dump, with proper buildings and gaps between them that could be described as streets. Here, there are just huts, mud and choking swirls of red dust. This dust—peppery, pungent, slightly rancid—is the smell of Africa: I cannot get it out of my nostrils.

The people here are Somalis, but they are governed by another tribe called Danakils, who control the trade routes and carry spears or swords. The whole place is under the aegis of a savage called Abou Bekr and his eleven sons. I do not use the word 'savage' here in its ethnic sense: the man has personally disembowelled over a hundred people. Needless to say, we are not going anywhere until we have his permission.

Every few days we are shown into his courtyard—a patch of red earth, surrounded by palisades. An elderly man with a wispy beard, he reclines under an awning on a couch of goatskins. He wears a dirty white robe and an enormous onion-shaped turban. His eyes are dead and weary.

To any question concerning the caravan, Abou Bekr answers, 'Insh'Allah'*—if it please God. We are waiting for something—some sign, some request: when we ask Abou Bekr what it will take to allow us to travel, he frowns; when we ask his courtiers, they shrug and repeat the same formula, 'Soon,* insh'Allah, *very soon.' We are told that Abou Bekr is well disposed towards us, that this interminable wait is simply a formality. There will also have to be an assembly of elders, which will debate our application, and sometimes Abou Bekr uses the difficulty of convening this as a reason why nothing is happening.*

In the meantime, we busy ourselves assembling our caravan. We have enlisted the help of one Desmond Hammond, a former military man who is now making his fortune trading ivory and other goods. He and his partner, a Boer called Tatts, vanish for a week at a time, laden down with Remingtons, Martini-Henrys and ammunition; when they return their camels are festooned with huge tusks.

Regards,
Wallis

Zeilah, 2nd August

My dearest Emily,

We hope to be leaving here soon. According to the latest reports, Ibrahim Bey, the coffee merchant, will be here in a few days. We are optimistic that, with his help, the administrative difficulty that has pinned us here will be resolved. Certainly Abou Bekr's courtiers seem to be full of happiness: they mention Bey's name and smile.

Poor Hector—he has been fretting about the rains. At one point he was thinking of leaving me here, making his way back to Aden and on to Ceylon before the bad weather comes, but apparently your father's instructions were that he must see me established at all costs. I do not find his company any easier, but I am grateful for it. To be here on one's own would be very harsh.

I have just been watching two cormorants—

AND THAT'S WHEN I saw her.

I was sitting on the deck of our boat, writing a letter, when another boat came round the bend in the river. A dhow, under human power—four pairs of oars rising and falling rhythmically, as one. On the deck, a large man in a white robe was seated on a throne-like stool, one hand on his knee. The sensual, heavy face was that of a potentate; the hooded eyes missed nothing as they scanned the jetty. Big, fleshy lips, an Arab's curving nose. Behind him stood a Negro: a tall man, or rather a tall boy, for despite his height there was something youthful in the black face. His hands were folded loosely over the pummel of a huge sword, its point sticking in the wooden deck.

And behind *him*, at the Arab's other shoulder, stood a girl. A saffron-yellow robe enveloped her, from her ankles to her hair. The face below the headscarf was delicate, fine-boned, and the body . . . As a breeze along the river ruffled the gown, I saw that she was strong and supple, like an athlete. She was, I realised with a start, breathtakingly beautiful, her skin so black that like a piece of split coal it seemed almost silver where it caught the light.

A whistle blew. The dhow raised its oars and drifted in towards the jetty. Its trajectory took it near to where our own craft was moored. People ran to and fro with ropes. The two men continued staring ahead, but as the dhow passed the girl turned a little and looked directly at me. It was all I could do to hold her gaze without flinching from that remarkable beauty.

The moment the boat docked, the Arab was on his feet. He was a heavy man, but nimble; he needed none of the offered hands to help him onto dry land. The Negro followed, holding his sword in front of him. Then the girl came ashore—a quick, confident stride as she stepped onto the gunwales, then jumped onto the jetty, balanced as a cat.

After that came the usual chaos and the unloading of cargo. I continued to watch her, mesmerised. Beneath the loose-fitting headscarf the hair, one could now see, was long and wiry. Tendrils and dark zigzags escaped. The yellow robe blew against her, outlining her body again, fleetingly . . .

The Arab gave an order, his voice booming; then the three of them walked up towards the village. I watched the saffron-yellow robe among the press of black heads—the way she moved: strong and light and easy, her shoulders pulled back like a runner. Something clicked in my brain, a key turning in a lock. I found I had been holding my breath, and when I released it the sound came out like a gasp. I looked down. In my hand was the half-finished letter to Emily. I crumpled it in my fist and threw it into the water, where it circled twice before drifting down the black, silent current towards the sea.

I WAS STILL SITTING there half an hour later when Hector hurried back.

'We're summoned,' he said. 'Ibrahim Bey has arrived, and now it seems the King will talk to us after all. It's damned impudence, if you ask me.'

I got up from my camp-chair and made to go ashore, but he stopped me.

'I think we should make a show of this, Robert. We're not just here as individuals; we're here as representatives of British Industry.'

And so it was that we walked into the court of Abou Bekr wearing as much regalia as we could muster: white tie, tails, cummerbunds and, in Hector's case, a rather splendid white hat surmounted with red cockatoo feathers.

Abou Bekr lay on his couch, eating dates. Ibrahim Bey stood in front of him. The Negro was at his master's shoulder; the girl was nowhere to be seen.

We were waved forward. Abou Bekr performed the introductions in a language none of us understood, though his gestures were clear. Bey, Hector and I all shook hands. The King spoke again; a document was brought; he dunked the royal seal in ink and pressed it to the paper. Then, staring fiercely, he held out a leathery hand to me. I shook it. We were dismissed.

'Have you been here long?' Bey enquired solicitously when we were outside. He might have been meeting us off a slightly delayed express train.

'Nearly a month,' Hector growled furiously.

'Oh. Not so bad, then.' Bey smiled. 'It's good to meet you both. You must be Crannach. And you'—he turned to me—'must be Robert Wallis. My good friend Samuel Pinker wrote to tell me you were coming. He asked me to help you in any way I can.' He bowed his head. 'I shall be honoured to do so.'

'What caused the delay?' Hector asked brusquely.

Ibrahim Bey's big face assumed an expression of bafflement. 'I have no idea. But in the meantime, there is still the council of elders to square. Will you make them a gift? A couple of goats should do it.'

'We don't have any goats,' I pointed out.

'And if we did,' Hector said ponderously, 'we wouldn't exchange them for travel permits in a country where we are already entitled to pass freely, as subjects of Her Britannic Majesty.'

'Of course,' Ibrahim Bey said thoughtfully. 'There is absolutely no obligation to give anything at all.' He caught my eye and winked. 'But you may find yourself stuck here for a very long time if you do not.'

'I am of the opinion,' Hector said, 'that whenever a white man resorts to bribery, he makes things worse for every other white man who follows.'

'Then I am fortunate not to be a white man—or at least, not quite,' Bey said, as if it were all a great joke. 'But assuming that the elders give their permission, will you agree to share the costs of a caravan with me? I too need to get to Harar, and the larger the group, the smaller the risk.'

'Why? Is it dangerous?' I asked.

'That journey is always dangerous, my friend. But we have guns. We would be unlucky to be killed.'

I felt strangely reassured. That was the charisma of the man, I suppose.

'But we will not bribe anyone,' Hector repeated doggedly.

'You would tip a waiter,' Bey suggested mildly. 'Why not a king?'

'A tip comes afterwards,' Hector said firmly. 'A bribe is before.'

'Then that's settled. A gift of two goats, to be given *after* the meeting. I'm sure they will accept your word on that: an Englishman's promise is notoriously reliable.' Bey clapped his hands. 'And now, may I offer you coffee? I have made camp on the hill; it is a little cooler up there.'

Hector said disgustedly, 'I have some preparations to attend to.'

Bey looked at me. 'Thank you,' I said. 'I'd be honoured.'

PORTERS WERE FERRYING water and a goat was being skinned as I made my way through the encampment. At the centre, one tent was larger than the rest. The Negro youth was standing outside it. When he saw me he silently lifted the flap and motioned for me to go inside.

The interior was hung with patterned silks, and carpets covered the floor. There was a pungent, spicy scent of incense. In the middle of the space, on either side of a low table, were two throne-shaped stools.

'Robert—welcome.' Bey emerged from another chamber. He now wore a flowing pair of cotton trousers, with a matching shirt and a waistcoat of patterned silk. He stepped quickly towards me and clasped both my shoulders. 'Samuel has written to me of your venture—your *ad*venture, I should say. And of the Guide, too—I am looking forward to making the acquaintance of that extraordinary system. But first—some coffee. Mulu! Fikre!'

The Negro came into the tent and they exchanged a few words in Arabic. Bey pointed to a stool. 'Please, sit,' he said to me.

He sat on the other stool, watching me. After a moment the girl came in and for a moment I felt dizzy, such was her effect on me. Now she wore a brown cotton robe that ended at her hips, over trousers of pale silk embroidered with pearls; a long coiled bracelet of copper wound itself about her arm like a snake. Her eyes, I saw now, were extraordinarily pale, almost grey. They met mine for a moment—then dropped, as she knelt and lighted incense in a brazier. Tendrils of perfumed smoke filled the tent.

'The Abyssinian coffee ceremony,' Bey's voice said, 'consists of three cups, taken one after the other. The first is for pleasure, the second provokes contemplation, and the third bestows a blessing.'

The Negro returned with a copper tray. On it were cups, a black clay pot, a drawstring bag, a napkin and a dish of pink liquid. The girl dipped the napkin in the dish and came to kneel before me. Then, surprisingly, she reached forward and wiped the damp, scented napkin over my face. The aroma of rosewater filled my nostrils and I felt her fingers on the other side of the cloth. Her perfect face was very close then she moved away again. She pulled at the strings fastening the bag and held it up to me.

'Now you must smell the beans, Robert,' Bey's voice said.

I took the bag from her and raised it to my nose. I recognised the aroma instantly. 'I've had this coffee before,' I said. 'You sold some to Pinker.'

Bey smiled. 'He has trained you well. This is the coffee of the land beyond Harar—the land where you are to make your plantation. The world calls it mocca, though it is quite different from the moccas of my country. It comes down from Harar by the same ancient slave route that we will be following.'

I looked at him, surprised.

'You didn't realise? Yes, the trail has been used by slavers for centuries. That, not merely coffee, is the source of Harar's wealth, and the reason why they have not always invited the attentions of outsiders. The two trades—coffee and slavery—are connected in other ways as well.'

He is silent a moment. The beans hiss in their pot as they roast.

'How so?' I asked.

'To keep awake as they travelled at night, the slavers ate the beans of the kaffa bush mixed with a little butter. In more temperate regions the beans were sometimes discarded—thrown by the wayside whenever the slavers stopped. Where they took root, new areas of coffee production started.'

'Then it was fortunate the traders stopped.'

'Not for their captives. It was at these halts that the boy slaves would be castrated. Then they were buried up to their waists in the hot sand to cauterise the wound. For an unfortunate few, the wounds became infected and they were left there in the desert to die a painful death.'

Despite the heat, I shivered. 'But that's all in the past now.'

He did not reply. The beans had reached the point roasters call first crack, popping and rattling in their clay pot. The girl tipped them onto a plate. The smell intensified. Scorched tar, peat smoke and a triumphant blaze of sweet, honeyed, floral aroma. The girl handed me the plate and I inhaled. 'These are good,' I said to her politely, but her beautiful face was expressionless.

'I see she doesn't understand,' I said as I passed the plate on to Bey.

'There you are wrong, Robert. Fikre knows seven languages, including French, English, Amharic and Arabic. But she will not speak without my permission.' He lifted the plate to his own face and inhaled deeply. 'Ah!'

I looked into the girl's eyes and saw a silent plea of desperate intensity.

I frowned a little, as if to say, *I don't understand.*

After a moment she gave the minutest of shrugs. *I cannot tell you.*

I slid my eyes towards Bey. *Why? Because of him?*

Another tiny, almost imperceptible nod. *Yes.*

She busied herself pounding the beans in a mortar, then tipped them into a silver coffee pot. When she poured on the boiling water, the smell was like a fanfare: exultant, a mixture of honeysuckle and spices, lilies and lime.

She poured coffee in a thin, continuous stream into two cups. As she handed one to me she leaned forward, masking our hands from Bey. I felt something small and hard being pushed into my hand, surreptitiously. Casually, as I lifted my coffee to my mouth, I glanced down.

In my palm was a single coffee bean. What did it mean? I drank the coffee. It was as good as when I had it in Limehouse—perhaps better. My senses tingled with the heat, the incense and the presence of the girl.

She avoided my eyes as she dipped the napkin in the rosewater and washed my face in preparation for the next cup. But her hand lingered, minutely, as she smoothed the damp cloth across my face.

She dropped the napkin. We both reached for it at once. Our fingers touched. Her eyes widened, startled. *Please. Be careful.*

I squeezed her hand once, reassuring her. *Don't be frightened. Trust me.*

Bey talked of Harar. 'Getting the coffee out is hard, but it will get easier. Menelik, the Abyssinian Emperor, is talking of building a railway.'

The third cup. Now the coffee was a little salty: evaporation had thickened it. Fikre refreshed it with a sprig of herb that tasted like ginger.

Bey took the sprig and sniffed it. 'This is *tena adam*, Robert. The Abyssinians believed it to be an aphrodisiac. The coffee ceremony, you see, has many meanings. Between friends, it is a gesture of friendship; between merchants, a symbol of trust. But between lovers it is a ritual of a different kind. When a woman gives a man coffee, it is a way of showing her desire.'

In my left hand, my fingers rotated the bean, small and hard and round.

'And that is the coffee ceremony. Now I know you will never cheat me. Ha!' His booming laughter filled the tent.

Fikre took the empty cups and placed them carefully on the tray. At the flap of the tent, just beyond his sight, she glanced back at me. A flash of white teeth, lips the colour of pomegranates. Then she was gone.

'How long has Fikre been in your service?' I asked, as casually as I could.

Bey looked at me thoughtfully. 'She's very lovely, isn't she?'

I shrugged. 'Yes, she is rather.'

He was silent for a moment, then he said abruptly, 'She isn't in my service, Robert. I own her. She's a slave.'

I had half suspected it. But it was still a shock—an outrage.

'I am telling you this,' Bey said, fixing me with a fierce look, 'because I will not lie to you. But I promise you that it is not what it seems. Some day I will tell you how I came to buy her. But not today.'

'What about Mulu?'

'Him too. He is her *lala*—her maid, her protector. He is a eunuch, taken from his tribe as a child and castrated on the journey, just as I described.'

I shuddered. It explained something that had been puzzling me about the way Mulu looked: the height of a man, the hairless face of a boy . . .

Bey said gently, 'Of course, for you British slavery is the great evil. But things are different here—it is not a question of simply saying to someone, "Now you are released, go home." Where could they go? Even if they knew who their own people were, they would not be accepted—they have no status. I give them a better life than they could otherwise hope for.'

I nodded; a part of me was appalled at what he was saying. But another part of me was horribly, furiously envious.

Six

We left Zeilah four days later—a caravan of thirty camels, consisting not only of ourselves and Ibrahim Bey but also Hammond and Tatts. Fikre and Mulu walked behind us with the other servants.

At Tococha we stopped for water. We filled the *gherbes*, giant goatskin bottles, two tied to each camel. The water had a rancid, animal taste that worsened after a day in the sun. Ten miles on, at the rim of the desert, we turned inland. In the moonlight—we travelled from late afternoon to dawn—the sand was brilliant and glistening, like a vast plain of quartz. If you licked your lips they tasted of salt. Sometimes there were steam vents, *fumaroles*, in the sand. The only living thing we saw all night was a thorn tree.

I found myself daydreaming about Emily, replaying scenes from our courtship—the way she stamped her foot when we had an argument in the street; lunch at the pub in Narrow Street . . . But then I caught a glimpse of Fikre, the moonlight catching on her slate-grey skin, and I was instantly aroused. The hypnotic rhythm of the camel, a constant nudging, rocking motion, did nothing to dispel the fantasies flitting through my head.

When the sun rose—soaring like a Montgolfier balloon over the sands—we were still in the same featureless desert. But eventually a tiny village came into view: Ensa, our destination for the day. There were a dozen ramshackle huts, a few goats and a well. We had covered forty miles.

THE FOLLOWING NIGHT I rode a little shamefully—it did not seem right to be sitting on a camel when a woman was walking. But I could hardly offer my camel to a slave.

Ibrahim Bey saw me glancing at Fikre and steered his camel alongside mine. 'I said I would tell you how I found her. Would you like to hear now?'

I thought, I am riding a stinking camel through the desert. I have barely slept in days. I am going to a place without civilisation. An Arab trader is going to tell me about his slave. Surely this is all a terrible dream.

'Please,' I said.

Bey talked for nearly an hour. It was an accident, it seemed, which began with a slave sale in Constantinople to which Bey was dragged along by a friend, against his better judgment.

'Please understand, Robert: it was not some squalid bazaar where labourers were sold by the gross. This was a sale of the most valuable specimens—girls who had been selected in infancy for their beauty, nurtured in the harem of a prestigious dealer, taught mathematics, music and languages.' He stared into the darkness. 'There were twenty or so of us there. A scribe sat at a table, preparing to record the payments. The trader made a short speech, then introduced the first girl, a Russian by birth. There was a certificate of virginity from a midwife: these were harem girls, not prostitutes.'

The caravan slowed as the animal negotiated some boulders that lay across our path. I glanced back. Mulu was helping Fikre across the rocks.

'The bidding started. Almost immediately some kind of record was broken. Girls like this came onto the market rarely, and for these wealthy men, nothing compared to the thrill of buying one. The sums being thrown around were far beyond my means, of course. I was a mere coffee trader, an observer, who by rights should not even have been present.

'After perhaps half a dozen girls had been sold, a temporary halt was called, and while we were taking coffee the girls came out to play instruments, or to play each other at chess. That was when I became aware of a whisper being passed around that a wealthy young courtier there was intent on buying the very best girl to present to the Sultan, in the hope of some preferment. The other buyers were speculating about which girl it would be.

'I looked around the room. I thought perhaps he would favour the fair-haired Hungarian girl. Then I noticed an African girl, very dark, very beautiful, sitting at one of the chess tables. She wore a jacket of shimmering red silk, and her expression as she moved the pieces was sombre. I paused as I passed by her table. Her opponent was a poor player, and when she had been beaten, in no more than half a dozen moves, I stepped forward. "I would be very honoured," I said, "if I could join you in a game."

'The African shrugged and reset the pieces. I made a couple of easy opening moves. The etiquette of the harem demanded that she lose to me, to flatter my ego. For a couple of turns, I thought she might. But then a spark of determination came into her eye and she began trying to beat me. I studied her face. It was obvious that she was seething with anger at the way she was being disposed of. Beating me was a tiny statement of her defiance.

'I became aware that someone else had come to stand by the table. It was the young courtier. He watched us, and his stillness made me think that he too had seen something extraordinary in this African girl.

'After we had returned to our seats, the trader announced the next lots. First was the African. The trader listed her many accomplishments. Two men bid against each other in a desultory sort of way, running the price up to a fairly generous figure. With a bored wave of his hand, the rich young courtier entered the sale. He was trying to suggest that this was an afterthought, that his real interest lay elsewhere, but he did not fool me. I understood the young man's motives well—because I shared them.

'In that brief time, over the chess table, I had fallen under Fikre's spell. It was remarkable—a visceral, all-consuming thing. I simply *knew* that I could not let that man, or any man, take her from me and break her spirit.

'There was a brief flurry of bidding. The young courtier shrugged—named a vast price. The other bidders bowed and withdrew. The hammer fell once. And then my hand was in the air. The courtier raised his eyebrows and lifted his hand again to signal that battle was joined. The onlookers sat up. The courtier frowned and doubled his bid. The price was already more than my annual income. Again I raised my hand. Again the other man doubled the bid. I knew that if I were successful I would have to mortgage everything I owned—even her. It did not stop me. I raised my finger, and called out a figure so large it meant almost nothing. The auctioneer turned to the other man for a response. Again, the price doubled. Again, the bidding was against me—until, without a moment's thought, I doubled again.

'Suddenly, the courtier shrugged and shook his head. It was over. The auction moved on. Fikre, seated on a chair in the middle of the room, glanced at me. I will never forget that look. It was a look of utter contempt.

'I had risked everything to become her owner, yet she displayed no more interest in the matter than if I had been a foolish young suitor calling compliments after her in the street. Yes, I was her owner,' Bey muttered, almost to himself. 'But think, if you can, what that meant. The responsibility—the decisions I had to make. What a dilemma I now faced.'

'Why?' I asked.

'That, my friend, will have to be a story for another occasion.'

ANOTHER STOP, another day of attempting to sleep through the heat. When the sun finally ripened to a deeper red, we loaded up the camels. The sand was no longer quartz-coloured but black; we were in volcanic country now.

Desmond Hammond rode alongside me, a Bedouin shawl wrapped round his neck to protect it from the drifting sand.

'Forgive me, Wallis, but you don't seem much like a planter.'

'Two months ago I would have taken that as the highest praise.'

He grunted. 'Well, there won't be many Europeans where you're going. Let alone many Englishmen. If you have problems . . . you could try getting a message to us via the Bedouin. They're reliable, if a little slow.'

'Thank you,' I said, with genuine gratitude.

'We could do some trading, if you want. I hear there's ebony, gold, diamonds, up there. Anything you need, just send me word.'

'I suppose Bey will be my nearest neighbour in Harar. I expect I'll do some trading through him.'

'Bey . . .' Hammond nodded to where Fikre was walking by Bey's camel, one hand on his stirrup. 'Do you know the story about that woman of his?'

'Yes. He told me last night, in fact. How he bought her in a sale.'

'The Bedouin say Bey is a sentimentalist. They believe he bought the girl for the worst of reasons—because he fell in love.'

'Is that so terrible?'

'It's mixing business and pleasure. Think about it. So he buys her—and don't forget, he paid a fortune for her—what then? Her value depends on two things: one is her virginity. The moment he has her, she loses her value.'

'What's the other thing?'

'Her youth,' Hammond said. 'Rich Arabs buy their wives at puberty, or not much older. By the time a woman's eighteen, she's lost most of her value. At twenty-five, she's worth nothing. So think what it must be like to be Ibrahim Bey. All your wealth is invested in this girl. You're her owner; you can do with her what you like. But you know that the moment you do, she's worthless. So you wait, paralysed, trying to decide. She's losing her value, day by day. A year passes. By now everyone knows of your predicament. You've become a laughing stock—and for a merchant, that's a terrible thing. You can't get credit—how could you, when everyone knows you can't bring yourself to sell your only asset? You know that the only way out is to grasp the nettle and sell her. But something stops you . . . sentiment.'

'He talked about his dilemma,' I said. 'That must be what he meant.'

We trudged through the shifting black scree all night. Sometimes I could imagine that we were trudging through a desert of roasted coffee beans.

THERE WAS NO MOON that night; it was necessary to go slowly. Gradually we became aware of a vibration in the air, which resolved itself into a sound, like distant thunder. It was drums. In the absolute darkness I realised that it was all around us, echoing across the empty desert. We fell silent.

'It must be a raiding party sent by the Galla,' Hammond said at last.

We kept going, but cautiously. Then, out of the darkness, came the sound of chanting. We drew together and travelled four abreast, the camels on the outside. The Bedouin loosened their daggers. Hammond checked his rifle.

'What are they singing?' I asked.

Hammond shrugged. 'It's in Galla.'

Fikre said suddenly, 'It is a war song. They are singing, "Love without kisses is not love, a spear without blood is not a spear."'

It was the first time I had heard her speak English. Her speech was heavily accented—like the English a Frenchman would speak.

'I'll spook them.' Hammond raised his rifle and fired four shots into the air. The camels, alarmed, broke into a trot, then slowed.

The chanting stopped abruptly. Now there was only the squeaking, sighing rustle of the black sand underfoot.

AN HOUR AFTER DAWN we reached Biokobobo, a village of sand-coloured houses nestled among palm trees. Beside it lay three pools of sparkling cobalt blue. The desert beyond sloped up towards the mountains. We were to stay here several days, to recuperate and to let the Galla war party move on. There was a small market—we ate dates, nuts, coconuts, flat breads, goat's cheese. Hector and I swam in one of the wadis; then we found a place to put up the camp beds and unpacked a few essentials.

I tried to write to Emily, but I could not. I could not even remember her properly. I got the Guide out from the luggage and carefully, in the shade of a house, unstopped a fragrance or two. They seemed insipid, insubstantial.

We ate roasted goat sprinkled with *berberi*, a powder made of chilli: once you got the taste it became quite an addiction. Fikre and Mulu did not eat with us, but sat slightly apart. Sometimes Mulu combed Fikre's hair with a steel comb, and at these times they chatted, quietly but animatedly, in a language I did not recognise. I saw her laugh, and deliberately bump his shoulder with hers, as if they were two schoolgirls. He only smiled shyly.

Once or twice she glanced at me, but at those times her eyes were expressionless: there was no sign, now, of that silent despair I had sensed before.

ON THE SECOND MORNING at Biokobobo I woke early. With a sigh I got up, stretched, went outside. In the half-light I saw a slim figure hurrying towards the wadi, wrapped in a blue shawl. Fikre. She went between the palm trees and was lost to sight. Of course: she had been unable to bathe yesterday, when the men were in the pool, so she had come now, for privacy. I skirted round to the other side of the wadi in time to see her unwinding the shawl.

The iron-coloured skin seemed to glow in the early sunshine. She scooped up water to wash her face, droplets of it glittering like diamonds, then dipped under the water. She surfaced, spluttering, and swam directly towards where I was standing.

I stepped forward, deliberately, so she could see me. Just as deliberately, she stood up. The pool was waist deep. The water streamed off her, polishing the black skin. The jewels dripped from her breasts. I felt the thudding of my heartbeat in my neck. For a long moment we looked at each other. Then, on the morning air, there was the sound of goat bells. She turned and slowly waded back to where she had left her robe.

Love without kisses is not love; a spear without blood is not a spear.

I could hear her speaking those words again with that strange, French inflection she had, and I knew that I was becoming obsessed.

'WOULD YOU LIKE some coffee, Robert?'

I looked up. It was Bey. I had been trying to read, but in truth I was unable to concentrate, even before this interruption. 'You have some here?'

'Of course. I never travel without a sack of beans.' He clapped his hands. 'Fikre, Mulu. Coffee, if you please.'

They came hurrying. In no time they had constructed a fire, unloaded the coffee, found the clay pot and the cups, ground the beans. The fire was lit, and from somewhere a tiny dish of rosewater was produced.

All this, I thought, so that we might have coffee.

'Hector?' Bey called.

'Aye, if yer making some I'll join ye.'

Fikre was sweating by the time she came to wash our faces—tiny, silvery beads on her black skin. I stared into her eyes. But they were unreadable.

Then I felt it—a coffee bean, slipped into my hand.

I reached down and touched the only part of her that was out of sight of Bey and Hector, sliding my hand round her ankle, squeezing for a moment.

There was still absolutely nothing in her eyes. But suddenly I notice that she was trembling, as if maintaining this composure cost a terrible effort.

WE BEGAN TO CLIMB towards the mountains. Sometimes we passed strips of land under cultivation. Tall Negroes strolled across the landscape, always in the same posture—a walking stick sideways across their shoulders, both arms crooked over it. The women were wrapped in gauzy robes of scarlet, green or turquoise. The children were naked. Their huts were humps of skins and rugs.

The endless travelling was becoming tedious now, and the mountains seemed as far away at the end of each night's march as at the beginning.

Dear Emily . . . I stared at the page. It was like a salt desert—a white glare from which the sun bounced, dazzling me. I closed my eyes. Her face floated in front of me. She was frowning. 'Robert, pay attention,' she said. I smiled, opened my eyes. But there was the page still, blank and unyielding.

Bey called, 'Coffee!'

I folded the paper and slipped it into an inside pocket. 'Coming.'

Was it my imagination, or was Bey watching Fikre and me with more than usual concentration today as she prepared the coffee? The hooded eyes were solemn, unreadable. Fikre washed our faces, then handed us the cups. There was no chance to pass anything.

But in the bottom of the cup, as I finished, I found it. A single bean, nestling among the grounds.

I spent many hours trying to puzzle out what these gifts meant. Finally, it struck me. The beans were not the message: it was the passing of them secretly that was. She was telling me that she was giving me her trust—the only thing she possessed, the only thing she had to give.

THE NEXT NIGHT, when Bey's attention was distracted by a long discussion with Hector, I dropped back gradually to the rear of the caravan where Fikre was walking. She glanced around, then she too fell back. We were now among the Bedouin, their camels hiding us from the others at the front.

We spoke in code, or rather in trivialities and nonsense.

'Your English is very good,' I murmured.

'My French is better.'

'*Je suis Robert. Robert Wallis.*'

'*Oui. Je sais. Je m'appelle Fikre.* In Abyssinian my name means "love".'

'My name, I'm afraid, doesn't mean anything at all.'

'But at least it's your real name,' she said with a twisted smile. 'Fikre was what my master called me. Like a dog I own nothing, not even my name.'

For the first time I felt the force of what had Bey called her defiance. This tiny girl was like a fierce coil of compressed resentment and fight.

Suddenly she darted forward. Bey was looking back along the caravan with a frown. Within moments there were ten yards between us.

I saw now that I had misjudged her trembling as fear. But the dominant emotion in this girl's life was not terror. It was a deep, all-consuming anger. This girl was filled with loathing for the man who had bought her, and what drew her to me, partly, was the sweet possibility of revenge.

THE DINNER IS a great success. As well as Arthur Brewer, Pinker has invited a number of free marketeers. Emily finds herself sitting directly on the MP's left. When the soup has been cleared, he starts to talk to her. Inevitably the conversation turns to political matters.

'Tell me—as a Liberal,' she says, 'is there not an inherent contradiction within Free Trade?'

He raises his eyebrows. 'In what way?'

'If the price of, say, sugar is being kept artificially high, does that not allow men such as Sir Henry Tate to look after his workers better?'

'It does,' he agrees, 'although it does not oblige him to.'

'Still, if the market has its way, the workers will always be paid the bare minimum. So Free Trade might work against the individual liberty of the workers, by denying them the opportunities that their freedom should bestow. They will not be free of poverty, disease or moral degradation, nor will they have the opportunity or incentive to rise above their current station.'

He looks at her, delighted. 'Miss Pinker—Emily—you have summed up in one eloquent nutshell the debate that is preoccupying our party.'

'Really?' She is absurdly pleased by his compliment.

'Gladstone, of course, thought that if you simply left everything alone—laissez-faire—it would all work out for the best. But what some of us are talking about now is something called constructive liberalism—government safeguarding the freedoms and well-being of the individual.'

'Meaning what, in practical terms?'

He spreads his arms. 'The state would take on many of the responsibilities of enlightened employers. For example, why shouldn't all workers be entitled to some sort of medical care? To sick pay? To a pension, even?'

It is all she can do not to gasp. 'How will it be paid for?'

'We are discussing a sort of national insurance scheme, into which every worker would pay.' He smiles, and glances down the table. 'Some of those whose support we need to enlist are not yet convinced.'

'How can I help?' she cries. It is what she has always believed in: not some dreary compromise but a completely new way forward.

'Would you be prepared to do constituency work?' he asks doubtfully.

'Yes! Please! Anything!'

'What's that?' Pinker calls genially from the head of the table. 'Brewer, what are you scheming with my daughter?'

Arthur keeps his eyes fixed on her. 'She is volunteering, Samuel. I had no idea she was so interested in politics. Of course, with your permission . . .'

Pinker smiles indulgently. 'What she does in her spare time is up to her. If Emily can be useful to you, Arthur, by all means rope her in.'

So now Emily adds Liberal political work to her other interests. Three afternoons a week she takes the train from Waterloo to Ealing to help in Arthur's constituency office. Among the volunteers there are several other suffragists. It is thrilling, this sense of comradeship and endeavour, these people with their different backgrounds all joining forces in the service of an ideal.

For all ideals are linked. That is what she sees now. If you want to change the world for the benefit of all, you make common cause with other idealists. Whether your particular interest is suffrage, prison reform, the poor law or pensions, you are all on the same side.

Arthur is the leader of their little group, but he wears his leadership lightly, always remembering to thank the volunteers for their efforts. Sometimes he takes small groups of helpers to tea at the House of Commons. When he invites Emily, he shows her up to the Ladies' Gallery, where women are allowed to watch the House at work from behind an iron grille. The debate is about the war and Emily is amazed by the boisterous atmosphere.

Arthur asks a question. He makes himself heard with dogged courtesy, and sits down to a grave chorus of 'Here, here'. Afterwards, when she meets him in the lobby, he is flushed with triumph. 'Did you see how I harried the Admiralty?' he cries. She congratulates him.

A group of men hurries past; then one of them turns back. 'Good work, Brewer,' he says, punching him on the arm.

'Thank you, sir,' Arthur says proudly.

The man's twinkling eyes turn to Emily. 'And who is this?' he says.

'Miss Emily Pinker, Sir Henry Campbell-Bannerman. A great reformer.'

'And what do you think of our Parliament, Miss Pinker?' Sir Henry asks.

'It is wonderful,' she says truthfully. 'There seem to be so many people here who are trying to get things done—to move forward.'

'Indeed, although there are almost as many trying to do the reverse,' he says, shaking his head comically. The other men laugh easily.

'Miss Pinker has a special interest in female suffrage,' Brewer says.

'Ah! And as you may have noticed'—Sir Henry indicates the men around him—'all of us here at present are male. We call it the mother of parliaments but exclude those who may be mothers. Perhaps, Miss Pinker, we will see a day when you not only have the vote, but might even be voted for.'

Then with a nod and a smile he has gone, the retinue following in his wake. She can sense the force of his optimism lighting her up like a bulb.

After Arthur has said goodbye to her, escorting her to the Underground station to catch a train back to Limehouse, she feels suddenly bereft.

Now we were climbing into the mountains. Ruined castles perched on inaccessible rocks, their battlements patrolled by eagles and kites. We saw cattle with tall horns in the shape of lyres. Even the villages had changed. Instead of the nomads' humped tents there were settlements built of wood and straw, and the people were round-faced and flat-nosed.

We made camp by a highland lake and bought fish from a villager. Fires were lit; the fish were speared on twigs and roasted. The Bedouin murmured to each other as they ate, then one by one they went to sleep.

The night was cold. I got up and moved closer to the fire. A sudden flare illuminated a face opposite me. She was staring into the embers, her fierce eyes reflecting the flames. Beneath the headcloth, a face of elfin beauty.

'I can think about nothing but you,' I whispered.

'Don't say that,' she said sharply in her lilting accent. 'It's what *he* says.'

'Perhaps it's true.'

She made a scornful noise. 'Did he tell you how he got me?'

'Yes.'

'He likes that story. I don't suppose it ever occurred to him that I would rather have been bought by the other man.'

'Would you?'

She looked at me. 'Before the sale I found a piece of broken glass tile and wrapped it in my clothes. When my new owner tried to take what he had paid for, I planned to use it to cut first his throat and then my own.'

Her eyes turned back to the flames. 'Night after night I waited. But Bey did not come. That could only mean he was going to sell me. But he did not do that either. I was puzzled . . . and then I began to see. He wanted to own me, but he also wanted to preserve me, like some precious object that he alone may take out of its box, to gloat over and then put back.'

She turned to look at me, raising her chin. In the half-light I could see her teeth, very white, behind her open lips.

I leaned towards her. A moment's hesitation, and then my mouth touched hers. She took my head in her hands, whispered breathlessly, 'They can buy me and sell me. But my heart is my own.'

We kissed again, more deeply. She looked around at the sleeping shapes. 'We must be careful,' she whispered. 'People have died for less.' She took our blankets and pulled them over our heads, covering us.

There, in the darkness—in the cave of the blankets, like a child's game—there was the smell of her breath: myrrh, cinnamon, musk . . . and the taste of her skin, the sweet warmth of a kiss, the sounds she made, her gasps.

And the words she whispered breathlessly as she nuzzled my lips: 'I have been waiting all my life for you.'

ANOTHER DAY'S TRAVEL. But the landscape had changed again. Now the hillsides were terraced for agriculture. From the high passes, looking down, it was as if someone had run a giant comb over the earth.

Sometimes I glimpsed a stand or two of a bush with dark, waxy leaves. Hector nudged me and grunted with satisfaction. 'See that? Coffee.'

Intrigued, I rode my mount alongside a bush to examine it more closely. The plant was dotted with tiny white blossom, the petals plump with perfumed sap. When I crushed them between my fingers, the aroma was of coffee, but with a faint note of honeysuckle and jasmine. Underneath each branch hung pendulous yellow cherries, fat and full of pulp. I pulled one off and bit it experimentally. But the flesh was bitter, astringent.

The scent, I discovered, was strongest in the evening. As night fell, so tendrils of that distinctive coffee-bush aroma seemed to hang in the darkness, and float, gossamer-like, from place to place on the still air.

THE DAYS WERE HOT, stifling, windless. My eyelids drooped as if under the effect of some drug. At the next stop, I could talk to Fikre only once. As we were unloading, we found ourselves hidden from the others by the camels.

'In Harar there is a warehouse Bey is trying to sublet,' she said urgently. 'It used to belong to a French coffee merchant. Say that you will take it.'

'Very well.'

The camels wheeled about, and before anyone could see us she was gone.

I WAS TOWARDS the back of the column, so I did not see at first why the caravan had halted. I join the others, who had drawn up on a ridge.

Below us, nestled in the bowl of a fertile plain, was a great lake. Beyond the lake was a town. Even at that distance we could see the walls and fortifications that surrounded it, the ragged flags fluttering from its rooftops, the brown clay houses and the white onion-shaped minarets—and the scavenging birds that wheeled over it endlessly, like flies circling a rotten fruit.

'Harar,' Bey said unnecessarily. 'We have arrived.'

YOU SMELT IT as soon as you entered through the wooden gate: the pungent, earthy smell of roasting beans, wafting from a dozen windows. In the bazaar, stalls were piled high with jute sacks, their contents spilling from them like polished beads. This was a city of coffee.

Ibrahim took me round the French merchant's house, a fine two-storey building overlooking the market. According to Bey, the merchant had arrived in Africa as a young man, eager to make his fortune in the coffee business, but got mixed up in some dubious schemes. Eventually he had gone back to Marseilles. His sister had later written to say that he had died, and Bey was only too pleased when I said I would take on the lease.

Meanwhile, Hector engaged a headman, Jimo, with experience of coffee farming. My Scottish companion refused to stay in Harar a moment longer than was absolutely necessary.

'We'll leave tomorrow. As soon as we've bought our seeds.'

'A few days won't make any difference, surely?'

'That's where you're wrong. You're a farmer now, Robert, you have to start working to the seasons. The rains—'

'Oh, the rains. I keep forgetting the rains.'

He muttered an expletive under his breath as he turned away.

In the market I found not only coffee but saffron, indigo and civet musk, along with a dozen fruits I had never seen before. I also found Fikre, buying food. She was wearing a dark red robe, the top looped over her hair. She turned her head, and my pulse quickened at the sight of that perfect profile.

'You must not be seen with me,' she murmured, picking up a mango and pressing it with her slim, dark fingers.

'I've taken the French merchant's house,' I said. 'Can you meet me there?'

She gave the seller some coins. 'I'll try to come at dusk.'

Then she was gone—a dark red robe slipping into the shadows.

AT DUSK I WAITED. I passed the time by wandering around. There were dozens of small wasps' nests in the corners of the rooms and a parrot was nesting under one of the ceilings, the floor below spattered with its guano.

A sound. I looked round. She was there, hurrying towards me, her feet bare on the wooden floor. Her eyes, under the red hood, were bright. She stopped. For a moment we stared at each other. Then I opened my arms and with a gasp she ran to me. She had been working among Bey's sacks all day, and her lips and neck still carried the smoky flavour of roasting coffee beans.

Eventually she pulled away. 'I didn't realise it would be like this.' She placed a hand on my cheek. 'That I would want you so much. Like hunger.'

I felt her fingers slipping under my shirt, cool on my bare skin.

'I can't stay,' she said. 'I have only a few minutes, but I had to see you.'

We kissed again and I pushed against her, on fire.

'We have to wait,' she said, almost to herself.

'Wait for what?' I gasped.

The words were slipped in between kisses. 'For him to go away. Back to the coast with his coffee. Then I shall give myself to you. It's the only way.'

Her expression was triumphant. She had it all worked out. She was going to sleep with me—to shatter her precious virginity. Bey's investment would be wiped out. This would be her grand revenge on the man who bought her.

'When he finds out, he'll be furious.'

'Yes,' she said. 'He will kill me. But he's killing me anyway, keeping me like this. And if we can have one night . . .' she looked into my eyes . . . 'it will be worth it. At least I will die knowing what love is.'

I was sick with apprehension. 'There must be a less dangerous way.'

She shook her head. 'Don't worry, he will never know it was you. Even if they torture me before I die.'

'You don't have to die,' I said urgently. 'Listen, Fikre. No one has to die.'

'A night of love, and then death. It's enough,' she whispered.

'No. Fikre, I promise I will think of something—'

'Kiss me,' she said. I did. 'I am ready for what he will do to me. We have to wait until he goes away. Just until then.'

With a groan I released her. She stepped away from me, looked back one last time. Then all that was left was her scent—coffee, rosewater and spice.

Seven

Dawn rises over the jungle, light and sound sweeping through the canopy together, the first glimmers of day greeted by a cacophony of calls, screeches, roars and rattles. Up on the hill, the white men snore on their camp beds. In the native village, the women put wood on the communal fire, then pound coffee before waking their husbands. The dawn is chilly: breakfast is taken squatting round the fire, wrapped in blankets.

There is only one topic of conversation: the visitors. White men have passed through the valley before, but these are different: they have built a house. True, it is a bad house—too close to the stream, so it will be infested with ants when the rains come, and too close to the ravine, so their animals will break their legs—but still a house. What do they want? No one knows.

One among them is particularly uneasy. Kiku, the medicine woman, sits on her own, deep in thought. It is true that the white men do not seem aggressive, but their arrival might herald something. Perhaps her foreboding comes from the *ayyanaa*, the spirits of the forest, who sometimes tell her things that cannot otherwise be known. So she sits apart, trying to listen to the forest.

'I will tell you what it is,' a young man called Bayanna says. 'They have come to kill the leopard.'

There is a general nodding. Of course—the leopard. For months now there have been sightings of a leopard in the valley, causing those with young children great anxiety. If the white men kill it, everyone will be safer. The only person in the village who has killed a leopard is Tahomen, their headman, and that was twenty years ago, when he was a young man. Because they want the leopard to be the reason the white men have come, this hope quickly turns to agreement, and agreement to certainty, so that soon everything is settled except who will show the strangers where best to hunt.

Suddenly they hear a crashing sound, followed by an irregular thumping on the path as two people wearing boots, and a third who is not wearing boots but who is equally unused to walking through the forest, approach the village. Some of the women take their children and hurry into their huts for safety; others take their children and hurry outside, the better to see what is going on. The crashing has by now been augmented by the sound of voices, booming and guttural, speaking words the villagers cannot understand.

'It be here somewhere, sah,' one voice is saying.

'I expect they'll have fled intae the trees, in any case,' another says confidently. 'Your native mind, Wallis, does not function like your working man's back home. It has been proven that their blood is thinner and their methods consequently more lethargic. Och, what's that in there?'

'It looks to me as if we have found their habitation, Hector.'

The villagers watch, nonplussed, as three men stride into the clearing. Two are immensely tall, white-skinned, with outlandish clothes; one of these is rendered even more alarming by his bushy red beard, while the other is wearing a green suit and a white pith helmet. The third man, a dark-skinned Adari, is wearing a robe of patterned cloth and carrying a long stick.

'Berrah well,' he says, gazing contemptuously at the villagers. 'Who be headman this savage place?'

'Just a minute, Jimo,' the red-haired man says. He strides forward. 'Nae listen, all of ye,' he booms. 'We have come here'—he points at the ground—'to grow coffee.' He points at the coffee that one of the villagers has been drinking from a wooden cup. 'If you work for us, you will be well paid.'

There is a short silence. Bayanna says, 'I think he wants coffee before he goes to shoot the leopard.' The villagers nod, relieved. Of course! Bayanna says helpfully to the visitors, 'I will lead you to the beast.' Aware that they do not understand what he is saying, he points to Tahomen's leopard tunic and mimes throwing a spear. 'Dish-dash?' he says hopefully.

'Dish-dash, is it?' the red-haired man chuckles. 'Excellent. I thought we would be able to strike a deal with these fellows. Tell them: tomorrow we chop forest.' He begins miming the actions of a man chopping a tree, or possibly beating a mortally wounded leopard to death with a club.

Another young man is by now disputing Bayanna's right to lead the white men to the leopard. 'Me! Me! I take you to the leopard!' he interrupts, jumping to his feet. He points at himself, then begins enthusiastically miming the clubbing of leopards.

'Capital,' the red-haired man booms. 'It appears we have our first woodsman. And you, sir? Yes? And you?'

Other young men now push themselves forward, eager to be handsomely rewarded for leading the white men to the leopard. 'You see, Wallis,' the red-haired man says, turning to his companion, 'how the universal language of Commerce breaks down barriers? Is it not wonderful to behold?'

'Absolutely,' the other white man says doubtfully. 'Er . . . should we explain to them that we have bought this land? That we are now, so to speak, their landlords?'

'I doubt whether that'll be a concept their primitive minds can grasp.' The red-haired man points to the woods. 'Forest—all of it—chop!' he shouts.

Jimo starts to move among the young men, dispensing cards. Each card, he explains, is divided into thirty days. Each day the men chop trees, they will have their card marked, and when they have accumulated a full month's worth of marks, they will be paid. The young men of the hunting party understand him perfectly—these are the tickets that prove you have been chosen as a champion leopard tracker. Some of them break into a dance, in which they jump up and down energetically and mime the leopard's death.

'Aha!' the red-haired man cries. 'We have been here just a few moments, but see how we have galvanised them! This forest will be cleared in no time!'

THE NIGHT WE ARRIVED, the young men of the village held some kind of dance. They were half a mile away from our camp, but it seemed as though they were deliberately making as much noise as possible.

'Christ, what a din,' Hector grumbled in his camp bed. 'Don't they realise they'll be working tomorrow?'

In my own camp bed, I was silent for a moment, thinking. 'Odd, isn't it,' I said at last, 'that they've never tried to cultivate this coffee themselves?'

'Odd? Not really. They've never had anyone like us to show them how.'

'But nothing they do is remotely like farming, is it?' I persisted. 'They don't seem to have any desire to . . . tame the jungle. I'm just wondering why not. Whether perhaps they might have tried it, and found it hasn't worked. You know—almost as if they might know something we don't.'

Hector snorted. 'You're looking at it the wrong way round, Wallis. It's us that knows something they dinnae.' He reached out to the pressure lamp that burned dimly on the packing case between us. 'Time to turn in.'

The hiss of the lamp died; darkness filled the mud hut. The drums and shouts from the native village seemed louder than ever.

'Good night, Hector.'

'Gu'night.'

I dreamed of Fikre, of her slender black body crouching above me, her clear pale eyes holding mine. 'Soon,' she whispered. 'Very soon. When Bey leaves Harar.' I half woke. In the darkness, an animal laughed at me. Down in the village, the endless throb of the drums was like a heartbeat.

THE VILLAGERS are getting drunk on fermented beer. The young men enthusiastically dance the dance of leopard-killing, but really they are dancing to impress the young women, who in turn are dancing the great cheer that the women make when the body of a leopard is brought back to the village, which was really a dance of encouragement to the men. Kiku sits to one side, watching. Her husband comes over and sits down next to her.

'You do not dance,' Tahomen says.

'I'm too old to dance,' she answers.

Tahomen grunts. 'Of course you're not. That's ridiculous.' They sit in silence for a little while. Then he says, 'This leopard. Do you really think the white men have come all the way here just to help us kill it?'

She shrugs noncommittally.

'It bothers me too,' he says. He spits into the fire. 'In any case, I'm glad they don't want the leopard. I'm rather hoping to take care of that myself.'

'You!'

'Yes. Why not?'

'People in your age-clan should leave the hunting to the younger men.'

'You think I'm too old?' Tahomen says in mock astonishment. 'Is that what people say, that I'm too old to kill another leopard?'

She sighs.

Tahomen spits expertly into the fire again. 'There's more than one way to catch a leopard, in any case,' he says thoughtfully.

'Yes. And all of them end in the people trying them getting killed.'

'Well, we shall see.'

WELL BEFORE DAYBREAK, a line of hung-over villagers waits with Jimo outside the white men's camp. Many have daubed themselves with magical patterns; some have even painted their faces to represent the whiskers and spots of the leopard. Some carry axes, some clubs, some spears.

'Like children,' the red-haired man sighs as he steps towards them. 'Spears to chop trees! Imagine! Jimo, get some more axes out of the store.'

When all the men have been equipped, the chopping party files into the jungle, the red-haired man leading them uphill until he reaches the highest point. He points at the trees. 'Here! Cut these!'

The villagers look at each other. If they stop to cut these trees down, there will certainly be no hope of finding the leopard today.

'Come on, boy,' Jimo says, roughly pushing one of the younger men towards a tree. Reluctantly, he hoists his axe and begins to chop.

'Good! Next boy! Chop!' Jimo shouts, leading the next man to the adjacent tree. Soon he has a line of villagers all hard at work chopping trees.

When the trees are almost chopped through, the red-haired man has Jimo move the men on to the next row down. Again they chop until the trunks are almost severed, then stop. The villagers work sullenly now—they have realised there is to be no leopard hunt after all. They grunt to each other: what can all this wood be for? Why are they leaving the trees half severed?

They move forward another row. Now one of the trees is a *qiltu*, a sycamore. Automatically the villagers part, moving to left and right.

'Over there!' the red-haired man calls. 'They missed one.'

Jimo leads one of the men to the sycamore tree. 'Chop!' he commands.

The man looks puzzled, then alarmed. The other villagers halt their own work to speak to the white men. This, they explain, is a *qiltu*—a tree sacred to women, from which the women's *siqqee*, or ritual sticks, are made.

'Make them stop jabbering,' the red-haired man says to Jimo, who drives the protesting villagers back to their own trees. 'Robert! Time to show them that we don't ask them to do anything we're not prepared to do ourselves.' He points to the base of the tree. 'You take that side.'

The villagers watch in appalled silence as the white men's axes split wood. Both men are sweating profusely by the time the job is done—or rather, almost done: once again, a narrow cone is left at the heart of the tree.

It is early afternoon when the red-haired man finally calls a halt. By now some forty trees have been half chopped. They all trudge back up the hill, where the cutters are ordered to finish off the very first tree they worked on. With a great crash it falls—but its way is impeded by the tree below, which somehow bears its weight. That tree too is felled, and that too leans against its neighbour on the downhill side. The third tree is tall and top-heavy. As it comes crashing down, the trunk splinters; men leap away as its vast bulk kicks into the air. Its branches slam into the next tree down and, with a crack, that tree gives under its weight—and then the next does the same, and the next, the hillside turning into a tidal wave of tumbling trunks and churning branches. The sound ripples like thunder away from the cutters, then echoes from every side of the valley. Birds fling themselves upwards: dust explodes through the falling branches: everything seems to settle in slow motion.

'Now tha',' says the red-haired man, gazing with satisfaction at the exposed hillside, 'is the best damn sight in the whole damn world.'

THAT NIGHT the villagers sit round the fire and discuss what happened. It is plain to everyone that there is to be no leopard hunting; it is the forest itself that the white men have come to slay. Yet what does it mean when a whole forest is destroyed? When a person dies, their spirit climbs into a tree: when a tree is felled, its spirit joins the spirits of the other trees around it: what will happen now to the thousands of spirits the white men have set loose?

Some of the older men believe that the young men should withdraw their labour. For the younger men, though, what is important is that the white men have promised to reward them for their help. They can sense that everything is about to change, and see that it might be to their advantage. Instead of being at the mercy of the jungle, now they will be able to control it, just like the white men. That they can work for people with such powers, and become rich at the same time, is an unimaginable piece of good fortune.

WITHOUT THE PROTECTION of the big trees, the delicate shoots and creepers of the forest floor quickly shrivelled in the sun, and the fallen wood was soon ready for burning. When the wind was coming from the right direction, Hector organised the men to light fires along the northern edge of the valley.

If the felling had been spectacular, the burning was something else again. The fire ran back and forth across the cleared land, filling it with a blazing, crackling forest of flame that reached almost as high as the original canopy.

The natives watched with expressions of terror, and they carried out our instructions with increasing reluctance. Whatever I thought of Hector personally, I was glad he was there. I would have been incapable without him.

After the burning, the hillsides seemed covered in smoking grey snow. Charred trunks poked out here and there, while a couple of giant trees that had somehow survived stood alone, their lower branches shrivelled like lace.

'Best fertiliser in the world,' Hector said, reaching down into a drift of ash and rubbing some in his hands. 'Coffee exhausts even the best ground, Robert: you're lucky to have plenty of land here. Come on, let's go home.'

Home was 'Wallis Castle', a squalid hut of mud and grass thatch, about fourteen feet in diameter, in which Hector and I were living like two tinkers. The thatch rustled all night long, and occasionally small poisonous wriggling things dropped out of it to visit us.

Our chief enemy was boredom. Darkness came early in the tropics, and we had only enough fuel to use our kerosene lamps for an hour each night. Hector surprised me by asking me to read aloud from my small library. I began with *The Importance of Being Earnest*, and eventually he took the book from me and performed a rather fine Gwendolyn. Heaven knows what Jimo, Kuma and the other natives must have made of it, the strange Scottish falsetto emerging from our hut, the nocturnal gales of laughter, and the rapturous applause with which he greeted my Lady Bracknell.

After the lamps had been turned off for the night, and the hut filled with the music of the jungle at night, Fikre would appear in my imagination, stepping towards my bed on silent feet, whispering, 'Soon . . .'

Emily was—quite literally—a distant memory. It was like my pocket watch, which I had tried to keep to European time. Once it wound down, there was no easy way to reset it. It seemed easier to adapt to the local hours, then to abandon the use of a watch altogether. I did not suddenly fall out of love with Emily, but the part of my heart that should have kept ticking away with the thought of her ran down and somehow never got restarted.

I dropped various hints to Hector that I would need to go into Harar soon, all of which he ignored. Then one night, soon after we had turned in, we heard a great commotion outside. Jimo came running into the hut, gabbling, 'Massa come one time, one time. *Marrano* eat coffee babies.'

We grabbed our rifles and headed outside. There was a little moon, and we could see shapes crashing around in the nursery beds. As we got closer we made out a whole family of warthogs, grunting ecstatically as they grubbed through our precious seedlings.

We chased them off and set Jimo to stand guard. In the morning we could see that they had wrecked the crop. Hector blamed himself for the disaster.

'I should have made fences.' He sighed. 'Well, it looks as if ye'll get your trip to Harar after all, Robert. This will all need to be replaced.'

'What a pity,' I said, although inwardly I was exultant. 'I'll go tomorrow.'

ONCE IN HARAR, I alerted Fikre to my presence by sending her a note, claiming to need her help with some translation. A servant brought her reply—something equally innocuous. There was no reference to Bey: that meant he was away. The gods were smiling on us.

The anticipation was unbearable. I passed the time improvising a bed from sacks of coffee, spread with silk shawls. It was surprisingly comfortable.

And then—so lightly I barely caught the sound—the door downstairs opened. I heard soft footsteps on the stairs.

Her beauty, each time I saw her, was still a shock. Now that we were finally together, it was as if we neither of us wanted to begin. She made me coffee as she had done in the desert, watching me as I drank the first cup.

Desire suddenly overwhelmed me. I unwound the robe from her body, spinning her round until she was naked before me. I, who had made love to many women, had known nothing like this: what it was to love someone whose passion was as great as my own, who gasped with pleasure at my every touch. She smelt of coffee: there was the taste of it in every kiss . . .

Later there was more love, and then she lay in my arms and we talked. The expression in her eyes was one of mingled triumph and fury as she said, 'Whatever happens now, I have won.'

'But Bey must never hear,' I said. Now that the madness of our coupling was over, it was hard not to be fearful. I had taken another man's woman, violated his property and ruined his investment. Bey would know that the only way to regain credibility would be to exact an impressive revenge.

I was struck by the fact that what we had done could not be undone. It was no use saying, 'We must stop this before it is too late.' It already was too late. We had done the single, terrible thing that would condemn us both.

We made love again, slowly, all urgency gone. Afterwards we slept, and woke together, and lay in an unspoken union of smiles and silence.

'We will think of something,' she said, breaking into my thoughts. She stroked my stomach with the backs of her fingers, lightly. 'When I first saw you, my only thought was that it would be a wonderful revenge on Ibrahim. But now . . .' one finger circled my navel gently . . . 'now that I have you—now that I've got this—I don't want it to end.'

'Nor do I. But it's hard to see how we can stop him from finding out.'

'Perhaps I can seduce him. Then he will think that *he* deflowered me.'

I frowned. 'He would know you were not a virgin.'

'There are ways of pretending. It wouldn't fool a doctor, but it would fool a man in lust, a man who believed what he wanted to believe.'

'Too risky. Besides, imagine if it didn't work—if he refused you. He'd know for sure that something was up.'

'What, then?'

'I don't know. I'll think of something.' It was like a refrain—one or other of us was always saying it: *I'll think of something.* The words reassured, like a mother's soothing comforts: *Don't worry. Go back to sleep. It'll be all right.* It would not be all right, but the words worked their magic all the same.

'I MUST SAY,' Hector observed one morning, weeks later, as we walked between the work gangs, 'you're taking this remarkably well, Robert. I confess I thought you'd be pining for your old Regent Street haunts by now.'

'Regent Street? I don't miss Regent Street in the slightest. In fact, my old life in England seems remarkably dull, compared with here.'

'Is that so? Then we'll make an adventurer of you yet.'

'Speaking of which, though,' I said casually, 'I'll need to go into Harar again soon. It'll be difficult to leave the farm after you've shipped out, so I should do as much trading as I can before you go, wouldn't you say?'

Reluctantly he said, 'I suppose so.'

'Good. That's settled, then—I'll go on Sunday.'

We had reached the brow of the hill. Below us, the gangs—each group wearing smocks of a specified colour—were digging the planting pits, one every six feet, along the lines of white tape we had marked out. Hector gazed down at them. 'Look at those lines, Robert. When all's said and done, Civilisation is just straight lines and white paint.'

A sound came towards us through the jungle—the low, desultory chanting of men who sing to keep a marching rhythm. Everyone stopped work.

'No stop!' Jimo shouted. The villagers turned back to their digging.

Through the trees, two long lines of men were coming towards us. No, not just men—there were women too, laden down with cooking pans, bags of maize, even small children tied in papooses round their backs. They were all short and swarthy, with wavy hair and heavy eyebrows.

'The coolies,' Hector announced. 'I wondered when they'd get here.'

The front man of each column gave a command and the newcomers stopped, swinging their packs to the ground and crouching beside them.

'Where have they come from?' I asked, puzzled.

'Ceylon. They're Indians—Tamils. Fantastic workers.'

'But how have they got here?'

'We ordered them, of course.' Hector strode up the slope towards the men's leader. He was standing waiting for us, his head lowered respectfully.

'You had them shipped over?'

Hector extended his hand to the head Tamil, who placed in it a sheaf of grubby papers. 'I had them recruited. They pay their own passage.'

'I'm surprised they could afford it.'

'They can't.' Hector sighed impatiently. 'There is no work for them now in Ceylon. So they have signed on with a gang-master to be shipped here. The cost of their sea-passage will be deducted from their earnings. Now we will buy their contracts from the gang-master, so that his expenses are covered, and the Tamils will get work and food, and everyone will be happy.'

'I see,' I said, though in truth I still did not understand.

The Tamils, it turned out, were a surly lot. But I could not deny that they were remarkable workers. Within days they had erected three large huts—one for the men to sleep in, another for the women and one where the coffee beans would be sorted. When they started digging planting pits they managed three hundred yards for every sixty covered by the locals.

'It is because they are indentured,' Hector said. 'They work hard because they have to—because they owe money.'

A few days later he assembled the African villagers in our camp.

From the crate that held our farm tools, he took out a couple of European-made axes. 'These are good axes—very expensive,' he said. 'They cost hundreds of rupees. Ordinarily, none of you would be able to afford one.'

Jimo translated this: there was a general nodding.

'But if you agree to work until our coffee harvest comes, we will give each of you an axe of your own, or for women, a hoe.'

Jimo translated again. This time there was a puzzled silence.

'You do not have to give us any money now,' Hector explained. 'You will pay us back one rupee a week, from your wages.'

Jimo translated. Now there was a hubbub of noise. Those who had grasped the concept were explaining it to their slower neighbours. Others leapt up to examine the axe, touching the smooth, lathe-turned haft, the mirror-like surface of the head, the greased cutting edge, murmuring with amazement.

'There is more,' Hector shouted over the noise. 'See! Over here!' He went to the crate containing our trade goods. 'Fish-hooks! Mirrors! They are all available on credit to those who sign up!' He held up a glass necklace and shook it. 'See?' It was plucked from his hand by a wondering villager.

He turned to me with an expression of satisfaction. 'They'll all agree. How can they not? From their point of view, it's the best offer they've ever had.'

IN THE VILLAGE tonight there is plenty to talk about.

'What will happen to the forest, once we all have these axes?' Kiku asks plaintively. 'What will happen to the trees? We will lose *saafu*,' she says, speaking of the balance and reciprocity that is so vital to their people.

'But there are many trees, and so few of us,' someone says. 'It seems only right that we should be able to chop them down. Then we will have made more *saafu*, not less, because the numbers will be more evenly balanced.' It is Alaya, Tahomen's new wife, who speaks, and to Kiku's annoyance the others seem to be impressed by Alaya's logic.

'Saying that we shouldn't use axes to chop trees—isn't that like saying that we shouldn't use pots to carry water?' someone else adds. 'We have enough work to do already without making life more difficult.'

The other women nod. Kiku knows that you cannot stop these changes, any more than you can stop water when it wants to flow downhill. But she is uneasy: she does not know where it will all end.

The next day they all sign up for the new contracts, even Tahomen. But as she looks at the necklaces that now adorn each woman's neck, Kiku cannot help thinking that they look more like the chains worn by slaves than anything the villagers have ever fashioned from the forest.

Eight

Pinker's has employed an American advertising agency, J. Walter Thompson, to help sell its coffee to the female market. In one of the advertisements, the headline reads: 'EVERY HUSBAND'S RIGHT—EVERY WOMAN'S DUTY.' In smaller type below, it says: 'Don't disappoint him! Make the right choice—choose Castle!' Rather to Emily's irritation, the campaign is a great success. Whether it is the condescending message or simply that Pinker's has drawn attention to itself, she is not certain, but Castle Coffee is now the best-selling packed coffee in the grocers' stores. There has been a massive expansion in that sector, with people like Thomas Lipton and John James Sainsbury opening vast new emporia as aggressively as Pinker's is expanding its coffee business, and the new way of marketing suits all parties. Sainsbury can place an order for Castle knowing he will get exactly the same product in every one of his shops, while Pinker knows the demand his advertising is creating can be satisfied through sufficient outlets. When Lipton suggests a version of Castle that is pre-ground, Pinker readily agrees.

'But pre-ground coffee will not last as long, or taste so good, as beans freshly prepared,' Emily points out.

'Perhaps there is a small difference—but not every woman has leisure to grind coffee these days. So many women have jobs, Emily. You would not want women to be penalised for working, would you?'

Of course she would not, so she drops her objections—not that he would take much notice of her opinion anyway. Her father has an army of advisers now. From the ledgers, she can tell that the expansion is being fuelled by ever-increasing quantities of the cheaper stuff, leavened with a sprinkling of good arabica. True, the product is cheaper too—just enough to undercut Howell's—but most of the money they save on raw materials is going to fund the new advertisements. Expansion, not profit, has become the objective.

The only part of their empire that does not thrive is the Temperance Taverns. Sometimes Emily accompanies her father on visits to these establishments, trying to puzzle out the problem.

'It cannot be the concept,' Pinker says, looking around at one almost deserted coffee house. 'Look at Lyons—their cafés seem always to be full.'

'But Lyons tea shops are on busy streets, so women can stop off for a few minutes during shopping trips. Our taverns are in residential areas.'

'That is because they were converted from public houses.' Her father sighs. 'Still, if they cannot make money, we shall have to close them down.'

'But I thought the taverns were the reason—the reason for everything?' she says, puzzled. 'Or is Temperance no longer your aim?'

Pinker purses his lips. 'Temperance is the objective, of course. But perhaps the means will be different—perhaps it will be packet coffee that will change the working man's habits.'

'While there are public houses, there will be drunks,' she reminds him.

He shrugs. 'Perhaps. But a business that does not make money cannot be the instrument of change. We will do nothing yet. The market may turn.'

I LAY IN FIKRE'S ARMS, sated. Every time either of us moved it released new wafts of scent—she had perfumed her skin with myrrh smoke before she came to meet me, standing naked over a brazier as the Bedouin women did, and now the fragrance mingled with the liquors of our lovemaking, the smell of sackcloth and the aroma of coffee beans from our impromptu bed.

'I've had an idea,' Fikre said.

'Hmm?' I was drifting off to sleep.

Something hard and light and dry dribbled between my teeth. I spluttered and opened my eyes. She was pouring coffee beans into my mouth from her hand. She grinned and ate the rest herself, chewing them straight from her palm with quick, fierce movements of her teeth, like a cat crunching bones.

'You eat unground beans?' I said.

She nodded. 'They're good.'

I tried some. She was right—they were good: the pure taste of coffee.

'And besides, you needed to wake up.' She paused. 'My idea. I've decided we must kill Ibrahim. It's the only way.'

'How would we do a thing like that?'

'You must hire a gang of *bashibazuks*—the mercenaries. They will kill him and then you and I can be together.'

'Unfortunately, you're mortgaged. He told me so in the desert. Even if he died, the moneylenders would take you to cover the debt.'

Her eyes flashed. 'How I hate him.' She reached out to stroke my face. 'Now that I have you—now I've got *this*—I want to live. To be with you.'

'I'll think of something,' I promised. That comforting lie again.

IN THE QUIET of the night there is a scream. Kiku rushes out of her hut.

Alaya is stumbling down the path from the white man's camp, one hand clutched to her mouth. They help her inside one of the huts, and little by little the story comes out.

A man approached her, saying he had a gift for her, and sure enough he gave her a necklace. But she did not want to give him what he wanted in return, so he knocked her to the ground, then took what he wanted by force.

'What man was this?' Kiku asks. 'Who did this thing to you?'

'Vanyata Ananthan,' Alaya whispers.

It is the Tamils' foreman. This complicates the situation. The workers fear the foremen more than they fear Massa Crannach or Massa Wallis. It is the foremen who assign jobs, who dock your wages if you do not do as they want.

Kiku knows that if the villagers do not act together, their lives will become impossible. She goes into her hut and finds her *siqqee* stick.

Every woman has a *siqqee* made of *qiltu*—the women's tree. She is given it by her mother, and through it flows all the power of the women who came before her. Just to hold it gives her the strength to endure. If a woman needs help in an emergency, all she has to do is to take her stick, step out of her hut and shout *siqqee*. It is a kind of alarm.

Kiku touches her stick to her forehead, gathering its strength. Then she goes outside and shouts, 'Daughter of woman, do you hear?'

There is silence. Then, from one hut, an answering shout, 'I have heard!'

'I have heard!' another voice shouts.

From every direction women are coming at a run. They gather round Kiku and Alaya in a group, facing outwards with their sticks raised, chanting, 'Daughter of woman, do you hear?' until every woman in the village is there. The men gather round them, shaking their heads.

Silence falls as they wait for Kiku to speak. '*Saafu* has been lost,' she says. 'First the forest was violated. Some of the men have said it is a good thing to control the trees with axes. But how will that restore *saafu*? *Saafu* means us and the forest living together, with neither having the upper hand.'

Some of her audience are nodding, but Kiku can tell that the younger men are not convinced. 'Now my sister Alaya has been attacked,' she says. 'Today it was Alaya; tomorrow it could be the wives or daughters of any of you. And that is why you must say to the white man that we will not work for him any more. Instead of teaching us his bad ways, he must let us teach him the way of *saafu*. Until then, the women are going to cross the water.'

Crossing the water—that is ritual language. It means that the women are going to withdraw from the life of the village. There will be no childcare, no cooking, no family life until peace is re-established.

Kiku leads the women away, into the jungle. As they pass the men, Tahomen stands up and says formally, 'Without women the fire will go out. We men will do what we need to restore *saafu*.'

I RETURNED FROM HARAR to find the plantation in a state of uproar. It seemed the African workers had called some kind of strike.

Hector was keen to restore order quickly. 'That man should not have done what he did, of course, but it's actually quite timely,' he said. 'We must show these people that their obligation is what matters, not their own feelings.'

A court was assembled. The shamefaced Tamil was brought before it and readily confessed what he had done. For this he was fined ten rupees.

'So,' Hector said, looking round at the watching villagers, 'this matter is settled. You can all return to work.'

Even when this had been translated, the villagers did not move.

'What's the difficulty now, Jimo?' Hector demanded.

After some conferring, Jimo reported that the villagers wanted the fine to be paid to them, rather than to the court.

'Absolutely not,' Hector said. 'That is not how our justice system works.'

'And they want the man sent away, sah,' Jimo said softly.

'What? Out of the question. He has paid his fine. That is an end to it.'

It seemed it was not. Even when Hector angrily dismissed the court, the villagers refused to return to work.

'Find me the lassie,' Hector said impatiently.

Alaya was brought before him and ordered to shake the Tamil's hand to show that there were no hard feelings. She stood there, eyes lowered, refusing to do any such thing. When the man took her limp hand and shook it, the watching villagers looked even more mutinous than before.

Hector strode angrily into the circle of villagers. 'Justice has been done,' he shouted. 'If you do not work, you will be in breach of your contracts.' He took a hoe and thrust it into the girl's hand. 'Now go. Back to work.'

No one moved.

'Jimo—beat her,' Hector snapped. 'Twelve lashes with the whip. Then choose one of the men and give him the same.'

Jimo motioned to two of the Tamils, who held Alaya while he struck her across the back. She screamed but made no attempt to move. When she was released she sank to her knees. The Tamils dragged a man into the circle. He too was given a dozen strokes. Then another villager was seized—

'Hector,' I said, repulsed. 'For God's sake, man. You can't beat them all.'

'Of course I can.' He turned to me. 'Robert, this is your plantation. How will you keep order when I'm gone if you won't show them who's in charge?'

Jimo looked from one to the other of us, waiting for orders.

'It's time you took some responsibility for this place, Robert. What's it to be? Will you beat them, or do you have a better idea?' Hector demanded.

I hesitated. Emily would have had a better idea—would have thrown herself between the beater and his victim if necessary. But what did I know of plantation work? I relied on Hector to show me how it should be done.

'Very well,' I said heavily. 'If you have to beat the wretches, beat them.'

'Carry on, Jimo.'

Jimo raised his stick and brought it down on the man's back, whipping him for the allotted number of blows. When he went to the next villager, the man raised his hands in a gesture of submission and muttered something.

'He says he will work, sah,' the overseer reported.

'Good.' Hector turned to the villagers. 'Who's next? You—will you work? You? And you? Excellent.'

In two weeks, I thought, I will be back in Harar with Fikre.

AFTER THE BREAKING of the strike, Hector instituted some changes. The villagers' round huts were taken down, and the flat area on which they had stood was cleared for use as a drying floor. The villagers were installed in long wooden huts like the Tamils', the men in one hut and the women in another, so that, as Hector said, there were no Africans and Indians any more, only plantation workers.

As soon as I could I returned to Harar. But when Fikre came to the house her face was clouded with fear.

'Bey is here,' she said as she slipped through the door. 'I cannot stay; it is too dangerous. But I had to see you. He means to sell me.'

'What?'

'He lost money on his last shipment. Now he can't afford to pay for the coffee in his warehouse. He was weeping when he told me. He said he loved me, that he cannot bear to sell me, but he has no choice. I told him I didn't care who owned me,' she said scornfully. 'A slave is a slave.'

'But this means you'll be sent away—'

She laughed hollowly. 'No, it doesn't, Robert. Before I'm sold, I will be examined by a midwife. Any buyer will insist on that. So I will be discovered. And then they will certainly kill me, unless I do it myself first.'

'You're not to kill yourself.'

'It will be better than the alternative. At least I will be free to choose the moment of my death. Now I must go. Will you kiss me?'

'You're not to die,' I said, pulling away and holding her. 'No one is going to die. I promise I'll think of something.'

HECTOR STEPS SILENTLY through the jungle, his rifle raised. In front of him Bayanna raises his hand. Both men freeze.

'There, sah,' Bayanna breathes.

Hector peers into the trees. The stripes of sunlight and shadow are very like a leopard's coat. He thinks he sees a flicker of movement . . .

'This way, sah,' Bayanna whispers, moving forward on silent feet.

Hector has not told Wallis that, when the other man goes off on his jaunts to Harar, he is hunting a leopard. He plans to shoot the thing first, then leave the animal's skin on the floor of their hut to await Wallis's return. 'Oh, aye,' he'll say casually. 'Thought I might as well have a little sport while I'm here.'

Behind them a twig snaps. Kuma the cook pads to Hector's side. He is carrying the second gun and a box of bullets.

'I don't think it dere, sah,' he says, peering ahead of them.

'Quiet, Kuma.'

'Yes, sah. Sorry, sah.'

If only it were not so dark, here under the canopy. The three men advance a little further. There is a small stream, and then a group of rocks. It is, Hector thinks, just the sort of place a leopard would choose to—

There is a sound like a huge chain rattling. A shape leaps at them, curving through the air, claws slashing. Hector brings the gun to his shoulder and fires in one smooth, practised movement. The leopard falls to the forest floor, writhing. Hector watches—the fewer bullets he uses, the less damage will be suffered by the pelt. Finally the animal stiffens and is still.

'By God,' Hector says, approaching it warily. 'The brute's enormous.' He feels a surge of excitement. Wallis can sneer all he likes—this victory, and the spoils, are his alone. He might even—

There is a screech, another roar, and something else flies through the air. The second leopard is smaller, but fiercer. Hector reaches back for his second gun, but Kuma has recoiled involuntarily, and Hector's hand finds only air before the creature is on him. The enormous jaws lock into his neck, tugging. He hears someone yell. The animal recoils as Bayanna hits it with his stick, then Kuma too is pounding it with the base of the rifle. As the animal opens its jaws to snarl, Hector manages to free himself. The leopard snaps at his face twice more, and Hector's vision seems to shrink into a tiny dot.

ON MY RETURN I found him in our hut, still in his bush clothes, the camp bed stained with his blood. Hector's left cheek looked as if it had been sliced open with a filleting knife, and there were three deep gouges from his right ear all the way down his neck. It was quite dreadful, and probably hopeless.

As I was looking at the damage, Hector opened his eyes.

'Oh, Robert. It's ye.'

'I'm here, Hector. I'm going to patch you up and fetch a doctor.'

He chuckled—or rather, tried to: a thin wheeze was all that escaped his lips. 'Wha' doctor, man? Nearest doctor's in Aden.'

'I'll think of something.'

'Aye.' He closed his eyes. 'Dinnae let them eat me. After I'm dead. Ye promise, now? Make sure I'm . . . properly buried.'

'Talk of burial is somewhat premature,' I said, 'since you're not dying.'

He tried to smile. 'You're a foolish pup, Wallish.'

'I find it extraordinary that even on your'—I almost said 'deathbed' but caught myself—'sickbed, Hector, you insult me. Now, I'll patch you up as best I can. Then we'll get you to Harar. Someone there will be bound to help.'

I opened up our medicine chest and told Jimo to boil some water while I located waxed thread and needles. I got four spoonfuls of Chlorodyne down Hector's throat and, when Jimo returned, I got to work. It quickly became apparent that even that potent mixture of laudanum, tincture of cannabis, chloroform and alcohol was incapable of entirely dulling the sensations of my needlework. I had to get Jimo and Kuma to hold him down. The screaming made it hard to concentrate, and the job was not one I would want to boast about, but at least it was done.

Afterwards I took a long draught of Chlorodyne myself. I fell immediately into a multicoloured sleep, in which I dreamed that I was back in Limehouse, analysing coffee with Emily, Ada and the Frog. In my dream Emily turned to Ada and said, 'What is the next liquid we must cup?' to which her sister replied, 'Oh, blood, I think.' I was then served three tiny porcelain dishes of dark red liquid, which I cupped daintily with a spoon.

THAT EVENING, Hector seemed a little better. He managed to swallow some stew, which Kuma spooned between his lips, but by the next morning he was running a fever. I gave him Dover's Powder as a sudorific. He was soon streaming with perspiration and his face swelled up severely.

'Kuma,' I said, 'fetch Kiku, the medicine woman. Perhaps she can help. And start the boys making a stretcher.'

The medicine woman brought herbs and barks with which she prepared a poultice. She applied it to Hector's wounds, then chanted over him in a high voice while making ritual flicks and movements of the hands. For a while this seemed to be efficacious—towards evening Hector regained consciousness. But he could open only one eye now: the other was too swollen.

'Robert?'

'I'm here.'

'Plant the seeds.'

'What are you talking about, Hector?'

'The new coffee berries—ye got them in Harar?'

'Yes, I have them. But don't exert yourself—'

'Keep the seedlings shaded with banana leaves. And keep them weeded. Don't use the Red Gang, they're idle bastards.'

'Very well, Hector.'

'Ye've made a good start here. It'll be civilised one day, if ye only keep going. That's the important thing—Civilisation. Not us. We're dispensable.'

There was a long silence, broken only by the medicine woman's murmurs and the painful see-sawing of Hector's breath.

'Tell Emily I'm sorry.'

'Emily?'

'Aye. Look after her, Wallis. She's a grand lassie.'

'Of course,' I said, mystified. I went to the door of the hut. 'Kuma? Where's that stretcher? We'll start for Harar as soon as Massa is well enough.'

I turned back to the bed. The medicine woman was bent over Hector's head, gesturing, as if she were miming pulling a rope out of his mouth, hand over hand. When she reached the end of her imaginary rope, she seemed to take something off and throw it up into the air.

Hector sighed. 'Thank ye.'

A kind of shudder seemed to pass through him. Again the medicine woman mimed the pulling out and throwing off. This time Hector just nodded, faintly, and then with a sudden violent groan he was still.

MORE WOMEN came up from the village to prepare the body, while I had the men dig a grave. I waited outside the hut.

The medicine woman came out with Hector's bloodstained clothing. I nodded towards the fire. 'Burn it.'

She hesitated, then took something from one of the pockets and handed it to me. It was a small sheaf of letters, tied up with very old, faded ribbon.

'Thank you. They may be something that should be sent back to his people.' I pulled the ribbon and looked at the topmost letter. For a moment, I thought I must have been hallucinating. The sender's address was one I recognised. The letter began: *My darling Hector . . .*

I turned it over. It was signed: *Your loving Emily.*

I hesitated—but not for long. Hector was dead and Emily was thousands of miles away. In those circumstances, scruples hardly seemed to matter.

My darling Hector,

By the time you get this I suppose you will be in Ceylon! I cannot tell you how much I wish I could be with you. Four years—it seems for ever—but I know that you will be such a success, and that my father will surely drop his objections before the end of your time there. In the meantime, write to me and tell me everything you see, so that I can experience it through your eyes. How I long to be married properly, so that I can be there by your side! I have an atlas, and every day I calculate how far your little boat must have travelled and try to imagine what you must be seeing . . .

Hector and Emily. Engaged. The evidence was in front of my eyes. And there was more, much more. What came through in those love letters, above all, was the passion, the longing with which she looked forward to their union. How different from the friendly but guarded tone of her letters to me.

Reading between the lines, it seemed there had been some sort of scandal. I leafed through the letters until I found what what I was looking for:

If we were impetuous, it was only from a surfeit of affection; we are not the first, nor will we be the last, to have 'jumped the gun' a little—or at least, it would have been a little, had my father not intervened . . .

She had slept with him. Behind the euphemisms, the truth was clear. Emily Pinker, brought up in the modern style—too modern, Pinker might have reflected—had thrown herself away on this dour, unprepossessing Scot.

Certain things made sense now: the time Pinker said that they must avoid not a scandal, but *another* scandal. I had thought nothing of it at the time, but he must have feared her reputation would not survive another battering.

I plunged on through the letters. Gradually one became aware of a change of tone—Emily was not so gushing or so girlish; she seemed to be responding more frequently to comments or objections made in Hector's half of the correspondence. And then, finally, after more than a year, there it was:

I do not see how you could be said to be 'releasing' me, since I am hardly bound to you by anything more than love—a love I thought was mutual. I never saw you as being under any kind of obligation. But if the attractions of travel and adventure are really so much more delightful than family and domesticity, as you say, then of course we must not be married . . .

It was strange how everything suddenly swung round. I hadn't liked Hector, yet he had somehow become my friend. It turned out I barely knew him. Emily I knew more about now than I had done in London.

There was one more letter, not so faded.

Dear Hector,

I hardly know how to respond to your last letter. I am delighted, of course, that you are considering settling down, and flattered that you still think of me, but I have to say that after so long apart I can hardly consider you as a potential husband. Indeed—if I may be blunt—the manner of our separation, the sentiments you expressed at the time, caused me no little anguish. I cannot stop you coming to England, and doubtless my father will invite you to the house, so let us try to remain friends, at least . . .

That was dated 7th February. Eight weeks before she had started working with me on the Guide. So much hurt and misery, and I had been completely unaware of it.

THAT NIGHT, the drums started up in the village. When we came to bury Hector the next morning, I discovered that his eyes and testicles had been taken. 'It is for *ju-ju*,' Jimo said mournfully. 'White man's body big magic.' I changed my mind about burial and had them fill the pit with kindling . . .

Afterwards, I entered a kind of numb daze. As well as the Chlorodyne, I tried some of Jimo's *khat*. It was bitter, and brought on a faint tingling sensation, as if I had become too big for my body and were somehow seeping out of every pore, like a gas. I maintained this state of intoxication for about a week, chewing a little more every time the effects wore off, before eventually falling asleep and waking with a terrible headache.

Somewhere in that drugged ethereal haze, however, I came to a decision.

Dear Emily,

I am afraid I have some tragic news. Poor Hector is dead. He was attacked by a leopard, and although I did what I could to save him, the wounds became infected almost overnight.

He expressed a wish to be cremated, a wish I carried out immediately after his death. While sorting through his things, I came across the enclosed letters from you. I have read them—probably I should not have done so, but there it is. Given what they reveal, you will not be surprised to learn that I do not intend to marry you after all. However, I should make clear that this was something I had begun to consider even before I read this correspondence. Briefly, I have fallen in love with someone else.

I wish you the best of happiness in your future life.

Yours sincerely,

Robert Wallis

So now I was free.

'LET ME BE SURE I have understood this correctly,' Ibrahim Bey said with a frown. 'You wish to buy Fikre from me?'

'I do.'

'But why?'

'I am in love with her.'

'One cannot love a slave. This I have learned through bitter experience.'

'Nevertheless, I wish to buy her,' I said stubbornly.

'Robert, Robert . . . ' He clapped his hands. 'Let us take coffee and I will endeavour to explain to you why this is a foolish course of action.'

We were in Bey's house, in a room filled with rugs and filigree lanterns.

I said, 'I am perfectly serious, Ibrahim. And I assure you I will not change my mind. But of course I shall take coffee, if you wish.'

Mulu brought us tiny cups of arabica. Bey's eyes were on me as he drank.

'So,' he said, putting down his cup, 'does this strange idea have anything to do with poor Hector's death?'

I shook my head.

'But your business is coffee, Robert. Not slavery.'

'This is not a business matter, Ibrahim. I heard you were thinking of selling. I want to buy. That's all there is to it.'

He sighed. 'It is true that I am compelled to sell her. I wish it were not so. But you realise that for you to sell her on would be impossible? While the Emperor tolerates the buying of slaves, no one but an Arab may sell them.'

'It makes no difference—I do not intend to sell.'

He gave me an anguished look. 'Robert . . . I think I told you I had to mortgage everything I owned to buy her. It was a moment of madness, one I deeply regret. If I could stop you making the same mistake, I would.' He paused. 'Perhaps you do not appreciate just how costly a girl like that actually is.'

'Name your price.'

He said softly, 'One thousand pounds.'

I reeled. 'I must admit, I had not realised it would be so much.'

'I told you it was extortionate. And I am certainly not trying to profit by the deal. One thousand pounds is what I paid.'

'She is worth less now, though, because she is older.'

'True.' He sighed. 'What price do you think is fair?'

'Eight hundred. It is all I have.'

He said heavily, 'I accept your offer, although it will leave me considerably out of pocket. Will you want to have her examined?'

'Of course not. You are not the only man of honour here. Will Austro-Hungarian dollars be acceptable?'

He nodded helplessly. 'Indeed.'

'I'll have the money brought round tomorrow.'

'And I will instruct my lawyer to draw up the necessary papers.' He shook his head. 'I fear that when you come to your senses you will somehow blame me for this. And you will no longer be my friend.'

'I can assure you that I am going into this with my eyes wide open.' I held out my hand. 'We have an agreement?'

Still he hesitated. 'They say that when you have shaken an Englishman's hand, there can be no going back on the deal.'

'That is correct.'

He took my hand in both of his. 'Then I will shake your hand, Robert, but I tell you frankly that it is with a heavy heart.'

EIGHT HUNDRED POUNDS. It meant using not just my advance from Pinker, but all the money for the expenses of the plantation, and what little I had made from my own trading. It was the money that, had things turned out differently, would have enabled me to marry Emily Pinker.

But I would still have fifty or so left. It was not much, but the coffee seeds were planted and paid for, there was enough to pay the villagers, and my other needs were few. Once the crop was growing, I might be able to borrow against its eventual sale. We would be able to survive. Then, once we had some money coming in, Fikre and I could leave—not for England, of course, but to some other part of Europe: Italy, perhaps, or the south of France. We would exist outside society, free from the strictures of conventional morality.

THE CHEST OF DOLLARS was too heavy for one man, so I went into the market to find two soldiers to carry it. I took my pistol, in case of robbers, and together we threaded our way through the maze of brown streets.

Darkness rose up around us as if it were being poured into the city from some gigantic pot. But Bey's house, when we finally got there, was full of lights—tiny candles in filigree lanterns, flickering like stars.

The lawyer was waiting in the first-floor sitting room. He asked me some questions to make sure I understood what I was doing, then presented me with a document in Arabic. 'This is her provenance—a bill of sale from the house that last sold her. Do you wish to show it to a lawyer of your own?'

'There is no need.'

He shrugged. 'And this is a document certifying that she was a virgin when she was sold.' He placed another document in Arabic in front of me. 'I understand you do not wish to have her examined?'

'There is no need,' I repeated.

'Very well.' He laid a third document on the table. 'You will have to sign this, to say that you accept her as she is.'

I signed. This time there was also a translation, in poor but tolerable

English. *I, the undersigned, do hereby accept the slave known as Fikre, in recompense whereof* . . . I scanned it and signed that too.

'And finally, the bill of sale.' The lawyer looked at Bey. 'Will you count the money?'

'Robert would not cheat me,' Bey said firmly.

Again I signed my name, while Bey signed the receipt.

'She is yours,' the lawyer said, handing me a last piece of paper—a simple certificate bearing a few lines of Arabic text. 'This is to confirm it. If you ever set her free, you must tear this up.'

I nodded. The lawyer finally left us.

'Robert,' Bey said seriously, 'I believe you will regret this one day. When that day comes, remember that you insisted that I sell her to you.'

'I understand.'

Fikre came into the room, on bare feet, her face sullen. Mulu was behind her, carrying a coffee sack. 'I have given her some clothes and so on,' Bey explained. 'As a slave she cannot own anything, but they go with her.'

'Thank you.' There were tears in Mulu's eyes as he handed the sack to me.

I held out my hand to her. 'Fikre—will you come with me?'

'Do I have a choice?' she said furiously.

We maintained the pretence until we were round the first corner. Then I could stand it no longer. I pulled her into a doorway, running my hands round her waist, reaching up for her head, pushing it against my lips.

At last we pulled apart. 'So now I am yours,' she said, grinning.

WHAT I REMEMBER of the days that followed is the sense of physical delight, the playful intoxication of a world reduced to a room, two bodies and a bed, our lovemaking interrupted only by rare forays to the market for food.

Eventually, however, the banquet of our senses reached its final course. We were sated. And our minds began to turn at last to the future.

'What do you mean to do?' Fikre asked.

'I'll have to go back to the plantation. The seedlings will need to be transplanted. It isn't fair to let Jimo deal with it on his own.'

'Shall I come with you?'

'I warn you, it's pretty rough. There are no feminine comforts.'

'I can do without those.' She paused. 'Robert, do you . . . have any plans for me? I mean, my . . . status.'

I laughed. 'Are you asking me to marry you? A white dress, church, all the ceremonies of the bourgeois?'

She shook her head. 'I don't want to be married. I want to be free.'

'We are free.'

She looked at me intently. 'Robert, what I've done with you—I do it willingly: not because you have a piece of paper, but because I want to. You know that, don't you?'

She was waiting, I knew, for me to say that I would tear up the papers. Why did I not? It would have proved my love. And yet something held me back. Deep down, I think I still needed to feel that I had that power over her—as if the love and the ownership were somehow linked.

I made a joke of it. 'But I fully intend to sell you just as soon as I find someone better'—something like that, or possibly it was even clumsier, I can't now recall. Whatever, I saw something harden for a moment behind her eyes. Then she nodded meekly, and the subject was dropped.

She mentioned it only one other time. We were in bed, and she suddenly took my head in her hands and said fiercely, 'If you give me my freedom, I will give myself back to you. All of me. I will be utterly yours.'

I groaned and said, 'I love you.'

Not quite the same thing, you see.

A COUPLE OF DAYS before we left for the plantation we came back from the market to find Mulu sitting on the doorstep. Fikre embraced him so happily that it was several moments before he could hand me Bey's letter.

My dear Robert,

Mulu is pining without Fikre, and I have no work for him here, so I have taken the liberty of sending him to you. He needs only his food and lodging. You will find him a good servant so long as he is allowed to tend to Fikre's needs as well as yours. If you do not want him, send him back. If you keep him, there is no need to pay me—unlike Fikre, his value is very small.

Your friend,

Ibrahim

There was no question of returning him. Fikre was overjoyed to see him, and he her. But I was not used to having a eunuch around—it made me uncomfortable, if the truth be told, the way the two of them were together, almost like two girls, chattering away in a language I could not understand. Sometimes he would help her dress, or bathe, and that too seemed strange to me, the intimacy that was more like that of a lady and her maid than that between a man and a woman.

Nine

The post from Harar is slow, and it is several weeks before Robert's letter arrives. It is the Frog who brings it, running from the hallway to deliver her prize, panting, into Emily's hands.

'Please may I read it?' she begs. 'Please?'

'I haven't read it myself yet. Besides, Robert's letters to me are private.'

'Please may you read me the bits that aren't private?' the Frog says hopefully. 'Look—it's got something in it. Has he sent you a present?'

Emily does not answer. She has opened the letter, which is more of a package, containing as it does her old letters to Hector. For a moment she does not understand; then she goes white. She scans the note.

'What is it?' the Frog demands. 'Is everything all right?'

'No, it isn't,' Emily says. She gets to her feet. 'I had better find father. I have some very bad news about Hector. And Robert—Robert has . . .' Words fail her, and then the Frog is treated to the extraordinary sight of her capable, efficient, all-powerful older sister bursting into tears.

SOME TIME LATER, Pinker comes out of his study to find the Frog waiting.

'Philomena,' he says, 'I'm afraid your sister has had a shock.'

'I know. Robert has jilted her. Ada told me.'

'I see. Well, you must be especially nice to Emily now. For example'—he hesitates—'it would not be nice, perhaps, to use the word "jilted". They have simply decided that their future lies apart.'

'But if he hasn't jilted her, why is she crying?'

'The other bad news,' he continues, 'is that Hector became very ill in the jungle. Sadly, he has passed away.'

The Frog thinks about this. 'Who will Emily marry now?'

'Well, in due course she will meet someone else she likes, and that is the person she will marry.'

Something suddenly strikes the Frog—a thought so appalling that it forces her froglike eyes open as wide as they will go. 'Robert will go on writing to me, though, won't he?'

'I doubt very much if he will,' her father says, shaking his head.

To his astonishment, he finds he has not one daughter in tears but two.

Fikre, Mulu and I found the plantation in a bad way, the workers nowhere to be seen. The digging of planting pits had slowed to five feet a day. Without Hector's iron discipline, the place seemed incapable of functioning. But the worst of it was the nursery beds. The leaves of the new seedlings were discoloured with faint rust-coloured circles. It was some kind of fungus.

Hector would have known what to do. Instead, I had to turn to the pages of Lester Arnold, who advised washing the affected plants with a solution of soap and strong coffee. When that failed, we had to decide what to do next. There was money to buy another lot of seed, but only one; after that we would be unable to pay the workers.

I explained all this to Fikre one evening as we ate. 'If the next lot die,' I concluded, 'there won't be any more—there's simply no more cash.'

She was silent a moment. 'Do you blame me?'

'Of course not.'

'But if you hadn't bought me, there would be more money.'

'There's no point in going down that road. What's done is done.'

It was not the most tactful thing I could have said.

'So you do regret it,' she persisted.

'Fikre, can you stick to the point? I have to decide what to do.'

For a moment her eyes flashed again. Then she seemed to check herself. 'Have you thought of growing coffee as the natives do?'

'They don't grow coffee. They just pick the wild berries in the forest.'

'Quite. Perhaps you don't need all this.' Her arm took in the cleared hillsides, the nursery, the rows of planting pits. 'You could turn your diggers into foragers. They could bring you the wild coffee, and then you could pay them for it and take it to market at a profit.'

'It's not how Lester Arnold says to do it, and his book is the only guide I've got. I can't disregard his proven commercial methods for—for coffee grown willy-nilly in the jungle.'

Fikre dropped her eyes. 'Very well. I was only trying to help.'

From then on, it was as if the plantation were jinxed. The seedlings that were not diseased were attacked by black ants. A warthog got into the nursery beds and wreaked havoc. The workers became increasingly truculent. The rust disease spread. I replanted the diseased seedlings in more spacious beds, redug the nursery with fresh soil, and planted new seeds. Some days I fell asleep without even taking my boots off.

And yet . . . every night, as evening fell, kingfishers and parrots flashed to and fro in the dusk, colobus monkeys swung effortlessly through the trees overhead, and fireflies tumbled through the darkness like magic. Fikre and I ate together, the hissing lamp our only companion. It was hard not to feel a sense of satisfaction. Whatever I had thought I might end up doing when I was sent down from Oxford, never had I imagined anything like this.

IF THE PAIN were a coffee, Emily thinks, she would be able to enumerate its components. Heartbreak is only one element of what she feels now. There is humiliation, too—the knowledge that for the second time in her life she has made a fool of herself. Her father and Ada love her too much to say, 'I told you so,' but they did tell her, and she ignored them. It turns out they were right about Robert. Failure—she feels stupid, incompetent. How can she hope to change the world when she can't even pick a husband? Anger—how dare he: betraying her like this with just a few casual lines, as if he were cancelling a newspaper subscription? Loneliness—she misses him, she would give anything to have him back. She remembers afternoons cupping coffees here in her father's office, the descriptors bouncing back and forth between them like musical phrases, a private, sensual language conveying so much more than the taste of coffee . . . And then there is an emotion for which there is no word: the terrible wrenching amputation of a physical desire that will now never be expressed . . . Damn you, Robert Wallis, she thinks to herself as she collects suffrage petitions. Damn you, she thinks as she takes minutes for Arthur's constituency meetings, and again as she wakes in the night and remembers suddenly why her eyes are sore and her nose inflamed, and waits for the tears to come yet again.

'I'LL HAVE TO GO to Harar,' I told Fikre. 'I need to replace those seeds.'

'Of course. Do you want me to come with you?'

I hesitated. 'Could you bear to stay here? The boys will work better if there's someone to keep an eye on them.'

'Of course. I'll give you a list of other things to get, for the house.'

'That would be grand.' I looked at her. 'You know I love you?'

'Yes, I know it. Come back soon.'

My business in Harar, as it turned out, was swiftly concluded, so I thought I would look in on Bey. There was something different about his house. The filigree lamps that had hung from the balcony were gone, that was it. I knocked on the door. It was opened by a man I did not recognise.

'How can I help you?' he asked in French.

'I am looking for Ibrahim Bey.'

He smiled mirthlessly. 'As we all are. Bey is gone.'

'Gone? Where?'

'To Arabia, perhaps. He left suddenly, to avoid his creditors.'

It made no sense. 'Are you sure?'

The man laughed. 'Certainly—I was one of them. I was lucky: I had this house as my security. The scoundrel had been planning this for some time—there was nothing left to sell.'

A thought struck me—a thought so awful that I could not bring myself to think it through. 'Do you by any chance read Arabic?' I asked slowly.

He nodded. 'Yes, a little.'

'May I show you some documents?'

He shrugged. 'If you wish.'

I went back to the French merchant's house and found the papers I had signed when I bought Fikre. Retracing my steps through the streets, I knocked again on the ornate door of the house where Bey had lived.

The man spread the papers by the window and looked through them. 'This is a bill of sale,' he said. 'A receipt for ten crates of the finest pistachios in Cairo. And this one'—he tapped another document—'is a loading bill for a consignment of coffee. And this'—he held up the certificate of ownership—'is a letter. A note, rather. It seems to be addressed to you.'

If you ever set her free, you must tear this up . . .

'Are you all right?' he enquired solicitously. 'Perhaps you would like some coffee.' He called out, and a servant entered with a pot.

'No. Please—what does it say?'

'It says, "My friend, do not judge us too harshly. It is surprisingly hard to make money in coffee these days, and my debts are mounting. As for the girl, forgive her. She is in love, and this was the only way."'

What did it mean? What way was the only way? For what was I having to forgive Fikre? How did he know that she was in love with me?

Unless . . . Something else flitted into my brain, a series of separate memories that suddenly joined together and made a coherent pattern.

I had to get back to the farm.

IT WAS IMPOSSIBLE to hurry that journey—the jungle clutched at you; it caught at your feet and tangled them with vines; it placed its hand on your chest and said, Wait; it sapped your strength and exhausted your will.

Besides, I already knew what I would find.

Fikre gone. Mulu gone. A note, fluttering on the camp bed.

Don't try to find us.

And then, in a slightly different hand, as if she had turned back to write it at the final moment: *He is the only man I have ever really loved.*

I will not try to describe how I felt. Perhaps you can imagine it. Not just despair, but grief—a complete, crushing, suffocating horror, as if the whole world had collapsed around me. As if I had lost everything.

But then, you see, I had.

They must have planned it long before they met me. But the coming of an Englishman must have galvanised them—and such an Englishman: young, naive, impetuous, with a strongbox full of money, and oblivious to everything except the sap roaring through his veins. The lure was so perfect, so *delectable* that I couldn't help but swallow it.

Tales told in the desert. Webs spun to ensnare an unsuspecting fly Perhaps some of them were even true. For example, I think Fikre probably had been brought up in a harem; it would explain her languages, her education. Whether she really had been a virgin I have no idea. I suppose it was unlikely—she certainly knew how to give a good performance in bed.

I could not know exactly how the story played out. But I could start to thread together possibilities. At the slave sale, during the game of chess, Bey must have seen how clever Fikre was, how agile her wits were even under pressure. But whose idea was it? Fikre's, I imagine. Perhaps she muttered even as she beat him, *If you help me, I will help you.*

What do you want?

To be free.

How can I possibly help with that?

Buy me.

With what? He will easily outbid me.

However much it costs, I will make sure you profit on the deal.

She would have looked at him then, with that level gaze I had come to know so well. But she would not have known it was going to work until Bey came into the bidding at the last minute.

And then the years of planning. Mulu, I imagine, joined them later, although it is possible he came from the same household. Mulu and Fikre loved each other completely—I could see that now. It was a kind of love between a man and a woman that I, in my ignorance, had not even conceived of. A love that was nothing to do with sex.

And yet, and yet . . . If it was Mulu she loved, why give herself to me so enthusiastically? Why those weeks of passion?

He is the only man I have ever really loved . . .

But Mulu was not a man, was he? Not in one sense. So perhaps she had simply wanted to know what love was really like, or rather *sex*, before accepting a life without it. Or perhaps . . . perhaps it was not just sex she had wanted. There was one other thing a eunuch could not provide: a child.

What a fool I had been. I had not just wandered into their trap; I had embraced it, tying its threads around myself with joy, blinded by lust.

ARTHUR BREWER comes into his constituency office, a letter in his hand. 'This one will have to be answered, I'm afraid. Some Poor Law guardian who knows for a fact that anyone in his parish who doesn't work is a malingerer —' He stops. 'Emily. Are you all right?'

'Hmmm?' She starts to turn towards him, then realises he will see that her eyes are red. 'Yes, of course,' she says, turning back to her typewriter.

'Perhaps you could dash off something placatory and noncommittal.' He places the letter on the table next to her. 'Are you quite sure you're well?'

To his amazement she takes a great shuddering gasp. Her hand flies to her mouth. 'I'm sorry. I shall be fine in just a—' But she cannot go on. Great gasping, racking sobs convulse her body.

'My dear,' he says, appalled. He offers her a handkerchief.

She takes it, buries her face in its comforting folds. A hand touches her shoulder, then descends to her back, patting her gently while she weeps.

When she has recovered enough to speak, he says gently, 'What is it?'

'Nothing,' she says. 'A disappointment, that's all.'

'But you're upset. You must take the rest of the afternoon off.' His face lifts. 'I know—we'll go to a moving picture. Have you seen one yet?'

She shakes her head.

'You see!' he cries. 'We are surely the last two people in London not to have been. I have been working you too hard.'

She manages a smile. 'It is we who have been working *you* too hard.'

'Well, whichever it is, the remedy is in our own hands.'

As he escorts her to the door, his arm protectively round her shoulders, she realises she has forgotten how pleasant it feels to be looked after.

TAHOMEN CROUCHES in the trees, very still. The mud streaked on his chest and shoulders echoes the pattern of the sunlight as it splashes through the canopy, making him invisible. His fingers are lightly curled round an axe, its head dulled with mud, lest sunlight catching on steel give him away.

He has been waiting like this for three hours, not far from where Massa Crannach was attacked. The leopard may have already moved on, but he does not think so. A *gongololo*, a huge orange millipede, makes its way along a twig, drops onto his leg, then rolls onto the forest floor, where it vanishes.

Distracted momentarily, Tahomen looks up. A shadow in the nearby trees flashes white and pink as a leopard yawns, showing its teeth.

Tahomen's fingers tighten involuntarily on the axe. The leopard's head swings up, its nostrils flaring. For long minutes they both wait.

In one lithe movement the leopard gets to its feet, picking its way delicately over the twigs and saplings. Its coat glows in the green gloom of the forest like the embers of a fire. Tahomen forces himself to be still. When it gets a little closer, he will strike.

The leopard mews quietly. From somewhere behind her, two cubs amble forward. When they reach their mother, one dives under her stomach and begins to suckle: the other, braver, leaps for a passing blue butterfly.

So that's why the leopard attacked Massa Crannach. Tahomen has suspected it all along. She was protecting her young.

The leopard bats away the cub that wants to suckle and the group moves on through the forest. When they have gone, Tahomen stands up stiffly.

He is no longer as young as he was, he thinks ruefully as he starts walking back. This was probably his last chance to kill a leopard.

As Tahomen nears the village, he hears a strange sound. It is coming from within a thicket of thorn trees. Carefully, he separates the branches with the haft of his axe and peers inside.

Massa Wallis is lying among the tangled thorns. He seems to be weeping.

Tahomen hacks his way into the thicket and pulls Massa Wallis out. But it is clear that there is something more deeply wrong than just having got stuck in a thorn tree. His eyes will not focus and he is moaning and mumbling under his breath. Putting the axe in his belt, Tahomen gets his arms round the white man and helps him towards the village.

ARTHUR BREWER meets Samuel Pinker at his club. They discuss certain issues of interest to them both—including the war in South Africa and how it will affect the Empire. They have much to talk about.

Eventually they are done, and sit puffing at cigars while they finish their drinks. But something, Pinker can tell, is still troubling the younger man.

'Mr Pinker,' Arthur begins.

'Samuel, please.'

'Samuel . . . there is something I have been meaning to ask.'

Pinker makes an encouraging gesture with his cigar.

'It's about Emily,' Arthur says with a diffident smile.

Pinker's eyes narrow, though he says nothing.

'I have said nothing to her, of course, and would not do so without your permission. But I find that she and I have many interests in common, and she is such delightful company—a credit to you, if I may say so.'

Pinker raises his eyebrows.

'I was wondering if I might be permitted to get to know her a little better.'

'Permitted?' Pinker says, barking cigar smoke like some furious dragon. 'Permitted? You want my permission to woo my daughter?'

Arthur, holding his nerve, nods. 'That is correct.'

Abruptly Pinker's face creases into a smile. 'My dear fellow, I was hoping that you already were.'

THE RAINS HAVE COME at last, a great deluge of grey water that pours from the sky as if from a gigantic waterfall.

The villagers discuss the question of what to do with Massa Wallis. The Tamils take little part in these discussions. Now that the farm has no master, and they have no guarantee of being paid, they slip off into the jungle in ones and twos, looking for other plantations to work on.

The water gets into the farm buildings, so the villagers take them apart and use the wood to construct round huts with thatched roofs, which they know will be waterproof. The rain softens the ground, so they take up some of the diseased coffee seedlings and put down yams and maize. After all, there is plenty of coffee in the jungle already, and a man cannot fill his belly with coffee alone.

One man, it seems, is going to try. Massa Wallis stays in Kiku's hut, existing only on coffee and *khat*, sleeping for a few hours before waking again, sobbing and banging his head against the ground in his madness.

'Why must we give him shelter?' those from the younger age—clans want to know. 'What has he done for us, except allow us to be beaten, and destroy our homes? He cannot even run the farm to make us money.'

'He is no different from ourselves,' Kiku tells them. 'You would not send a visitor away without giving him food or shelter, would you?'

'Will he die?' Tahomen asks her.

'If he wants to. It's not like having a curse put on you by a sorcerer. Massa Wallis has cursed himself, and only he can decide if he will let it be lifted.'

At a table in Arthur Brewer's constituency office, Mary, a middle-aged volunteer, is folding leaflets and placing them in a neat stack. Emily comes and takes each stack to her own table, where she puts the leaflets in envelopes.

After a while, Mary looks up. 'I have cut my fingers three times on these dratted leaflets. Shall we stop for some tea?'

'Yes, you must certainly stop,' Arthur says, entering the room. 'It will be our first piece of legislation—no one shall fold constituency leaflets for more than two hours without a tea break.'

'In that case we shall have to work on. Because we have only been doing this forty minutes,' Emily says drily. She smiles at him.

'I'll put the kettle on,' Mary says. As she passes the younger woman she murmurs, 'I may be a while—that kettle is a slow one.'

'There is a meeting tonight,' Arthur says when she has gone. 'I am afraid I am expected to attend, but I was wondering—if you are not too tired—if you could bear to come with me, as my guest.'

'What is the subject?'

'Home Rule.' He spreads his arms. 'We must find a way to get a bill through the Lords. As it stands, the landowners have made it clear they will block any attempt to settle the Irish question.'

'I should like that very much, Arthur,' she says. 'Will Sir Henry be there?'

He nods. 'He is the main speaker.'

'I will look forward to it, then. They say he is a wonderful orator, and, in any case, it will be a pleasure to accompany you.'

It is a strange courtship, not least because much of it takes place in the run-up to a general election. There is all the intense activity of a political campaign: writing, printing and folding leaflets, going from door to door delivering leaflets, attending meetings, organising debates, lobbying, touring the constituency . . . It is thrilling, but they are rarely together for more than a few minutes at a time; he is the general and she among the foot soldiers. Arthur demonstrates his affection by enquiring, tenderly, if she is working too hard, and by insisting that she takes a short break now and then, with him. Her frailty becomes a kind of convenient myth between them.

It grows clear to the others that the two of them have an understanding. His chivalry and his gallantry are focused on Emily. When, at a public meeting, he talks about the Vulnerable, his eyes seek out hers in the audience. When he talks about the Role of Woman, it is one particular woman he favours with a smile. When he talks about the Liberals as the Party of the

Family, he catches her eye and looks grave, so that she cannot stop herself smiling, and has to stare at the floor for fear she will make him grin too.

She does not think about Robert Wallis. Or if she does, it is only anger, of all those initial emotions, that she still feels. At such times she is not at all the frail little woman Arthur believes her to be; she feels like finding that feckless, self-centred young man and giving him a thump on the nose.

THE ELECTION COINCIDES with the return of troops from South Africa and the Conservative Government organises victory parade after victory parade. Sometimes, it is hard to tell the election and the war celebrations apart.

The Conservatives retain power by a comfortable margin. Afterwards, Pinker is enraged to discover that William Howell, of Howell's Coffee, has been knighted, ostensibly for his services to philanthropy, but actually—everyone knows—for his contribution to Conservative Party funds.

Senior Liberals complain that support for female suffrage is keeping them out of office. They need policies designed to appeal to *electors*, they argue, rather than to those who do not have a vote to cast. Sick pay, pensions, unemployment benefit—these are the way to appeal to the working man.

In London, the Suffrage Union redoubles its efforts to win influence. Emily works as hard for them as she ever did for Arthur's constituency. For Arthur, the disappointment at his party losing the election is tempered by the fact that in his own constituency his share of the vote has gone up. He is an important man now among the Liberals, a future minister. Luckily, he has found the perfect minister's wife: hard-working, right-thinking and wealthy. Nothing is more natural than to make a proposal of marriage.

He takes her to the terrace of the House of Commons one evening, and impresses upon her that this is not a step he takes lightly, that no one has a higher regard for the sanctity of love, expressed in its purest form as a life-long union between two people, than he does. 'In conclusion,' he says, 'I should like your permission to ask your father for your hand.'

'Oh, Arthur,' she says. 'The answer is yes—of course it is yes.'

Of course it is yes. How can it not be? She is a Rational person: to walk away from everything she has ever envisaged for herself would be a deeply irrational thing to do. If, over the coming weeks, she has doubts—and she does—then those, too, are only natural. It is a big step. And if, when he speaks of marriage, it sometimes seems to her that he means by it something more abstract and rather nobler than she does, then that too is only to be expected. He is an idealist: it is one of the things she most admires in him.

MASSA WALLIS, although he is still not speaking much, is eating again and working every day in the forest, picking coffee. Kiku judges that the time had come to settle the question of what to do about him. She waits until the council of the age-clans has gathered to discuss village matters then she raises her *siqqee* stick to indicate that she has something to say.

'Sons of woman, daughters of woman,' she begins.

Tahomen nods to her. 'Speak, and we will listen.'

'You will recall,' she says, 'that when the white men came, *saafu* was broken. The forest was unhappy. Now the fields they cleared are full of weeds and bushes; the trees are growing back. But do not think that everything is going back to the way it was before. Already, traders are coming to this place, looking for things to buy or exchange. The forest can grow back, but it cannot defend itself against the next white man who wants to tear it down and plant straight lines. We can tell the white man his plants will die, that warthogs will eat his seeds and the sun will shrivel his seedlings, but the white man will not listen to us, because that is his nature.'

'What do you suggest?' somebody asks. 'Or are you like the dog who barks when the hyena is gone?'

She shakes her head. 'What I suggest is this. We have been paid money by the white man, money for our work. We must give it back to him.'

There is a long silence as the villagers ponder this odd proposal.

'Massa Wallis cannot stay here,' she explains. 'Until he goes, there will not be *saafu*. To get back to his own valley he needs money—a lot of money. If we give him back what we have earned, he will have enough.'

'But then all our work will have been wasted,' a listener objects.

'Yes—but when he has gone, we will still be able to pick the wild coffee berries from the forest and take them to Harar to be sold. They will be worth more than before, because the white men showed us how to wash off the pulp and dry them in the sun. Then we will all share the money that we make. Most importantly, no other white man will be able to come and say, "I will have this land now." That is not how it works; they would have to find Massa Wallis and buy the land back from him, and he will be a long way away.'

'Surely the forest already belongs to us,' someone objects.

'It should do, but it does not. There is nothing we can do about that now.'

'And why should we help this man?' somebody else asks. 'Why does he deserve our generosity?'

'We should help this man,' Kiku says, 'because he is a man, the son of a woman, just as we are the sons and daughters of women.'

There is a long silence. Then Tahomen clears his throat. 'Thank you, Kiku,' he says. 'You have given us much to think about.'

They talk for days. That is their way: what may look like aimless chatter is actually a slow process of examining an issue from many points of view, testing each against the proverbs that constitute their received wisdom, until at last a consensus emerges. It is a very different decision-making process to the white man's, which assumes that the most crucial thing in any situation is speed, not agreement, and therefore allows orders to be imposed on the unwilling in the name of discipline. The villagers have no discipline, but they do have something far more powerful: the need for *saafu*.

I WAS SITTING in my hut as dusk fell. Below me in the valley, clouds gathered. Tropical birds darted in the tree canopy, flashes of colour against the gloom.

Tahomen appeared, walking slowly up the hill towards me, dressed in his chief's finery: my old alpaca jacket, worn over a piece of cloth wrapped at the loins. Behind him was Kiku. The medicine woman's hair had been coloured with red dye, and at her throat was a necklace of ebony beads. Behind her was Alaya, and behind her, a silent procession of villagers.

Tahomen stopped in front of me. 'Massa go home,' he said. Solemnly, he placed two coins, thalers, on the ground by my feet. Then he walked on a little way and squatted down to watch.

Kiku said something. She, too, placed a couple of coins at my feet.

Alaya smiled at me and gave me one thaler. The person behind her did the same, and the person after that . . . Those who had no money donated a mirror, or a necklace, or some other trinket given to them by Hector and me.

To an outsider, it might have looked as if they were giving me tribute—I was sitting there in my camp-chair like a king on my throne, and they were filing past me one by one, making obeisance. But it is I who was humbled, who bowed my head as each passed, my hands clasped together, tears flowing from my eyes, saying over and over, '*Galatoomi*.' Thank you.

The next day, Jimo, Kuma and I loaded my few possessions onto a mule. I took only what I could sell in Harar; the rest I left for the villagers.

The very last thing I came across was a stout mahogany box containing a number of glass tubes of scent and a pamphlet headed *The Wallis–Pinker Method Concerning the Clarification and Classification of the Various Flavours of Coffee*. It was too heavy to fit on the mule, and quite worthless, but I was pleased, nevertheless, to see that both the samples and the text had defied Hector's prediction and survived the terrible heat of the tropics.

Ten

'They say the price of coffee will soon be double what it was last year,' Arthur Brewer remarks, glancing from his paper to his wife. 'In New York, apparently, investors who speculated on a fall are throwing themselves off skyscrapers rather than pay their debts.'

'You make it sound as if suicide were an economy measure,' Emily says sharply, pushing her eggs to the side of her plate and laying down her knife and fork. 'Presumably the poor creatures thought they had no choice.'

Arthur frowns. He had not really meant to initiate a conversation, only to fill the silence over the breakfast table with an occasional observation. Mainly he does this to show that he is not actually neglecting his wife by reading the paper—in fact, it is almost as if he were reading it for both of them, filleting out the titbits that are appropriate for her consumption. The glance of silent reproach she gives him every morning when he picks up *The Times* while they eat is surely unjustified. And the way she coughs ostentatiously when he lights his pipe . . .

He turns back to the paper, looking for something with which to change the subject. 'I see there is a move to have Oscar Wilde's remains moved to the cemetery at Père Lachaise. They're even talking about a memorial.'

'That poor man. It's a disgrace that he was sent to prison in the first place. When his only crime—'

'My dear,' Arthur says mildly, '*pas devant les domestiques*.' He nods to where the junior maid, Annie, is clearing the sideboard.

Emily seems, he thinks, to sigh a little, but she says nothing. He sips his tea and turns the page. The doorbell rings and the maid goes to answer it. Both of them, without appearing to, listen to see who it is.

'Dr Mayhews is in the drawing room,' Annie announces.

Immediately Arthur is on his feet. 'I will go and explain matters to him first,' he says. He does not add 'man to man', but it is clear that that is what he means. 'If you wait here, my dear, I will send Annie up when he is ready to see you.'

So Emily waits. Occasionally the rumble of male voices penetrates from the drawing room next door, although they are too indistinct for her to catch the words. It hardly matters. She knows what Arthur will be saying.

'WE HAVE BEEN MARRIED almost two years,' Arthur explains. 'And she is—' He stops. 'This is somewhat difficult for me.'

Dr Mayhews, a bony man in his early fifties, says, 'You may be sure that you can tell me nothing I have not heard many times before.'

'Yes, of course. Even so . . .' Arthur hesitates again. 'After our marriage, my wife seemed to undergo a change. On our honeymoon she was delightful, but since then she has become increasingly . . . opinionated. Shrewish, one might almost say. She is easily distressed and kicks against the restrictions of married life. She has always been spirited; that I have no problem with. But this present mood of hers—she can be silent one hour, then so vociferous it is hard to get a word in edgeways. And this is not just women's chatter; she will converse on radical ideas, politics . . . Sometimes she barely makes sense.' He stops, aware that he is perhaps mixing up a medical history with his own resentments. But Dr Mayhews is nodding gravely.

'Is there conjugal incompatibility?' he enquires delicately.

'Well, of course— Oh.' Arthur realises what Dr Mayhews is asking and blushes. 'Not on the honeymoon. But afterwards.'

'Is she wanton?'

Reluctantly, Arthur nods. 'Sometimes, yes. Shockingly so.'

'And does she suffer from nervous inefficiency or exhaustion?'

'I suppose she does, at times.'

'Have you ever suspected hysteria?' the doctor asks quietly.

'She has never screamed blue murder, or fainted in company, or run down the street in her nightgown, if that is what you mean.'

Dr Mayhews shakes his head. 'The word "hysteria" is a diagnosis, not a description of a kind of behaviour. It applies to malaises emanating from the female parts—hence the term, from the Greek *hustera*, or womb. From your description, I am almost sure hysteria may be the problem here. Does she overindulge in coffee?'

Arthur stares at the doctor. 'Yes, she does. Her father is a coffee merchant. She has always drunk copious amounts.'

Dr Mayhews shakes his head again. 'The female reproductive force is so strong that it can irradiate every part of the frame. When it becomes disordered, as it may easily do—even from something as simple as an excess of coffee—it can carry its confusion into every department, even into the deepest recesses of the mind itself. Are you familiar with the work of Dr Freud?'

'I have heard of him.'

'He has proved that these complaints are generally hysteroneurasthenic in origin. Passion and hysteria are close cousins,' the doctor adds darkly.

'Can it be cured?'

'It can be treated. But don't worry, Mr Brewer. There are a number of excellent practitioners dealing with this sort of malady. And it may become less acute with time. Generally women are less prone to these problems once they have a child, the body having fulfilled its natural function.'

THREE DAYS LATER the motor car drives Emily to Harley Street for her appointment with the specialist. She asks the chauffeur to wait, and alights onto the pavement. It is thronged with people going in and out of the imposing doorways. Most, she notices, are women.

She enters Number 27 and gives her name to a doorman. He indicates a row of chairs. 'Please, take a seat. Dr Richards will be with you shortly.'

She sits and waits, closing her eyes. God, she is tired. It is exhausting, this constant struggle with Arthur. She has tried so hard to be the wife he wants her to be, to manage him by hints and suggestions rather than by nagging or needling. But the truth is that she likes a good argument, always has done. Arguments between friends, it seems to her, are simply the quickest way for two intelligent people to exchange strongly held opinions.

To Arthur, an argumentative wife is a challenge to his authority. He desires silence, order, acquiescence, while she desires . . . she isn't sure quite what, but certainly not the suffocating boredom of the house in Eaton Square, and all the important issues of the world reduced to 'the woman's sphere'.

It was one thing, apparently, for her to deliver leaflets and sample coffees when she was single; as an MP's wife her function, suddenly, is ceremonial. She is expected to be at Arthur's side for every social visit, every tea party, every debate—never to speak, but simply to applaud him indulgently, a visual embodiment of the Approval of Woman.

Yet, simultaneously, he has betrayed her. The Liberals, for whom she and other suffragists have worked tirelessly over the years, have decided to drop female suffrage. Campbell-Bannerman himself—the jovial, kindly leader she met in the House of Commons—pronounced it a 'distraction'. And Arthur, to whom by this time she was engaged, went along obediently—no, enthusiastically—with his party's new line. 'It is politics, my dear. And politics is simply a question of priorities. Would you really put Votes for Women ahead of pensions for miners? Come,' he added, 'we must not let this change anything between us.' He does not appreciate that her feelings for him and her political principles sprang from the same impulse.

Arthur is not a cruel man, but he is a conventional one, and if the conventions are cruel, then the man will be as well. In the House, Arthur expresses his political personality through a fanatical devotion to that institution's myriad regulations and points of order; at home, he expresses it with disapproval and sniping . . . and now this ridiculous business with Dr Mayhews.

Strangely, though, her being told she was ill has brought out a tenderness in Arthur that had previously been absent. He knows what role to slip into at last: the protective husband. He has started bringing her cups of tea and enquires solicitously after her health at every opportunity. It is driving her mad. And if she professes the slightest opinion on any subject, his face adopts an anxious expression as he reminds her that Dr Mayhews has left instructions that passion is, for the time being, best avoided.

Passion! It is a lack of passion that is the problem, not a surfeit of it—God knows she tried to show him that. When the honeymoon ended, so too did Arthur's inclination to continue its pleasures. Relations took place, but they were perfunctory, and any enjoyment she got entirely coincidental. And so she resigned herself to remaining unfulfilled in that respect.

She knows perfectly well that no visit to a doctor's is going to change anything, but to have refused to go, in the face of Dr Mayhews's diagnosis, would have put her in the wrong. So here she is.

'Mrs Brewer?'

Emily turns. The speaker is a good-looking young man in a smart suit. 'I'm Dr Richards,' he says, shaking her hand. 'Will you follow me?'

ARTHUR HAS NOTICED a change in his wife since her visit to the specialist. They are having breakfast together in a companionable silence later that week when he laughs out loud at something he has read.

'This writer. Most amusing,' he says. 'The things he saw in Africa . . .'

'Would you like to read me some of it?'

'Well, you have to know the context. About the French. At Teruda.'

'Really.'

'Name of Wallis. Robert Wallis.' He puts the paper down to pick up his pipe. 'Are you all right, my dear? You seem a little pale.'

'I do feel a bit off colour. And the room is quite stuffy.'

'Would you like me to wait a few minutes before I smoke?'

'Thank you.'

'Or you could always go into the sitting room.'

She gets to her feet. 'Perhaps if I sit near a window I will feel better.'

'Well, be careful not to catch a chill.'

'If I do catch one, I shall be sure to release it again immediately.'

He stares at her. 'What?'

'I was joking, Arthur. I don't know why. I was thinking of something else at the time.'

'Good heavens,' he says, returning to his paper.

Later, at dinner, there is another incident. He is explaining to their guest, a visitor from France, that the Liberals were the most reforming government that the country has ever seen; that they transformed the lives of the working classes beyond recognition—

'If you are a man, that is,' his wife interjects. 'For the women, there is to be no change.'

Their visitor smiles. Arthur shoots his wife an anxious glance, fearing that she is about to mount her hobbyhorse. 'Remember your condition, my dear,' he murmurs, as Annie helps their guest to some vegetables.

His wife looks at him; then, somewhat to his surprise, she nods meekly and remains silent for the rest of the meal. It is extraordinary, he thinks to himself, what a difference a medical diagnosis can make.

AFTER HER SECOND visit to Dr Richards, Emily instructs the chauffeur to drive home without her. 'I shall walk to John Lewis,' she tells him.

She walks down Harley Street into Cavendish Square, then on towards Oxford Street. She does not go into John Lewis; it is the walk she wanted. She passes beneath a billboard advertising Castle Coffee: a bride and groom, in wedding clothes, are toasting each other with cups of Castle. The headline reads: 'I VOW to give him Castle. What every husband wants!'

If only marriage were so simple, she thinks.

A noise on the other side of the road catches her attention. A small group of women has gathered and one of them holds a placard: 'DEEDS NOT WORDS!' For a moment it feels as if someone has written it just for her. Then she sees that they are suffragists. Two of the others are unfurling a banner on which is written in black paint: 'VOTES FOR WOMEN.' The group raises a ragged cheer, causing passers-by to stop and stare. Rather than be seen gawking, Emily turns to watch their reflection in a shop window.

'Are you shopping here, sister?' asks a woman standing beside her.

'I am not, no. I am walking home.'

'Then you will not mind if I do this. Please step back.' The woman raises her hand and makes a stabbing motion at the window.

Emily jumps, then sees that the woman is merely scrawling the downstroke of a huge V with a lipstick concealed in her hand. In a few moments, the same slogan that is on the placard has been written in three-foot high oxblood letters across the window.

Up and down the street come shouts and cries of outrage as other windows suffer the same fate. There is the crash of breaking glass. A policeman's whistle sounds. Nearby, someone yells. 'Down there!' A man is pointing in their direction. 'That's one of 'em!' The woman looks panicked.

'Quick, take my arm,' Emily says. She takes a step forward and hooks the woman's arm in hers. Then she swings her round to face the street. 'Look down there, as if you can see something too,' she urges her companion. 'But whatever you do, don't move.' Sure enough, a group of four men rush past them, going in the direction the two women are looking, their feet pounding on the pavement. She feels the other woman's body relax.

Emily says, 'I think they've gone.'

'Thank you.' The woman's eyes are shining with triumph. 'We have struck a blow for freedom.'

'What have shop windows to do with votes?'

'We have had enough of talk. We have a new group: we are going to make a nuisance of ourselves. Unless we do that, we shall never get anywhere.'

'But if you are a nuisance, you may annoy the men so much they never give us anything.'

'*Give?*' They are walking down towards Piccadilly now, the woman striding along confidently as if she knows where she is going. 'You make equality sound like a treat—like a new hat. It is our right, and the longer we go on asking for it politely, the more we give men the false impression that they can choose to deny it to us. Do you have money?'

'I'm married.'

'But you had money of your own, before? Then you pay taxes. There isn't a politician alive who believes in taxation without representation—until it comes to women. Why should they be allowed to take our money from us when we can't tell them how to spend it?'

'Believe me,' Emily says, 'I am strongly in favour of Votes for Women. I'm just not sure about being a nuisance.'

'Then come to a meeting and let us persuade you. Tonight, if possible. Here, I'll write down the address.' She scribbles something on a card and hands it to her. 'We will awaken the feminine force!'

Emily feels a surge of excitement. 'Very well,' she says. 'I'll come.'

It took me two years to get back. Perhaps fortuitously, my attempt to travel up through Sudan coincided with a small military stand-off between Britain and France, subsequently known as the Teruda Incident. I discovered I had some ability as a foreign correspondent, and starvation was averted for the time being. From Egypt I wandered up to Italy, and spent the summer on the shores of Lake Como, where I finished, and destroyed, a novel about a man who falls in love with a slave. It was a terrible book, but writing it was part of putting all that behind me, and once the flames had eaten into the last page of the manuscript I knew, finally, that I was free of her.

I discovered something important, during that long return. I had loved Fikre with an absolute physical passion, and even something a bit more besides. Despite what had happened, I found that I hoped she was happy. That may not seem like much of a discovery, compared to the naming of Lake Victoria or pinpointing the source of the Nile. But for me it was new territory, to be marked in full on the hitherto blank atlas of the heart.

In the time I had been away, London had reinvented itself yet again. Oscar Wilde, John Ruskin and Queen Victoria had all died within a few months of each other, just as the century ended, all those redoubtable Victorian queens escorting each other to the grave. Now, instead of Pater and Tennyson, people spoke of J. M. Barrie and H. G. Wells. The streets were full of what had been called autokinetics, but were now known as motor cars. The electrophone had become the telephone, and one could use it to speak to anywhere in the country. The mood of the city had changed too. London was well lit, well run and well regulated. The bohemians, the decadents and the dandies were all gone, chased from the half-shadows by the new electric streetlights, and the respectable middle classes had taken over.

I had written a few articles on my travels, and I managed to place them with the *Daily Telegraph*, leaving their offices in Fleet Street with a cheque for twelve pounds in my pocket. For a few weeks after the articles appeared in print, I knew what it was to be fêted. There were invitations to private houses—soirées at which I was expected to thrill the company with tales of bloodthirsty savages and the exotic otherness of Africa, all neatly wrapped up with the platitude that Trade would one day turn the place into another Europe. I disappointed. In my articles I had been forced to water down my opinions, but in the drawing rooms of Mayfair and Westminster I was less circumspect. I pointed out that the only bloodthirsty savages I had met were wearing white skins and khaki uniforms; that what we now called Trade was a continuation of slavery by more devious means; that the natives I had lived among were as sophisticated in their way as any society in Europe. People listened to me politely, shooting each other meaningful glances, then said things like, 'But in that case, Mr Wallis, what is to be Done With Africa?'

And I answered, 'Why, nothing. We should clear out—admit we don't own any part of it, and just go. If we want African coffee, we should pay Africans to grow it. Pay a bit more, if necessary, so that they have a chance to get themselves started. It'll be to our benefit in the long run.'

It was not the answer they wanted to hear, and generally those who had started the evening hanging on my every word had let go their grasp long before the end. That suited me: I was not there to make myself popular.

EMILY PINKER was a chapter in my life that I knew was closed, but her father was another matter. Finally, I could put it off no longer. I went down to Limehouse and sent my card in to his office.

He made me wait—of course. As I sat in one of the anterooms I watched a procession of porters and storemen with jute sacks on their shoulders, marching past me out to where a line of lorries waited in the street. I wondered why they did not store them in the warehouse.

Then I saw a face I recognised—Jenks, the secretary, although he was clearly rather more than a secretary now: he had two assistants running after him as he hurried back and forth directing the loading. 'Jenks,' I called out.

'Oh, hello, Wallis. We heard you were back. And wondered when we would see you.' He continued moving as he spoke, so that I was obliged to get to my feet and follow him. 'There,' he said to one of his assistants. 'Up there, on the second floor. Do you see? Space for at least another five hundred.'

I stopped, silenced by what I saw in front of me. The warehouse was not just full: it was crammed. On every side, walls of coffee sacks reached up to the roof. There were no windows—just a couple of arrow slits in the endless heights, where sacks had been piled up against the real windows and a sliver or two of light sneaked past. Between the great stacks were tiny pathways and winding corridors, staircases made of sacks, wormholes . . . There must have been over fifty thousand bags in that warehouse alone.

There was an open sack near where we stood. I reached down and pulled out a few beans, sniffing them. 'Indian typica, if I'm not mistaken.'

Jenks nodded. 'Your palate was always accurate.'

I looked up at the towers of sacks. 'Is it all the same? What's it for?'

'You had better come upstairs,' Jenks said.

PINKER WAS SITTING at his desk. The ticker-tape machine was chattering softly; he was holding the tape, reading the fast-flowing symbols.

'Oh, there you are, Wallis. Back at last,' he said, as if I had just been down to the West End for lunch. 'How was Africa?'

'Africa was not a success.'

'So I surmised.' He was still looking at the machine's strange rubric.

'The warehouse is very full,' I commented when he said nothing further.

'That?' He sounded surprised. 'That is nothing. You should see the bonded stores. I have four now; all larger than this, all filled to capacity. I am having to rent extra space until it is over.'

'Until what is over?'

Pinker explained that he had had a revelation: he had grasped, finally, that the coffee market was cyclical. If the price went up, plantation owners planted more, but the seedlings took four years to produce a crop. Four years after a price rise, therefore, a glut occurred, which caused the price to fall. Plantation owners went out of business or switched to other crops. Four years later, this caused a shortage; prices rose, and the planters expanded again.

'An eight-year cycle, Wallis. As immutable, as inexorable, as the waxing and waning of the moon. The cartel can mask it, but they cannot eradicate it. And once I realised that, I knew I had him.'

'Had who?'

'Howell, of course.' He smiled tightly. 'He'll be howling soon enough.'

Pinker had been waiting years for the cycle to come round to the point at which the price would be lowest. 'The Brazilian Government is taking out vast loans to buy up their farmers' coffee, and so smooth its passage onto the market. But it cannot last. The market is like a river: you can only dam it for so long. When the dam bursts, it will take everything with it.'

He crossed to a map of the world that dominated one wall. 'I have been making alliances, Robert. Arbuckle on the West Coast. Egbert's in Holland. Lavassa in Milan. We act together.'

'You have formed a cartel?'

'No!' He spun round. 'We have formed the opposite of a cartel—an association of companies who believe in freedom, the free movement of capital. You rejoin us at an auspicious moment.'

'I have not come to ask for my job back. I just wanted to apologise.'

'Apologise?'

'For letting you down.'

He frowned. 'But all's well. Emily is satisfactorily married. Hector's death, of course, was a tragedy—but it was an accident of his own making. And now, Robert, I am in need of someone with your knowledge of coffee.'

'What you have in your warehouse now is barely coffee.'

'Yes. And do you know something? Thanks to our advertising, the customer believes it tastes better than the finest arabica. If you put a cup of Castle and a cup of Harar mocca side by side, it is the Castle they would prefer. The average housewife's nose, it seems, is easily led.'

'You despise your customers,' I said, surprised.

He shook his head. 'I do not despise them. I have no feelings for them whatsoever. In a successful business there is no room for sentiment.'

'Be that as it may, I intend to make my living by my pen from now on.'

'Ah, yes—I read your articles. They were amusingly written, if a little misguided. But, Robert, you can continue to write for the newspapers as well as work for me. In fact, it might be useful; I could suggest some avenues for you to explore, set you right about certain matters—'

'That isn't quite how it works.'

'Then you will want to settle up.' His voice had barely changed, but there was now a dangerous glint in his eye. 'Three hundred a year, wasn't it? And you managed—what? Six months? Let us say you owe a thousand, and not bother with the small change.' He held out his hand. 'A cheque will do.'

'I cannot pay you,' I said quietly.

He smiled thinly. 'Then you had better stay with us until you can.'

ON MY WAY OUT, I encountered Jenks again.

'Well?' he said.

'He seems to want me on the staff again.'

'I'm glad to hear that, Wallis.'

'Are you?'

'Yes.' He sighed. 'The old man—I sometimes think he has gone a little odd, you know. Perhaps together we might be able to . . . well, to calm him.'

THE CURIOUS THING was that Pinker seemed to have no real use for me. Occasionally he would seek me out and deliver a lecture about the evils of price-fixing or the iniquities of the Exchange.

Once, when he had delivered himself of a particularly biting critique of his opponents, he glanced at me and said, 'Make a note of it, Robert. You will never remember it precisely unless you do.'

'But I am unlikely to have occasion to need to.'

'Write it all down,' he insisted. 'That way, when you come to tell the story, you will not have to guess—you will have the proof.'

Then I realised why he wanted me around.

'He means me to be his biographer,' I said to Jenks when we were alone.

He nodded. 'He thinks he is making history. He always has done. Emily used to record his utterances. Since she married, he has had no one.'

'Speaking of Emily, do you ever hear from her?' I asked, casually.

'Why would I?' he said coldly. 'She is married now; she has her own concerns. She does not need to mix with the likes of you and me.'

After that, I kept a note of my employer's observations. I picked up some snippets of Pinker family news, too. Ada had stayed in Oxford and married a don; Philomena had 'come out', as the phrase had it, going to society parties and mixing with artistic types in Bloomsbury. There was no longer any reason for them to come to their father's offices. As for Emily, since her marriage she was effectively barred from taking part in the business.

'Her job is to be a wife, and a politician's wife at that,' Pinker said testily, the only time I mentioned her. 'Doubtless she will soon have her own family to concern herself with. In the meantime, we have a business to run.'

Pinker began to instruct Jenks and me in the workings of the Exchange, the mysterious alchemy by which wealth is created in the City.

'We sold half a million sacks of coffee this month, and made a profit of two shillings on each. What if we'd had ten million bags under contract?'

'There is not so much coffee in the supply chain,' Jenks said, baffled.

'Yes. But suppose our bags are hypothetical. What then?'

'Then we would have made twenty times the profit,' I said.

'Exactly.' Pinker nodded. 'Where shall we find those ten million bags?'

Jenks threw up his hands. 'It is a riddle—a nonsense. The coffee does not exist, and nothing we can say will make it otherwise.'

'But it will exist in the future,' Pinker insisted. 'What if we could bring it back here to the present, where it will be more use?'

I said slowly, 'If someone had a contract to supply it at a later date, at a specified price . . .'

'Yes?' Pinker said eagerly. 'Go on, Robert.'

'And if you could buy that contract . . . Well, its value would go up or down, depending on the current price. A grower could take out insurance against a future fall in prices. He could buy a contract that assumed they would fall, and make a small profit to offset the greater loss from his crops.'

'Exactly,' Pinker said with satisfaction.

'But what does this have to do with us?' Jenks said plaintively. 'We have a coffee—Castle Coffee. People drink it. We have a duty to ensure that it continues to be there, on the shelves, not merely in some hypothetical sense.'

'Yes,' Pinker said, with a sigh. 'We have a coffee. And you are right, Simon—we must not be unduly distracted by fascinating possibilities.'

I think Jenks saw himself as the practical one, the diligent servant who ensured that his eccentric master always had a clean shirt to wear and socks on his feet. It was Jenks who dealt with the advertising agency now, Jenks who negotiated terms with Sainsbury and Lipton. In that commonsense world he was completely at home. It was the more philosophical, notional world of the Exchange that flummoxed him.

Pinker said to me one day, 'You have an affinity for finance, Robert.'

'That seems unlikely, given that I have never managed to stay out of debt for more than a day or two in my life.'

'I'm not talking about money. I'm talking about finance—a completely different matter. And I suspect it is precisely your attitude to debt that is the reason. Simon cannot shake off the idea that borrowing is a bad thing, that creditors must be paid off. But in this new hypothetical world, one can buy and sell debts and contracts just as profitably as one can sell beans.'

BY NOW the articles and the invitations had almost dried up, but there was an at-home in Pimlico to which I went, more to fill myself up with canapés and wine than because I wanted to tell, yet again, of my adventures.

And there she was.

She had her back to me, but I knew her instantly. When she half turned away from the person she was talking to, I saw that she had changed. There was more sharpness to her face and less bloom on her cheeks.

She was not one of the group who hung on my words, but her husband was, and he called her over. 'May I introduce my wife?' he said. 'Emily has a particular interest in Africa, Mr Wallis.'

Her handshake was brief, her expression unreadable.

'Indeed,' I said, 'Miss Pinker and I are old acquaintances. We both worked for her father.'

At that the man flushed. 'She is not Miss Pinker now.'

'Of course. My apologies, Mrs . . .?'

'Brewer,' she said. 'Mrs Arthur Brewer.'

'And she was never actually employed by her father,' Brewer said nervously, looking around to see who might be listening. 'She used to lend a hand with his papers, but these days being my wife gives her plenty to do.'

'Indeed,' I said, 'there is nothing wrong with employment.'

She raised her eyebrows a little. 'Do you have employment, Mr Wallis?'

'Not enough. Your father keeps me on his staff, but I have little to do.'

'Oh, but you are a writer,' Brewer said. 'I read several of your pieces on Africa—they were most evocative; one could almost smell the dust . . .' And he was off, chattering away, while my eyes remained locked on his wife.

Yes, she had changed. Her eyes had a slightly bruised quality, and there was a belligerence in her gaze that had not been there before.

Brewer was still rattling on. Clearly he had no idea that she and I had once been engaged. I wondered at that. Why had she not told him?

It was hopeless. I could not speak to her with him there and, besides, people were starting to stare and whisper. I said to Brewer, 'Sir, I agree with everything you have said, and since that leads me to believe that I will agree with everything else you say, there seems little point in prolonging our conversation.' I nodded at his wife. 'Mrs Brewer. It was good to see you again.'

I moved to the other side of the room. Behind me I heard Brewer say, 'Well!' in a hurt tone. I did not care that I had offended him: I cared only whether his wife would come after me.

She did not, directly. I circumnavigated the room, talking briefly to this person, then that, allowing myself to be swept, as if by accident, into quiet corners. Still she did not come. Until, finally, as the room was beginning to thin, I turned and found her behind me, replacing an empty glass on a tray.

'Tell me one thing,' I said quietly. 'Are you happily married?'

She stiffened. 'You're very direct.'

'There's no time for diplomacy. Are you happy with that man?'

She glanced over at where Arthur was holding forth. 'Is happiness the purpose of a marriage?'

'I'll take that as a no. May I see you?'

'Come to Castle Street tomorrow at four.' She put the glass down. 'You know, Robert, you've become really quite fierce,' she said as she moved away.

Fierce: that was one word for it. What I had felt when I looked across that room and saw her profile—even before I met the look of tired accusation in her eyes—was a fierce emotion, certainly. But it was more than that.

Love without kisses is not love, the Galla warriors sang. What was it, then? What was this thing that remained after mere desire had departed? What was the name for this thing without kisses that burned more fiercely than a kiss—this thing more terrible than love?

THE NEXT DAY I was there at four, and she was not. The café was closed up, its windows shuttered, and from the air of decay it had clearly been that way for some time. I paced up and down, waiting. It was after five when she finally appeared, walking purposefully down the street towards me.

'In here,' she said, producing a key.

I followed her inside. Dustsheets covered the marble tables, but the coffee-maker behind the bar looked clean.

Emily went to a cupboard and pulled out a jar of coffee beans. 'These are fresh. Kenyan. I brought them here myself, last week.'

I did not understand. 'Why?'

'I come here sometimes on my own to drink good coffee—what we have at home is awful. And occasionally I need a quiet place to meet . . . certain people. Somewhere my husband is not aware of.'

'I see.'

She glanced at me sharply. 'Do you?'

'I shan't judge you for taking lovers, Emily. God knows I've had my share.'

She ground the coffee and the aroma filled the room.

'Is there anyone at the moment?' I asked.

She smiled. 'You're very blunt these days. No, I don't have a lover at the moment. I find myself rather too busy for that.'

When the coffee was done she carried it to one of the tables. I picked up my cup; there was a lemony sharpness and a rich, blackcurrant depth.

'It has been a long time,' I said at last, 'since I had a cup as good as this. I'm surprised you still own these cafés, actually.'

'We don't. They lost money and had to be sold. But when I found out that the new owners intended to turn them back into public houses, I insisted on keeping this one. I don't think Arthur has even realised it exists—he is only interested in the stocks and shares, the ones that make money.' She sighed. 'It's the law of the jungle, isn't it—survival of the strongest?'

'Having spent some time in a jungle,' I said, 'I can tell you that its laws are considerably more complex.'

She put down her cup. 'Robert? Will you tell me how Hector died?'

So I told her the whole thing. She wept silently as I spoke.

'Thank you for telling me,' she said when I had finished. 'And for what you did. I know you weren't fond of Hector, but I'm glad you were there.'

'You loved him.'

'I was very young.'

'But you loved him . . . fully. Not as you loved me.'

She turned her head away from me. 'What do you mean?'

'You and I were friends. Not lovers.'

Outside, there was a sudden rattle as a noisy knot of children ran down the street, running sticks along the railings. Then they were gone again.

'What I told my father,' she said, 'was that I wanted to marry you. That should have been enough, surely?'

'But you were in love with Hector.'

'That was already long over, as you are presumably aware, since you read the letters. He preferred his bachelor freedom. And you'—she turned to me at last, her eyes accusing—'you fell in love with someone else.'

'Yes. I am sorry for that.'

'And did you'—she made an ironic gesture—'"love her fully"?'

'I suppose I did.'

'I see.'

'Emily, I have done a lot of thinking these past few years. I asked to meet you today because I wanted to apologise. For my letter. I was . . . discourteous.'

'Discourteous!'

'It would mean a great deal to me if you were able to forgive me.'

'Let me get this straight, Robert,' she said, setting her cup down rather firmly in its saucer. 'You are asking my forgiveness for the manner in which you broke off our engagement, and for nothing else?'

'I am aware that there are probably other things—'

'Well, let us think what those other things might be,' she said. 'You asked my father for my hand in marriage, without telling me you were thinking of doing so. You spent every evening when we were together in the fleshpots of Covent Garden—did you think I didn't know? You went off to Africa in a fearful sulk, and you wrote me those horrid letters in which you made it clear that you felt trapped, even before you fell in love with someone else—'

'Believe me, I would do anything—anything—to make amends. To put all that behind us. To start again.'

She said incredulously, 'You mean, to be your . . . to be what that woman was to you?' Two spots of colour had appeared in her cheeks.

I said slowly, 'Until we have done that—until our bodies have been together—it's like smelling without tasting. I want us to feel . . . Well, I can't explain it. But learning to feel the pleasure of love is like learning to taste—your palate changes, just as it does when you learn to cup coffee.'

There was a long silence. 'And this is what you have learned on your travels, is it?' she said furiously. 'How to insult women?'

'I had rather thought that the continuation of my feelings for you after so long was a compliment,' I muttered.

'Anyway, it's quite impossible.'

'Because of Arthur?'

'No. You don't understand. I am not that sort of woman. Don't protest, Robert, there's nothing either of us can do about it.'

'But what about the others? The men you meet here?'

'Those I meet here are women. We need somewhere private to plan our criminal actions.'

'Oh . . .' I said, puzzled.

'I am what's called a suffragette,' she explained. 'It is a name we loathe. An attempt by the newspapers to make us sound silly and ineffectual.'

'Ah.' I thought about it. 'There's been some criminal activity, hasn't there? Slogans on walls, women trying to demonstrate in the Commons—'

'That was us. At least, some of it.'

'But what will happen if you're caught?'

'We'll go to prison. And it isn't "if"; it's "when". There'll come a time when the Movement will need prisoners—martyrs, if you like. Imagine it, Robert, these "silly girls", these "suffragettes", actually prepared to be imprisoned for our cause. They won't be able to call us the feeble sex then.'

'And your husband? Does he know?'

She shook her head. 'But he's bound to find out sooner or later.'

'Perhaps he'll divorce you.'

'Not him. It would look bad.'

'And why is it so important, the chance to elect an MP, to send some pompous oaf like Arthur to the House? Is it really worth risking prison for?'

She looked at me with utter certainty. 'It is the only way left. They promised it to us so many times and every time they lied. They deny us the vote, the recognition that we have rights as great as men's. Voting—representation—is where they have made their stand. The House of Commons is their citadel. And so we must storm it, or accept for ever that we are not their equals.'

'I see.'

'Will you help us?'

'Me!' I said, astonished. 'How?'

'I've thought for some time that if our group is to grow we'll need a place where meetings can be held, and where people who are interested can come to find out more. A place like this café. I've been looking out for someone to manage it. Yesterday, when you said you were at a loose end, it struck me that you would do it very well. I could ask my father to release you, for the afternoons at least—I'm sure he would agree to that. And you could live in the rooms above the shop—it would save you paying rent.'

I shook my head. 'I'm flattered, Emily, but surely you can see it's impossible. I've had articles published, things are starting to happen for me.'

'Oh, yes. I see perfectly,' she said with a rush of anger. 'When you said just now you would do anything to make amends—that was just another pose, I take it?' She glared at me. 'You had better go.'

There was a long silence. 'Oh, very well,' I said. 'I'll run your blasted café.'

'Really?' She sounded surprised.

'I said so, didn't I? Don't ask me why. I seem to have a ridiculous inability to say no to anyone in your family.'

Her eyes narrowed. 'You do realise I will never sleep with you?'

'Yes, Emily. I do understand that.'

'It would be a considerable undertaking. Once it became known that this is where we gather . . . you'll have to keep a pickaxe handle behind the bar. And the salary will be quite small. You will not be able to afford your usual cohorts of whores and concubines. Why are you smiling?'

'I was recalling a previous negotiation with a Pinker over the terms of my employment. I am sure that my pay will be sufficient for my modest needs. However, I do have one condition. No blends. I'm damned if I'll take coffees from all over the world, only to mix them up into one nameless sludge.'

She put out her hand. 'In that case, Robert, we have ourselves a deal.'

Eleven

Pinker's reaction was not, initially, favourable. I assumed it was the impropriety that bothered him—his married daughter employing someone who had once been close to her. But eventually he relented.

For the next few weeks I was busy. There were builders to oversee, staff to hire, a brief legal skirmish when it became apparent that we could no longer call it Castle Coffee. We renamed it the Castle Street Coffee House, and everyone was satisfied.

I met Frederick Furbank, the importer who had supplied Emily with her Kenyan coffee. 'Robert Wallis!' he cried, pumping my hand. 'I have to tell you, sir, that a modified version of the Wallis–Pinker Method has now been adopted by all the smaller merchants. Wait until I tell the others that I am buying coffee for Wallis!'

Furbank and I tasted some coffees together and made an initial selection. We talked coffee-trade jargon happily for several hours, and by the end of it I knew Emily had a supplier who would not cheat her.

Once the café opened, I was busy supervising the waiters, attending to the Toselli machine, even washing cups and dishes when the occasion required. And almost from the start, there was a steady stream of women who came there looking for information. You could always tell those ones—their expressions both determined and anxious as they slipped through the door.

The militant Suffrage Movement—the Cause, as they called it—was growing quickly now. Emily and her co-conspirators spent long hours in the back room debating everything—their constitution, their ethics, what was legitimate action and what was not, how to make their case. For a movement whose avowed slogan was 'deeds not words', there certainly seemed to be an awful lot of the latter.

There were times, in fact, when I thought it was all just a girlish adventure. But then, at the end of their interminable meetings, they would put on their hats, tie up their boots, and head off in ones and twos to daub slogans on government buildings with buckets of whitewash, or to flypost walls with their manifesto. These escapades, I admit, filled me with misgivings.

'Don't stand there glowering,' Emily said one night, as she prepared to go and plaster bills on Chelsea Bridge. 'If you're worried, come along.'

'What makes you think I'm worried?'

'You've polished that cup so thoroughly you've almost punched a hole in it. Really, I shall be perfectly all right, but come if you want—it would be useful, actually; you could hold the bucket while I apply the paste.'

'Very well. If you need me, I'll come.'

'I didn't say I needed you, Robert; I said you would be useful.'

We hailed cabs in the street—five ladies with proclamations under their arms, each carrying a bucket of wallpaper paste and a brush—and me.

Emily and I alighted on the Embankment. She began to unroll the posters, but there was a brisk wind and it was no easy matter to paste them.

'You would never have managed this alone,' I said as a bill rolled across the bridge for the fourth time. I sprang to retrieve it.

'Yes, well, you have the satisfaction of knowing that you were needed after all,' she said crossly, clutching at her hat.

'You're annoyed!'

'Of course I am. I can't get the dratted things to stay on the brickwork.'

I glanced across the bridge. Two policemen were strolling across from the Lambeth side towards us. 'Run!' I shouted.

We hurried back towards the Embankment. There was a whistle; then thudding feet echoed across the bridge.

'Faster!' I urged, taking her by the elbow.

We worked our way towards Parliament Square, flyposting any public buildings we passed on the way. Then, by Westminster Bridge, we saw a motor car parked by the side of the road. On the bonnet was a government flag.

'That's the Home Secretary's car,' Emily said. 'Come on, let's flypost it.'

'But, Emily—you can't. It's a lovely machine. A thing of beauty.'

'Oh, in that case,' she said sarcastically, 'let's wander around until we find something ugly and flypost that instead, shall we? Robert, I can't help the fact that the Home Secretary has chosen a particularly nice machine to be driven around in. The message is what counts,' she added, sloshing paste onto the backs of four or five bills. 'Keep a lookout, will you?'

'This isn't fair play,' I protested, even as I did as she asked.

'The thing about women, Robert,' she said as she applied the greasy back of the first bill to the car's pristine metalwork, 'is that we are not gentlemen. And we are not playing a game; we are fighting the fight.'

'Oi!' There was a shout. I turned. The policemen had spotted us again.

We pelted down numerous side streets, until at last I drew her into a quiet, darkened doorway. We waited, listening. The streets were silent.

'I think we've lost them,' I said. 'We should give it five minutes, to be sure.'

'Isn't this wonderful?' she said. 'You always wanted to be a rebel.'

I could not help it—those flashing eyes; the panting lips; the rise and fall of her chest as she caught her breath . . . I kissed her.

She kissed me back—I was sure of it: deeply, lingering, with a sigh of pleasure. But when I went to kiss her a second time she stopped me with a hand on my chest. 'We must find you a wife, Robert,' she said quietly.

'What do you mean?'

'You and I—we are friends now, aren't we? We have thrown over the trivialities of romance for the deeper bonds of comradeship.'

'Don't mock me, Emily.'

She sighed. 'I'm sorry for making light of it. But I meant what I said. You and I are pals. If you want any more you must find someone else.'

'I don't want anyone else,' I said, letting go of her shoulders.

The Government had learned from the suffragettes' successes in Manchester, and, in London, decided on a different policy—that of belittling them. The impression they gave was that the militants were over-excitable females with nothing better to do, rather than the threat to natural order they had been portrayed as in the north. In the back room of the café, the suffragettes decided to make a show of force by holding a procession.

The procession was planned for Easter Monday. The newspapers called it the 'Ride of the Valkyries' and 'the charge of the petticoat soldiers', but all that was water off a duck's back to Emily by this time.

'Would you like me to come with you?' I asked.

'Why not?'

'Shall I bring my pickaxe handle?'

'Oh, I doubt you will have any need of that. The pitched battle can wait until another occasion.'

We were to march—or rather process—from Trafalgar Square to Westminster, where the women would present their petition to the House of Commons. When we got to the square, my first thought was that Emily had done well—the place was crowded. Then with a sinking feeling I saw how many of those milling about were men. Looking vulnerable in the middle of the square, fifty or sixty women and a few male supporters stood waiting.

We set off, with a mob of about two hundred on either side. Some shook their fists, some howled abuse, most just eyed the women with an interest that was openly sexual. Occasionally hostility turned to violence. I saw three men run towards an embroidered banner, tear it from the women's arms and stamp on it until all that was left were some broken sticks and a few sodden rags. More policemen were standing not twenty feet away, watching.

Few of us in the procession were men, but we were a particular target. To begin with I did not understand why I kept hearing a peculiar clucking sound, until I also heard the shouts of 'Henpecked! Henpecked!'

I felt Emily push her arm through mine as we walked. 'Just ignore it.'

'On the contrary,' I said, 'I was thinking what a pleasure it is to be mistaken for your husband.'

As we entered Westminster Square the crowd pushed in behind us. In front of us, blocking the way to the House, was a line of mounted policemen. It seemed that we were not to be allowed to present our petition after all.

All around us the chanting intensified, and then, quite without warning, there was a commotion on our right as a group of men rushed into the marchers, grabbing the women and wrestling them to the ground.

'Why don't the police do something?'

'They are moving at last. Look.'

It was true—the police had drawn their truncheons. But with a sickening sensation I saw that it was the suffragettes who were their targets. Screams filled the air. We could not escape. The press of the panicking crowd all around us was too thick, and although we were pushed this way and that, we always got swept back to the same place. The blue uniforms and their truncheons were within touching distance. I could see the sweat on the red face of the policeman nearest to me as he knocked a woman to the ground.

'Get behind me,' I said to Emily. I clasped her to me, turning my back on that blue wave as it prepared to break over us.

I WAITED IN A CELL for hours, bloodied, bruised and thoughtful.

Allegiance is a strange thing. It can be intellectual—but it can also be visceral, a decision forced on you by events. I had stood alongside the women as they were attacked, and I suddenly saw the natural justice of what they were trying to do. If their demands were as trivial as the newspapers claimed, why go to such lengths to deny them? If females were such gentle, precious creatures, why club them to the ground at the first signs of dissent?

As I pondered these questions, the door opened. A policeman looked in and said, 'Come with me.'

Still handcuffed, I was led down the corridor into a gloomy room lined with white tiles, like a bathroom. Emily's husband was sitting at a steel table. Next to him was a dour-looking fellow in a black suit.

'Wallis,' Brewer said, looking me contemptuously up and down. 'I suppose I should have known.'

'Known what?'

He leaned back. 'When they told me that my wife and I had both been arrested, I was naturally concerned. To be in two places at once is difficult enough, but to have been making a civil disturbance outside the House while simultaneously denouncing it inside is surely quite remarkable.'

'That particular mistake was not of my making, I assure you.'

'No. It was mine. I should have realised that someone—or something—had infected my wife with this filth.'

'Where is she?'

'She is to be released on medical grounds.'

'What? Is she hurt?'

'She suffers from hysteria,' Brewer said calmly. 'Were you aware of that?'

'Hysteria? Says who?'

'I do,' said the man in the black suit.

'Dr Mayhews is her principal physician. It turns out that she has not been attending her appointments with the specialist for some time.' Brewer eyed me with distaste. 'In any case, she will now get the treatment she requires.'

'If you have harmed her—'

'I am sending her to a private sanatorium in the country,' he interrupted. 'And *you* will never make contact with her again. Do I make myself clear?'

I said, 'I intend to write a full account of today's procession—including the illegal activities of the police—and submit it to a newspaper.'

'Please do so. You will find that no editor in this country will publish it. Take him back,' he said to the policeman.

With deliberate insolence I said, 'I doubt very much that you will want my association with your wife to become common knowledge, Brewer.' I gave the word *association* a particular intonation. I knew what he would take it to mean. His face froze. 'If you have her locked up, I will publicise our relationship in every club and coffee shop in London.'

He recovered himself. 'The suffragists cannot afford that kind of scandal.'

'Perhaps. But I am not the suffragists. And I will stop at nothing—absolutely nothing—to have Emily released.'

'And if I do release her?' he said slowly. 'What do I get then?'

'My discretion.'

He snorted disbelievingly.

I shrugged. 'It is the only guarantee you will get.'

There was a long silence. 'Throw this man out,' he said at last. 'Doctor, we will make alternative arrangements for my wife's treatment in London.'

'YOU DID WHAT?' Emily cried.

'I told him I'd keep quiet about the affair we are having if he let you go.'

'I saw him just now,' she said, appalled, 'and he never mentioned it.'

'Perhaps he was too embarrassed.'

'No,' she said. 'I think we underestimate men like Arthur. How good they are at keeping their true feelings hidden. It is why they will never give us power unless they are forced to.' She looked at me. 'So you struck a deal over me. You had no right to. Even if it had been true about the affair.'

'I'm sorry. I could think of no other way.'

'And now I will have to face Arthur every day, and he will never say anything, but he will think he knows . . .' She sighed. 'Well, I have lost the moral high ground, but perhaps it will do me good to be a little humbled.'

'There is one possible compensation,' I said. 'If your husband thinks we are sleeping together, then we might as well be guilty as charged.'

'Might as well? What a romantic you are, Robert.'

'But you see my point? What is there to stop us?'

'Apart from the little matter of you having given your word. Oh, and your slight propensity to go and fall in love with other women. I'm sorry, Robert. Even put so irresistibly, I find I am able to refuse that offer.'

As THE PRICE of coffee climbed ever higher, so the quantities pouring out of Brazil and other South American countries turned to a flood. Now there was a new shadow on the horizon: overproduction. Who would drink all this coffee? True, standardisation had kept down the price of the finished article in the shops, but there was surely a limit to the demand? The price wobbled briefly, and still the supply rose, fuelled by planting decisions made four or five years earlier. Pinker watched the markets, waiting to pounce.

The Brazilian Government announced that it would deal with any oversupply by destroying the surplus itself, before it reached the market. The stock markets approved, and the inexorable rise of coffee, and the various bonds and currencies associated with it, continued unabated.

One of Pinker's contacts telegraphed from Brazil to report that a convoy of barges scheduled to dump sacks out at sea had been spotted unloading their cargo onto a freighter. The freighter's name was the SS *Nastor*.

My researches told me that the *Nastor* was registered to a shipping syndicate and was bound for Great Britain by way of Arabia. Jenks then tracked down a consignment of coffee from one of her previous trips. It was as we suspected: the sacks were labelled mocca, but their contents were Brazilian. The SS *Nastor* had been shipping beans to Arabia, where after a brief interval they were reloaded and sent on to Britain, to be sold at what was a low price for mocca but a rather good price for Brazilian.

Pinker was exultant—once again his instincts had been proved correct. 'You must tell the world, Robert. Your Fleet Street contacts—have lunch with a few of them, and let them know how Brazil honours its commitments. But do it subtly. It should not look as if it comes from us; people will say we have an interest.'

I did as he asked, and when articles appeared criticising the Brazilian Government, he professed himself well pleased. The market wobbled—and we milked the fluctuation for all it was worth.

THE SUFFRAGETTES had changed their tactics and were now heckling politicians at public meetings. I accompanied Emily on one of these outings, a mission to the Wigmore Hall to interrupt a speech by a senior government minister. Perhaps he got wind that something might occur. Anyway, after we had been waiting for half an hour, a spokesman announced that the Great Man had been delayed on parliamentary business and that his place would be taken by the MP Mr Arthur Brewer.

I glanced across at Emily. She had gone quite pale.

'You need do nothing,' I said. 'There are enough others to make a show.'

She shook her head. 'A principle is hardly a principle if it is dropped at the first sign of adversity. The others will be looking to me to do my part.'

The debate began. Arthur spoke well. His theme was Liberty and Security, and the balance that must be kept between the two; how the hard-won freedoms of Great Britain must not be thrown away—

To my right, a small figure in a smart green dress rose from her seat. Molly Allen, fearless as ever. 'If you think so much of Liberty,' she said in a high, loud voice, 'don't keep it just for the men.' She took out her banner and shook it. 'Votes for Women!'

Uproar. Instantly three stewards were pushing towards her, but she had quite deliberately seated herself in the middle of a row. A furious clergyman sitting behind her tore the banner from her hand. She promptly unrolled another. 'You may pass that one around,' she said. 'I have more, if anyone would like one.' Then the stewards reached her—one on either side, and there was a tug of war as to which would manage to yank her to him.

On the platform, Arthur was watching all this with an expression of amused tolerance. 'I see we have been graced by the presence of the ladies,' he said with a smile. 'But as I was saying—'

Geraldine Manners got to her feet. Geraldine was frail, passionate and nearly fifty years old—it was she who had first been responsible for recruiting Emily to the militants, after the episode in Regent Street. 'Answer the question!' she shouted. 'Will a Liberal Government give votes to women?'

Stewards charged furiously towards her. She barely had time to unfold her first banner before she was dragged backwards from the hall.

On the platform, Arthur's composure did not waiver. As soon as he could make himself heard over the hubbub, he raised his hand and said, 'The lady herself has had to rush off'—laughter—'but I will address her question. The answer is no.' Much applause. 'Now, to return to the real issue of the day, one that is close to the hearts of many in this room: employment—'

From the back of the hall I heard Edwina Cole's voice. 'Why do you take taxes from women when you won't let them vote?' She waited until they were all looking before she got to her feet, banner in hand. 'Votes for Women!'

In their haste to reach her the stewards were climbing over the chairs.

'Show some respect for your Member of Parliament,' a man shouted.

'He is not my Member of Parliament,' she retorted. 'I am a woman: I have no member.' One or two people laughed at that, though others winced at the coarseness of the joke. Then she was pulled down. There was a shriek; it sounded as if someone had punched her.

Emily was still deathly pale. 'There is no need,' I said quietly.

She did not answer. Shaking, she got to her feet. She pulled out a banner. 'What about the women?' she called. 'Why no votes for us?'

Brewer looked at her and his face froze. More stewards—those who had been unsuccessful in the race to get to Edwina—thundered towards us.

'Very well,' Arthur said slowly. 'I am for Free Speech: I will answer this question.' There was a ripple of applause, and one or two boos. 'Madam, your friends have illustrated far better than I could how dangerous it would be to give the vote to people like you—people who would abuse the democratic process without a second thought. They remind us that women who resort to this sort of behaviour in seeking the vote would, if they were successful, resort to the same methods to obtain any other political objective. Those who will not behave as citizens cannot expect the rights of citizens.'

Applause and cheers from the audience, over which Emily could just be heard, shouting, 'Other methods have failed! It is precisely because—'

But the crowd had ears only for Brewer, who was in full flow. 'Not only do they use hysterical methods; they would incorporate that hysteria permanently in the political life of the nation. They seek Votes for Women, yet are prepared to betray womanhood and all the virtues of their sex to get it. What does that say about them? What kind of example do they set their children?'

The meeting gave him a standing ovation, just as the stewards were laying violent hands on his wife.

'Get off me,' she cried at the men as they pushed and pulled her along the aisle, but there was no question of them letting her go now.

She had dropped her banner on the seat. Without thinking, I got to my feet. No one looked at me to begin with. We were all on our feet, clapping the glorious protector of our liberties. I shouted, 'Votes for Women!' to get their attention and, as soon as there was a lull in the noise, called out, 'What does it say about your marriage, Brewer, that your own wife is a militant?'

There was a pause. For a moment he seemed uncertain how to answer. Then he said languidly, 'I have already given this subject far more time than it deserves. Do we want to talk about women—or work?'

The cry came back 'Work!' but by then I too was already being manhandled out of the hall by the stewards.

THAT EVENING, of course, she has to confront him. He has arranged himself in their sitting room with his papers around him and he is waiting for her when she returns—the master in his domain, seemingly quite composed.

At last he says, 'I was surprised to see you at the meeting this afternoon.'

She takes a deep breath. So they *are* going to talk about it. And she is going to tell him why she did what she did—why she will not stop. This is hard—harder even than the meeting.

She matches the even modulation of his voice. 'You were already aware, I think, of my political views.'

'I was aware that you supported extremism. I had not known that you were now actively engaged in attacking the democratic process.'

'It is not a democratic process. Democracy requires the enfranchisement of the whole population, not just the male half—'

'Please,' he says acidly. 'We have both had enough speeches for one day. What you forget is that when you behave like this it is my name you are trampling in the dirt. As a Brewer, the reputation of the family is in your hands. And as my wife, your actions reflect on me. If you attack me in public, people will think I behave badly to you in private.'

'That is ridiculous.'

'Oh? You were not there, I think, when your friend Wallis made that very point to several hundred of the electorate.'

'He had no right to do that,' she mutters. 'I did not ask him to.'

'Perhaps you have less control over him than you think. People like that will use your movement for their own ends. Just as he uses you.'

'Arthur—you misunderstand. There is nothing between us.'

'Well, it hardly matters now. Emily, I have made some decisions. I have decided that you must give up Wallis completely. And you must give up Votes for Women. You must no longer be involved. Not in any form.'

'Arthur, I cannot agree to that.'

'I am no longer seeking your agreement. I am overruling you. This is my decision, and as your husband I expect you to abide by it.'

'And if I do not?'

'I would remind you of your marriage vows—'

'Is that what this about?' she cries. 'As if I have broken a contract of sale, and you would be recompensed?'

'For my part,' he says quietly, 'I meant every word of those vows.'

'It did not feel that way when you spoke to me in that horrid fashion in front of all those people.'

'The time and place was not of my choosing,' he says drily. 'Besides, if I had not addressed you when I did, the stewards would have treated you far more roughly. As it was, they were forced to wait. It calmed them down.'

She is not sure whether to believe him, or if this is just a politician's way of retelling events to his own advantage.

'In any case,' he adds, 'there is something else I wish to say. What Wallis shouted out . . . He asked what it said about my marriage, that my wife was a militant. It was offensive and personal. But he may have a point. Our relations . . . Perhaps I have not been as attentive to domestic matters as I ought.'

She is silent, unsure where this is going.

'Dr Mayhews is of the opinion that your hysteria will be eased when you are fulfilling the purpose for which nature intended you. Certainly I have noticed that few of these militants seem to be young mothers—'

'That is because young mothers cannot leave their children—'

'Be that as it may. I have decided it is high time we started a family.'

'What!'

'Dr Mayhews is in full agreement. Although you are somewhat delicate, he observes that it is frequently nature's way to strengthen the female frame during pregnancy, with corresponding benefits for mental robustness.'

'Arthur,' she says, aghast, 'I am too busy to have children just now.'

'But you are not going to be busy, because you are going to give all that other business up,' he says reasonably. 'We will start immediately.' He stops. 'You would not refuse me this?'

'Of course not,' she says dully. 'If you will excuse me, I will go and ask Annie to draw me a bath.'

'And I shall be up presently.' He gestures at the papers. 'I have some work to finish, but I will not be long.'

THE FOLLOWING DAY Emily told me briefly about Arthur's reaction to their encounter at the meeting. Finally she said—with a little gasp that was trying to be a laugh—'We are trying for a child.'

'Are you serious?'

'Arthur is very serious. You cannot imagine how seriously . . . Well, never mind.' She sighed. 'I am not certain whether he means to punish me with pregnancy, or whether he genuinely believes it will cure me of the Cause.'

'But you will let him?'

'I have no choice. As he reminded me, I made certain vows.'

'It was when you made them that you had no choice. After all, one cannot call in one's lawyer to rewrite the wedding vows clause by clause.'

'No. Perhaps it would be better if one could. But in any case, it is not quite as simple as you put it.'

'Why not?' I said, then saw what she was getting at. 'You want a child?'

'A family. Yes. Why do you look surprised? It is what most women want.'

'But you cannot be a mother and a militant.'

'Why not, exactly?' she demanded.

'Well, take yesterday. When those stewards manhandled you. Imagine if you had been pregnant.'

'Perhaps then they would have seen the brutishness of their actions.'

'In principle you are quite right, Emily—but what use will your principles be when you are lying in a hospital?'

'When will you get into your thick skull, Robert, that principles are not things to be put on and taken off again like one of your stupid jackets.'

'Actually,' I said, 'I possess very few jackets these days, a consequence of the low wages for which I labour. My employer is—'

'In any case, it is all your fault,' she snapped. 'It was the insult you hurled at Arthur that prompted all this in the first place.'

'Ah.'

'Ah, indeed. Though a slightly more abject "Ah" would be appreciated.'

'Emily, I'm so sorry. I should not have said what I did. I wanted to rile him—it was seeing you being roughly treated, and by him of all people.'

She sighed. In a different tone, she said, 'And I have to give you up. You and the Cause. He insists on it.'

'I see. Well, this is even more serious. What are you going to do?'

'I cannot give up the Cause,' she said briskly. 'I could give you up, I suppose, but since you and the Cause are now a job lot, and since I have already decided to defy him over the political side, I suppose you are here to stay.'

'Does that mean—'

'No, Robert. It does not.'

'How do you know what I was going to ask?'

'Because it is what you always ask. And the answer is always no.'

Twelve

Pinker made more money out of the movements in the coffee price after the revelations about the *Nastor* than Castle had generated in six months. The mood in Narrow Street was one of quiet triumph—and also shock. I think we had all surprised ourselves by how effortless this new way of generating money was. It required no warehouses, no machinery, no porters or menials, just a few signatures on some time contracts. It was profit without expense; it seemed to transform itself from a thought in Pinker's head to cash in the bank without any intermediary except his will.

He was generous towards his staff: they were all given bonuses according to their length of service. Those like Jenks, who had worked for him for many years, were now wealthy men.

To me, too, he was far kinder than he needed to be. Called into his office, I found him sitting in front of some ledgers.

'Ah, Robert. I am just going through the books, clearing up some anomalies.' He smiled. 'What a pleasure that is, to be able to cancel one's old mistakes with a stroke of a pen.'

I nodded, though I was not entirely sure what he meant.

'I am writing off the Ethiopian enterprise,' he explained. 'It is time to put all that behind us and look to the future again. A clean balance sheet—a blank slate, waiting to be filled with new endeavours.' He pushed the ledgers to one side. 'You owe me nothing, Robert. Your debts are annulled.'

'Thank you,' I said. 'But . . . '

'From now on, you will be paid the same salary as Jenks. And like him, you will be given a bonus every year, dependent on how well we fare.'

'That is very generous. But . . .'

He held up his hand. 'You are about to say, but you are an artist. I know. And that, Robert, is precisely why I value you so much. Some of the others do not see the big picture. Or they see it, but fail to appreciate its beauty. I wonder if they have the imagination to take this company forward. You and I understand that it is not enough to have a product. One must have a *vision*.'

'You're referring to your political ambitions? Temperance, Social Reform?'

He made a dismissive gesture. 'In part. But those are small fry, Robert. Art is neither moral nor immoral: it exists for its own sake. Well, then— why not business for business's sake? Why should an enterprise not simply exist, with no other purpose than to stand for ever, to be admired, and thus to change the way men think, or work, or live . . . You will understand, Robert, in time. You will see how great this company of ours can be.'

He seemed to be waiting for me to speak. 'Indeed,' I said politely.

'Let me be clear: I am offering you a job as one of my right-hand men. It is customary to say either yes or no.'

There was really no decision to be made. I needed a job and no one else was going to offer me one. I had no illusions about Pinker's visions. The man was a Napoleon, but he was a damned capable one, who paid handsomely.

'I accept with pleasure,' I said.

'Good. Then that is settled. And, Robert—move out of Castle Street soon, hmm? You can afford better accommodation on the salary I am paying you. And my daughter will soon have other things on her mind besides coffee.'

IF PINKER THOUGHT he was forcing me to choose between him and his daughter, he was mistaken. Although I had no intention of moving out of Castle Street until I had to, I barely saw Emily now. All her energies were directed towards her political work.

As the suffragettes' struggle became more intense, so their organisation became more autocratic. Previously there had been a constitution and elected officers, with decisions taken after a show of hands. Now the constitution was torn up and decisions by vote were replaced by orders from the top. 'The leaders must lead: the rank and file must carry out their orders,' wrote Mrs Pankhurst, their chairman—or, as she now styled herself, 'Commander in Chief of the Suffragette Army'.

'But isn't this the exact opposite of what you believe in?' I said to Emily on one of the rare occasions when we managed to have a cup of coffee together. 'How can you have an organisation fighting for democracy that bans democracy from its own workings?'

'It is the result that counts,' Emily said, 'not the methods.'

She was ordered to shout slogans at a certain minister; she did so. She was ordered to deliver handbills in a certain district; she did so. She was ordered to speak outside a factory in the East End; she did so, even though she was pelted with rotten eggs for her trouble.

One tactic of those who opposed them was to release mice or rats onto the stage when a suffragette was speaking, in the hope of provoking a girlish scream. I was present at the Exeter Hall when they tried that with Emily.

Without breaking stride she reached down and picked up the mouse, holding it up so the audience could see. 'I was a mouse too, once,' she said. 'Now it is Asquith who is the mouse. And look!' She pointed to a large rat that was scurrying across the stage. 'There is Mr Churchill!' It got her a cheer.

But then, a few minutes later, I saw her stagger. At first I put it down to the heat. Turning to the organiser, she said, 'May I have a glass of water?'

Water was fetched, but as she took the glass she staggered again, spilling some over her dress. I could hear the organiser saying to her in a concerned voice, 'Are you all right? You look done in,' and her answer, 'I am a little faint.' No sooner had she said it than she collapsed.

She was helped off. I hurried round to the side door and found her sitting on a chair, being fanned. 'It's just the heat,' she said, shooting me a warning glance. 'It is very stuffy in there.'

I did not dispute it, but we both knew that she was pregnant.

'WILL YOU STOP? If you go on like this, you will damage yourself.'

'What nonsense, Robert. Women have been giving birth for millions of years, and they have had to do much more arduous things during their pregnancies than making a few speeches. The sickness will pass in a few weeks.'

'Have you told Arthur?'

'Not yet. He and Dr Mayhews will almost certainly try to hospitalise me. So for the moment I intend to keep mum, as it were.'

'I am not at all happy about this.'

'I cannot stop now, Robert. We are at a critical stage—one more push and I do believe the Government will crumble.'

Personally, I thought the opposite—one more push and the Suffrage Movement would burn itself out. But I did not say so, for her sake.

I TOOK MY NEW-FOUND wealth down to Sotheby's, where I bought a number of fine drawings by a Renaissance master. I spread my rooms at Castle Street with Turkish rugs and frequented the more expensive departments of Liberty once again. It seemed, finally, that my life had settled on its course. I was a coffee merchant, working for the greatest concern in London.

I noticed, however, that there was a darker tone to Castle advertisements these days. As well as the pliable women of the early posters, they featured rebellious wives who got their just desserts. Women who had failed to give their husbands Castle were shown being scolded, spanked—or in one case having the offending liquid poured over her head—by husbands who demanded obedience in coffee as in everything else. One even showed a woman holding a placard, with the caption 'Who's in charge? Men, assert yourselves! If she's not serving Castle Coffee, it certainly isn't you!'

Doubtless the copywriters of J. Walter Thompson would claim that they were only reflecting the new mood, not amplifying it, but there was no doubt that battle lines were being drawn.

'THERE IS TO BE another march,' Emily said. 'The biggest yet. All the suffrage societies are coming together to organise it. They are calling for a million people to fill the streets all the way from Hyde Park to Westminster.'

'And I suppose you intend to go, despite your condition?'

'Of course. There are women who will make incredible sacrifices to be at that march. The least I can do is walk alongside them.'

'Let me take your place.'

'What?'

'I mean it. If you agree to stay safely at home, I will go instead. And if you insist on going, I will not. So the numbers will be exactly the same.'

'Do you really not see why it would not be the same thing at all?'

I shrugged. 'Not really.'

'We are not tokens to be counted. We are people who must be heard.' She stared at me helplessly. 'Robert, you have grown so cynical and bitter. What happened to the happy-go-lucky show-off my father met in the Café Royal?'

'He fell in love,' I said. 'Twice. And both times he failed to see that he was making a fool of himself.'

She caught her breath. 'Perhaps my husband is right. Perhaps you and I should stop seeing so much of each other. It cannot be easy for you.'

'I can't give you up,' I said shortly. 'I'm free of the other one but I can't be free of you. I hate it but I can't stop it.'

'If I really make you so unhappy, then you should go.' Something about her voice had thickened. I looked at her: the corner of her eye was glistening. 'It must be the baby,' she gulped. 'It is making me tearful.'

Seeing her crying, I could not quarrel with her. But neither could I go on as we were. She was right: the situation was becoming impossible.

AT NARROW STREET I found the porters unloading sacks from the warehouse. 'What's going on?' I asked Jenks.

'It seems we are selling our stocks,' he said drily.

'What—all of them? Why?'

'I have not been privileged with that information. Perhaps he'll tell you.'

'Ah, Robert!' Pinker called, spotting me. 'Come along—we are off to Plymouth. Just you and I—the train leaves in an hour.'

'Very well. But why Plymouth?'

'We are meeting a friend. All will become clear in due course.'

On the train, we sat in first class and watched the countryside go by. Pinker was strangely quiet, although I had noticed that he was more relaxed when he was in motion, as if the furious headlong impetus of the train somehow soothed his own restless need for activity.

Eventually we reached Buckley, a small country station near Plymouth, where a car was waiting. The doors bore a discreet monogram, a heraldic H.

'That's Howell's monogram,' I said, surprised.

Pinker nodded. 'We are going to his English home. We both felt it would be more discreet than meeting in London.'

Howell's English home was an Elizabethan manor house. Sheep grazed on either side of the long drive, and there were glimpses of the distant sea.

'A fine estate,' Pinker commented. 'Sir William has done well for himself. Ah! There is our host, come out to greet us.'

I recognised Sir William Howell from the portrait on packs of Howell's Planter's Premium. In the flesh he seemed leaner, more intimidating.

He and Pinker closeted themselves together in a drawing room for half an hour before I was called in. The space between them was strewn with papers.

'Come and join us, Robert! Sir William has brought us a gift.' Pinker held out a large envelope. 'Take a look.'

I slid out the pages and scanned them. It made no sense to me at first—a list of foreign names, figures and a series of subtotals at the bottom.

'Those are this year's output figures from the fifty largest estates in Brazil,' Sir William said. 'You had best not ask how I got them.'

I looked at the figures again. 'But this alone comes to more than Brazil's entire annual output.'

'Fifty million bags,' Pinker agreed. 'Whereas the Brazilian Government declares only thirty million.'

'What happened to the rest? Has it been destroyed?'

Sir William shook his head. 'It is an accounting trick—or rather, a series of tricks. They have built in false figures for wastage, downgraded certain estates, created losses that do not exist—anything, in short, to make it look as if they produce less coffee than they actually do.'

'If the Exchange knew about this . . .' I muttered.

'Exactly,' Pinker said. 'Robert, I think you should have a lunch or two with your journalist friends. We need the news to start coming out next week. You must say only that there is to be a great scandal. Then, when a statement is made in the House of Commons next Wednesday—'

'How do you know a statement will be made then?'

'Because I know who will be making it, and why. But that is only the start of it. There will be a Trade and Industry investigation announced, and the monopolies committee will call for sanctions against Brazil—'

My mind was racing. 'Trade and Industry—that's Arthur Brewer's ministry, isn't it? And he is the chairman of that committee.'

Pinker's eyes twinkled. 'What use is a son-in-law in the Government if one cannot provide him information on matters of national interest? But even then we will not release all the figures. You must feed different parts of the document to different newspapers, so that no one has the whole picture—they will all be speculating and the speculation will feed on itself—'

'The markets will stampede.'

'The markets will realise the truth, that they have been too trusting. The Brazilians release their own figures on Thursday. They will be another fiction—a gross underestimate. The difference is, this time people will be able to see it.' He leaned back in his seat. 'This is the moment, Robert,' he said softly. 'I have waited seven years for this.'

He was perfectly calm—they both were. I knew then that everything Pinker had done had been directed to this end.

I turned to Sir William. 'If the market crashes, it will ruin you.'

'I used to think so,' he said quietly. 'Like every other damn fool producer, I used to think we needed to support the price of coffee. But it is not so. It is the less efficient producers who will go to the wall first. When it is all over, and the price settles, my plantations will still make a profit—a small amount per acre, perhaps, but healthy when taken across the operation as a whole.' He nodded at Pinker. 'It was your employer who did the sums.'

'Why should Sir William's efforts support farmers less successful than himself?' Pinker demanded. 'The future is a smaller number of bigger companies, I am certain of it.'

Howell nodded. 'Life will be easier when only the big *fazendas* are left.'

I said slowly, 'But what about all those smaller producers? For twenty years they have been encouraged to plant coffee—to root up crops they can eat in favour of a crop they can only sell. What will happen to them?'

Both men looked at me blankly.

'They will starve,' I said. 'Some of them will die.'

'Robert,' Pinker said easily. 'We have an opportunity to free the markets from the grip of foreign control. Those people you speak of will find more efficient ways to make a living. They will turn to new enterprises, some of which may fail, but some of which will enrich their countries as coffee never could. Remember Darwin: improvement is inevitable.'

I said, 'There was a time when I might have swallowed that nonsense.'

Pinker sighed. 'Think what this opportunity could mean for you, Robert. Sir William and I are old men. Our time will soon be over; then a new generation will come to the fore. Why not you among them? You understand the need for bold decisions. Oh, you are young, and sometimes misguided, but we would be there to steer you.'

'And then there are the investors,' I said. 'All those who have put their savings into coffee bonds. They will lose everything too.'

Pinker shrugged. 'Speculation involves risk. They have profited handsomely from our labours. It is not them I am thinking of; it is you.'

They looked at me, waiting. I thought of Emily, defying her own husband to do what she thought was right. I thought of Fikre, bought and sold like a sack of beans, simply because of where and what she had been born. And I thought of my villagers picking coffee berries in the cloud forests of the Abyssinian highlands—coffee that would soon be almost worthless.

'I cannot help you,' I said.

'You cannot stop us,' Sir William said threateningly.

'Perhaps not. But I will not be part of this.' I got up and left the room.

I WALKED BACK to the station, down that long, elegant drive, past the grazing sheep—that idyllic English scene paid for by the sweat of a hundred thousand Brazilian workers. Pinker still had my return ticket: I travelled back to London third class, on seats that stained my fine suit with coal dust.

Pinker's plan was simple. In the parlance of the Exchange, he was taking a short position. He would sell not only the coffee he had, but coffee he did not have—making contracts to supply it in the future, in the expectation that by then the price would have fallen and he would be able to buy it in at a lower price than he had committed to sell for.

But short selling is not simply a bet on which way the market will go. In large enough volumes, it puts pressure on the price. There is no more coffee in the world, of course, but suddenly there are more sellers than buyers for it, and traders will take whatever they can get to close their positions.

If that pressure combined with a market panic, with ordinary investors rushing to sell, not even a government could buy enough to maintain the price. Pinker would bankrupt the Brazilian economy. And the world price of coffee, from Australia to Amsterdam, would tumble.

Currency speculators and other city men would all be in on it too. It was as straightforward as a game of poker. Pinker and his allies would sell coffee they did not own: the Brazilian Government would buy coffee they did not want: the winner would be the one who held his nerve the longest.

BACK AT CASTLE STREET, I found Emily preparing a banner. 'Your father is going to crash the market,' I said. 'He is in league with Sir William Howell. Your husband too. They are conspiring to cause a panic on the Exchange.'

'Why would they do that?' she said calmly, tying up her banner.

'They will all make fortunes. But I think that's only part of the reason—your father is obsessed with making his mark on history. Whether he destroys or creates, makes money or loses it—I don't believe anything really matters to him except that it is Pinker who is behind it.'

She rounded on me. 'That is wholly unfair.'

'Is it? When I first met you, it was Temperance he claimed to champion—how will crashing the price help that? And then he used to talk of Africa, and how coffee would turn the savages to God—when did you last hear him speak that way? They were just ideas, plucked from the air and squeezed dry. He never really believed in anything except himself.'

'Do not tar him with your own brush, Robert,' she said furiously.

I sighed. 'I know I have not been much use to the world, but neither have I done it much harm. What they are doing now will cause untold misery.'

'The markets must be free,' she said doggedly.

'Is freedom about destroying peoples' lives?'

'How dare you, Robert!' she snapped. 'You have achieved nothing, so you belittle him. You have always been jealous of my admiration for him!'

We quarrelled then—not argued, but quarrelled, both of us saying things that were designed to wound. But what hurt her the most, I think, was the accusation that her father was acting without any thought or principle.

'I will not stand for it, do you hear? He is a great man, a brilliant man. He cares. I know he cares. Because if he did not . . .' And then she was gone, the door slamming on its hinges as she went.

I thought, She will come back soon enough.

I had not reckoned with her stubbornness.

PINKER, SO JENKS told me later, went back to Narrow Street, gave Howell's figures to Jenks and instructed him to call the newspapers. The journalists were eager to help spread the rumours that would destroy the market. Were Howell's figures true? The more I thought about it, the more I doubted it.

Jenks told me that when Pinker had taken care of that, he went into his warehouse. It was empty by then—every bean he owned committed to the battle. He walked into that vast, echoing space and called, 'Jenks?'

'Here, sir.'

'Sell them, will you? Sell them all.'

'Sell what, sir?'

'All this, man.' Pinker's hands took in every empty corner of the store.

'There is nothing here, sir.'

'Can't you see them? My invisibles! My hypotheticals! Every alliance and coffee future, every contract we are good for. Prepare to sell them all.'

ON THE DAY of the march, it rained—not a light spring shower, but a downpour so heavy that it was as if the gods were hurling marbles down at London's streets. Westminster was a stinking quagmire. The endless ranks of bedraggled women set off anyway, but they had their heads down. Every marcher was blind to everything but the clinging mud around her own feet.

At 2.30, in the House of Commons, Arthur Brewer rose to ask a question. In his hand were Sir William's crop figures. Even in the House, the noise of the rain made it almost impossible to be heard without shouting. When the lobby journalists realised what he was saying, that the rumours were confirmed, they rushed to the telephones . . . The honourable members too, those with investments in coffee, were busy trying to reach their brokers. Even Pinker could not have predicted how swiftly the panic would grow.

She should not have been there. That much was obvious to everyone, in hindsight. When she collapsed in the mud, no one noticed at first: they were all falling over, slithering and slipping in their boots and petticoats, and the streets were coming to a standstill in the confusion.

Perhaps if she had been more careful she would not have lost the baby. But we can never know.

AT CASTLE STREET, I watched the weather turn from sunny to stormy—black clouds, the colour of a dark roast, gathering over the City. It may seem fanciful, but when the deluge started, it seemed to me, as if it was not rain but coffee beans that poured down from the heavens, drowning us all.

I had no desire to witness Pinker's victory in the Exchange, but the importer Furbank went. He told me later that when it was all over—when the Brazilian Government finally admitted defeat, and the numbers went into freefall—he was watching Pinker's face. He had expected to see the merchant exultant. But there was nothing in his expression, Furbank said, but a mesmerised, polite interest as he watched the numbers tumble.

THE RAIN HAD STOPPED. As Furbank and I crossed the river by Tower Bridge, the ships at Hay's Wharf were unloading their cargoes. But instead of taking the sacks of coffee into the warehouse, the porters were making a vast pile in the open area in front of the buildings.

'What are they doing?' Furbank asked, puzzled.

'I am not certain.'

Then, as we watched, a twist of smoke came from the far side of the pile.

'They have set fire to it. Look!' The stack must have been doused in petroleum spirit: within moments it was completely alight, the flames encircling it like a giant Christmas pudding. 'But why are they burning it?'

With a sickening sensation I realised what had happened. 'The new price—it is not worth the cost of storing it now. It is cheaper to burn it, and free up the ships for other goods.' I looked down the river. From other quays along the bank—Butler's Wharf, St Katherine's Dock, even Canary Wharf—came similar plumes of smoke. I smelt coffee on the wind—that bitter, beguiling perfume spreading like a thin, fragrant fog over London.

'They will burn it all,' I said wonderingly.

I will never forget that smell, or those days. I walked the streets of East London hour after hour, unable to tear myself away. I smelt Brazilian, Venezuelan, Kenyan, Jamaican, even mocca, all going up in those fires. A million cups of coffee, burned as if in offering to some terrible new god.

I DID NOT GO BACK to Pinker's, but a fortnight afterwards, as I was locking up the café, I heard a knocking on the door. 'We're closed,' I shouted.

'It's me,' a tired voice said.

I let her in. She had a coat on, and on the pavement was a valise.

'I came by cab,' she said, 'and now I have sent it away. May I come in?'

'Of course.' I looked at the bag. 'Where are you going?'

'Here,' she said. 'If you'll have me, that is.'

I made coffee while she told me what had happened.

'Arthur and I had a row. Both of us said such things—well, you know how angry I can get. I told him he was nothing more than my father's creature, and for once he lost his self-control.'

'He hit you?'

She nodded. 'Not even particularly hard—but I cannot stay with him now. I'll stay here, if you really don't mind.'

'Mind? Of course not. I should welcome it.'

'You do understand, though, don't you, Robert—there must be no impropriety. People can say what they like, but we must know we have nothing to reproach ourselves for.'

I sighed. 'Very well.'

'Oh, don't look like that. In any case, I suspect between Arthur and the baby I have been rather wrecked for all that.'

'You'll recover. And when you do . . .'

'I do not want to give you false hope, Robert. If you find it difficult simply to be my friend, then you must say so and I will stay somewhere else.'

SOMETIME THAT NIGHT, very late, I woke up and heard the sound of crying. I went to her, and put my arm round her, and said, 'It will be all right.'

'I have failed,' she sobbed. 'I have failed at everything. I am no good as a wife, no good as a mother, no good as a suffragist.'

'Shh,' I said, 'it will be all right,' and I held her, very still and quiet, while she sobbed her poor heart out until morning.

Thirteen

Four weeks later Pinker holds an Extraordinary General Meeting of his board. Since the board consists of himself, Emily, Ada and Philomena, the meeting takes the form of a lunch—a lunch of celebration, the daughters assume, to toast their father's successes in the Exchange.

The sisters have not seen each other recently, and there is much family news to catch up on. Only Emily is a little quiet.

It is over coffee that Pinker finally brings up the business of the day. 'My dears,' he says, looking around the table. 'This is a family occasion, but there are also one or two company matters we are obliged to discuss. I have asked Jenks to take the necessary minutes.'

The secretary comes in and sits to one side, greeting the sisters with a smile. He balances a folder on his knee and takes out a pen.

'We are a family business,' Pinker begins. 'That is why we are able to have these meetings in this way. It is now seen as a rather old-fashioned way of doing things, I'm afraid. Public companies, listed on the Exchange, who open up their stock to the opportunities of the market—these are the companies that will have the resources and the flexibility to expand across the world. These companies, you may have observed, can also buy and sell each other. Old enemies are having to forge new alliances. Lyle and Tate, for example—two long-time rivals who are now forming a single entity.'

He pauses. 'I have been having discussions with one of our competitors. A combination of our interests would suit both parties: in Castle we have the better market share, while he has a greater expertise in the production of the raw material. He is rich in assets; we are rich in cash. Together, I believe, we will create a company capable of taking on the world.'

'Who is this person, Father?' Ada asks.

'It is Howell,' Pinker says. 'Sir William Howell.'

There is a stunned silence. Philomena says, 'But you hate each other.'

Pinker smiles. 'Somewhat to our surprise, we find we have much in common. I doubt we will ever be friends, but we can certainly do business.'

This time the silence goes on for some time.

'This company will be listed on the Exchange. An announcement will be made tomorrow morning. This will mean the end of Pinker's as a family firm. The new company will have to be run in a different way. All the shareholders, for example, will be eligible to attend the General Meetings.' He looks round the room. 'I doubt they will all fit into our dining room.'

Nobody smiles.

'Will we be shareholders?' Ada asks.

'You will have some shares, yes. But they will not be voting ones.'

'So we are being asked to sell?' That is Philomena's voice.

'Yes. You will all receive money—a great deal of money—from the sale of your shares to the new company.'

'I don't know . . .' Emily says.

'If we are not to be swallowed up by one of the big American firms, we must become a big firm ourselves,' Pinker says firmly. He pauses. 'There is something else that has influenced my decision. Sir William has a son.'

They stare at him.

'Jock Howell has been educated in all aspects of his father's business.

After we have formed the company he will need to come and run this side of things for a while, under my auspices of course. Then, when Sir William and I retire, he will be well positioned to take over the combined operation.'

'You would give away your business—to Howell's son?' his eldest daughter says, aghast.

'What choice do I have?' Pinker says quietly. 'He has a son. I do not.'

'So if one of us had been a boy—' Emily says with sudden fury.

'No, no, no,' Pinker says soothingly. 'It is not like that at all. But you are married, and to an MP. Ada and Richard have Oxford. Phil is more than occupied with parties and dances. Of course it cannot be any of you.'

'I would have taken it over, if you had only asked me,' Emily says. 'I would have avoided marriage altogether, if that had been the alternative—'

'That's enough,' her father says sharply. 'I do not want to hear any criticism of your husband. There has been quite enough scandal as it is.'

She bites her lip.

He gestures down the table. 'Jenks, thank you, you may go.'

Jenks closes his file and gets to his feet.

'Wait,' Emily says. 'We should have a vote.' She looks around the table, at her sisters. 'If we all have shares, we should vote on this.'

'Don't be ridiculous,' her father says. 'This is not some suffragette meeting. This is my company.'

'You will not be able to argue with your shareholders like this when you are listed,' she points out. 'They may not even approve of your Jock Howell. Or perhaps he will have *you* voted off—have you thought of that?'

He hesitates.

'All those against the proposal,' she says, raising her hand.

'Enough,' her father snaps, recovering himself. 'Jenks, you may go. Record that the proposal was carried with no opposition.'

'Yes, sir,' Jenks says. He leaves the room. There is a long, weighted silence, and then with a sudden cry Emily does the same.

SHE KEPT A ROOM at Castle Street, and as the tempo of the unrest accelerated she spent more and more time there. In all that time I hardly heard her speak of her husband or her father at all. She and I were almost a household, albeit of a somewhat unconventional kind.

'Robert?'

I looked up. On the counter was a mahogany box. Emily opened it. Inside were rows of glass phials, and a number of cups and spoons for cupping.

The Guide.

She placed four packets of coffee on the table and began to unwrap them. 'These are Furbank's best new coffees—two from Guatemala and two from Kenya.' When she had prepared the first set of grinds, she poured water carefully over them and looked at me expectantly. 'Well?'

I sighed. 'There is no point.'

'There is every point, Robert. Furbank says these are good, distinctive coffees. The people who produced them should not go under just because they are forced to sell them at the same price as Howell's industrial product. There are still enough people in the world who care about coffee. They simply need a way to distinguish the good from the poor, and the Guide cannot do that unless you keep it up-to-date.' She pushed a cup towards me.

I groaned. 'What do you want me to do?'

'Taste them. Aspirate, aerate and ultimately expectorate. Ready?'

Together we pushed down the grounds and slurped a little of the coffee into our mouths.

'Interesting,' she said thoughtfully.

I nodded. 'An aroma of bananas.'

'And on the tongue, a little natural roughness . . .'

'Even a touch of muscat grapes.'

The same tastes in both our mouths, our tongues, our lips: the sensations passing back and forth between us, like kisses.

'Blackberry, or peach?'

'Plums, I rather think. Or possibly damsons. Taste it again.'

'I would say rather, the crust of a freshly baked loaf.'

'Very well—I'll make a note. Will you change the cups?'

I said later, 'You know, we could start by asking Furbank to source the coffees we sell here from African farms, instead of big plantations. It would make little difference in itself but, if enough people did it, it might give a few small farmers an alternative to working for the white man.'

'I think it's an excellent idea.'

'Of course, it will make the coffee more expensive.'

'Will we make a loss?'

'I haven't the foggiest.'

'Dear Robert—you really have no idea how to run a business, do you?'

'It's businessmen who have no idea how to do that, in my experience.'

Out of the ashes of those fires rose a tiny wisp of something worth preserving—not hope, exactly, nor even love, but something fragile, delicate, ethereal as smoke: something that she and I shared in that room, and which was then shared with others, with Furbank and other importers, with a few passionate customers, and then a few more, growing little by little, like a series of tiny messages that flickered around the world.

AND THEN, as Emily had predicted, there came a time when her movement needed martyrs. In September, she was instructed to throw a stone through the window of the House of Commons.

'You need not go,' I said.

'Of course I need not. But I want to.' She shook her head. 'You don't understand, Robert. If it is my fate to be imprisoned; it will not be a sacrifice. It will be a privilege—the fulfilment of everything I have worked for.'

She was arrested on her first attempt. I wondered, afterwards, if she had waited until she was certain the policeman was watching.

Her trial was remarkably quick. Since she was not denying the charge, there were no speeches for the defence. The arresting officer read his notes; the prosecutor said a few words; the stipendiary magistrate declared the sentence—ten shillings or three weeks in jail.

Emily said calmly, 'I will go to jail.'

'Do you refuse to pay your fine?'

'I refuse to recognise the authority of this court, which is paid for out of my taxes without my consent.'

'Very well. Take her down.'

I TRIED TO SEE HER in the cells, but they would not let me. So I hung around outside with the rest of the crowd, hoping to get a glimpse of her as they moved her to Holloway. I spotted Brewer, dressed as if for a funeral.

'Happy now, Wallis?' he bellowed as he pushed his way through the crowd. 'Or is there any further degradation you would wish upon my wife?'

'I have no more desire to see her in prison than you do,' I said miserably.

Just then the Black Maria left the court, moving slowly through the crush, its bell ringing to clear a way. There was nothing to be seen of Emily in the back, but we set up a great cheering and clapping to try to encourage her.

Then I saw another face I recognised. 'Ada?' I called. 'Ada Pinker?'

She turned. 'Why, it's Robert.' She stepped towards me, and so did the woman she was with. 'I didn't know you'd be here.'

'Nor I you. Have you come down from Oxford? Emily told me you had married a don.'

'Yes, the movement is very robust there, but we haven't had the violence they've had here in London.' Ada sighed. 'I have a terrible feeling about this.'

'As do I. I suspect Emily may be fixed on hunger-striking.'

'We hope to be able to visit her,' Ada said. 'We're family, after all.'

I turned to her companion—a young woman a few years younger than Ada. 'I don't believe I've had the pleasure.'

'Oh, you have, Mr Wallis,' she said. 'Though I doubt it was a pleasure. I suspect your recollections of me will not be favourable ones.'

My bafflement must have shown on my face, because Ada said, 'Philomena is rather grown up since you saw her last.'

'Good Lord—the Frog?'

The young woman nodded. 'Not many people call me that these days.'

Now I looked at her more carefully I could just see an echo of the childish features I remembered. But the pouched, froglike eyes had changed—or rather, her face had changed around them. Now they gave her an unusual appearance, like someone who has just woken up.

'I kept all your letters,' she added. 'I drove my sisters mad, demanding to know when the next one was going to come. I used to learn them by heart.'

'I doubt very much they were worthy of repeated reading,' I said. We were walking away from the court now, along with the crowd.

We reached the Underground station and she stopped. 'We are going west. Shall I let you know if we hear anything from Emily?'

'Please.' I handed them my card. 'And it was a pleasure to see you both again, despite the circumstances.'

'You too,' Ada said earnestly, and we all shook hands.

As I took Philomena's gloved hand in mine she said, 'Did you write any more of your nonsense poems, Mr Wallis?'

I shook my head. 'I had hoped to have left nonsense behind. Although these days there seems to be plenty being spouted by the Government.'

'Yes,' Ada said, looking anxious. 'They are very determined not to give in. I do hope Emily will be all right.'

HER CELL is twelve feet by eight, the walls painted grey. There is a gas lamp, a small window too high to see out of, a plank bed and a chair. On the bare wood are two folded sheets and a pillowcase. Two buckets with tin lids stand under a corner shelf. The shelf holds a prayer book, a card of rules, a piece of slate and a chalk. In the door is a small hatch. There is nothing else.

She spreads the sheets on the bed and examines the buckets. One contains water, the other has clearly been used as a commode. The pillowcase is filled with straw; sharp golden shards prick between the weave.

Sounds seem to boom and bounce back and forth down the corridors. She hears a distant rolling thunder of noise that gradually comes closer: doors, shouts and footsteps. The hatch opens. A voice says, 'Dinner's here.'

'I am not eating,' Emily says.

A tin bowl of soup appears at the hatch. She doesn't move. After a moment it disappears again, leaving a faint greasy smell of warm root vegetables. The thunder rolls away. Eventually the gas light dims.

The next morning she lies on her bed, in defiance of the printed rules. The hatch opens. 'Aren't you up yet?' a voice says. 'Breakfast's here.'

'I'm on hunger strike.'

The hatch closes again.

Then the stream of visitors begins. The chaplain, the matron, the work supervisor—they all offer platitudes. 'It is to be hoped,' the chaplain explains, 'that you can use this time for reflection, to improve yourself.'

'But I do not want to improve myself. It is the Prime Minister I hope to improve.' He seems taken aback, and cautions her against disrespect.

She is taken for a bath—the cubicle has a two-foot door across it and the wardress comes and looks at her every minute.

When she is back in her cell the governor visits. 'Don't think you can make trouble in here,' he warns her. 'We know what we're about. But if you don't give us any difficulty, you shall soon have your freedom again.'

She replies, 'You can release me from this place, but you cannot give me my freedom. Only when women have the vote will I have that.'

He sighs. 'You will address me as sir, while you are in my charge.' He eyes her. 'Your husband is a Member of Parliament, isn't he?'

She nods.

'If there are any small comforts you require, let me know. Soap for example, or a better pillow—'

'I insist on being treated the same as any other prisoner.'

'Very well.' He hesitates. 'Mrs Brewer, if you are successful—if women get the vote—it will destroy all chivalry between the sexes, have you thought of that? Why should men treat women as any different from themselves?'

'Was it chivalry that prompted you to offer me soap?' Emily says quietly. 'Or my husband's position?'

Lunch arrives. More soup, though the trusty who brings it calls it stew. She refuses it. A doctor comes and asks her when she last ate. She tells him.

'Eat your dinner tonight,' he says. 'The alternative is to be forcibly fed.'

'I will not cooperate.'

'A lot of these people who talk about hunger strikes only last a couple of days. After that their bodies tell them not to be so stupid.'

He too leaves her. She waits a long time. There is an hour of exercise, walking round an outdoor yard in single file and in silence.

At dinner time—which is actually midafternoon—the wardress asks her if she will eat. Emily says she will not.

At dusk the lights are turned off. She lies on her bed, by now quite dizzy with hunger. She tries to sleep, but hunger pangs make it impossible to rest for more than a few minutes at a time.

The next day she refuses breakfast. The pain seems to be getting less now, not more. Sometimes she feels despair; sometimes without warning great waves of exhilaration wash over her. I can do this, she tells herself. I can starve myself. They can control everything else, but my body is my own.

By the evening she is almost delirious with hunger. I am lighter than air, she tells herself, and the phrase seems to reverberate round and round inside her empty frame. *I am lighter than air . . . I am lighter than air . . .*

The doctor comes. 'Will you eat?' he says shortly.

'I will not.' Her voice comes out strangely.

'You are starting to stink. Did you know that? It is the smell of ketosis—the body feeding off itself. If you go on with this, you will do irreparable damage to your reproductive organs, your digestive system, your lungs . . .'

'I am not going to change my mind.'

He nods. 'Very well. Then we must save you from yourself.'

SHE IS HALF PUSHED, half dragged along the wing by four wardresses, and taken into a large room. The doctor she met earlier is there, along with another, younger man; both wear rubber aprons over their suits. On the desk is a length of tube, a funnel and a jug of what looks like sloppy porridge.

'Put her in the chair,' the doctor says.

The women manoeuvre her into a large wooden chair. The younger doctor goes behind her to hold her head back, while the other picks up the length of tubing. 'Hold her steady now,' he says.

She clenches her teeth shut. But it is not her mouth he goes for. Instead, he pushes the tube into her right nostril. The sensation is so repulsive that she opens her mouth to scream, but she finds she can barely gasp.

Another inch, then another. She can feel it in the back of her throat now, making her gag. She tries to shake her head but the younger doctor has her too firmly in his grasp. She feels a sharp pain in her windpipe, and then with a final sickening slither the thing is fully inside her.

'That should do it,' says the older man, standing back. He fits a funnel onto the end of the tube. Taking the jug of porridge, he begins to pour it into the funnel, raising the whole assembly into the air as he does so.

Warm, choking liquid fills her windpipe. She coughs and retches, but the hot, thick liquid will not budge. It is like trying to vomit when you cannot.

'That's a square meal's worth,' the doctor says.

The tube is pulled from her nostril—a long, agonising withdrawal. As it leaves her she vomits.

'We shall have to replace that,' the doctor said. 'Hold her still.'

So the whole ghastly thing is repeated.

THAT NIGHT she sets fire to her cell, pulling apart her pillow and pushing straw onto the gas burner. Then she barricades herself in, wedging the plank bed under the door handle. They have to chisel the hinges off to get to her. After that she is moved to a cell that has an iron bed, screwed to the floor.

That night, and all the next day, someone comes and looks at her every ten minutes. At first she thinks they are coming to gawp, and shouts at them.

'You are being close-watched,' a voice answers coldly. 'We are charged with making sure that you cannot do yourself harm.'

At lunchtime the matron comes with a glass of milk, which she refuses.

Now that she knows what it is like, she is dreading the feeding. By the time they come to get her she is ready to vomit from sheer fright. But they know what they are about now, and the tube is pushed in quickly. Then she faints.

When she comes round the doctor is looking at her anxiously. 'You had better give this over,' he says. 'You are not fit for this sort of thing.'

'Is anybody?' she says bitterly. 'You are a doctor. You should refuse to do it.'

'Nobody cares,' he says suddenly. 'That's what I don't understand. You are sitting in here doing this to yourself and nobody on the outside has the faintest idea. What's the point of it?'

'To show that you can only govern with the consent of the governed—'

'Save me your slogans.' He waves at the wardresses. 'Take her away.'

As they escort her to her cell, one of the women says quietly, 'They take taxes on my pay, so I don't see what right they have to say I can't vote.' She glances at Emily sideways. 'And you were brave in there.'

'Thank you,' she manages to say.

'It's not true what he told you, anyway. You're in all the papers. Not the details, but people know what's going on.'

That night she cannot breathe properly—there is something lodged in her windpipe. She is sick again, and there are streaks of blood in her vomit.

She cannot face the tube the next day. She accepts a glass of milk and then a little soup. After that she goes back on hunger strike.

I WAS IN THE CAFÉ, cleaning the coffee-maker, when her husband came. It was midmorning—a quiet time. I suppose he had chosen it for that reason.

'So this is where you disseminate your poison, Wallis,' a voice said.

I looked up. 'If you are referring to my coffee, it is the finest there is.'

'I was not referring to your coffee.' He placed his hat on the counter. 'I have come to talk to you about my wife. The doctors tell me that if she keeps this up it will kill her.'

'Would these be the same doctors who once pronounced her hysterical?'

'This is different.' He paused. 'She has been hurt. An attempt at forcible feeding that went wrong. It appears to have damaged her lungs.'

I stared at him, appalled.

'We need to get her out of prison,' he said. 'Or at least, out of danger.'

I found my voice. 'Then prevail upon your Government to give women the vote.'

'You know that's not going to happen.' Suddenly I saw how tired he looked. 'This Government will never give in. Apart from anything else, it would send the wrong message to our enemies. The Empire may look impregnable, but there are those in Europe who would take advantage of any domestic crisis. What Emily is doing is dangerous for all of us.'

'And why are you telling me this?'

'I thought perhaps she might listen to you, even if she will not to me.'

It must have taken some courage, I thought, to come here like this.

'I doubt that,' I said, shaking my head.

'Do you love her?'

It was strange to be discussing such a thing, and with him of all people. But they were strange times. I nodded. 'Yes.'

'Then help me save her. Write to her,' he urged. 'Tell her she has done enough, that you don't want her to throw away her life like this.'

'If I do write, and it weakens her resolve, she may never forgive me.'

'But it must still be done. For her sake, if not for ours.' He picked up his hat. 'You should know that the Government is talking about enacting a new piece of legislation. It will allow them to release hunger strikers on licence.'

'But if they release them, they will go out and create more unrest.'

'Only if they are well enough. And if they are well enough, they will be re-arrested and returned to prison. That way, if they die, they will not do so in prison, as martyrs, but in hospital, as invalids. So you see, her protest will not make any difference in the end. You must write that letter.'

'I make no promises. I will think about it tonight—'

'One final thing,' he interrupted. 'If you can get her to stop all this, I will give her a divorce.'

I said slowly, 'I don't believe she wants a divorce.'

'It's not her I'm talking to. It's you.' He looked at me levelly. 'If you can persuade her to stay alive, Wallis, she's yours. I'm washing my hands of her.'

When he had gone I thought about what he had said. I was under no illusions about his motives. He was a man for whom love was indistinguishable from his own interests. If what he had told me was true, and Emily died, it would reflect badly on him. Better, from his point of view, to divorce her. He had known the best way to make his appeal to me. But it did not alter the fact that he was right. A letter from me saying she had done enough, couched in the right way, might change Emily's mind.

I could not contemplate a world without her in it. I loved her, and I wanted her to live. As to whether she would ever marry me . . . I knew her too well to take that for granted, but I could hope. Finally, after so long, we had a chance at happiness.

I stayed up late, drinking cup after cup of coffee. I took a piece of paper and a pen, and by the time dawn came I had written my letter.

Fourteen

Emily died in Paddington Hospital, four weeks later. Just as Brewer had predicted, the Government released her on medical grounds rather than allow her to die in prison. There had been some hope that with proper medical care she might improve. But it was too late.

By the time of her death, the Suffrage Movement had, despite all the Government's efforts, achieved the unthinkable: a conciliation bill supported by the majority of MPs. The militants declared a truce. But even as it seemed that victory was finally within their grasp, Emily was fading.

I managed to see her a couple of times in hospital, but she was very weak by then. She never regained the weight she lost in prison: her beautiful face was reduced to angles, like something that had been hacked about with a knife, and her skin, when you looked closely, was like a piece of old muslin.

I had brought flowers. 'Thank you,' she said hoarsely, as I held them up for her to smell. 'They're lovely, Robert, but next time bring me something else. Cut flowers die so quickly; they make me think of death.'

'What shall I bring you?'

'Bring me some coffee beans, and a grinder to grind them.'

'Will the doctors allow it?'

'Not to drink. But I can smell the aroma of the grounds, and perhaps you could drink a cup for me.'

I laughed. 'That's the strangest order I've ever taken.'

'How is the café?' she asked.

'It does well. The new Kenyan is very good, just as you predicted.'

She closed her eyes. Then she said, 'I got your letter. Thank you.'

'Did it make a difference?'

She nodded.

'Then I am glad.'

Her hand reached for mine. 'It must have been hard to write.'

'It was the easiest thing in the world.'

'Liar.' She sighed. 'I have written a letter to you, in return. You will get it when I die.'

'There's no question—'

'Please, Robert. Don't insult me by pretending. The doctors have been quite honest. My lungs have almost gone. They give me laudanum to dull the pain. They'll give me my drops when you've gone.'

'Then I will go soon.'

'Perhaps you had better. I am a little tired.'

'But I'll come back. And next time I'll bring that coffee.'

She died the next night, in her sleep.

IT ARRIVED a few weeks after the funeral, in a small packing crate along with some legal papers relating to the shop and a solicitor's letter, explaining that in full and final discharge of the estate of Mrs Emily Brewer, deceased, he was obliged to inform me . . . et cetera.

The letter was written in her own hand, the writing small and purposeful.

My dear Robert,

I wanted you to know that I am leaving the café to my sisters. It is not much of a bequest, given how little profit it makes, but I was never able to be as unsentimental about business as my father, and I have been happy there. I hope you will decide to stay on, at least for the time being. The Cause needs Castle Street, and Castle Street needs you.

Robert, I believe that men and women will only be able to communicate with each other properly when they are equal. That is why there is something I must tell you, however difficult it is for me to set it down . . . You recall that morning when I told my father that I wanted to marry you, and why? I think you have always assumed that the reasons I gave him then were my real ones. They were not. I told him only what I thought would persuade him most readily. There had already been one potential scandal with Hector . . . How could I stand there and tell him what I really felt, how much I desired you? But it is true. How I have always longed to feel your body against mine, imagined what it must be like to be in bed with you. There—I have said it. I have always wanted more than anything to share that experience with you, then wake up in the morning and know that if I just reach around you will be there . . .

I was ashamed of it. And so I left too much unsaid.

You will fall in love again—of course you will. When you do, there is one thing you must promise me. Tell her everything—about me, and about you, and what happened in Africa. Tell her your true feelings, and perhaps one day she will be able to talk to you about her desires.

There is something else I want you to do for me: I want you to write it all down. To tell our story. It must not be forgotten. Tell the truth, Robert, and tell it kindly. In the end, that is all any of us can do.

Sometimes, when the longing for you was almost too much to bear, I reminded myself that men and women have been sleeping together for thousands of years; that millions of them do it every day. But a friendship between a man and a woman is still a rare and precious thing. Robert, I love you—but most of all I am glad to have been your friend.

Your loving Emily

The only other things in the crate were another letter and a small mahogany box. I recognised the box at once: it was probably the last surviving example of the original Wallis–Pinker Method.

The letter was the last one I had written to her, with a note from the solicitor: *Mr Brewer has asked that this be returned to you.*

Castle Street, April 28th

My dear Emily,

Your husband has been to see me. He is worried about your health—we all are. That will not surprise you: what may come as a surprise is that he made me an offer concerning your welfare.

He said that if you will give up your hunger strike, he will give you up—will stand aside so that you can divorce him. He does this, of course, in the mistaken belief that you and I are lovers, and that we will marry if you are free. He wants me to persuade you to follow this course of action.

My darling Emily, when I think of what joy it would be to be married to you, you must know that I cannot conceive of anything more wonderful. And yet I am not going to try to persuade you one way or the other. I do not tell you to give it over, or to continue with the strike. All I will say is that it is a great thing you have done, and that whatever you decide to do now, I will be proud of you. And I will never stop loving you.

The decision is yours.

With all my love,

Robert

AS BREWER had suggested, Emily's sacrifice made little difference in the long run. At the last minute the Government dropped its support for the new conciliation bill. The militants, outraged, responded by calling for England to be made ungovernable.

What followed was chaos. Burning linen was pushed into letterboxes; government buildings and shops had their windows smashed; cricket pavilions and even churches were set on fire. Years later, the suffragettes liked to claim that theirs had been a peaceful insurrection, but that was not how it looked at the time. Asquith was a particular target. They tried to tear off his clothes while he was playing golf, and were prevented only by his daughter Violet, who beat them off with her bare fists. An Irish MP sitting next to him in a carriage was wounded in the ear by a hatchet. Meanwhile, almost two hundred women were on hunger strikes.

To begin with, like many others, I thought the Government deserved whatever they got. We male supporters had been organised into a separate body by now. I broke a few windows and burned a few empty buildings myself, and each time I thought with a burst of satisfaction that I was doing it for Emily. But, again, like many others I eventually found that I did not have the same appetite for conflict that the movement's leaders had.

A YEAR PASSED. I visited Emily's grave; I ran the café and maintained the Guide; I paid no attention to politics and still less to the arts. In truth, I paid little attention to the café either. There were hardly any customers now, and I made no particular effort about those few who still came.

And then one day Ada and Philomena paid me a visit. I came in late, and found them looking around the place with a faintly perplexed air. Ada in particular was running her gloved hand over the counters, inspecting the result with a fastidious expression on her face.

'Can I help you?' I said sourly.

'Oh, Robert, there you are,' Ada said. 'Perhaps you had better make us some coffee.'

I sighed. 'I'll get some Java. The mocca is too stale.'

They exchanged glances, but said nothing until the coffee was prepared.

'You're aware we own this café now?' Ada said.

I nodded.

'From what few accounts have been kept, it seems to be losing money.'

'The location is wrong,' I said brusquely. 'This is a residential area. Nobody needs a place like this on their doorstep.'

Again the two women exchanged glances.

'The thing is,' Philomena said, 'it seems such a shame to close it.'

I thought so too, but I could see no reason to keep it open. I said nothing.

'Phil has some ideas,' Ada said. 'Would you like to hear them?'

I said with a shrug, 'I suppose I had better.' I pulled up a chair.

Philomena said, 'You are right, I think, that this is not the best place for a café. But people do not only drink coffee in cafés. There is also the home.'

I snorted. 'No one drinks coffee at home either now, as far as I can see. It's all packaged rubbish. Like Castle. The cheapest coffees, pre-roasted and pre-ground, then stored in paper packets on the shelves of Messrs Lipton and Sainsbury until what little flavour it possesses finally evaporates.'

'Well, quite,' Philomena said. She regarded me with those sleepy, just-woken-up eyes. There seemed to be a trace of amusement in them.

'We were wondering,' Ada said, 'why we can't sell people a quality coffee.'

I looked at them, puzzled.

'You see, we grew up with fine coffee,' she explained. 'The sort of coffee that is now almost impossible to get hold of.' She shrugged. 'It seems to us that if we are finding it hard to get then there must be others in a similar predicament. Not a vast number, but'—she allowed her eyes to travel around the run-down café—'perhaps enough to support a business.'

'So what you are suggesting—'

'Is a small operation, not unlike Pinker's used to be,' Philomena finished for her. 'Essentially, it would be a shop with a couple of roasting ovens, the roasters not hidden away but proudly on display for all to see.' Almost unconsciously she pointed with a delicate finger towards the end wall, where, I could now see, there was just room for two small roasters side by side. 'It will be the drama of the roasting that makes the difference—'

'And the smell . . .' Ada said.

'Of freshly roasted mocca!' Philomena inhaled deeply. 'Imagine!'

'And the chimney,' Ada said, pointing to a currently chimneyless corner.

Philomena nodded. 'Wafting said aroma down the street . . .'

'So that even if you don't want a pound of Bogota to take home . . .'

'You might decide to call in and buy a cup instead . . .'

'Or a jug.'

'A jug?' I said, puzzled.

Philomena turned her eyes on me. The sleepiness, I now saw, was an illusion. Her eyes were sharp and shrewd and quick. 'Like buying a jug of beer for your supper. Why not a jug of coffee for your breakfast?'

'They do something similar in Africa,' I admitted. 'The coffee sellers wander the streets of Harar; everyone comes to their door to buy from them.'

Philomena clapped her hand on top of Ada's. 'You see? Robert is already seeing how it could work.' She grinned at me. 'And we won't be spending money on advertising, Just on good beans—African beans, if you wish it.' She opened her bag and took out some sketches. 'We will make it look nice.' She placed them in front of me. 'These are some tea rooms I visited recently in Edinburgh. The style is Art Nouveau. I thought perhaps something similar here.' She waved her gloved hand at the space. 'With your palate and our investment, there is no reason why this place should not be a success.'

I studied the sketches. 'We'd need to close. This refit will take months.'

'Three weeks,' Philomena corrected me. 'We start the day after tomorrow.'

'Good Lord. Er—"we"?'

Philomena put the sketches away. 'We are going to be quite involved as employers. I hope that will not cause you any problems—working for a woman, I mean.'

'But—this is hardly fitting work for Samuel Pinker's daughters, surely? You must be wealthy women now.'

'Really, Robert, have my sisters taught you nothing? We will decide for ourselves what is fitting.'

'Your father won't be happy about it.'

'On the contrary. You underestimate him, Robert. He likes nothing better than to see his daughters succeed.' She paused. 'He sent his regards, by the way. There is not a bean of coffee in Narrow Street now. The warehouse has even been painted—it is a great big office, with desks instead of sacks. But I think he rather misses the old days. You should talk to him sometime.'

'You really think he'll help you?'

The two sisters looked at each other. 'Why would we want his help?' Philomena asked. 'This is business.'

At the door, just as they were leaving, she turned. 'Are you writing something about Emily?'

'What makes you think so?'

'Because she asked you to. I know—she told me.'

'I suppose I am trying. Why?'

'Because I should very much like to read it, Robert,' she said simply. 'So get on with it, will you?'

I WENT TO THE WINDOW to watch them as they walked away. Philomena evidently already had some further ideas; she was pointing to the street corner, and then back to the café, talking animatedly to her sister as she turned. I caught her face in profile, the edge of that sleepy smile—

And I suddenly felt something stir in me, something I had not expected to feel. Oh, no, I thought. Please no. Not that. Not again.

Epilogue

We opened the shop; we fell in love. But that is another story—a story with its own plot, its own surprises, its prologues and choruses and sudden reverses of fortune; a story that cannot be told only because, unlike the story of Emily and me, as yet it has no ending.

Having reached the end of this memoir, I find the Victorian in me will not be satisfied without a moral—or perhaps, it is fairer to say, a conclusion.

What have I learned? I have learned what every man must learn, and no man can be taught—that despite what poets may tell you, there are different kinds of love.

Just as a good coffee might smell of, perhaps, leather and tobacco and honeysuckle all at once, so love is a mixture of any number of feelings: infatuation, idealism, tenderness, lust, the urge to protect, the desire to ravish, comradeship, friendship and a thousand more besides.

There is no chart or code to guide you through these mysteries. Some must be sought at the end of the world, and some in a stranger's glance. Some can be found in the bedroom, and some in a crowded street. Some will burn you like a moth in their flames, and some will warm you with a gentle glow. Some will bring you pleasure, some will bring you happiness, and some—if you are lucky—will even bring you both.

The laugh of a woman, the smell of a child, the making of a coffee—these are the various flavours of love.

I WAS GOING to leave it there, but Phil, having read over these pages, has some comments. That is the problem with having your wife double up as your employer: you are under her thumb twice over.

So, for the record, it is apparently not true that I was once promised 'a very advantageous proposition—three aways for two poems'. She also claims that the poem I then composed for her was not as good as the one I actually give here; it did not even rhyme properly, apparently.

She also says that Hector was a far more sympathetic character than I have made him out to be—'a rather dashing, romantic type, a sort of restless adventurer-hero, well read, fluent in several languages, an anthropologist before the term was invented'. So perhaps I have done him a disservice.

She feels, too, that my portrayal of Emily may be a little slanted, but for opposite reasons: love may have blinded me to her faults. 'My sister was admirable in many ways,' Phil has scribbled in a margin, 'but she could also be inflexible and strict. I think she was attracted to the militants partly because she admired their absolute autocracy—the way those suffragettes always referred to Emmeline Pankhurst as "the Leader" always made me feel slightly nauseous.'

'Tell them about Arthur,' she has written under the last page. Actually, I had intended to do so, but somehow it didn't fit anywhere. After Emily's death Arthur Brewer, MP, had a rather extraordinary change of heart, and began making speeches in support of suffrage. It would be easy to be cynical, and say that he had finally seen which way the wind was blowing; it would also be easy to take a more forgiving view, and say that her death, and the circumstances of it, made him realise that he had done his wife a great wrong.

Castle Coffee was for a time the most successful packaged brand in the country. But when Jock Howell took over the company, he made some bad decisions. In particular, he failed to anticipate the way that instant coffee would transform the market. The Castle name was eventually sold to another concern, who embarked on an aggressive price war with a competitor that ultimately destroyed them both.

Meanwhile, several small importers were developing their own versions of the cupping guide, improving on the work that Emily and I began. The Wallis–Pinker Method is no longer unique, nor even among the most comprehensive of those systems. But I like to think that, had it never existed, those later versions would never have become quite what they are today.

The coffee shop has gone from strength to strength. The Pinker sisters were not being entirely honest when they visited me that day. I would refer you to a small but significant slip Phil made, when she asked me if I would find it difficult working for *a woman*—note the use of the singular. It quickly became clear that the plans were all Phil's; she had asked Ada to come along with her for moral support, and because—she admits it now—she already suspected that her relationship with me was going to be charged with feelings that were more than just professional.

After two years we opened a second branch, and then another, and another, and then we realised that, unless we were careful, we would have just the sort of business we both abhorred, in which you start to rely on numbers to tell you what is going on rather than on the aroma of a roasting Java, or the mouthfeel of a Kenyan, or the bright taste of a freshly brewed Guatemala . . . So we stopped, and there are no plans to open any more.

And then, five years after the events I have written about here, Phil and I produced a blend of our own. It smelt intensely of vanilla and meringues, burnt cream and crusty bread, and that faint, far-off whiff of sex that perfumes all newborn skin when it first emerges from the womb. She is absolutely perfect, and she rejoices in the name of Geraldine Emily Wallis.

ANTHONY CAPELLA

Date of birth: December 6, 1962
Home: Oxfordshire
Writes: novels, screenplays, travel features

RD: I'm sure many readers will wonder if it was a Starbucks or other coffee-drinking experience that triggered your new novel . . .

AC: I do remember thinking that, having written about someone who abandons duty for pleasure in *The Wedding Officer*, I wanted to put the case for the opposite point of view, i.e. to write about someone who, in the course of growing up, realises the limitations of unfettered sensuality and hedonism. I also wanted to write a story about business, as it is the dramatic backdrop to most of our lives today but doesn't feature much in fiction. Yet business brings together so many great themes: conflict and struggle, families, change, ethics . . .

RD: There's so much information in the story about coffee-growing and different types of bean—how did you do your research?

AC: Well, it was a curious process, because it had to be coffee-growing as it would have been understood by someone at the turn of the century. I had to try to see the business through that lens. Reading old books helped—in particular a coffee-growing manual from the 1880s called *Coffee: Its Cultivation and Profit*.

RD: Was there any aspect of the book that you found particularly challenging?

AC: The plotting. This is a big, epic book—it takes place over three continents and thirty years, at a time of huge change. But it's a love story, not a historical novel. I wanted to have a sense of historical events without it feeling as if history was the subject of my story. Finding a structure for that took a little while.

RD: Was it difficult to write as convincingly as you do about the uncharted heart of the African continent at the turn of the century?

AC: Well, the difficult thing was to avoid trying to turn everything into *Heart of Darkness*! The truth is, there was more than one sort of African experience back then—so, again, reading memoirs helped, such as *Out of Africa* and *The Flame Trees of Thika*.

RD: Do you have a favourite coffee?

AC: Ethiopian coffee is undoubtedly the best in the world—that's partly why I set the African section of the book in Ethiopia. In Sidamo and Yrgacheffe, the Bordeaux and Burgundy of single-estate coffees, you can still find coffee growing wild. Sidamo is strong and dark, a classic chocolate-flavoured mocha. Yrgacheffe is a light, fragrant, slightly smoky-tasting coffee, with notes of blueberry and lemon.

RD: Robert Wallis's two loves, the African slave Fikre and the very sensible Emily Pinker, are a study in contrast. Which do you think you'd have fallen for?

AC: Both! And that's why I enjoyed writing them both, I think. I can understand why Robert becomes sexually obsessed with Fikre; I can understand, too, why he's surprised to find himself falling in love with Emily. I hope I would have recognised Emily's qualities rather sooner than he does, though . . .

RD: Was Emily's involvement with the suffragettes something that you planned for her from the start, or did her character lead her in that direction?

AC: That was one of those rather annoying things that happen to an author when you create a character. I knew from the start that Emily would be a political idealist, but it only became clear to me after I started to research the period that she would therefore have to be a suffragette. So much has already been written about the suffragettes that I knew I would have to get it absolutely right, or people would spot the errors and all my authority as their guide through the story would evaporate. So it necessitated months of extra research.

RD: The ending of the novel is extremely moving—did you find it so when you were writing it? And did you feel that Emily had to die?

AC: I hadn't originally meant her to die, in all honesty. What became clear, though, as I rewrote and rewrote, was that Robert had to be offered a moment of choice, in which he chooses an unselfish course for the first time in his life. In some way, he had to make a sacrifice of his love. Did I find it moving? Yes. That must sound a bit bizarre, but I absolutely had a sense of Emily as a real person by the time I wrote those scenes. And I suppose I identified with Robert by then, too, so I felt some of what he must have felt. That doesn't always happen!

RD: All your novels are supremely sensual, full of delicious tastes and aromas, and sizzling passion. Is that a reflection of your character, or do you think it's just something that comes through in the type of stories you like to write?

AC: Both. I am a hedonist, and I do like to write about sensual things, but I try not to write about them in a self-indulgent way. Just listing or describing pleasure becomes very boring. . . What interests me is what pleasure does to people, awakening their senses, perhaps, or making them selfish or blind, as happens to Robert.

RD: And what is your idea of a perfect day?

AC: It varies. In fact, that's the number one requirement—variety. So I would say it is one that is pleasantly and surprisingly different to the one before. Being at home in the country is nice, but I also like to travel and discover new cultures. Unfortunately, as a writer, far too much of my time is spent at a keyboard.

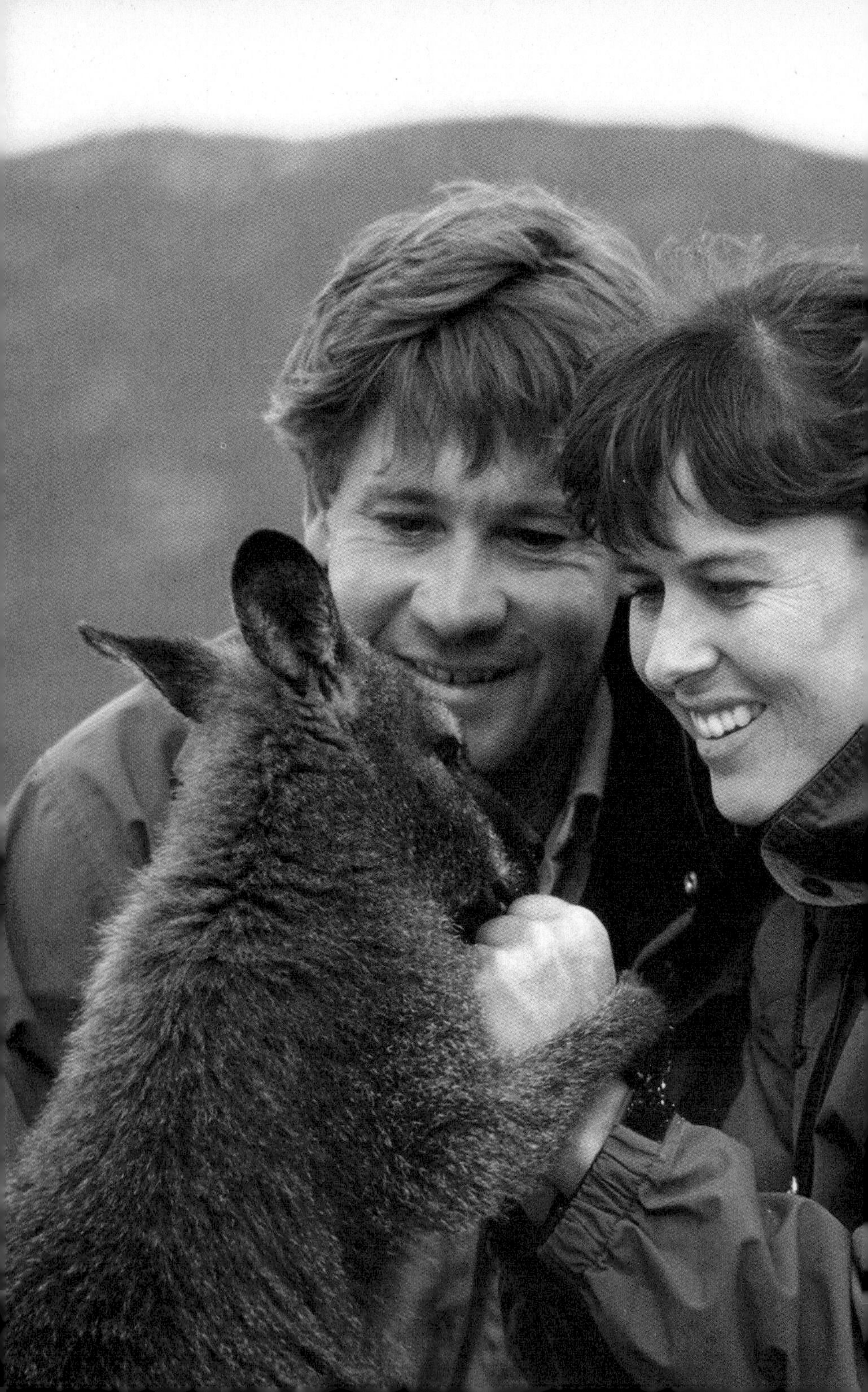

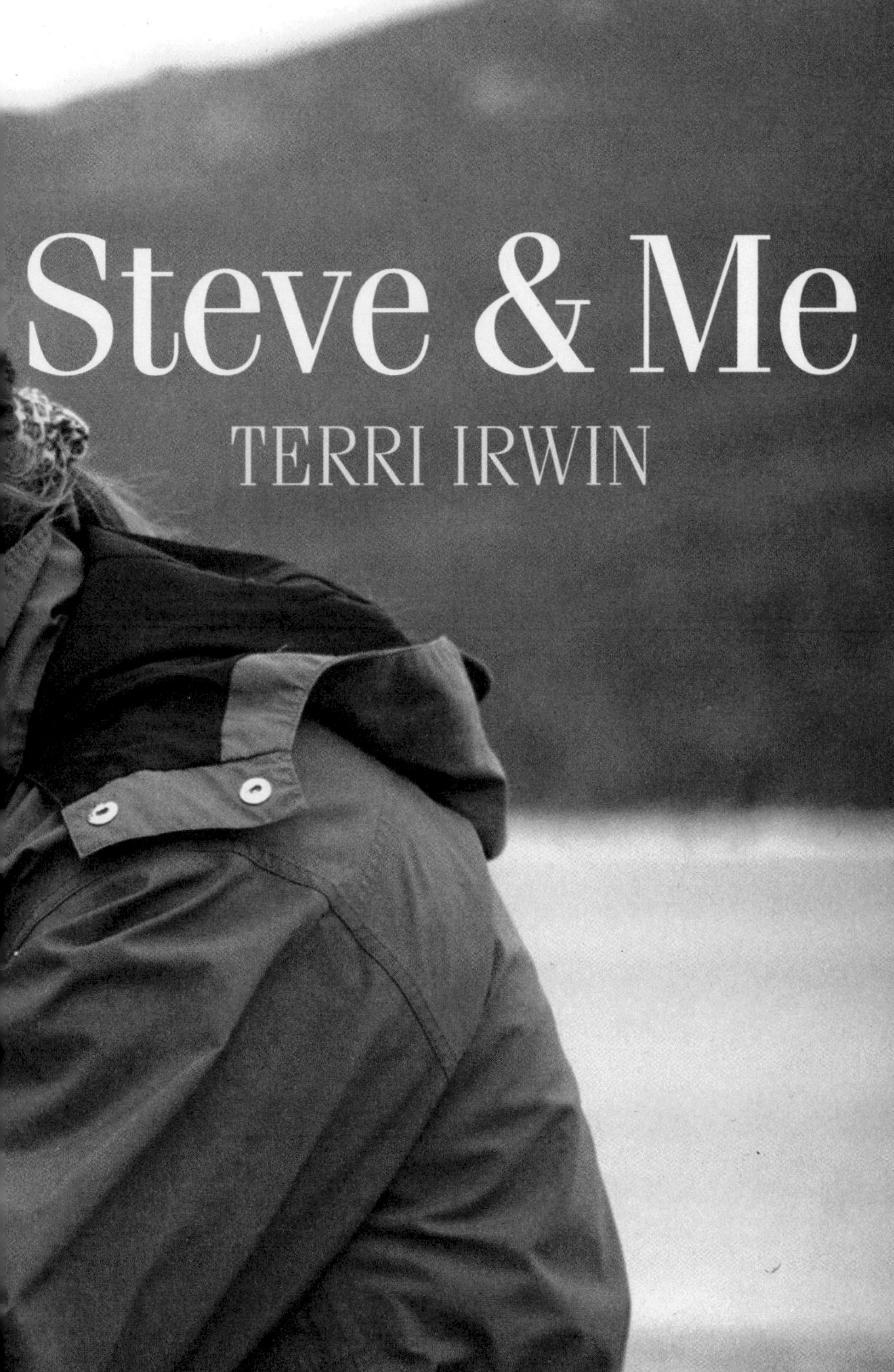

Steve & Me
TERRI IRWIN

In 1991, young animal-rescue worker Terri Raines left the United States bound for a holiday in Australia, little knowing that the trip would change her life. While visiting a Queensland wildlife park, she met and fell head over heels in love with a tall, blond force of nature named Steve Irwin. Steve & Me *is an inspiring account of their happy years together; a passionate tribute to a man adored by everyone he met and worked with, written by the woman who shared his adventures and loved him best of all.*

Chapter One

The name of the zoo was the Queensland Reptile and Fauna Park. As I crossed the parking area, I prepared myself for disappointment. *I am going to see a collection of snakes, lizards and miserable creatures in jars, feel terribly sorry for them, and leave.*

It was October 1991. I was Terri Raines, a twenty-seven-year-old Oregon girl in Australia on an unlikely quest to find homes for rescued American cougars. A reptile park wasn't going to be interested in a big cat. I headed through the pleasant spring heat towards the park thinking pessimistic thoughts. But the prospect of seeing new species of wildlife drew me in.

I walked through the modest entrance, only to be shocked at what I found on the other side: the most beautiful, immaculately kept gardens I had ever encountered. Peacocks strutted around, kangaroos and wallabies roamed freely, and palm trees lined all the walkways. It was like a little piece of Eden.

I saw that the reptile enclosures were kept perfectly clean—the snakes glistened. I kept rescued animals myself at home and I knew the kinds of nightmares zoos can fall into. But I saw not a sign of external parasites on these animals, no old food rotting in the cages, no faeces or shed skin.

So I enjoyed myself. I toured around, learned about the snakes and fed the kangaroos. It was a brilliant, sunlit day.

'There will be a show at the crocodile enclosures in five minutes,' a voice announced on the PA system. 'Five minutes.'

I noticed the crocodiles before I noticed the man. There was a whole line of crocodilians: alligators, freshwater crocodiles and one big saltie—a saltwater crocodile. Amazing, modern-day dinosaurs. I didn't know much about them, but I knew that they had existed unchanged for millions of years. They are among the most ancient creatures on the planet.

Then I saw the man. A tall, solid twenty-something (he appeared younger than he was, and had actually turned twenty-nine that February), dressed in a khaki shirt and shorts, barefoot, with blond flyaway hair underneath a large Akubra hat and a black-banded wristwatch on his left wrist. Even though he was big and muscular, there was something kind and approachable about him, too.

I stood and listened to him talk.

'They can live as long as or even longer than us,' he said, approaching the water's edge with a piece of meat. The crocodile lunged out of the water and snapped the meat from his hand. 'This male croc is territorial,' he explained, 'and females become really aggressive when they lay eggs in a nest.' He knelt beside the croc that had just tried to nail him. 'Crocodiles are good mothers.'

Every inch of this man, every movement and word exuded his passion for the crocodilians he passed among, and he made sure his audience admired the crocs, not himself. I recognised his passion, because I spoke the same way about cougars as this Australian zookeeper spoke about crocs. When I heard there would be a special guided tour of the Crocodile Environmental Park, I was first in line for a ticket. This man was on fire with enthusiasm, and I felt I really connected with him, like I was meeting a kindred spirit.

What was the young zookeeper's name? Irwin. Steve Irwin.

STEVE TALKED about the crocodiles' courting rituals: the males are very gentle as they nudge up and down alongside the female until she is receptive. He explained that they seemed to develop real affection for each other.

Affection for each other but not for Steve. I watched the still, murky water erupt with an enormous ton of saltwater crocodile. The croc nearly snapped the buttons off Steve's shirt as he neatly deposited a piece of meat into its mouth. The reverberation of the jaws coming back together sounded like a rifle report.

'Sometimes just seeing a croc in the wild can scare the daylights out of people,' he said, passing by sub-adult crocodiles. 'But if you follow some simple rules, these little tackers pose no threat at all to human life.

'If we get a report about a particularly naughty little crocodile bothering people,' Steve explained, 'I go out with my dog, Sui, in a dinghy. We'll capture the croc so it won't get shot.'

Then he described what he meant by 'capture'. As he told the story I was totally captivated, and so were the other zoo visitors. 'If the croc is young, six feet long or smaller,' he said, 'I'll catch it by hand. We go out at night with a million-candlepower spotlight, shining bright across the water. That way, I can pick up the eye-shine of the crocodile. Their eyes glow bright red, right at the surface of the water. The croc thinks he's camouflaged by the darkness. He doesn't understand that my spotlight is revealing his location.'

Idling the dinghy, quietly bringing it in closer and closer to the croc, Steve would finally make his move. He'd creep to the front of the boat and hold the spotlight until the last moment. Then he would leap into the water.

Grabbing the crocodile round the scruff of the neck, he would secure its tail between his legs and wrap his body round the thrashing creature. Crocodiles are amazingly strong in the water. But Steve would hang on. He knew he could flip the croc into his dinghy and pin the snapping animal down.

'Piece of cake,' he said.

That was the most incredible story I had ever heard. And Steve was the most incredible man I had ever seen—catching crocodiles by hand to save their lives? This was unreal. I had an overwhelming sensation. I wanted to build a big campfire, sit down with Steve next to it, and hear his stories all night long. Eventually the tour was over; I felt I just had to talk to this man.

Steve had a broad, easy smile and the biggest hands I had ever seen. He came up and with a broad Australian accent said, 'G'day, mate.'

I had never, ever believed in love at first sight. But I had the strangest, strongest feeling that it was destiny that took me into that little wildlife park that day.

Steve started talking to me as if we'd known each other all our lives. My friend Lori took a picture of us and the moment I first met Steve was forever captured. The zoo was about to close, but we kept talking.

Finally, I could hear Lori honking her horn in the car park. 'I have to go,' I said to Steve, managing a grim smile. I felt a connection as I never had before, and I was about to leave, never to see him again.

'Why do you love cougars so much?' he asked, walking me towards the park's front gate.

There were many reasons. 'I think it's how they can actually kill with their mouths,' I finally said. 'They can conquer an animal several times their size, grab it in their jaws and kill it instantly by snapping its neck.'

Steve grinned. 'That's what I love about crocodiles,' he said. 'They are the most powerful apex predators.'

Apex predators. Meaning that both cougars and crocs were at the top of the food chain. On opposite sides of the world, this man and I had the same passion.

'Call the zoo if you're ever here again,' Steve said. 'I'd really like to see you.' Could it be that he felt the same way I did? As we drove back to Brisbane, I was contemplative. I had no idea how I would accomplish it, but I was determined to figure out a way to see him. The next weekend, Lori was going diving with a friend, and I took a chance and called Steve.

'What do you reckon, could I come back for the weekend?' I asked.

'Absolutely. I'll take care of everything,' came Steve's reply.

My heart was pounding as I drove up the coast again a few days later. There was the familiar little sign, the modest entrance. And there he was, as large as life—six foot tall, broad shoulders, a big grin, and a warm and welcome handshake. Our first real touch.

Right away, I was extremely self-conscious about a hurdle I felt that we had to get over. I wasn't entirely sure about Steve's marital status. I started asking him questions about his friends and family.

He lived right there at the zoo, he told me, with his parents and his sister Mandy. His sister Joy was married and had moved away.

'Would you like to meet my girlfriend?' he asked.

Ah, I felt my whole spirit sink into the ground. 'Yes, I'd love to.'

'Sue,' he called out. 'Hey, Sue.'

Bounding round the corner came this little brindle Staffordshire bull terrier, Sui, his dog.

'Here's me girlfriend,' he said with a smile.

This is it, I thought. There's no turning back.

We spent a wonderful weekend together. I worked alongside him at the zoo from sunup to sunset. During the day it was raking the entire zoo, gathering up the leaves, cleaning up every last bit of kangaroo poo, washing out lizard enclosures, keeping the snakes clean.

The first afternoon of that visit, Steve took me in with the alligators. They came out of their ponds like sweet little puppies—puppies with big sharp teeth and frog eyes. I didn't know what to expect, but with Steve there I felt a sense of confidence and security. The next thing I knew, I was feeding the alligators big pieces of meat as if I'd done it all my life.

That evening, Steve put me up at a motel, a few miles from the zoo. I met his parents and had dinner with the whole family.

The next night, Steve and I went to dinner in Caloundra, a nearby town.

He took me to a resort that featured an all-you-can-eat buffet dinner—seafood banquet, my favourite. I loaded my plate high with prawns, crab, oysters and everything I loved. I didn't know it then, but Steve was a bit worried that I was going to eat more than he did.

And then, suddenly, the weekend was over. Steve drove me back down to Brisbane. I had the biggest ache in my heart. I had fallen hard. As we said goodbye, he put his arms round me for the first time, and I felt all his strength and warmth in that embrace. But it was over. I was going back to my side of the world. I had no idea if I would ever see Steve Irwin again.

Chapter Two

COUGAR CUBS FOR SALE.

Four words jumped out at me from the classified ads in the *Oregonian*, one of the main newspapers in my home state of Oregon. It was 1986; I was twenty-two years old, living on my own, running a pilot car business I had inherited from my father.

Cougar cubs, I thought. That's strange. How can that be possible or legal when we've got cougars living in the wild in Oregon? How can you buy and sell them like pets?

I tried to put the thought out of my mind, but I couldn't shake it. Finally I decided I had to drive up and check out the situation. The address was a residence in Hillsboro, a small suburb to the west of the city of Portland.

The owner of the place came out to meet me—a reed-thin smoker, with aviator glasses and thinning hair.

'I'm here to see the cougar cubs,' I said.

'Only got one left,' he said, and led me into a garage. A small portable pet carrier sat pushed up against one wall. I peered inside. A bone-thin baby cougar stared blankly back out at me. She looked about three months old and her eyes were dull and lifeless. She had tried so hard to get out of the cage that she had rubbed a large patch of fur off her forehead. I detected the painful swelling of the joints that indicated rickets, the result of a poor or incorrect diet.

'How much are you selling her for?'

'Thirteen hundred,' he replied flatly.

Thirteen hundred dollars. A lot of money for me to come up with. 'Well, thank you for showing her to me,' I said.

I turned to leave, but I knew I had to do something.

EUGENE, OREGON, the 'Emerald City', is beautifully situated at the end of the Willamette Valley. It's an outdoorsy, friendly kind of place, perfect for a soccer-playing, horse-riding, cheerleading young student at the Eugene Christian School, which is what I was. My mom, Julia, was a teacher. I was the baby of the family. My sister Bonnie lived with us until I was six weeks old, when she moved out and got married. I knew my sister Tricia better, since she didn't get married until I was six. As I was growing up, I was well and truly the only child.

My father, Clarence, worked a variety of jobs and being a heavy-haul trucker was one of them. He also ran the pilot cars that preceded and followed extra-wide loads on the highway. Driving his truck one day, my dad saw a mother merganser duck that had been hit by a car. Her baby ducks were with her, running around frantically back and forth at the side of the road.

'Look,' he said to me when he arrived home that evening. He opened his jacket to reveal half a dozen little ducklings.

I was ecstatic. Merganser ducks are fish-catchers and have sharp beaks with a serrated edge, totally unlike the flat, shovel-like bills of mallard ducks. They also have funny little haircuts: the feathers on top of their heads flip up at the back. To my eight-year-old eyes, they were beautiful.

We had a small stream, which we called a slough, that ran behind our house. It was full of minnows, small fingerlings that were grey and under an inch or two long. I'd help my dad catch a couple of hundred every day, and the ducklings ate them with relish.

That small flock of mergansers was so special to me because we didn't have any pets. They would come up to me when I called and they would nuzzle me with their tiny beaks. I wanted to keep them for ever. But I had to learn an important lesson. My dad used my room as an example.

'Look around,' he said. In my bedroom was everything that I loved—my nice soft bed, my favourite toys and great big sunny windows. 'I want you to imagine something,' Dad continued. 'Imagine if you could never leave this room. We'd bring in all your favourite food, and you could have a TV in here, but you still couldn't ever leave. Would you be happy?'

I knew what he was getting at. 'Maybe for a little while,' I said.

'For a little while,' he repeated.

We introduced the ducks back into the wild. Afterwards, I thought about how it all made sense to me. No matter how nice the place is where you live, you need to experience life and the world.

It wouldn't be long before I'd learn another lesson that was a real turning point. I saw a dog scrounging around in the school parking lot, a dirty and scrawny mutt. Some of the kids and I shared a bit of food with the dog at recess. I suddenly felt an unusual responsibility towards the stray. I didn't feel it was enough just to give it something to eat and say that I'd helped it, and then move on. I needed to make sure that dog was in a safe place.

'We've got to do something to help,' I explained to my teacher.

'The school's already called animal control,' my teacher said. She assured me that if the owners were looking for the stray, they would have the best chance of finding it through animal control.

'But if the dog isn't claimed, they'll put it to sleep, right?'

My teacher sighed. 'I suppose. But there aren't any other options, Terri.'

What happened to the stray dog, I'll never know. But with the fierce determination of a child to right injustice, I resolved that when I grew up, I would not walk past a problem. I would stop and fix it. The stray dog and the ducklings were just minor incidents in the life of a young girl growing up in the Pacific Northwest. But they formed two vital threads in the fabric of who I am today: when you help an animal, do your absolute best to make sure you don't harm it at the same time. And, never walk past a problem with an animal—fix it.

These were the lessons I remembered when I encountered a sick, emaciated cougar in a plastic pet cage.

I STARTED BY CONTACTING the Oregon State Fish and Wildlife Department. 'Is it legal to keep a cougar?' I asked. It turned out that it was perfectly legal, provided the animal was born in captivity.

'Once they are in captivity,' said the voice on the line, 'they fall under the jurisdiction of the United States Department of Agriculture.'

I called the USDA. There was only a single official, Dr Overton, who was in charge of all of Northern California and the entire 97,000 square miles of Oregon. I described the baby cougar's situation to him.

'The best we could do for the animal,' he said, 'is to issue a warning and check up on her in a few months.'

'In a few days that cougar will be dead,' I replied.

'I apologise,' Dr Overton said. 'I don't have any other options.'

I felt bad for him, and I shared his frustration at being stretched so thin. It reminded me of what my teacher had said about the stray dog. Back then, I swore that if there were no other options, then *I* would be the option. Now I was an adult with the opportunity to fix the glitch in this system.

I drove back up to Hillsboro, laid my money down and took possession of one very sick, very pitiful cougar, pet pack and all.

My very first hurdle was my dog, Shasta, whom I dearly loved. Shasta was most perturbed when I showed up at 'her' house with a baby cougar. But after a few days the two had an uneasy truce.

The baby cougar stayed in the garage. I played with her in the back yard and rolled around with her in the house. After a few days of eating good food she started coming round and immediately began acting like a cougar. This turned out to be both good and bad.

Her favourite game was hiding until my back was turned. Then she'd pounce ferociously and grapple me round the backs of my legs. Cougars are superb stalk-and-ambush predators. Her cub-level version of it was a cute enough trick, unless I happened to be sitting down, not paying attention.

When I was doing paperwork, watching TV or had relaxed in any sort of seated position, she would sneak up on me very quietly with her big soft padded feet on the carpet. She would leap through the air and land on my back, grabbing the back of my neck with her jaws.

She would clamp down on me, refusing to let go, with a guttural growl coming out between her clenched teeth. The whole process left me rather unsettled. I never knew when I was going to be pounced on.

I began doing more thorough and appropriate research. I learned that no official regulations existed for housing a cougar. Several governmental agencies had opinions as to what might be required. In the end, I figured it would be best to go along with the strictest guidelines.

I wound up having a mini-Fort Knox built in my back yard, which cost about $6,000. The den box was huge, made of wood, bolted down off the ground, with a big rubber top. I put in a large picnic table. The cougar enjoyed that, since it was wood and she could leap up in two little steps to get on top. Then I hired another builder to put a roof over half the enclosure.

The money disappeared quickly. I learned that it cost about $5 a day to feed this 'pet' and that the bigger she got, the more she enjoyed the pouncing game. I didn't have to name her, since she already came with a beautiful one—Malina. Instead of letting her jump on my head whenever she felt like it, I sought guidance on how to discipline her. I would let her play with me until she gave me a nip or grabbed me with her big feet and pulled me in for a good bite. Then I would scold her and pop her gently on the nose. We got to know each other, and Malina began to respect me. She soon became very territorial about her enclosure, and that's where Shasta came in.

Shasta was a brilliant sidekick. She would go into Malina's enclosure and find any little scraps of meat that might be left over after dinner. Malina didn't appreciate this much, but every time she tried to defend her territory, Shasta would bark, growl and snap, quickly putting the cougar in her place. Soon Malina realised she wasn't top dog, and her attitude problems were quickly resolved.

Malina also learned that it was fun to go out for walks on her leash. Early in the morning we would hit the local playground. The fences of the tennis courts were high enough that I could let her run around freely. Utilising a thirty-foot lead, I'd also take her to the beach. Malina crawled on her belly and hid in the beach grass, flattening her ears to the side, and would sit absolutely motionless. People strolled by, and we would exchange 'hellos', but they never knew that three feet away from them was a crouching cougar.

Soon I was taking Malina out for events to educate people about cougars. She came with me to schools—everything from small classrooms to universities—and I would take her to various community events too. She loved it! She'd sit behind a roped-off area, flicking her tail, people-watching.

I began taking my cougar with me to court hearings. I'd join environmentalist attorneys and people concerned about the cruelty of certain hunting practices, such as bear-baiting and hunting cougars with dogs. By taking Malina into the courtroom, I not only got press, I also brought the hunters face to face with the animal they were trying to persecute. Instead of the snarling, terrifying demon of the night that they imagined stalking their children, they would see a beautiful, noble spirit of the wilderness.

Malina marked the beginning of my affinity for predatory mammals. After an internship with the Fish and Wildlife Department, I earned my certificate as a wildlife rehabilitator. I had found my purpose.

SOON, MORE ENCLOSURES began to sprout up in my back yard. As a wildlife rehabilitator, I took in foxes, bobcats, raccoons and possums. All sorts of animals came into my care, but I seemed to have a knack with predatory mammals above all others—with the exception of wolves.

One timber wolf I was called to rescue was beautiful but extraordinarily thin. She'd just had a litter of pups and was nursing them. Even though the kennel was seven feet wide and fourteen feet long, and had a roof on it, she started tugging until she pulled the cage partially off the concrete pad. At sixty pounds, probably half her normal weight, and lactating, the wolf was still demolishing her enclosure. I wasn't going to be able to hold her.

I didn't have many options. I thought of the one place she couldn't escape—my very own Fort Knox.

Wolf and cougar switched places. I enticed the mama wolf away with some food so I could check on her puppies. The tiny wolf pups, whose eyes weren't even open yet, growled menacingly at my approach.

Malina didn't like her new small enclosure, but I was too busy to notice. After all, it was only going to be a few days until I placed the wolf and her puppies with a rescue group that specialised in wolves. That weekend, I drove up the coast and left them in much better hands than mine.

It had been a big day. I returned home after dark, and went in to feed and brush Malina, our usual evening routine. She sat up on her den box inside the small enclosure. As I was brushing her, she put her forehead down to me as she always did, asking for a rub. As part of this process, Malina would usually bump her head into mine. It always hurt a bit, but it was a sign of affection, so I bumped heads back.

When I turned round to walk out of the enclosure, without warning, Malina pounced. All of a sudden, I felt her muscular forearms enveloping my shoulders. She grabbed the back of my head so that her upper teeth dug into the top of my skull, with her bottom canines hooked neatly under the lip of my skull at the back of my neck.

Malina began to bite down. I could feel her canines puncturing my scalp. My head was going to explode. Her arms braced my shoulders, squeezing tightly. I started swinging wildly backwards with the brush in my hand, hitting her on the top of the head. She didn't budge. The pressure grew so great that I knew something was going to give.

'NO, NO, NO!' I yelled at the top of my lungs. She loosened her grip for a moment and I quickly twisted away. She dropped down to the floor of the kennel but immediately pounced again, grappling me round the front and biting at my chest. I beat her away a second time and backed for the door.

I felt the adrenaline surging through my arms and into my fingertips as I reached behind me and fumbled with the latch. It was tricky, but I didn't dare turn round. I managed to unlatch the door and slam it behind me. I collapsed. I had not an ounce of strength left. I felt sick.

With a huge booming bang, Malina crashed into the door just after it shut. She turned round, gave me a dirty look over her shoulder, and sulked back to her den box.

I learned a few valuable lessons that night. First, I needed to be really careful about working with wild animals when I was by myself. Second, never take an animal that is used to one enclosure and put it in a smaller one. And last, a wild animal is just that. I could work with them and develop some level of mutual respect. But I could never forget they were wild.

I WAS MORE OR LESS prepared for the physical aspects of wildlife rescue. I never shied away from hard work. But I found myself less prepared for the emotional challenges of the rescue work I was taking on. The way some people treat wildlife is beyond comprehension.

A cougar hunted by dogs is put through unbelievable trauma. Instead of just hating the hunters, I tried to learn from them. I went to hunting exhibitions and fairground events. I learned that a mother cougar will climb a tree when a hunter approaches, leaving her cubs to be torn apart by hunting dogs. A cougar's fear of humans is so great it outweighs her instinct to protect her young. The stories were heartbreaking. Still, the more I learned, the more determined I became to stop these perpetrators of crimes against wildlife. I would even sit in on court cases to show support and encouraged others to do the same, especially with truly heinous crimes against wildlife. For one memorable trial, the judge moved the venue three times to increasingly larger courtrooms, because there were 300 of us who showed up.

On trial were two men, one in a plaid shirt and the other with a long, ZZ Top-style beard. Plaid Shirt was the main perpetrator, charged with animal cruelty. He had brought his young son along during the bear-killing for which he was on trial. The reason the state managed to bring charges is that the hunters had made a videotape of their gruesome acts. They showed the video in court. ZZ Top and Plaid Shirt cornered the bear cub. In order to preserve the integrity of the pelt, they attempted to kill the cub by stabbing it in the eyes.

It was absolutely gut-wrenching to watch. The bear struggled for its life, but Plaid Shirt kept thrusting his knife, moving back as the animal twisted frantically away, then moving forward to stab again. The bear cub screamed, and it sounded eerily as though the bear was actually crying 'Mama,' over and over. Plaid Shirt and ZZ Top sat unfazed in court. From my place in the gallery, I watched as a towering man in a police uniform burst into tears and walked out of the courtroom. At the end of the video, Plaid Shirt brought his nine-year-old son over to stand triumphantly next to the dead bear cub.

'Clearly, you deserve jail,' the judge told Plaid Shirt. 'Unfortunately, the jails are filled with people even more heinous than you. So I am going to sentence you to three thousand hours of community service.'

I approached the judge after the trial, furious that this man might end up collecting a bit of rubbish along the highway as his penance.

'I want him,' I said, referring to Plaid Shirt. I said that I ran a wildlife rehabilitation facility and could use a volunteer.

The first day Plaid Shirt showed up, he actually looked scared of me. He cleaned cages, fed animals and worked hard. I asked him every question I could think of: where he hunted, how he hunted, why he hunted. I felt as though I was in the presence of true evil.

For months he helped. He had some skills, like carpentry, and he could lift heavy things. He fulfilled his community service. In the end, I couldn't tell if I had made any difference or not.

THE EMOTIONAL ROLLER COASTER of rescue work never seemed to end. I named my facility 'Cougar Country' to highlight my focus, but I found myself called to help many different animals—in vets' offices, in the field, in classrooms and courtrooms. Somehow I kept it all together, and ran my pilot car company, Westates Flagman, too. My day had forty-eight hours. Life was rewarding, but hectic, and it helped that I had no social life.

After a particularly long day, I got a phone call out of the blue.

'I'm going to Australia to scuba dive the Great Barrier Reef,' my friend Lori said to me in September 1991. 'You ought to come along. We'd have a great time. You *need* a good time.'

A lot of things argued against this trip. My back yard was full of rescued animals that needed care and attention, 24/7. And I knew the key to running my business was being there every single day. I loved my life, but maybe Lori had a point. I had been burning the candle at both ends.

'I've got a girlfriend over there,' Lori continued, trying to convince me. 'We'd have someone to hang out with who knows the country.'

I'd been to Australia in my early twenties, journeying up the coast from Sydney to Brisbane. It was the most wonderful place. I had fallen in love with the wildlife, the wild places and the open, friendly people.

And there were the cougars. In the back of my mind I thought I might be able to combine my passion for rescue work with my love of Australia. Cougar Country was taking in cougars from everywhere: pets discarded when they grew too dangerous and those orphaned by hunters. I couldn't keep them all myself. I needed responsible facilities to take them. Completely naive about Australia's importation and quarantine regulations, I thought that there might be some opportunities 'down under' for people doing educational work with wildlife, who might be able to take a cougar.

Chapter Three

After meeting Steve for the first time in the Queensland heat, I arrived back home to a cool, foggy Oregon in the autumn of 1991. Malina and Cougar Country were waiting, and my old life quickly swept me up. But the world had changed. I had changed.

A week passed, then two. By the third week I was pretty sure I wasn't going to hear from my Australian action hero again. But there wasn't a day that went by when he wasn't the first thing on my mind as I woke up, and the last thing on my mind as I went to sleep. After four weeks of waiting for a call from Australia, I became convinced that it wasn't going to happen.

In mid-November a call came in late at night.

'G'day, mate,' said the voice on the other end of the line. 'It's Stevo calling from Australia. How are you going?'

Well, for starters, I was going without breathing for a few moments. 'Good,' I stammered.

'I'm coming to Oregon in ten days,' he said. 'I'd love to see you.'

Yes! I was floored. Ten days. That would be . . . Thanksgiving.

'Steve,' I said. 'Do you know about the American holiday of Thanksgiving? We all get together as a family. We eat our brains out and take walks and watch a lot of football—American football, you know, gridiron, not your rugby league football.' I was babbling. 'Do you want to come and share Thanksgiving with my family?'

Steve didn't seem to notice my fumbling tongue. 'I'd be happy to,' he said. 'That'd be brilliant.'

'Great. Send me all the details, your flight and everything,' I said.

'I will,' he promised. Then he hung up.

THANKSGIVING DAY finally arrived. I remember feeling so proud to have my family meet my Aussie man. We had just eaten an epic feast of devilled eggs, turkey and stuffing, lots of gravy, cranberry sauce and sweet potatoes. We took a break before the desserts came out and the menfolk headed into the living room to watch football. But Steve wandered back into the kitchen to talk to each of my sisters and my mom, getting to know the whole family.

I thought he was very considerate, because I knew instinctively that he was a bit shy and totally out of his element. He had never visited the United States before, or been this serious about a girl. We had only spent a few days with each other, but both of us seemed to know that his visit was more than just a casual meeting. Being together felt more and more like destiny.

We went everywhere. I gave him the grand tour, the best the Pacific Northwest can offer, which is nothing short of spectacular. Everything revolved round wildlife. We hiked the Coastal Range out of my parents' beach cabin to look for black bears, and travelled to eastern Oregon to see white-tailed deer, coyotes and the Eastern Oregon antelope, animals that Steve had never experienced before.

Then, too soon, our time was over. I felt the familiar ache, the pressure in the middle of my chest. Ever since I'd met Steve, I had experienced the same ache whenever I left him. It was a very real pain, one I'd never felt before.

'I have to see you again,' I said. For the first time, I was very open about my feelings for him. As he was leaving, I was already making plans to see him again in Australia.

I LEFT THE ICEBOX-COLD of Oregon for the tropical heat of Cairns in early January 1992. As I got off the plane to catch my connecting flight to Brisbane, I found it almost difficult to breathe, it was so hot and muggy.

My mind was working in funny ways. *It's just too hot here*, I thought. *I could never live here*. Then I caught myself. *Hang on a minute. Why would that even be an option? I'm just coming over to see this guy.* But that Cairns moment was the first time I actually thought about leaving my Oregon life behind to join Steve in his Australian one.

I stepped out into the airport in Brisbane. There was Steve, back in his khakis. It was nice to see him in those familiar shorts, after having to bundle up in Oregon against the cold.

We embraced, and I had the sense that we were one person. Apart, we weren't whole, but together, we were OK again. We immediately got lost in conversation. The crocodiles were nesting, Steve said. It was stinking hot, the perfect time of year for all things reptilian. Steve Irwin's time.

Twenty-four hours after I stepped off the plane in Brisbane, Steve was showing me how to raid croc nests to retrieve the eggs so they wouldn't just die in the nest. He showed me how to feed venomous snakes that were hot and loaded, how to get in with the cassowaries and retrieve their food bucket without getting kicked in half.

I slowly got to know the staff, who were more like extended family, and Steve's remarkable parents, in whose home I was staying. They had founded the zoo nearly a quarter of a century before. Steve's father, Bob, still did the books. His mom, Lyn, ran the food kiosk. Steve's best mate, Wes, was working as his right-hand man.

As much as I enjoyed it, we weren't going to stay at the zoo. I was about to experience a life-changing event: Steve Irwin in the Australian bush.

Our destination was the Burdekin River, on the coast, 800 miles north of Brisbane. The Burdekin is dependent on the wet season, which brings floods of epic proportions. The rainfall is massively unpredictable and wholly cyclone-dependent. The Burdekin was the closest habitat to the zoo for the big saltwater crocs, so off to the river we went.

Dams were planned, Steve explained. The river wasn't terribly well known, and its crocodile populations weren't well understood. He wanted to go up and survey the crocs, see where their nesting sites were, and gauge the success of their breeding.

Parts of the Burdekin were dangerously remote, and these, of course, were the parts where we were headed. Steve had to pack his own fuel, water, food, spare tyres, boat, engine and extra parts. He loaded up the Ute, the pick-up truck. Swags—sleeping-bags—went in, but no tent. We would be sleeping under the stars.

My first hurdle came before we left. Steve's little dog, Sui, was coming with us, and she realised that I would be taking her place next to Steve in the front of the truck.

'Move over, Sui,' I said. She turned and glared at me, for all the world like a jealous woman. I couldn't help but laugh.

As we headed out, it came to light that this would be a sixteen-hour trip—and the driving would be shared.

After several hours, Steve climbed into the back under the canvas canopy and stretched out on top of one of the swags. I wasn't worried about falling asleep while I was driving. I was too nervous to be sleepy.

STEVE DROVE the next morning as we made the turn for the Burdekin River. The single-lane dirt road, as small as it was, ended there—but we had another two or three hours of four-wheel driving to go.

As we pounded and slammed our way deep into the bush, Steve talked about the area's Aborigines. The landscape was alive to him, not only with human history, but also with the complex inter-relatedness of plants, animals and the environment. He pointed out giant 150-year-old eucalypts, habitats for insectivorous bats, parrots and brush-tailed possums.

After hours of bone-jarring terrain, we reached the Burdekin, a beautiful river winding through the tea trees. We set up camp—by which I mean Steve did—at a fork in the river, where huge black boulders stood exposed in the middle of the water. I tried to help, but I felt completely out of my depth. Steve unpacked the boat and the motor, got it tied and moored on the river, rolled out the swags, and lined up containers of fuel, water and food.

Then he started stringing tarps. What a gift Steve had for setting up camp. I watched him secure ropes, tie knots and stretch canvas like he was expecting that we'd have to withstand a cyclone. It was hot, more than 100° Fahrenheit, but Steve didn't seem to notice.

Sui found a little shallow place at the edge of the river and immediately plopped herself in. I saw Steve look over at her as if calculating her chances of being snatched by a croc. Crocodiles are the ultimate camouflage attack predators, striking from the water's edge.

There would never be 'down time' for Steve. We were off in an instant. We grabbed Sui, jumped in the boat and headed upstream. White Burdekin ducks startled up, their dark neck-rings revealed as they flew over us. Cormorants dried their feathers on the mid-river boulders, wings fully open. It was magical and unspoilt, as if we were the first visitors there.

Steve knew the area intimately. As part of the East Coast Crocodile Management Program in the 1980s, he had been commissioned to remove problem crocodiles. Crocodiles helped to maintain the ecological balance, which meant that wherever there were crocodiles, there was great fishing. Therein lay the conflict. Fishermen didn't seem to like sharing their favourite spot with a crocodile. All through the 1980s, Steve caught and relocated numerous Burdekin River crocs. He even had some at the Queensland Reptile and Fauna Park that he'd rescued from this very river.

Burdekin crocodiles were special, and physically different from other salties, a bit more sleek and streamlined. Many of them had only four nuchal scutes, the osteodermal plates on the neck, while most saltwater crocs had six. As we motored up the river, Steve pointed out slides and footprints left behind by crocodiles that had been sunning on the bank. The further upstream we went, the bigger the slides got. Steve explained the social hierarchy of the crocodile. Females would inhabit a specific area to nest, and then there would be big male salties. The sub-adult crocs dwelt on the fringe, staying out of the way of the big dominant crocs. There were also 'crèche areas', where the baby crocs would grow up, catching small insects, fish, frogs or baby birds.

We returned to camp. Steve seemed calmer now that he'd got his bearings and revisited familiar places. Just downstream from the camp, we hopped from one exposed boulder to the next, getting out into the middle of the river. As we sat together on a mid-river boulder, the shadows crossed the water and the sun sank lower. We looked into each other's eyes and talked about all the things we loved. I realised then that I had fallen in love with Steve. We made our way back across the boulders before it got dark.

'Night-time is croc time,' Steve said. 'It's important to get off the water before they are active and hunting.'

Back in camp, Steve started cooking. I asked if I could help. He waved me off. 'My trip, my treat,' he said.

I sat watching the river as it changed with darkness coming on, and enjoyed the smell of cooking. I could hear the soft flapping of the fruit bats overhead. At first there were just a few, then dozens, finally hundreds, crossing above the crowns of paperbark trees and honey myrtles. They looked surreal, spooky and beautiful, gliding across the darkening sky.

We finished dinner, jumped into the boat and headed back up the river. This was Steve's favourite time. I hadn't understood what he was doing on our trip earlier that afternoon. He had memorised where he had seen the slides. During the day we hadn't spotted a single croc. After getting on the water, Steve shone his spotlight across the inky blackness and picked up the red eye-shine of crocs. As we slowly idled the boat upstream, the red orbs would blink and then vanish as the crocodiles submerged on our approach. Suddenly I felt terribly exposed in the little dinghy. The beautiful melaleuca trees that had looked so spectacular during the day now hung eerily over the water, as their leaves dipped and splashed in the black water. Fish came alive, too. Everything made more noise in the dark.

Some of the crocodiles allowed us to get close. Steve could gauge a croc's total size based on the length of its head. He showed me how to hold the spotlight right under my chin, so that I could look directly over the beam and pick up the eye-shine of the crocs.

'Look, look, look,' Steve whispered excitedly, 'there's another one.' There was something strange about this one, only a single red eye reflected. Perhaps the other one had been shot out, Steve suggested.

'He's big,' he whispered. 'Maybe five metres.'

We edged closer. The engine coughed and suddenly ground to a stop. Steve leaned over the back of the dinghy, reaching in up to his shoulder in the water, to clear the weeds from around the propeller.

The single red eye blinked out. The big croc had submerged. Submerged where? I wondered. I am in the middle of nowhere, surrounded by crocodiles. Steve finally cleared the weeds, yanked the ignition cord and the engine started.

The heat hadn't really broken when we got back to camp. It was still well over ninety degrees. The insects that had been attracted to my spotlight were stuck and struggling in the sweat running down my back.

'How about a quick tub?' Steve said. I'd learned that was Australian for bath. Somehow, the words 'bath' and 'crocodile' refused to go together in my mind. But into the Burdekin we went, in our shorts, barefoot, picking our way through the stones, sticks and burs until we got to the smooth rocks of the river. Steve jumped in. As I edged towards deeper water, he blocked my path and moved himself in front of me.

'What are you doing?'

He laughed. 'I caught the last big male crocodile around here last year, but I can't be too sure another one hasn't moved in.'

ON OUR RETURN from the bush, we went back to work at the zoo. A sixty-foot tree by the Irwin family home had been hit by lightning some years previously, and a tangle of dead branches was in danger of crashing down on the house. Steve thought it would be best to take the dead tree down.

He looked like a little dot high up in the air, swinging through the branches, working the chainsaw. After he pruned off all the limbs, the last task was to fell the massive trunk. Steve climbed down, secured a rope two-thirds of the way up the tree and tied the other end to the bull bar of his Ute.

My job was to drive the truck. Steve cut the base of the tree. As the chainsaw snarled, Steve yelled, 'Now!' I put the truck in reverse, slipped the clutch, and went backwards at a forty-five degree angle as hard as I could. With a groan and a tremendous crash, the tree hit the ground.

Steve cut the downed timber into lengths and I stacked them. The whole project took us all day. As the long shadows crossed the yard, Steve said four words very uncharacteristic of him: 'Let's take a break.'

We sat under a big fig tree in the yard with a cool drink. We were both covered in little flecks of wood, leaves and bark. Steve's hair was unkempt, a couple of his shirt buttons were missing and his shorts were torn. I thought he was the best-looking man I had ever seen.

Steve turned to me. 'So, do you want to get married?'

Casual, matter-of-fact. I nearly dropped the glass I was holding. I had twigs in my hair and dirt caked on the side of my face.

My first thought was what a mess I must look. My second, third and fourth thoughts were lists of every possible excuse for why I couldn't marry Steve Irwin: I could not leave my job, my house, my wildlife work, my family, friends, pets—everything I had worked so hard for back in Oregon.

Steve never looked concerned. He simply held my gaze.

As all these excuses flashed through my mind, a little voice from somewhere above me spoke. 'Yes, I'd love to.'

With those four words my life changed for ever.

Chapter Four

My head was still spinning from the ceremony and the celebration. The four months between February 2, 1992—the day Steve asked me to marry him—and our wedding on June 4 had been a blur.

The first challenge was how to bring as many Australian friends and family as possible over to the United States for the wedding. None of us had a lot of money. Eleven people wound up making the trip from Australia, and we held the ceremony in the Methodist church my grandmother attended.

It was more than a wedding, it was saying goodbye to everyone I'd ever known. I invited everybody, including people who may not have been intimate friends. I even invited my dentist. The whole network of wildlife rehabilitators came too—400 people in all.

The ceremony began at 8 p.m. As the minister started reading the vows, I could see that Steve was nervous. His dinner jacket looked like it was strangling him. Poor Steve, I thought. He'd never been up in front of such a big crowd before.

'The scariest situation I've ever been in,' Steve would say later of the ceremony. This from a man who wrangled crocodiles!

Then, just as we were to leave on a honeymoon in the beautiful Pacific Northwest, a call came from Australia. 'It's a big one, Stevo, maybe fourteen or fifteen feet,' John Stainton said over the phone. 'I hate to catch you right at this moment, but they're going to kill him unless he gets relocated.'

John was one of Australia's award-winning documentary makers. He and Steve had met in the late 1980s, when Steve had helped John to shoot commercials that required a zoo animal. But their friendship had not really taken off until 1990, when a beer company had hired John to film a tricky shot involving a crocodile.

He had called Steve. 'They want a bloke to toss a coldie to another bloke, but a croc comes out of the water and snatches at it. The guy grabs the beer right in front of the croc's jaws. You think that's do-able?'

'Sure, mate, no problem at all,' Steve had said with his usual confidence. 'Only one thing, it has to be my hand in front of the croc.'

John agreed. He journeyed up to the zoo to film the commercial. It was the first time he had seen Steve on his own turf, and he was impressed. He was even more impressed when the croc shoot went off flawlessly. As John left the zoo after completing the shoot, Steve gave him a collection of VHS tapes he had shot himself. He simply propped his camera in a tree, or jammed it into the mud and filmed himself single-handedly catching crocs.

John watched the tapes when he got home to Brisbane. He told me later that the footage was unbelievable. 'It was Steve. The camera loved him.'

He rang up his contacts in television and explained that he had a hot property. The programmers couldn't use Steve's original VHS footage, but one of them had a better idea: he gave John the green light to shoot his own documentary of Steve.

That led to John's call to Oregon on the eve of our honeymoon.

'I know it's not the best timing, mate,' John said, 'but we could take a crew and film a documentary of you rescuing this crocodile.'

Steve turned to me. Honeymoon or crocodile? For him, it wasn't much of a quandary. But what about me?

'Let's go,' I replied.

TWO WEEKS AFTER WE SAID, 'I do', Steve and I were on a river system called Cattle Creek, near Ingham, 700 miles up the Australian coast from Brisbane. John Stainton was there as well, together with a soundman and a cameraman. Steve's best mate, Wes, was there too.

The big saltie in Cattle Creek was in great danger. When we arrived, we discovered cartridge casings and other evidence that people had been shooting at him. Steve worked up and down the river system in the dinghy, finding the areas the crocodile had been frequenting, mentally marking the slides, and searching for the right spot to set the trap.

At the end of an exhausting first day, the six of us gathered wearily round the fire. I looked up and realised that five pairs of eyes were looking at me. Oh, I get it: I'm the only woman here. I'm supposed to be cooking dinner.

The camp 'kitchen' consisted of a collection of odd, alien-looking utensils such as a jaffle iron and a camp oven. I had no idea how to use any of them. Steve came to the rescue: he made toasted sandwiches in the jaffle iron and cooked up a stew in the camp oven. We realised it was going to work best if I was the assistant and he was the chef.

As I chopped vegetables that first night, a big lacy showed up.

'Grab it,' Steve said to me. I picked up the lizard. John and his crew went into action. I told the camera everything I knew about lace monitors.

'Lace monitors are excellent tree climbers,' I said. 'They can grow up to seven feet long.' I spoke about the lizard's predatory nature and diet. Meanwhile, the star of the show flicked his forked tongue in and out. After we got some footage, I put the huge lizard down, and Steve leaned his head into the camera frame to have a last word.

'And they've also got teeth like a tiger shark, mate,' he said with relish. 'They can tear you to ribbons!'

'Thanks a lot,' I said, laughing, after John stopped filming. 'You should have told me that before I picked the bloody thing up!'

Steve was a natural in front of the camera. John had to give him only one important piece of advice.

'Stevo,' John instructed, 'there are three people in this documentary. There's you, Terri and the camera. Treat the camera just like another person.'

Steve's energy and enthusiasm took over. He completely relaxed, and managed to just be himself—which was true of his entire career.

This wasn't just a film trip, it was also our honeymoon. Steve would sometimes escape the camera crew and take us up a tributary to be alone. We watched the fireflies come out. The magical little insects glowed everywhere, in the bushes and in the air. The darker it got, the brighter their blue lights burned on and off.

I had arrived in a fairyland.

Mostly, though, we worked. To successfully trap crocs, meat was needed for bait. This was where Sui came into her own, rounding up pigs. Feral pigs are not native to Australia, but were introduced when Europeans first arrived. They root up native vegetation and raid freshwater crocodile nests, feeding on everything from plants to turtles.

Over the years, Steve and Sui had become the ultimate pig-catching team. It was an amazing process to watch. Since there was no way to pack and store large slabs of fresh meat, we were off to some local cane fields at first light to catch pigs. Steve then kept them in makeshift corrals until he needed them.

The cane fields are dangerous. Taipans, the third most venomous snake on earth, follow rats into the cane. As we crashed through, intent on catching pigs, it was impossible to scan the ground for snakes.

Steve signalled to me by pointing to his nose that he could smell pigs. Sniffing the air, I caught a heavy, musky odour. We soon saw tracks and heard the rustling of bushes up ahead.

Steve whispered, 'Up front, Sui.' She exploded forward, disappearing in the thick cane. Steve was right behind her. Suddenly I heard crashing sounds all around me. I realised the pigs had doubled back.

A large boar burst through the bush right in front of me. Sui and Steve came up quickly behind. The big boar decided that it was time to turn and fight. Sui started yapping at the pig, dancing in front of its nose. The boar's tusks stuck out at odd angles. It slashed at Sui, who moved like a boxer in the ring, weaving in and out, deftly manoeuvring the pig.

Steve was on the pig in a flash. He grabbed it by the back legs, lifted it up wheelbarrow-style, and rolled it on its side. Sui was beside herself with joy, dashing in and out, her barking shrill and excited. The pig that Steve had so quickly overturned clearly weighed more than he did.

'Come over here quick,' he said.

Steve directed me to grab Sui. Mission accomplished.

Day after day, Steve checked the traps for the big croc. Now it was a waiting game.

The Cattle Creek ecosystem teemed with life. It was a favourite spot for fishermen, because wherever you have crocs, you have a healthy fish population. Crocs manage a river system by culling out everything that shouldn't be there: creatures that are weak, old or sick.

There was plenty of wildlife to film: water pythons, venomous snakes, numerous beautiful birds, koalas, possums and all kinds of lizards. But the big croc remained elusive.

Finally we found him. But as we approached, he failed to submerge. We were horrified to discover that the poachers had beaten us, and shot him. It was likely he had been killed some time ago. Crocs often take a long while to die. They have the astonishing ability to shut off blood supply to an injured part of their body. The big croc had shut down, finally succumbing to his wound. He was huge, some fifteen feet long, fat and in good shape.

Steve was beside himself; he felt as if the croc's death was a personal failure. We filmed the croc and talked about what had happened. But eventually, Steve simply had to walk away. When I went to him, there were tears in his eyes. This death wasn't abstract to Steve. It was personal, as though he had lost a friend, and it fuelled his anger towards the poacher who had killed such a magnificent animal.

Steve knew there was another croc in the area that was also in potential danger. 'Maybe if we save that one,' Steve said with resolve, 'we can salvage something out of this trip.'

That night we cruised Cattle Creek again to film the trap sites. The next morning, Steve got up before me and left to check the traps. The fire was already going when I crawled out of my swag. I heard the boat's motor so I ran down to the riverbank to meet Steve.

'We got one in a trap,' he said, breathless. Then he turned and yelled up to the guys. The whole camp erupted into action. The film crew grabbed their gear, and we went to rescue the crocodile before a poacher's bullet could claim it.

I didn't know what to expect. As we approached the trap, the crocodile heard the boat's motor and started thrashing. In the dim, early-morning light, all I could see was the net moving violently back and forth, a large, muddy-coloured croc caught within. It was a magnificent animal.

Steve had secured the trap to a tree. The crocodile was cinched up inside, since the mouth of the trap drew shut when the weight bag dropped. Steve needed to secure the weight bag separately and get the trap stabilised, while still avoiding those jaws. He retied several knots in quick succession. Once he was satisfied that it was safe, he could take into consideration the film crew and me. He explained that the object would be to get the crocodile out of the trap. We needed it completely unencumbered to be able to relocate it.

The mesh trap was tangled in the croc's teeth and claws. We needed to carefully untangle it. As we approached the croc, my adrenaline surged. I could feel my fingertips tingling and my mouth went dry.

Steve positioned the camera crew so they could have the best vantage point without risk of getting nailed. Then he turned to me.

'Right,' he said. 'You jump on its head and I'll get the net off.'

Um . . . what? I thought. Surely I misunderstood?

'Right,' Steve shouted. 'Now!'

So I jumped on the crocodile's head. I lay down as flat as possible and flung my arms round its head. The croc struggled. As it swung round with me on top, I hung on for grim death, hoping I wouldn't feel those teeth on my arms. I was finally able to pin down its head.

Steve began at the tail end, rolling the trawler mesh back, working the net under the croc's massive tail. Half a crocodile's body length is taken up by its tail. Steve slipped one back leg out of the net, then the other. He pushed the mesh up further, now working directly underneath me.

I slid from one side of the crocodile to the other, always keeping my arms round the head so the croc couldn't swing round and nail Steve. As we worked, the sweat dripped off my face and my heart pounded. I hung on as tightly as possible. I pressed my cheek against the top of the croc's head, and got a close-up view of the head shields and calcium deposits on top of its skull. The croc would exhale and I felt its warm, odourless breath blowing up into my fringe, brushing across my face. I felt so special as I closed my eyes to experience each breath. I was beginning to understand Steve's spiritual connection with these ancient reptiles.

Every once in a while, the crocodile would let out a guttural growl. Even though its jaws were partially held by the mesh, it was daunting to be in such close proximity to over 3,000 pounds per square inch of jaw pressure.

Steve gathered the mesh of the trap round the crocodile's head. This was the most dangerous part. He traded places with me and worked his hands under the net, wrapping his hands round the croc's jaws as he eased its head out of the trap.

The croc was free, with only Steve's hands clamping shut its jaws. We bound its snout and slipped on a blindfold to settle it. Next, we determined that it was a female and measured her. She wasn't even ten feet long, but when I was lying on top of her, it felt like I was holding down a dragon. As we motored up the river I could feel Steve's reverence for her. He didn't just like crocodiles. He loved them.

We finally came to a good release location. We got the crocodile out onto a sandbar and slipped the ropes and blindfold and trappings off her. She scuttled back into the water.

'She'll be afraid of boats from now on,' Steve said. 'She'll never get caught again. She'll have a good, healthy fear of humans, too. It'll help keep her alive.'

For ever afterwards, Steve and I referred to the Cattle Creek rescue as our honeymoon trip. It also marked the beginning of Steve's filming career. He was gifted with the ability to hunt down wildlife. But he hunted animals to save them, not kill them. That's how the Crocodile Hunter was born.

Chapter Five

In spite of the death of the big croc, I felt that our time at Cattle Creek had been superb. Even before we got back to the zoo and saw the footage, there was a hint in the air that something special had been accomplished.

We were elated at saving one crocodile and bitterly disappointed at the one that had been shot. Steve felt the failure to save the Cattle Creek croc from poachers more strongly than I did. I wasn't used to him being gloomy or fixated on mortality. But he kept asking me to promise him that I'd keep the zoo going if something happened to him.

I solemnly promised him that I would keep the zoo going. 'But nothing's going to happen,' I said lightly, 'because the secret to being a great conservationist is living a long time.'

On the drive back to the zoo, we had talked for a long time, a marathon conversation. We didn't know whether our Cattle Creek documentary would make a huge difference or not. But we agreed that through our zoo and our shared life together, we would try to change the world.

There was a big wide world out there. We were just a small wildlife park in Australia. It was absurd to think the two of us could change the world. But our love seemed to make the impossible appear not only possible, but inevitable. Side by side we could face anything.

Back at the zoo, while the documentary was being edited and before it was aired on Australian television, our sense of purpose became more firmly settled than ever. We officially took over stewardship of the zoo from Steve's parents, who had founded it in 1970 as the Beerwah Reptile Park.

The new name would be simply Australia Zoo. We would build and expand. We wanted to increase viewing access to the croc enclosures so more people could see and appreciate these wonderful animals. We had grand plans.

We worked to make ends meet. We judged it a good Sunday if we had 100 visitors, perhaps $650 in gross receipts. But running a business isn't just monitoring income, balancing the books and ensuring quality. Part of any business person's plan has to include a vision for the future and hard work. I would watch Steve planting trees, moving earth and landscaping. He milled his own timber to build enclosures. He worked from dawn until well after dark, when he rigged spotlights to be able to keep working. I had never seen anything like it. He was a machine. He would go past human endurance.

Running a zoo meant being able to work with wildlife, yes. But I discovered there was so much more to it. Steve had an apprenticeship in diesel fitting, so he could operate and repair the backhoes, vehicles and machines necessary to run the zoo. He laid brick and concrete, designed enclosures, and had an eye like an interior decorator for the end result of all his work. It didn't just have to be sturdy and well-built, it had to look good, too.

Over the course of the years in the early 1990s, I helped as Steve developed and expanded the zoo. Funds were limited. Steve did much of the work himself, making what little money we had stretch that much further. He wouldn't even have one project finished before he would already be dreaming up visions of another.

It seemed like there weren't enough hours in the day, no matter how hard we worked. Luckily, we had at the zoo an amazing creature that always gave us an instant reality check, putting all our ambitions in perspective.

Harriet was a giant Galápagos land tortoise. She fascinated me. We tracked her story with tortoise expert Scott Thompson, piecing together an amazing biography that would never be conclusively proved, but was eminently plausible.

We believed Harriet had been collected in 1835 by Charles Darwin himself. She was brought to Australia from England in 1841 by Captain Wickham aboard the *Beagle*. In fact, three Galápagos tortoises were donated to the Brisbane Botanic Gardens, after Darwin realised they did not flourish in England, where he had originally taken them in 1835.

How could we determine if Harriet was one of the Darwin Three? Scott Thompson found a giant tortoise in the collection of the Queensland Museum that had been mislabelled an Aldabran tortoise. Carved on the carapace was the animal's name, 'Tom', and '1929'. We now had potentially found two of the three Darwin tortoises. In living memory people had seen Harriet and Tom together. The third tortoise was never found and is presumed buried somewhere in the botanic gardens. Harriet lived on.

Steve and I both became very excited at this news. It was amazing to learn what a special resident we had at the zoo.

Despite her impressive background, Harriet remained attractively modest. She had a sweet personality like a little dog. She loved hibiscus flowers, and certain veggies were her favourites. Steve carried on a practice that his parents had implemented: whatever you feed animals should be good enough for you to eat. Thus Harriet got the most beautiful mustard greens, kale, aubergines, courgettes and even roses.

In return, Harriet gave us all a lesson in how to live a long life. Don't worry too much. Take it easy. Stop and munch the flowers.

It was a lesson Steve noted and understood, but could never quite take to heart. He was a meteor. Harriet was more of a mountain. In this world, we need both.

STEVE WANTED to help me feel as comfortable with snakes as I was with my mammal friends, since I was living every day with about 150 snakes, in a country that was home to the top eleven most venomous snakes in the world.

He knew just the right teacher. 'Let me introduce you to Rosie,' Steve said to me one day, bringing out a beautiful boa constrictor. She was eight feet long and as fat as my arm. I was more nervous than I wanted to admit.

'The first step is to get to know each other,' Steve said.

While Steve cooked dinner, I sat at one end of the sofa. Rosie lay coiled at the other. I eyed her suspiciously. She eyed me the same way. Finally, there came a revelation. I watched her, curled up on her end of the sofa, and I realised Rosie was more wary of me than I was of her. That's when I started to understand the thought process of the snake. Snakes are logical: *If it's bigger than me, I'm afraid of it; if it's smaller than me, I will eat it.* Fortunately, I was way too big for Rosie to think of me as a snack.

I inched closer to her. Rosie tentatively stretched her neck out, flicked her tongue a few times and slid into my lap. It was a monumental moment and a huge new experience for me. We began to check each other out. I stroked her soft, smooth skin. She smelled every little bit of me, and since snakes smell with their tongue, this meant a lot of flicking and licking. As she approached my face, I felt myself instinctively recoil. Incredibly, Rosie seemed to sense my anxiety and hesitated. As I relaxed, she relaxed.

As time went by, I was able to tolerate Rosie round my shoulders. Soon I did the dishes with Rosie round my neck, and paperwork with her stretched out on the table. We began doing most of my household chores together. She preferred small indoor spaces where she felt secure, but became braver and braver as she trusted me more.

Rosie enjoyed exploring. She stretched her head out and flicked her tongue at anything I showed her. Soon she was meeting visitors at the zoo. Children derived the most delight from this. Some adults had their barriers and suspicions about wildlife, but most children were very receptive. They would laugh as Rosie's forked tongue tickled their cheeks or touched their hair.

Rosie soon became my best friend and my favourite snake. I could always use her as a therapist, to help people with snake phobia get over their fear. She became a great snake ambassador at the zoo, and I became a convert to the wonderful world of snakes.

Through Rosie's ambassadorship, I was able to participate more in the hands-on running of the zoo. Steve gave me my own area to work in. I had baby crocodiles (saltwater and freshwater). It was wintertime when I first took over their care. I had to be careful about feeding them. If baby crocs ate too much and it wasn't warm enough, they wouldn't be able to digest their food. All reptiles rely on the temperature of their surroundings to regulate their bodily functions. I had to crank up the heaters in their rooms, keep their tubs clean and monitor them closely.

A consistent theme of operating the zoo was money management. Although we were in the subtropics, it did get cool in winter. We couldn't afford the specific type of expensive heater we needed to keep the animals warm. I remember the triumph we felt when we located two paraffin heaters for only A$85. They held enough fuel to burn for twelve hours, so we were able to keep the baby crocodiles and lizards at comfortable temperatures.

I was the one-woman marketing department for the zoo. There was no email or fax machine. Everything had to be done on the phone. Steve didn't even own a typewriter. Filing system? No way. The Irwins had a simple but effective tool for keeping track of zoo business: a calendar diary. I used a calculator for doing payroll and instituted a filing-card system for keeping track of people with whom we did business.

Life was simpler then. Steve's sister Mandy worked with us, and we employed three full-time staff and one part-time. That was the whole zoo crew.

AS PRECIOUS AS OUR MONEY WAS, I had two holes into which I poured quite a lot of it. Their names were Shasta and Malina. I was determined to bring my two best animal friends from Oregon and make them part of my new life.

I made the appropriate contacts with the Australasian Regional Association of Zoological Parks and Aquaria (ARAZPA) and initiated the paperwork for the various government department approvals, in order to bring Malina to the zoo. I also worked to bring my dog Shasta to Australia. Time, effort and money went into vet checks, special transportation boxes, a four-month quarantine in Hawaii and a five-month one in Sydney. Quarantine worked out at $26 per day. Steve loved Sui so much that he understood completely why it was worth it to me.

The process took for ever and I spent my days tangled in red tape. I despaired. I loved my life and I loved the zoo, but there were times during that desperate first winter when it seemed we were fighting a losing battle.

Then our documentaries started to air on Australian television. The first one, on the Cattle Creek croc rescue, caused a minor stir. There was more interest in the zoo, and more excitement about Steve as a personality. We hurried to do more films with John Stainton. As those hit the airwaves, it felt like a slow-motion thunderclap. Croc Hunter fever began to take hold.

Although the first documentary was popular and we were continuing to film more, it would be years before we would see any financial gain from our film work. But Steve sat down with me one evening to talk about what we would do if all our grand plans ever came to fruition.

'When we start to make a quid out of Crocodile Hunter,' he said, 'we need to have a plan.'

That evening, we made an agreement that would form the foundation of our marriage in regard to our working life together. Any money we made out of Crocodile Hunter, whether it was through documentaries, toys or T-shirts (we barely dared to imagine that our future would hold spin-offs such as books and movies), would go right back into conservation. We would earn a wage from working at the zoo like everybody else. But everything we earned outside it would go towards helping wildlife. That was our deal.

As a result of the documentaries, our zoo business turned from a trickle to a steady stream. When we did $3,500 worth of business one Sunday, and then the next Sunday upped that record to bring in $4,500, we knew our little business was taking off.

Things were going so well that it was a total shock when I received a stern notice from the Australian immigration authorities. It appeared that not only was it going to be a challenge to bring Shasta and Malina to my new home, I was encountering problems with my own immigration, too.

USING TYPICAL BUREAUCRATIC LOGIC, the Australian Consulate in San Francisco informed me that it would not process my application for permanent residency in Australia unless I was residing in the United States. I flew back in December 1992 with conflicting emotions. I was excited to see my family and friends. But I was sad to be away from Steve.

The process didn't seem to make any sense. First, I had to show up in the States and prove I was actually present, or I would never be allowed to emigrate back to Australia. Cheques for processing fees went missing, as did passport photos and certain signed documents. I had to obtain another set of medical exams, blood work, tuberculosis tests and police record checks—and in response, I got lots of 'maybe's' and 'come back tomorrow's'. It would have been funny, in a surreal sort of way, if I had not been missing Steve so much.

A month stretched into six weeks. When my visa finally came through, it felt like Christmas morning. That night we had a goodbye party at the restaurant my sister owned, and my whole family came. Although I knew I would miss everyone, I was ready to go home. Home didn't mean Oregon to me any more. It meant, simply, by Steve's side.

When I arrived back at the zoo, we fell in love all over again.

STEVE AND I had to shift an alligator to a new enclosure, and John came to film. Working with these large crocodilians was still pretty new to me. Steve jumped in and grabbed the full-grown female alligator, which immediately started heading for the water, dragging Steve with her.

'Grab her back legs!' he called to me.

I grabbed one of the alligator's back legs and her tail, trying to slow her down. Steve swung to the side to try to thwart her moving away. His knee twisted, and then I heard it pop. I felt terrible. If I had done a better job at holding the gator, he might not have wrenched his knee.

'Don't worry about it, babe,' he told me that night. He could tell I thought it was my fault. 'My knee's been giving me curry since high school.'

There never seemed to be a dull moment. Steve came running into the house one morning before the zoo opened. 'Throw on your robe, quick,' he said. I followed Steve to the alligator enclosure and couldn't believe my eyes. Two of our adult females, known as the 'Fang Sisters', had decided to battle over the same nesting spot in their enclosure. They were locked together, their teeth tearing through each other's skulls. Blood pooled on both their heads.

'Get in!' Steve shouted. 'We've got to get them apart.' He told me to jump one while he jumped the other. Once we had them more or less secured, he began the agonising process of prising their jaws apart.

Mud and blood splattered over both of us. I watched Steve struggle with the duelling alligators. They seemed intent on killing each other, and he was intent on saving them both. It took both of us, with all our strength, to hold them apart. We sat there for some time in the mud, each holding a blood-soaked alligator, knowing that if either of us let go, it would happen all over again. It was early in the morning and no one else was at the zoo. It seemed like an eternity that we sat there, in a stalemate.

I didn't think I could hold on much longer. Finally Steve got his arm under his alligator and swung her round. He jumped up, grabbed a fence panel, and stuck that between the two alligators to manoeuvre them apart. Steve kept the two alligators separated while I ran to get building materials so he could improvise a barrier.

I SLOWLY BECAME familiar with the personalities of all the zoo's crocodilians. They were as individual as people. I got to know them intimately during nesting season. Saltwater crocodiles deposit around sixty eggs a season. If you leave them all in the nest, some will break, and the rotten-egg smell becomes overpowering—so one of the tasks of the zoo crew was to remove the eggs.

Mary, our oldest female croc, was easy to work with because she would tear after anyone who approached, leaving her nest unprotected. Cookie sat directly on top of her nest and would not leave. Steve had to get in close in order to coax her away. Whenever she came off the nest to make a flying lunge at Steve, my job was to sneak in and madly grab as many eggs as I could. On my first raid, I took sixty-six eggs out of Cookie's nest.

The zoo crocs were stars. Mary got to appear in *Endless Summer 2*, the sequel to the legendary 1960s surfing travelogue. In the movie, Steve played a surfer carrying his board past a billabong with a crocodile in it.

The $1,000 Steve earned for his cameo helped to fund a huge wedge-tailed eagle enclosure at the zoo, with logs suspended from the roof for easy perching. It provided a home for two injured eagles, and it was also a great educational exhibit. We were keeping our promise to put every cent the Crocodile Hunter earned right back into conservation.

Around the time Steve finished the eagle enclosure, we got our first blast of bad press. An Australian programme ran a so-called exposé on the zoo, on our documentaries and on Steve. There it was, on national television for all of Australia to see. Steve's wildlife work wasn't real. He was a magician, and what people saw on screen was sleight of hand.

The programme cut deep for Steve, who had spent his whole life cultivating relationships with wild animals, and wanted to share his passion with the world. It hurt his feelings deeply, and I suffered to see him suffer.

SHASTA WAS OVERJOYED to see me. After unending paperwork and nine months of quarantine, she had finally arrived in Brisbane. When I first spotted her at the airport, she was growling at the air-freight personnel. As soon as she saw me, her entire expression changed. It was a magic moment.

At that point in time, between Steve and myself, I was the cash-rich one. I had around $120,000 in the bank after selling my Oregon house and my business, Westates Flagman. We both wanted to expand the zoo and were looking at adjacent properties. A two-acre tract was up for sale, but the owners were asking $60,000 for it. If we purchased the land, the zoo would be enlarged from four acres to six. At the time, it seemed like an enormous step to take. That evening we argued back and forth. We talked, dreamed and planned.

Steve always seemed to worry about the future. 'If anything happens to me, promise that you'll take care of the zoo.'

'Of course I will,' I said. 'That's easy to promise, but nothing is going to happen to you. Don't worry.'

Steve was convinced that he would never reach forty. That's why he was in such a hurry to get as much done as he could. He didn't feel sad about it. He only felt the motivation to make a difference before he was gone.

Tonight, he was unusually contemplative. 'None of our petty problems really matter,' he said.

I agreed. 'In a hundred years, what difference is it going to make, worrying about this two acres of land? We need to focus on the real change that will make the world a better place for our children and grandchildren.'

Steve gave me a strange look. Children? We had never discussed having children much. The thought of filming more documentaries, running the zoo *and* raising a family was just too daunting. But that evening we did agree on one thing: we would spend some of my savings and make the leap to enlarge the zoo. We were both so happy with our decision.

Around that time, Steve managed to secure a piece of posterity in a way he never expected. While shooting a film called *Hidden River*, he and I were rowing past the camera to get a particular shot. Steve suddenly leapt to his feet and flung himself out of the boat.

He vanished beneath the water. After what seemed like a great deal of time, he hoisted a large, pale turtle to the surface and hauled it into the boat. It had a light-coloured head, an almost pink nose, and beautiful, delicate colouring. Its watery, saucer-shaped eyes craned up and looked at Steve.

'Crikey, I've only ever seen this species once before, with my dad,' Steve marvelled. As it turned out, Steve had discovered a new species of turtle right there in the middle of the river. We photographed his find, filmed it, measured it and weighed it.

The Queensland Museum verified that it was an undescribed species that would be called Irwin's turtle: *Elseya irwini*, for ever named after Steve.

BACK AT THE ZOO, now that we had decided to buy an additional two acres, Steve was determined to open the whole of the original four acres to the public. The Crocodile Environmental Park had always been a separate part of the zoo, with separate admission, open only for croc shows. But now, as the crowds increased as a result of our documentaries, he wanted to showcase the crocs.

Steve planned the grand opening of the Crocodile Environmental Park for the Christmas school holidays. That meant building extra walkways, ramps and grandstands for visibility, and erecting double fences all round the enclosures so people couldn't come in close proximity to the crocodiles. It was a tremendous amount of work.

Steve spent the spring feverishly concreting crocodile ponds. He shifted the animals around so that each croc was in a good position to be viewed. He worked tirelessly—nearly sixteen weeks of backbreaking labour.

His focus was always on the animals he loved. I knew that he didn't want people showing up at the zoo just to see him, the Crocodile Hunter. He wanted people to come to see his crocs. That's what Steve was all about. Working so hard was his way of making sure that visitors would have the best opportunity to love crocodiles like he did.

Steve ended up with terrible concrete burns on his arms and hands. His wrist had to be splinted. He never complained. We opened for Christmas and the school holidays, and the new layout was a huge success. The zoo visitors streamed in, and everyone was thrilled to see crocs just like they would in the wild. They left the zoo with a new appreciation for Steve's favourite animal.

Chapter Six

I missed my cougar, Malina, so much that I decided to resume my efforts to bring her over to Australia. I was crestfallen when the Australasian Regional Association of Zoological Parks and Aquaria (ARAZPA) would not support my application. In addition, ARAZPA's Taxon Advisory Group (TAG), an accrediting organisation for zoos, was of the opinion that because cougars were not endangered in most of their range in America, there was no need to make them a priority species in Australia. Therefore, Malina would have to remain in the United States.

Their decision left me feeling very uncomfortable. All apex predators survive precariously. It is extraordinarily difficult to bring a predatory mammal species back after it lands on the endangered list. I felt it was better to keep it off the list in the first place. Malina could have served as the 'spokes-cat' for everything from Sumatran tigers to cheetahs.

It was taking too long to get Malina to Australia, so I needed to find her more permanent housing in the States. Fortunately, I had fantastic friends at Wildlife Images near Grants Pass, Oregon. They agreed to take Malina and house her in a beautiful enclosure, complete with shady trees and grass under her feet. Steve came with me to Oregon, and we filmed her move to the new luxury accommodation.

Sadly, Malina never made it to Australia. About a year after her move to Wildlife Images, she got sick. She was taken to a vet and sedated for a complete examination. It turned out her kidneys were shutting down. It could have been a genetic problem, or just old age. Either way, she never woke up.

ONE NIGHT, as I cooked dinner in our home on the zoo grounds, I heard Steve come thundering up the front stairs. He burst wild-eyed into the kitchen. For a second I thought he'd been nailed by a snake.

'I know what we have to do!' he said, extremely excited.

He pulled me into the living room, sat me down and took my hands in his. Looking intently into my eyes, he said, 'We've got to have children.'

'OK-aaay,' I said.

'You don't understand, you don't understand!' he said, trying to catch me up to his thoughts. 'Everything we've been working for, the zoo that we've been building up, all our efforts to protect wildlife, it will all stop with us!'

We'd talked about having children before, but for some reason it hit him that the time was now.

'We have got to have children,' he said. 'I know that if we have kids, they will carry on when we're gone.'

I said, 'You know, there is no guarantee that we won't have a son who grows up to be a shoe salesman in Malaysia.'

'Come on,' Steve said. 'Any kid of ours is going to be a wildlife warrior.'

WE WERE in far north Queensland, enjoying one of our many trips to Cape York Peninsula. We spent a lot of time with crocs in the wild there, and at the end of the trip, Steve had an idea. 'I want to show you something,' he said, inviting me along on a drive. He was uncharacteristically quiet and subdued as we drove, and when we arrived at our destination, I understood why.

A croc farm.

It was vast. A single one of the enclosures on the farm could have held our whole zoo. The breeding ponds were immense, and overcrowded.

As soon as we arrived, Steve headed straight for the crocodile enclosures. Once inside, there were no fences or barriers to separate us from the big, territorial male crocs or the nesting females. There were only narrow, vehicle-wide tracks between the breeding ponds. The sense of exposure and vulnerability had me on edge. It was so different from the careful, respectful relationship we maintained with our own zoo crocs.

'See these clubs, babe?' he said, picking one up from a whole collection that lay alongside the track. 'They use these to belt the crocs.'

As we walked the narrow strip of land between the ponds, Steve and I dodged strikes from male salties over fifteen feet long, and from the aggressive, nesting females. We could be ambushed virtually anytime from any direction. We visited the farm's nursery, where the eggs were hatched after collection and the babies were raised. It was the equivalent of the most heinous POW camp you could imagine. Steve and I entered a large shed filled with rows of lidded boxes. Rock'n'roll music spilled full blast from speakers mounted on the ceiling. The room was completely dark. One of the workers switched on the lights and lifted up one of the lids.

Inside the box were a dozen or more small crocodiles, one or two feet long. So far, they had spent the whole of their existence inside such boxes. The baby crocs cowered pathetically as soon as the light hit their eyes.

The worker lashed out with his stick. He bashed the crocs to force them into the corners of the box, striking them repeatedly, hard, wherever the stick happened to land. It took all my will-power not to scream 'Stop!' and rip the stick out of his hands. What did he think he was doing?

Steve looked at me, and I could tell he felt the same urge. 'We're on their turf now, mate,' he said to me quietly, meaning the croc farmers. The business of crocodile farming was perfectly legal.

The little crocs had no fight left in them. As they cowered, the worker tossed meat to them. Then he slammed shut the lid of the box, immersing the baby crocodiles in darkness once more. That is how farm-raised crocs exist for the first three years of their lives, in pitch black, with constant, blaring music, then a sudden blast of light, a beating and some food.

When the babies graduated up to the sub-adult pond, they lived among an overcrowded, tangled mass of three-, four- and five-foot crocodiles. In these stagnant, putrid ponds, Steve and I saw injuries suffered from fighting over food and space: severed limbs, parts of jaws torn off and great chunks bitten out of their tails.

The prevalence of birth defects horrified me: knots and stumpy burls where a tail was supposed to be, flippers instead of feet. After half a dozen miserable years, the farm crocs would cop a bullet to their skulls. In another corner of the farm, the carcasses were processed. Their skins were sent out to adorn people for clothing, and their flesh was sold bush meat-style.

I'd seen Steve in countless situations that required great physical and emotional strength. He suffered the rigours of the bush without complaint. But seeing him in that croc farm that day made me realise he needed every ounce of his strength to witness the animals he loved so much being treated in such a sadistic, inhumane manner.

How crocodile farming could be allowed in a country that was fighting to stop whaling and the bear bile trade was beyond me. I could not understand how anyone could proudly wear reptile-skin boots considering the torturous conditions under which the skins were obtained.

I left the farm that day shaken and confused.

'Why did you bring me there?' I asked. But I knew the answer without Steve saying anything. He was doing me a favour. It's much easier to talk about something that you've actually seen and experienced.

'It's the farming that is evil,' Steve said. 'Not the people involved. Not all of them are wicked monsters, you know. Those blokes beat the crocodiles because they're afraid of them, or because that's what they were told to do.'

Steve told me that a lot of crocodile behaviour research, scientific studies and filming was done at croc farms.

'It's an easy place to access crocodiles in great numbers,' he said.

'But there's no way on earth you could ever observe any form of natural behaviour there,' I said.

Steve nodded grimly. While we had been at the farm, we had witnessed females who were defending their nests being beaten back into submission, something that would never happen in the wild. The farm had some of the biggest crocs I'd ever seen. They were beautiful animals, living in squalor.

Croc farmers were fiercely protective of their livelihood and ignored efforts to control or regulate the industry, or provide alternatives, such as ecotourism. A few of them arrogantly described themselves in public as 'crocodile conservationists'. I found this disgustingly deceptive. Killing crocs for money is not conservation.

We drove off and Steve didn't say anything for a long time.

I heard a small exhalation from his side of the truck. I couldn't see his face in the gloom. I realised he was crying.

WORD OF THE CROCODILE Hunter spread, and we discovered that people overseas were starting to notice Steve as well. Peter Jennings, the respected anchor of *World News Tonight* on America's ABC network, happened to see one of our documentaries. Every week, Jennings featured a different individual as his 'Person of the Week'. Jennings chose to honour Steve, featuring him in a long segment and naming him the person of the week.

As an American I knew the significance of this recognition. Steve was appreciative, but humble about it all. His hard work was finally getting some recognition. It took a while, but that first glimmer of visibility led to increased interest in our documentaries in America. The Discovery Channel, the gold standard of documentary cable television in the States, came calling.

Our partnership had evolved to the point where I was taking on more and more of the business side of the enterprise, both at the zoo and with our film work. I recall the first meeting I ever had with the programming executives at the Discovery Channel. I arrived at their offices in Bethesda, Maryland, the sleek, modern headquarters of what was becoming one of the fastest-growing cable channels of the mid-1990s.

I was intimidated by the building, the big city and the men in suits. I didn't know what I was supposed to do. I kicked myself for not preparing a whole presentation. So I did the only thing I knew how to do. I talked about wildlife, our love for it, and our commitment to its conservation.

'I'm excited to have the opportunity to work with Discovery,' I concluded. 'Steve and I have always loved the channel. You do such quality shows. We want to be part of your family.'

Then the lights went down and we all stared at an enormous TV monitor to watch a Crocodile Hunter documentary. When it ended, the lights came back up, and it was clear that the programmers at the Discovery Channel were a bit hesitant about Steve.

One of the executive producers was a woman named Maureen. 'Terri, you see, there's a specific format for documentary filming,' she said carefully. 'The main focus is not on the host, but rather on the show's subject.'

Maureen was right. Up until that time, wildlife documentaries were made up of eighty per cent wildlife, twenty per cent host. What I had just shown her was a documentary where Steve was in almost every single shot.

'If you just put one of our shows on,' I pleaded, 'I know it will rate really well.'

Maureen gave me a patient smile. Everyone else in the room nodded thoughtfully. They all rose to their feet at once.

So, I figured, no go.

Then something interesting happened. Discovery had a subsidiary channel called Animal Planet. It had launched in 1996. And the executives at Animal Planet had a different reaction to our show.

'We want to air your documentaries, all of them, in the same form as you aired them in Australia,' Animal Planet's president and general manager, Clark Bunting, told us, genuinely excited.

Sold. Just getting our shows on television in America was a big deal.

DATELINE IS A MAJOR prime-time news show in America, reaching millions of viewers on the NBC network. So it should have been very good news when the show's producers informed us that they wanted to do a segment on Steve, and they wanted to film it in Queensland.

'We want to experience him first-hand in the bush,' the producer told me cheerfully over the phone.

The producers were looking for two totally different environments in which to film. We chose the deserts of Queensland with the most venomous snake on earth, and the Cape York mangroves—crocodile territory. 'Great!' responded *Dateline*. 'Perfect!'

Only . . . the host was a woman, who had to look presentable, so she needed a generator for her blow-drier. And a Winnebago, because it wasn't really fair to ask her to throw a swag on the ground among the scorpions and spiders. This film shoot would mean a bit of additional expense. But the exposure we would get on *Dateline* would be good for wildlife conservation, our zoo and tourism. We scraped up the money, and off we went with the *Dateline* crew into the bush.

We searched and searched for fierce snakes, but to no avail. Then Steve's sixth sense kicked in. At 5.30 one morning, after days of fruitless searching, he said, 'Hurry up, let's get going.'

Our *Dateline* host was keen. 'Where are we heading?' she asked.

'We've got to get out on the black soil plains,' Steve said. 'We are going to see a fierce snake at seven thirty.'

The host looked surprised. Even I teased him. 'Oh, yeah, seven thirty, Stevo. We are going to see a fierce snake at *exactly* seven thirty, right.'

But off we trundled to the black soil plains: camera crew, host, Winnebago, Ute—the whole convoy. Steve scanned the landscape. I monitored the temperature (and the clock). Seven thirty came and went.

After a little bit of teasing, Steve gave a good-natured grin, but then a look of determination passed over his face. No lie: precisely at 7.32 a.m. he spotted a fierce snake. We ended up filming not one but two that morning. The rest of the NBC crew looked upon Steve with new respect. This guy says we're going to see a snake at 7.30 and he's off by two minutes? They were checking their watches and shaking their heads.

We pulled up stakes and headed north to croc country. Lakefield National Park is one of my favourite places in Australia. Steve considered it the most beautiful place on earth. He gave the NBC people everything they wanted. Not only did we spot numerous saltwater crocodiles, but Steve also found one that had submerged under the overhanging branch of a tree. We were able to crawl out on the limb and film straight down over a magnificent twelve-foot croc.

ONLY A SHORT TIME after we'd been croc hunting with *Dateline* in Cape York, Steve and I found ourselves out of our element entirely, at the CableACE Award banquet in Los Angeles.

Steve was up for an award as host of the documentary *Ten Deadliest Snakes in the World*. He lost out to the legendary Walter Cronkite. After the ceremony, we got roped into an after-party that was not our cup of tea.

We got separated, and I saw Steve across the room looking quite claustrophobic. I sidled over.

'Why don't we go back up to our room?' I whispered in his ear. This proved to be a terrific idea. It fitted in nicely with our plans for starting a family!

After our stay in Los Angeles, Steve flew back to the zoo, while I went home by way of Fiji. We were very interested in working there with crested iguanas, a species under threat. I did some filming for the local TV station and checked out a population of the brilliantly patterned lizards on the Fijian island of Yadua Taba.

When I got back to Queensland, I discovered that I was expecting. Steve and I were over the moon. I couldn't believe how thrilled he was. We named the life growing inside me 'Igor'. Steve and I were both sure we were having a boy. With Igor on board, it was ironic that our first documentary journey, to Tasmania, involved a family tragedy of epic proportions. Tasmania, the island off the southern coast of Australia, has unique wildlife and spectacular, temperate-zone rain forests. But as soon as we arrived, Steve and I were swept up in a harrowing whale beaching.

In a remote area on the western side of the island, near the town of Marrawah, a pod of sperm whales was stranded on the beach. One big male came to shore first. Over the next twenty-four hours, another thirty-four whales stranded themselves, including calves and pregnant mothers.

Whale stranding is one of the heartbreaking mysteries of the animal world and is little understood. At this moment no scientific reasoning mattered as we encountered the tragedy unfolding on that Tasmanian beach.

I felt so helpless. All I could do was be there as the huge, gorgeous sea mammals fought pitifully to stay alive. The weather was cold and the seas were too rough to get a boat out to help the whales. We put our arms round the dying animals, spoke to them, and looked into their eyes to share in their pain and grief. Physically, emotionally and even spiritually, it had been an exhausting day.

I pondered what communication the baby inside me would have got from the event. The dying whales had sung among themselves. Steve and I spoke back and forth over their stranded bodies. What did baby Igor pick up on? Through our experiences, we were beginning to form our very own tiny wildlife warrior, even before the baby was born.

Igor had only just begun his education. We left the beach to track Tasmanian snakes inland. Steve was feeling particularly protective of me.

'Whatever you do, don't grab any of these snakes,' he said. 'They are all venomous here in Tasmania. You've got to be careful.'

'No problem,' I said. But it did turn out to be difficult just to watch. Over and over again, Steve got to wrangle a gorgeous venomous snake as the crew filmed. I wanted some of the action!

After a few days of this, we tramped through the bush and encountered a great big tiger snake. Steve turned round and motioned to the cameraman to start rolling. We approached the tiger snake as it drank in the stream. It raised its head slightly. It knew we were there. My heart started pounding, but I had made a decision. I knew we had one take with this snake. Once we disturbed it, it would never go back to drinking, and the shot would be lost.

I moved forward, waddling my pregnant body in behind the snake, and tailed him. He was a huge snake, but slow and gentle, just as I had anticipated. I told the camera all about tiger snakes, how they could give birth to thirty young at once, and how the Tasmanian tiger snakes are special, tolerating some of the coldest weather in the country.

As I let the snake go, I looked sheepishly back at Steve. He didn't say a word. I'm not entirely sure if he was angry with me. I think he realised that I was still the same old Terri, even though I was pregnant.

Maybe it was my condition, but I was even more sensitive about cruelty to wildlife. When we journeyed to New Zealand to protest against whale hunts, we viewed a documentary about whales attacking the whaling ships, trying to defend the females and their young. Whales have family structures, mannerisms and habits that are similar to our own. In the midst of this very emotional work in Wellington, I felt the baby move for the first time. Soon the baby was dancing around inside me both day and night.

There was still stacks of filming to be done. We filmed sharks just off the Queensland coast, near where Steve's parents had retired. We then headed for the Galápagos Islands, my last international trip before giving birth.

When we reached the Galápagos Islands, we stayed on the water in a catamaran. I was completely unprepared for the heat. Even on the boat there wasn't a breeze. The crew slept above deck. I was so hot that somehow Steve and John managed to negotiate for some ice. They'd take turns filling a tea towel with ice to cool down my giant tummy. There was a whole day when the baby didn't move. I was worried. But everything was fine the next day, and I think Igor had just spread out like the rest of us, trying to keep cool.

The last filming I did while pregnant with baby Igor was off the Australian coast again, for a documentary on sharks. I was almost at the point where I couldn't go out on the boat any more. I felt incredibly uncomfortable on the rolling seas. I went out for one last trip and spent most of the time lying on my side, holding my enormous belly.

Steve knew the sharks intimately by now. 'The big tiger sharks will show up at eleven o'clock,' he said. And sure enough, they did, right on the dot. We had the shark cage and the dinghy, with myself, Steve and Sui.

I sat in the dinghy and watched the enormous tiger sharks as they circled round. They had to be more than fourteen feet long. I quickly figured out that because of my great belly I was very unbalanced. I had to be careful not to tip the boat. Sui was an old hand at all of this. She planted herself in the centre of the boat and lay down, sticking to the safest spot possible.

Steve enjoyed going into the cage. The sharks came up to him, trying to open this strange container and get to the nice yummy food inside.

'They have a childlike curiosity,' he told me, breaking to the surface. 'They're really trying to figure out how to get me!'

While Steve lowered himself down again, I got to experience the sharks on the surface, in the dinghy. Tiger sharks don't feed only under the water. They readily take food off the surface, too, and even lift themselves partially out of the water. Huge tiger sharks came up to taste the boat, taste the motor, and put their heads all the way over the back of the dinghy.

I was fascinated. Steve was right. Bringing people into close proximity to wildlife was all you had to do. I fell in love with tiger sharks that day.

That was the last documentary of my pregnancy. For the next few weeks I'd be restricted to working at the zoo.

One evening, I noticed that I was a bit leaky, but when you are enormously pregnant all kinds of weird things happen with your body. I didn't pay any particular attention. The next day I called the hospital.

'You should come right in,' the nurse told me over the phone. Steve was fairly nearby, on the Gold Coast south of Brisbane, filming bull sharks.

I won't bother him, I thought. I'll just go in for a quick checkup.

'If everything checks out OK,' I told them at the hospital, 'I'll head back.'

The nurse looked to see if I was serious. She laughed. 'You're not going anywhere,' she said. 'You're having a baby.'

I called Steve. When he arrived at the hospital, I saw that he had brought the whole camera crew with him. John Stainton was just as flustered as anyone, but suggested we film the event.

'It's OK with me,' Steve said. I was in no mood to argue. Each contraction took every bit of my attention.

When they finally wheeled me into the delivery room at about 8 p.m., I was so tired I didn't know how I could go on. Steve proved to be a great coach. He encouraged me as though it were a footy game.

'You can do it, babe,' he yelled. 'Come on, push!'

At 9.46 p.m., a little head appeared and Steve was beside himself with excitement. I was in a fog, but I clearly remember the joy on his face. He helped turn and lift the baby out. I heard both Steve and doctor announce simultaneously, 'It's a girl.'

Steve cut the umbilical cord and cradled her, gazing down at his newborn daughter. 'Look, she's our little Bindi.'

She was named after a crocodile at the zoo, and it also fitted that the word 'bindi' was Aborigine for 'young girl'. Here was our own little Bindi.

I smiled up at Steve. 'Bindi Sue,' I said, after his beloved dog, Sui.

Steve handed her gently to me. We both looked down at her in utter amazement. I said, 'I couldn't have done it if you hadn't been here.'

'Yes, you could have.'

'No, I really needed you here.'

Once again, I had that overwhelming feeling that as long as we were together, everything would be safe and wonderful. Steve gazed down at Bindi and smiled, tears rolling down his cheeks, with such great love for his new daughter. The world had a brand-new wildlife warrior.

Chapter Seven

Stephen Robert Irwin was born in Upper Ferntree Gully, outside Melbourne, in 1962, on his mother's birthday, February 22.

Lynette and Robert Irwin—Lyn and Bob—exposed him to wildlife at an early age. Steve always described his household when he was growing up as harbouring a 'menagerie'. That meant an ever-expanding collection of tanks, terrariums and cages with a growing population of snakes and lizards.

Lyn and Bob moved their family north from the Melbourne area to Queensland in 1970. They purchased the original four-acre zoo property in Beerwah after a snake-finding trip. Eight-year-old Steve and his sisters, Joy and Mandy, helped to install the family menagerie in what was at first called the Beerwah Reptile Park. Joy was the older sister, Mandy the younger, and Steve was in the middle. Steve got along well with his sisters, and the usual sibling rivalry expressed itself in who could better care for the menagerie of animals taken in by the family. Bob loved all reptiles, even venomous snakes. Lyn took in the injured and orphaned. They made a great team, and Steve was born directly from their example and teaching.

'Whenever we were driving,' Steve told me, 'if we saw a kangaroo on the side of the roadway that had been killed by a car, we always stopped.' Mother and son would investigate the dead roo and, if it was female, check its pouch. They rescued dozens, maybe hundreds, of live kangaroo joeys this way, brought them home and raised them.

Bob's knowledge of reptile and especially snake behaviour made him an invaluable resource for academics. The Queensland Museum wanted to investigate the ways of the secretive fierce snake, and Bob shared their passion. When the administrators of the Queensland National Parks and Wildlife Service wanted to relocate problem crocodilians, they called Bob.

Meanwhile, Lyn became, in Steve's words, 'the Mother Teresa of animal rescue'. She designed a substitute pouch for orphaned roo and wallaby joeys. She came up with appropriate formulas to feed them, too. Lyn created the warm, nurturing environment that made Steve's dreams, goals and aspirations real and reachable. Steve was always a boy who loved his mum, and Lyn was the matriarch of the family, a pioneering wildlife rehabilitator who set the mark for both Steve and myself.

Steve's childhood was 'family, wildlife and sport', he told me. He played rugby league for the Caloundra Sharks in high school and was picked to play rugby for the Queensland Schoolboys and represent the state, but chose to go on a field trip with his dad to catch reptiles instead.

Lyn's passion for rehabilitation and Bob's passion for crocodiles meshed together to prompt a new effort to save 'problem' crocodiles by relocating them to areas where they would not bother humans.

Bob pioneered a kinder, gentler way to do it. At that point in time, the accepted method of croc capture was a cruel one. Park rangers and animal control officers would sink a barbed harpoon into the animal's hide. They would then reel in the thrashing, bleeding croc. Often, the harpoons would go astray and miss their mark, or the barbs would tear themselves out during the struggle, leaving a gaping, jagged hole.

'The way they were doing it,' Steve said, 'there was maybe a one-in-five chance of success.'

His father's approach was quite different, and quite ingenious, involving such practices as jumping, soft-mesh trapping and netting. The approach grew out of Bob's knowledge of crocodilian behaviour. Crocs are ambush predators, snatching their prey by lunging onto land from the water. Bob lured them to a trap with fresh meat, usually a feral pig. He hung a fist-sized piece of meat as lead-in bait in front of a trawler-mesh trap.

Saltwater crocs are very intelligent and wary of traps. The 'free' feed would give them a sense of security, and they wouldn't worry about the new thing in their territory. Then, after the lead-in bait disappeared a few nights in a row, Bob placed fresh meat deep within the trap.

The target crocodile would enter and pull on the meat; this released a trigger mechanism and tripped a weight bag. When the weight bag fell, it pulled the mouth of the trap shut like a drawstring, preventing the crocodile from escaping. Then came the tricky part. Bob and young Steve had to pin the croc by laying themselves on top of it. Bob would peel back the mesh, blindfold the animal and duct-tape its jaws, then transport it in the trap or in a croc box.

The process developed by trial and error over the course of many years. Steve would later perfect it. There was no doubt that it was vastly superior to a harpoon barb, and there was nothing, of course, more invasive than a bullet. The crocs Bob captured faced two options: they would be shot by their angry, fearful human neighbours, or relocated to safer environments. Bob preferred to see the momentary discomfort of the captured croc to seeing it lying dead on a riverbank.

He brought his young son along on his crocodilian relocation work. 'I got so I could work the spotlight, and Dad would jump the smaller ones,' Steve said. 'He tossed them into the bottom of the boat, and I would dive on top to pin them. They used to thrash me, putting up a good fight.' Steve didn't officially perform his first capture until he was nine years old. Father and son had been working together on croc relocation for a couple of years by then.

The Queensland National Parks and Wildlife Service was confident that Bob's croc-catching expertise could help to remove a group of freshwater crocs on the Leichhardt River. Freshies are smaller, with long, narrow jaws, and less aggressive than the saltwater variety, but they still have a fearsome set of teeth and can lash out when cornered.

Steve and Bob worked together for several nights, moving one freshie after another out of a section of river that was about to be dammed. On their last night, while Bob wrangled one croc in the boat, Steve caught the red eye-shine of another with his spotlight. He alerted his father.

'Get up in front,' Bob said. 'Hold him with your spotty.'

That's when Steve realised this capture was going to be different. He was in the front of the boat—which meant that he would be the one leaping on top of the croc in the water.

Bob made him wait until the last possible moment to jump. Steve kept his light shining into the croc's eyes.

'OK, I got him,' Bob said. He turned his own torch on and shined the croc. That was Steve's signal to drop his own spotty and get ready to jump.

'Wait, wait, wait,' Bob cautioned, and the dinghy moved closer. Bob could barely contain his son, who was bursting with excitement. 'Now!'

Steve leapt. As soon as he did, he realised that he had misjudged the croc's size. It wasn't a three-footer. It was more like four or five feet long, easily matching his weight.

The croc dived. No matter what, I'm not letting go, Steve thought. There was no way he was going to let his dad down. Just as Steve was about to run out of air, he felt his father's strong arm reach down to bring both Steve and the croc into the boat.

Steve told me that when he looked at Bob's face, he could see both worry and pride. Worry because Steve had been out of sight in the murky water—and pride because he had made a perfect capture, his first time out.

'Dad started grinning from ear to ear,' Steve recalled. 'I had jumped my first croc. It was one of the biggest moments of my life.'

Bob and Lyn set Steve on the path he travelled in life. What was incredible about Steve was how much he made it his own. He took the example of his parents and ran with it.

In 1980, Bob and Lyn decided to change the name of the Beerwah Reptile Park to the name under which I would first encounter it, the Queensland Reptile and Fauna Park. Angry at the senseless slaughter of crocodilians, Bob began to expand the zoo to create habitats for rescued crocs.

At the start of the 1980s, Steve was eighteen, a recent graduate from Caloundra State High School, and still under his father's tutelage. Ten years later, he had been transformed. He proved himself capable of doing some of the most dangerous wildlife work in the world, solo and with spectacular results. Years in the wilderness lent him a deep understanding of the natural world. More than that, he had reinforced a unique connection with wildlife that would stay with him throughout his whole life.

THE LEGEND of a giant black saltie in Cape York had been growing for years. It haunted a river system in north Queensland, and eluded all attempts at capture or death. In 1988 the East Coast Crocodile Management Program enlisted Bob and Steve to remove this 'problem' crocodile and relocate him back to their zoo.

It was a difficult assignment. At first, they could find no sign of the mythical black croc. For months, Bob and Steve surveyed the mangrove swamps and riverbanks, finally locating a telltale belly slide that betrayed the presence of a huge male.

Then Bob gave his son the ultimate vote of confidence. He left him alone. Bob went back to Beerwah. It was just Steve and his dog, Chilli. The huge saltwater crocodile had repeatedly outwitted 'professionals' from crocodile farms and hunters with high-powered rifles sent in to exterminate him. Steve took up a hunt that had already lasted for years. Only he planned to save this modern-day dinosaur rather than kill it.

One night the saltie almost took him instead. Steve spotted a smaller female and set a net across the river to snare her. An incredible force pulled the net upstream, against the current and against all logic. Steve started his outboard, but it didn't help. The bow of his boat pitched downwards, taking on water. He rushed to cut the net free before the croc swamped the boat. He needn't have bothered. The bow of the boat suddenly surged upwards and the net hung limp. Steve pulled it in and found a gaping hole as big as his dinghy. The heavy-duty trawler mesh had been torn straight through.

Another evening, Steve and Chilli watched half a dozen feral pigs swim across the river. As the animals clambered up the opposite bank, the hindmost pig seemed to slip suddenly back into the water and disappeared, without a thrash or squeal. Steve didn't even see the big croc.

Stalking the black ghost, Steve became one with the river. He spent months at a time in the bush. He disregarded the mangrove mud that covered him until he was camouflaged as he sat silently in wait. He learned the river systems of the area like the back of his hand.

Then the croc made his move. Steve discovered that the lead-in bait for one of his traps had been eaten, grabbed down with such force that its nylon cord had wound up high in a mangrove tree. He chose a particularly smelly chunk of meat to bait the trap the next night. He placed it downstream and made his way through the swamp on foot, so he would leave no sign of his approach on the riverbank.

For the next two days, nothing. Steve rebaited the trap, this time using the carcass of a whole boar. He woke in the night. Chilli had alerted him that something had disturbed the peace of the mangroves. Steve would have to wait until daylight to check the trap.

The following morning he took his boat out and saw that the big male had triggered the trap and was snared in the mesh—sort of. Even though the rectangular-shaped net was the biggest he had, the croc's tail and one back leg stuck out. But the black ghost had finally been caught.

At Steve's approach, the animal thrashed wildly, smashing apart mangrove trees on either side of the trap. Steve tried to top-jaw-rope the croc, but he was fighting too violently. Normally Chilli acted as a distraction, giving Steve the chance to secure the croc. But the dog cowered on the floor of the dinghy. Steve was on his own.

He finally secured a top-jaw rope and tied the other end to a tree. With a massive 'death roll'—a defensive manoeuvre in which the reptile spins its enormous body—the big croc smashed the tree flat and snapped it off. Steve tried again; the croc thrashed, growling and roaring in protest at the trapper in khaki, lunging again and again to tear Steve apart.

Finally, the giant croc death-rolled so violently that he came off the bank and landed in the boat, which immediately sank. Chilli had jumped out and was swimming for shore as Steve worked against time. With the croc underwater, Steve lashed the animal, trap and all, in the dinghy. But moving the waterlogged boat and a ton of crocodile was simply too much. Steve sprinted several miles in the tropical heat to reach a cane farm, where he hoped to get help. The cane farmers were a bit hesitant to lend a hand, so Steve promised them a case of beer, and a deal was made.

With a sturdy fishing boat secured to each side of Steve's dinghy, they managed to tow it downriver, where they could winch croc and boat onto dry land to get him into a crate. By this time a crowd of spectators had gathered and Steve soon won the locals over to see just how special this old crocodile really was.

He brought the croc back to Beerwah, named him Acco, and gave him a beautiful big pond that Bob had prepared, with plenty of places to hide.

We were in the Crocodile Environmental Park at the zoo when Steve first told me the story of Acco's capture. I just had to revisit him after hearing his story. There he was, the black ghost himself, magnificently sunning on the bank of his billabong.

Standing there next to this impressive animal, I tried to wrap my mind round the idea that people had wanted him dead. His huge, intimidating teeth made him look primeval, and his osteodermal plates gleamed black in the sun—a dinosaur, living here among us. I felt so emotional, contemplating the fear-based cruelty that prompted humans to hate these animals.

For his part, Acco still remembered his capture even though it had happened nearly a decade before. Whenever Steve went into his enclosure, Acco would stalk him and strike, exploding out of the water with the intent of catching Steve unawares.

When I met him in 1991, Steve had just emerged from a solid decade in the bush, either with Bob or on his own, with just his dog Chilli, and later Sui. Those years had been like a test of fire. As a boy all Steve wanted to do was to be like his dad. At twenty-nine he'd become like Bob and then some.

He had done so much more than catch crocs. In the western deserts, he and Bob helped researchers from the Queensland Museum to understand the intricacies of fierce snake behaviour. Steve also embarked on a behavioural study of a rare and little-understood type of arboreal lizard, the canopy goanna, scrambling up into trees in the rain forests of Cape York Peninsula in pursuit of herpetological knowledge.

As much as Steve had become a natural for television, over the course of the 1980s he had become a serious naturalist as well. His hands-on experience, gleaned from years in the bush, meshed well with the more abstract knowledge of the academics. No one had ever accomplished what he had, tracking and trapping crocodiles for months at a time on his own.

STEVE AND I brought Bindi home in July 1998. The dead of winter on the Sunshine Coast is not exactly Antarctica. There is never any snow. But the old Queenslander house we lived in on the zoo grounds, built on stumps and with its large double doors opening onto verandahs, was draughty and hard to heat, with high ceilings. It also had a lot of steps leading up to the front and back doors. The combination of steps and a new baby made me nervous. Even keeping Bindi warm was challenging, but we made do. We brought in space heaters and bundled her up constantly.

We had been looking at some land adjoining the zoo and decided to purchase it in order to expand. There was a small house on the new property, nothing too grand, just a modest home built of brick, with three bedrooms and one bathroom. We liked the seclusion of the place most of all. The builder had tucked it in behind a macadamia orchard, but it was still right next door to the zoo. We could be part of the zoo yet apart from it at the same time. Perfect.

'Make this house exactly the way you want it,' Steve told me. 'This is going to be our home.'

He dedicated himself to getting us moved in. I knew this would be our last stop. We wouldn't be moving again. We never entertained. The zoo was our social place. Living so close by, we could have easily got overwhelmed, so we made it a practice never to have people over. It wasn't unfriendliness, it was simple self-preservation. Our brick residence was for our family.

Almost as soon as we got our baby home, we packed her up to leave. Bindi was six days old when she embarked on her first film shoot (actually, her second, if you count filming her birth). Steve, Bindi and I headed off for the States, with a stop first at Australia's Double Island to film turtles.

We drove through the Double Island sand dunes, spending a day filming on the area's spectacular beaches. Bindi did marvellously. On location, she was absolutely content. Fraser, one of the assistants on the shoot, stayed with Bindi while Steve and I filmed. Then we'd walk round behind the camera to hug and kiss her, and I could feed her. She didn't squeak or squawk. I swear she seemed to keep quiet when John called out, 'Rolling!'

It felt fantastic to be back filming again, and it made me realise how much I'd missed it. The crew represented our extended family. I never once caught a feeling of annoyance or impatience at the prospect of having a six-day-old baby on set. On the contrary, the atmosphere was one of joy. I can mark precisely Bindi Irwin's introduction to the wonderful world of wildlife documentary filming: Thursday, July 30, 1998, in the spectacular subtropics of the Queensland coast, where the brilliant white sand meets the turquoise water. This is where the sea turtles navigate the rolling surf each year to come ashore and lay their eggs.

Next stop: America, baby on board. Bindi was so tiny she fitted on an airline pillow. Steve watched over her almost obsessively, fussing with her, and guarding to see if anything would fall out of the overhead bins whenever they were opened. Such a protective daddy.

Our first shoot in California focused on rattlesnakes and spiders. In Texas, Bindi got to meet toads and Trans-Pecos rat snakes. Steve found two stunning specimens of the non-venomous snakes in an abandoned house. I watched as two-week-old Bindi reacted to their presence. She gazed up at the snakes and her small, shaky arms reached out towards them.

I laughed with delight at her eagerness. Steve looked over at me, as if to say, See? Our own little wildlife warrior!

In Florida, we got to hang out with some of America's finest at Eglin Air

Force Base. The Army Rangers there had been clearing a section of bush for doing operations, and encountered a huge eastern diamondback rattlesnake. Diamondbacks grow to be the largest rattlers anyway, but this one was big for another reason: she was pregnant. Not long after the Rangers' reptile handlers had transported her back to a holding facility, she gave birth.

We watched as the newborn rattlers worked their way out, lay still for a short moment, and then began striking at everything and anything nearby. Although it was a great defence mechanism, in case a predator was about to eat them, it appeared pretty comical. They were all fang, and trying to look tough. An interesting way to greet the world. Even the Rangers laughed.

Once the Rangers had completed their training mission, all the dangerous wildlife they collected (including the rattlers) would go right back where it came from.

Steve was in his element during the Florida shoot. He spotted a coral snake at Eglin, and another huge diamondback. It was stinking hot, like most summers in the southeast. Bindi spent a lot of her time sitting in the air-conditioned vehicle, while one of the crew stayed with her. I would move far enough away so that the camera's microphone couldn't pick up the sound of the truck running, film like mad, and then run back to be with her.

Bindi always enjoyed being close to Steve. He seemed to both excite her and keep her calm at the same time. He showed her everything that entered his world, all the wildlife, the landscapes and the people. Even at just a few weeks old, Bindi turned her head when Steve walked past her. Then she fussed until he came and picked her up.

The bond between father and daughter continued to grow stronger.

As much as he influenced her, Bindi changed Steve, too. After our Florida trip, Bindi and I went home, while Steve flew off to the Indonesian island of Sumatra. We couldn't accompany him because of the malaria risk. At one point, Steve was filming with orang-utans when his newfound fatherhood came in handy.

A local park ranger who had worked with the national park's orang-utans for twenty-five years accompanied Steve into the rain forest, where they encountered a mother and baby orang-utan.

'She reminds me of Bindi,' Steve exclaimed, seeing the infant ape. It was a mischievous, happy baby, clinging to her mother way up in the top branches of a tree.

'This will be great to film,' Steve said. 'I'll climb into the tree and then you can get me and the orang-utans in the same shot.'

The ranger waved his hands, heading Steve off. 'You absolutely can't do that,' he said. 'The mother orang-utans are extremely protective. If you make a move anywhere near that tree, she'll come down and pull your arms off. She won't tolerate you in her tree.'

'I won't climb very close to her,' Steve said. 'I'll just go a little way up. Then the camera can shoot up at me and get her in the background.'

The ranger looked doubtful. 'OK, Steve,' he said. 'But I promise you, she will come down out of that tree and pull your head off.'

'Don't worry, mate,' Steve said confidently, 'she'll be right.'

He climbed into the tree. Down came the mother, just as the ranger predicted. Tugging, pulling and dragging her baby along behind her, she deftly made her way right over to Steve. He didn't move. He sat on his branch and watched her come towards him.

The crew filmed it all, and it became one of the most incredible shots in documentary film-making. Mama came close to Steve. She swung onto the same branch. Then she edged her way over until she sat right beside him. Everyone on the crew was nervous, except for Steve.

Mama put her arm round Steve's shoulders. While hanging on to her baby, she pulled Steve in tight with her other arm, looked him square in the face, and . . . puckering up her lips, she looked lovingly into Steve's eyes.

'You've got a beautiful little baby, sweetheart,' Steve said softly. The baby scrambled up the branch away from them, and without taking her eyes off Steve, the mother reached over and grabbed the tot back down.

'You're a good mum,' Steve cooed. 'You take good care of that bib-bib.'

'I have never seen anything like that,' the park ranger said later. The encounter was further evidence of the uncanny connection Steve had with the wildlife he loved so much, as well as one proud parent recognising another.

MEANWHILE, MY LIFE back at home was made much easier with the help of Steve's sister Joy and her husband, Frank Muscillo. Tall and dark-haired, with an open, friendly face, Frank began at the zoo by working half-days, helping me with payroll and paperwork. If it hadn't been for Frank coming to the rescue during that period when I was trying to juggle work with a new baby, I don't know what I would have done.

Frank was brilliant at bookkeeping, an exceptional businessman and a dad as well. With two kids of his own, he understood that no matter how busy work got, family came first. Eventually he became general manager of the zoo, and a vital component to its success.

Bindi was blossoming. At just six weeks old, she held her head up and reached for objects. When Steve came home from Sumatra, it was obvious how much he had missed his little girl. I had to smile when Steve sat down on the couch with Bindi, telling her of his adventures moment by moment, while she stared intently at him.

Steve shared everything with her. He took her round the zoo and introduced her to the wildlife. One day he took her into the enclosure with Agro, one of our biggest crocodiles. A school group had come to the zoo, and assembled in their neatly pressed uniforms around the enclosure. Bindi squealed with delight and looked intently at Agro. That afternoon Steve did the crocodile demonstration with his daughter cradled in his arms.

After the croc show, I noticed Bindi was as alert as I had ever seen her. She was so thrilled. Joining her daddy for the croc demo became something she looked forward to. Sometimes Bindi and I would sit in the enclosure to watch Steve with the crocodiles, and she would cry until he picked her up so she could be part of the action.

On Bindi's first birthday in July 1999, we began a tradition of our own. We threw open the doors of the zoo with free admission to all children. We offered free birthday cake and invited cockatoos, camels, snakes and lizards to party with us. It poured with rain all day but it didn't matter. A crowd of 300 had shown up to celebrate.

Steve's mother, Lyn, looked on that day with a proud smile. I could read on her face how important it was to her that Steve had started a family. And Bindi had a great day wearing a small pink sweater that her gran had made.

That night, Bindi, Steve and I all curled up in bed. 'As long as we're together,' Steve said, 'everything will be just fine.'

It was spooky, and I didn't want to think about it, but it did indeed seem that Steve got into trouble more when he was off on his own. Every time we were together on a trip, we knew we'd be OK. When we were apart, though, we shared a disconcerting feeling that was hard to put into words.

FOR THE NEXT DOCUMENTARY we took a DC-10 all the way across the country, from the east coast to the west. Together we flew into 'the red centre', the interior of the continent and the location of Uluru, or Ayers Rock, one of Australia's most recognisable icons.

'Have a look at it,' Steve said when we arrived. 'It's the heart of Australia.'

I could see why. A huge red mountain rose up out of the flat, sandy landscape. The rock appeared out of place in the great expanse of the desert.

We respectfully filmed only the areas we were allowed to access with the local Aborigines' blessing. As we approached the rock, Steve saw a lizard nearby. He turned to the camera to talk about it. I was concentrating on Steve, Steve was concentrating on the lizard, and John was filming. Bindi was with us, and she could barely take two steps on her own at this point, so I knew I could afford to watch Steve.

But after John called out, 'Got it,' and we turned back to Bindi, we were amazed at what we saw. Bindi was leaning against the base of Uluru. She had placed both her palms against the smooth stone, gently put her cheek up to the rock, and stood there, mesmerised.

'She's listening,' Steve whispered. It was an eerie moment. The crew stopped and stared. Then Bindi suddenly seemed to come out of her trance. She plopped down and started stuffing the red sand of Uluru into her mouth.

I HAD PLANNED a visit to Oregon; Steve would join us after Bindi and I promoted our new Crocodile Hunter toy line at the big annual toy fair in New York City. So Bindi and I flew to the States ahead of Steve. We drove down to the Oregon coast, where my sister and I share a small beach cabin. We couldn't contact Steve because mobile phones weren't in range. There was no phone at the cabin, either, only a payphone across the street at a gas station. It was one of the rare periods when we were out of touch.

During this time, Steve's parents had decided to move closer to us at the zoo. They would manage our property on the Great Dividing Range, which we'd named Ironbark Station. This was our conservation land, and we were attempting to restore the native bush. We began planting eucalypts not long after we bought the property. Steve worked into the night planting trees. If the rain didn't come immediately, he would dutifully water each and every seedling. We had high hopes that one day the land would offer refuge to everything from koalas to phascogales.

This was the property Lyn and Bob were taking over. Lyn was particularly thrilled about being closer to the family. She and Bob had been living in Rosedale, on the Queensland coast, a four-and-a-half-hour drive from the zoo. Ironbark Station was only two hours away.

I was sound asleep at the Oregon beach cabin when there was a knock at the door. A woman who said she was from the Red Cross stood on the front porch. I was foggy-headed. 'I don't mean to alarm you,' she was saying. 'But you need to call home immediately.'

Terror struck me. My mind raced. Where was Steve? Bindi lay asleep in the bedroom. I asked the woman from the Red Cross to stay on the porch while I went across the street to the payphone. The international calling procedure seemed immensely complicated that morning, and terribly slow.

I heard Steve's voice on the other end of the line and I experienced an immediate flood of relief. But Steve was incoherent. Sobbing, he managed to choke out the words. His mother had been killed in a car accident.

I felt the blood drain from my face. I couldn't believe it. He tried to explain, but the next thing I knew, the line went dead.

It took a few frantic calls to find out what had happened. Lyn had left Rosedale to make one last trip with a few remaining family possessions, in the process of moving to their new home on our property. She drove with the family malamute, Aylic, in the passenger seat beside her, and Sharon, their bird-eating spider, in a glass terrarium in the back of the truck. Lyn left the Rosedale house at about three o'clock in the morning.

As she approached Ironbark Station, her Ute left the road travelling at sixty miles per hour. The truck hit a tree and she died instantly. Aylic died as well, and the tank holding the bird-eating spider was smashed to pieces.

Early in the morning, at the precise moment when the crash happened, Steve was working on the backhoe at the zoo. He suddenly felt as if he had been hit by something and fell off the machine, hitting the ground hard. He told me later that he knew something terrible had happened.

Steve got in his Ute and started driving. He had no idea what had happened, but he knew where he had to go. With uncanny precision, he drove towards where the accident occurred. His mobile phone rang. It was Frank. When his brother-in-law told him what had happened and where, Steve realised he was heading there.

I immediately packed up Bindi and went to catch the next plane home. The family was in free fall. Steve was in shock, and Bob was even worse off. Lyn had always acted as the matriarch, the one who kept everything together. She was such a strong figure, a leader. Her death didn't seem real.

I had never dealt with grief like this before. Lyn was only in her fifties, and it seemed cruel to have her life cut short. These were going to be her golden years. She and Bob could embark on the life they had worked so hard to achieve. They would be together, near their family, able to take care of the land and enjoy the wildlife they loved. Now Bindi's gran was gone just when they had most looked forward to spending time together.

My heart was broken. I couldn't imagine what Steve, his dad and his sisters were going through. Steve was inconsolable, and Bob was obviously unable to cope. Joy and Mandy were trying to keep things together, but were distraught and heartbroken. Everyone at the zoo was sombre.

Steve's younger sister Mandy performed the mournful task of sifting through the items from the truck. One of the objects Lyn had packed was Bob's teapot. As Mandy went to wash it out, she noticed movement. Inside was Sharon, the bird-eating spider, the sole survivor of the accident, who had managed to crawl into the teapot to hide.

After the funeral, time appeared to slow down and then stop entirely. It would be a long time before life returned to anything like normality. His mother's death was something that Steve would never truly overcome. Lyn Irwin was a pioneer in wildlife rehabilitation work. She had given her son a great legacy, and eventually that gift would win out over death. But in the wake of her accident, all we could see was loss.

Chapter Eight

After Lyn's death, Steve coped by throwing himself into working on the land. Up on the driver's seat of a backhoe or a bulldozer, he could be alone with his thoughts. He worked the property around the zoo to prepare it for expansion. His idea was to create a mini-Madagascar, an island habitat for the zoo. True to his ideal of getting wildlife into people's hearts, Steve thought zoo visitors shouldn't have to stare across the water at the animals. They would take a boat ride to adventure and disembark among land tortoises and lemurs. If the lemurs felt like coming down to play, they could. If they wanted to stay in the trees, they could do that, too. The island would be a place where they would roam free.

Just then Hollywood came calling. If you could design a place as far removed as possible from the real-life questions of grief and loss, Hollywood would be it. No one really noticed that it was an emotionally scarred Steve who showed up at the Emmy Awards ceremony that year.

Croc Files was a fun show, with each episode taking kids on a new adventure with stacks of exciting wildlife. It had been nominated in the category of Outstanding Children's Series. The awards were held in May 2000 at the Century Plaza in Los Angeles.

The hustle and bustle of the Emmys didn't impress Steve much. The big city wasn't where Steve wanted to be, even in the best of times, and now it was much harder because he would never again be able to share his achievements with his mum.

As it happened, the night belonged to Disney Channel's *Bill Nye, the Science Guy*, which took home four Emmys, including the one for Outstanding Children's Series. I felt badly for John Stainton and Judi Bailey, the *Croc Files* producers, but I knew it was a big deal to be nominated at all.

Hollywood wasn't through with us yet, though.

We entered into exploratory talks with MGM, one of the major Hollywood studios, about doing a Crocodile Hunter movie. Although the negotiations were tedious, Steve never wavered in his conviction that the movie would have a strong conservation message. He convinced John Stainton to agree that there would be no CGI (computer-generated imagery) wildlife in the movie. We didn't want to pretend to react to an animal in front of a green screen, and then have computer graphic technicians complete the shot later. That was how Hollywood would normally have done it, but that wasn't an option for Steve.

As talks ground on at MGM, we came up with a title: *Crocodile Hunter: Collision Course*. But mostly we had phone calls and meetings. The main sticking point was that no underwriter would write a policy for a project that required Steve to be working with real live crocodiles.

As negotiations seemed to be grinding to a halt, we were all feeling frustrated. Along with John and Judi, we took a big risk and started filming on the movie before we had a contract signed. There didn't seem to be any choice. I imagined all the insurance underwriters across the world reacting to the phrase 'live crocodiles'. So we began shooting with our zoo crocodiles, but without signatures on the dotted line for the movie.

A particular scene in the script—and a good example of an insurance man's nightmare—had a crocodile trying to lunge into a boat. Only Steve's expertise could make this happen, since the action called for both Steve and me to be in the boat. If the lunging crocodile happened to hook his head over the boat's edge, he would tip us into the water. That would be a one-way trip.

'How are you going to work it?' I asked Steve.

'Get the crocs accustomed to the dinghy first,' he said. 'Then I'll see if I can get them interacting with me while I'm in the boat.'

We decided to try with Charlie. He definitely had attitude. He spent a lot of his time trying to kill everything within range. Steve felt good about the possibility of Charlie having a go.

Because he was filming a movie and not shooting a documentary, John had a more complex set-up than usual, utilising three 35mm cameras. Each one would film in staggered succession, so that the magazine changes would never happen all at once. There would never be a time when film was not rolling. We couldn't very well ask a crocodile to wait while a fresh film magazine was loaded into a camera.

'You need to be careful to stay out of Charlie's line of sight,' Steve said to me. 'I want Charlie focusing only on me. If he changes focus and starts attacking you, it's going to be too difficult for me to control the situation.'

Right. Steve got no argument from me. Getting anywhere near those bone-crushing jaws was the furthest thing from my mind. I wasn't keen on being out on the water with a huge saltwater crocodile trying to get me. I would have to totally rely on Steve to keep me safe.

We stepped into the dinghy, which was moored in Charlie's enclosure, secured front and back with ropes. Charlie came over immediately to investigate. It didn't take much to encourage him to have a go at Steve. Steve grabbed a top-jaw rope. He worked on roping Charlie while the cameras rolled.

Time and time again, Charlie hurled himself straight at Steve, a half-ton of reptile flesh exploding up out of the water only a few feet away from me. I tried to hang on and keep the boat counterbalanced. I didn't want Steve to lose his footing and topple in. Charlie was one angry crocodile. He would have loved nothing more than to get his teeth into Steve.

Steve continued to deftly toss the rope. Then, all of a sudden, Charlie swung at the rope instead of Steve, and the rope went right over Charlie's top jaw. A perfect toss, provided that had been what Steve was trying to do. But it wasn't. We had a roped croc on our hands that we really didn't want.

Steve immediately let the rope go slack. Charlie had it snagged in his teeth. Because of Steve's quick thinking and prompt manoeuvring, the rope came clear. We breathed a collective sigh of relief.

Steve looked up at the cameras. 'I think you've got it.'

To the applause of the crew, Steve got us both out of the boat. He gave me a big hug. He was happy. This was what he loved doing best, being able to interact and work with wildlife. Never before had anything like it been filmed in any format, much less on 35mm film for cinema.

Steve wanted to portray crocs as the powerful apex predators they are, keeping everyone safe while he did it. Not once did he want it to appear as though he were dominating the crocodile, or showing off by being in close proximity to it. He wished for the crocodile to be the star of the show.

With the live-croc footage behind us, the insurance people came on board, and we were finally able to sign a contract with MGM. We were to start filming in earnest—first stop, the Simpson Desert, with perentie lizards and fierce snakes.

The day before we headed out was an unusually warm one. Shasta had a hard time of it. Bindi wrapped her in wet towels to help her cool off. Every few minutes she would raise her head and bark a bit.

The last couple of years, Shasta's back had been out so badly that I would wheelbarrow her around. She always liked sleeping in the car. I think it made her excited to be going on a trip. That night, she seemed so restless that I put her in the car and kissed her good night. I knew she'd be happiest there.

In the morning, we were off to our first official day of filming the movie. Steve put the last few things together in the zoo. I went out to get Shasta organised for staying with a friend. Sometime during the night, Shasta had died. She was seventeen and a half years old, the only dog I'd ever had. She went through nine months of quarantine to join me in Australia. She had been a loyal friend and an excellent guard dog.

Bindi and I said goodbye to Shasta together. We discussed the circle of life and collected a few of Shasta's favourite things. She would be buried with her favourite blanket.

STEVE ALWAYS HAD a feeling that he wouldn't live a long life. He would sometimes say that he hoped a croc wouldn't get him, because he felt it would undo all of his hard work convincing people that crocs are wonderful animals worth protecting. After losing his mother, he seemed even more focused on accomplishing as much as possible in the time he had here on earth.

Steve didn't fear death. Maybe that was part of his secret for being so gifted with wildlife. He had such perfect love for every animal, and especially crocodiles, that there didn't seem to be any room left over for fear.

But this didn't mean that Steve didn't have his share of close calls.

One day I was feeding Cookie, Wes was feeding Mary, and our crew member Jan was backing Wes up. Steve was talking to the zoo visitors about our big male, Agro, partially submerged in the water near him.

Steve was so intent on getting his message across about crocodiles that he might have been a bit distracted. It had poured with rain that day, leaving the grass wet and slippery. Agro took full advantage when Steve's back was to the water. He powered forward like a missile, out of the water and halfway up the bank. As he came out, Wes yelled.

Agro had Steve backed against the fence. Steve couldn't move. I looked across the enclosure and saw the look on Steve's face—it wasn't fear, it was resolve. A big male saltwater croc was about to grab him. But for some unknown reason, Agro hesitated for a split second. Maybe he was distracted by Wes, running over to save his best friend.

Steve darted sideways and ran down the fence line. He was safe.

That night we lay in bed and I stroked his face, tracing the lines that were starting to form round the corners of his eyes. 'I thought for a minute there he had me,' Steve said softly in the dark.

DURING CYCLONE SEASON in March 2001 a massive low-pressure system lay off the coast of Queensland. The morning daylight took on a yellowish cast. By four o'clock that afternoon, the rain started.

Steve told anyone who was not working outside with the animals to go home. At 4.15, Steve announced an official storm watch, which meant that all staff who remained needed to prepare for the potential of a flood.

During a storm, we needed to check fences. As water flowed through the enclosures at the zoo, it would push debris up against the fences, putting pressure on them that they were not designed to resist. With enough pressure from floodwaters, the fences would give, releasing the crocs and other animals from their enclosures.

By 4.30, Steve announced that the situation had escalated to 'cyclone watch'. The winds howled, and a deluge broke from the sky.

Our house was located on high ground. I got Bindi home safely with her nanny, Thelma, and then I rushed back to the zoo.

All the watercourses in the zoo were designed with storm grates. Steve had opened them to let the water through. Now it was time to divide the staff up into teams to quickly remove debris from the bulging fences.

Animals in areas where the flooding was severe had to be moved. We shuffled the kangaroos to high ground and put the dingoes in special night quarters. We checked Harriet and the other giant tortoises to make sure they had lumbered up to the top part of their enclosures, out of the rushing water.

The rain came down like a waterfall, and the winds were absolutely deafening. As darkness descended upon the zoo, we found it impossible to keep our equipment dry. The first to fail were the walkie-talkies. We broke into smaller groups. Even lights that were designed for use in water were succumbing to the rain. Head torches sputtered and blinked off.

I teamed up with Rebecca, one of the staff who had volunteered to stay and help. We cleared debris from the dingo enclosure. Although the dingoes were locked safely in their warm and dry night quarters, we wanted to make sure that their fence line didn't buckle and need repairs the next day.

We posted ourselves along the fence. Wading through waist-deep rushing water, we cleared armloads of leaves, sticks and debris. It became hard to keep our bearings with deep water covering everything.

There were several enclosures where it was a matter of security not to let the fences buckle. The number-one priority was the croc enclosures. If a fence buckled and a crocodile floated loose, everyone working in the zoo would be in jeopardy.

The storm wasn't an entirely new situation. The zoo flooded almost every year. But this storm was horrendous. The chaos was illuminated by lightning flashes, as well as the spotlights from vehicles the staff had parked nearby, trying to keep the work areas visible.

Wes, Steve and other staff battled the flood in Graham the crocodile's home. One man stood on the fence to spot the croc. He had to shout to Wes and Steve as they cleared the fence line inside the enclosure in waist-deep, dark waters. With the vehicle spotlights casting weird shadows, he had to try to discern the crocodile from among the floating bits of debris.

If Graham submerged, Wes and Steve had to be warned immediately. They had worked together like this for years and were synchronised with their every move. They jumped into the enclosure, cleared three armloads of debris, then jumped back out and re-evaluated the situation.

Graham's female, named Bindi, was nesting, which added another dangerous dimension to the job, since Graham was feeling particularly protective. The men were also keenly aware that night-time meant croc time—and Graham would be stalking them with real intent.

They reached down for their three armloads of debris. Steve scooped up his first load and flung it out. Suddenly, Wes slammed into the fence with such force that his body was driven in an arc right over the top of Steve.

It only took a split second for Steve to realise what had happened: as Wes had bent over to reach for an armload of debris, he had been hit from behind by over twelve feet of reptile, weighing close to 900 pounds.

In near pitch blackness, Steve seized a pick handle that rested near the fence. He turned towards the croc. Wes was on his side now, in water that was about three feet deep. Steve could see the crocodile in the spotlights of a Ute. As Graham moved in, Steve reached into the water and grabbed his back legs. He thought Graham was holding Wes under the water. Steve pulled with all his strength, managing to turn the crocodile round to focus on him.

As Graham lunged towards Steve, Steve drove the pick handle into the crocodile's mouth and started hammering at his head. Wes saw what was happening and scrambled up the fence.

'I'm out, mate, I'm out!' Wes yelled, blood pouring down his leg.

Steve looked up to see Wes on top of the fence. He understood that even though Wes was wounded, he was poised to jump back down into the water to try to rescue his best mate.

'Get out!' Steve shouted. 'I'm all right.' Steve and Wes both toppled over the fence and crashed down.

In the dim light, Steve could see how badly Wes had been torn open. 'Mate,' Steve said. 'Let me carry you back to the compound.'

'It's OK!' Wes yelled through the downpour. 'I can make it myself.' Both men pushed their way through the water towards the compound. No one else knew what had happened. We continued working in the rain.

Somehow Frank got word of the incident to the dingo enclosure. When I got to the compound, I was shocked. Wes was conscious and standing up. I had a look at his wounds. He was badly torn up.

We decided we would take Wes to the hospital ourselves. Wes was fluctuating between feeling euphorically happy to be alive and lashing out in anger. He was going into shock, and had lost a lot of blood.

Steve drove. A trip that would normally have taken half an hour took less than twenty minutes. Steve and I were both very emotional. We realised again how much we loved Wes. The thought that we had almost lost him terrified us. It was a horrible, emotional Friday night. Over the course of the weekend we learned that Wes would most likely make a full recovery. He would keep his leg and probably regain most movement. There was still some doubt as to whether he was going to need skin grafts.

Steve laid his life on the line to defend Wes. And as severely injured as Wes was, he stopped at the top of the fence to turn back and help Steve. That was mateship; that was love.

AFTER THE STORM and Wes's accident, we re-evaluated the safety procedures at the zoo. But the circumstances had been so unusual that night, there wasn't anything we could have done differently.

The bond between Wes and Steve only grew stronger. I don't think there is a similar concept in the rest of the world as the traditional Australian ideal of 'mateship'. 'Best friends' just doesn't do it. Mateship is deeper.

Wes started working at the zoo when he was fourteen and Steve was already in his twenties. Wes backed him up on croc captures. It was a friendship tested and retested in the bush. Through the years both men had numerous opportunities to save each other's life. But nothing had ever happened as dramatically as that night during the flood.

Even after Wes's full recovery, the close call seemed to set Steve back emotionally. The devastation of losing his mother and then nearly losing his best friend weighed heavily on his mind. Steve wasn't worried about his own mortality and was always very open about it, but the recent events only gave him more cause to think about life and death.

It never ceased to amaze me how tough Steve was on the outside, but how deeply loving he was on the inside. He showed his feelings more than any man I have ever met. During our night-time conversations we spoke at great length about spirituality and belief. Steve's faith had been tremendously tested. At times he would lash out and blame God, and sometimes he would proclaim that he did not believe in God at all. When bad things happened it shook Steve to the core. His strong feelings demanded deep spiritual answers, and he searched for them all his life.

Hearing the footsteps of his mortality made Steve all the more focused on family. We had a beautiful daughter. Now we wanted a boy.

I had read about how, through nutrition management, it was possible to stack the odds for having either a boy or a girl. I met with a nutritionist. She gave me all the information for 'the boy-baby diet'.

Chapter Nine

Our ongoing Hollywood education included the lesson that movie-making is not finished once you actually make the movie. Before we could sell *Crocodile Hunter: Collision Course* to audiences, we had to sell it to the theatre-owners who were going to show it to the public. So the first stop for our promotional efforts was a gathering of movie theatre exhibitors called Show West, in Las Vegas. Our presentation featured live wildlife, organised wonderfully by Wes.

We embarked on a twelve-city North American promotion tour, and then hit London, Dublin and Glasgow. To buzz us around, MGM provided the corporate jet, with a crocodile painted on the side. It was a whirlwind tour.

My sister Bonnie came with us to care for Bindi while Steve and I did interviews, one after another, from the morning shows to late-night television. We also spoke with reporters from newspapers, magazines and radio programmes. Over the course of six weeks, we did 1,200 interviews.

Once again, Wes organised animals for the Los Angeles premiere of *Crocodile Hunter: Collision Course*. We had a red carpet like no other. Steve, Bindi and I came down it on an elephant. Wes brought in a giraffe, cheetahs and an alligator. Steve climbed up on the elephant alone, and the trainer persuaded her to rear straight up in the air. The pictures were priceless.

All our promotional work paid off. *Crocodile Hunter: Collision Course* grossed more in the first weekend than the cost of filming. The movie promotion had been a hard slog but, even on the road, we continued our efforts to conceive. Part of our boy-baby effort was the need to try right at the time of ovulation. I packed an ovulation kit. When the strip turned blue, it meant we had a twenty-four- to forty-eight-hour window to get busy.

Upon returning to Australia, we headed out to the Brigalow Belt, an endangered bush habitat that stretches from New South Wales north into Queensland. It's named after a wattle, or tree species, but because of intense land-clearing, the whole region was in trouble.

We had purchased 80,000 acres to help protect this fragile environment. Steve wanted to check up on our dams, which had been built 100 or more years ago. These dams had never before dried out. Now we were battling a severe drought that the land hadn't seen in ages. Decades' worth of silt had built up in the dams, and was fifteen feet deep in places.

While there was still water in the middle of the pools, animals attempted to reach it through the silt but would get bogged. We spent day after day checking dams, finding about eight to ten animals hopelessly mired in the silt at each and every one, primarily kangaroos and wallabies.

We had to get to the dams early in the morning. Some of the kangaroos had been struggling all night. Steve engineered planks and straps to rescue them. The silt would suck us down just as fast, so we had to be careful going out to rescue the roos. Some of them were too far gone and couldn't recover, but we saved quite a few.

It was after this trip that I discovered I was pregnant. With the news that he would soon be a daddy again, Steve seemed inspired to work even harder. Our zoo continued to get busier, and we had trouble coping with the large numbers. The biggest draw was the crocodiles. Crowds poured in for the croc shows, filling up all the grandstands. The place was packed.

Steve came up with a monumental plan. He sketched out his idea for me on a piece of paper.

'Have a go at this, it's a coliseum,' he declared, his eyes wide with excitement. He drew an oval, then a series of smaller ovals at the back of it. 'Then we have crocodile ponds where the crocs could live. Every day a different croc could come out for the show, swim through a canal system,' he sketched rapidly, 'then come out in the main area.'

'Canals?' I said. 'Could you get them to come in on cue?'

'Piece of cake!' he said. 'And get this! We call it . . . the Crocoseum!'

His enthusiasm was contagious. Steve was determined to take the excitement and hype of the ancient Roman gladiators and combine it with the need to show people just how awesome crocs really are.

It was a huge project. Nothing even remotely similar had ever been attempted anywhere in the world. The arena would seat 5,000 and have space beneath it for museums, shops and a food court. The centre of the arena would have land areas large enough for people to work round crocodiles safely and water areas large enough for crocs to be able to access them easily.

These were heady times. As the Crocoseum rose into the sky, my tummy got bigger and bigger with our new baby.

The Crocoseum debuted during an Animal Planet live feed, its premiere beamed all over the world. The design was a smashing success.

One night, at the end of November, my waters broke and immediately the contractions started. I had been sleeping in Bindi's room because I was so awkward and uncomfortable that I kept waking everybody up. Plus, Bindi loved being able to snuggle down in bed with her daddy.

I crept into their room. As I stood beside the bed, I leaned in next to Steve's ear. When I whispered his name, he opened his eyes without moving. Bindi slept on at his side. It was about midnight and I told Steve that we didn't have to leave for the hospital yet, but it would be soon. Once he was satisfied that I was OK, I headed back to Bindi's bed to get some rest.

Steve came to my bedside not long after I lay down, and said, 'I'm putting my foot down. The baby is going to be named Robert Clarence

Irwin if it's a boy.' Robert, after his dad, Bob, and Clarence, after my dad.

'You don't need to put your foot down,' I whispered to him. 'I think it's a beautiful name.'

When my contractions were four minutes apart, I knew it was time to head to the hospital. It was five o'clock in the morning. Steve got everything organised. Thelma, Bindi's nanny, came over to get her off to school.

At the hospital, the birth progressed a lot faster than it had with Bindi. I wasn't worried because I had Steve with me, and I knew everything would be fine, as long as we were together.

The baby came. Steve said, 'It's a boy!' and brought him to me. I remember my son's tiny pink mouth. He looked like a baby bird with his eyes closed and his mouth open. Steve cried tears of joy.

Once we got settled, the proud papa headed for Sunshine Coast Grammar School to tell Bindi the news. Steve brought her to the hospital, where she took her little brother in her arms and looked at him lovingly.

It was December 1, 2003, and we had all just received the best Christmas present ever. Robert Clarence Irwin. Baby Bob. When we brought him home, all the zoo staff welcomed the new arrival.

We had always had a good relationship with a group of Buddhist monks from Tibet. They had blessed Bindi when she was a newborn. As Robert celebrated his one-month birthday, we decided to hold a fundraiser for a Buddhist convent where the well had dried up. We invited the nuns to stay at Australia Zoo, and planned to hold the fundraiser at our brand-new Crocoseum, doing our part to help raise some money for the new well.

The nuns wished to know if we wanted them to bless the animals while they were at the zoo. 'Would you please bless Robert?' we asked.

Bindi had been blessed along with the crocodiles when she was a month old. Now we would do the same for Robert. The nuns came into the Crocoseum for the ceremony. I brought a sleepy little Robert, adorned with his prayer flag and a scarf. We invited press to help publicise the plight of the nuns. Robert was peaceful. The nuns sang and gave him their special blessing.

The ceremony was over, and the croc show was about to begin. Just as we had done with Bindi at this age, we brought Robert out for the show. Steve talked about how proud he was of his son. He pointed out the crocodile to Baby Bob. Although Robert had been in with the crocodiles before, and would be again, this was an event where we could share the moment with everybody.

When the croc show was over, Steve brought Robert back underneath the Crocoseum and I put him in his stroller. His eyes were big and he was waving his arms. Bindi was a regular during the croc shows, and now it looked as though Robert would be joining in as well.

Later that day, a message was forwarded to us. One of the television channels covering the event at the Crocoseum had decided to put a negative slant on the story.

'How crazy could that be?' I said to Steve. 'What negative aspect could you possibly find in such a beautiful event?'

Then the news broke like a tidal wave. It wasn't just one television station that had picked up the story. There appeared to be a collective decision to crucify Steve for having Robert at the crocodile show with him.

The story had gone out all over the world. Steve was portrayed as an evil, ugly monster who had exploited his son in some kind of stunt show. Part of the problem was the infamous Michael Jackson 'baby-dangling' incident, when the pop star hung his baby out of a hotel window in Berlin, to adoring fans waiting below. The press played the two stories off against each other. Steve and Michael, a couple of baby danglers.

We didn't know what to do. I knew beyond certainty that the most important part of Steve's life was his family. His children meant everything to him. All of a sudden, my wonderful, sharing, protective husband was being condemned. His crime was sharing wildlife experiences with Robert exactly as he had done for the last five and a half years with Bindi.

The media circus escalated. Helicopters hovered over the zoo, trying to catch a glimpse of the crazy Irwin family. We soon realised we couldn't go anywhere. There would be no visits to the zoo, no answering the phone, no doing croc shows. The criticism and the spin continued.

I stood by Steve's side and watched his heart break. I couldn't believe the mean-spirited, petty, awful people in the world. Editors manipulated film footage, trying to make the croc look bigger or closer to Robert than it actually had been. What possible motivation could they have?

THE SAME NIGHT the Baby Bob controversy hit, a police officer stopped by. The governor-general, the officer said, required Steve to contact him.

When Steve called the number the police gave, the governor-general's secretary answered. She was quite terse and to the point. She indicated that we would be investigated by Children's Services.

I could hear the sharp edge in the woman's voice even though Steve held the phone. 'Be very careful, Mr Irwin,' she said. 'We have the capacity to take your children.'

Could the social workers come and take our children away? Children who were so desperately loved, well taken care of and cherished?

This was a media beat-up at its very worst. All of those officials reacting to what the media labelled 'The Baby Bob Incident' failed to understand the Irwin family. This was what we did—teach our children about wildlife from a very early age. It wasn't unnatural and it wasn't a stunt. It was who we were. To have the press fasten upon the practice as irresponsible made us feel that our very ability as parents was being attacked.

This is why Steve never publicly apologised. For him to say 'I'm sorry' would mean that he was sorry that Bob and Lyn raised him the way they did, and that was simply impossible. The best he could do was to sincerely apologise if he had worried anyone. The reality was that he would have been remiss as a parent if he didn't teach his kids how to coexist with wildlife. After all, his kids didn't just have busy roads and hot stoves to contend with. They literally had to learn how to live with crocodiles and venomous snakes in their back yard.

Steve and I struggled to get back to a point where we felt normal again. Sponsors spoke about terminating contracts. Members of our own documentary crew sought to distance themselves from us, and our relationship with Discovery was on shaky ground.

But gradually we were able to hear what people were saying. We read the emails that had been pouring in, as well as faxes, letters and phone messages. Real people helped to get us back on track. Their kids were growing up with them on cattle ranches and could already drive tractors, or lived on horse farms and helped to handle skittish stallions. Other children were training to be gymnasts, a sport that was physically rigorous and held out the chance of injury. The parents and kids had sent us messages of support.

So many parents employed the same phrase: 'I'd trust my kids with Steve any day.'

I knew Steve was starting to cope when he proposed one of his most ambitious documentaries with John Stainton. They would journey to Antarctica and document conditions for wildlife there. It was summer in the Southern Hemisphere, and that's the only practical time to go to Antarctica, but the continent was still no place for small children. Steve went south with a camera crew. I went to Florida with the children.

Steve discovered that the Antarctic wildlife had little fear of humans. There were no hunting parties out terrorising the wildlife, so they didn't perceive people as a threat. The penguins were among the friendliest. In fact, he found if he mimicked their actions, they would often repeat them in response. He maintained a respectful distance, but often the penguins came to him. Steve was really interested in learning more about the penguins' main predator, the leopard seal. The seals had a fierce reputation.

Steve watched them emerge from the holes in the ice.

'They're like great big caterpillars,' he told me. As with crocs, they could be dangerous in the water, or lunging out from the water's edge. But once the seals were out of the water, they resembled gigantic inchworms coming at you. There was really no threat of them chasing a human down.

The best approach to a leopard seal was to give it a wide berth. Steve was able to talk about leopard-seal behaviour while sitting on the ice with one nearby. The seal didn't fling itself at Steve. In fact, it listened as Steve told its story, then slipped back into the water.

Antarctica has definite rules about approaching wildlife. Penguins, for example, have a specific distance restriction, meaning all humans have to stay at least that distance away—unless the penguin approaches them. The reality was a little different. Researchers had to proceed through great numbers of the birds just to walk to the lavatory. Tourist boats ploughed through penguins when approaching ports, actually killing them in droves.

Steve was determined to focus on the positive aspects of his experience. Humpback whales came up to the side of the boat, lifting their huge heads out of the water, having a look round. There was no need to go searching for them—the natural curiosity of the humpbacks made them come to him. Steve donned his dry suit to do some filming in the water. The whales approached. Because Steve's dry suit had a small leak in it, he climbed up on a growler—a small iceberg—and was able to hang on to complete filming.

The resulting footage represented what Steve was all about. He was able to bring his experience with these beautiful whales into people's living rooms. This is why he did what he did—to get wildlife into our hearts.

Steve came back from his Antarctica trip with renewed determination. In his last documentary, he showed how penguins actually play. He tried to demystify the fierce reputation of the leopard seal. He talked about how humpback whales have a family structure similar to ours, that they are mammals, they love their children and they communicate.

But in the wake of the Baby Bob incident, reporters seemed to be lying in wait for Steve. This time he was attacked for filming with the wildlife of Antarctica. Commentators characterised Steve sliding down the slippery slopes with penguins as 'interfering', and sitting near a leopard seal to demonstrate that it wasn't a horrible monster as 'displacing wildlife'. Most ludicrous of all, when Steve sat on the growler, a report claimed he was riding a whale.

Australian authorities launched an official investigation. Laws regulated procedures of filming Antarctic wildlife, and the charges, if proven, carried potential jail time. Just months after being devastated by claims that he wasn't a good father, Steve faced charges that he was a wildlife harasser, instead of a wildlife warrior. We found ourselves spending money on lawyers that should have been going to wildlife conservation.

In the end, the investigation determined that Steve had done nothing wrong on the Antarctic documentary trip. Once again, the thoughts and prayers of ordinary people around the world who believed in Steve sustained us. But not since he'd lost his mother had I seen him so low. He had taken two hits in quick succession, first Baby Bob, then the Antarctica allegations.

'Crocodiles are easy,' Steve said, 'they try to kill and eat you. People are harder. Sometimes they pretend to be your friend first.'

PROFESSOR CRAIG FRANKLIN of the University of Queensland mounted a crocodile research partnership with Steve. The idea was to fasten transmitters and data loggers on crocs to record their activity in their natural environment. But in order to place the transmitters you had to catch the crocs first, and that's where Steve's expertise came in.

Steve never felt more content than when he was with his family in the bush. 'There's nothing more valuable than human life, and this research will help protect both crocs and people,' he told us. The bush was where Steve felt most at home. It was where he was at his best. On that one trip, he caught thirty-three crocs in fourteen days.

He wanted to do more. 'I'd really like to have the capability of doing research on the ocean as well as in the rivers,' he told me. 'I could do so much for crocodiles and sharks if I had a purpose-built research vessel.'

When we got back from our first trip to Cape York Peninsula with Craig Franklin, Steve immediately began drawing up plans for his boat. He wanted to make it as comfortable as possible. As he envisioned it, the boat would be somewhere between a hard-core scientific research vessel and a luxury cruiser.

He designed three berths, a plasma screen television for the kids and air-conditioned comfort below deck. He placed a big marlin board off the back, for jet skis, shark cages or hauling out huge crocs. One feature he was really adamant about was a helicopter pad. He designed the craft so that the helicopter could land on the top. Steve's design plans went back and forth to Perth for months.

'I want this boat's primary function to be crocodile research and rescue work,' Steve said. 'So I'm going to name her *Croc One*.'

Croc One was his baby. But for some reason, I felt tremendous trepidation about this boat. I attributed this to feelings of concern for Bindi and Robert. It made me uncomfortable to think about being 200 miles out at sea with two young kids.

We had had so many wild adventures together as a family that, ultimately, I had to trust Steve. But my support for *Croc One* was always, deep down, halfhearted at best. I couldn't shake off my sense of foreboding.

Over the course of two years, from June 2004 to June 2006, two separate deaths did nothing to ease my overall anxiety. Steve's beloved dog, Sui, died of cancer in June 2004. He had set up his swag and slept beside her all night, talking to her, recalling old times in the bush catching crocodiles, and comforting her.

Wes, the most loyal friend anyone could have, was there for Steve while Sui passed from this life to the next. He shared in Steve's grief. They had known Sui longer than Steve and I had been together.

Two years after Sui's death, in June 2006, we lost Harriet. At 175, Harriet was the oldest living creature on earth. She had met Charles Darwin and sailed on the *Beagle*. She was a living museum and an icon of our zoo.

The kids and I were headed to Fraser Island with Joy, Steve's sister, and her husband, Frank, our zoo manager, when I heard the news. An ultrasound had confirmed that Harriet had suffered a massive heart attack.

Steve called me. 'I think you'd better come home,' he said.

'I should talk to the kids about this,' I said.

Bindi was traumatised. 'I don't want to see Harriet die,' she said resolutely. She wanted to remember her as the healthy, happy tortoise with whom she'd grown up.

I was worried about Steve, but told him that Bindi couldn't bear to see Harriet dying. 'It's OK,' he said. 'Wes is here with me.' Once again, it fell to Wes to share his best mate's grief.

Even in the midst of loss, Steve still managed to concentrate on future projects. One included plans to work with Philippe Cousteau Jr, the grandson of one of Steve's heroes, the pioneering oceanographer Jacques Cousteau, on a documentary called *Ocean's Deadliest*.

Chapter Ten

On July 25, 2006—the day after Bindi's eighth birthday celebration—we headed out to Cape York Peninsula on a five-week croc research trip. Once again, we partnered with the University of Queensland's Professor Craig Franklin. Steve's instincts, experience and scientific curiosity about crocodiles married well with the academic world.

He certainly put his Crocodile Hunter money where his heart was. We spent hundreds of thousands of dollars on the scientific equipment, travel costs, trapping gear and the infrastructure to support the big research team. For the first time, we would employ time-depth recorders as well as satellite tracking to trace croc behaviour.

This would be the first croc research trip where both Bindi and Robert were old enough to participate. Robert was two and a half, and walking and talking like a serious little man. Bindi, of course, had been involved in croc research trips before. But now she had new motivation. We were in the middle of filming her own nature show, *Bindi the Jungle Girl*.

This was important for Steve. 'There'd be nothing that would make me happier than having Bindi just take over filming and I could take it easy and run the zoo, do my conservation work,' Steve would say.

It might have seemed like an unusual thing to say about a kid who had just turned eight, but Bindi was no ordinary kid. Bindi had a calling. I would sense it when I was around her, just as I sensed it when I first met Steve.

Bindi would participate in the filming in such a way that she always made sure a certain conservation message came through, or she'd want to do a take again to make sure her words got the message across properly.

As soon as we reached the campsite, where we would launch the boat and start setting the traps, Steve was into it immediately. He would scan up and down the river system for an hour and a half, dozens of miles, getting to know where the crocs hung out. He was able to match a croc to each slide, each track, belly print and footmark in the mud.

As he set the traps, Steve specifically targeted different-sized animals that he and the other scientists had agreed to catch: big males, breeding females and sub-adults. He set floating traps and soft-mesh traps. Steve would often catch more crocs in a single day than the team could cope with.

We trapped several smaller females, all around the nine-foot mark. That's when Steve stepped back and let the all-girl team take over: all the women in camp, zoo workers mainly, and myself. We would jump on the croc, help secure the tracking device and let her go.

At one point Steve trapped a female that he could see was small and quiet. He turned to Bindi. 'How would you like to jump the head?'

Bindi's eyes lit up. This was what she had been waiting for. Once Steve removed the croc from the trap and secured its jaws, the next step was for the point person to jump the croc's head. Everybody else on the team followed immediately afterwards, pinning the crocodile's body.

'Don't worry,' I said to Bindi. 'I'll back you up.'

Steve was nervous as he slipped the croc out of its mesh trap. 'Ready, and now!' he said. Bindi flung herself on the head of the crocodile. I came in right over her back. The rest of the girls jumped on immediately, and we had our croc secured.

As we idled back into camp, Robert said, 'Can I please drive the boat?'

'Crikey, mate, you're two years old,' Steve said. 'I'll let you drive the boat next year.'

But then, quite suddenly and without a word, Steve scooped Robert up and sat him next to the outboard. He put the tiller in his hand.

'Here's what you do, mate,' Steve said, and he began to explain how to drive the boat.

Robert spent the trip jumping croc tails, driving the boat and tying knots. Steve created a croc made of sticks and set it on a sandbar. He pulled the boat up next to it, and he, Robert and Bindi went through all the motions of jumping the stick-croc.

'I'm going to say two words,' Robert shouted, imitating his father. '"Go" and "now". First team off on "go", second team off on "now".' Then he'd yell 'go, now' at the top of his lungs. He and Steve jumped up as if the stick-croc was about to swing round and tear their arms off.

'Another croc successfully caught, mate,' Steve said proudly. Robert beamed with pride, too.

Watching Steve around the camp was to witness a man at one with his environment. Steve took all the knowledge he'd acquired over the years and added his own experience. Nothing seemed to daunt him. On Cape York, we faced the obvious wildlife hazards, including feral pigs, venomous snakes and huge crocodiles. I never saw Steve afraid of anything, except the chance of harm coming to someone he loved.

FILMING WILDLIFE DOCUMENTARIES couldn't have happened without John Stainton, our producer. Steve always referred to John as the genius behind the camera, and that was true. The music orchestration, the editing, the knowledge of what would make good television and what wouldn't—these were all areas of John's clear expertise.

But on the ground, under the water or in the bush, while we were actually filming, it was 100 per cent Steve. He took care of the crew and eventually his family as well, while filming in some of the most remote, inaccessible and dangerous areas on earth.

Steve kept the cameraman alive by telling him exactly when to shoot and when to run. He orchestrated what to film and where to film, and then located the wildlife. Steve's first rule, which he repeated to the crew over and over, was a simple one: film everything, no matter what happens. 'If something goes wrong,' he told them, 'you are not going to be of any use to me lugging a camera and waving your other arm around trying to help. Just keep rolling. Whatever the sticky situation is, I will get out of it.'

Steve had the smooth and steady movements of someone who was self-assured after years of practice. He'd get into the boat, fire up the engine and start immediately. There was never any hesitation. His physical strength was unsurpassed. He could chop wood, collect water and build many things with an ease that was obvious when anybody else (myself, for example) awkwardly struggled with the same task.

Every morning and evening at Lakefield National Park, the fruit bats would come and go from the trees around our campsite. During the day, you could hear them in the distance as they squabbled over territory. Each fruit bat wanted to jockey for the best position on a branch. But when evening came, as if by silent agreement, all the bats knew to fly off at the same time.

Steve grabbed me and the kids one evening, and we went out onto the river to watch the bats. I would rank that night as one of the most incredible experiences of my life. We were sitting at dusk with the kids in the boat, and all of a sudden the trees came alive. The bats took flight, skimming over the water to delicately dip for a drink, flying directly over our heads. It was as if we had gone back in time and pterodactyls flew once again.

It was such an awe-inspiring event that we all fell quiet, the children included. The water was absolutely still. All we heard were the wings of these ancient mammals in the darkening sky.

We lay back quietly in the boat, floating in the middle of this paradise. We knew that we were completely and totally safe. We were in a small dinghy in the middle of some of the most prolifically populated crocodile water, yet we were absolutely comfortable, knowing that Steve was there with us.

'One day, babe,' Steve said softly to me, 'we'll look back on wildlife harvesting projects and things like croc farming the same way we look back on slavery and cannibalism. It will be simply an unbelievable part of human history. It will be something we will never, ever return to.'

That trip was epic. Every day was an adventure. Bindi sat down for her formal schooling at a little table under the big trees by the river, with the kookaburras singing and the occasional lizard or snake cruising through the camp. She had the best scientists from the University of Queensland around to answer her questions.

I could tell Steve didn't want it to end. We had been in bush camp for five weeks. Bindi, Robert and I were now scheduled for a trip to Tasmania. Along with us would be the children's teacher, Emma, and Kate, her sister, who worked at the zoo. It was a trip I had planned for a long time. Emma would celebrate her thirtieth birthday, and Kate would see her first snow.

Steve and I would go our separate ways. He would leave Lakefield on *Croc One* and go directly to rendezvous with Philippe Cousteau for the filming of *Ocean's Deadliest*. We had tried to figure out how we could all be together for the shoot, but there just wasn't enough room on the boat.

Steve drove us to the airstrip at the ranger station. One of the young rangers there immediately began to bend his ear about a wildlife issue. I took Robert off to pee on a bush before we had to get on the plane. It was just a tiny prop plane and there would be no lavatory until we got to Cairns.

When we came back, all the general talk meant that there wasn't much time left for us to say goodbye. Bindi pressed a note into Steve's hand and said, 'Don't read this until we're gone.' I gave Steve a big hug and a kiss. Then I kissed him again.

Steve was his usual enthusiastic self as we climbed into the plane. We knew we would see each other in less than two weeks. I would head back to the zoo, get some work done, and leave for Tasmania. Steve would do his filming trip. Then we would all be together again.

The pilot fired up the plane. Robert had a seat belt on and couldn't see out of the window, so he wasn't able to see his daddy waving goodbye. But Bindi had a clear view of Steve, who had parked his Ute just outside the gable markers and was standing on top of it, legs wide apart, a big smile on his face, waving his hands over his head.

I could see Bindi's note in one of his hands. He had read it and was acknowledging it to Bindi. She waved frantically out of the window. As the plane picked up speed, we swept past him and then we were into the sky.

WE WERE HEADING for Cradle Mountain to show Kate her first snow. On the way to the mountain, we would stop at a beautiful little wildlife park near Launceston. We had rented a pair of small cottages. Bindi, Robert and I snuggled down in one, while Emma and Kate had their own cottage nearby.

The next day was Sunday and it was Father's Day, so it was natural for us to try to get in touch with Steve. I knew he was filming somewhere off the Queensland coast.

On board *Croc One*, along with Steve and Philippe Cousteau, was Jamie Seymour, a toxicologist. They planned to study several dangerous sea species, with the double goal of understanding their place in the environment and teaching people how to frequent Australia's waters more safely.

We tried to get through to Steve on the phone, but of course he was out filming. I spoke via satellite phone to Kate Coulter, a long-time zoo employee, along with her husband, Brian. We all took turns talking to her.

'Steve captured a huge sea snake,' Kate said. 'He said it was the biggest he had ever seen. He said, "Thick as my arm, no, thick as my leg."'

Kate knew Steve well, and she conveyed his enthusiasm perfectly. She told us she would pass along our messages.

'Tell Daddy how much I love him and miss him,' Bindi said, and Kate told her she would. Robert wanted to go and see the big sea snake his father had caught. He didn't grasp that the Cape was thousands of miles away.

At the Launceston wildlife park, we met the new generation of baby devils. They were tiny, smaller than guinea pigs, and just starting to emerge from their mothers' pouches.

The park reminded me of our own Australia Zoo when it first started out. It was a family operation run by Dick and Judi Warren. They were both warm and friendly and eager to talk.

We toured the park, seeing parrots, wombats and tiger snakes. 'Koalas and primates,' Dick said. 'We'll get some koalas and primates and then we'll be set.'

I thought back to how many times Steve and I had said something similar. 'Just one more species and then our zoo will be done.' I was coming to realise that Australia Zoo would never be done. There were too many species in the world that needed our help.

We didn't hurry ourselves the next day. We meandered west, stopping at a raspberry farm and at the Honey Factory in Chudleigh. The Honey Factory also featured a plethora of bee-themed products. Bindi sampled every single flavour of honey that they had. She bought a wristwatch with a bee on it. Robert picked out a backpack.

As we walked out of the door, Bindi looked at her newly purchased watch and said, 'It's twelve o'clock.' We all stopped for a moment and considered that it was twelve o'clock. Then we got in the car and left.

Our destination that day was Cradle Mountain National Park where we had booked rooms. We wanted to climb the mountain to the snow line.

We drove into the Cradle Mountain resort still munching on raspberries. Emma and Kate waited with the kids in the car while I went in.

'Where's all the snow?' I asked the woman behind the desk.

'It snowed this morning,' she said.

Then she passed me a note. She said, 'Frank called from the zoo. Why don't you take the call in the office?' she said. I thought that was a little odd, since when I had been there before I'd always used the payphone near the pub at the resort. But I entered the office and sat down in a big, comfortable chair. I could see the car park out of the window.

'How you going, Frank?' I said into the phone.

He said, 'Hi, Terri. I've been trying to get hold of you for a while.' His voice had a heavy, serious tone.

'Well, I've just got here,' I said. 'Sorry about that. What's up?'

'I'm sorry to say that Steve had a bit of an accident while he was diving,' Frank said. 'I'm afraid he got hit in the chest by a stingray's barb.'

I'm sure there wasn't much of a pause, but I felt time stop.

Then Frank said the three words I did not want him to say. 'And he died.'

I took a deep breath and looked out of the window. The world stopped. I took another breath.

'Thank you very much for calling, Frank,' I said. I didn't know what I was saying. I was overwhelmed, already on autopilot. 'You need to cancel the rest of our trip, you need to contact my family in Oregon and you need to get us home.'

I knew the one thing I wanted to do more than anything was to get to Steve. I needed to bring my kids home as fast as possible. I didn't understand what had been going on in the rest of the world. Steve's accident had occurred at eleven o'clock in the morning. The official time of death was made at twelve noon, the exact time that Bindi had looked at her watch and said, for no apparent reason, 'It's twelve o'clock,' on September 4, 2006.

Now I had to go out to the car and tell Bindi and Robert what had happened to their daddy. The person they loved most in the world was gone, the person they looked up to, relied upon and emulated. I had to tell them that they had lost this most important person, on this most beautiful day.

Emma came in and I told her what had happened. Suddenly I felt very sick. I didn't know if I could stand up, and I asked to use the rest room. Then I realised this was the exact time for me to be strong. For years, I had counted on Steve's strength. At six feet tall and 200 pounds, he was a force to be reckoned with. But he always told me there were different kinds of strength. Steve said he could count on me to be strong when times were hard.

I thought about that, and I suddenly understood there must be a reason that I was here and he was gone. I needed to help his kids, to be there for our children. All I wanted to do was run and run and run. But I had to stay.

With Emma at my side, I went outside and climbed into the car. Robert was asleep. Bindi knew instantly by my face that something was wrong.

'Did something happen to one of the animals at the zoo?' she asked.

'Something happened to Daddy,' I said. 'He was diving, and he had an accident.' I told her everything that I knew about what had happened. She cried. We all cried. Robert still slept.

It was back and forth, in and out of the resort now, making phone call after phone call. The challenge was getting home. I couldn't comprehend the massive response by the press—we were being tracked down like prey, the helicopters already hovering in the air. Taking a commercial flight home was out of the question, so we managed to find a charter plane.

'We can drive,' Emma said gently, meaning herself and Kate. We had to get to the airport and run the gauntlet of the media. I suddenly felt a real desire to take charge and not to fall in a heap. I knew I needed to be strong.

'I can drive,' I said.

It was on an impossibly narrow, winding section of road that Robert decided to wake up. So I had to drive and at the same time tell my son what had happened. He asked me to explain everything again, and I did for a second time.

Robert stopped talking. He held on to Piggy, his little plush friend, staring out of the window. For half an hour he didn't say a word.

When we got close to the airport, the reality of the public reaction to Steve's death began to sink in. Members of the media were everywhere. We drove straight through the gates to pull up right next to the charter plane.

The last thing I felt like at that moment was talking to anyone about what had happened. I just wanted to get to Steve.

As I walked towards the plane, I turned back to thank the police who had helped us. The tears in their eyes shocked me out of my own personal cocoon of grief. This wasn't just a job for them. They genuinely felt for us, and suffered Steve's loss. So many other people loved him, too, I thought.

All during the endless, three-hour plane ride to Maroochydore, I kept flashing back through our fourteen years of adventures together. Part of me wished we could have flown for ever, never landing, never facing what we were about to. I concentrated on Bindi and Robert, getting them fed, and making sure they were comfortable.

The plane landed at Maroochydore in the dark. We taxied in between hangars, out of public view. As I came down the steps of the plane, Frank, Joy and Wes stood there. We all hugged one another. Wes sobbed. We managed to help each other to the hangar, where we all piled into two vehicles for the half-hour drive back to the zoo.

Chapter Eleven

Chance. Fate. Destiny. These were words I lived by. I believed my life had been shaped for a special purpose. But with Steve's death my faith was tested. Was it pure chance that Steve, a man who cheated mortality almost every single day of his adult life, died in such a bizarre accident?

During the decade and a half I knew him, I don't think a week went by when he didn't get a bite or injury of some kind. His knee and shoulder plagued him from years of jumping crocs. As Steve erected a fence at our Brigalow Belt conservation property, a big fence-post driver he was using slipped and landed on his head, compressing the fifth disk in his neck. Even injured, he still managed to push on—at the zoo, filming, and doing heavy construction. He went at work like a bull at a gate. He climbed trees with orang-utans. He traversed the most remote deserts and the most impossible mountains. He packed his life chock-a-block full with risks of all kinds.

I had no regrets for Steve's glorious life, and I know he couldn't have lived any other way.

When Bindi, Robert and I got home on the evening of Steve's death, Wes, Joy and Frank came into the house. We never entertained, we never had anyone over, and now suddenly our living room seemed full.

We had to make arrangements to bring Steve home. I tried to keep things as private as possible. One of Steve's former classmates at school ran the funeral home in Caloundra that would be handling the arrangements. He had known the Irwin family for years, and I recall thinking how hard this was going to be for him as well.

Our guests decided on their own to leave and let us get on with our night. I gave the kids a bath and fixed them something to eat. I got Robert settled in bed and stayed with him until he fell asleep. Bindi looked worried. Usually I curled up with Robert in the evening, while Steve curled up with Bindi. 'Don't worry,' I said to her. 'Robert's already asleep. You can sleep in my bed with me.'

Little Bindi soon dropped off to sleep, but I lay awake. It felt as though I had died and was starting over with a new life. I kept going over and over what had happened. I wanted to talk to everyone who had been there with Steve on the day of his accident.

I lay there while the clock ticked on. *Here is another minute I have survived without Steve.* I consoled myself with the thought that the clock was ticking for all of us. None of us could know when it was going to be our time. I resolved that I would celebrate the people who were still here, and apply myself to the work that still had to be done. But what really sustained me during those dark, lonely hours of the night was another deeper, more persistent thought. With every tick of the clock, I was one moment closer to being with Steve again. As strong as Steve was in this life, I knew without a doubt he would be a force to be reckoned with in the next.

The first morning was especially hard. Usually, our morning routine involved listening with one ear for the sound of a motorbike approaching the house. Steve never slept more than a few hours a night. He was always up before us, and would go about his zoo business and then come back, riding up to the house and bursting through the door. He'd tell the kids about something new and exciting going on in the zoo, and then he would bundle them up, with me protesting that they needed hats or coats—and no matter what I said, he would spirit them out of the door and onto the motorbike.

That first morning, the realisation sank in that he wasn't going to come bursting in any more.

Using the satellite phone connection, I finally reached *Croc One*. The captain, Kris, was in tears. I tracked down John Stainton, and he assured me that he hadn't left Steve's side.

'I've got a charter plane coming,' John said. 'I'll get him home, Terri.'

As John arranged to bring Steve home, the media pressure steadily increased. I told Wes I wanted to go to meet the plane, but that I wouldn't take the kids. This was my time to be with my soul mate, and I needed to do it on my own. I headed out with a police escort.

Wes accompanied me. It was night. As the seaplane came in, the ranks of police stood at attention. Many of them had met Steve previously. Once again, I was overwhelmed to see the looks of grief on their faces.

The plane landed, and I had a moment to sit with Steve on my own. It was a bit of an effort to clamber up into the back of the plane. A simple wooden casket rested inside, still secured. I knew that who Steve was, his spirit and his soul, were no longer there, but it was strange how I couldn't cry.

I sat down and leaned my head against the wooden box that held his body and felt such strange peace.

In some way, we were together again.

As I write this, I am still waiting for Steve to walk through the door. His sarong still hangs on the bed. His toothbrush is in the bathroom.

Reality is sinking in more and more. Bindi and I have a lot of heart-to-heart talks. These seem to help her, and I feel thankful that over the years I had set the foundation of faith in Bindi.

Robert is like a pitiful puppy, and still waits patiently for his daddy to come home from heaven. I hadn't been prepared for how devastated Robert would be. Some nights he sits in the bathtub and cries. 'I want my daddy,' he says, over and over. It absolutely tears my heart out.

We have a dear friend, a wonderful psychologist who has helped a great deal—he suffered a loss in his own family recently, and we both felt sad. He explained that grief is your own process. You can't compare your grief to anyone else's. It is something that is uniquely yours. People outside our immediate circle murmured concern that perhaps Bindi was coping a little too well with her grief, and I wasn't immune to comments in the press about her remarkably composed speech at Steve's memorial service. It was nice to have my friend's professional opinion to put my mind at ease.

'That's what you are aiming for,' he told me. 'You are trying to raise children who can cope with life and not fall apart. That's the goal. Understanding that where there is love there is grief, and where there is life there is death, and that a person's spirit and soul never die and that their love never ends—these are important lessons to impart to our children.'

Bindi does do well. It will take more time with Robert. I have learned that as Bindi gets older and reaches adolescence, there may be another period when grief revisits her.

Because of the constant media surveillance, I could not venture out to see the countless tributes that mourners laid down in front of the zoo. But all the items were collected and stored safely, and we now display a lovely memorial selection.

The public response to Steve's death would have overwhelmed him most of all—the kind thoughts, prayers, sympathy and tears. I wasn't facing this grief on my own. So many people from around the world were trying to come to terms with it as well. The process seemed particularly difficult for children who had not had the opportunity to experience the circle of life as Bindi had. I felt it was important to get a message out to them. When your hero dies, everything he stood for does not end. Everything he stood for must continue.

There was never a doubt in my mind that I'd keep working towards stopping the destruction of our environment and wildlife. There were so many triumphs that Steve had already worked so hard for.

I sat down with Wes. 'First, we're going to work on everything Steve wanted to achieve,' I said. 'Then we'll move on to everything that we were collectively working towards. And finally, I want to continue with my own goals, in terms of our conservation work.'

We strategised about the expansion of the zoo. I didn't want to just maintain the zoo as it was, I wanted to follow Steve's plans for the future. Wes and I took the stacks of plans, blueprints and manila folders from Steve's desk. I assembled them and laid them out on a conference table.

'This was Steve's plan for Australia Zoo over the next ten years,' I said. 'I want to do it in five.'

This winter, we christened *Steve's Whale One*, a whale-watching excursion boat that will realise another of his long-held dreams. He always wanted to expand the experience of the zoo to include whales. *Steve's Whale One* is a way for people to see first-hand some of the most amazing creatures on earth. The humpbacks in Australian waters approach whale-watching boats with curiosity and openness. It is a delightful experience, and one that I am confident will help to inspire people and end the inhumane practice of whaling.

Bindi the Jungle Girl aired on July 18, 2007, on ABC-TV in Australia, and we were so proud. Bindi's determination to carry on her father's legacy was a testament to everything Steve believed in. He had perfectly combined his love for his family with his love for conservation and leaving the world a better place. Now, this love was perfectly passed down to his kids.

The official beginning of Bindi's career was a fantastic day. All the time and effort, and joy and sorrow of the past year culminated in this wonderful series. Now everyone was invited to see Bindi's journey, first filming with her dad, and then stepping up and filming with Robert and me. It was also a chance to experience one more time why Steve was so special and unique, to embrace him, to appreciate him and to celebrate his life. Bindi, Robert and I would do our best to make sure that Steve's light would continue to shine as we worked together to protect all wildlife and all wild places.

After Bindi's show launched, it seemed so appropriate that another project we had been working on for many months came to fruition. We found an area of 320,000 acres in Cape York Peninsula, bordered on one side by the Ducie River and on the other side by the Wenlock River—some of the best crocodile country in the world. It is one of the top spots in Australia, and the most critically important habitat in the state of Queensland. Prime Minister John Howard, along with the Queensland government, dedicated $6.3 million to obtaining this land, in memory of Steve.

On July 22, 2007, the Steve Irwin Wildlife Reserve became official. This piece of land means so much to the Irwin family, and I know what it would have meant to Steve. Ultimately, it means the protection of his crocodiles, the animals he loved so much.

What does the future hold for the Irwin family? Each and every day is filled with incredible triumphs and moments of terrible grief. And in between, life goes on. We are determined to continue to honour and appreciate Steve's wonderful spirit. It lives on with all of us. Steve lived every day of his life doing what he loved, and he always said he would die defending wildlife. I reckon Bindi, Robert and I will all do the same.

God bless you, Stevo. I love you, mate.

STEVE & ME

5

Left page: 1 As a boy, Steve was often 'either on the roof or up in some tree'. **2** Wedding day, June 4, 1992: left to right: Terri's mother Julia Raines, Bob Irwin, Terri, Steve, Lyn Irwin and Clarence Raines. **3** Steve and Terri on the day they met. **4** 'I'd like to be remembered as a good dad.' **5** Their final trip together—crocodile research in Queensland: from left: Robert, Terri, Steve and Bindi. **Right page: 6** With Harriet, the giant Galápagos land tortoise. **7** Steve grapples with a crocodile. **8** Soul mates. **9** The Irwins aboard Steve's research vessel, *Croc One*.

THE BONE GARDEN

TESS GERRITSEN

Teacher Julia Hamill is digging in the garden of her home when she is shocked to find a human skull—that of a female who died from unnatural causes in the early 1800s.

As she delves into an archive of letters from the period, Julia reads about a dark time of disease and primitive medicine, and of a shadowy figure who was terrorising the streets of Boston.

March 20, 1888

Dearest Margaret,

I thank you for your kind condolences, so sincerely offered, for the loss of my darling Amelia. Every month seems to bring the passing of yet another old friend. Now it is with deepest gloom that I must consider the rapidly evaporating years left to me.

I realise that this is perhaps my last chance to broach a difficult subject. I know that your aunt felt it wisest to keep it from you. She did it solely out of love, as she wanted to protect you. But I have known you from your earliest years, dear Margaret, and have watched you grow into a fearless woman. And so I believe that you would want to know this story, however disturbing you may find it.

Fifty-eight years have passed since these events and, indeed, I myself had almost forgotten about them. But this past Wednesday, I discovered an old news clipping and I realised that unless I speak of it soon, the facts will almost certainly die with me. Since your aunt's passing, I am now the only one left who knows the tale.

The details are not pleasant. But there is nobility in this story, and heartbreaking courage as well. No doubt your aunt seemed no more extraordinary than any other grey-haired lady whom one passes on the street. But I assure you, Margaret, she was most worthy of our respect. Worthier, perhaps, than any woman I have ever met.

I enclose the news clipping. If you have no desire to learn more, please tell me, and I will never again mention this. But if indeed the subject of your parents holds any interest for you, then I will once again pick up my pen. And you will learn the story, the true story, of your aunt and the West End Reaper.

With fondest regards, O.W.H.

ONE

The Present

So this is how a marriage ends, thought Julia Hamill as she rammed the shovel into the soil. Not with sweet whispers goodbye, not with the loving clasp of arthritic hands forty years from now, not with children and grandchildren grieving round her hospital bed. She lifted a scoop of earth and flung it aside, sending stones clattering onto the growing mound. It was all clay and stones, barren soil, like her marriage, from which nothing had sprouted.

She stamped down on the shovel and heard a clang, as the blade hit a stone—a big one. She repositioned the blade, but she could not prise it loose. Demoralised and sweating in the heat, she stared down at the hole. All morning she had been digging like a woman possessed, and she had stirred up a cloud of mosquitoes that whined round her face and infiltrated her hair.

Suddenly the task seemed hopeless. She dropped the shovel and slumped to the ground. Why had she ever thought she could restore this garden, salvage this house? She looked across at the weathered clapboards. *Julia's Folly*—that's what she should name it. Bought when she hadn't been thinking straight, when her life was collapsing after her divorce. At thirty-eight years old, she would finally have a house in her own name, a house with a past, a soul. When she had first walked through the rooms with the real estate agent, and had gazed at the hand-hewn beams and antique wallpaper, she'd known this house was special. And it had called to her, asking for her help.

'The location's unbeatable,' the agent had said. 'It comes with nearly an acre of land, something you seldom find any more this close to Boston.'

'Then why is it still for sale?' Julia had asked.

'You can see what bad shape it's in. When we first got the listing, there were boxes and boxes of books and old papers, stacked to the ceiling. It took a month for the heirs to haul it all away. Obviously, it needs bottom-up renovations, right down to the foundation.' The agent hesitated. 'There's another issue I should tell you about. The previous owner was a woman in her nineties, and she died here. That makes some buyers a bit squeamish.'

'In her nineties? Of natural causes, then?'

'That's the assumption. It was summertime. And it took almost three weeks before one of her relatives discovered . . .' The agent's voice trailed off. Suddenly she brightened. 'But hey, the land alone is special. You could tear down this whole place. Get rid of it and start fresh!'

The way the world gets rid of old wives like me, Julia had thought. This splendid, dilapidated house and I both deserve better.

That same afternoon, Julia had signed the purchase agreement.

Now, as she sat on the mound of earth, slapping at mosquitoes, she thought: What did I get myself into?

She swiped a hand over her eyes, and looked down at the hole again. How could she possibly expect to get her life in order when she couldn't even summon the strength to move one stupid rock?

She picked up a trowel and, leaning into the hole, began to scrape away soil. More of the stone emerged, like an iceberg's tip. She kept digging, deeper and deeper. Suddenly the rock symbolised every obstacle, every challenge that she'd ever wobbled away from. *I will not let you defeat me.*

With the trowel, she hacked at the soil beneath it, tunnelling deeper into the hole. She had two months before she'd have to face another classroom. Two months to uproot these weeds, nourish the soil, put in roses.

She dropped onto her belly and hacked away. Her trowel collided with something solid. Shoving back her hair, she stared down at what her tool had just hit. She brushed away soil and pebbles, exposing an unnaturally smooth dome. She felt her heart thudding against the earth, but she kept digging, with both hands now, gloved fingers scraping through stubborn clay. More of the dome emerged, curves knitted together by a jagged seam. Deeper and deeper she clawed, her pulse accelerating as she uncovered a small dirt-filled hollow. She pulled off her glove and prodded the caked earth with a bare finger. Suddenly the dirt fractured and crumbled away.

Julia stared down at what she had just revealed. A breeze feathered the grass, stirring the sweet-syrup smell of Queen Anne's lace. Julia's gaze lifted to her weed-ridden property, a place she had hoped to transform into a paradise. She'd imagined a vibrant garden of roses and peonies, an arbor twined with purple clematis. Now when she looked at this yard, she no longer saw a garden. She saw a graveyard.

'YOU COULD HAVE ASKED for my advice before you bought this shack,' said her sister, Vicky, sitting at Julia's kitchen table.

Julia stood at the window, staring out at the multiple mounds of earth that had sprung up in her back garden. For the past three days, a crew from the medical examiner's office had practically camped out in her yard.

Outside, the medical examiner, Dr Isles, had just arrived and was crossing towards the excavation site. Julia thought her an unsettling sort of woman, calm and collected with ghostly pale skin and Goth-black hair.

'It's not like you to just jump into something,' said Vicky. 'An offer on the first day you saw it? Did you think anyone else would snatch it up?' She pointed to the crooked cellar door. 'This place has to be a hundred years old.'

'It's a hundred and thirty,' Julia murmured. 'It's not such a bad property,' she insisted. 'It's got an acre of land. It's close to the city.'

'And it's got a dead body in the back yard.'

Vicky was right. Julia thought: I've poured my bank account into this house, and now I'm the proud owner of a cursed property. Through the window, she saw another newcomer arrive. It was an older woman with short grey hair, dressed in blue jeans and heavy work boots.

'Did you talk to Richard before you bought it?' Vicky asked. The change in her voice—suddenly quiet—made Julia turn to look at her sister.

'No, I didn't talk to him. Why are you asking?' said Julia.

'You were married to him. Don't you call him every so often, just to ask if he's forwarding your mail or something?'

Julia sank into a chair. 'I don't call him. And he doesn't call me.'

For a moment Vicky just sat in silence as Julia stoically stared down. 'I'm sorry,' she said finally. 'I'm so sorry you're still hurting.'

Julia gave a laugh. 'Yeah, well. I'm sorry, too.'

'It's been six months. I thought you'd be over him by now. You're bright, you're cute, you should be back in circulation.'

Vicky *would* say that. Suck-it-up Vicky who, five days after her appendectomy, had charged back into a courtroom to lead her team of attorneys to victory. She wouldn't let a little setback like divorce trip up her week.

Vicky sighed. 'To be honest, I didn't drive all the way over here just to see the house. You're my baby sister, and there's something you should know—' She stopped. Looked at the kitchen door, where someone had just knocked.

Julia opened the door to see Dr Isles, looking cool despite the heat.

'I wanted to let you know that my team will be leaving today,' Isles said. 'We've found enough to determine this is not an ME case. I've referred it to Dr Petrie, from Harvard.' Isles pointed to the older woman who had just arrived. 'She's a forensic anthropologist. She'll be completing the excavation, purely for research purposes. If you have no objection, Ms Hamill.'

'So the bones are old?'

'It's clearly not a recent burial. Why don't you come out and take a look?'

Vicky and Julia followed Isles down the sloping garden to where the remains were laid out on a tarp.

Dr Petrie sprang easily to her feet from a squat and came forward to shake their hands. 'You're the homeowner?' she asked Julia.

'I just bought the place. I moved in last week.'

Dr Isles said, 'We sifted a few items from the soil. Some old buttons and a buckle, clearly antique.' She reached into an evidence box sitting beside the bones. 'And today, we found this.' She pulled out a small ziplock bag. Through the plastic, Julia saw the glint of multicoloured gemstones.

'It's a regard ring,' said Dr Petrie. 'They were quite the rage in the early Victorian era. The names of the stones are meant to spell out a word. A ruby, emerald and garnet, for instance, would be the first three letters in the word *regard.* This ring is something you'd give as a token of affection.'

'Are these actually precious stones?'

'Oh, no. They're probably just coloured glass. The ring isn't engraved—it's just a mass-produced piece of jewellery.'

'Would there be burial records?'

'I doubt it,' Dr Petrie said. 'This appears to be something of an irregular interment. There's no gravestone, no coffin fragments. She was simply wrapped in a piece of hide and covered up.'

'Maybe she was poor.'

'But why choose this particular location? There was never a cemetery here. Your house is about a hundred and thirty years old, am I right?'

'It was built in 1880.'

'Regard rings were out of fashion by the 1840s.'

'What was here before 1840?' Julia asked.

'I believe this was part of a country estate, owned by a prominent Bostonian family. Most of this would have been open pasture. Farmland.'

Vicky stared down at the bones. 'Is this—one body?'

'A complete skeleton,' Dr Petrie said. 'She was buried deep enough to be protected from scavengers. Plus, it looks like she was wrapped in animal hide, and the leaching tannins are something of a preservative.'

'She?'

'Yes.' Dr Petrie looked up, sharp blue eyes narrowed against the sun. 'This is a female. Based on dentition, she was fairly young, certainly under thirty-five. All in all, she's in remarkably good shape.' Dr Petrie looked at Julia. 'Except for the crack you made with your trowel.'

Julia flushed. 'I thought the skull was a rock.'

'It's not a problem distinguishing between old and new fractures. Look.' Dr Petrie picked up the skull. 'The crack you made is right here, and it doesn't show any staining. But see this crack on the parietal bone? And there's another one here, under the cheek. These surfaces are stained brown from long exposure to dirt. That tells us these are pre-morbid fractures.'

'Pre-morbid?' Julia looked at her. 'Are you saying . . .'

'The blows almost certainly caused her death. I would call this a murder.'

IN THE NIGHT, Julia lay awake, listening to the creak of old floors and the rustle of mice in the walls. As old as this house was, the grave was even older. While men had been hammering together these beams, laying down the floors, only a few dozen paces away the corpse of an unknown woman had been mouldering in the earth.

Did no one know she was here? Did no one remember her?

She kicked aside the sheets and lay sweating atop the mattress. Even with both windows open, the bedroom felt airless. A firefly flashed in the darkness above her, its light winking as it circled the room. She sat up in bed and turned on the lamp, wondering how to catch it without killing it.

The phone rang. At eleven thirty, only one person would be calling.

'I hope I didn't wake you,' said Vicky. 'I just got home from one of those endless dinners.'

'It's too hot to sleep anyway.'

'Julia, there was something I wanted to tell you earlier, when I was there. But I couldn't, not with all those people around.'

'No more advice about this house, OK?'

'This isn't about the house. It's about Richard. I hate to be the one to tell you this, but you shouldn't have to hear through the grapevine.'

'Hear what?'

'Richard is getting married.'

Julia gripped the receiver so tightly her fingers went numb. In the long silence, she heard her own heartbeat pounding in her ear.

'So you didn't know.'

Julia whispered, 'No.'

'What a little shit he is,' Vicky muttered with enough bitterness for them both. 'It's been planned for over a month, that's what I heard. Someone named Tiffani with an *i.* I mean, how cutesy can you get?'

'I don't understand how this happened so quickly.'

'Oh, honey, he had to be running around with her while you were still married. Did he suddenly start coming home late? And there were all the business trips. A man doesn't ask for a divorce out of the blue.'

Julia swallowed. 'I don't want to talk about it right now.'

'Hey. Hey, are you OK?'

'I just don't want to talk.' Julia hung up.

For a long time, she sat motionless. Above her head, the firefly kept circling. She climbed up onto the mattress. As the firefly darted closer, she caught it in her hands. Palms cupped round the insect, she walked to the kitchen and opened the back door. There, on the porch, she released it.

Did it know she'd saved its life? One puny thing she was capable of.

She lingered on the porch, breathing in gulps of night air. Richard was getting married. Her breath caught in her throat, spilled out in a sob. She gripped the porch railing and felt splinters prick her fingers.

And I'm the last to find out.

November 1830

Death arrived with the sweet tinkling of bells. Rose Connolly had come to dread the sound, for she'd heard it too many times already as she sat beside her sister's hospital bed, dabbing Aurnia's forehead and holding her hand. Every day those cursed bells, rung by the acolyte, heralded the priest's arrival on the ward to administer the ritual of extreme unction. Though only seventeen years old, Rose had seen many lifetimes' worth of tragedy these last five days. On Sunday, Nora had died, three days after her wee babe was born. On Tuesday, after four days of feverish agonies following the birth of a son, Rebecca had mercifully succumbed, but only after Rose had been forced to endure the stench of the putrid discharges crusting the sheets. The whole ward smelt of sweat and fevers and purulence.

'The bells again,' Aurnia whispered. 'Which poor soul is it this time?'

Rose glanced down the lying-in ward, to where a curtain had been hastily drawn round one of the beds. She could hear the priest murmuring.

'Through the great goodness of His mercy, may God pardon thee . . .'

'Who?' Aurnia asked again. In her agitation, she struggled to sit up, to see over the row of beds.

'I fear it's Bernadette,' said Rose. She squeezed her sister's hand. 'She may yet live. Have a bit of hope. Her baby is healthy.'

Aurnia settled back against the pillow with a sigh, and the breath she exhaled carried the fetid odour of death. 'There's that small blessing, then.'

Blessing? That the boy would grow up an orphan? That his mother had spent the last three days whimpering as her belly bloated from childbed fever? If this was an example of His benevolence, then she wanted no part of Him. But she uttered no such blasphemy in her sister's presence. It was faith that had sustained Aurnia all these days as she laboured in vain to give birth to her first child.

'Rose?' Aurnia whispered. 'I'm greatly afeard 'tis time for me as well.'

'Time for what?'

'The priest. Confession.'

'And what small sins could possibly trouble you? God knows your soul, darling. Do you think He doesn't see the goodness there?'

'Oh, Rose, you don't know all the things I'm guilty of! All the things I'm too ashamed to tell you about! I can't die without—'

'Don't talk to me of dying. You can't give up. You have to *fight*.'

Aurnia responded with a weak smile and reached up to touch her sister's hair. 'My little Rosie. Never one to be afraid.'

But Rose was afraid. Terribly afraid that once Aurnia received the final blessing, she'd stop fighting and give up.

Aurnia closed her eyes and sighed. 'Hasn't Eben come?'

Rose's hand tensed round Aurnia's. 'Do you really want him here?'

'We're bound to each other, himself and me. For better or worse.'

Mostly for worse, Rose wanted to say, but held her tongue. Rose could scarcely abide the man's presence. For the past four months, she had lived with Aurnia and Eben in a Broad Street boarding house, her cot squeezed into a curtained alcove in their bedroom. She had tried to stay out of Eben's way, but, as Aurnia had grown heavy with pregnancy, Rose had taken on more and more of her sister's duties in Eben's tailor shop. In the back room, she had spied Eben's sly glances, had noticed how often he stood too close, inspecting her stitches as she laboured over trousers and waistcoats.

Rose wrung out a cloth over the basin and, as she pressed it to Aurnia's forehead, she wondered, Where has my pretty sister gone? Not even a year of marriage and already the light had left Aurnia's eyes, the sheen gone from her flame-coloured hair, her face a dull mask of surrender.

Aurnia lifted her arm from beneath the sheet. 'I want you to have this,' she whispered. 'Take it now, before Eben does.' Aurnia touched the heart-shaped gold locket that hung round her neck. A gift from Eben, Rose assumed. Once, he had cared enough about his wife to give her such a fancy trinket.

'Please. Help me take it off.'

'It's not the time for you to be giving it away,' said Rose.

But Aurnia managed to slip off the necklace by herself and she placed it in her sister's hand. 'It's yours. For all the comfort you've given me.'

'I'll keep it safe for you, 'tis all.' Rose placed it into her pocket. 'When this is over, darling, I'll put it back round your neck.'

Aurnia smiled. 'If only that could be.'

The receding tinkle of bells told her the priest had finished his ministrations to the dying Bernadette, and Nurse Mary Robinson scurried over to pull back the curtain in preparation for the next visitors, who had just arrived.

Dr Chester Crouch walked onto the lying-in ward, accompanied by the hospital's head nurse, Miss Agnes Poole, as well as an entourage of four medical students. Dr Crouch started his rounds at the first bed, occupied by a woman who had been admitted after two days of fruitless labour at home. The students watched as Dr Crouch slipped his arm under the sheet to discreetly examine the patient. She gave a cry of pain as he probed deep between her thighs. His hand re-emerged, fingers streaked with blood.

'Towel,' he requested, and Nurse Poole promptly handed him one. Wiping his hand, he said to the four students, 'This patient is not progressing. The cervix has not fully dilated. How should her physician proceed? You, Mr Kingston! Have you an answer?'

Mr Kingston, a handsome and dapper young man, answered without hesitation, 'I believe that ergot in souchong tea is recommended.'

'Good. What else might one do?' He focused on the shortest of the four students, an elf-like fellow with large ears to match. 'Mr Holmes?'

'One could try a cathartic, to stimulate contractions,' Mr Holmes promptly answered.

'Good. And you, Mr Lackaway?' Dr Crouch turned to a fair-haired man whose startled face instantly flushed red. 'What else might be done?'

'I—that is—I would have to think about it.'

'*Think* about it? Your grandfather and father were both physicians! Your uncle's dean of the medical college. Come now, Mr Lackaway! Have you nothing to contribute?'

Helplessly the young man shook his head. 'I'm sorry, sir.'

Sighing, Dr Crouch turned to the fourth student, a tall dark-haired young man. 'Your turn, Mr Marshall. What else might be done in this situation? A patient in labour, who is not progressing?'

The student said, 'I would urge her to sit up or stand, sir. And if she is able, she should walk about the ward.'

'And what of bleeding the patient as a treatment?'

A pause. Then, deliberately, 'I am not convinced of its efficacy.'

Dr Crouch gave a startled laugh. 'You—*you* are not convinced?'

'On the farm where I grew up, I experimented with bleeding, as well as cupping. I lost just as many calves with it as without it.'

'On the *farm*? We are dealing with human beings here, not beasts, Mr Marshall,' said Dr Crouch. 'A therapeutic bleeding, I've found in my own experience, is quite effective for relieving pain.'

He handed the soiled towel back to Nurse Poole and moved on, to Bernadette's bed. 'And this one?' he asked.

'Though her fever has abated,' said Nurse Poole, 'the discharge has become quite foul. She spent the night in great discomfort.'

Again, Dr Crouch reached under the sheet to palpate the internal organs. Bernadette gave a weak groan. 'Yes, her skin is quite cool,' he concurred. He looked up. 'She has received morphine?'

'Several times, sir. As you ordered.'

His hand came out from beneath the sheet, fingers glistening with yellowish slime, and the nurse handed him the same soiled towel. 'Continue the morphine,' he said quietly. 'Keep her comfortable.' It was as good as a death pronouncement.

Bed by bed, patient by patient, Dr Crouch made his way down the ward. By the time he reached Aurnia's bed, the towel he used to wipe his hands was soaked with blood.

Rose stood to greet him. 'Dr Crouch.'

He frowned at her. 'It's Miss . . .'

'Connolly,' said Rose, wondering why this man could not seem to remember her name. She had been the one to summon him to the lodging house where, for a day and a night, Aurnia had laboured without success.

Dr Crouch reached beneath the sheet, and as he probed the birth canal, Aurnia gave a moan of agony.

He straightened and looked at Nurse Poole. 'She is not yet fully dilated.' He dried his hand on the filthy towel. 'How many days has it been?'

'Today is the fifth,' said Nurse Poole.

He took Aurnia's wrist and felt the pulse. 'Her heart rate is rapid. And she feels a bit feverish today. A bleeding should cool the system and—'

'You have bled her enough,' cut in Rose.

Dr Crouch glanced up, clearly startled. 'What relation are you again?'

'Her sister. I was here when you bled her the first time, Dr Crouch. And the second time, and the third.'

'And you can see how she's benefited,' said Nurse Poole.

'I can tell you she has not.'

'Do you wish me to treat her or not?' snapped Dr Crouch.

'Yes, sir, but not to bleed her dry!'

'I have no time to bleed her today, anyway.' Dr Crouch pointedly looked at his pocket watch. 'I'll stop in to see the patient first thing in the morning. Perhaps by then, it will be more obvious to Miss, er—'

'Connolly,' said Rose.

'—to Miss Connolly that further treatment is indeed necessary. Gentlemen, I shall see you at the morning lecture, nine a.m.' He strode away, the four medical students trailing after like obedient ducklings.

Rose ran after them. 'Sir? Mr Marshall, isn't it?'

The tallest of the students turned. It was the dark-haired young man who'd said he'd grown up on a farm. One look at his ill-fitting suit told her that he indeed came from humbler circumstances than his classmates. As his colleagues continued out of the ward, Mr Marshall stood looking at her expectantly. He has such a weary face for a young man, she thought. Unlike the others, he gazed straight at her, as though regarding an equal.

'I heard your words to the doctor,' she said. 'About bleeding.'

The young man shook his head. 'I spoke too freely, I'm afraid.'

'And am I wrong, sir? Should I allow him to bleed my sister?'

He glanced, uneasily, at Nurse Poole, who was watching them with clear disapproval. 'I'm not qualified to give advice. I'm only a first-year student. Dr Crouch is my preceptor, and a fine doctor.'

'I've watched him bleed her three times, but to tell God's truth, I see no improvement. Every day, I see only . . .' Rose stopped, her voice breaking. She said softly, 'I only want what's best for Aurnia—'

Nurse Poole cut in, 'You're asking a *medical student*?' She gave a snort and walked out of the ward.

For a moment Mr Marshall was silent. Only after Nurse Poole was out of the room did he speak again.

'I would not bleed her,' he said quietly. 'It would do no good.'

'What would you do? If she were your own sister?'

The man gave the sleeping Aurnia a pitying look. 'I would apply cool compresses for the fever, morphine for pain. I would see that she receives sufficient nourishment and fluids. And comfort, Miss Connolly,' he said sadly, and turned away.

Rose walked back to Aurnia's bed. Was I wrong to bring her here? she wondered. Should I have kept her at home? The room in their boarding house was cramped and cold, and Dr Crouch had recommended Aurnia be moved to the hospital, where he could more easily attend her. 'For charity cases such as your sister's,' he'd said, 'the cost will be what your family can bear.'

Rose looked down the row of suffering women. Her gaze stopped on Bernadette, who lay silent. The young woman who, only a few days ago, had laughed as she'd held her newborn son in her arms, had stopped breathing.

TWO

'How long can this blasted rain keep up?' said Edward Kingston, staring at the steady downpour.

Wendell Holmes blew out a wreath of cigar smoke that drifted from beneath the hospital's covered verandah and fractured into swirls in the rain. 'Why the impatience? Anyone would think you have a pressing appointment.'

'I do. With a glass of exceptional claret.'

'Are we going to the Hurricane?' said Charles Lackaway.

'If my carriage ever shows up.' Edward glared at the road, where horses clip-clopped and carriages rolled past, wheels throwing up clots of mud.

Though Norris Marshall also stood on the hospital verandah, the gulf between him and his classmates would have been apparent even at a casual glance. Norris was new to Boston, a farm boy from Belmont who had taught himself physics with borrowed textbooks, who'd bartered eggs and milk for lessons with a Latin tutor. He had never been to the Hurricane Tavern. His classmates, all Harvard graduates, gossiped about people he did not know and shared inside jokes he did not understand. He was not part of their social circle.

Edward sighed. 'Can you believe what that girl said to Dr Crouch? The gall of her! If any of the Bridgets in our household ever spoke that way, my mother would slap her. It's important that the Irish know their place.'

'Her sister may well be dying,' said Norris.

The three Harvard men turned, obviously surprised that their usually reticent classmate had spoken up.

'Five days in labour and already she looks like a corpse. Her prospects do not look good. The sister knows this and she speaks from grief.'

'Nevertheless, she should remember where charity comes from,' said Edward.

'And be grateful for every crumb?'

'Dr Crouch is not bound to treat the woman at all. Yet that sister acts as though it's their right,' Edward said. 'A little gratitude wouldn't kill them.'

Norris felt his face flush. He was about to offer a sharp retort in defence of the girl when Wendell smoothly redirected the conversation.

'I do think there's a poem in this, don't you? "The Fierce Irish Girl".' He paused. 'Here stands the fiercest warrior, this true and winsome maid . . .'

'Her sister's life the battlefield,' added Charles.

'She—she—' Wendell pondered the next verse in the poem.

'Stands guard, unafraid!' Charles finished.

Wendell laughed. 'Poetry triumphs again!'

'While the rest of us suffer,' Edward muttered.

All this Norris listened to with the acute discomfort of an outsider. How easily his classmates laughed together.

Wendell peered through the rain. 'That's your carriage, isn't it, Edward?'

'About time it showed up,' Edward said. 'Gentlemen, shall we?'

Norris's three classmates headed down the steps. Edward and Charles splashed through the rain and clambered into the carriage. But Wendell paused, glanced over his shoulder at Norris, and came back up.

'Aren't you joining us?' he said.

Startled by the invitation, Norris didn't immediately answer. Though he stood a full head taller than Wendell Holmes, there was much about this diminutive man that intimidated him. It was more than Wendell's dapper suits, his famously clever tongue; it was his air of utter self-assurance.

'Wendell!' Edward called from the carriage. 'Let's go!'

'We're going to the Hurricane,' said Holmes. 'Seems to be where we end up every night.' He paused. 'Or have you other plans?'

'It's very kind of you.' Norris glanced at the two men who were waiting in the carriage. 'But I don't think Mr Kingston was expecting a fourth.'

'Mr Kingston,' said Wendell with a laugh, 'could use more of the unexpected in his life. Anyway, he's not the one inviting you. I am.'

Norris looked at the rain, falling in sheets, and longed for the warm fire that would almost certainly be burning in the Hurricane. More than that, he longed for the chance to slip in among his classmates, to share their circle.

'Wendell!' Now it was Charles calling from the carriage. 'We're freezing!'

'I'm sorry,' said Norris. 'I'm afraid I have another engagement.'

'Oh?' Wendell's eyebrow lifted in a mischievous tilt. 'I trust she's a charming alternative.'

'It's not a lady, I'm afraid. But it's simply something I can't break.'

'I see,' said Wendell, though clearly he didn't, for his smile had cooled and already he was turning to leave. 'Another time, perhaps.'

There won't be another time, thought Norris as he watched Wendell dash into the street and climb in with his two companions. He imagined the conversation that would soon take place in that carriage. Disbelief that a mere farm boy from Belmont had dared to decline the invitation.

While they sit warm in the Hurricane, thought Norris, I shall be engaged in quite a different activity. One I would avoid, if only I could. He braced himself for the cold, then stepped into the downpour and splashed resolutely towards his lodgings, there to change into old clothes before heading out, yet again, into the rain.

The establishment he sought was the Black Spar, a tavern in Broad Street near the docks. Norris knew many of the patrons, and they merely glanced up as he stepped in the door. He moved to the bar, where moon-faced Fanny Burke was filling glasses with ale. She looked up at him with small, mean eyes. 'You're late and he's in a foul mood. He's round the back.'

Norris had not had time for supper and he glanced hungrily at the loaf of bread she kept behind the counter but didn't bother to beg a slice. Fanny Burke gave nothing away for free, not even a smile. With stomach rumbling, he pushed through a door and stepped outside.

The rear yard smelt of wet straw and horse dung, and the rain had churned the ground into a sea of mud. Beneath the stable overhang, a horse gave a nicker, and Norris saw that it was already harnessed to the dray.

'Not going to wait for you next time, boy!' Fanny's husband, Jack, emerged from the shadows of the stable. He carried two shovels, which he threw in the back of the wagon. 'Want to be paid, get here at the appointed hour.' With a grunt, he hoisted himself up and took the reins. 'You comin'?'

Norris scrambled up into the dray beside Jack, who gave the horse an impatient flick of his whip. They rolled across the yard and out of the gate.

'How far are we going this time?' asked Norris.

'Does it matter?' Jack hacked up a gob of phlegm and spat into the street.

No, it didn't matter. As far as Norris was concerned, this was a night he simply had to endure.

The dray rocked over the cobblestones, and in the back of the cart the two shovels rattled, a reminder of the unpleasant task that lay ahead. He'd prefer to be studying or at the Hurricane, but this was the bargain he'd struck with the college, a bargain he'd gratefully agreed to. This is all for a higher purpose, he thought, as they rolled out of Boston, moving west.

'Came by this way two days ago,' said Jack, and spat again. 'Stopped at that tavern there.' He pointed and, through the veil of falling rain, Norris saw the glow of firelight in a window. 'The proprietor said there's a whole family in town, two young ladies and a brother, ailing from the consumption. All of 'em doing quite poorly.' He made a sound that might have been a laugh. 'Have to check again tomorrow, see if they're getting ready to pass on. Any luck, we'll have three at once.' Jack looked at Norris. 'I'll be needing you for that one.'

Norris gave a stiff nod, his dislike of this man suddenly so strong he could scarcely abide being seated next to him.

'Oh, you think you're too damn good for this,' said Jack. 'Don't you?'

Norris didn't answer.

'Too good to be around the likes of me.'

'I do this for a greater good.'

Jack laughed. 'Some high-and-mighty words for a farmer. Think you're going to make a fine living, eh? You think this will make you one of those gentlemen? You think they'll invite you to their fancy oyster parties?'

Norris sighed. 'Today, any man can rise above his station.'

'Do you s'pose *they* know that? Those Harvard gentlemen?'

Norris went silent, wondering if perhaps Jack had a point. He thought once again of Wendell Holmes and Kingston and Lackaway, sitting in the Hurricane. A world away from the filthy Black Spar, where Fanny Burke reigned over her foul kingdom of the hopeless.

Jack snapped the reins and the dray jolted ahead through mud and ruts. 'Still a ways to go,' he said and gave a snorting laugh.

By the time Jack finally pulled the rig to a stop, Norris's clothes were soaked through. Stiff and shaking from the cold, he climbed out of the cart. His shoes splashed ankle-deep in mud.

Jack thrust the shovels into his hands. 'Make quick work of it.' He grabbed trowels, a lantern and a tarp from the cart, then led the way across sodden grass, weaving among the headstones until he stopped at a muddy mound of bare earth.

'Buried just today,' said Jack, taking a shovel. Eyeing the grave, he muttered, 'Head should be at this end,' and scooped up a shovelful of mud.

'Came through here a fortnight ago,' he said, flinging the mud aside. 'Heard this one was near to giving up the ghost.'

Norris set to work as well. Though it was a fresh burial and the dirt had not settled, the soil was soaked and heavy.

'Someone dies, people talk about it,' panted Jack. 'They order coffins, buy flowers.' He flung aside another scoop and paused, wheezing. 'Trick is not to let 'em know you're interested.' He resumed digging, but at a slower pace. Norris did the lion's share. Rain continued to fall, puddling in the hole, and Norris's trousers were caked with mud all the way up to his knees. Soon Jack climbed out of the hole to squat at the edge, his wheezing now so loud that Norris glanced up, just to be certain the man was not on the verge of collapse. This was the only reason the old miser ever brought along an assistant: he could no longer do it alone. He knew where the prizes were buried, but he needed a young man's muscles to dig them up.

Norris's shovel hit wood.

'About time,' grunted Jack. Beneath the cover of the tarp, he lit the lantern, then grabbed his shovel and slid back into the hole. The men scraped away mud from the coffin, revealing the head end of it.

Jack slipped two iron hooks under the lid and handed a rope to Norris. They climbed out of the hole and together pulled against the lid, both of them straining as the wood groaned. The lid suddenly splintered and the rope went slack, sending Norris sprawling backwards.

'That's it. That's good enough,' said Jack. He lowered the lantern into the hole and looked down upon the coffin's occupant.

The corpse was a woman, her skin pale as tallow. Golden ringlets of hair framed her face, and resting upon her bodice was a bunch of dried flowers. So beautiful, thought Norris. An angel, too soon called to heaven.

'Fresh as can be,' said Jack with a happy cackle. He slipped his hands under the girl's arms. She was light enough that he could drag her, unassisted, out of the coffin and onto the tarp. 'Let's get her clothes off.'

Norris, suddenly feeling nauseated, didn't move.

'What? Don't want to touch a pretty girl?'

Norris shook his head. 'She deserves better.'

'You didn't have no problem with the last one we dug up.'

'That was an old man.'

'All I know is that she'll fetch the same price.' He pulled out a knife, slipped the blade under the neckline of the corpse's dress and tore the gown open down the front to reveal a gossamer-thin chemise beneath it.

Methodically, he ripped open the skirt and pulled off the tiny satin slippers. Norris could only watch, appalled by the violation of this young woman's modesty. Yet he knew it must be done, for the law was unforgiving. To be caught with a stolen corpse was serious enough; to be caught in possession of a corpse's stolen property was to risk far worse penalties. So Jack stripped away the clothes, removed the rings from her fingers, the satin ribbons from her hair. He tossed them all into the coffin, then glanced at Norris.

'You gonna help carry her back to the wagon or not?' he growled.

Norris stared down at the naked corpse, her skin white as alabaster. She was painfully thin, her body consumed by some unforgiving illness.

'Who's out there?' a distant voice shouted. 'Who trespasses?'

At once Jack doused the lantern and whispered, 'Get her out of sight!' Norris dragged the corpse back into the open grave, then both he and Jack scrambled into the hole as well. Pressed close to the corpse, Norris felt his heart pounding against her chilled skin. He listened for the footsteps of the watchman, but all he could hear was the beating rain and the thump of his own pulse. It was Jack who finally dared to raise his head and peer out of the hole. 'I don't see him,' he whispered. 'Best we move her quick.'

They did not relight the lantern. While Jack lifted the feet, Norris gripped the nude body beneath the arms, and he felt the corpse's damp hair drape across his arms as he lifted her shoulders from the hole.

The rain slowed to a drizzle as they quickly refilled the hole, shovelling mud back onto the now vacant coffin. When the last of the earth had been replaced, they smoothed over the ground as best they could with their shovels. In time, the grass would grow in, a headstone would be planted, and loved ones would continue to lay flowers on a grave where no one slept.

They wrapped the corpse in the tarp, then Norris carried her to the cart and set her down gently. Jack tossed the shovels in beside her.

As they rode back to town, Norris found no reason to exchange words with Jack, so he kept his silence, longing only for the night to be over so he could part ways with this repellent man.

By the time they turned onto the cobblestoned street behind the apothecary shop, Jack was whistling. Anticipating, no doubt, the cash that would soon line his pocket. They rumbled to a stop on the paving stones. Jack jumped down from the dray and knocked on the shop's back door. A moment later the door opened and Norris saw the glow of a lamp shining through the crack.

'We got one,' said Jack.

The door opened wider, revealing the bearded, heavyset man holding the lamp. 'Bring it in, then. And be quiet about it.'

Norris lifted the tarp-covered body and carried her through the open doorway. The man with the lamp met his gaze with a nod of recognition. 'Upstairs, Dr Sewall?' asked Norris.

'You know the way, Mr Marshall.'

Yes, Norris knew the way, for it was not the first time he had carried a corpse up this narrow stairway. He reached the first floor and paused in the dark. Dr Sewall squeezed past him and led the way up the hall. Norris followed him through the last doorway, into a room where a table waited to receive its precious merchandise, and laid the corpse down. Jack had followed them up the stairs and stationed himself at one end of the table.

Sewall approached the body and pulled back the tarp. 'Yes, she's in good condition,' he murmured as he peeled away the tarp, exposing the naked torso. Sewall straightened and gave a nod. 'She'll do, Mr Burke.' He produced a small cloth bag, which he handed to Jack. 'Your fee.'

'There's only fifteen dollars in here. We agreed on twenty.'

'You required Mr Marshall's services tonight. Five dollars is credited towards his tuition. That adds up to twenty.'

'I know damn well what it adds up to,' said Jack, ramming the money into his pocket. 'And for what I provide, it's not nearly enough.'

'Twenty dollars per specimen is what I pay. Whether or not you need an assistant is your decision. But I doubt that Mr Marshall here will work without adequate compensation.'

Jack shot a resentful look at Norris. 'He's my muscle, that's all. I'm the one who knows where to find 'em.' He turned to leave. In the doorway, he paused and reluctantly looked back at Norris. 'The Black Spar, Thursday night. Seven o'clock,' he snapped, and walked out. His footsteps thumped heavily down the stairs and the door slammed shut.

'Is there no one else you can call on?' asked Norris. 'He's the worst kind of filth.'

'All resurrectionists are alike. If our laws were more enlightened, then vermin like him would not be in business at all. Until that day, we're forced to deal with the likes of Mr Burke.'

'I'd happily choose any employment but this, Dr Sewall. Is there no other task I could perform?'

'There's no need more pressing to our college than the procurement of specimens.'

Norris gazed down at the girl and said softly, 'I don't think she ever imagined herself as a *specimen*.'

'We are all specimens, Mr Marshall. Take away the soul, and any body is the same as another. Heart, lungs, kidneys. It's always a tragedy, of course, for one so young to die.' Briskly, Dr Sewall pulled the tarp over the corpse. 'But in death, she will serve a nobler purpose.'

THE SOUND OF MOANING woke Rose. Sometime in the night she had fallen asleep in the chair beside Aurnia's bed. Now she lifted her head and suddenly saw that her sister's eyes were open, her face contorted in pain.

Rose straightened. 'Aurnia?'

'I cannot bear this any longer. If only I could die now.'

Rose focused on Aurnia's bedsheet. On the stain of fresh blood. She shot to her feet in alarm. 'I'll find a nurse.'

'And the priest, Rose. Please.'

Rose hurried from the ward. Oil lamps cast their weak glow against the shadows and the flames wavered as she ran past. By the time she returned to her sister's bed with Nurse Robinson and Nurse Poole, the stain on Aurnia's sheet had spread to a widening swath of bright red. Miss Poole snapped to the other nurse, 'We move her to surgery at once!'

There was no time to send for Dr Crouch; instead, the young house physician, Dr Berry, was roused from his room in the hospital grounds. He stumbled sleepily into the surgery room where Aurnia had been rushed. Instantly he paled at the sight of so much bleeding.

'We must evacuate the womb,' he said, and fumbled through his bag of instruments. 'The baby may have to be sacrificed.'

Aurnia gave an anguished cry of protest. 'No. No, my baby must live!'

'Hold her down,' he ordered. 'This will be painful.'

'Rose,' pleaded Aurnia. 'Don't let him kill my baby!'

Aurnia writhed as a fresh contraction gripped her, and her moan rose to a scream. 'Oh God, the pain!'

'Tie down her hands, Miss Poole,' ordered Dr Berry. He looked at Rose. 'And you, girl! Come here and help hold her down if need be.'

Shaking, Rose moved closer to the bed. His surgical instruments were soon scattered across a low table as he frantically rummaged for the right tool. The instrument he picked up was a frightening device, by all appearances designed to maim and crush.

'Don't hurt my baby,' Aurnia moaned. 'Please.'

'I'll try to preserve your child's life,' said Dr Berry. 'But I need you to lie perfectly still, madam. Do you understand?'

Aurnia managed a weak nod.

The two nurses tied down Aurnia's hands, then stationed themselves on either side of the bed, each grasping a leg.

'You, girl! Take her shoulders,' Nurse Poole ordered Rose. 'Keep her pressed to the bed.'

Rose moved to the head of the bed and placed her hands on Aurnia's shoulders. Her sister's milk-white face stared up at her, long red hair spilling across the pillow, green eyes wild with panic. Suddenly her face contorted in pain and she tried to rock forward, her head lifting off the bed.

'Hold her still! Hold her!' ordered Dr Berry. Grasping his monstrous forceps, he leaned in between Aurnia's thighs and Aurnia shrieked as though her very soul was being wrenched from her body. A burst of red suddenly splattered the young doctor's shirt and he jerked away.

Aurnia's head flopped back against the pillow and she lay panting, her screams now reduced to whimpers. In the sudden quiet, another sound rose. A strange mewing that steadily crescendoed to a wail.

The child. The child is alive!

The doctor straightened, and in his arms he held the newborn girl, the skin bluish and streaked with blood. He handed the baby to Nurse Robinson, who quickly wrapped the crying infant in a towel.

Rose stared at the doctor's shirt. So much blood. Everywhere she looked—the mattress, the sheets—she saw blood.

Nurse Robinson brought the swaddled infant to Aurnia's bed. 'Here's your little girl, Mrs Tate. See how lovely she is!'

Aurnia struggled to focus on her new daughter. 'Margaret,' she whispered, and Rose felt the sudden sting of tears. It was their mother's name. *If only she were alive to see her first grandchild.*

'Tell Eben,' Aurnia whispered. 'He doesn't know.'

'I'll send for him. I'll *make* him come,' said Rose.

'There's too much bleeding.' Dr Berry thrust his hand between Aurnia's thighs. 'But I can feel no retained placenta.' Pressing his hands on Aurnia's belly, he vigorously massaged the abdomen. The blood continued to soak into the sheets, seeping in a wider and wider stain. 'Cold water,' he ordered. 'As cold as you can get it! We'll need compresses. And ergot!'

Nurse Robinson set the swaddled infant in the crib and scurried from the room to fetch what he had asked for.

'He doesn't know,' Aurnia moaned.

'She *must* lie quiet!' Dr Berry ordered.

'Before I die, someone must tell him he has a child . . .'

The door flew open and Nurse Robinson hurried back in, carrying a basin of water. 'It's as cold as I could make it, Dr Berry,' she said.

The doctor soaked a towel, wrung it out, and placed the frigid compress on the patient's abdomen. 'Give her the ergot!'

In the cradle, the newborn cried harder, her wail more piercing with each breath. Nurse Poole looked at Rose. 'For pity's sake, take that baby out of here! We need to attend to your sister.'

Rose took the screaming infant and reluctantly crossed towards the door. There she stopped and looked back at her sister. The last remnants of colour were slowly draining from Aurnia's face as she whispered silent words.

Please be merciful, God. If You hear this prayer, let my sweet sister live.

Rose stepped out of the room. There in the gloomy hallway, she rocked the crying infant. She slipped her finger into little Margaret's mouth, and toothless gums clamped down as she began to suck.

In the dark passage, only a single flame glowed. Standing beneath it, Rose studied the baby's pale and downy hair. She examined five little fingers and marvelled at the hand's plump perfection. She placed her hand on the tiny chest and felt the beating of her heart, quick as a bird's. Such a sweet girl, she thought. My little Meggie.

At that moment, the door swung open, spilling light into the hall. Nurse Poole came out of the room, closing the door behind her. She halted and stared at Rose, as though surprised to see her still there.

Fearing the worst, Rose asked, 'My sister?'

'The bleeding has stopped, that's all I can tell you,' snapped Nurse Poole. 'Now take the baby to the ward. It's warmer there. This hall is far too draughty for a newborn.' She turned and hurried away down the corridor.

Rose carried the baby back to the lying-in ward and sat down in her old chair beside Aurnia's empty bed. As the night wore on, the baby fell asleep in her arms. Wind rattled the windows and sleet ticked against the glass, but there was no word of Aurnia's condition.

From outside came the rumble of wheels over cobblestones. Rose crossed to the window. In the courtyard, a horse and phaeton rolled to a stop. The horse suddenly gave a panicked snort, its hoofs dancing nervously as it threatened to bolt. A second later Rose saw the reason for the beast's alarm: merely a large dog, which trotted across the courtyard.

'Miss Connolly.'

Startled, Rose turned to see Agnes Poole. The woman had slipped into the ward so quietly Rose had not heard her approach.

'Give me the baby.'

'But she sleeps so soundly,' said Rose.

'Your sister cannot possibly nurse the baby. She's far too weak. The infant asylum is here to fetch her. They'll provide a wet nurse.'

Rose stared at the nurse in disbelief. 'But she has a mother!'

'A mother who most likely will not live.' Nurse Poole held out her arms, and her hands looked like unwelcoming claws. 'Give her to me.'

'Did Aurnia agree to this? Let me speak to her.'

'She's unconscious. She can't say anything.'

'Then I'll speak *for* her. This is my niece, Miss Poole, my own family.' Rose hugged the baby tighter. 'I'll give her up to no stranger.'

Agnes Poole's face had gone rigid in frustration and she appeared ready to wrench the baby from Rose's arms. Instead, she turned and swept out of the ward, her skirt snapping smartly with every stride.

Rose went back to the window and watched as Agnes Poole materialised from the shadows of the walkway and crossed to the waiting phaeton to speak to the occupant. A moment later the driver snapped the whip and the horse clopped forward. As the vehicle drove out of the gate, Agnes Poole stood alone, her silhouette framed by the glistening stones of the courtyard.

Rose looked down at the baby in her arms. *No one will ever take you from me. Not while I still breathe.*

THREE

The Present

'Thank you for seeing me on such short notice, Dr Isles.' Julia took a seat in the medical examiner's office. 'You probably don't get many requests like mine, but I really need to know. For my own peace of mind.'

'Dr Petrie's the one you should be talking to,' said Isles. 'The skeleton is a forensic anthropology case.'

'I'm not here about that skeleton. I've already spoken to Dr Petrie and she had nothing new to tell me.'

'Then how can I help you?'

'When I bought my house, the real estate agent told me that the previous owner was an elderly woman who'd died on the property. Everyone assumed it was a natural death. But a few days ago, my neighbour mentioned there'd been several burglaries in the area. Now I'm starting to wonder if . . .'

'If it wasn't a natural death?' said Isles bluntly.

Julia met the medical examiner's gaze. 'Yes.'

'I'd have to know the name of the deceased.'

'I have it right here.' Julia handed a bundle of photocopies to Isles. 'It's her obituary, from the local paper. Her name was Hilda Chamblett.'

'So you've already been digging into this.'

'It's been on my mind.' Julia gave an embarrassed laugh. 'Plus, there's that old skeleton in my back yard. I'm feeling a little uneasy that two women have died there.'

'At least a hundred years apart.'

'It's the one last year that really bothers me.'

Isles nodded. 'I suppose it would bother me, too. Let me find the report.' She left the office and returned moments later with the file. 'The autopsy was done by Dr Costas,' she said, as she sat down at her desk. She opened the file. '"Chamblett, Hilda, age ninety-two, found in the back yard of her Weston residence. Remains were found by a family member who had been away and had not checked on her for three weeks."' Isles flipped to a new page and paused. 'The photos aren't particularly pleasant,' she said.

Julia swallowed. 'Maybe you could just read me the conclusions?'

Isles once again began to read aloud. '"Body was found in a supine position, surrounded by tall grass and weeds . . . No skin or soft tissue is found intact on any exposed surfaces. Shreds of clothing still adhere to parts of the torso. In the neck, cervical vertebrae are clearly visible and soft tissues are lacking. Large and small bowel are largely missing, and remaining lungs, liver and spleen have defects with serrated margins. Noted around the corpse are numerous bird droppings."' Isles looked up. '"Assumed to be from crows."' She closed the folder. 'That's the report.'

'You haven't told me the cause of death.'

'Because it was indeterminable. She was ninety-two. It was a hot summer, and she was out alone in her garden. It's reasonable to assume she had a cardiac event.'

'But you can't be sure. So it could have been . . .'

'Murder?' Isles's gaze was direct. 'This particular death just doesn't ring any alarm bells for me. In the case of a ninety-two-year-old woman found dead in her own back yard, murder isn't the first thing that comes to mind.'

Julia sighed. 'I'm sorry I ever bought the house. I haven't had a good night's sleep since I moved in. I've been having dreams.'

'What sort of dreams?'

'It's been three weeks now and I keep hoping they'll go away, that it's just from the shock of finding those bones in my garden.'

'That could give anyone nightmares.'

'I don't believe in ghosts. Really, I don't. But I feel as if she's trying to talk to me. Asking me to *do* something.'

'The deceased owner? Or the skeleton?'

'I don't know. *Someone*.'

Isles's expression remained utterly neutral. But her words left no doubt where she stood on the matter. 'I'm not sure I can help you with that. I'm just a pathologist and I've told you my professional opinion.'

'And in your professional opinion, murder is still a possibility, isn't it?' insisted Julia. 'You can't rule it out.'

Isles hesitated. 'No,' she finally conceded. 'I can't.'

THAT NIGHT, Julia dreamed of crows. Hundreds of them were perched in a dead tree, staring down at her with yellow eyes. Waiting.

She startled awake to the noise of raucous caws and opened her eyes to see the light of early morning through her uncurtained window. A pair of black wings glided past like a scythe wheeling through the sky. Then another. She climbed out of bed and went to the window.

The oak tree they occupied was not dead, as in her dream, but was fully leafed out in the lush growth of summer. At least two dozen crows had gathered there, perched like strange black fruit among the branches. She turned away and thought. I have to hang some curtains on this window.

In the kitchen, she made coffee and spread butter and jam on toast. Outside, there was a noisy eruption of cawing and flapping wings. She looked out of the window to see the crows suddenly lift simultaneously into the air and fly away. Then she focused on the far corner of her yard, down near the stream, and she understood why the crows had fled so abruptly.

A man stood on the edge of her property. He was staring at her house.

She jerked away so he couldn't see her. Slowly, she eased back towards the window and peered out. He was lean and dark-haired, dressed against the morning chill in blue jeans and a brown sweater.

He took two steps towards her house.

She ran across the kitchen and snatched up the cordless phone. Darting back to the window, she looked out to see where he was, but could no longer glimpse him. Then something scratched at the kitchen door.

'McCoy!' a voice called out. 'Come on, boy, get away from there!'

Glancing out of the window again, she saw the man suddenly pop up from behind tall weeds. Then a golden labrador trotted into view and crossed the yard towards the man. He bent down to clip a leash onto the dog's collar. As he straightened, his gaze met Julia's through the window and he waved.

She put the phone down, opened the kitchen door and stepped outside.

'Sorry about that!' he called out. 'I didn't mean to trespass, but he got away from me. He thinks Hilda still lives there. She used to keep a box of dog biscuits just for him.'

She walked down the slope towards him. He no longer frightened her. She could not imagine a rapist or murderer owning such a friendly animal. The dog was practically dancing at the end of the leash as she approached, eager to make her acquaintance.

'You're the new owner, I take it?' he said.

'Julia Hamill.'

'Tom Page. I live right down the road.' He started to shake her hand, then remembered the plastic bag he was holding and gave an embarrassed laugh. 'Oops. Doggy doo. I was trying to pick up after him.'

So that's why he'd crouched momentarily in the grass, she thought.

The dog jumped up on his hind legs, begging for Julia's attention.

'Down, boy!' Tom yanked on the leash and the dog reluctantly obeyed.

He was maybe in his early forties, she thought. Through her kitchen window, his hair had appeared black; now that she was closer, she could see threads of grey mingled there, and his dark eyes, squinting in the morning sunlight, were framed by well-used laugh lines.

'I'm glad somebody finally bought Hilda's place. She really couldn't keep it up. This garden was too much for her, but she'd never let anyone else work in it. If she had, they might've found that skeleton a long time ago.'

'You've heard about it.'

'The whole neighbourhood has.' He looked at her, his eyes so direct it made her feel uneasy. 'How do you like the neighbourhood?' he asked. 'Aside from the skeletons?'

She hugged herself in the morning chill. 'I don't know. I love Weston, but I'm a little spooked by the bones. I wish I knew who she was.'

'The university couldn't tell you?'

'They think the grave's early nineteenth century. Her skull was fractured in two places, and she was buried as if they were in a hurry to dispose of her.'

'That sounds an awful lot like murder to me.'

She looked at him. 'I think so, too.'

They said nothing for a moment. In the trees, birds chirped. Not crows this time, but songbirds, flitting gracefully from twig to twig.

'Is that your phone ringing?' he asked.

Suddenly aware of the sound, she glanced towards the house. 'I'd better get that.'

'It was nice meeting you!' he called out as she ran up the steps to her porch. By the time she made it into her kitchen, he was moving on, dragging the reluctant dog after him.

It was Vicky on the phone. 'So what's the latest instalment of *Home Improvement*?' she asked.

'I tiled the bathroom floor last night.' Julia's gaze was still on her garden, where Tom's brown sweater was now fading into the shadows beneath the trees. That old sweater must be a favourite of his, she thought. You didn't go out in public wearing something that ratty unless you had a sentimental attachment to it. Which somehow made him even more appealing.

'. . . and I really think you should start dating again.'

Julia's attention snapped back to Vicky. 'What?'

'I know how you feel about blind dates, but this guy's really nice.'

'No more lawyers, Vicky.'

'They're not all like Richard. Some of them do prefer a real woman to a blow-dried Tiffani. Who, I just found out, has a daddy who's a big wheel at Morgan Stanley.'

'I have to go, Vicky. I've been in the garden and my hands are all dirty. I'll call you later.' She hung up and immediately felt guilty for that little white lie. But just the mention of Richard had thrown a shadow over her day and she didn't want to think about him. She'd rather shovel manure.

THAT NIGHT, she was too exhausted to prepare anything more elaborate than a grilled cheese sandwich and a bowl of tomato soup. She ate at the kitchen table with the photocopied news clippings about Hilda Chamblett spread out in front of her. The articles were brief, reporting only that the elderly woman had been found dead in her back yard and that foul play was not suspected. At ninety-two you are already living on borrowed time.

She read the obituary:

> Hilda Chamblett, lifelong resident of Weston, Massachusetts, was found dead in her back yard on July 25. Her death has been ruled by the medical examiner's office as 'most likely of natural causes.' Widowed for the past twenty years, she was a familiar figure in gardening circles. She is survived by her cousin Henry Page of Islesboro, Maine, as well as two grand-nieces and a grand-nephew.

The ringing telephone made her splash tomato soup on the page. Vicky, she thought, probably wondering why I haven't called her back yet.

Julia picked up the phone. 'Hello?'

A man's voice, gravelly with age, said, 'Is this Julia Hamill?'

'Yes, it is.'

'So you're the schoolteacher who bought Hilda's house.'

Julia frowned. 'Who is this?'

'Henry Page. Hilda's cousin. I hear you found some old bones in her garden.'

Julia turned back to the kitchen table and quickly scanned the obituary.

. . . her cousin Henry Page of Islesboro, Maine . . .

'I'm interested in those bones,' he said. 'I'm considered the family historian, you see.' He added, with a snort, 'Because no one else gives a damn.'

'What can you tell me about the bones?' she asked.

'I've been looking into it,' he said. 'When Hilda died, she left about thirty boxes of old papers and books to me. I admit, I just shoved them aside. But then I heard about your mysterious bones and I wondered if there might be something about them in these boxes.' He paused. 'Is this interesting to you?'

'I'm listening.'

'I've come across some letters and newspapers with historical significance. I'm wondering if I've found the clue to who those bones belong to. You can look at the documents any time you want to come up to Maine.'

'That's an awfully long drive, isn't it?'

'Not if you're really interested. It doesn't matter to me one way or the other whether you are. But since this is about your house, about people who once lived there, I thought you might find the history fascinating. Certainly I do. There's an article here about the brutal murder of a woman.'

'Where? When?'

'In Boston. It happened in the autumn of 1830. If you come up to Maine, Miss Hamill, you can read the documents for yourself. About the strange affair of Oliver Wendell Holmes and the West End Reaper.'

1830

Rose draped her shawl over her head, wrapped it tight against the November chill and stepped outside. She had left baby Meggie nursing greedily at the breast of another new mother in the lying-in ward, and tonight was the first time in two days she'd left the hospital. Though the night air was damp with mist, she breathed in deeply to wash the miasma of illness from her lungs.

She walked swiftly, her footfalls echoing as she navigated the warren of streets, towards the wharves. Her breath seemed unnaturally loud, magnified by the thickening fog that grew ever denser as she moved towards the harbour. Then, through the rush of her own breathing, she heard footsteps behind her. She stopped and turned. The footsteps moved closer.

She backed away, her heart hammering. In the swirling mist, a dark form slowly congealed into something solid.

A voice called out, 'Miss Rose! Miss Rose! Is that you?'

She released a deep breath as she watched the gangly teenager emerge from the fog. 'Dash it all, Billy. I should box your ears!'

'For what, Miss Rose?'

'For scarin' me half to death.'

'I didn't mean to,' he whimpered. And of course it was true; the boy couldn't be blamed for half of what he did. Everyone knew Dim Billy, but no one wanted to claim him. He was a constant and annoying presence in Boston's West End, wandering from barn to stable in search of a place to bed down, begging scraps from pitying housewives and fishmongers.

'What're you doing out and about at this hour?'

'Lookin' for my pup. He's lost. Where're *you* going?'

'To fetch Eben. He needs to come to the hospital.'

'Why?'

'Because my sister is very ill. She has a fever, Billy.' And after a week in the lying-in ward, Rose understood what lay ahead. She had seen so many of the other new mothers on the ward die of childbed fever.

'Is she going to die?'

'I don't know,' she said softly. 'I don't know.'

'I'm afraid of dead people. When I was little, I saw my own da dead. They wanted me to kiss him, even though his skin was all burned off.'

'Can you tell me about it later, Billy? I'm in a hurry. Go look for your pup now, why don't you?' She quickened her pace.

'Mr Tate's not at Mrs O'Keefe's lodging house.'

She stopped. 'How do you know? Where is he?'

'I seen him over at the Mermaid. Mr Sitterley gave me a spot of lamb pie. I saw Mr Tate go in, and he didn't even say hello.'

'Are you sure, Billy? Is he still there?'

'If you pay me a quarter, I'll take you.'

She waved him away and walked on, her mind on Eben, on what she would say to him. All the anger that she'd been holding in against her brother-in-law was now rising to a boil. She pushed through the door, into the tavern. She paused near the entrance, gazing round the room at patrons gathered at tables, huddled at the bar. At a corner table, a woman with dark hair and a green dress was laughing loudly.

'You want to be served?' a man called out to her from behind the bar. This must be Mr Sitterley, she thought, the barkeep who'd given Dim Billy a taste of lamb pie, no doubt to shoo the boy out of his establishment.

She said, 'It's a man I'm looking for.' Her gaze came to a stop on the woman in the green dress. Sitting beside her was a man who now turned and shot Rose a resentful look.

She crossed to his table. The woman's mouth gaped open, revealing rotting teeth. 'You need to come to the hospital, Eben,' said Rose.

Aurnia's husband shrugged. 'Can't you see I'm busy grieving?'

'Go to her now, while you can. While she still lives.'

'Who's she talking about, darlin'?' the woman said.

Eben grunted. 'My wife.'

'You didn't tell me you had a wife.'

'How can you be so heartless?' said Rose. 'It's been seven days since you've been to see her. You haven't even come to see your own daughter!'

'Already signed over my rights to her. How'm I supposed to care for the brat? Let the ladies at the infant asylum have her. She's the only reason I married your sister. Baby on the way, I did my duty. But she was no cherry, that one.'

'She belongs with her family. I'll raise her myself, if I have to.'

'You?' He laughed. 'You're just months off the boat from Ireland, and all you know is a needle and thread.'

'I know enough to look after my own flesh and blood.' Rose grabbed his arm. 'Get up, you bastard. You *will* come with me.'

He stumbled to his feet. 'She has but a few hours left,' Rose said. 'Even if you have to lie to her, you *will* tell her you love her!'

He shoved her away and stood swaying, drunk and unsteady. The tavern had fallen silent, save for the crackle of flames in the fireplace. Eben glanced around at all the eyes watching him in disapproval.

He drew himself up straight and managed a civil tone. 'No need to rail at me like a harpy. I'll come. I was only finishing up my drink.'

With head held high, he walked out of the Mermaid. She followed him outside, into the penetrating mist. They'd walked only a dozen paces when Eben abruptly turned round to face her.

His blow sent her reeling backwards. She staggered against a building, her cheek throbbing, the pain so terrible that for a few seconds the world went black. She did not even see the second blow coming. It whipped her sideways and she fell to her knees, felt icy water soaking into her skirt.

'That's for talking back to me in public,' he snarled. He grabbed her by the arm and dragged her across the cobblestones, into a narrow alley.

Another blow slammed into her mouth and she tasted blood.

'And that's for the four months I've had to put up with you. Always taking her side, always lined up against me, the two of you. My prospects ruined, all because she got herself knocked up. You think she didn't beg me for it? You think I had to seduce her? Oh, no, your *saintly* sister wanted it. She wasn't afraid to show me what she had. But it was spoilt goods.'

He wrenched her to her feet and shoved her up against a wall.

'So don't play the innocent with me. I know what kind of trash runs in your family. I know what you want. The same thing your sister wanted.'

He rammed up against her, pinning her against the bricks as his mouth closed over hers. He clawed at her petticoat, her stockings, to reach naked flesh. At the touch of his hand on her bare thigh, her spine snapped taut.

Her fist caught him beneath the chin and she felt his jaw slam shut. He screamed and staggered backwards, his hand clapped to his mouth.

'My tongue! I've bit my tongue!' He looked down at his hand. 'Oh God, I'm bleeding!'

She ran. Hiking her skirt above her knees, she bolted headlong into the disorientating mist. She did not know which street she was on, or in which direction she was headed. He was too drunk to keep up, much less navigate the maze of narrow streets. She rounded a corner and came to a halt. Through the rush of her own breathing, she heard the clattering wheels of a passing carriage, but no footsteps. She realised she was on the Cambridge road and that she'd have to double back to return to the hospital.

She started walking north, pausing every few paces to listen for footsteps. She knew the hospital was straight ahead of her, on North Allen, but she could not yet see it through the fog. Eben was almost certainly there, waiting to pounce. She turned. There was another way into the building, but she would have to trudge across the damp grass of the hospital common to the rear entrance. Eben would not expect her to hike across this dark field.

She waded into the grass and icy water soaked into her shoes. The lights from the hospital intermittently faded out in the mist and she had to stop to regain her bearings. There they were again—off to the left. The fog thinned as she climbed the slope towards the building. By the time she stumbled out of the grass, onto cobblestones, she was clumsy on cold-numbed feet.

Chilled and shivering, she started up the back stairway. Suddenly her shoe slid across a step slick with something black. She stared up at what looked like a dark waterfall that had cascaded down the stairs. Only as her gaze lifted to the source of that waterfall did she see the woman's body draped across the steps above, her skirts splayed, one arm flung out.

At first Rose heard only the drumming of her own heart. Then she heard the footstep, and a shadow moved above her like an ominous cloud blotting out the moon. The blood seemed to freeze in Rose's veins. She looked up.

What she saw was the Grim Reaper himself.

She stumbled backwards and almost fell as she hit the bottom step. Suddenly the creature swooped towards her, black cape billowing like monstrous wings. She whirled to flee, pivoted right and sprinted alongside the building. She could hear the monster in pursuit.

She darted into a passage and found herself in a courtyard. She ran to the nearest door, but it was locked. Pounding on it, she shrieked for help.

I am trapped.

Behind her, gravel clattered across the stones. She spun round to face her attacker. In the darkness she could make out only the movement of black on black. She backed up against the door, her breaths coming out in sobs. Cringing, she turned her face in anticipation of the first slash. Instead she heard a voice, asking a question that she did not immediately register.

'Miss? Miss, are you all right?'

She opened her eyes to see the silhouette of a man. Behind him, through the darkness, a light winked. It was a lantern, swaying in the grasp of a second man, now approaching.

'Who's out here? Hello? Wendell! Over here!'

'Norris? What's all the commotion?'

'There's a young woman here. She seems to be hurt.'

The lantern swung closer. Rose blinked and focused on the faces of the two young men who were now staring at her. She recognised them both, just as they recognised her.

'It—it's Miss Connolly, is it not?' said Norris Marshall.

She gave a sob. Her legs suddenly went out from under her and she slid down the wall to land on her rump against the cobblestones.

FOUR

Though Norris had never before met Mr Pratt of Boston's Night Watch, he had known other men just like him, men too puffed up on authority to ever acknowledge the undeniable fact that they are stupid. Though not a large man, Mr Pratt gave the impression that he thought he was. His only impressive feature was his moustache, the bushiest Norris had ever seen. As Norris watched the man taking notes with a pencil in the hospital dissection room, he could not help staring at it.

Pratt finally looked up from his pad of paper and regarded Norris and Wendell, who stood beside the draped body. Pratt's gaze moved on to Dr Crouch, who was clearly the medical authority in the room.

'You say you have examined the body, Dr Crouch?' he asked.

'Only superficially. We took the liberty of bringing her into the building. It did not seem right to leave her lying there on the cold steps. The victim, Miss Agnes Poole, is the head nurse of this institution.'

Wendell interjected, 'Miss Connolly must have told you that. Didn't you already question her?'

'Yes, but I find it necessary to confirm everything she's told me. You know how it is with these flighty girls. Irish girls in particular.'

Norris said, 'I'd hardly call Miss Connolly a flighty girl.'

Watchman Pratt fixed his narrowed gaze on Norris. 'You know her?'

'Her sister is a patient here. We've spoken. In regard to her sister's care.'

Pratt eyed Norris's clothing. 'You have blood on your shirt.'

'I helped move the body from the steps. And I assisted Dr Crouch earlier in the evening.'

Pratt glanced at Crouch. 'Is this true, Doctor?'

Dr Crouch said, 'Mr Holmes and Mr Marshall are my apprentices. They assisted me earlier this evening on Broad Street, at a difficult delivery.'

'What were you delivering?'

Dr Crouch stared at Pratt, clearly thunderstruck by the man's question. 'What do you think we were delivering? A cart of bricks?'

Pratt slapped his pencil down on the pad. 'There is no need for sarcasm. I simply wish to know everyone's whereabouts tonight.'

'This is outrageous. I am a physician, sir, and I have no need to account for my activities. We *summoned* the Night Watch, for God's sake.'

The moustache twitched. 'I see no need for blasphemy,' he said coldly, and slipped his pencil into his pocket. 'Now then. Show me the body.'

Dr Crouch said, 'Shouldn't Constable Lyons be present?'

Pratt shot him an irritated look. 'He will get my report in the morning.' He pointed to the draped body. 'Uncover her.'

Pratt had assumed a nonchalant pose, but when Dr Crouch pulled off the sheet he could not suppress a gasp. He flinched away from the table, shocked by the mutilations performed on Agnes Poole.

'As you can see,' said Dr Crouch, 'the trauma is horrific. The killer has not merely sliced open the torso. He has done far, far more.' He glanced at Pratt. 'If you wish to see the damage, you'll have to step up to the table.'

Pratt swallowed. 'I can . . . see it well enough from here.'

'I doubt that.' Crouch pulled on an apron and tied the strings behind his back. 'Mr Holmes, Mr Marshall, I'll need your assistance. It's a good opportunity for you both to get your hands dirty.'

Growing up on his father's farm, Norris was no stranger to the smell of blood or the butchering of pigs and cows. He knew what death looked like and smelt like. But this was a different view of death. Reluctantly, he took an apron from the wall hooks, tied it on, and took his place at Dr Crouch's side. Wendell stood on the other side of the table, his face revealing no revulsion, only a look of intent curiosity.

Dr Crouch soaked a cloth in a basin of water and gently sponged blood away from the incised skin. 'As you can see here, gentlemen, the blade must have been quite sharp. These are clean cuts, very deep. And the pattern—the pattern is most intriguing.'

'What do you mean? What pattern?' asked Pratt.

'If you would approach the table, I could show you.'

'I'm busy taking notes, can't you see? Just describe it for me.'

'Description will not do it justice. Perhaps we should send for Constable Lyons? Surely *someone* in the Watch has the stomach to do his duty?'

Pratt flushed an angry red. Only then did he finally approach the table, to stand beside Wendell. He took one glimpse into the gaping abdomen and quickly averted his gaze. 'All right. I've seen it.'

'But do you see the pattern, how bizarre it is? A slice straight across the abdomen, from flank to flank. And then a slice straight up the midline, towards the breastbone, lacerating the liver. They are so deep, either one of these cuts would have caused death. The blade had to be quite long. It has sliced all the way to the backbone and nicked the top of the left kidney.' Crouch looked up. 'She would have died quickly, from exsanguination.'

'Ex—what?' asked Pratt.

'Quite simply, sir, she bled to death.'

Pratt swallowed hard. 'You said it had to be a long blade. How long?'

'To penetrate this deep? Seven, eight inches at the least.'

'A butcher's knife, perhaps?'

'I would certainly classify this as an act of butchery,' said Dr Crouch. 'It is indeed a most curious pattern. Two separate slashes, perpendicular to each other. Almost as if the killer were trying to carve the sign of . . .'

'The cross?' Pratt looked up with sudden interest. 'The victim wasn't Irish and a papist, was she?'

'No,' Crouch said. 'Most definitely not. And just because the wound resembles a cross doesn't mean the killer is a papist.'

'How well acquainted were you with Miss Poole, Doctor?' Pratt asked.

'She administered to many of my patients. She was competent and efficient. And most respectful,' Dr Crouch said.

'Had she any enemies that you're aware of?'

'Absolutely not. She was a nurse. Her role here was to ease suffering.'

'And Rose Connolly? Had she any disagreements with Nurse Poole?'

'She may have had. The girl is headstrong. Nurse Poole did complain to me that she was demanding.'

'She was upset about her sister's care,' said Norris.

'Upset enough to commit violence?'

'I didn't say that.'

'How, exactly, did you happen to find her tonight? She was outside in the courtyard, was she not?'

'Dr Crouch asked us to meet him in the lying-in ward. I was on my way here, from my lodgings. I was almost at the hospital when I heard screams.'

'Miss Connolly's? Or the victim's?'

'It was a woman. That's all I know. I followed the sound and discovered Miss Connolly in the courtyard.'

'And did you see this creature she so imaginatively describes?' Pratt glanced at his notes. '"A caped monster like the Grim Reaper, with a black cape that flapped like the wings of a giant bird."' He looked up.

Norris shook his head. 'I saw no such creature. I found only the girl.'

Pratt looked at Wendell. 'And where were you?'

'I was inside, assisting Dr Crouch. I heard the screams as well and ventured outside with a lantern. I found Mr Marshall in the courtyard, along with Miss Connolly, who was cowering there. She was clearly frightened.'

'Did you notice anything else unusual about her? Other than the fact she appeared frightened?'

'She *was* frightened,' said Norris.

'Did you not notice her dress was badly ripped?'

'She'd just fled a killer, Mr Pratt,' said Norris. 'She had every right to be dishevelled. Why don't you just ask her how her dress was torn?'

'I have. She claimed it happened earlier in the evening. When her sister's husband attempted to molest her.' He shook his head in disgust. 'These people are like animals, breeding in the tenements.'

Norris heard the ugly note of prejudice in the man's voice. *Animals*. Oh, yes, he'd heard that name used for the Irish, those immoral beasts who crammed the tenements and were always whoring, always procreating.

Norris said, 'Miss Connolly is hardly an animal.'

'For a man who scarcely knows her, you rise quickly to her defence.'

'I feel sorry for her. Sorry that her sister is dying.'

'Oh, that. *That* is over with,' said Pratt, and he closed his notebook. 'Rose Connolly's sister is dead.'

We had no chance to say goodbye.

Rose washed Aurnia's body with a damp cloth, gently wiping away the smudges of dirt and dried sweat and tears from her face. If there was a heaven, she thought, surely Aurnia was already there and could see the trouble Rose was in. *I am afraid, Aurnia. And Meggie and I have nowhere to go.*

Aurnia's neatly brushed hair gleamed in the lamplight, like coppery silk draped across the pillow. In a little basket beside the bed, baby Meggie slept soundly, unaware of her mother's passing, of her own precarious future. For two days, Meggie had been nursed on the ward by three new mothers, who had willingly passed the child among them.

Rose glanced up as a nurse approached. It was Miss Cabot, who had assumed authority since Nurse Poole's death.

'I'm sorry, Miss Connolly, but it's time to transfer the deceased. We need the bed.' She handed a small bundle to Rose. 'Your sister's belongings.'

Here were the pitifully few possessions: Aurnia's soiled night frock and a hair ribbon and her cheap little ring of tin and coloured glass.

'Those go to the husband,' Nurse Cabot said. 'Now she must be moved.'

Rose heard the squeaking of wheels and she saw the hospital groundsman pushing in a wheeled cart. 'I've not had enough time with her.'

'The coffin is ready in the courtyard. Have arrangements been made for burial? If you are unable to pay, there are options for a respectful interment.'

A pauper's burial was what she meant. Crammed into a common grave with nameless pedlars and beggars and thieves.

'How much time do I have to make arrangements?' asked Rose.

Nurse Cabot glanced impatiently up the row of beds. 'By tomorrow noon,' she said, 'the wagon will come to pick up the coffin.'

The groundsman lifted Aurnia from the bed. As he placed the corpse into the handcart, a sob escaped Rose's throat.

'There's another issue,' said Nurse Cabot. 'The child. You can't possibly take adequate care of it, Miss Connolly.'

The woman in the next bed said, 'Someone from the infant asylum came when you were out, Rose. Wantin' to take her. But we wouldn't allow it.'

'Mr Tate has signed away his parental rights,' said Nurse Cabot. 'You're far too young to raise the baby yourself. Be sensible, girl! Give it to someone who can.'

In answer, Rose snatched up Meggie from her basket and held her tightly. 'Give her to a stranger? I'd have to be on my deathbed first.'

Nurse Cabot gave a sigh of exasperation. 'Suit yourself. It'll be on your conscience when the child comes to grief.' She looked at the groundsman, who still waited with Aurnia's body on his cart. 'Remove her.'

Still holding tightly to Meggie, Rose followed the man out of the ward to the courtyard. There, by the glow of his lamp, she stood vigil as Aurnia was laid into the pine box. She watched him pound in the nails. The coffin now sealed, he picked up a lump of charcoal and scrawled on the lid: *A. TATE*.

'Just so there's no mix-up,' he said, and straightened to look at her. 'She'll be here till noon. Make your arrangements by then.'

Rose laid her hand on the lid. *I'll find a way, darling. I'll see you properly buried.* She wrapped her shawl round both herself and Meggie, then walked out of the hospital courtyard.

She did not know where to go. She didn't want to go back to the lodging house room that she'd shared with her sister and Eben. Eben was probably there now, sleeping off the rum, and she had no wish to confront him.

Force of habit sent her in a familiar direction, the same street that she had walked earlier that evening. A carriage clattered past, pulled by a sway-backed horse with a drooping head. As it rolled by, she saw a figure she recognised standing across the street from her.

'Did y'hear the news, Miss Rose?' said Dim Billy. 'Nurse Poole's been killed, over at the hospital!'

'Yes, Billy. I know.'

'They said she was slit right up her belly, like this.' He slashed a finger up his abdomen. 'Cut off her head with a sword. And her hands, too.'

'You're repeating nonsense and you should stop it. Not everything you hear is the God's truth. Some people lie. You can't trust them all, Billy.'

She began to walk again. Perhaps Mrs Combs down the street from Mrs O'Keefe's would grant her and Meggie a corner in her kitchen.

'I told the Night Watch everything I saw,' said Billy, practically dancing up the street beside her. 'The Watch says I'm a good one to talk to.'

'That you are.'

They walked together, past darkened windows, past silent houses. The boy stayed with her until she came, at last, to a stop.

'Aren't you going in?' said Billy.

She gazed up at Mrs O'Keefe's lodging house. Up the stairs would be her narrow bed, tucked into the curtained alcove in the room she'd shared with Aurnia and Eben. She remembered Eben's hands groping at her thighs tonight, and with a shudder she turned and walked away.

'Aren't you going home?' Billy said as he caught up to her.

'I can't go there tonight, Billy. Mr Tate is angry with me. Very, very angry. And I'm afraid he might . . .' She halted and stared at the mist. 'Oh God, Billy,' she whispered. 'I'm so tired. Where am I to go with the baby?'

'I know a place you could take her,' he said. 'A secret place. But you can't tell anyone about it.'

DAWN HAD NOT yet lifted the darkness when Jack Burke harnessed his horse and climbed up onto the buckboard. He guided the dray out of the stable yard and onto the icy cobblestones. At this hour, his was the only wagon on the street, and the clip-clop of the horse's hoofs, the rattle of the wheels, were unnervingly noisy in the otherwise silent street.

In the fog ahead, a crouching figure suddenly materialised right in front of the horse. Jack pulled up sharply on the reins and the horse halted with a snort. A teenaged boy scampered into view.

'Bad pup! Bad pup, you come to me now!'

The dog gave a yelp as the boy pounced and grabbed him round the neck. Straightening, the struggling dog now firmly in his grip, the boy stared wide-eyed as he suddenly saw Jack glaring at him through the mist.

'You damn half-wit, Billy!' snapped Jack. 'Get outta the road!'

The boy grinned stupidly, the mutt struggling in his arms. 'He doesn't always come when I call. He needs to behave.'

'Can't even look after yourself, and you got a damn dog?'

'We're out lookin' for a bit o' milk. Babies need milk, y'know, and she drank up all I got for her last night.'

What *was* the fool boy babbling about? 'Get outta my way,' said Jack. 'I got business to attend to.'

He snapped the reins and the wagon lurched forward. The horse took only a few paces before Jack abruptly pulled him to a stop. He turned to look back at Billy's spindly figure, half hidden in the mist. He'd be an extra pair of hands. And he'd be cheap.

'Hey, Billy!' Jack called. 'You want to earn ninepence?'

The boy hurried up to him. 'What for, Mr Burke?'

'Leave the dog and climb in.'

Billy dropped the dog and scrambled aboard. 'Where are we going?'

Jack snapped the reins. 'You'll see.'

The wagon rolled on through drifting fingers of mist, past buildings where candlelight was starting to appear in windows.

Billy glanced behind him. 'What's under the tarp, Mr Burke?'

'Nothing.'

Daylight was gaining on them, but the fog still hung thick. When at last they pulled to a stop, Jack could not see more than a few yards ahead of him, but he knew exactly where he was.

So did Billy. 'Why are we at the hospital?'

'Wait here,' Jack ordered the boy. He swung open the gate and walked into the hospital's rear courtyard. He needed to go only a few paces before he spotted what he'd been hoping to find: a coffin, with the lid newly nailed on. The name *A. TATE* had been scrawled on it. He got to work prising up the lid, then pulling it off to reveal the shrouded body within.

He returned to the wagon, where the boy was still waiting, and whisked off the tarp. 'Help me move this.'

Billy slithered down and came round to the rear. 'It's a log.'

'You are so clever.' Jack grabbed one end and dragged it from the wagon.

'Is it firewood?' asked Billy, grabbing the other end.

'Just move it, eh?' They carried the log to the coffin and set it down. 'Now help me lift this out,' Jack ordered.

Billy took one look into the coffin and froze. 'There's somebody in there—someone *dead*.'

'You want your ninepence or not?'

Billy looked up at him. 'I'm afraid o' dead people.'

'They can't hurt you, idiot.'

The boy shuffled away, moving towards the gate.

'Billy. You get your arse back here.'

Instead, the boy turned and fled from the courtyard into the mist.

'Useless,' grunted Jack. He took a breath, hauled up the shrouded body and rolled it out of the coffin. It thudded onto the cobblestones.

Daylight was brightening fast. He had to work quickly. He heaved the log into the coffin, and with a few swings of a hammer nailed the lid back into place. May you rest in peace, Mr Log, he thought. Then he dragged the corpse, still sewn into its shroud, across the courtyard to his wagon.

Moments later he was back on the dray, guiding his horse down North Allen Street. Glancing over his shoulder, he checked his tarp-covered cargo. He had not laid eyes on the corpse itself, but it was fresh, and that was all that mattered. And this time, the fee didn't have to be shared.

FIVE

Rose woke to find Meggie sleeping beside her, and she heard the clucking of chickens, the rustle of straw. It took her a moment to remember where she was. To remember that Aurnia was dead. Grief seized her in its fist, squeezing so hard that she could not breathe.

Something nearby beat a steady tattoo, and she turned to see a black dog staring at her, its wagging tail slapping against a bale of hay. It trotted over to lick her face. Pushing it away, she sat up. The dog gave a bored whine and headed down the stairs. Peering over the edge of the hayloft, she saw it trot past a stabled horse and disappear through the open barn door.

She looked around the loft and wondered where Billy had gone.

So this was where he sheltered. A depression in the straw marked where he had slept last night. A chipped cup and saucer and trencher were set upon an overturned crate. She had to smile at his resourcefulness. Last night, Billy had disappeared for a short time and returned with a precious cup of milk, no doubt squeezed furtively from someone's cow or goat. Rose hadn't questioned his source as Meggie had sucked on the milk-soaked rag.

In a corner of the loft, she spotted a little wooden box. She lifted the hinged lid. Inside were pretty pieces of glass, a seashell and two whalebone buttons, treasures that Billy had collected as he roamed the streets of the West End. Every day was a treasure hunt for Dim Billy, and a pretty button was enough to make him happy.

Billy's treasure box suddenly reminded her of something she'd put in her pocket, something she'd completely forgotten until now. She pulled out the locket and chain and felt a sudden flash of grief at the sight of Aurnia's necklace. The chain was feathery light and she remembered how the gold locket had gleamed on Aurnia's creamy white skin.

This was gold. It would buy Aurnia a proper burial.

She heard voices and peered out through the window. A wagon filled with bales of hay had just rolled into the yard, and two men stood dickering over the price. It was time to leave.

She scooped up the sleeping baby and made her way down the steps. Quietly, she slipped out of the barn door.

A FREEZING MIST clung to the ground of St Augustine's cemetery. Holding Meggie in her arms, Rose stood in a forlorn corner, beside the newly turned mound of earth.

'She's 'bout deep enough, miss.'

Rose turned to look at the two gravediggers. The older one dragged a sleeve across his face, leaving streaks of mud on his cheek.

'Will there be no one else to see her laid to rest?' he asked.

'No one else,' she said, and looked down at Aurnia's coffin. She fought the sudden impulse to tear off the lid, to gaze once again on her sister's face.

'Shall we finish, then?'

She swallowed her tears and gave a nod.

The old man turned towards his partner, a blank-faced teenager, who had shovelled with lackadaisical effort. 'Help me put her in.'

Ropes creaked as they lowered the coffin, dislodging clots of dirt that thudded into the hole. Their task almost completed, the boy worked with more alacrity as they filled the hole, shovel after shovel full of soggy earth landing on the coffin.

Rose turned away from the grave and only then did she see the ghostly figure approaching them through the fog. She recognised the face peering out from beneath the hood of the cape. It was Mary Robinson, the young nurse from the hospital.

'I didn't know where else to find you,' said Mary. 'I'm sorry for your sister. God rest her soul.'

'You were kind to her, Miss Robinson.'

As Rose blinked away tears, Mary moved closer and her voice dropped to a whisper. 'There are people enquiring about the child.'

Rose gave a weary sigh and looked down at her niece, who lay serene in her arms. Little Meggie had inherited Aurnia's sweet temperament, and she was content to lie quietly and study the world with her wide eyes. 'I've given them my answer. She stays with her own people. With me.'

'Rose, they're not from the infant asylum. I promised Miss Poole that I'd say nothing, but now I cannot remain silent. The night the baby was born, after you left the room, your sister told us . . .' Suddenly Mary fell still, her tense gaze riveted not on Rose, but on something in the distance.

'Miss Robinson?'

'Keep the child safe,' Mary said. 'Keep her hidden.'

Rose turned to see what Mary was looking at, and when she saw Eben stride out of the fog, her throat went dry. As he drew closer, Rose saw that he was carrying her satchel, the same bag she'd brought with her to Boston four months ago. Contemptuously, he threw it at her feet.

'I took the liberty of packing your belongings,' he said, 'since you are no longer welcome at Mrs O'Keefe's establishment. And don't come begging for my charity.'

She picked up the bag from the mud. 'Was that what you forced on me last night? Charity?'

Straightening, she met his gaze, and felt a thrill of satisfaction at the sight of his bruised lip. *Did I do that? Good for me*. Her cold retort clearly enraged him, and he took a step closer, then glanced at the two gravediggers still at work filling in the hole. He halted, his hand balled in a fist.

His lips peeled back, like an animal baring its teeth, and his words came out in a whisper. 'You had no right to talk to the Night Watch. They came round this morning. All the other lodgers are gossiping about it.'

'I only told them the God's truth. What you did to me.'

'As if anyone believes *you*. You know what I told Mr Pratt? I told him what you really are. A little cock-tease. I told him how I took you in, fed you, housed you, to please my wife. You'd have starved without our charity.'

'Do you not even care that she's gone?' Rose saw no grief in his eyes, only wounded vanity. She looked down at the grave. 'Maybe I'll go hungry,' she said. 'But at least I look after my own. I see to my sister's burial. I'll raise her child. What kind of a man do you think people will call you when they hear you didn't pay a penny to bury your wife?'

His face flushed scarlet, and he glanced at the two diggers. Tight-lipped, he reached into his pocket and withdrew a handful of coins. 'Here,' he snapped, and held them out to the diggers. 'Take it!'

The older man glanced uneasily at Rose. 'The lady paid us already, sir.'

'Goddamn it, take the bloody money!' Eben grabbed the man's dirt-stained hand and slapped the coins into his palm. Then he looked at Rose. 'Consider my obligation fulfilled. And now you have something that belongs to *me*.'

'You don't care a whit about Meggie. Why would you want her?'

'It's not the brat I want. It's Aurnia's things. I'm her husband, so her possessions come to me. The hospital told me they gave you her belongings.'

'Is that all you want?' She removed the small bundle she'd tied round her waist and handed it to him. 'It's yours, then.'

He opened the bundle and the night frock, ribbon and ring fell to the ground. 'Where's the gold locket? Never told me how she got it, and all these months she refused to sell it, even though I could've used the money.'

'I pawned it to pay for this grave and you're not welcome here. You gave my sister no peace while she was alive. At least allow her to rest in peace.'

Eben glanced at the old gravedigger, who was glowering at him. He had to struggle to keep his abusive tongue in check. All he said was, 'You'll hear more about this later, Rose.' Then he turned and walked away.

'Miss? Miss?'

Rose turned to the old digger, who met her gaze with a look of sympathy. 'I expect you'll want this. It should keep you and the baby fed for a time.'

She stared at the coins that he'd placed in her hand. And she thought, For a while, this will hold off our hunger. It will pay for a wet nurse.

The two labourers gathered up their tools and left Rose standing beside the fresh mound of Aurnia's grave. Once the dirt settles, she thought, I will buy you a stone marker with a carving of an angel.

Only then did she remember Mary Robinson. She glanced round, but did not see her anywhere. The arrival of Eben must have driven her off.

Drops of rain splashed her face. She lingered, clutching Meggie as rain muddied the earth. 'Sleep well, darling,' she whispered.

Rose picked up Aurnia's scattered belongings. Then she and Meggie left St Augustine's and headed towards the slums of South Boston.

'MIDWIFERY IS THE BRANCH of medicine which treats of conception and its consequences. And today, you have heard some of those consequences. Many of them, alas, tragic . . .'

Even from the grand stairway outside the auditorium, Norris could hear the booming voice of Dr Crouch. He hastened up the steps, vexed that he had arrived so late for morning lectures. But last night he had once again been in the gruff company of Jack Burke, an expedition that had taken them south to Quincy. They had returned to Boston well after midnight, carting only one specimen in such poor shape that Dr Sewall, upon peeling back the tarp, had grimaced at the stink.

Norris could still smell that stink on his hair, his clothes, as he climbed the stairs to the auditorium. He pulled open the door and slipped quietly into the lecture hall, where Dr Crouch was now pacing the stage.

'. . . though distinct from surgery and physic, midwifery requires knowledge of anatomy and physiology, pathology and . . .' Dr Crouch paused, his gaze fixed on Norris. The audience turned like a many-eyed beast and looked at Norris, who was pinned in place by all the stares.

'Mr Marshall,' said Crouch. 'We're honoured you've chosen to join us.'

'I'm sorry, sir. I have no excuse.'

'Indeed. Well, find a seat.'

Norris spotted an empty chair and quickly sat down, in the row just ahead of Wendell, Charles Lackaway and Edward Kingston.

On stage, Crouch cleared his throat and continued. 'And so to conclude, gentlemen, I leave you with this thought: The physician is sometimes all that stands in the way of darkness. When we enter the gloomy chambers of sickness, we are there to offer divine hope and courage. Be true to the calling. Be true to those who place their lives in your most worthy hands.'

The audience sat utterly silent for a few seconds. Then Edward Kingston rose to clap. Others joined in, until the whole hall echoed with applause.

'Well. I'd call that a Hamlet-worthy performance,' said Wendell, his dry appraisal lost in the din of clapping hands.

Dr Crouch left the stage and sat down in the front row with the other faculty members. Now Dr Aldous Grenville, who was both dean of the medical college and Charles Lackaway's uncle, stood to address the students. Though his hair was already silver, Dr Grenville stood tall and unstooped, a striking figure who commanded the room with just one look.

'Thank you, Dr Crouch. Now we move on to the final segment of today's programme, an anatomical dissection presented by Dr Erastus Sewall.'

In the front row, portly Dr Sewall rose to his feet and strode on stage.

'Before I proceed,' said Sewall, 'I wish to call on a volunteer. Perhaps a gentleman from among the first-year students would assist me?'

There was a silence as five rows of young men discreetly stared down at their own shoes.

'Come now, you've only just begun your medical studies and you must get your hands bloody if you're to understand the human machine. If one of you will just be bold enough?'

'I will,' said Edward, and he stood. As he headed up the aisle, he shot a cocksure grin at his classmates.

Wheels rumbled across the wooden stage as an assistant pushed a table out from the wings. Dr Sewall shed his coat and rolled up his sleeves as the assistant next brought out a small table with a tray of instruments. 'The art of dissection,' he said, as he slipped on an apron, 'is like that of a sculptor, coaxing a work of art from a block of marble, revealing the beauty of every muscle and every organ, every nerve and blood vessel.' He turned to the table where the body lay, still draped. 'Let us reveal today's subject.'

Norris felt anticipatory nausea as Dr Sewall reached for the shroud. He dreaded the unveiling of the half-rotten corpse he and Jack had unearthed last night. But when Sewall swept off the sheet, it was not the stinking man. It was a female. And even from his seat in the auditorium, Norris recognised her. Curly red hair cascaded over the edge of the table. Her head was turned slightly, so that she faced the audience with half-closed eyes and parted lips. Norris could hear his own heartbeat pounding in his ears. *That corpse is Rose Connolly's sister.* How in God's name had the girl's beloved sister ended up on the anatomist's table?

Dr Sewall calmly picked up a knife. He seemed oblivious to the shocked silence that had fallen over the room. He looked at Edward, who stood frozen at the foot of the table. No doubt he, too, had recognised the body.

'I advise you to slip on an apron.'

Edward did not seem to hear him.

'Mr Kingston, unless you wish to soil that very fine coat you're wearing, I suggest you remove it and put on an apron.'

Even arrogant Eddie, it appeared, had lost his nerve.

Dr Sewall made the first cut. It was a brutal slash, from breastbone to pelvis. As the skin parted, loops of bowel spilled out from the open belly.

'The bucket,' said Sewall. He looked up at Edward, who was staring down in horror at the gaping wound. 'Will *somebody* position the bucket? Since my assistant here seems incapable of any movement whatsoever.'

Uneasy laughter rippled through the audience at the spectacle of their overbearing classmate being so publicly yanked down a few notches. Flushing, Edward snatched up the bucket and set it down on the floor.

'Lying atop the bowel,' said Dr Sewall, 'is a caul of tissue called the omentum. I have just sliced through it, releasing the intestines. In this young female subject, I find sparse deposits of fat in the omentum.

'Next, I shall clear away this bowel, which obstructs our view of the organs beneath.' He leaned in with his knife, and his hand came up holding one severed end of the bowel. 'Now I shall free it at the other end, where the small bowel becomes large bowel, at the ileocaecal junction.' Again he reached in with his knife. He straightened, holding up the severed end.

'Mr Kingston, the bowel can go into the bucket. Next, we shall see what the heart and lungs look like.' Dr Sewall reached for an ugly-looking instrument and clamped its jaws round a rib. The sound of snapping bone echoed through the hall. He looked up at the audience. 'You cannot get a good view of the thorax unless you look straight into the cavity. I believe it might be best if the first-year students move closer for the rest of the dissection. Come, gather round the table.'

Norris was closest to the aisle, so he was one of the first to reach the table. He stared down at the face of the woman whose innermost secrets were now being revealed to a room full of strangers. She was so lovely, he thought. Aurnia Tate had been in the full bloom of womanhood.

'I should first like to point out an interesting finding in her pelvis,' said Dr Sewall. 'Based on the size of the uterus, I would conclude that this subject has quite recently given birth. You will note the particularly foul odour, and the obvious inflammation of the peritoneum. Taking these findings into account, I'm willing to offer a conjecture as to the likely cause of her death.'

There was a loud thud in the aisle. One of the students said, alarmed, 'Is he breathing? Check if he's breathing!'

Dr Sewall called out, 'What is the problem?'

'It's Dr Grenville's nephew, sir,' said Wendell. 'Charles has fainted.'

In the front row, Professor Grenville rose to his feet, looking stunned. Quickly he made his way up the aisle towards Charles.

'He's all right, sir,' Wendell announced. 'Charles is coming round now.'

Grenville knelt at his nephew's side and patted Charles on the face. 'Come come, boy. You've just gone a bit light-headed.'

Groaning, Charles sat up and clutched his head. 'I feel sick.'

'I'll take him outside, sir,' said Wendell. 'He could use the fresh air.'

'Thank you, Mr Holmes,' said Professor Grenville.

We are all unnerved, even the most seasoned among us, thought Norris, looking around the auditorium at the ashen faces. What normal human being could watch this morning's butchery and not be appalled?

The Present

Julia drove north, fleeing the heat of the Boston summer, and joined the weekend stream of cars headed north into Maine. By the time she crossed into Maine, the air was starting to feel chilly. Soon her views of forest and rocky coastline vanished behind a bank of fog.

When she finally arrived at the beach town of Lincolnville that afternoon, she could barely make out the massive outline of the Islesboro ferry docked at the pier. Henry Page had warned her that there'd be limited space aboard for vehicles, so she left her car in the terminal lot, grabbed her overnight bag, and walked onto the waiting vessel.

She walked off the boat into a disorientatingly grey world. Henry Page's house was just a mile from the island's terminal. In the thick fog, she stayed well to the side of the road as she walked, to avoid being hit by a car.

A mailbox suddenly appeared in front of her. Staring closely, she could just make out the faded word on the side: STONEHURST. Henry Page's house.

A track climbed steadily through dense woods. The house appeared so suddenly that she halted, startled. It was made of stone and old wood that, over the years, had turned silvery in the salt air. Though she could not see the ocean, she knew it was nearby because she could hear waves slapping against rocks and seagulls crying.

Julia climbed the worn granite steps to the porch and knocked. Mr Page had told her he would be home, but no one came to the door. She left her bag on the porch and had started to walked back down the steps when she heard a noise behind her.

Henry Page looked ancient, his hair as white as the mist, his eyes squinting through wire-rimmed spectacles. He stood at the open door with stooped shoulders, his gnarled hand gripping a cane.

'I'm Henry Page,' he said. 'You're Ms Hamill, I presume.'

'Yes. I thought you weren't home.'

'You think I can just sprint down the stairs? I'm eighty-nine years old. Next time, try a little patience.' He gestured for her to come up the steps. 'Come in. I have a nice sauvignon blanc chilling.'

She followed him into the house. It smelt of dust and old carpets. And books. Thousands of old books were crammed in floor-to-ceiling shelves. An enormous stone fireplace took up one wall. The space felt dark and claustrophobic. It did not help that there were a dozen boxes stacked up in the centre of the room beside a massive oak dining table.

'These are a few of Hilda's boxes,' he said.

He thumped over to the dining table, where the contents of one of the boxes were spread out across the battered tabletop. 'As you can see, the moving company I hired just threw things willy-nilly into boxes. These old newspapers here have dates anywhere from 1840 to 1910. It could take us weeks to go through them all.'

Julia suddenly registered the fact he'd used the word *us*. She looked up. 'I'm sorry, Mr Page, but I wasn't planning to stay very long. Could you just show me what you've found concerning my house?'

'Oh, yes. Hilda's house.' To her surprise, he walked away from her, his cane thudding across the wood floor. 'Built in 1880,' he yelled back. 'For an ancestor of mine named Margaret Tate Page.'

Julia followed Henry into a 1950s kitchen. He rummaged around in the refrigerator and pulled out a bottle of white wine.

'The house was passed down through generations. Pack rats all of us, just like Hilda,' he said, twisting a corkscrew into the bottle. 'Which is why we're left with this treasure trove of documents.' The cork popped out of the bottle and he pulled down two wineglasses from a cabinet.

'The bones in my garden were probably buried before 1880,' Julia said. 'What you've found in these boxes isn't going to tell us anything about them.'

'How can you say that? You haven't even looked at the papers yet.' He filled the glasses and held one out to her.

'Isn't it a little early in the day to be drinking?' she asked.

'Early?' He snorted. 'I'm eighty-nine years old and I have four hundred bottles of excellent wine in my cellar, all of which I intend to finish. I'm more worried that it's too *late* to start drinking. So, please, join me.'

She took the glass. He picked up his own glass and shuffled back into the library where he rifled through the papers on the table and plucked out one of them. He set it in front of her. 'Here, Ms Hamill. Here is the clue.'

She looked down at the handwritten letter, dated March 20, 1888.

Dearest Margaret,

I thank you for your kind condolences, so sincerely offered, for the loss of my darling Amelia . . .

Julia looked up. 'This was written in 1888. That's well after the bones were buried.'

'Keep reading,' Henry said. And she did, until the final paragraph.

I enclose the news clipping. If you have no desire to learn more, please tell me, and I will never again mention this. But if indeed the subject of your parents holds any interest for you, then I will once again pick up my pen. And you will learn the story, the true story, of your aunt and the West End Reaper.

With fondest regards, O.W.H.

'Do you realise who *O.W.H.* is?' asked Henry. His eyes, magnified by the lenses of his spectacles, gleamed with excitement.

'You told me over the phone it was Oliver Wendell Holmes. He was a writer, wasn't he?'

'Oliver Wendell Holmes Senior was more than just a literary figure. Yes, he was a poet and a novelist and a biographer, a lecturer and a philosopher. And he was a physician. One of the finest of his age.'

She looked at the letter with more interest. 'So then this is historically significant?'

'And the Margaret whom he addresses in the letter—that's my great-great-grandmother, Dr Margaret Tate Page, born in 1830. She was one of the first women physicians in Boston. That's *her* house you now own.'

'Who is this aunt he speaks of in the letter?'

'I have no idea.' He glanced at the dozen boxes stacked beside the dining table. 'I've only searched these six so far. Nothing's in order. But here is the history of your house, Ms Hamill.'

'He said that he enclosed a clipping. Did you find it?'

Henry reached for a scrap of newspaper. 'I believe this is what he referred to.' It was dated November 28, 1830.

West End Murder Described as 'Shocking and Grotesque'

At 10 p.m. Wednesday, officers of the Night Watch were called to Massachusetts General Hospital after the body of Miss Agnes Poole, a nurse, was discovered dead on the back steps of the hospital. Her injuries, according to Officer Pratt of the Watch, left no doubt that this was an attack of the most brutal nature. The lone witness remains unidentified to this reporter, out of concern for her safety, but Mr Pratt confirms that it is a young woman, who described the assailant as 'cloaked in black like the Grim Reaper, with the wings of a bird of prey'.

'This murder took place in Boston,' said Julia. 'I see no connection to my house.'

'Oliver Wendell Holmes may be the connection. He writes to Margaret, who's living in your house. He makes this puzzling reference to her aunt, and to a killer known as the West End Reaper. Somehow, Holmes became involved in this murder case—a case he felt compelled to tell Margaret about over fifty years later.'

The distant bellow of a ship's horn made Julia look up. 'I wish I didn't have to catch the ferry.'

'Then don't leave. Why not spend the night? I saw your overnight bag by the front door and I have a guest room with quite a spectacular view.'

She glanced at the window, at fog that had grown even thicker.

'But perhaps it's not really worth your trouble.' He sighed. 'Oh, well. What does it matter? Someday, we'll all be just like her. Dead and forgotten.'

She didn't move. She was thinking about what he'd said. About forgotten women. 'Mr Page?' she said.

He looked back, a bent little gnome of a man clutching his knobby cane.

'I think I will spend the night.'

For a man his age, Henry could certainly hold his drink. By the time they'd finished dinner, they were well into a second bottle of wine, and Julia was having trouble focusing. Night had fallen, and in the glow of lamplight everything in the room had blurred to a warm haze.

Henry refilled his glass and sipped as he reached for another document, one of an endless collection of correspondence addressed to Margaret Page. He glanced at her over the rim of his glass. 'You've given up already?'

'I'm exhausted. And a little tipsy, I think.'

'It's only ten o'clock.'

'I don't have your stamina,' she said. 'Tell me about your cousin Hilda.'

'She was a schoolteacher, like you.' He flipped over a letter. Added, absently, 'Never got around to having any children of her own.'

Julia sank back in the chair, looking at the stack of boxes, the only legacy that Hilda Chamblett had left behind. 'So that's why she was living alone. She didn't have anyone.'

'Why do you think I live alone? Because I want to, that's why! I want to stay in my own house, not some nursing home. It's a consequence of liking one's privacy. You live alone, so you must know what I mean.'

She stared at her glass. 'It isn't my choice,' she said. 'My husband left me.'

'Why? You seem like a pleasant enough young woman.'

Pleasant enough. Right, that would bring the men running. His remark was so unintentionally insulting that she laughed. But somewhere in the middle of that laugh, the tears started. She dropped her head in her hands, struggling to control her emotions. Henry made no attempt to comfort her. He simply studied her, the way he'd studied those old newspapers.

She wiped her face and abruptly stood. 'I'll clean up,' she said. 'And then I think I'll go to bed.' She turned towards the kitchen.

'Julia,' he said. 'What's his name? Your husband.'

'Richard. And he's my ex-husband.'

'Do you still love him?'

'No,' she said softly.

'Then why the hell are you crying over him?'

'Because I'm an idiot,' she said.

SIX

1830

A haze of cigar smoke hung over the dissection room, the welcome odour of tobacco masking the stench of the cadavers. On the table where Norris worked, a corpse lay with its chest split open, and the resected heart and lungs rested in a bucket on the floor.

Their instructor, Dr Sewall, paced through the dissection room, past tables of cadavers where young men worked four to a corpse. 'I want you to complete the removal of all the internal organs today,' he instructed.

Norris glanced across the table at Charles, whose pale face was wreathed in smoke while he frantically puffed on his cigar.

Sewall paused at Norris's table and examined the organs lying in the bucket. 'Which one of you resected the heart and lungs?' he asked.

'I did, sir,' Norris said.

'Fine job. Finest I've seen in the room.' Sewall looked at him. 'You've done this before, I take it.'

'On the farm, sir. Sheep and pigs.'

'I can tell you've wielded a knife.' Sewall looked at Charles. 'Your hands are still clean, Mr Lackaway.'

'I—I thought I'd give the others a chance to start.'

'Start?' He looked down at the corpse and grimaced. 'By the smell of this one, it'll rot before you even pick up your knife, Mr Lackaway. What are you waiting for? Get your hands dirty.'

'Yes, sir.'

As Dr Sewall walked out of the room, Charles reluctantly reached for the knife. As he gathered his nerve, a bloody chunk of lung flew across the table and smacked him in the chest. He gave a yelp and jumped back.

Edward laughed. 'You heard Dr Sewall. Get those hands dirty!'

Now that Dr Sewall had left, the students turned boisterous. A flask of whisky began making its rounds. The team at the next table propped up their corpse and shoved a lit cigar in its mouth.

'This is disgusting,' said Charles. 'I can't do this.' He set down the blade. 'I never *wanted* to be a doctor.'

'Come on, Charlie,' encouraged Wendell, and he held out a knife to him. 'It's not so bad once you get started. You can resect the small bowel.'

As Charles stared at the offered knife, someone jeered from across the room, 'Charlie! Don't faint on us again!'

Flushing red, Charles took the knife. Grim-faced, he began to cut. But this was no skilful resection; these were savage slashes, his blade mangling the bowel, releasing a stench so awful that Norris lurched backwards, lifting his arm to his face to stifle the smell.

'Stop,' said Wendell, grabbing Charles's arm. 'You're making a mess of it!'

'You told me to cut! You told me to get my hands bloody! That's what my uncle keeps telling me.' Charles threw down the knife. Its thud was lost in the high-spirited bedlam of young men let loose upon a task so gruesome, the only sane response was perverse frivolity.

Norris picked up the knife and asked, 'Are you all right, Charles?'

'I'm fine.' Charles released a deep breath. 'I'm perfectly fine.'

A student stationed at the door hissed suddenly, 'Sewall's coming back!'

Instantly the room fell quiet. Cadavers resumed their positions of dignified repose. When Dr Sewall walked back into the room, he saw only diligent students and serious faces. He crossed straight to Norris's table and came to a halt, staring at the slashed intestines.

'What the devil is *this* mess?' Appalled, he looked at the four students.

Charles appeared to be on the verge of tears.

Edward said, too eagerly, 'Mr Lackaway was trying to resect the small bowel, sir, and—'

'It's my fault,' Norris cut in. 'It was a bit of horseplay. Charles and I—well, it got out of hand, and we sincerely apologise. Don't we, Charles?'

Sewall regarded Norris for a moment. 'In light of your obvious skill as a dissector, this conduct is doubly disappointing. Do not let it happen again.'

'It won't, sir.'

'I'm told that Dr Grenville wishes to see you, Mr Marshall. He waits in his office.' Sewall turned to the class. 'As for the rest of you, there will be no more tomfoolery. Proceed, gentlemen!'

'PROFESSOR GRENVILLE?' The dean looked up from his desk. Backlit by the gloomy daylight through the window behind him, his silhouette resembled a lion's head, with its mane of wiry grey hair. As Norris paused on the threshold, he felt Aldous Grenville studying him, and he wondered what blunder on his part could have precipitated this summons.

'Do come in, Mr Marshall. And please close the door.'

Uneasy, Norris took a seat. Grenville lit a lamp and the flame caught, casting its warm glow across the gleaming desk, the cherry bookshelves.

'You were at the hospital,' said Grenville. 'The night Agnes Poole died.'

Norris was taken aback by the abrupt introduction of this grim subject, and he could only nod. The murder had been six days ago, and since then there had been wild gossip in town about who—or what—could have killed her. The *Daily Advertiser* had described a winged demon.

'You were the first to find the witness. The Irish girl,' said Grenville. 'Have you seen her since that night?'

'No, sir.'

'You are aware that the Night Watch is looking for her?'

'Mr Pratt told me. I know nothing about Miss Connolly.'

'The girl hasn't been seen at her lodging house since that night,' said Grenville. 'Her sister's husband, a tailor named Mr Tate, told the Night Watch she was unstable. She'd even accused *him* of base acts against her.'

'I saw nothing unsound about her,' Norris said.

'She made some rather startling claims. About that creature in the cape.'

'She called it a *figure*, sir. She never said that it was in any way supernatural. It was the *Daily Advertiser* that called it the West End Reaper. She may have been frightened, but she was not hysterical.'

'You can't tell Mr Pratt where she might be?'

'Why does he think I can?'

'He suggested that you might be better acquainted with her . . . people.'

'I see.' Norris felt his face tighten. *So they think that a farm boy in a suit is still just a farm boy.* 'May I ask why it's so urgent that he find her?'

'There is a matter concerning an item of jewellery. A locket that was briefly in the possession of Miss Connolly, before it found its way to a pawnshop. By all rights, it should have gone to her sister's husband.'

'You are saying that Miss Connolly is a thief?'

'I'm not saying it. Mr Pratt is. How did she strike you?'

'A clever girl. And forthright. But not a thief.'

Grenville nodded. 'I'll pass along that opinion to Mr Pratt.'

Norris, believing the interview to be over, started to rise, but Grenville said, 'A moment more, Mr Marshall.'

Norris settled uncomfortably back into the chair.

'You are satisfied thus far with your course of study?' asked Grenville. 'And with Dr Crouch?'

'He's an excellent preceptor. I'm grateful he took me on. I've learned a great deal about midwifery at his side.'

'I understand you have strong opinions of your own on the subject.'

Suddenly Norris was uneasy. 'I did not mean to question his methods,' he said. 'I certainly don't have Dr Crouch's experience.'

'No. You have a farmer's experience.' Norris flushed, and Grenville added, 'I mean you've had practical experience. You've observed the process of gestation and birth.'

'But as Dr Crouch quite plainly pointed out to me, a cow cannot be compared to a human being.'

'Of course not. Cows are far more companionable. Your father must agree, or he would not hide himself away on that farm.'

Norris paused, startled. 'You are acquainted with my father?'

'No, but I know of him. He must be proud of you, pursuing such a demanding course of study.'

'No, sir. He's unhappy with my choice. He had thought to raise a farmer.

He considers books a waste of time. I would not even be here, at the medical college, were it not for the generosity of Dr Hallowell.'

'Dr Hallowell in Belmont? The gentleman who wrote your letter of recommendation?'

'Yes, sir. Truly, there's no kinder man. He and his wife always made me feel welcome in their home. He tutored me in physics and encouraged me to borrow books from his own library. Books were my salvation.'

Norris was suddenly embarrassed that he'd used a word so revealing. But salvation was precisely what books had meant to him during the bleak nights on the farm, nights when he and his father had little to say to each other. When they did speak, it was about whether the hay was still too wet, or how close the cows were to calving. They did not speak of what tormented them both.

'It's a pity that your father did not encourage you,' said Grenville. 'Yet you've come so far with such little advantage.'

'I've found . . . employment here, in the city.' Disgusting though his work with Jack Burke might be. 'It's enough to pay for tuition.'

'Your father contributes nothing?'

'He has little to send.'

'I hope he was more generous with Sophia. She deserved better.'

Norris was startled by the mention of that name. 'You know my mother?'

'While my wife Abigail was still alive, she and Sophia were the dearest of friends. But that was years ago, before you were born.' He paused. 'It was a surprise to us both when Sophia suddenly married.'

And the biggest surprise of all, thought Norris, must have been her choice of a husband, a farmer with little education. Though Isaac Marshall was a handsome man, he had no interest in the music and books that Sophia so treasured. Norris said, hesitantly, 'You do know that my mother is no longer living in Belmont?'

'I'd heard she was in Paris. Is she still there?'

'As far as I know. She hasn't corresponded. Life on the farm was not easy for her, I think. And she . . .' Norris stopped, and the memory of his mother's departure was like a fist suddenly closing round his chest. She'd left on a Saturday, a day he scarcely remembered, because he'd been so ill. And weeks later, he was still weak and wobbly on his feet when he'd come down to the kitchen to find his father, Isaac, standing at the window, staring out at the mist of summer. His father had turned to face him, his expression as distant as a stranger's.

'Your mother just wrote. She won't be coming back,' was all Isaac had said, before walking out of the house and heading to the barn to do the milking.

As time went by without other letters, Norris had come to accept a truth that no eleven-year-old boy should have to face: that his mother had abandoned her son to a father who lavished more affection on his cows than on his own flesh and blood. Though his father refused to speak of it, Norris had been forced to come to the inevitable conclusion that surely a man was involved. Sophia had been barely thirty, a bright and lively beauty. On which of her trips to Boston had she met him? What promises had he offered to compensate for the abandonment of her son?

Norris took a breath and, as he exhaled, he imagined his pain being released as well. But it was still there, the old ache for just one glimpse of the woman who had broken his heart. 'I should return to the dissection room,' he said abruptly. 'Is that all you wished to see me about, sir?'

'There is one more thing. It's about my nephew, Charles. He looks up to you. He was quite young when his father died of a fever, and my sister thoroughly coddled him when he was a boy, so he's grown up on the sensitive side. He is finding the studies difficult and he receives little encouragement from his friend Mr Kingston. Only ridicule.'

'Wendell Holmes is a good and supportive friend.'

'Yes, but you are perhaps the most skilled dissector in your class. That's what Dr Sewall tells me. So I'd appreciate it, should you see that Charles needs any extra guidance . . .'

'I'd be happy to look out for him, sir.'

'And you won't let Charles know we spoke of this?'

'You can trust me.'

Both men stood. For a moment, Grenville studied him. 'And so I shall.'

DR CHESTER CROUCH had invited his four students to join him at the Hurricane for an evening round of drinks. Norris drank too much that night and he could feel the effects as he walked unsteadily home along the river. He thought of his three classmates, bound for their own far superior lodgings, and pictured the cheery fires and the snug rooms that awaited them.

I must study, he thought. There's still time tonight. But when he climbed the stairs to his freezing attic room, he was too exhausted to even open a textbook. To save on candlelight, he undressed in the faint glow of the window, staring out across the hospital common. Shivering, he climbed under the blanket and fell asleep almost instantly.

And almost instantly was woken by a knocking on the door.

'Mr Marshall? Mr Marshall, are you there?'

Norris rolled out of bed and stumbled in a daze across the attic. Opening the door, he saw the hospital groundsman, his face lit eerily by a flickering lantern. 'They need you, up at the hospital,' he said. 'A carriage has turned over near the Canal Bridge. We've got injured comin' in, and we can't find Nurse Robinson. They've sent for other doctors, but with you being so close, I thought I should fetch you, too. Better a medical student than nothing.'

'I'll be right there,' said Norris, ignoring the unintended slight.

He dressed in the dark, fumbling for trousers and boots and waistcoat. He pulled on a greatcoat against the chill and made his way down the dark steps, into the night. He cut directly across the common. An overturned carriage, he thought. Multiple injuries. Would he know what to do? He was so focused on the crisis ahead that at first he did not understand what he was hearing. But a few paces later he heard it again, and stopped.

It was a woman's moan, and it came from the riverbank. The sound came again, and he ran to the riverwalk and called out, 'Hello? Who's there?' Staring down at the river's edge, he saw something dark lying close to where the water lapped. *A body?*

He scrambled over the rocks and his shoes sank into black mud. As he slogged towards the water, his heart pounded faster, his breaths accelerating. It *was* a body. In the darkness, he could just make out the shape of a woman. She was lying on her back, her skirts submerged to the waist in the water. Hands numb with cold, he grabbed her beneath the arms and dragged her up the bank. Gasping from exertion, he crouched down beside her and felt her chest for a heartbeat, a breath, any sign of life. Warm liquid bathed his hand. He stared down and saw the oily gleam of blood on his palm.

Behind him, a pebble clattered on rocks. He turned, and a chill lifted every hair on the back of his neck.

The creature stood on the bank above him. Its black cape fluttered like giant wings in the wind. Beneath the hood, a death's-head stared, white as bone. Hollow eyes looked straight at him. So frozen in fear was Norris that he could not have fled, even if the creature had swooped at him.

Then, suddenly, it was gone. And Norris saw only a view of the night sky.

On the riverwalk, lamplight appeared. 'Hello?' the hospital groundsman shouted. 'Who's down there?'

His throat shut down by panic, Norris could produce only a choked, 'Here.' Then, louder, 'Help. I need help!'

The groundsman came down the muddy bank, lantern swaying. Holding up the light, he stared down at the dead body. At the face of Mary Robinson. Then his gaze lifted to Norris, and the look on the old man's face was unmistakable. It was fear.

NORRIS STARED DOWN at his hands, where the coat of dried blood was now cracked and flaking off his skin. Only as he'd carried Mary Robinson into the building, into the light, had he seen the full horror of her injuries. He'd brought her into the hall, dripping a trail of blood, and a shocked nurse had mutely pointed him towards the surgery room. But as he'd laid Mary on the table, he already knew that she'd passed beyond the help of any surgeon.

'How well did you know Mary Robinson, Mr Marshall?'

Norris looked up and focused on Mr Pratt from the Night Watch. Behind Pratt stood Constable Lyons and Dr Aldous Grenville. They hung back in the shadows, beyond the circle of light cast by the lamp.

'She was a nurse. I've seen her, of course.'

'Did you have any relationship with her outside your work at the hospital?'

'I'm studying medicine, Mr Pratt. I have little time outside of that.'

Mr Pratt turned to Dr Grenville. 'You have examined the body, sir? Can you render an opinion?'

'I can, but I should like Dr Sewall to examine it as well.'

Norris said softly, 'It's the same killer. The same pattern.' He looked up. 'One cut straight across the abdomen. Then a twist of the blade and a slash straight up, towards the sternum. In the shape of a cross.'

'But this time, Mr Marshall,' interjected Constable Lyons, 'the killer has taken it a step further.'

Norris focused on the senior officer of the Night Watch. Though he had never before met Constable Lyons, he knew of the man's reputation. Unlike bombastic Mr Pratt, Constable Lyons was soft-spoken. For the past hour, he had allowed his subordinate Pratt complete control of the investigation. Now Lyons moved into the light and Norris saw a compact gentleman of about fifty, with a trim beard and spectacles.

'Her tongue is missing,' said Lyons.

Watchman Pratt turned to Grenville. 'The killer sliced it out?'

Grenville nodded. 'It would not be a difficult excision with a sharp knife.'

Norris didn't like the way Pratt turned to look at him. 'And, Mr Marshall, you say you saw a creature with a cape? With a face like a skull's?'

'He was exactly as Rose Connolly described him. She told you the truth.'

'Yet the hospital groundsman saw no such monster. He told me he saw only you, bending over the body. And no one else.'

'It was standing there for only an instant. By the time the groundsman came upon me, the creature was gone.'

Pratt studied him. 'Why do you think the tongue was taken?'

'I don't know.'

'It's a monstrous thing to do. But if one were a student of anatomy, it might make sense to collect a body part. For scientific reasons, of course.'

'Mr Pratt,' cut in Grenville, 'you have no grounds to suspect Mr Marshall.'

'A young man who happened to be in the proximity of both murders?'

'He's a medical student. He *would* be found near this hospital.'

Pratt looked at Norris. 'You grew up on a farm, did you not? Have you any experience slaughtering animals?'

'These questions have gone far enough,' said Constable Lyons. 'Mr Marshall, you're free to go.'

Norris stood and crossed to the door. There he paused and looked back. 'I know you didn't believe Rose Connolly,' he said. 'But now I've seen the creature, too. Whether you believe me or not, *something* is out there. Something that chilled my very soul. And I hope to God I never see it again.'

SOMEONE WAS POUNDING on his door once more. What a nightmare I've had, thought Norris as he opened his eyes and saw daylight shining through his window. This is what comes from drinking too much brandy.

'Norris? Norris, wake up!' called Wendell. 'Norris, we must talk!'

Norris threw off his blanket and sat up. Only then did he see his greatcoat, draped over the chair, the fabric stained with broad smears of blood.

Norris opened the door to find Wendell standing in the dim stairway.

'You look awful,' said Wendell.

Norris crossed back to the bed and sat down. 'It was an awful night.'

Wendell stepped inside and shut the door. He looked around at the wretched little garret, taking in the rotting beams, the straw-filled mattress set atop the bed frame of weathered planks, and the stained copy of Wistar's *Anatomy* that lay on top of the desk.

'I imagine you're wondering why I didn't turn up at rounds,' said Norris. He felt painfully exposed, sitting only in his shirt.

'We know why you didn't turn up. It's all they're talking about at the hospital. What happened to Mary Robinson.'

'Then you know that I'm the one who found her.'

'That's one of the versions. There are all sorts of hideous rumours flying.'

Norris stared down again at his bare knees. 'Would you hand me my trousers, please? It's bloody freezing in here.'

Wendell tossed him the trousers, then turned and looked out of the window. As Norris dressed, he noticed bloodstains on the turn-up of his trousers.

'What are they saying about me?' he asked.

'What a coincidence it is that you came so soon upon both death scenes.'

'I wasn't the one who found Agnes Poole's body.'

'But you were there,' Wendell said.

'So were you.'

'I'm not accusing you.'

'Then what are you doing here? Come to take a peep at where the Reaper lives?' Norris rose to his feet, pulling on his shirt. 'It makes for good gossip, I imagine, to share with your Harvard chums over Madeira.'

Wendell crossed towards him. He was far shorter, and he stared up at Norris like an angry little terrier. 'You've had a chip on your shoulder since the day you arrived. The poor farmer's boy, always on the outs. Charles and I have made every attempt to include you, yet you hold us at arm's length, as though you've already decided any friendship is destined to fail.'

'We're classmates, Wendell. Nothing more. We share a preceptor and perhaps we share a round of drinks now and then. But take a look around this room. You can see we have little else in common.'

'I have more in common with you than I have with Edward Kingston.'

Norris laughed. 'Oh, yes. Just look at our matching satin waistcoats. Name one thing we have in common.'

Wendell turned to the desk, where Wistar's lay open. 'You've been studying, for one thing, in this freezing attic. I think you study for the same reason I do. Because you believe in science. I recognise a man of science when I see one. And I've seen your generosity as well.'

'My generosity?'

'In the anatomy room, when Charles made such a bloody mess. You stepped forward and covered for him when Edward and I didn't. You're not like most of the others in our class. You have the *calling*. Charlie Lackaway is here only because his uncle expects it of him and he hasn't the spine to resist. And Edward, he doesn't even bother to hide his lack of interest. Half the students are here to please their parents, and most of the others just want to earn a comfortable living.'

'And why are *you* here? Because *you* have the calling?'

'I admit, medicine was not my first choice. But one can hardly make a living as a poet. Though I have been published in the *Daily Advertiser*. But medicine has *become* my calling. I know it's what I'm meant to do.'

Norris reached for his greatcoat and paused for a heartbeat, his gaze on the bloodstains. He pulled it on anyway. 'If you'll excuse me, I need to explain my absence to Dr Crouch. Is he still at the hospital?'

'Norris, if you go to the hospital, I must warn you what to expect. People are wondering about you. They're afraid.'

'They think I killed her?'

'The trustees have been speaking with Mr Pratt.'

'They aren't listening to his rubbish?'

'They have no choice but to listen. They are responsible for enforcing order in the hospital. They can discipline any doctor on the staff and they can certainly ban a lowly medical student from the wards.'

'Then how would I learn? How would I pursue my studies?'

'Dr Crouch is trying to reason with them. And Dr Grenville has argued against the ban as well. But there are rumours.'

'What are they saying?'

'The fact that her tongue was removed has convinced some that the killer is a medical student.'

'Or someone who's butchered animals,' said Norris. 'And I am both. Why aren't *you* afraid of me? Why do *you* assume I'm innocent?'

'I don't assume anything.'

Norris gave a bitter laugh. 'Oh, *there's* a loyal friend.'

'Damn it, this is *exactly* what a friend would do! He'd tell you the truth. That your future's in jeopardy.' Wendell turned towards the door. There he paused and looked at Norris. 'You have more bull-headed pride than any son of wealth I've ever met.' He yanked open the door.

'Wendell, I'm sorry,' said Norris. And he sighed. 'I'm not accustomed to assuming the best of people.'

Wendell closed the door. 'What are you going to do?'

'Against rumours? What can I do? The more I insist I'm innocent, the more guilty I look.'

'You have to do something. This is your future.'

And it hung by a thread. All it took were a few whispers, and the hospital trustees would ban him permanently from the wards. The only path left to him would be back to his father's farm.

'Until the killer is caught,' said Wendell, 'everyone's eyes will be on you.'

SEVEN

Jack Burke guided his dray through the thickening dusk, the wooden wheels crackling over a thin crust of frozen mud. At this hour, on this lonely road, he met no one. This was further than he liked to journey on such a bitter night, but grave watchers were now stationed at the Old Granary burying grounds, and at Copp's Hill on the North Side.

Once, he could make a good living. But new snatchers were coming into the trade. And they were younger, quicker, and more daring. Tonight, instead of a quick snatch, Jack was forced to drive on this endless back road, dreading the labours ahead. And all alone, too; with so few pickings these days, he was loath to pay a partner. He only hoped that any fresh grave he found was the work of diggers too lazy to bury their charge the full six feet.

The low wall of the cemetery was ahead. He pulled his horse to a halt and paused in the road, scanning the shadows. He reached back for his shovel and lantern, and jumped off the dray. His boots crunched onto frost-heaved earth. His legs were stiff from the long ride and he felt clumsy as he scrambled over the stone wall, the lantern and shovel clanging together.

It did not take long for him to locate a fresh grave. He sank his shovel in the soil where the head would be. After only a few scoops of earth, he had to pause, wheezing in the cold, regretting that he had not brought along that young Norris Marshall. Once again he sank the shovel into the soil and was about to lift the next scoop when a shout made him freeze.

'There he is! Get him!'

Three lanterns were bobbing towards him, closing in fast. In panic, he abandoned his lamp and fled, carrying only the shovel. Darkness hid his path, and every gravestone was an obstacle waiting to trip him like bony hands.

'Over there!' came a shout.

A gun fired, and Jack felt the bullet hiss past his cheek. He scrambled over the wall, abandoning the shovel wherever it had fallen. As he climbed into the dray, another bullet whistled by so close he felt it flick his hair.

'He's getting away!'

One crack of the whip and the horse took off, the dray rattling wildly behind it. Jack heard one last gunshot and then his pursuers fell behind, their lights fading into the darkness.

By the time he got back to the Black Spar, he could barely climb out of the wagon. He stabled the horse and walked wearily into the tavern, wanting nothing more than a seat by the fire and a glass of brandy. But as he sank into a chair, he felt Fanny eyeing him from behind the counter. The establishment was almost empty; one man stood at the bar, digging desperately in his pockets for coins. In a corner, another man had laid down his head, and his snores were loud enough to rattle the glasses that littered his table.

'You're back early.'

Jack looked up at Fanny, who stood over him, her gaze narrow.

'Not a good night,' was all he said. He drained his glass.

'You think I've had a good night here? With this lot?' She snorted.

'Another flip!' the man at the bar yelled.

'Show me your coins first,' shot back Fanny.

'Have a little pity, missus. It's a cold night.'

'And you'll be out in it straight away if you can't pay for another drink.' She looked back at Jack. 'You came home empty-handed, didn't you?'

He shrugged. 'They had watchers.'

'You didn't try some other place?'

'Couldn't. Had to leave behind the shovel. And the lamp.'

She leaned in closer and said softly, 'There are easier ways to make money, Jack. Let me put out the word and you'll have all the work you need.'

'And get hanged for it?' He shook his head.

'You come home empty-handed more often than not these days.'

'The pickings aren't good. They just get worse.'

'Missus?' the man at the bar called. 'Just one more and I promise I'll pay you next time.'

Fanny wheeled round at him in fury. 'Your promise is worthless! You can't pay, you can't stay. Get out.' She stomped towards him and grabbed him by the jacket. 'Go on, get out!' she roared.

She hauled the man across the room, yanked open the door and shoved him out into the cold. She slammed the door, then turned, her gaze landing on the remaining customer, the man who had fallen asleep at the corner table.

'You, too! It's time to leave!'

The man did not stir.

'We're closed! *Go!*' She crossed to the man and gave him a hard cuff on the shoulder. He rolled sideways and toppled off his chair onto the floor.

For a moment, Fanny just stared down in disgust at his gaping mouth, his lolling tongue. A frown creased her forehead and she leaned in close.

'He ain't breathing, Jack,' she said, looking up.

'What?' Jack hauled himself out of the chair and knelt beside the man. He looked into the man's open eyes. When had he stopped snoring? Death had crept in so furtively they hadn't even noticed its entrance.

He looked at Fanny. 'You know who he is?'

'Just some blow-in from the wharves. Walked in alone.'

Jack straightened, his back aching. 'I'll go harness the horse.'

Fanny met his gaze with a nod, a canny glint in her eye.

'We'll earn our twenty dollars after all,' he said.

The Present

'Resurrectionist,' said Henry, 'is an old word, no longer used. Most people today have no idea it refers to a grave robber or a body snatcher.'

'And Norris Marshall was one of them.'

'Only by necessity.'

They sat at the dining table, the pages of another letter from Oliver Wendell Holmes spread out beside their coffee cups and muffins. Although it was well past midmorning, the fog still hung thick outside the windows, and Henry had turned on all the lamps to brighten the murky room.

In the distance, the ferry's horn bellowed. Julia looked at her watch and stood. 'I need to get going, Henry, if I'm to catch the next boat.'

'When you come back, you can help me bring up the boxes from the cellar.'

'Is that an invitation?'

'I thought it was understood.'

She looked at the stack of unopened boxes and thought of the treasures inside them, still unexplored, the letters still to be read. She had no idea if the identity of the skeleton in her garden might lie inside those boxes. What she did know was that the story of Norris Marshall and the West End Reaper had already lured her into its spell.

IT WAS CLOSE to dinnertime when she finally arrived home in Weston. Here at least, the sun was shining, and she looked forward to lighting up the barbecue and sipping a glass of wine in the back garden. As she stepped inside the house, she heard her phone ringing. The answering machine kicked in. 'Julia, I've just found something. When you get home, call me and I'll—'

She picked up the phone. 'Henry?'

'Oh. You're there.'

'I just got home.'

'It was in box number six,' he said. 'The last will and testament of Dr Margaret Tate Page. It's dated 1890, when she would have been sixty. In it, she leaves her possessions to various grandchildren. One of them is a granddaughter named Aurnia. I think this confirms without a doubt that Margaret Tate Page is our baby Meggie, grown up.'

'Then the aunt whom Holmes mentioned in his first letter . . .'

'Is Rose Connolly.'

1830

The light through the grimy window had faded to little more than dull pewter. There were never enough candles in the workroom, and Rose could scarcely see her stitches as her needle plunged in and out of white gauze. It was a fine gown meant for a ball, and as Rose worked, she imagined how the skirt would rustle when its wearer stepped onto the dance floor.

She struggled to see the thread in the feeble light. Someday, she would look like the other women sewing in this room, their eyes fixed in perpetual squints, their fingers callused and scarred from repeated needle pricks.

The needle lanced Rose's finger and she gasped, dropping the gauze on the worktable. She brought her throbbing finger to her mouth and tasted blood, but it was not the pain that vexed her; rather, she was worried that she had stained the white gauze. Holding up the fabric, she could just make out a tiny fleck. Both my stitches and my blood, she thought, I leave on this gown.

'That will be enough for today, ladies,' the foreman announced.

Rose folded the pieces she had worked on, and joined the line of seamstresses waiting to collect their pay for the week.

'You, girl! Rose, isn't it? I need a word with you.'

Heart sinking, Rose turned to face the foreman.

'Yes, Mr Smibart?' she asked.

'It has happened again,' he said. 'And it cannot be tolerated.'

'I'm sorry, but if my work's unsatisfactory—'

'Your work is perfectly adequate,' he said. 'It's the other matter. I cannot have outsiders disturbing me, enquiring about matters that you should deal with in your own time. Tell your friends you are here to *work*.'

Now she understood. 'I'm sorry, sir. Last week, I told Billy not to come here, and I thought he understood. I'll explain it to him again.'

'It wasn't the boy this time. It was a man.'

Rose went very still. 'Which man?' she asked quietly.

'Some beady-eyed fellow, asking all sorts of questions about you. This is a business, Miss Connolly, and I will not tolerate such interruptions.'

'I'm sorry,' she murmured.

'You keep saying that, yet the problem remains. No more visitors.'

'Yes, sir,' she said meekly, and turned to leave.

Rose shivered as she fought the piercing wind. She walked alone, the last of the women to leave the building. It must be that horrid Mr Pratt from the Night Watch asking about me, she thought. Billy had told her the man was enquiring about her around town, and all because she had dared to pawn Aurnia's locket. All Eben's doing, thought Rose. I accused him of attacking me so he retaliates by accusing me of being a thief.

She moved deeper into the warren of tenements until, at last, she reached a door with a low arch and knocked. It was opened by a child with filthy cheeks, his blond hair hanging like a ragged curtain over his eyes. He stood mutely, staring at the visitor.

A woman's voice yelled, 'Fer God's sake, Conn, the cold's gettin' in! Shut the door!'

The silent boy scuttled off into some dark corner as Rose stepped in, closing the door against the wind. In the dimness of the room, she began to make out the chair by the hearth, where the fire had burned down, and the table with its stacked bowls. Then, all around her, the moving shapes of little heads. So many children. Rose counted eight at least, but surely there were others that she could not see, curled up and sleeping in the shadowy corners.

'You brought yer payment fer the week?'

Rose focused on the enormous woman seated in the chair. Now that her eyes had adjusted, Rose could see Hepzibah's face, with its bulging double chin. No matter what time of day or night Rose visited, she'd always found Hepzibah sitting like a fat queen on her throne, her little charges crawling about her feet like grimy supplicants.

'I've brought the money,' said Rose, and she placed half her week's pay in Hepzibah's waiting hand.

'I just fed 'er. A greedy girl, that one, 'bout emptied me breast with just a few sucks. I should charge you more fer 'er.'

Rose knelt to lift her niece from the basket. Little Meggie stared up at her, and Rose was sure that her tiny lips curled into a smile of recognition.

There were no other chairs in the room, so Rose sat down on the filthy floor, among toddlers waiting for mothers to return from work and rescue them from Hepzibah's indifferent supervision. If only I could take you home to a snug, clean room, she thought. But the room on Fishery Alley where Rose slept, a room she shared with twelve other lodgers, was even more grim, infested with rats and foul with disease. Far better that Meggie stay here with Hepzibah, whose fat breasts never ran dry. Here at least she'd be warm and fed. As long as Rose could keep the money coming.

It was only with the greatest reluctance that she finally laid Meggie back in the basket and stood to leave.

'I'll be back tomorrow,' Rose said.

'And same again next week,' Hepzibah answered. Meaning the money, of course. For her, it was all about the money.

'You'll have it. Just keep her safe.' She stepped out of the door. The streets were dark now, and the only source of light was the glow of candles through grimy windows. She rounded the corner and her footsteps slowed, stopped.

In the alley ahead waited a familiar silhouette. Dim Billy waved and came towards her, his impossibly long arms swinging like vines. But it was not Billy she focused on; it was the man standing behind him.

'Miss Connolly,' said Norris Marshall. 'I need to speak to you.'

'He said he's your friend,' said Billy.

She shot an irritated look at Billy. 'Do you believe *everything* you're told?'

'I *am* your friend,' said Norris. 'Do you know that Mr Pratt is searching for you, what he's saying about you?'

'He's been saying I'm a thief. Or worse.'

'Mr Pratt is a buffoon.'

That brought a grim smile to her lips. 'An opinion we have in common.'

'We have something else in common, Miss Connolly,' he said quietly. 'I've seen it, too. The Reaper.'

She stared at him. 'When?'

'Last night. It was standing over the body of Mary Robinson.'

'Nurse Robinson?' She fell a step back, the news so shocking it felt like a physical blow. '*Mary* is dead?'

'The news is all over town,' said Norris. 'I wanted to speak to you before you hear some twisted version of what happened. Is there someplace warm and private where we can talk?' he asked.

She did not know if she could trust this man. But at her sister's bedside, he had been courteous to her, the only student who had met her gaze with any real regard. Gazing up the alley, she considered where to go.

'Come with me,' she said.

A few streets away, she turned up a shadowy passage and stepped through a doorway. In the hallway, a lone lamp burned in its sconce, the flame shuddering wildly as she swung the door shut against the wind.

'Our room's upstairs,' said Billy, and he scampered up ahead of them.

Norris looked at Rose. 'He lives with you?'

'I couldn't leave him sleeping in a cold stable,' she said. She lit a candle at the sconce and Norris followed her up a dozen creaking steps to the dim and stinking room that housed the thirteen lodgers. Sagging curtains hung between straw mattresses like a regiment of ghosts. One of the lodgers was resting in a dark corner and they could hear the man's ceaseless hacking.

Ducking his head beneath the low rafters, Norris picked his way across the mattress-strewn floor and knelt beside the sick lodger.

'Old Clary's too weak to work,' said Billy. 'So he stays in bed all day.'

Norris made no comment, but he understood the significance of the blood-flecked bedclothes. Clary's pale face was so wasted by consumption that his bones seemed to gleam through his skin.

Without a word, Norris rose back to his feet.

'Over here's my bed!' declared Billy, and he plopped down on a pile of straw. 'If we shut the curtain, we'll make a pretty room all to ourselves. You can sit there, sir. Old Polly won't notice that anyone's been using her bed.'

Norris did not look at all eager to settle onto the bundle of rags and straw. Rose slid the curtain across to give them privacy from the dying man in the corner, and only when she settled onto her own bed did he resignedly sit down as well. The three of them formed a circle round the flickering candle, which cast spindly shadows on the curtain.

'Now tell me,' she said. 'Tell me what happened to Mary.'

He stared at the light. 'I'm the one who found her,' he said. 'Last night, on the riverbank. She'd been cut, Miss Connolly, the same way Agnes Poole was cut. The same pattern, slashed into her abdomen.'

'In the shape of a cross?'

'Yes.'

'Does Mr Pratt still blame papists?'

'I can't imagine that he does now.'

'And who would Mr Pratt's unlucky suspect be this time?'

'I am.'

In the silence that followed, she stared at the shadows playing on Norris's face. Billy had curled up and lay dozing, each breath rustling the straw.

'So you see,' he said, 'I know what it's like to be unfairly accused. I know what you've gone through.'

'*You* know, do you? Yet it's myself who's looked at with suspicion every day of my life. *You* have no idea.'

'Miss Connolly, last night I saw the same creature you did, but no one believes me. No one else saw it. The hospital groundsman saw *me* bending over her body. I'm looked at with suspicion by the nurses, the other students. The hospital trustees may banish me from the wards. All I've ever wanted was to be a doctor. Now everything I've worked for is threatened.' He leaned closer, and the candle's glow painted his face with gaunt shadows. 'You've seen it, too. I need to know if you remember the same things I do.'

'I told you that night what I saw. But I don't think you believed me then.'

'I admit, at the time your story seemed far-fetched. But you were overwrought and clearly terrified.' He added quietly, 'Last night, so was I.'

She looked at the candle flame. And whispered, 'It had wings.'

'A cape, perhaps. Or a dark cloak.'

'And its face glowed white.' She met Norris's gaze. 'White as a skull. Is that what you saw?'

'I don't know. The moon was on the water. Reflections can play tricks.'

Her lips tightened. 'I'm telling you what I saw. And in return, you offer explanations. "It was just the *moon's reflection*"!'

'I'm a man of science, Miss Connolly. I seek logical explanations.'

She swallowed and said softly, 'I'm afraid he knows my face.'

'And this is why you hide?' Norris asked.

'I hide to avoid trouble, Mr Marshall. From everyone.'

'Including the Night Watch? They're saying you pawned an item of jewellery that wasn't yours.'

'My sister gave it to me.'

'Mr Pratt says you stripped it from her body while she lay dying.'

She gave a snort. 'My brother-in-law's spreading rumours about me. Even if I *did* take it, how else was I supposed to pay for Aurnia's burial?'

'Her burial? But she . . .' He paused.

'What about Aurnia?' she asked.

'Nothing. It's just . . . an unusual name, that's all. A lovely name.'

She gave a sad smile. 'It was our grandmother's name. It means "golden lady". She deserved better,' Rose said softly. 'But in the end, the only one standing at her grave was me. And Mary Robinson.'

'Nurse Robinson was there?'

'She was kind to my sister, kind to everyone.' She shook her head sadly, thinking of the last time she had seen Mary Robinson, at St Augustine's cemetery. She remembered the woman's darting glances and jittery hands. And how she had suddenly vanished without saying goodbye.

Billy stirred and sat up, scattering pieces of dirty straw from his hair. He looked at Norris. 'Are you sleeping here with us, then?' he asked.

Rose flushed. 'No, Billy. He's not.'

'I can move my bed to make room for you,' said Billy. 'But I'm the only one gets to sleep next to Miss Rose. She promised.'

'I wouldn't dream of taking your place, Billy,' said Norris. He stood and brushed straw from his trousers. 'Thank you for speaking to me, Miss Connolly.' He pulled aside the curtain and started down the stairs.

'Mr Marshall?' Rose scrambled to her feet and followed him. 'I must ask that you not enquire at my place of work again,' she said.

He frowned. 'I'm sorry? I've never been to your place of employment.'

'A man was there today, asking where I lived.'

'I don't even know where you work.' He opened the door, letting in a blast of wind. 'Whoever enquired about you, it wasn't me.'

EIGHT

'You wished to speak to me, Dr Grenville?' said Norris.

Dr Grenville gazed across his desk, his face giving away nothing. The blow is about to fall, thought Norris.

'You have seen the latest article in the *Daily Advertiser*?' asked Grenville. 'About the West End murders?'

'Yes, sir.' Why delay it any longer, he thought. 'I wish to know the truth, sir. Am I or am I not to be expelled from this college?'

'That's why you think I've called you here?'

'It is a reasonable assumption. Considering . . .'

'The rumours? Ah, yes, they are flying thick and furious. I've heard from the families of a number of our students. They're all concerned about the reputation of this college. Without our reputation, we are nothing.'

'And they think I am a threat.'

'You can understand why, can't you?'

Norris looked him straight in the eye. 'All they have to convict me is circumstance. This medical college prides itself on its scientific method. Isn't that method all about seeking answers based on facts, not hearsay?'

Grenville leaned back in his chair, but his gaze remained fixed on Norris.

'I'm not the only one who's seen the killer,' said Norris. 'Rose Connolly has seen him, too.'

'A monster with black wings and a skull's face?'

'There is *something* evil at work in the West End.'

'Attributed by the Night Watch to the work of a butcher.'

'And that's the real charge against me, isn't it? That I'm the son of a farmer. If I were the son of any prominent gentleman, would I be a suspect?'

After a silence, Grenville said, 'Your point is well taken.'

'Yet it changes nothing.' Norris turned to leave. 'Good day, Dr Grenville. I see I have no future here.'

'Why would you *not* have a future here? Have I dismissed you?'

Norris turned back. 'You said my presence was a problem.'

'It is indeed a problem, but it's one that I'll deal with. I'm fully aware that you face a number of disadvantages. Unlike so many of your classmates, you did not come straight from Harvard. You're self-taught, yet doctors Sewall and Crouch are impressed by your skills.'

For a moment Norris could not speak. 'I—I don't know how to thank you.'

'Don't thank me yet. Things may still change.'

'You won't regret this.'

'There's one more thing. When did you last see young Dr Berry?'

This was a completely unexpected question and Norris paused, perplexed. 'It was yesterday evening. As he was leaving the hospital.'

Grenville turned his troubled gaze to the window. 'That was the last time I saw him, too,' he murmured.

'THOUGH THERE has been much speculation as to its aetiology,' said Dr Chester Crouch, 'the cause of puerperal fever remains open to debate. This is a most evil disease, which steals the lives of women just as they achieve their heart's desire, the gift of motherhood . . .' He stopped and stared.

So did everyone else, as Norris walked into the auditorium. Yes, the infamous Reaper had arrived.

'Do find a seat, Mr Marshall,' said Crouch.

'Over here.' Wendell stood. 'We've saved a seat for you, Norris.'

Norris squeezed his way up the row, past young men who seemed to flinch as he brushed past. He settled into the empty chair between Wendell and Charles. 'Thank you, both,' he whispered.

'We were afraid you might not be coming at all,' said Charles. 'You should have heard the rumours this morning. They were saying—'

'Now. *If* you will allow me to continue,' Crouch said. He began once again to pace the stage. 'We are, at this moment, experiencing an epidemic of childbed fever in our lying-in ward. Though her child might be safely delivered, the new mother still faces danger. It may manifest during labour, or it may develop hours, even days after the delivery. First, she feels a violent chill. This is followed by a fever that causes the skin to flush, the heart to race. But the true torment is the pain. It begins in the pelvic area and progresses to excruciating tenderness as the abdomen swells. There is often a bloody discharge, too, of a most foul nature. But the worst is yet to come.'

Crouch paused, and the audience was utterly silent.

'The pulse grows more rapid,' Crouch continued. 'Respirations become laboured. The pulse grows irregular. At which point, there is little left to offer except morphine and wine. Because death inevitably follows.' He looked round the room. 'Some claim it's an epidemic contagion like smallpox. But if this is so, why does it not spread to women who are not pregnant? What other explanation might there be to account for the thousands of women dead of this illness in France? In Hungary? In England?

'Here, too, in Boston, we are seeing many more of them. My colleagues cite alarming numbers. One doctor has lost five patients in quick succession. And I have lost seven, in this month alone.'

Abruptly Wendell stood. 'A question, sir. If I may?'

Crouch glanced up. 'Yes, Mr Holmes?'

'Is there also such an epidemic in the tenements in South Boston?'

'Not yet.'

'But so many of the Irish live in filth there. Their diet is inadequate. Under those conditions, shouldn't there be many such deaths?'

'The poor have a different constitution. They're made of sturdier stock.'

'I've heard that women who suddenly give birth in the fields seldom come down with the fever. Is that also because of a stronger constitution?'

'That is my theory.' He paused. 'But now we move on to Dr Sewall's anatomical presentation. His specimen is, I regret to say, one of my own patients, a woman who perished from the illness I have just described.'

As Dr Crouch sat down, Dr Sewall climbed to the stage, the steps creaking beneath his massive weight.

'What you have just heard,' said Sewall, 'is the classic description of childbed fever. Now you shall see the pathology of this disease.' He paused and gazed round the auditorium. 'Mr Lackaway. You have yet to volunteer for any anatomical demonstration. Will you come down here and assist me?'

'Sir, I don't think I'm the best choice—'

Edward said, 'Oh, go *on*, Charlie.' He gave him a clap on the shoulder. 'I promise, someone will catch you this time when you faint.'

Swallowing hard, Charles reluctantly made his way down to the stage.

Sewall's assistant rolled out the cadaver from the wings and removed the drape. Charles recoiled, staring at the young woman. Black hair cascaded from the table, and one arm, white and slim, dangled over the side.

On stage, Sewall handed a knife to Charles. 'This will not be a complete autopsy. We'll focus only on the pathology of this particular disease.'

Edward murmured, 'I give him ten seconds before he hits the ground.'

'Hush,' said Wendell.

Charles approached the body and Norris could see his hand shaking.

'The abdomen,' said Sewall. 'Make your cut.'

Grimacing, Charles made a slice down the belly, but his cut was shallow.

'You'll have to be bolder than that,' said Sewall. 'Cut deeper.'

Charles paused, gathering up his nerve. Again he sliced. Again it was too shallow. A stuttering incision that left parts of the abdominal wall intact. He raised his sleeve to his forehead and wiped away sweat. Then, using one hand to stretch the belly wall taut, he sliced a third time. The putrid smell that rose from the ever-widening gap made him turn away, pale with nausea.

'Watch it. You've nicked the bowel!' barked Sewall.

Charles flinched, and his knife fell from his hand and thudded to the stage. 'I've cut myself,' he whimpered. 'My finger.'

Sewall gave an exasperated sigh. 'Oh, go on, then. Sit down. I'll finish the demonstration myself.'

Flushing with humiliation, Charles returned to his seat beside Norris.

Dr Sewall refocused on the cadaver. 'You see here the peritoneal membrane, and its appearance is abnormal. In cases of childbed fever, the peritoneum lacks lustre and there are pockets of pale, creamy fluid. We cannot explain the reasons for these changes and I am no more than an anatomist. I can only show you what I have laid bare with my knife.'

Dr Sewall split open the chest and lifted out a lung. Glancing at his classmates, Norris saw a range of expressions from boredom to concentration. A few weeks of medical study had stiffened their spines so they could watch without disgust as Sewall excavated the heart and remaining lung. We've lost our sense of horror, thought Norris. It was a necessary step in their training.

EARLY IN THE EVENING, Jack Burke had already singled him out. The sailor sat alone at a table, talking to no one, his gaze fixed only on the rum that Fanny set before him. Three drinks was all he had money for. He downed the last drink and, as Fanny waited, he rummaged through his pockets for more coins, but came up empty-handed. Jack could see Fanny's lips tighten, her eyes narrow. As far as she was concerned, if a man took up space at a table, he had better be able to afford to keep the rum flowing. That was why the Black Spar was a failing enterprise, thought Jack, watching Fanny's face turn ugly. Walk a ways down the street, into that new tavern, the Mermaid, and you'd find a laughing young barmaid and a generous fire. You'd also find a crowd, many of them Fanny's old regulars who'd fled the Black Spar.

Before she could speak, Jack caught her gaze. He gave her a warning shake of his head. *Leave that one alone, Fanny.*

She stared at Jack for a moment. Then, with a nod, she went behind the bar and poured a glass of rum. She came back to the sailor's table and set the glass before him. The drink did not last long. Fanny silently set another drink before him. No one counted the number of times Fanny whisked away an empty glass and replaced it with a full one. No one cared that the man began to slump forward, his head resting on his arms.

One by one, as their pockets emptied, the customers staggered out into the cold, until only the snoring seaman at the corner table was left.

Fanny crossed to the door, barred it shut, and turned to look at Jack.

'How much did you give him?' he asked.

'Enough to drown a horse.'

The seaman gave a great rattling snore. They stared down at the sleeping man, watching drool spill from his lips.

Jack gave the shoulder a nudge; the man snored on, unaware.

Fanny snorted. 'You can't expect them all to keel over nice and easy.'

'He's a young one. Healthy looking.' *Too healthy*. Jack gave a harder shove. Slowly, the man tumbled out of the chair and thumped onto the floor. Jack rolled him onto his back. Damn it all. He was still breathing.

'I can't leave any marks on his neck. It has to look natural.'

'Then we'll make it look natural.' Fanny stared down at the man for a moment, her eyes narrowed. 'Wait here,' she said.

He listened to her footsteps thumping up the stairs to their bedroom. A moment later she returned, carrying a threadbare cushion and a filthy rag. He understood at once what she had in mind, but he didn't move. He had dug up corpses with flesh falling off their bones. But actually *making* a corpse was always a different matter. A hanging matter.

Still. Twenty dollars was twenty dollars, and who would miss this man?

He lowered himself onto creaking knees beside the drunken seaman. The jaw had fallen slack and he shoved the rag into the gaping mouth. The man jerked his head. Jack lowered the cushion and pressed it over the mouth and nose. All at once the man came awake and clawed at the pillow.

'Hold his arms! Hold his arms!' yelled Jack.

'I'm trying, damn it!'

The man bucked and twisted, boots pounding against the floor.

'I'm losing my grip!' Jack panted. '*Sit* on him.'

Fanny pulled up her skirts and planted her hefty bottom on the squirming man's hips. Sheer terror had given the victim supernatural strength and he clawed at Jack's arms, leaving bloody tracks with his nails. With a roar of pain, Jack pressed down with all his weight, yet still the man fought him. How long did it take a man to die, for pity's sake?

Jack scrambled on top of the chest and sat on the ribs. Now they were both riding him and their combined weight at last immobilised him. Only his feet were moving now, the heels of his boots battering the floor in a panicked tattoo. As his strength drained, the feet slowed their tempo. Jack felt the chest give one last shudder and then the arms went slack and slid away.

It was another moment before Jack dared to lift the pillow. He stared down at the mottled face.

They stripped him together, peeling away his clothes and boots.

'Let's get 'im in the wagon,' said Jack. He grabbed the naked man under the arms, startled by the unfamiliar heat of a newly dead corpse.

Outside, in the stable yard, they swung the body into the dray and left it uncovered in the cold, as Jack harnessed the horse. Wouldn't do to deliver too warm a corpse, though Sewall had never been one to ask questions.

Nor did he ask them this time. After Jack dropped the body onto Sewall's table, he stood by nervously as the anatomist peeled back the tarp. For a moment Sewall said nothing, though he must have registered the extraordinary freshness of this specimen. Holding a lamp close, he inspected the skin, peered into the mouth. No bruises, Jack thought. Just some poor unfortunate sot he'd found collapsed dead on the street. That was the story.

Dr Sewall set down the lamp and left the room. It seemed to Jack that he was gone a long time. Then he returned, holding a bag of coins.

'Thirty dollars,' he said. 'Can you bring me more like this?'

Thirty? This was better than Jack had expected.

'As many as you can find,' said Sewall. 'I've got buyers.'

'Then I'll find more.'

The bag of coins made a pleasant jingle in Jack's pocket as he steered the empty dray over the cobblestones. It was more than any other specimen had brought him. Visions of sacks bulging with coins shimmered in his head all the way home. He rounded the corner into the alley that led to his stable-yard gate. Suddenly he yanked on the reins, drawing the horse to a stop.

A black-caped figure stood before him, silhouetted against the ice-slick gleam of cobblestones.

Jack squinted to make out a face. The features were shadowed by the hood, and all he could see was the pale gleam of teeth.

'You've been busy tonight, Mr Burke.'

'I don't know what you mean.'

'The fresher they are, the more they fetch.'

Jack felt the blood freeze in his veins. *We were watched.* He sat still, heart thumping, his hands clutching the reins.

Jack shuddered. 'What do you want?'

'A small service, Mr Burke. I want you to find someone.'

'Who?'

'A girl. Her name is Rose Connolly.'

IN THE LODGING HOUSE on Fishery Alley, Rose lay awake, listening to the crackling of straw beneath restless bodies. She badly needed to urinate, but she was cosy beneath her blanket, and did not want to leave it. She thought of baby Meggie. *Thank God you are not breathing in this foul air. I'll see you grow up healthy, girl, even if my eyes go blind from threading needles.*

She thought of the white gauze gown she had completed yesterday. By now it would have been delivered to the young lady who had ordered it. Miss Lydia Russell, the daughter of the distinguished Dr Russell. Rose had worked feverishly to complete it on time, since she'd been told that Miss Lydia needed it for the medical college reception tomorrow night, at the home of the dean, Dr Aldous Grenville. Rose imagined the laughter and the candlelight, the doctors in their fine topcoats. She imagined the ribbon-bedecked ladies taking their turns at the piano, each vying to display her skills to the young men.

Would Norris Marshall be there? She felt a sudden twinge of jealousy that he might admire the young lady who wore the gown Rose had laboured over. She knew that he was a man of only modest means, but he was beyond her reach. Even a farmer's son, if he carried a medical bag, could one day be welcomed into the best parlours in Boston. The only way Rose would ever set foot in those parlours was with a mop in her hand.

Billy turned over, bumping up against her. Resigned, she sat up. Her full bladder could no longer be ignored. The piss bucket was at the far end of the room, across all those sleeping bodies. Better to go outside.

She pulled on her shoes and cloak, crawled across Billy's sleeping body, and made her way down the stairs. Outside, the slap of cold wind made her suck in a startled breath. Glancing up and down Fishery Alley, she saw no one, and squatted right there on the cobblestones. With a sigh of relief, she stepped back inside and was about to climb the stairs when she heard the landlord call out, 'Who's there? Who's come in?'

Peering through his doorway, she caught sight of Mr Porteous, sitting with his feet propped up on a stool.

'It's me,' said Rose.

'Come in here, girl. There's a gentleman to see you.'

Norris Marshall has come back was her first reaction. But when she stepped into the room and saw the visitor standing by the fireplace, bitter disappointment silenced any greeting from her lips.

'Hello, Rose,' said Eben. 'I've had a hard time tracking you down. I've come to make amends.'

'The person you should make amends to is no longer here.'

'You have every right to reject my apologies. I'm ashamed of how I behaved and I did not deserve your sister.'

'No, you did not.'

He came towards her, arms outstretched. 'This is the only way I know how to make it up to Aurnia,' he said. 'By being a good brother to you, a good father to my daughter. Go, fetch the baby, Rose. Let's go home.'

Old Porteous watched raptly. This was probably the best entertainment he'd been treated to in weeks.

'Your old bed is waiting for you,' said Eben. 'And a crib, for the baby.'

'I'm paid up here for the month,' said Rose.

'Here?' Eben gave a laugh. 'You can't possibly prefer *this* place!'

'Now then, Mr Tate,' cut in Porteous, suddenly realising he'd just been insulted. 'I give them fresh straw, sir. Every month.'

Eben took a breath, then said, 'Rose, please consider what I'm offering. If you're not happy, you can always return here.'

She thought of the boarding house where Eben lived. It was not grand, but it was clean, and she would not be sleeping on straw.

'Go up and fetch her. Let's go.'

'She's not here. She stays with a wet nurse. But my bag is upstairs.' She turned towards the steps.

'Unless it has something of value, leave it. Let's not waste time.'

She had no desire to return to the fetid room upstairs. She looked at Porteous. 'Please tell Billy to bring my bag round tomorrow to the tailor's shop. I'll pay him for it.'

Eben took her arm. 'The night gets colder by the hour.'

Outside, snowflakes had begun to swirl down from the darkness, stinging flakes that settled treacherously onto icy cobblestones.

'Which way to this wet nurse?' Eben asked.

''Tis a few streets over.' She pointed. 'Not far.'

Eben picked up the pace, urging her far too quickly on such precarious ground. Why such haste? she wondered. Why, after that impassioned appeal for her forgiveness, had he suddenly fallen silent? She'd never trusted Eben before; why should she trust him now?

She did not stop at Hepzibah's building, but walked past it, kept leading Eben away from Meggie as she considered why he had really come tonight.

'Where is this place?' he demanded. 'You said it was close by.'

'It's so late, Eben! Must we fetch her now? We'll wake the household.'

'She's my daughter. She belongs with *me*.'

'And how will you feed her?'

'It's all arranged.'

'What do you mean "all arranged"?'

He gave her a hard shake. 'Just take me to her!'

Rose had no intention of doing so. She continued to lead him away.

Abruptly Eben jerked her to a stop. 'What game are you playing with me, Rose? We've gone twice past this very street!'

She yanked away from him. 'A short time ago, you cared nothing about your daughter. Now suddenly you can't wait to get your hands on her. Well, I won't give her up now, not to you.'

'There's someone else who might convince you.' He grabbed her arm again and pulled her up the street, heading towards the harbour.

'Where are we going?'

'To a man who could change your life. If you're nice to him.' He led her to a building she did not know and knocked on the door.

It opened, and a middle-aged gentleman peered out at them over the light of a flickering lamp. 'I was about to give up and leave, Mr Tate,' he said.

Eben gave Rose a shove, forcing her ahead of him over the threshold. She heard the bolt slide home behind her.

'Where is the child?' the man asked.

'She won't tell me. I thought you could convince her.'

'So this is Rose Connolly,' the man said, and she heard London in his voice. An Englishman. He was shorter than Eben, and his thick side-whiskers were mostly grey. His topcoat was fashionably cut of fine fabric. 'So much fuss over this mere girl.'

'She's cleverer than she looks,' said Eben.

'Let's hope so.' The man started down a hallway. 'This way, Mr Tate. We'll see what she can tell us.'

Eben took her arm in a firm grip. They followed the man into a room where she saw roughly made furniture and a floor scarred by gouges. In the hearth were only cold ashes. The room did not match the man, whose air of prosperity were better suited to one of the fine homes on Beacon Hill.

Eben pushed her into a chair and gave her a dark look.

The older man set the lamp down on a desk, stirring up a puff of dust. 'You've been in hiding, Miss Connolly,' he said. 'Why?'

'What makes you think I've been hiding?'

'Why else would you call yourself Rose Morrison? That is, I believe, the false name you gave to Mr Smibart when he hired you as a seamstress.'

She glared at Eben. 'I didn't wish to encounter my brother-in-law again.'

'That's why you changed your name? It had nothing to do with this?' The Englishman reached into his pocket and pulled out something that gleamed in the lamplight. It was Aurnia's necklace. 'I believe you pawned this several weeks ago. Something that did not belong to you.'

She could not let that charge go unanswered. 'Aurnia gave it to me! She deserved a decent burial. I had no other way to pay for it.'

The Englishman glanced at Eben. 'You didn't tell me that. She had a good reason to pawn it.'

'It still wasn't hers,' said Eben.

'And it sounds like it wasn't yours either, Mr Tate.' The man looked at Rose. 'Did your sister ever tell you where she got this necklace?'

'Why does it matter?' she shot back.

'This is a valuable piece of jewellery, Miss Connolly. Only someone of means could have afforded it.'

'Now you'll claim Aurnia stole it. You're with the Night Watch, aren't you?'

'I'm not with the local authorities, if that's any reassurance. I work for a client who shall remain nameless. I'm charged with the gathering of information. Information that, I'm afraid, only you can provide.' The Englishman moved towards Rose. 'Where is your sister's child? Where is the baby?'

'He doesn't deserve her.' She glanced at Eben. 'What sort of father signs away the rights to his own daughter? Instead o' paying a pretty penny for a fancy lawyer, he could've bought his girl milk and a warm crib.'

'Is that what you think? That I'm in Mr Tate's employ?' The Englishman gave a startled laugh. 'I work for someone else, Miss Connolly. Someone who wants very much to know where the child is. Where is the baby?'

Rose sat silent, suddenly thinking of that day in St Augustine's cemetery, when Mary Robinson had appeared like a ghost from the mist. *There are people enquiring about the child. Keep the child safe. Keep her hidden.*

'What a shame that a girl with your intelligence is forced to live so close to the edge. Your shoes look as if they're falling apart. And that cloak—surely, you deserve better.'

'So do many others.'

'Ah, but *you* are the one being offered an opportunity here. A thousand dollars. If you bring me the child.'

She was stunned. That much money could buy a room in a fine lodging house with hot meals every night. New clothes and a warm coat, not this cloak with its tattered hem. *All I have to do is surrender Meggie.*

'I can't help you,' she said.

Eben's blow came so quickly that the other man had no time to intervene. The impact made Rose's head snap sideways.

'That was not necessary, Mr Tate. You can get more cooperation with a carrot than with a stick.'

'Well, she just turned down the carrot.'

Rose lifted her head and stared at Eben with undisguised hatred.

'I apologise for that.' The Englishman looked at Eben. 'Leave the room.'

Eben shot Rose a poisonous look, then walked out, slamming the door.

The man reached for a chair and dragged it over to Rose's. 'Now, Miss Connolly,' he said, sitting down to face her. 'You know it's only a matter of time until we find her. Save us all the trouble and you'll be well rewarded.'

'Why is she so important to you?'

'Not to me. To my client, who wants the child to stay alive and healthy.'

'Are you saying Meggie's in danger?'

'Our concern is that *you* may be. And if something happens to you, we'll never find the child.' He leaned forward, his face deadly serious. 'Both Agnes Poole and Mary Robinson are dead. You do know that?'

She swallowed. 'Yes.'

'You were a witness the night Agnes Poole died. You saw the killer. And he certainly knows that.'

'Everyone knows who the killer is,' she said. 'I heard it yesterday, on the streets. Dr Berry has fled town.'

'Yes, that's what the newspapers have reported. Dr Nathaniel Berry lived in the West End. He knew the two victims. Now Dr Berry's gone missing, so of course he must be the Reaper.'

'Isn't he?'

'Do you believe everything you hear on the street?'

'But if he isn't the killer . . .'

'Then the West End Reaper may still be in Boston, and he could well know your identity. After what happened to Mary Robinson, I'd be looking over my shoulder if I were you. We were able to find you, and so could anyone else. Which is why I'm so concerned about your niece's welfare. You're the only one who knows the baby's whereabouts . . .' He paused. 'A thousand dollars, Miss Connolly. Give us the child, and the money's yours.'

She said nothing. Weary of her silence, the man finally stood. 'Should you change your mind, you can find me here.' He placed a calling card in her hand, and she stared down at it: *Mr Gareth Wilson, 5 Park Street, Boston*.

'You'd do well to consider my offer,' he said. 'And to consider, too, the welfare of the child. In the meantime, Miss Connolly, do be careful.' He walked out, leaving her alone in the room, her gaze still fixed on the card.

'Are you insane, Rose?' Eben was standing in the doorway. 'That's more money than you'll ever see! How dare you refuse it?'

Staring into his eyes, she suddenly understood why he cared. 'He promised you money, too, didn't he?' she said. 'How much?'

'Enough to make it worth it.'

'Worth giving up your child?'

'Haven't you figured it out? She's not *my* child. I thought it was mine, and that's the only reason I married Aurnia. But time tells the truth, Rose. It told me what kind of woman I really married.'

She shook her head, not willing to believe it.

'Whoever the father is,' said Eben, 'he wants that child. And he has enough to pay whatever it takes. Accept the money.'

She stood. 'I'd starve before I give her up.'

He followed her out of the room, to the front door. As she stepped outside, he yelled, 'This time they were gentle with you, but next time you won't be so lucky!'

To her relief, Eben didn't follow her. The night had grown even colder, and she shivered as she retraced her steps to Fishery Alley, hoping that old Porteous had not already barred the door. Even her poor pile of straw seemed a luxury this night, and she should not have so easily surrendered it.

NINE

The Present

The journey was familiar to Julia now, the same road north, the same ferry ride, even the same dense fog hiding her view of the crossing to Islesboro. This time, though, she was prepared for the damp weather, and was dressed in a sweater and jeans as she dragged her small roll-aboard suitcase up the track to Stonehurst.

She knocked on the door, resolving to be patient and wait until he appeared. After a few moments, she tried the front door and found it unlocked. Poking her head inside, she called out, 'Henry?'

She brought her suitcase into the house and yelled up the stairs, 'Henry, I'm here!'

She heard no answer. She walked into the library, where she saw papers scattered across the table. Then she spotted the cane lying on the floor and the two skinny legs that poked out from behind the stack of boxes.

'*Henry!*'

He was lying on his side, his trousers soaked in urine. Frantic, she rolled him onto his back and bent close, to see if he was breathing.

He opened his eyes. And whispered, 'I knew you'd come.'

'I THINK HE MAY have had an arrhythmia,' said Dr Jarvis. 'I find no signs of a stroke or heart attack and his EKG looks normal at the moment.'

'At the moment?' asked Julia.

'Arrhythmias can come and go without warning, which is why I want to keep him on a monitored unit for the next twenty-four hours. I've already called his family. His grand-nephew's driving up from Massachusetts, but he won't get here till midnight at the earliest. Until then, maybe you can talk Henry into staying in that bed.'

'Where else is he going to go? The ferry's stopped running.'

'Ha, you think that'd stop Henry? He'd just call some friend with a boat to bring him home.'

'You sound like you know him pretty well.'

'The whole medical staff knows Henry. I'm the only doctor he hasn't fired yet. And I may be about to lose that exclusive status.'

Through the curtain round Henry's bed came his complaining voice. 'Dr Jarvis told you I didn't have a heart attack. So why am I still here?'

'Mr Page, don't you dare disconnect that monitor.'

'Where is she? Where's my young lady?'

'She's probably left by now.'

Julia took a deep breath and crossed to his bed. 'I'm here, Henry,' she said, and stepped through the curtain.

'Take me home now, Julia.'

'You know I can't. The ferry stopped running at five.'

'Call my friend Bart in Lincolnville. He has a boat with radar. He can get us across in the fog.'

'No, I'm not going to. I refuse. You can't make me.'

He stared at her. 'Well,' he huffed, 'someone's grown a spine.'

'Your grand-nephew's on his way. He'll be here later tonight.'

'Maybe he'll do what I want.'

'If he gives a damn about you, he'll say no.'

THROUGH THE CLOSED curtain, Julia heard a doctor and nurse conferring, and she sat up, rubbing the sleep from her eyes. She had dozed off in the chair by Henry's bed. She glanced at him. He was sleeping comfortably.

'This is his most recent EKG?' a man asked.

'Yes. Dr Jarvis said they've all been normal.'

The sound of shuffling paper. 'His blood work looks good. Oops. His liver enzymes are up a little. He must be into that wine cellar again.'

'Do you need anything else, Dr Page?'

'Other than a double shot of Scotch?'

The nurse laughed. 'Good luck with him. You'll need it.'

The curtain parted and Dr Page stepped in. Julia stood to greet him, and her gaze fixed on a startlingly familiar face.

'Tom,' she murmured.

'Hi, Julia. I hear he's been giving you a hard time. On behalf of our whole family, I apologise.'

'But you—' She paused. '*You're* his grand-nephew?'

'Yeah. Didn't he tell you I lived in your neighbourhood?'

'No. He never mentioned it.'

Tom glanced in surprise at Henry, who was still sound asleep. 'Well, that's bizarre. I told him that you and I had met. That's why he called you.'

She motioned to him to follow her through the curtain away from the bed. 'Henry called me because of Hilda's papers. He thought I'd be interested in the history of my house.'

'Right. I told him that you wanted to know more about the bones in your garden. Henry's sort of our family historian, so I thought he might be able to help you. Well, he *is* eighty-nine. He might forget things.'

'He's sharp as a tack. That's why it was such a shock for me when I found him on the floor. He seems so indestructible.'

'I'm glad you were there. Thank you for everything you did.' He touched her shoulder and she flushed at the warmth of his hand.

'I feel responsible. I'm the reason he's digging through those boxes. Maybe it's too much for him and that's why he collapsed.'

'You can't make Henry do anything he doesn't want to do. When I spoke to him last week, he sounded more excited than I've heard him in years. Usually he's crotchety and depressed. Now he's just crotchety.'

From behind the curtain came Henry's voice. 'I heard that.'

Tom grimaced. He opened the curtain round Henry's bed. 'You're awake.'

'Took you long enough to get here. Now let's go home. Julia and I have work to do. Twenty more boxes at least. Where is she?'

She joined Tom at the curtain. 'It's too late to go home now. Why don't you go back to sleep?'

'Only if you promise you'll take me home tomorrow.'

She looked at Tom. 'What do you think?'

'If Dr Jarvis clears it, I'll help you get him home in the morning,' he said. 'And I'll hang around for a few days to make sure everything's OK.'

'Oh, good!' said Henry, clearly delighted. 'You'll be staying! Now *you* can bring up all the boxes from the cellar.'

IT WAS LATE the next afternoon when they brought Henry home on the ferry. Dr Jarvis had ordered him to go straight to bed. Instead, Henry stationed himself at the top of the cellar steps, shouting orders as Tom carried boxes up the stairs. By the time Henry finally retired to his bedroom that night, it was Tom who was exhausted.

With a sigh, he sank into an armchair by the fireplace and said, 'He may be eighty-nine, but he can still make me jump through hoops.'

Julia looked up from a box of papers. 'Has he always been this way?'

'As long as I can remember. Which is why he lives alone. No one else in the family wants to deal with him. He never had a child. By default, I guess I'm it.' Tom looked at her hopefully. 'Want to adopt a used uncle?'

'Not even if he comes with four hundred bottles of vintage wine.'

'Oh. So he's introduced you to his wine cellar.'

'We made a good dent in it last week. But the next time a man gets me drunk, I'd like him to be on the other side of seventy.' She turned her attention to the old newspapers and documents they'd pulled out of box number fifteen that afternoon. Here were old editions of the *Boston Post* and the *Evening Transcript* and letters, dozens of them, addressed to Margaret. Dr Margaret Tate Page had lived a long and eventful life, judging by the letters.

'Anything interesting?' asked Tom. She was startled to find him standing right behind her, looking over her shoulder.

'This should all be interesting to you,' she said, trying to focus on the letter and not on his hand, which was now resting on the back of her chair. 'Since it's about your family.'

He went round the table and sat down across from her. 'Are you really here because of that old skeleton?'

'You think there's another reason?'

'This must be taking a lot of time away from your own life. Digging through all these boxes, reading all these letters.'

'You don't know what my life's like right now,' she said, staring down at the documents. 'This has been a welcome distraction.'

'You're talking about your divorce, aren't you?' When she looked up at him, he said, 'Henry told me about it.'

'He got me drunk. I talked.' She slumped back in her chair. 'I think Henry has the right idea. Stay single and collect wine instead. Or get a dog.'

'Or plant a garden?'

She set down the letter she'd been reading and looked at him. 'Yes. Plant a garden. It's better to watch something growing, not dying.'

Tom leaned back in his chair. 'You know, I get the strangest feeling when I look at you. I feel like we've met somewhere before.'

'We did. In my garden.'

'No, before that. I swear, I remember meeting you.'

She stared at the reflected firelight dancing in his eyes. *A man as attractive as you? Oh, I would have remembered.*

He looked at the stack of documents and pulled a few pages off the top. 'You said we're looking for any reference to Rose Connolly? You think those were her bones in your garden?'

'I just know that her name keeps popping up in those letters from Oliver Wendell Holmes. For a poor Irish girl, she left quite an impression on him.'

Tom sat back to read. Outside, the wind had risen and waves were breaking on the rocks. In the fireplace, a downdraught made the flames shudder.

Tom's chair gave a sudden creak as he rocked forward. 'Julia? Did Oliver Wendell Holmes sign his letters with just his initials?'

She stared at the page that he'd slid across to her. 'Oh my God,' she said. 'We have to tell Henry.'

1830

Tonight, it did not seem to matter that he was a farmer's son.

Norris handed his hat and greatcoat to the parlour maid and felt a twinge of self-consciousness about the missing button on his waistcoat. But the girl gave him the same curtsy that she'd given to the well-dressed couple ahead of him. And just as warm a welcome awaited him when he stepped forward to be greeted by Dr Grenville.

'Mr Marshall, we're delighted you could join us this evening,' said Grenville. 'May I present you to my sister, Eliza Lackaway.'

That the woman was Charles's mother was immediately apparent. She had his blue eyes and pale skin, flawless as alabaster even in middle age.

'You're the young man my Charles speaks so highly of,' she said.

'I wouldn't know why, Mrs Lackaway,' Norris answered modestly.

'He said you're the most skilled dissector in his class.'

It was an inappropriate topic for genteel company, and Norris glanced at Dr Grenville for guidance.

Grenville merely smiled. 'Eliza's late husband was a physician. Our father was a physician. She's quite accustomed to the most grotesque conversations around our supper table.'

'I find it all quite fascinating,' said Eliza. 'When we were growing up, our father often invited us into the dissecting room. If I were a man, I, too, would have pursued the study of medicine.'

'And you would have been splendid, dear,' said Grenville.

'So would any number of women, if we had only the opportunity.'

Dr Grenville gave a resigned sigh. 'A topic that you will no doubt raise again tonight. Please, Eliza, let the poor boy have a glass of champagne.'

Norris looked Eliza in the eye and saw fierce intelligence there. 'I was raised on a farm, Mrs Lackaway, so my experience is with livestock. I have never observed a stallion to be cleverer than a mare, or a ram cleverer than a ewe. And if the welfare of offspring is threatened, it's the female of the species who's far more formidable. Even dangerous.'

Eliza gave an approving nod. 'I shall remember that answer next time I'm drawn into debate on the issue. Your mother must be proud of having raised such a forward-thinking son. I certainly would be.'

Norris managed to maintain his smile. 'I'm sure she is.'

'Eliza, you remember Sophia?' said Grenville. 'Abigail's dear friend.'

'Of course. She used to visit us often in Weston.'

'Mr Marshall is her son.'

Eliza's gaze swung back to Norris with sudden intensity, and she seemed to recognise something in his face. 'You're Sophia's boy?'

'Yes, ma'am.'

'Why, your mother hasn't visited us in years, not since poor Abigail died. I do hope she is well?'

'She's very well, Mrs Lackaway,' he said, but even he could hear the lack of conviction in his own voice.

Grenville gave him a clap on the back. 'Go and enjoy yourself. Most of your classmates are already here and well into the champagne.'

Norris walked into the ballroom and paused, dazzled by what he saw. Young ladies glided by in butterfly-bright gowns. A massive chandelier glittered overhead and, everywhere, crystal sparkled. Against the wall was a long table with a lavish display of food. So many oysters, so many cakes!

'Finally you're here! I was wondering if you would come.' Wendell held two glasses of champagne. He handed one to Norris. 'Is it as excruciating as you feared? Have you been snubbed, insulted or otherwise abused yet?'

'After all that's happened, I didn't know how I'd be received.'

'The latest issue of the *Gazette* should put you safely in the clear. Did you read the latest? Dr Berry spotted in Providence.'

Indeed, if one was to believe the rumours flying around town, the fugitive Dr Berry was hiding in a dozen places at once.

'I can't believe he could be the one,' said Norris. 'I never saw it in him.'

'Isn't that often the case? Murderers look like everyone else.'

'I saw only a fine physician.'

'Even I have to agree with the ridiculous Mr Pratt on this one. Dr Berry must be the Reaper. And if it's not him, I'm afraid there's only one alternative suspect.' Wendell eyed him over his glass. 'That would be you.'

Uneasy under Wendell's gaze, Norris turned to survey the room. How many people were, at that moment, whispering about him?

'Why the face?' said Wendell. 'Are you trying to look guilty?'

'I wonder how many here think that I am.'

'Grenville wouldn't have invited you if he had any doubts.'

Norris shrugged. 'The invitation went out to all the students.'

'You know why, don't you? All these young ladies searching for husbands. Not to mention all their desperate mamas. You can see there aren't enough medical students to go around.' He noticed that Norris's gaze was not on the girls, but on the buffet table. 'But I think that ladies are not your first priority.'

'That juicy-looking ham over there definitely is.'

'Then shall we make its acquaintance?'

Near the oysters, they met up with Charles and Edward, who were considering the wide array of choices.

Charles took out a kerchief and dabbed his brow. His face was a bright pink. 'I'm afraid I have no appetite. It was freezing in here just a while ago. Mother had them build up the fire and I think they've overdone it.'

'It feels perfectly comfortable to me.' Edward turned and beamed at a slender brunette in a pink gown as she glided past. 'Wendell, you know that girl, don't you? Won't you introduce me?'

As Edward and Wendell drifted away in pursuit of the brunette, Norris frowned at Charles. 'Are you unwell? You look feverish.'

'I don't really feel up to being here tonight. But Mother insisted.'

'I'm quite impressed by your mother.'

Charles sighed. 'Yes, she has that effect on everyone. I hope you didn't have to suffer through her *women should be doctors* speech.'

'A bit of it.'

'Uncle says there'd be riots if he ever admitted a woman to the college.'

The musicians were now tuning their instruments, and already couples were pairing up and single men were searching out dance partners.

'I think it's time for me to retire,' said Charles. 'I'm not feeling well.'

'What's wrong with your hand?'

Charles looked down at the bandage. 'Oh. It's that cut from the dissection. It's swollen up a bit.'

'Has your uncle seen it?'

'If it gets any worse, I'll show it to him.' Charles turned to leave, but his path was blocked by a pair of smiling young ladies. The taller one said, 'We're quite annoyed with you, Charles. When *will* you visit us again? We were *so* disappointed when your uncle showed up in Providence without you.'

'I'm sorry. Next time, I promise,' said Charles, impatient to retreat. 'If you'll excuse me, ladies, I'm afraid I have a touch of fever. But let me introduce you to one of my most brilliant classmates, Mr Norris Marshall from Belmont. These are the Welliver sisters from Providence. Their father is Dr Sherwood Welliver, one of my uncle's friends.'

'One of his *dearest* friends,' the taller girl amended. 'We're visiting Boston. I'm Gwendolyn. She's Kitty. Do you dance, Mr Marshall?'

'Not well, I'm afraid,' Norris admitted.

The girls both smiled at him. Kitty said, 'We are *splendid* instructors.'

The sisters were, indeed, fine instructors. Norris danced every dance and drank too much champagne. And he allowed himself, just for this one night, to imagine a future of many such evenings.

He was one of the last guests to pull on his coat and leave the house. Snow was falling, fat luxurious flakes like soft blossoms. He stood outside on Beacon Hill and breathed in deeply, grateful for the fresh air.

'Mr Marshall?' a voice whispered.

Startled, he turned to see a figure emerging from the curtain of white.

'I was afraid I'd missed you,' said Rose Connolly.

'What are you doing here, Miss Connolly?'

'I don't know who else to turn to. I've lost my job and I have nowhere to go.' She glanced over her shoulder. 'They're looking for me.'

'The Night Watch has no interest in you now. You don't need to hide.'

'It's not the Watch I'm afraid of.' Her chin snapped up as Dr Grenville's front door opened, spilling light from the house as a guest departed.

Norris quickly turned and began to walk away, afraid that someone might see him speaking to this ragged girl. Rose followed him. Only when they were well down Beacon Hill, did she fall into step beside him.

'Does someone threaten you?' he asked.

'They want to take my sister's child from me.'

'Who wants her?'

'I don't know who they are, but I know they're vicious, Mr Marshall. I think they're the reason Mary Robinson is dead. And Miss Poole. Now I'm the only one still alive.'

'You needn't worry. I've heard it on the best authority that Dr Berry has fled Boston. They'll find him soon enough.'

'But I don't believe Dr Berry is the killer. The day my sister was buried, Mary Robinson came to see me in the cemetery. She asked about the baby. She told me to keep her safe, keep her hidden.'

'She was speaking of your sister's child?'

'Yes.' Rose swallowed. 'I never saw Mary again. The next I heard, she was dead. And *you* were the one who found her.'

'What is the connection between her murder and your niece?'

'I think her very existence is living proof of a scandalous secret.' She turned and scanned the dark street. 'They're hunting us. They've driven me from my lodgings. I can't go to my job so I can't pay the wet nurse.'

'They? These vicious people you speak of?'

'They want her. But I won't give her up, not for anything.'

The girl's gone mad. He stared into her eyes, burning in the darkness, and wondered if this was what insanity looked like.

'I'm sorry, Miss Connolly. I don't see how I can help you,' he said, backing away. He started walking again, in the direction of his lodgings.

'I came to you because I thought you were different. *Better*.'

'I'm only a student. What can I do?' He walked on, hoping that she would tire of pursuing him. But she trailed after him as he headed north.

'You yourself *saw* the creature. You found poor Mary's body.'

He turned to face her. 'And do you know how close I came to losing my position because of that? I'd be insane to raise any new questions about the murders. All it takes is a few whispers, and I could lose everything I've worked for. My future. I'd be back on my father's farm.'

'Is it so terrible to be a farmer?'

'Yes! When my ambitions are so much higher!'

He gazed in the direction of Dr Grenville's house. Tonight he'd glimpsed possibilities he'd never dreamed of.

'I thought you would care,' she said. 'Now I find that what really matters to you are your grand friends in their grand houses.'

Sighing, he looked at her. 'It's not that I don't care. There's simply nothing I can do about it. I have no business getting involved. I suggest you walk away from it as well, Miss Connolly.' He turned from her.

'I can't walk away,' she said. Her voice suddenly broke. 'I don't know where else to go . . .'

He took a few steps and slowed. Stopped. Behind him, she was crying softly. Turning back, he saw her slumped wearily against a gate.

'Have you no place to sleep?' he said, and saw her shake her head. He reached into his pocket. 'If it's a matter of money . . .'

Straightening, she glared at him. 'I ask nothing for myself! This is all for Meggie.' Angrily, she swept her hand across her face. 'I came to you because I thought we had a bond, you and I. We've both seen the creature.' She took a deep breath and hugged her cloak tighter. 'I won't trouble you again.'

He watched her walk away, a small figure receding into the curtain of falling snow. My dream is to save lives, he thought. Yet when a single friendless girl pleads for my help, I cannot be bothered.

'Miss Connolly!' he called. 'My room is a short walk from here. For tonight, if you need a place to sleep, it might serve you.'

THIS WAS A MISTAKE. Norris lay in bed, considering what he would do with his guest come morning. In one moment of reckless charity, he had taken on a responsibility he did not need. It's only temporary, he promised himself. The girl had slipped silently up the stairs behind him, then curled up like an exhausted kitten in the corner and almost immediately fallen asleep.

When he rose the next day, she was still sleeping. By the light of day, her clothing looked even more ragged, but poor though she was, her face was fine-boned and flawless, and her chestnut hair reflected the sun's pale gleam in coppery streaks. Were she resting on a pillow of fine lace instead of rags, she would rival any beauty from Beacon Hill. Though he could scarcely spare the money, he left a few coins beside her.

Norris had never attended a service by the Reverend William Channing, but he had heard of the man's reputation. Last night, at Dr Grenville's reception, the Welliver sisters had sung Channing's praises. 'That's where you'll find anyone of consequence on a Sunday morning,' Kitty Welliver had gushed. 'His sermons are so profound. Truly, he makes one *think!*'

While Norris doubted that a single profound thought ever crossed Kitty Welliver's mind, he could not ignore her suggestion that he attend. Last night, he had glimpsed the circle in which he one day hoped to circulate, and that same circle would be seated that morning in the pews of the Federal Street church.

As soon as he stepped inside, he spotted familiar faces. Wendell and Edward sat near the front, and he started to make his way towards them, but he suddenly found himself flanked on either side by the Welliver sisters.

'We hoped you'd come,' said Kitty. 'Wouldn't you like to sit with us?'

'Yes, do,' said Gwendolyn. 'We always sit upstairs.'

So upstairs he went, and found himself seated in the balcony, wedged between Kitty on the left and Gwendolyn on the right. Here the sisters were free to gossip straight through the Reverend Channing's sermon. 'There's Rachel. I didn't know she was back from Savannah,' said Kitty.

'Where?'

'Sitting next to Charles Lackaway. You don't suppose the two of them . . .?'

'I can't imagine. Don't you think Charles looks sickly today?'

Kitty leaned forward. 'He did claim he had a fever last night. Maybe he was telling the truth after all.'

Gwendolyn giggled. 'Or maybe Rachel is just *too* much to bear.'

Norris tried to focus on the Reverend Channing's sermon, but it was impossible with these silly girls chattering away. He thought of Rose Connolly, dressed in rags and curled up exhausted on his floor.

By the time the Reverend Channing finally ended his sermon, Norris was desperate to escape the sisters and their gossiping, but they remained seated, trapping him between them as the congregation began to file out.

'Oh, we can't leave yet,' said Kitty, tugging him back down into his seat when he tried to rise. 'You can see everything so much better from up here.'

'See what?' he asked in exasperation.

'Rachel has practically draped herself over Charles.'

'She's been pursuing him since June. Oh. They're getting up now. See how . . .' Kitty paused. 'What on earth is *wrong* with him?'

Charles staggered from his seat into the aisle and caught himself on the back of a bench. Then slowly he sank to the floor.

The Welliver sisters gave a simultaneous gasp and jumped up. There was chaos below as parishioners crowded around the fallen Charles.

'Let me through!' called Wendell.

By the time Norris had hurried downstairs and made his way through the crowd, Wendell and Edward were already kneeling beside their friend.

'I'm fine,' Charles murmured. 'Really I am.'

'You don't look fine, Charlie,' said Wendell. 'We've sent for your uncle.'

Norris suddenly focused on the bandage encasing Charles's left hand. The fingertips that protruded from it were red and swollen. He knelt and slowly removed the dressing. When at last the blackened flesh beneath was revealed, he rocked back on his heels, horrified.

'We need to get you home, Charlie,' said Norris. 'Your uncle will know what to do.'

'IT'S BEEN A FEW DAYS since he nicked himself at the anatomy demonstration,' said Wendell. 'He knew his hand was getting worse. Why the blazes didn't he tell anyone? His uncle at least.'

'And admit how clumsy and incompetent he is?' said Edward.

'Poor Charlie. He has no aptitude for medicine and we all know it. You'd think his uncle would accept it.' Wendell stood at Dr Grenville's parlour window, gazing out as a carriage and four rolled past.

They heard a knock at the front door. Mrs Furbush, the housekeeper, scurried down the hall to greet the new visitor. 'Oh, Dr Sewall. Thank heavens you've arrived, Mrs Lackaway is frantic.'

Norris glimpsed Dr Sewall as he walked past the parlour doorway, carrying his instrument bag, and heard him climb the stairs to the first floor. From upstairs came the sound of voices and Mrs Lackaway's sobbing.

Wendell sank into an armchair and stared with fierce concentration into the fire. 'She had childbed fever,' he said suddenly. 'The cadaver he dissected that day, when he cut himself. Dr Sewall said she died of childbed fever.'

'So?' said Edward.

'You saw his hand.'

Edward shook his head. 'A most gruesome case of erysipelas.'

'That was gangrene, Eddie. Now he's febrile and his blood is poisoned, by something acquired with one small nick of the knife. Is it only by chance, do you think, that the woman, too, died of a fulminating fever?'

Edward shrugged. 'Many women die of it. There've been more this month than ever.'

'And most of them were attended by Dr Crouch,' said Wendell quietly.

They heard footsteps descend the stairs and Dr Sewall appeared, his hulking frame taking up the entire doorway. He looked over the three young men gathered in the parlour, then said, 'You, Mr Marshall. And Mr Holmes and Mr Kingston, too. Come upstairs. I need you to hold down the patient.'

The three young men followed Sewall up the stairs, and with every step Norris's dread mounted, for he could guess what was about to happen. Sewall led them along the upstairs hallway and into Charles's room.

The sun was setting, and the wintry afternoon light glowed in the window. Round the bed, five lamps were burning. At their centre lay a ghostly pale Charles, his left hand concealed beneath a drape. In a corner, his mother sat rigid, her eyes aglow with panic. Dr Grenville stood at his nephew's bedside, his head drooped in resignation. A row of surgical instruments gleamed on a table: knives and a saw and silk sutures and a tourniquet.

Charles gave a whimper. 'Mother, please,' he whispered. 'Don't let them.'

Eliza turned desperate eyes to her brother. 'Is there no other way, Aldous? Tomorrow he might be better! If we could wait—'

'If he had shown us his hand earlier,' said Grenville, 'I might have been able to arrest the process. But it's far too late now.'

'He said it was just a small cut. Nothing of significance.'

'I have seen the smallest cuts fester and turn to gangrene,' said Dr Sewall. 'When that happens, there is no other choice.'

Norris knew what had to be done. He stared at the knives and bone saw laid out on the table and thought, Dear God, I don't want to watch this. But he stood firm, for he knew his assistance was vital.

'If you cut it off, Uncle,' said Charles, 'I'll *never* be a surgeon.'

'I want you to take another draught of morphine,' said Grenville, lifting his nephew's head. 'Go on, drink it, Charles. All of it.'

Charles settled back on the pillow and gave a soft sob. 'All I ever wanted,' he moaned, 'was that you would be proud of me.'

'I am proud of you, boy. Let's do it, Dr Sewall.'

Eliza rose and tugged desperately at her brother's arm. 'Could you not wait another day? Please, just another day.'

'Mrs Lackaway,' said Dr Sewall, 'another day will be too late.' He lifted the drape, revealing Charles's grotesquely swollen hand. The skin was greenish black and even from where Norris stood he could smell the rotting flesh. 'This is wet gangrene. The poison is spreading and by tomorrow, nothing, not even amputation, will reverse it.'

Eliza stood with her hand pressed to her mouth. 'He is my only child,' she whispered through her tears. 'I cannot lose him, or I swear I shall die.'

'Fate is always in God's hands, madam.' He paused. When he spoke again, his voice was softer, gentler. 'The loss of a hand is not the loss of a soul. With luck, you will still have your son, madam.' He glanced at Grenville. 'Perhaps it would be best if Mrs Lackaway stepped out of the room.'

Grenville inclined his head. 'Go, Eliza. Please.'

'Let nothing go wrong, Aldous,' she said. Stifling a sob, she left the room.

Sewall turned to the three medical students. 'Mr Holmes, you will hold down the right arm. Mr Kingston, the feet. Mr Marshall and Dr Grenville will take the left arm. The draughts of morphine Mr Lackaway has had will not be enough to mask this pain and he will fight us. The only merciful way to do this is quickly. Do you understand, gentlemen?'

The students nodded.

Wordlessly, Norris moved to Charles's left side.

'I'll try to preserve as much of the limb as possible,' said Dr Sewall. 'But I'm afraid the infection has advanced too far for me to preserve the wrist.' He looked at Norris. 'You will have a vital role in this, Mr Marshall. I want you to take hold of the forearm, right above where I make my incision. Dr Grenville will control the hand. First the skin is cut, then it's detached from the fascia. After I have divided the muscles, I will need you to apply the retractor, so that I can see the bones. Is all this clear?'

Norris could barely swallow, his throat was so dry. 'Yes, sir,' he murmured.

'If you think this is beyond your ability, say it now.'

'I can do it.'

Sewall gave him a long, hard look. Satisfied, he reached for the tourniquet.

A FIRE BURNED BRIGHTLY in the parlour hearth, and Norris had gulped down several glasses of Dr Grenville's excellent claret, but he could not seem to shake the chill that still lingered after what he had witnessed. Wendell and Edward, too, seemed to feel chilled, for they had pulled their chairs close to the hearth where Dr Grenville was seated. Only Dr Sewall seemed not to notice the cold. He sat facing the fire, his generous girth filling the chair.

'There are so many things that may yet go wrong,' he said as he reached for the bottle and refilled his glass. 'The days ahead are still dangerous.' He looked at Grenville. 'She does know that, doesn't she?'

They all knew he spoke of Mrs Lackaway. They could hear her voice upstairs, singing a lullaby to her sleeping son. Since Sewall had completed his terrible operation, she had not left Charles's room.

'Eliza is not ignorant of the possibilities. My sister has been around physicians all her life. She knows what can happen.'

They could hear the creak of floorboards as Eliza paced Charles's bedroom above them. If a mother's love alone could save a child, there would be no medicine more powerful than what Eliza now dispensed with every agitated step, every anxious sigh.

There was a knock on the front door. They heard the parlour maid scurry down the hall to answer it, and a few moments later Mr Pratt of the Night Watch appeared.

'Dr Grenville,' the maid said. 'I did tell him you were not taking visitors.'

'That's all right, Sarah,' said Grenville. 'Clearly Mr Pratt feels the matter is urgent enough to warrant this intrusion.'

'I do, sir,' said Pratt.

'Then what's the reason for this interruption?' asked Grenville.

'This afternoon,' said Pratt, 'two young boys playing under the West Boston Bridge found what looked like a bundle of rags. When they took a closer look, they saw it was the body of a man.'

'The West Boston Bridge,' said Dr Sewall, straightening in his chair at this disturbing news.

'Yes, Dr Sewall,' said Pratt. 'Dr Crouch was on the wards when the body was carried into the hospital. A fortunate circumstance, actually, because he also examined Agnes Poole. He saw at once the similarities in the injuries. The peculiar pattern of the cuts.' Pratt looked at Norris. 'You would know what I'm talking about, Mr Marshall.'

Norris stared at him. 'The shape of a cross?' he asked softly.

'Yes. Despite the . . . damage, the pattern is apparent.'

'What damage?' asked Sewall.

'Rats, sir. Perhaps other animals as well. It's clear that the body has been lying there for some time. It's logical to assume that his death coincided with the date of his disappearance.'

It was as if the temperature in the room had suddenly plunged. Though no one said a word, Norris could see stunned realisation on all the faces.

'Then you have found him,' Grenville finally said.

Pratt nodded. 'The body is Dr Nathaniel Berry's. He did not flee, as we all believed. He was murdered.'

The Present

Julia looked up from Wendell Holmes's letter. 'Was he right, Tom? Did that case of childbed fever have anything to do with Charles's blood poisoning?'

Tom stood at the window, staring out at the sea. 'Yes,' he said quietly. 'It was almost certainly related. What he described in his letter barely begins to touch on the horrors of childbed fever.' He sat down at the table, across from Julia and Henry. 'In Holmes's era,' said Tom, 'it was so common that during epidemics one in four new mothers died of it. And you know the worst part of all? They were killed by their own doctors. Through ignorance. In those days, they had no concept of germ theory. Doctors used their bare hands to examine women. They'd perform an autopsy on a corpse that was putrid with disease, then they'd go straight to the maternity ward, with filthy hands. They'd examine patient after patient, spreading infection right down the row of beds.'

'It never occurred to any of them just to wash their hands?'

'No. Women were dying and no one in America could figure out why.' He looked down at the letter. 'No one, that is, until Oliver Wendell Holmes. That's what makes these letters so valuable. This is medical history, straight from the pen of one of the greatest doctors who ever lived.'

TEN

1830

Sheltered in a nook beneath a doorway, Rose gazed across the hospital common, her eyes fixed on Norris's attic window. She had been watching for hours. Why hadn't he come back? What if he did not return tonight? She hoped for a second night under Norris's roof, for a chance to see him, to hear his voice. This morning, she'd woken to find the coins he'd left for her. In return for his generosity, she'd mended two of his threadbare shirts.

She saw candlelight flicker to life in a window. His window.

She moved across the hospital common, then eased open the door to his building, peeped inside, and quietly slipped up the two flights of stairs to the attic. At his door she paused, patted her hair, straightened her skirt, feeling foolish even as she did it. Why would Norris bother to look at her after dancing with all those fine ladies last night?

She knocked and heard his footsteps approach the door. Suddenly he was standing before her. 'There you are! Where have you been?'

She paused, confused. 'I thought I should stay away until you came home.'

'You've been gone all day? No one has seen you here?'

His words stung her like a slap in the face. All day she'd been hungry to see him, and this was the greeting he gave her? I'm the girl he wants no one to know about, she thought. The embarrassing secret.

She turned to leave.

'Where are you going? I've brought food for you. Won't you stay?'

She paused on the stairs, startled by the unexpected offer.

'Please,' he said. 'There's someone here who wishes to speak to you.'

She still felt the sting of his earlier comment, but her stomach was rumbling and she wanted to know who this 'someone' might be. She stepped into the attic and focused on the little man standing near the window. She remembered him from the hospital. He had eyes like a sparrow's, bright and alert, and while she studied him, she knew that he was studying her in kind.

'This is my classmate,' said Norris. 'Mr Wendell Holmes.'

The little man nodded. 'Miss Connolly.'

'I remember you,' she said. 'I'm the one you wished to see, Mr Holmes?'

'About the death of Dr Berry. You've heard about it?'

'I saw a crowd gathered near the bridge. They told me they'd found the doctor's body.'

'This new development greatly confuses the picture,' said Wendell. 'By tomorrow, the newspapers will be stoking terror. *West End Reaper still at large!* The public will once again see monsters everywhere. It puts Mr Marshall in a most uncomfortable position. Perhaps even a dangerous one.'

She turned to Norris. 'Ah, so that's why you're suddenly willing to listen to me. Because it now affects you.'

Norris gave an apologetic nod. 'I'm sorry, Rose. I should have paid more attention to you last night. My only excuse is that I had much to consider.'

'Oh, yes. Your *future*.'

He sighed, a sound so defeated that she almost felt sorry for him. 'I have no future, not any more.'

'And how can I change that?'

'What matters now,' said Wendell, 'is that we learn the truth.' He came towards her, his eyes so sharply focused on her that she felt he could see straight into her mind. 'Tell us about your niece, Rose. The little girl whom everyone is searching for.'

'I'll tell you,' she said. 'But first . . .' She looked at Norris. 'You said you brought me food.'

She ate as she told the story, pausing to rip into a chicken leg or stuff a chunk of bread into her mouth. Her last meal had been that morning, a shrivelled scrap of smoked mackerel that the fishmonger had planned to toss to his cat. She'd pressed the few coins that Norris had left her into Billy's hand and asked him to deliver the money to Hepzibah.

For another week, at least, little Meggie would be fed.

And now, for the first time in days, she, too, could eat her fill. So she did, leaving a mound of broken chicken bones, gnawed clean.

'You truly have no idea who fathered your sister's child?' asked Wendell.

'Aurnia said nothing to me. Though she hinted . . .' Rose paused. 'She asked me to fetch the priest for last rites. It was so important to her, but I kept putting it off. I didn't want her to stop fighting. I wanted her to live.'

'And she wanted to confess her sins.'

'Shame kept her from telling me,' Rose said softly.

'And the child's father remains a mystery?'

'Except to Mr Gareth Wilson.'

'Ah, yes, the mysterious lawyer. May I see the card he gave you?'

She reached in her pocket for the card, which she handed to Wendell.

'He lives on Park Street. An impressive address.'

'A fine address doesn't make him a gentleman,' she said. 'He used Eben to find me. Which makes Mr Wilson no better.'

'Would your brother-in-law know who his client might be?'

'Fool that he is, Eben wouldn't know a thing.'

'Have you told any of this to the Night Watch?'

'It's useless to speak to Mr Pratt.' Her tone of disdain left no doubt what she thought of the man. 'No one believes the likes of me. We Irish need to be watched all the time, or we'll pick your pockets and steal your children.'

'You're certain the child is safe?' Wendell asked.

'As safe as I can make her.'

'Where is she? May we see her?'

Rose hesitated.

Norris said, 'She seems to be at the centre of it all. Please, Rose. We only want to be sure she's well protected. And healthy.'

It was Norris's plea that convinced her. From their first meeting in the hospital, she had been drawn to him, had felt that, unlike the other gentlemen, he was someone she could turn to.

She looked out of the window. 'It's dark enough. I never go there in daylight.' She stood. 'It should be safe now. We can walk.'

IN HER ZEAL to keep warm, Hepzibah had nailed her shutters closed, turning her room into a dark little cave in which the fire was reduced to glowing coals and not even a single candle burned.

After they had entered, Rose swept Meggie from the basket with a joyful laugh and brought the little face up to hers, breathing in the familiar scent of her hair. Meggie responded with a wet cough, and tiny fingers reached out to grasp a handful of Rose's hair. Mucus gleamed on her upper lip.

'Ah, my darling girl,' said Rose, hugging Meggie to her. The two gentlemen standing behind her remained strangely silent, watching as she fussed over the baby. She turned to Hepzibah. 'Has she been ill?'

'Started coughing last night. You haven't been here in a few days.'

'I sent money today. Billy brought it, didn't he?'

By the faint glow of the hearth, Hepzibah looked like an enormous toad planted in the chair. 'Aye, but I'll be needing more.'

Norris said, 'May we take a look at the baby?'

Hepzibah eyed him and gave a grunt. 'Who might you gentlemen be?'

'We're medical students, madam.' Norris lit a candle at the hearth. 'Bring the baby here, Rose. So I can get a better look at her.'

Rose carried Meggie to him. The baby gazed up with trusting eyes as Norris examined her. Already he had the sure hands of a doctor, Rose observed, and she imagined him as he would one day look, his hair streaked with grey, his gaze sober and wise. He inspected Meggie thoroughly. She was coughing, and strands of clear mucus trickled from her nostrils.

'She seems to have no fever,' said Norris. 'But there is congestion.'

Hepzibah gave a dismissive grunt. 'All the little ones have it. Not a child in South Boston who doesn't have snot under his nose.'

Wendell reached into his pocket and withdrew a handful of coins, which he placed in the wet nurse's hand. 'There'll be more. But the child must stay well fed and healthy. Do you understand?'

Hepzibah stared at the money. And she said, with a new note of respect, 'Oh, she will, sir. I'll be sure of it.'

Rose stared at Wendell, stunned by his generosity. 'I'll find a way to pay you, Mr Holmes,' she said softly. 'I swear to you.'

'There's no need to talk of payment,' said Wendell. 'If you'll excuse us, Mr Marshall and I need to speak alone.' He looked at Norris, and the two men stepped outside, into the alley.

'THIS PLACE IS APPALLING,' said Wendell. 'Even if she keeps the child well fed, *look* at the woman! She's grotesque. And this neighbourhood—all these tenements—they're ridden with disease.'

They stood outside Hepzibah's door, shivering in the cold night air. 'The baby can't stay here,' Norris agreed.

'The question is,' said Wendell, 'what's the alternative?'

'She belongs with Rose. That's where she'll be best cared for.'

'Rose can't feed her. And if she's right about these murders, if she's truly being hunted, then she needs to stay as far away from the baby as she can get. She knows that.'

'And it's breaking her heart. You can see it.'

'Yet she's clear-eyed enough to realise it's necessary.' Wendell glanced down the alley as a drunken man came tottering out of a doorway. 'She's quite a remarkable girl. And a pretty one, too. Even under all those rags.'

So I've noticed.

'What are you going to do with her, Norris?'

Wendell's question brought Norris up short. What *was* he going to do with her? This morning, he'd been resolved to send her on her way with a few coins. Now he realised he couldn't turn her out on the street.

'No matter what you choose,' said Wendell, 'even if you send her away, your fates seem to be tied together.'

'What do you mean?'

'The West End Reaper haunts you both. Rose believes she's stalked by him. The Night Watch believes you *are* him. Until he's caught, you and Rose won't be safe. Nor will the child.'

THE NEXT MORNING, when he had walked into the auditorium for lectures, Norris had noticed the startled glances and heard the sharp intakes of breath. No one had directly challenged his attendance. How could they, when he had not been formally charged with any crime? No, the gentleman's way of dealing with scandal was with whispers and innuendo, both of which he must now endure. Soon his ordeal would end one way or the other. After the Christmas holiday, Dr Grenville and the school trustees would render their decision and Norris would know if he still had a place in the college.

When his lectures were at an end, he had made his way to Park Street, where Rose awaited him. For now he was reduced to this: skulking in the street, spying on the one man who might know the Reaper's identity.

He and Rose had been watching the house all afternoon, and now the fading light took with it the day's last blush of colour. Number Five was one of eight imposing terraced houses that faced the snow-blanketed common. So far they had caught not even a glimpse of Mr Gareth Wilson or of any visitors. Wendell's enquiries about the man had turned up little information, only that he'd recently returned from London.

The door to Number Five suddenly opened.

Rose whispered, 'It's him. It's Gareth Wilson.'

The man was warmly dressed in a black beaver hat and a voluminous greatcoat. He paused outside his front door to pull on black gloves, then began to walk briskly up Park Street in the direction of the State House.

Norris's gaze followed the man. 'Let's see where he goes.'

They allowed Wilson to reach the end of the block of terraced houses before falling into step behind him. At the State House, Wilson turned west towards the maze of the Beacon Hill neighbourhood.

Norris and Rose followed him past stately brick homes. It was quiet here, too quiet, and only an occasional carriage rattled past. Wilson turned into narrow Acorn Street and was almost invisible as he walked down the shadowy passage. He stopped at a door and knocked. A moment later the door opened, and they heard a man say, 'Mr Wilson! It's a pleasure to see you back in Boston after all these months.'

'Have the others arrived?'

'Not everyone, but they'll be here soon. This dreadful business has made us all quite anxious.'

Wilson stepped into the house and the door swung shut.

It was Rose who made the next move, walking boldly up the alley as though she belonged there. Norris followed her to the doorway and they stared up at the house. Above the door was a massive lintel, where, in the fading light, Norris could just make out the symbols carved in the granite.

'Someone else is coming,' whispered Rose. Quickly she looped her arm in his, and they turned and walked away, bodies pressed together like lovers. Behind them, they heard a knock on the door.

The same voice that had greeted Gareth Wilson said, 'We wondered if you'd make it.'

'I apologise, but I came straight from a patient's sickbed.'

Norris came to a halt, too shocked to take another step. Slowly, he turned. Though he could not see the man's face through the shadows, he could make out a familiar silhouette, the broad shoulders filling out the generous greatcoat. Norris stood rooted to the spot. *It cannot be.*

'Norris?' Rose tugged on his arm. 'What is it?'

He stared up the alley at the doorway through which the new visitor had just entered. 'I know that man,' he said.

DIM BILLY IS AN APT NAME for the boy who now shambles down the alley. A half-wit the boy might be, but he is not entirely useless. He is the key to finding Rose Connolly. The boy must know where to find her. And tonight, he will almost certainly talk.

The boy stops suddenly and his head jerks up. Somehow he's sensed the presence of another in his alley. 'Who's there?' he calls out. At the far end of the alley, a silhouette has appeared, backlit by the glow of a street lamp.

'Billy!' a man calls.

The boy stands still. 'What d'ya want with me?'

'I want to talk to you about Rose.' Eben moves closer. 'Where is she?'

'I don't know.'

'Come on, Billy. You do know. I only want to speak to her.'

'You hit her. You're mean to her.'

'There's money in it for you if you help me find her.'

'She says if I tell, they'll kill Meggie.'

'So you do know where she is.'

Billy backs away. 'I ain't talking to you.'

'Where is Rose?' Eben advances. 'Come *back here!*'

But the boy scrabbles away, quick as a crab. Eben makes a desperate lunge and stumbles in the dark. He goes sprawling facedown as Billy makes his escape, his footsteps receding into the darkness.

'Little bastard. Wait till I get my hands on you.' Eben grunts as he rises to his knees. He is still on all fours when his gaze suddenly fixes on the gleam of two leather shoes, planted almost in front of his nose.

'What? Who?' Eben scrambles to his feet as the figure emerges from the doorway, black cape sweeping across the icy stones.

'Good evening, sir.'

Eben gives an embarrassed grunt and pulls himself up straight, swiftly reclaiming his dignity. 'Well! This is not a place I'd expect to find—'

The thrust of the knife drives the blade so deep it strikes spine, and the handle transmits the impact against bone. Eben sucks in a breath, his eyes bulging in shock. He does not cry out; in fact, he makes no sound at all. The first stab is almost always met with the silence of the stunned.

The second slash is swift and efficient. Eben collapses to his knees, hands pressed to the wound as though to hold back the gout of entrails.

Eben's is not the face the Reaper expected to stare down upon this night. But though it's not Billy's blood that trickles between the cobblestones, there is a purpose yet for this harvest. Every death, like every life, has its use.

By now, Eben's heart has ceased to beat. Only a little blood spills as the blade slits into the scalp and begins to peel away its prize.

'THESE ACCUSATIONS are extremely dangerous,' said Dr Grenville. 'Before you take them any further, I advise you to consider the consequences.'

'Norris and I both saw him come out of that building last night, on Acorn Street,' said Wendell. He had joined Norris and Rose outside the house later on that evening. 'It *was* Dr Sewall. And there were others at that house, others we recognised.'

'And what of it? A gathering of gentlemen is hardly extraordinary.'

'Consider who those men were,' said Norris. 'One was Mr Gareth Wilson, recently returned from London. A most mysterious individual with few friends in town.'

'You've been enquiring into Mr Wilson's affairs, all because of what some silly girl told you? A girl I have yet to lay eyes on?'

'Rose Connolly strikes us both as a reliable witness,' said Wendell.

'I can't judge the reliability of a girl I've never met. Neither can I allow you to slander a man as respected as Dr Sewall.' Grenville rose from his chair and paced in agitation to the hearth. He said finally, 'Dr Sewall saved my nephew's life. I refuse to believe he's involved in any way with these murders.' He turned to Norris. 'You, better than anyone, know what it's like to be a victim of rumours. Do you think it's been easy for me to be your champion? To defend your place in our college? Yet I have done so because I refuse to be swayed by gossip.'

'Sir,' said Wendell, 'you haven't heard the names of the other men at that meeting. We took note of who came and went from Acorn Street. One of them was Mr William Lloyd Garrison. I recognised him, because I heard him speak this past summer, at the Park Street church.'

'Mr Garrison, the abolitionist? Do you feel it's a crime to advocate the freeing of slaves?'

'Not at all. I find his position a most noble one.'

'I'm in sympathy with the abolitionists, too,' said Norris. 'But there are disturbing things being said about Mr Garrison. A shopkeeper told us—'

'A shopkeeper? Now *that* is a reliable source indeed.'

'He told us that Mr Garrison is often seen out late at night, moving in a most furtive manner in the vicinity of Beacon Hill.'

'I, too, am often out late at night, due to the needs of my patients. Some might call my movements furtive as well.'

'But Mr Garrison is no physician,' Norris said. 'Acorn Street seems to attract visitors not from the neighbourhood. There are reports of eerie chanting heard in the night, and last month bloodstains were found on the cobblestones. When people in the neighbourhood complained to the Night Watch, Constable Lyons resisted any investigation. Even odder, he issued orders that the Watch is to avoid Acorn Street entirely.'

'Who told you this?'

'The shopkeeper.'

'Consider your source, Mr Marshall.'

'We would be more sceptical,' said Wendell, 'except there was one more familiar face that emerged from the house. It was Constable Lyons himself.'

Dr Grenville stared at the young men in disbelief.

'Whatever is going on is being shielded at the highest levels,' said Norris.

Grenville gave a sudden laugh. 'Do you realise, Mr Marshall, that Constable Lyons is the only reason you are not in custody? His dimwit associate, Mr Pratt, was ready to arrest you, but Lyons stayed his hand. Lyons has been under pressure from all sides—the public, the press, everyone is braying for an arrest. But he won't be rushed. Not without evidence.'

'I had no idea, sir,' said Norris quietly.

'If you want to remain at liberty, do not antagonise your defenders.'

'But, Dr Grenville,' said Wendell, 'why would men of such diverse occupations come together late at night at such a modest address? In fact, a detail of the residence is most interesting.' Wendell looked at Norris, who removed a folded sheet of paper from his pocket.

'These symbols are carved on the granite lintel above the doorway, sir,' said Norris. He gave the sheet to Grenville. 'You can see two pelicans facing each other. And between them, there's a cross.'

'You'll find many a cross on buildings in this city.'

'That's not just any cross,' said Norris. 'This one has a rose at its centre. It's the cross of the Rosicrucians, a society so secret that no one knows the identity of its members. There are reports, here and in Washington, that they indulge in sacrifices. That among their victims are children, whose innocent blood is spilled in secret rituals. This child that Rose Connolly protects seems to be at the centre of the mystery. We assumed the baby's sought by the man who fathered her. Now we witness these secret meetings and we wonder if another motive entirely is at work here.'

'Child sacrifice? This is thin evidence indeed, Mr Marshall. I am meeting the trustees after Christmas to defend you. How can I support your enrolment if my sole argument is an outlandish conspiracy theory, hatched by a girl I've never met? Where is she? Who shelters her?'

Norris was grateful when Wendell interjected smoothly, 'We have arranged for her lodgings, sir. I assure you, she's in a safe place.'

'And the baby?'

'She, too, remains hidden, sir,' said Wendell. 'She's fed and cared for, but in the most unclean surroundings.'

'Then bring her here, gentlemen. I assure you she'll be safe, and in the healthiest of households.'

Norris and Wendell exchanged glances. Norris said, 'Rose would never forgive us if we made such a decision without her. She must choose.'

'You would stake a child's life on this girl's judgment?'

'She may be only seventeen, but she deserves respect, sir. Against all the odds, she's survived, and she's kept her niece alive as well.'

'Then your *own* judgment is in question, Mr Marshall. A mere girl *cannot* be trusted with such a grave responsibility.'

A knock on the door made them all turn. Eliza Lackaway, looking concerned, stepped into the room. 'Is everything all right, Aldous?'

'Yes, yes,' Grenville said. 'We're just having a spirited discussion.'

'We could hear you upstairs, which is why I've come down. Charles is awake now and would dearly love to see his friends.' She looked at Wendell and Norris. 'He wanted to make sure you didn't leave without saying hello.'

'We wouldn't dream of it,' said Wendell. 'We were hoping to see him.'

'Go.' Brusquely, Grenville waved the young men out of the room. 'Our conversation is at an end.'

Eliza frowned at her brother's rude dismissal of their visitors, but she refrained from commenting on it as she led Norris and Wendell out of the parlour and up the stairs.

They found Charles looking pale, but with a smile on his face.

'I could hear my uncle's voice booming through the floor,' he said. 'It sounded like quite a lively discussion downstairs.'

Wendell drew up a chair to sit beside the bed. 'Had we known you were awake, we'd have come up sooner.'

Charles tried to sit up, but his mother protested, 'No, Charles. You need to rest.' She turned to Norris and Wendell. 'Gentlemen, please don't exhaust him.' She looked at Charles. 'I'll check on you in a bit, darling.'

Charles waited until his mother had left the room, then he gave an exasperated sigh. 'God, she smothers me!'

'Are you feeling better?' asked Norris. 'Is it still very painful?'

'My uncle says the signs are good. I haven't had a fever since Tuesday.' He regarded his bandaged wrist and said, 'Dr Sewall saved my life.'

At the mention of Dr Sewall's name, neither Wendell nor Norris spoke.

'So now, tell me the latest,' said Charles at last. 'What news is there?'

'We miss you in class,' said Norris.

'*Fainting Charlie?* No wonder you all miss me. I can always be counted on to make everyone else look brilliant by comparison.'

'You'll have all this time to study, lying here in bed,' said Wendell.

'When you come back to class, you'll be the most brilliant of us all.'

'You know I'm not coming back,' Charles said. 'I was never meant to be a doctor. I have neither the talent nor the interest. It's always been about my uncle's hopes, my uncle's expectations.'

'What *do* you want to be, Charlie?' asked Norris.

'Ask Wendell. He knows.' Charles pointed to his boyhood friend. 'He's not the only one prone to bursts of poetic verse.'

Norris gave a startled laugh. 'You want to be a *poet*?'

'My uncle hasn't accepted it yet, but now he's going to have to. The problem is that he thinks poems and novels are frivolous diversions.'

Wendell gave a sympathetic nod. 'Something my own father would say.'

The creak of a footstep announced Eliza's return to the room. 'Gentlemen,' she said, 'I think it's time for Charles to rest.'

Wendell stood. 'We do need to be going anyway.'

'Wait. You never told me why you came to see my uncle.'

'Oh, nothing really, Charlie. It's just about that West End business.'

'You mean the Reaper?' Charles's attention perked up. 'I hear they found Dr Berry's body.'

Eliza cut in. 'Who told you that?'

'The maids were talking about it.'

'They shouldn't have. I want nothing to upset you.'

'I'm not upset. I *want* to hear the latest.'

'Not tonight,' said Eliza. 'I'll see your friends out now.'

She accompanied Wendell and Norris down the stairs to the front door. As the two men stepped out, she said, 'While Charles welcomes your visits, I do hope that next time you'll keep the conversation on pleasant subjects.'

'We'll remember that, Mrs Lackaway,' Norris said. 'Good night.'

He and Wendell paused outside, their breath clouding in the cold.

'Dr Grenville is right, you know,' said Wendell. 'The child would be much better off here, with him. We should have taken him up on the offer.'

'It's not our decision. The choice is Rose's.' Norris stared up the street. 'I think she's the wisest girl I've ever met.'

'You *are* besotted with her, aren't you?'

'I respect her. And, yes, I'm fond of her—who wouldn't be?'

'The word is "besotted", Norris. Bewitched. In love.' Wendell gave a knowing sigh. 'And clearly she's just as besotted with you.'

Norris frowned. 'What?'

'Haven't you seen the way she looks at you, the way she hangs on your every word? She's in love with you. Open your eyes, man!' Wendell laughed and gave him a clap on the shoulder. 'I must go home for the holiday. I take it you're going to Belmont?'

Norris was still stunned by what Wendell had just said. 'Yes,' he said, dazed. 'My father expects me.'

'What about Rose?'

What about Rose, indeed?

She was all Norris thought about as he walked back to his lodgings. Rose in love with him? He'd been oblivious to it.

From the street below, he could see candlelight flickering in his attic window. She's still awake, he thought, and suddenly he could not wait to see her. He climbed the stairs, his heart pounding as much from anticipation as from exertion.

Rose had fallen asleep at the desk, her head resting on her folded arms, Wistar's *Anatomy* lying open before her. The candle had guttered down to a mere puddle of wax, and, as he lit another, Rose stirred awake.

'Oh,' she murmured, lifting her head. 'You're back.'

He watched her stretch, her neck arching, her hair tumbling loose. Looking into her face, he saw no artifice, no guile, just a drowsy girl trying to shake off sleep.

She looked up at him. 'Did you tell him? What did he say?'

'Dr Grenville wants to hear the story from your own lips.' He placed his hand on her shoulder. 'Rose, he offered to take in Meggie.'

She went rigid. Instead of gratitude, what flashed in her eyes was panic. 'Tell me you didn't agree! *You had no right!*' She shot to her feet. Staring into her eyes, Norris saw the primal fierceness of a girl prepared to sacrifice everything for someone she loved. 'You gave him *Meggie*?'

'Listen to me. *Listen.*' He took her face in his hands and forced her to meet his gaze. 'I told him I'd do only what *you* want. You're the one who knows best and I just want you to be happy.'

'You mean that?' she whispered.

'Yes. Truly.'

They stared at each other for a moment. Suddenly her eyes went bright with tears and she pulled away. How small she is, he thought. How fragile. Yet this girl has carried the weight of the world, and its scorn as well. *She's quite a remarkable girl. And a pretty one, too*, Wendell had said. Looking at her now, Norris saw a pure and honest beauty. *This is a girl who'd stand by me. Even if I don't deserve it.*

'Rose,' he said, 'it's time for us to speak of the future. What happens next to you and Meggie. I must be honest: my prospects at the college are dim. I don't know if I can afford to keep this room, much less keep us all fed.'

'You want me to leave.' She said it as a statement of fact, as if no other conclusion was possible. 'I can live with the truth. Just tell me.'

'Tomorrow, I go home to Belmont. My father expects me for Christmas. I can tell you it won't be a cheerful stay. He's not one for celebration.'

'You needn't explain.' She turned. 'I'll be gone in the morning.'

'Yes, you'll be gone. With me.'

She turned back to him, her eyes wide. 'Go to Belmont?'

'It's the safest place for you both. There'll be fresh milk for Meggie and a bed of your own. No one will find you there.'

Sheer delight sent her flying into his arms. Laughing, he caught her and twirled her round the room, and felt her heart beating joyfully against his.

Suddenly Rose pulled away and he saw the doubt in her face. 'But what will your father say about me?' she asked. 'About Meggie?'

He couldn't lie to her. 'I don't know,' he said.

ELEVEN

It was past three when the farmer stopped his wagon on the Belmont road to let them off. They still had two miles to walk, but the sky was blue and the ice-crusted snow glittered bright as glass in the afternoon sun. As they trudged down the road with Meggie in Rose's arms, Norris pointed out the neat house that belonged to Dr and Mrs Hallowell, the childless couple who had welcomed him into their home as if he were their own son. Dr Hallowell had opened his library to Norris and last year had written the glowing recommendation letter to the medical college. Rose took in all this information with a look of eager interest. When they crested the rise, and the Marshall farm appeared on the horizon, she stopped to stare, her hand shielding her eyes from the setting sun's glare.

'It's not much to look at,' he admitted. 'I couldn't wait to escape from it.'

'I wouldn't mind living here at all.' Meggie stirred awake in her arms and gurgled. Rose smiled at her and said, 'I could be happy on a farm.'

He laughed. 'I think you could be happy anywhere, Rose.'

'It's not the *where* that counts.'

'Before you say *it's the people you live with*, you need to meet my father. He's a bitter man. You just need to know that ahead of time.'

'Because he lost your mother?'

'She abandoned him. She abandoned both of us. He's never forgiven her.'

'Have you?' she asked, and looked at him, her cheeks pink from the cold.

'It's getting late,' he said.

They walked on, the sun sinking lower, bare trees casting their spindly shadows across the snow. The closer they got to the farm, the more Norris dreaded the coming reunion. But Rose showed no signs of apprehension, walking cheerfully beside him, humming to Meggie. How could any man, even his father, dislike this girl? Surely she and the baby will charm him? he thought. Rose will win him over, the way she's won me over, and we'll all laugh together at supper. Yes, it could be a good visit after all.

They stepped through the sagging gate into a front yard littered with a pile of logs still to be split into firewood. Rose hiked up her skirt and followed Norris through the hog-churned mud.

Before they reached the porch, the door opened and Norris's father stepped out. Isaac Marshall had not seen his son in two months, yet he merely stood on his porch, watching in silence as his visitors approached. He offered only the flicker of a smile as his son climbed the steps.

'Welcome home,' said Isaac, but made no move to embrace his son.

'Father, may I introduce you to my friend Rose. And her niece, Meggie.'

Rose stepped forward, smiling, and the baby gave a coo, as though in greeting. ''Tis good to meet you, Mr Marshall,' Rose said.

Isaac kept his arms at his side and his lips tightened. Norris saw Rose flush and, at that moment, he had never disliked his father more.

'She'll be staying the night?'

'I was hoping she could stay longer. She and the baby are in need of lodgings for a while. She can use the room upstairs.'

'I'll not be a bother, Mr Marshall,' said Rose. 'And I work hard.'

LONG AFTER ROSE and Meggie had gone to bed, Norris and Isaac sat together at the kitchen table, a lamp burning between them. Though Norris had drunk only sparingly from the jug of apple brandy, his father had been drinking it all evening. Isaac poured himself yet another glass and his hand was unsteady as he recorked the jug.

'So what is she to you?' said Isaac. 'Is she knocked up?'

Norris stared at his father in disbelief. *It's the brandy talking.* 'You have no right to say such things about her. You don't even know her.'

'How well do *you* know her?'

'I haven't touched her, if that's what you're asking. I hoped she'd be welcomed here. She's a hard-working girl, with the most generous heart I know. She deserves better than the reception you gave her.'

'I'm only thinking of your welfare, boy. Your happiness. She comes with a baby. You want to raise a child that isn't even your own?'

Abruptly Norris stood. 'Good night, Father.' He turned to leave the room.

'I'm trying to spare you the pain I knew.'

Norris stopped, and with sudden comprehension, he turned to look at him. 'You're talking about Mother.'

'I tried to make her happy.' Isaac gulped the brandy and set the glass down hard on the table. 'I tried my best.'

'Well, I never saw it.'

'Children don't see anything, don't know anything. There's a lot you'll never know about your mother.'

'Why did she leave you?'

'She left you, too.'

Norris could think of no retort for that painful truth. *Yes, she did, and I'll never understand it.* Suddenly exhausted, he returned to the table and sat down. 'What don't I know about Mother?' he asked.

'Things I should've known myself. Things I should've wondered. Why a girl like her would ever marry a man like me.' He lowered his head. 'I don't think she ever loved me.'

'Did you love her?'

Isaac lifted his damp gaze to Norris's. 'What difference did it make? It wasn't enough to keep her here. *You* weren't enough to keep her here.'

Those words, both cruel and true, hung in the air between them like spent gunpowder. They sat in silence, facing each other across the table.

'The day she left,' said Isaac, 'you were sick. You remember? It was a summer fever. You were so hot, we were afraid we'd lose you. Dr Hallowell went to Portsmouth that week, so we couldn't call on him. All night, your mother stayed up with you. And all the next day. And still your fever wouldn't break. And what does she do? Do you remember her leaving?'

'She said she loved me. She said she'd be back.'

'That's what she told me. That her son deserved the best and she was going to see that you got it. She put on her finest dress and walked out of the house. And she never came back. Not that night, or the night after. I was here all alone, with a sick boy, and I had no way of knowing where she'd gone. Mrs Comfort came to watch you while I searched. Every place I could think of, every neighbour she might have visited.' He paused. 'Then a boy turned up at the door one day, with Sophia's horse. And the letter.'

'Why have you never shown me that letter?'

'You were too young. Only eleven. It's long gone now. I burned it. But I can tell you what it said.' Isaac swallowed and looked straight at the lamp. 'She said she couldn't be married to me any longer. She'd met a man, and they were leaving for Paris. *Go on with your life*. That's all.'

'Was there nothing about me? She must have said something.'

Isaac said quietly, 'That's why I never showed it to you, boy. I didn't want you to know.'

'Why did you wait all these years to tell me?'

'Because of *her*.' Isaac looked towards the upstairs bedroom, where Rose was sleeping. 'She has her eye on you, boy, and you have your eye on her. You make a mistake now and you'll live with it for the rest of your life. The girl comes with a sweet enough face. But what does it hide?'

'You misjudge her. I love this girl. I plan to marry her.'

Isaac laughed. 'I married for love, and see what came of it!' He lifted his glass, but his hand paused in midair. He turned and looked towards the door.

Someone was knocking. They exchanged startled looks. It was deep into the night, not an hour for a neighbourly visit. Frowning, Isaac picked up the lamp and opened the door.

'Mr Marshall?' a man said. 'Is your son here?'

At the sound of that voice, Norris rose at once in alarm.

'What do you want with him?' asked Isaac. He suddenly stumbled backwards as two men forced their way past him, into the kitchen.

'There you are,' said Mr Pratt, spotting Norris. 'You're returning with us to Boston.'

'How dare you push your way into my home!' said Isaac. 'Who are you?'

'The Night Watch.' Pratt's gaze remained on Norris. 'The carriage is waiting, Mr Marshall.'

'You're arresting my son?'

'I'm not going until you tell me the charges,' said Norris.

'The charges are murder,' said Pratt. 'The murders of Agnes Poole, Mary Robinson and Dr Nathaniel Berry. And now, Mr Eben Tate.'

'Tate?' Norris stared at him. Rose's brother-in-law murdered as well?

'We have all the proof we need. It's now my duty to return you to Boston, where you will face trial.' Pratt nodded to the other Watchman. 'Bring him.'

Norris was forced forward, and had just reached the doorway when he heard Rose cry out, 'Norris?'

He turned and saw her panicked gaze. 'Go to Dr Grenville! Tell him what's happened!' he shouted just before he was shoved out of the door.

His escorts forced him into the carriage, and Pratt signalled the driver with two hard raps on the roof. They rolled away and headed down the Belmont road towards Boston.

'Even your Dr Grenville can't protect you now,' said Pratt. 'Not against the evidence in your room.'

Norris shook his head. 'I have no idea what you're talking about.'

'The jar, Mr Marshall. It's not every day one finds a human face sloshing about in a jar of whisky,' said Pratt. 'And in case there's any doubt left at all, we found your mask, as well. Still splattered with blood. Played it close to the edge with us, didn't you?'

The mask of the West End Reaper, planted in my room?

'I'd say it's the gallows for you,' said Pratt.

The other Watchman gave a chuckle, as though he looked forward to a good hanging. 'And then your good doctor friends can have a go at you,' he added. The bodies of executed criminals went directly to the autopsy table with the full approval of the law.

Through the window, Norris saw moonlit fields, the same farms along the Belmont road that he always passed on his journeys into Boston. This would be the last time he saw them. The road took them east from Belmont, and the farms became villages as they rolled ever closer to Boston. Now he could see the Charles River, glittering beneath moonlight.

The carriage wheels clattered onto the West Boston Bridge and Norris knew that, once over the bridge, it would be a short ride north to the city jail.

'Whoa! Whoa, there,' the driver said, and the carriage came to a stop.

'What's this?' said Pratt. He called to the driver, 'Why have we stopped?'

'Got an obstruction here, Mr Pratt.'

Pratt threw open the door and climbed out. 'Blast it all! Can't they get that horse out of the way?'

'They're trying, sir. But that nag's not getting up again.'

Through the carriage window, Norris could see the bridge railing. Below flowed the Charles River. He thought of cold black water. There are worse graves, he thought.

Pratt was opening the carriage door to climb back in. As it swung open, Norris threw himself against it and tumbled out.

Knocked backwards by the door, Pratt sprawled to the ground.

Norris caught a glimpse of his surroundings: the dead horse, lying in front of its overloaded wagon. And the Charles River, its moonlit surface hiding the turbid water beneath. He did not hesitate. Either I seize this chance or I give up any hope of life, he thought, as he scrambled over the railing.

'Catch him! Don't let him jump!'

Norris was already falling. Through darkness, through time, towards a future as unknown to him as the waters towards which he plummeted.

The plunge into the cold river was a cruel slap of welcome. He sank over his head into a thick blackness, then caught the glimmer of moonlight above and struggled towards it. As he took in a gasp of air, he heard voices.

'Where is he? Do you see him?'

'Call out the Watch! I want the riverbank searched!'

Norris dived back into icy darkness and let the current carry him. It bore him past Lechmere Point, past the West End, bringing him ever eastwards, towards the harbour. Towards the docks.

The Present

Julia stood at the ocean's edge and stared out to sea. The fog had finally dissipated and she could see islands offshore and a lobster boat, cutting across water so calm it might be tarnished silver. She did not hear Tom's footsteps behind her, yet somehow she knew he was there.

'I'm all packed,' he said. 'I'll be catching the four thirty ferry. I'm sorry to have to leave you with him, but he seems to be stable.'

'We'll be fine, Tom,' she said, her gaze still on the lobster boat.

'It's a lot to ask of you.'

'I don't mind, really. I'd planned to stay the whole week anyway, and it's so beautiful here. Now that I can see the water at last.'

They were silent for a moment, watching as the boat growled to a stop and the lobsterman pulled up his traps.

'You've been awfully quiet all afternoon,' he said.

'I can't stop thinking about Rose and how strong she must've been.'

'When people need to, they usually find the strength.'

'I never did. Even when I needed it most.'

They started to walk along the ocean's edge.

'You're talking about your divorce?'

'I assumed it was my fault that I couldn't keep him happy. That's what happens when you're made to feel inadequate.' She shook her head. 'Rose wouldn't have put up with it.'

'That's a good mantra for you from now on. *What would Rose do?*'

They watched as the lobsterman tossed his trap back in the water.

'I have to leave for Hong Kong on Thursday,' said Tom. 'I'll be there for a month.'

'Oh.' She fell silent. A whole month before she saw him again.

'I love my work, but it means I'm not home half the time. Instead, I'm chasing epidemics, tending to other people's lives while forgetting that I have one of my own. I'm forty-two and my housemate spends half the year at the dogsitter's.' He stared at the water. 'Anyway, I'm thinking of cancelling this trip.'

She felt her pulse suddenly quicken. 'Why?'

'Partly because of Henry. He's eighty-nine, after all, and he won't be around for ever.'

Of course, she thought. It's all about Henry. 'If he has problems, he can call me. He's a friend now, and I don't abandon my friends.'

'Well, he certainly likes you. He told me that if he was "just ten years younger . . ."'

She laughed. 'When he first met me, I think he could barely tolerate me.'

'Henry can barely tolerate anyone, but he ended up liking you.'

'It's because of Rose. We're both obsessed with her. I'm even having dreams about her. It's as if I'm there, seeing what she saw. The carriages, the streets, the dresses. It's because I've spent way too much time reading all those letters. It's all starting to seem so . . . familiar.'

'The way you seem familiar to me. I keep having this feeling that I know you. That we've met.'

'I can't think of any reason we would have.'

'No.' He sighed. 'I can't, either.' He looked at her. 'So I guess there's no reason for me to cancel my trip. Is there?'

There was more to that question than either of them was acknowledging. She met his gaze, and saw both possibility and heartbreak in his eyes. She was ready for neither.

Julia looked at the sea. 'Henry and I will do fine.'

THAT NIGHT, Julia once again dreamed of Rose Connolly. Except this time Rose was a sedate young woman with upswept hair and wisdom in her eyes.

She stood gazing down a slope towards a stream. It was the same gentle slope that would one day become Julia's garden, and on this summer day, tall grass rippled like water in the wind. From over the crest a young girl came running, her skirts flying behind her, her smiling face flushed from the heat. She flew towards Rose, who swept her up in her arms.

'Look, Meggie.' Rose set the girl back on her feet and gestured towards the stream. 'Isn't this a lovely spot? Someday, you should build your house here.' She reached for the girl's hand. 'Come. Cook's expecting us for lunch.'

They walked, the aunt and her niece, their skirts rustling through the tall grass as they strode together up the slope, until they went over the crest.

Julia woke up with tears in her eyes. *That was my garden. Rose and Meggie walked in my garden.*

She climbed out of bed and went to the window, where she saw the pink light of dawn. She tried not to wake Henry as she tiptoed down the stairs and into the kitchen to make coffee. On the way, she peeped into the library.

Henry was slumped in a chair at the dining table, his head drooping, a blizzard of paper spread out before him.

Alarmed, she ran towards him, fearing the worst. But when she grasped his shoulder, he straightened and looked at her. 'I found it,' he said.

Her gaze fell to the handwritten pages that lay on the table in front of him, and she saw the three familiar initials: *O.W.H.* 'Another letter!'

'I think it may be the last one, Julia.'

'But this is wonderful,' she said. Then she noticed how pale he was, and that his hands were shaking. 'What's wrong?'

He handed her the letter. 'Read it.'

TWELVE

1830

The gruesome object had been steeping for two days in whisky, and at first, all Rose saw was a flap of raw meat submerged in a tea-coloured brew. Mr Pratt held the jar up to Rose's face, forcing her to take a closer look.

'Do you know who this is?' he asked.

She gazed into the jar, and the object suddenly bobbed up against the glass, which magnified every feature. Rose recoiled in horror.

'It's a face you should recognise, Miss Connolly,' said Pratt. 'It was stripped from a body found two nights ago. The body of your brother-in-law, Mr Eben Tate.' He set the jar down on Dr Grenville's table. 'I think it's quite clear, Doctor, that your student Mr Marshall deceived you. He *is* the West End Reaper. It's only a matter of time before he's apprehended.'

'All you have is a specimen pickled in whisky,' said Grenville.

'And a bloodstained mask. A white mask, just as certain witnesses'—he looked at Rose—'have described.'

Rose said, 'He's innocent! I'll testify—'

'Testify to what, Miss Connolly?' Pratt gave a dismissive snort.

'You planted that jar in his room.'

Pratt advanced on her with a look of fury. 'You think your testimony will be worth anything? I know that you've been living with Norris Marshall. Did he kill Eben Tate as a favour to you? Oh, yes, a jury will certainly believe *your* testimony!'

Rose said to Grenville, 'This jar was not in his room. I swear to it.'

'Who authorised the search of Mr Marshall's room?' asked Grenville. 'How did the Night Watch even think to look there?'

For the first time, Pratt appeared uneasy. 'There was a letter, advising the Night Watch that we might find certain items of interest in his room.'

'A letter from whom?'

'I am not at liberty to say.'

Grenville gave a comprehending laugh. 'Anonymous!'

'We found the evidence, didn't we? It should be obvious by now, sir, that you've sorely misjudged the young man, and so has everyone else. Everyone but me.' He gave a curt nod. 'Good night, Doctor. I'll see myself out.'

They listened to Pratt's footsteps as he walked down the hall, and then the front door closed behind him. A moment later, Dr Grenville's sister, Eliza, swept into the parlour.

'Has that awful man finally left?' she asked.

'I'm afraid it looks quite grim for Norris,' Grenville said.

'Is there nothing you can do to help him?' asked Eliza.

'He counts on you, Dr Grenville!' said Rose. 'If both you and Mr Holmes defend him, they'll be forced to listen.'

'Wendell will testify in his defence?' asked Eliza.

'He's been in Norris's room. He knows that jar wasn't there. Or the mask.' She looked at Grenville. 'It's all my fault. It's all to do with me, with Meggie. The people who want her, they'd do anything.'

'Including send an innocent man to the gallows?' said Eliza.

'That's the least of it.' Rose approached Grenville, her hands outstretched. 'The night Meggie was born, there were two nurses in the room. Now they're both dead, because they learned the name of Meggie's father.'

'A name you've never heard,' said Grenville.

'I wasn't in the room. The baby was crying, so I carried her out. Later, Agnes Poole demanded I give her up, but I refused.' Rose swallowed and said softly, 'And I've been hunted ever since.'

'So it's the child they want?' said Eliza. She looked at her brother. 'She needs protection.'

Grenville nodded. 'Where is she, Miss Connolly?'

'Hidden, sir. In a safe place. And no one can make me tell.'

He met her gaze, taking her measure. 'I don't doubt you for an instant. You've kept her safe from harm this long.' Abruptly, he stood. 'I must go out.'

'Where are you going?' Eliza asked.

'There are people I need to consult in this matter.' He looked at his sister. 'Eliza, will you see to the girl's needs? Have Mrs Furbush make a bed for her in the kitchen. While she's under our roof, she must not come to harm.'

It was the grandest house Rose had ever set foot in. The kitchen was warm, the coals in the fireplace still aglow and throwing off heat. The briskly efficient housekeeper, Mrs Furbush, had insisted on tossing her cloak, along with the rest of Rose's worn clothing, into the fire. As for the girl herself, Mrs Furbush had called for soap and a great deal of hot water. Now bathed and wearing a fresh gown, Rose lay in unaccustomed comfort in a bed near the fireplace. She knew that Meggie, too, was warm and safe tonight.

But what of Norris? Where did he sleep tonight? Was he cold and hungry? Why had she heard no news?

Long after the rest of the household had retired, Rose lay awake. The coals in the hearth had lost their glow and, through the kitchen window, she could see a tree, silhouetted by moonlight, and hear the branches sway in the wind. And now she heard something else: footsteps creaking on the servants' stairway. She lay still, listening as the footsteps moved into the kitchen. She heard a chair tip over and a voice muttered, '*Blast* it all!'

Rose rolled out of bed and scrambled to the hearth, where she fumbled in the darkness to light a candle. As the flame flared to life, she saw the intruder was a young man in a nightshirt, his fair hair in a tangled swirl from sleep. He froze at the sight of her.

It's the young master, she thought. Dr Grenville's nephew, whom she'd been told was recuperating upstairs in his bedroom. A bandage encased the stump of his left wrist, and he swayed, unsteady on his feet. She set down the candle and ran forward to catch him as he sagged sideways.

'I'm all right, I'm fine,' he insisted.

'You should not be up, Mr Lackaway.' She righted the chair that he had just overturned and gently lowered him into it. 'I'll fetch your mother.'

'No, don't. Please! She'll only fuss at me,' he said. 'I'm tired of being trapped in my room, just because she's terrified I'll catch a fever.' He looked up at her with pleading eyes. 'Just let me sit here for a while.'

She sighed. 'As you please.'

She crossed to the hearth to stir the coals back to life and add more wood. Flames leapt up, throwing their welcome warmth into the room.

'You're Norris's friend,' he said.

She nodded. 'My name's Rose.'

'Well, Rose. I'm his friend, too. And from what I hear, he needs every friend he can get.'

Rose sank into a chair at the table. 'I'm so afraid for him,' she whispered. 'Even your uncle has his doubts now.'

'But you don't?'

'Not a one.' She looked Charles straight in the eye. 'I know his heart.'

'Well, Rose, if ever I face the gallows, I'll count myself lucky to have a friend like you.'

She shuddered at his mention of the gallows.

'I'm sorry, I shouldn't have said that. They've given me so much morphine, I don't know what I'm saying any more.' He looked down at his bandaged stump. 'I only came down for a nip of brandy.' He gave her a hopeful look. 'Would you fetch it for me? It's in that cupboard over there.' She suspected that this was not the first time he'd made a nocturnal raid on the brandy bottle. She poured him only a knuckle's worth, which he drank down in one gulp. She put the bottle back in the cupboard and said firmly, 'I'll help you back to your room.'

With her candle to light their way, she guided him up the servants' steps to the first floor. As she helped him down the hallway, she saw richly patterned carpet and a gleaming hall table. On the wall was a gallery of portraits of distinguished men and women. She guided Charles to his room and helped him to his bed. He flopped onto his mattress with a sigh.

'Thank you, Rose. He's a lucky man, Norris is. To have a girl who loves him as much as you do.'

She watched as his breaths deepened, as he sank into sleep. Carrying the candle, she left his room and stepped back into the hallway. There she halted, her gaze frozen on a face that stared back at her. In the gloom, with only the glow of the flame to illuminate the hall, she stood rooted before the portrait, stunned by the familiarity of those features. She saw a man with a mane of thick hair, and dark eyes that reflected a lively intelligence. So entranced was she by the image, she did not hear the approaching footsteps until they were a few feet away.

'Miss Connolly?' said Dr Grenville, frowning at her. 'May I ask why you are wandering about the house at this hour?'

'Your nephew came down to the kitchen, sir. I didn't think he was steady on his feet, so I helped him back to his bed.' She gestured at Charles's door.

Dr Grenville peered into the room at his nephew, who was sprawled uncovered on the bed and snoring loudly.

'I'm sorry, sir,' she said. 'I wouldn't have come upstairs if he didn't—'

'No, I'm the one who should apologise.' He sighed. 'It's been a most trying day and I'm weary. Good night.' He turned.

'Sir?' she said. 'Is there news of Norris?'

He stopped. Reluctantly he turned to look at her. 'I'm afraid to say there's little cause for optimism. The evidence is damning.'

'The evidence is false.'

'Norris Marshall lives in proximity to all four murders. He was found bending over the body of Mary Robinson. The excised face of Eben Tate was discovered in his quarters. He is a skilful anatomist as well as a butcher. When these points are presented in a court of law, his guilt will seem undeniable. Men have gone to the gallows for less.'

She stared at him in despair. 'I cannot see him hanged!'

'Miss Connolly, not all hope is lost. There may be a way to save him.' He took her hand and looked into her eyes. 'But I will need your help.'

'BILLY. OVER HERE, BILLY!'

The boy looked around in confusion, searching the shadows for whoever had just whispered his name. A black dog capered at his feet. Suddenly it gave an excited bark and came trotting towards Norris, who was crouched behind a stack of barrels.

'Who is it, Spot?' Billy asked.

Norris stepped out from behind the barrels. 'It's me, Billy,' he said. The boy began to back away. 'I won't hurt you. You remember me, don't you?'

The boy looked at his dog, who was now licking Norris's hand, clearly unconcerned. 'You're Miss Rose's friend,' he said.

'I need you to take her a message.'

'They're searching for you, all up and down the river.'

'Billy, if you're her friend, you'll do this for me.'

Spot had sat down at Norris's feet and was wagging his tail.

'I want you to go to Dr Grenville's house and find out if she's there. Give her this.' Norris handed him a folded scrap of paper. 'Put it into her hands. *Only* her hands. She'll be angry with you if you don't.'

That did it; Billy's biggest fear was of displeasing Rose. The boy stuffed the note into his pocket. 'I'd do anything for her,' he said.

'Don't tell anyone you saw me.'

'I'm not a half-wit, y'know,' Billy retorted. He walked off into the night, the dog trotting at his heels.

Norris did not linger, but quickly moved on, striding in the direction of Beacon Hill. The clothes he'd stolen were ill-fitting, but a heavy cloak, snatched from a tavern hook, concealed all. He turned into narrow Acorn Street, the same alley where Gareth Wilson and Dr Sewall had met, in the home with the pelicans carved on the lintel. Norris chose a dark doorway in which to wait, hidden in shadow. By now, the note should be in Rose's hand, a note on which he'd written only one line: *Tonight, under the pelicans*.

If it fell into the hands of the Night Watch, they'd have no idea what it meant. But Rose would know. Rose would come. He settled down to wait.

The night deepened. One by one, lamps inside houses were extinguished and the windows on Acorn Street fell dark. He hugged the cloak more tightly and watched his breath cloud in the darkness. He'd wait here all night, if he had to. His legs grew stiff, his fingers numb. The last of the windows on Acorn Street fell dark.

Then, emerging from round the corner, a figure appeared. A woman, framed from behind by lamplight. She paused in the middle of the alley.

'Norrie?' she called softly.

At once he stepped from the doorway. 'Rose,' he said, and she ran towards him. He swept her into his embrace and swung her round, so happy to finally see her again. In that moment he knew that the plunge into the Charles River had been both a death and a rebirth, and this was his new life, with this girl who had nothing to offer except love.

'I knew you'd come,' he murmured. 'I knew.'

'You must listen to me. This is important, Norris.'

He fell still. It was not her command that caused him to freeze, it was the silhouette of a burly figure moving towards them, from the other end of Acorn Street. The clatter of hoofs behind Norris made him swing round, just as a carriage pulled to a stop, blocking his other escape route.

'Norris, you have to trust them,' said Rose. 'You have to trust *me*.'

From behind him came a familiar voice. 'It's the only way, Mr Marshall.'

Startled, Norris turned to the man who stood facing him. 'Dr Sewall?'

'I suggest you get into that carriage,' said Sewall. 'If you want to live.'

'They're our friends,' said Rose. She reached for his hand and tugged him towards the carriage. 'Please, let's get in before anyone sees you.'

Whatever awaited him, Rose had willed it so, and he trusted her with his life. She led him to the carriage and tugged him in after her.

Dr Sewall, who did not climb in, swung their door shut. 'Godspeed, Mr Marshall,' he said through the window. 'I hope we'll meet again someday.'

Only as Norris settled back for the ride did he focus on the figure sitting in the carriage across from him and Rose. The glow of a street lamp illuminated the man's face, and Norris could only stare in astonishment.

'No, this is not an arrest,' said Constable Lyons, as the driver slapped the reins and the carriage rolled away.

'Then what is it?' asked Norris.

'It is a favour, to an old friend.'

THEY RODE OUT of the city, across the West Boston Bridge, and through the village of Cambridge. It was the same route by which Norris had been transported as a prisoner only a few nights earlier. The entire way, Rose's small hand stayed entwined with his, a silent reassurance that all was according to plan, that he need not fear betrayal.

The town of Cambridge gave way to dark countryside and empty fields. It was not until the outskirts of Medford that the carriage finally turned into a cobblestoned yard and slowed to a stop.

'You'll rest here for a day,' said Constable Lyons. 'Tomorrow, you'll receive directions to the next safe house, in the north.'

Norris climbed from the carriage. Constable Lyons led the way to the door and knocked twice, paused, then knocked once more.

After a moment the door opened and an elderly woman wearing a lace night bonnet peered out, holding up a lamp to see her visitors' faces.

'We have a traveller,' said Lyons.

The woman frowned at Norris and Rose. 'These two are unusual fugitives.'

'These are unusual circumstances. I bring them at the request of Dr Grenville. Both Mr Garrison and Dr Sewall have agreed to it, and Mr Wilson has given his assent as well.'

The old woman moved aside to let the three visitors enter.

Norris stepped into an ancient kitchen, the ceiling blackened from the soot of countless cooking fires. Norris felt Rose tug his hand, and she pointed up at the carved emblem, mounted on the crossbeam. A pelican.

Constable Lyons saw what they were staring at, and he said, 'That is an ancient symbol, Mr Marshall. The pelican represents self-sacrifice for the greater good. It reminds us that as we give, so shall we receive.'

The old woman added, 'It's the seal of our sisterhood. The Order of the Rose of Sharon. We're members of the Rose Cross, sir. And this is a way station for travellers. Travellers in need of sanctuary.'

Norris thought of the house in Acorn Street, with the pelicans carved into the lintel.

'They're abolitionists,' said Rose. 'This is a house of hiding.'

'A way station,' said Lyons. 'One of many stops the Rosicrucians have established between the south and Canada.'

'You shelter slaves?'

'No man is a slave, Mr Marshall,' said Constable Lyons. 'Now you understand why this house and the house on Acorn Street must never be spoken of. Dr Grenville assured us that you are a supporter of the abolitionist movement. If you are ever captured, you must not say a word about these outposts, for you'll endanger untold lives.'

'I swear to you, I'll reveal nothing,' said Norris. 'You are all members of the order? Even Dr Grenville?'

Lyons nodded. 'Again, a secret not to be revealed.'

'Why are you helping me? I'm not a fugitive slave. If you believe Mr Pratt, I'm a monster.'

Lyons gave a snort. 'In truth, Pratt is an imbecile. I would have him tossed out of the Night Watch if I could, but he has manoeuvred his way into the public eye. Your arrest was to be his crowning triumph.'

'And that is why you help me? Merely to deny him that triumph?'

'No. We help you because Aldous Grenville is utterly convinced of your innocence. And to let you be hanged would be a grave injustice.' Lyons looked at the old woman. 'I leave him here with you now, Mistress Goode. Mr Wilson will return with provisions for his journey tomorrow at nightfall.' He turned to Rose. 'Come, Miss Connolly. Shall we return to Boston?'

Rose looked stricken. 'Can I not stay with him?' she asked.

'A lone traveller moves more quickly and safely.'

'I've only just found him again! Can't I stay with him, tonight? You said Mr Wilson will come tomorrow. I'll return to Boston with him then.'

Norris grasped her hand more tightly and said, to Lyons, 'I don't know when I'll see her again. Please, allow us these last few hours together.'

Lyons gave a sigh and nodded. 'Mr Wilson will be here before noon tomorrow. Be ready to leave then.'

THEY LAY IN DARKNESS, their bed illuminated only by the moonglow through the window, but it was enough light for Rose to see his face. To know that he was looking at her as well.

'You promise you'll send for me and Meggie?' she said.

'As soon as I've reached a safe place, I'll write to you. The letter will come from another name, but you'll know it's from me.'

'If only I could go with you now.'

'No, I want you to stay safe in Dr Grenville's house. And what a comfort to know that Meggie's cared for. Truly, you've found the best place possible.'

'The one place I knew you'd tell me to hide her.'

'My clever Rose. You know me so well.'

He cupped her face, and she sighed at the warmth of his hands.

'You'll wait for me, won't you?' he whispered.

'Always.'

'I don't know what I can offer you except a life in hiding. Always looking over our shoulders. I'm so afraid that one day you'll wake up and regret this. I'd almost rather we never see each other again.'

Moonlight blurred through her tears. 'Is that truly what you want?' she whispered. 'That we live our lives apart?'

He said nothing.

'You must tell me now, Norrie. Because if you don't, I'll always be waiting for your letter. I'll wait until my hair is white and my grave is dug. And even then, I'll be waiting . . .' Her voice broke.

'Stop. Please stop.' He wrapped his arms round her and pulled her against him. 'If I were truly unselfish, I'd tell you to forget me. But it seems I'm not so noble after all. I'm jealous of any man who'll ever have you or love you. I want to be that man.'

'Then be him.' She reached up and clutched at his shirt. '*Be* him.'

She could not see into the future, and tonight might be all the future they'd ever have. So she took what time they had left together and wasted none of it. With feverish hands she pulled at the hooks and laces of her gown, her breaths quick and frantic with the need for haste. So little time; dawn would be upon them. Never before had she made love to a man, but somehow she knew what would please him, what would bind him to her for always.

Even before the night lifted, she heard the crowing of a rooster and opened her eyes to see that darkness had changed to a cold grey. In despair, she watched the day brighten, and though she would hold back the morning if she could, already she felt Norris's breathing change, felt him surface from whatever dreams had kept him so soundly entwined round her.

He opened his eyes and smiled. 'It's not the end of the world,' he said, seeing her mournful face. 'We'll live through this, too.'

She blinked away tears. 'And we'll be happy.'

'Yes.' He touched her face. 'So very happy. You just have to believe.'

Outside, a dog was barking. Norris rose and went to look out of the window. She watched him, his bare back framed in the morning light, and hungrily committed every curve, every muscle to memory.

'Mr Wilson is here to fetch you,' said Norris. He came back to the bed. 'I don't know when I'll have another chance to say this.' He knelt down on the floor beside her and took her hand in his. 'I love you, Rose Connolly, and I want to spend my life with you. I want to marry you. If you'll have me.'

She stared at him through tears. 'I will, Norrie. Oh, I will.'

A loud knock made them both stiffen. The old woman's voice called through the door, 'Mr Wilson has arrived. He needs to return at once, to Boston, so the young lady had best come downstairs.'

Norris looked at Rose. 'I promise you, this is the last time we'll ever part,' he said. 'But now, love, it's time.'

OLIVER WENDELL HOLMES sat in Edward Kingston's parlour, listening to Kitty Welliver on his left and to her sister, Gwendolyn, on his right, and decided that being imprisoned in Hell would be far more tolerable. Had he known that the Welliver sisters were visiting Edward today, he would have stayed away—at least ten days' ride away. But once he set foot in Edward's house, each sister had snagged an arm by which they pulled Wendell into the parlour, like hungry spiders hauling in their next meal. Now I'm truly done for, he thought, as he balanced a cup of tea on his lap.

The young ladies cheerfully sipped cup after cup of tea as they gossiped with Edward and his mother. Wendell suppressed a yawn and stared out of the window as the sisters rambled on. There's a poem in this somewhere, he thought. A poem about useless girls in pretty dresses.

'. . . and he assured me that bounty hunters will catch up with him eventually,' said Kitty. 'Oh, I *knew* there was something unsavoury about him.'

'So did I,' said Gwendolyn with a shudder. 'That morning in church, sitting beside him—why, it gave me the chills.'

Wendell's attention snapped back to the sisters. 'Are you talking about Mr Marshall?'

'Of course we are. You've been in Cambridge the last few days, Mr Holmes, so you've missed all the gossip.'

'I heard quite enough of it in Cambridge, thank you.'

'I've heard,' said Gwendolyn, her eyes bright with excitement, 'that he has an accomplice. An Irish girl.' She lowered her voice. 'An *adventuress*.'

'You have heard nonsense!' snapped Wendell.

Gwendolyn stared at him, shocked by his blunt rebuttal.

'Oh dear,' Edward's mother quickly interjected, 'the teapot's empty. I think I should call for more.' She picked up a bell and rang it vigorously.

'Wendell,' said Edward, trying to smooth things over. 'It's only idle talk.'

'*Only?* They are talking about Norris. You know as well as I do that he's incapable of committing murder.'

'Then why has he run away?' said Gwendolyn. 'Why did he leap from that bridge? If he's innocent, he should stay and defend himself.'

Wendell laughed. 'Against the likes of you?'

'Where *is* that girl?' said Mrs Kingston, sweeping to her feet. She crossed to the door and called out, 'Nellie, are you deaf? *Nellie!* We will have more tea at once!' She swung the door shut with a bang and thumped back to her chair. 'I tell you, it's impossible to find decent help these days.'

The sisters sat in resentful silence, neither one caring to look in Wendell's direction. He had crossed the boundary of gentlemanly behaviour.

Wendell set down his cup and saucer. 'I do thank you for the tea, Mrs Kingston,' he said. 'But I fear I must be going.' He stood; so did Edward.

'Oh, but a fresh pot is coming.' She glanced towards the door. 'If that scatterbrained girl will just do her job.'

'You're quite right,' Kitty said. 'There is no decent help these days. Why, our mother had a dreadful time this past May, after our chambermaid left. She was only three months with us when she ran off and got married.'

'How irresponsible.'

Wendell said, 'Good afternoon, Mrs Kingston. Miss Welliver, Miss Welliver.'

His hostess nodded a farewell, but the two girls did not acknowledge him and continued to chatter on as he and Edward started towards the door.

'Aurnia was hardly a jewel, but at least she kept our wardrobe in order.'

Wendell, turning, stared at Gwendolyn, who prattled on.

'It took us a whole month to find someone suitable to replace her.'

'Her name was Aurnia?' said Wendell.

Gwendolyn looked round.

'Your chambermaid,' he said. 'Was she young? Pretty?'

Gwendolyn met his gaze coolly. 'She was about our age, wouldn't you say, Kitty? As for pretty—well, that depends on one's standards.'

'And her hair—what colour was it?'

Gwendolyn shrugged. 'Red. Quite striking, really, though these flame-haired girls are all *so* prone to freckles.'

'Do you know where she went? Where she is now?'

Kitty said, 'I think Mother might know. Only she won't tell us, because it's not the sort of thing one talks about in polite company.'

'Wendell, you seem uncommonly concerned about a mere servant,' Edward said.

Wendell returned to his chair and sat down, facing the clearly flummoxed Welliver sisters. 'I want you to tell me everything you can remember about this girl, starting with her full name. Was it Aurnia Connolly?'

'Why, Mr Holmes,' said Kitty. 'However did you know?'

'THERE'S A GENTLEMAN here to see you,' said Mrs Furbush.

Rose looked up from the nightshirt that she had been mending. At her feet was the basket of garments that she had laboured over that day. Since returning to the household that morning, she had focused all her grief on a frenzy of mending and stitching, the one skill with which she could repay the kindness that Mrs Lackaway and Dr Grenville had shown her.

'The gentleman's at the back door,' said Mrs Furbush.

Rose placed the nightshirt in her basket and stood. As she crossed the kitchen, she could feel the housekeeper watching her curiously, and when she reached the door, she understood why.

Wendell Holmes was standing in the servants' entrance—a strange place for a gentleman to come calling.

'Mr Holmes,' said Rose. 'Why do you come the back way? Do come inside. Dr Grenville is at home.'

'This is a private matter, for your ears only. May we speak outside?'

She glanced over her shoulder and saw the housekeeper watching them. Without a word, she stepped out, pulling the kitchen door shut behind her.

'Do you know where Norris is?' he asked. When she hesitated, he said, 'This is urgent, Rose. If you know, you *must* tell me.'

She shook her head. 'I promised. I cannot break my word. Even for you.'

'Then you *do* know where he is?'

'He's safe, Mr Holmes. He's in good hands.'

He grasped her by the shoulders. 'Was it Dr Grenville? Is *he* the one who arranged the escape?'

She stared into Wendell's frantic eyes. 'We can trust him, can't we?'

Wendell gave a groan. 'Then it may already be too late. Grenville will never let Norris live to stand trial. Too many damaging secrets would come out. Secrets that will destroy this household.'

'But Dr Grenville has always defended Norris.'

'And do you wonder why a man of such influence would stake his reputation defending a student with no name, no family connections?'

'Because Norris is innocent! And because—'

'He did it to keep him out of the courtroom. I think he wants Norris tried in the court of public opinion. There, he's already been found guilty. All it takes is a bounty hunter to commit the execution. It will all end quite conveniently when the West End Reaper is tracked down and killed.'

'Why would Dr Grenville do this? Why would he turn against Norris?'

'There's no time to explain. Just tell me where Norris is, so I can warn him.'

She stared at Wendell Holmes, not knowing what to do. She'd never doubted him before, but now, it seemed, she must doubt everyone.

'At nightfall,' she said, 'he leaves Medford and travels north, on the Winchester road, to the town of Hudson.'

He nodded. 'With any luck, I'll catch up with him long before he reaches Hudson. Not a word to Grenville,' he warned.

She watched him run out of the side yard and an instant later heard horse's hoofs clatter away. A gust swept by, twirling dead leaves and dust, and she squinted against the sting. She caught a glimpse of a dog moving across the walkway. It sniffed at the bushes, then lifted a leg against a tree and headed back towards the Beacon Hill gate. As she watched it trot away, she suddenly remembered that she had lived through a moment like this before.

But it had been at night. With that image came a gnawing sense of sadness, a remembrance of terrible grief. She had stood at a window, holding her newborn niece and looking out into the night. She remembered a horse and phaeton arriving in the hospital courtyard. She remembered Agnes Poole stepping out from the shadows to speak to the phaeton's occupant.

And she remembered one more detail: the jittery horse, its hoofs clattering nervously as a dog had trotted past.

That was Billy's dog there that night. Was Billy there as well?

THIRTEEN

It was nearly midnight when the household at last fell silent. Lying in her bed in the kitchen, Rose waited for the creak of footsteps upstairs to cease. Only then did she rise and pull on her cloak. She eased out of the back door and made her way along the side of the house, but just as she was about to emerge into the front yard, she heard a carriage rattle to a stop.

Someone pounded on the front door. 'Doctor! We need the doctor!'

A moment later the door opened and Dr Grenville said, 'What is it?'

'A fire, sir, over near Hancock's Wharf. Two buildings are gone, and we don't know how many injuries. Dr Sewall asks for your assistance.'

'Let me get my bag.'

A moment later the front door slammed shut and the carriage rolled away.

Rose slipped out of the front gate onto Beacon Street. Ahead, on the horizon, the night sky glowed an alarming red. A wagon careered past her, bound for the burning wharf. She made her way up the quiet slope of Beacon Hill, towards the neighbourhood known as the West End.

Twenty minutes later, she slipped into a stable yard and eased open the barn door. In the darkness, she smelt horses and sweet hay.

'Billy?' she called softly. Somewhere above, in the hayloft, a dog whined.

She made her way through the shadows to the narrow staircase and crept up the steps. Billy's spindly silhouette was framed in the window. He stood staring at the red glow to the east.

'Billy?' she whispered.

He turned to her. 'Miss Rose, look! There's a fire! Do you think it could jump all the way here? Should I get a bucket of water?'

'Billy, I need to ask you something.'

But he paid no attention to her; his gaze was fixed on the fire's glow. She touched his arm and felt him trembling.

'It's over on the wharves,' she said. 'It can't come this far.'

'Yes, it can. I saw a fire jump onto my da, all the way from the roof. Burned him black, Miss Rose, like cooked meat.'

'Billy, I need you to remember something. This is important. The night Meggie was born, a horse and phaeton came to the hospital to take her away. Nurse Poole said it was someone from the infant asylum, but I think she sent word to Meggie's father. Meggie's *real* father. Billy, I saw your dog at the hospital that night, so I know you were there, too.' She grasped his arm. 'Who came to get the baby?'

At last he looked at her, and by the glow through the window she saw his bewildered face. 'I don't know. It was Nurse Poole wrote the note. Told me there'd be half a dollar if I delivered it quick.'

'Where did she send you with the note?' Rose asked.

His gaze was back on the flames. 'It's growing. It's coming this way.'

'Billy.' She shook him hard. 'Show me where you took the note.'

He nodded. 'It's away from the fire. We'll be safer there.'

He led the way down the steps and out of the barn. The dog followed them, tail wagging, as they headed up the north slope of Beacon Hill. Every so often, Billy stopped to see if the flames were following them.

'Where are we going?'

'This way. You know.'

They came down the hill onto Beacon Street. Again, Billy glanced east. Smoke was blowing towards them. 'Hurry,' he said. 'Fire can't cross the river.' He began to trot up Beacon Street, moving steadily towards the Mill Dam.

'Here it is.' He pushed through a gate and stepped into a yard. The dog trotted in after him.

She halted in the street and stared up in shock at Dr Grenville's house.

'I took it to the back door,' he said. He headed round the corner of the house and vanished into shadows. 'Here's where I brought it, Miss Rose.'

So this was the secret Aurnia told in the birthing room that night.

She heard the dog growl.

'Billy?' she said. She followed him into the side yard. The shadows were so thick she could not see him. She took a few steps forward then halted as the dog came creeping towards her, growling, the ruff of his neck standing up. What was wrong with him? Why was he afraid of her?

She stopped dead in her tracks as a chill screamed up her spine. The dog was not growling at her, but at something *behind* her.

'Billy?' she said, and turned.

'I WANT NO MORE blood spilled. And see you keep my carriage clean. There's already a mess here, and I'll have to mop up this path before daylight.'

'I'm not doing this alone. You want it done, ma'am, you'll have to take an equal part in it.'

Through the hammering pain in her head, Rose heard their muffled voices, but she could not see them, could not see anything. She opened her eyes and confronted a darkness as black as the grave. Something pressed down upon her, so heavy that she could not move, could barely draw in a breath.

'What if I'm stopped on the road?' the man continued. 'I have no reason to be driving this carriage. But if you're with me—'

'I've paid you quite enough to take care of this.'

'Not enough for me to risk the gallows.' The man paused at the growl of Billy's dog. 'Bloody mutt,' he said, and the dog yelped with pain.

Rose fought to take in a breath, and she inhaled the scent of dirty wool and an unwashed body, alarmingly familiar smells. She worked one arm free and groped at what was lying on top of her. She felt a jaw, slack and lifeless, a chin with the first pitiful bristles of an immature beard. And then something slimy coated her fingers with the smell of rust. *Billy*. She pinched his cheek, but he didn't move. Only then did she realise he was not breathing.

'. . . either you come with me, or I won't do it. I won't risk my neck.'

'You forget, Mr Burke, what I know about you.'

'Then I'd say we're even. After tonight.'

'How dare you.' The woman's voice had risen, and Rose suddenly recognised it. *Eliza Lackaway*.

There was a long pause. Then Burke gave a dismissive laugh. 'Go on, go ahead and shoot me. Then you'll have three bodies to dispose of.'

'All right,' said Eliza. 'I'll come with you.'

'Climb in back with 'em. Anyone stops us, I'll let you talk us out of it.'

Rose heard the carriage door open and felt the vehicle sag with the new weight. But the carriage did not move. Burke said softly, 'We have a problem, Mrs Lackaway. A witness.'

'What?' Eliza took in a startled breath. 'Charles,' she whispered, and scrambled out of the carriage. 'Go back into the house at once.'

'Why are you doing this, Mother?' asked Charles.

'There's a fire on the docks, darling. We're bringing the carriage round, in case they need to transport the injured.'

'I saw you, Mother, from my window. I saw what you put in the carriage. Why did you kill them?'

There was a long silence.

Burke said, 'He's a witness.'

'He's my *son*!' Eliza took a deep breath, and when she spoke again she sounded calmer. 'Charles, I'm doing this for your future.'

'What does killing two people have to do with my future?'

'I will *not* tolerate another one of his bastards turning up! I cleaned up my brother's mess ten years ago and now I'll do it again.'

'What are you talking about?'

'It's your inheritance I'm protecting, Charles. It came from my father, and I won't see one penny of it go to the brat of a chambermaid!'

There was a long silence. Then Charles said, 'The baby is *Uncle's*?'

'That shocks you?' She laughed. 'A saint my brother is not, yet every accolade goes to *him*. I was just the daughter, to be married off. *You* are my accomplishment, darling. I won't see your future destroyed.' Eliza climbed back into the carriage. 'Now let's go to Prison Point Bridge, Mr Burke.'

'Mother,' said Charles. 'If you do this, *none* of it is in my name.'

'But you'll accept it. And one day, you *will* appreciate it.'

The carriage rolled away. Trapped beneath Billy's body, Rose lay still. Let them think she was dead. It might be her only hope of escape. Through the rattle of the carriage wheels, she heard the clatter of another vehicle racing past. The fire was pulling crowds east; no one would notice this lone carriage moving west. She heard a dog's insistent barking—Billy's dog, running after his dead master.

With every rumble of the carriage wheels, Rose was being carried closer to Prison Point Bridge. There two bodies could be rolled into the water and no one would witness it. Panic made her heart pound. Already she felt as if she were drowning, her lungs desperate for air. Rose could not swim.

'AURNIA CONNOLLY,' said Wendell, 'was a chambermaid in the Welliver household in Providence. After only three months in their employ, she abruptly left that position. That was in May. Soon thereafter, she married a tailor with whom she was already acquainted. Mr Eben Tate.'

Norris stared anxiously at the dark road ahead. He was at the reins of Wendell's two-man shay and for the past two hours they had driven the horse hard. Now they were approaching the village of Cambridge and Boston was just a bridge crossing away.

'Kitty and Gwendolyn told me their chambermaid had flame-coloured hair,' said Wendell. 'She was young and said to be quite fetching. Dr Grenville visited the Wellivers back in March. He stayed there for two weeks, during which time the sisters noticed he would often sit up quite late, reading in the parlour, after the rest of the household had retired.'

In March. The month that Aurnia's child would have been conceived.

'This is madness for you to go back to the city,' said Wendell.

'I won't leave Rose with him.' Norris leaned forward as if by sheer will he could force their little shay to move more quickly. 'I thought I was protecting her. Instead, I've delivered her straight to the killer's house.'

The bridge was in front of them. Norris slowed the exhausted horse to a walk and gazed across the water at the orange glow in the night sky. Even this far from the blaze, the air was heavy with the smell of smoke.

A boy ran past their shay and Wendell called out, 'What's burning?'

'They say it's Hancock's Wharf! They're calling for volunteers!'

Which means there'll be fewer eyes elsewhere in town, thought Norris. Fewer chances I'll be recognised. Nevertheless, he lowered the brim of his hat as they started across the West Boston Bridge.

'I'll go to the door to fetch her,' said Wendell. 'You stay with the horse.'

Norris stared ahead, his hands tightening round the reins as the horse clopped off the bridge onto Cambridge Street. Once he and Rose were out of this city, they'd head west to collect Meggie. By sunrise, they'd be well away from Boston.

He turned the horse south, towards Beacon Street. Grenville's house now lay ahead, but, as they neared the front gate, the horse suddenly reared, startled by a moving shadow. Norris hauled on the reins and finally managed to regain control. Only then did he see what had panicked the animal.

Charles Lackaway, dressed only in his nightshirt, stood in the yard, staring at Norris with dazed eyes. 'You came back,' he murmured.

Wendell jumped out of the shay. 'Just let him take Rose and say nothing. Please, Charlie. Let her go with him.'

'I can't . . .' Charles's voice broke into a sob. 'I think she has killed her.'

Norris scrambled to the ground. Grabbing Charles by the collar of his nightshirt, he pinned him to the fence. 'Where is Rose?'

'My mother—she and that man took her—to Prison Point Bridge,' Charles whispered. 'I think it's too late.'

In an instant Norris was back in the shay. He did not wait for Wendell. He cracked the whip and the horse broke into a gallop.

'Wait!' Wendell called, running after him.

But Norris only swung the whip harder.

THE CARRIAGE STOPPED. Wedged into the floor of the carriage, trapped under the weight of Billy's body, Rose could no longer feel her legs. She heard the door open, felt the carriage sway as Eliza stepped out onto the bridge.

'Wait,' Burke cautioned. 'There's someone coming.'

Rose heard the steady clip-clop of a horse crossing the bridge. Billy's dog began to bark and she could hear it scratching at the carriage, trying to reach its dead master. Would the passing horseman mark that odd detail?

She tried to shout for help, but her voice was muffled beneath the heavy oilcloth draped over her and Billy. She heard the horse trot past, and then the sound of the hoofs faded as the rider moved on.

'Damn it, one of them is still alive,' Eliza said.

The door swung open. The oilcloth flew off. The man grabbed Billy's body and rolled it out of the carriage. Rose sucked in a deep breath and screamed. Her cry was immediately cut off by a thick hand over her mouth.

'Hand me my knife,' Burke said to Eliza. 'I'll shut her up.'

'No blood in the carriage. Just throw her in the water.'

'What if she can swim?'

His question was answered by the sudden rip of cloth as Eliza tore Rose's petticoat into strips and tied her ankles together. A wad of cloth was stuffed into Rose's mouth, then the man bound her wrists.

The dog's barking became frenzied. It circled the carriage now, howling, but it stayed just beyond the reach of their kicks.

'Throw her in *now*,' Eliza said. 'Before that bloody dog draws any more—' She paused. 'Someone else is coming.'

Rose gave a sob as the man hauled her out of the carriage. She squirmed in his arms, her hair whipping his face. As he carried her to the railing, Rose caught a glimpse of Billy, lying dead beside the carriage, his dog crouched beside him. She saw Eliza, her hair wild and wind-blown. And she caught a view of the sky, the stars muted by a haze of smoke. Then she fell.

NORRIS HEARD THE SPLASH. He could not see what had just fallen into the water, but he spotted the carriage stopped on the bridge ahead.

As he drew closer, he saw the boy's body sprawled beside the carriage. A black dog crouched beside it, teeth bared and growling as it held off the man and woman trying to get near the fallen man. *It's Billy's dog.*

'We couldn't stop the horse in time!' the woman called out. 'It was a horrible accident! The boy ran straight in front of us and . . .' She stopped, staring in recognition as Norris climbed out of the shay. 'Mr Marshall?'

Norris yanked open the carriage door but did not see Rose inside. From the floor, he plucked up a torn strip of cloth. *From a woman's petticoat.* That splash. They'd thrown something into the water. Norris ran to the railing and stared into the river. He saw rippling water, silvered by moonlight. And then a shudder, as something broke the surface, then sank again.

Rose.

He scrambled over the railing and flung himself off the bridge, stretching out his arms as though to seize this one last chance at happiness. He sliced into water so cold it made him suck in a startled gasp. He surfaced, coughing. Paused only long enough for several deep breaths, then he plunged, once again, underwater. In the darkness, he flailed blindly at anything within reach, his hands meeting only empty water. Out of breath, he popped to the surface again. This time he heard a man's shouts.

'There's someone down there!'

'I see him. Call the Night Watch!'

Three quick breaths, then once again, Norris dived down. With every passing second, Rose was slipping away from him. Arms churning, he clawed at the water, as frantic as a drowning man. A desperate need for air drove him back to the surface for another breath.

One last time he dived. The glow of the lanterns above faintly penetrated the dark water in shifting ribbons of light. He saw the shadowy strokes of his own arms, saw clouds of sediment. And drifting just below, he saw something else. Something pale, billowing like sheets in the wind. He lunged towards it and his hand closed round cloth.

Rose's limp body drifted towards him, her hair a swirl of black.

At once he kicked upwards, pulling her with him. But when they broke the surface and he gasped in lungfuls of air, she was limp. Sobbing, he hauled her towards the riverbank, kicking until his legs were so exhausted that, when his feet touched mud, he could not support his own weight. He crawled out of the water and dragged Rose onto dry land. She was not breathing.

He rolled her onto her stomach. *Live, Rose! You have to live for me.* He placed his hands on her back and leaned in, squeezing her chest. Water gushed from her lungs and spilled out of her mouth.

Frantic, he tore the bindings from her wrists and turned her onto her back. He pressed his hands against her chest, trying to expel the last drops of water from her lungs.

'Rose, come back to me! Please, darling. Come back.'

Her first twitch was so faint, it might only have been his imagination.

Then, suddenly, she coughed, a racking cough that was the most beautiful sound he'd ever heard. Laughing and crying at once, he turned her onto her side and brushed sopping hair from her face. Though he could hear footsteps approaching, he did not look up. His gaze was only on Rose, and when she opened her eyes, his face was the first thing she saw.

'Am I dead?' she whispered.

'No.' He wrapped his arms round her shivering body. 'You're right here with me. Where you'll always be.'

A pebble clattered across the ground and the footsteps came to a standstill. Only then did Norris look up to see Eliza Lackaway, her cape billowing in the wind. *Like wings. Like the wings of a giant bird.* Her gun was pointed straight at him.

'They're watching,' Norris said, glancing up at the people who stood on the bridge above. 'They'll see you do it.'

'They'll see me kill the West End Reaper.' Eliza shouted towards the crowd, 'Mr Pratt! It's Norris Marshall!'

Voices on the bridge rose in excitement. 'Did you hear that? It's the West End Reaper!'

Rose struggled to sit, clinging to Norris's arm. 'But I know the truth,' she said. 'I know what you did. You can't kill us both.'

Eliza's arm wavered. She had only one shot. Even as Mr Pratt and two men from the Night Watch gingerly worked their way down the steep bank, she was still standing there, her gun swinging between Norris and Rose.

'Your son told us,' said Norris. 'He knows what you did, Mrs Lackaway. Wendell Holmes knows, too. You can kill me here, now, but the truth is already out. Whether I live or die, your future has already been decided.'

Slowly, her arm dropped. 'I have no future,' she said softly. 'Whether it ends here, or on the gallows, it's over.' She raised her gun, but this time it was not pointed at Norris; it was aimed at her own head.

Norris lunged towards her. Grabbing her wrist, he tried to wrench the gun free, but Eliza resisted, fighting with the viciousness of a wounded animal. Only when Norris twisted her arm did she finally release her grip. She stumbled back, howling. Norris stood pitilessly exposed on the riverbank with the gun in his hand. In the space of a heartbeat, he realised what was about to happen. He saw Watchman Pratt take aim. He heard Rose's anguished scream of '*No!*'

The impact of the bullet slammed the breath from his lungs. The gun dropped from his hand. He staggered and sprawled backwards on the mud.

A strange silence fell over the night. Norris stared up at the sky but heard no voices, no footsteps crowding in. All was calm and peaceful. He felt no pain, no fear, only a sense of astonishment.

Then, as though from far away, he heard a sweet and familiar voice, and he saw Rose as though she gazed down from the heavens.

'Please, Wendell, you must save him!' she cried.

Now he heard Wendell's voice as well, and heard cloth rip as his shirt was torn open. 'Bring the lamp closer! I must see the wound!'

Light spilled down in a golden shower and, as the wound was revealed, Norris saw Wendell's expression, and read the truth in his eyes.

'Rose?' Norris whispered.

'I'm here. I'm right here.' She took his hand and leaned close as she stroked back his hair. 'You're going to be fine, darling.'

He sighed and closed his eyes. He could see Rose floating away from him, carried on the wind so swiftly that he had no hope of reaching her. 'Wait for me,' he whispered. He heard what sounded like a distant clap of thunder echoing through the gathering darkness.

JACK BURKE yanked up the floorboard in his bedroom, frantically scooped out the savings he had hidden there and threw it all into his saddlebag.

'What are you doing, taking all the money? Are you mad?' shouted Fanny. 'You can't take it all! That's mine, too.'

'You don't have a noose hanging over your head.' Suddenly his chin shot up and he froze. Someone was pounding on the door downstairs.

'Mr Burke? This is the Night Watch. You will open this door at once.'

Fanny looked at him with narrowed eyes. 'What did you do, Jack?'

'She's the one that did it,' said Jack. 'She killed the boy, not me.'

'What boy?'

'Dim Billy.'

'Then let her go to the gallows.'

'She's dead. Picked up the gun and shot herself with the whole world watchin'.' He rose to his feet and slung the heavy saddlebag over his shoulder. 'I'm the one'll be blamed for it all.' He headed for the stairs.

The front door crashed open and Jack froze at the bottom of the stairs as three men burst in. One of them stepped forward and said, 'You're under arrest, Mr Burke, for the murder of Billy Piggott, and the attempted murder of Rose Connolly.'

Jack was hauled forward so roughly that he dropped the saddlebag on the floor. In an instant Fanny darted in and snatched it up, hugging the precious contents to her chest. She made no move to help him, said not a word in his defence as he was led out of the tavern door.

Sitting in the carriage, Jack knew exactly how it would all turn out. Not just the trial, not just the gallows, but beyond. He knew where the bodies of executed prisoners invariably ended up. He thought of the money he'd saved for his precious lead coffin and the gravesitter, to defeat the efforts of resurrectionists like himself. Long ago, he'd promised himself that no anatomist would ever cut open his belly. Now he looked down at his chest and gave a sob. Already, he could feel the knife begin to cut.

IT WAS A HOUSE in mourning and a house shamed. Wendell Holmes knew that he was intruding upon the private agonies of the Grenville home, but no one asked him to depart. Indeed, Aldous Grenville did not even seem to notice that Wendell was in the parlour. He sat hunched in a chair, with his head bowed in grief. Constable Lyons sat facing him.

The housekeeper, Mrs Furbush, entered the parlour with a tray of brandy, which she set down upon the end table. 'Sir,' she said quietly, 'I gave Mr Lackaway that draught of morphine you requested. He's asleep now.'

Grenville said nothing, merely nodded.

Constable Lyons said to her, 'And Miss Connolly?'

'She won't leave the young man's coffin, sir. I don't know what we'll do with her when they come to take him in the morning.'

'Leave her be. The girl has every reason to grieve.'

Mrs Furbush withdrew and Grenville said softly, 'As do we all.'

Lyons poured a glass of brandy and put it into his friend's hand. 'Aldous, you cannot blame yourself for what Eliza did.'

'I do blame myself. I should have suspected.' Grenville sighed. 'I knew she would do anything for Charles. But to *kill* for him?'

'We don't know that she did it all herself. Jack Burke swears he's not the Reaper, but he may have been involved.'

'Then she most certainly instigated it.' Grenville stared down at his glass. 'I have no excuse for what I did. Only that Aurnia was lovely, so lovely. And I'm nothing but a lonely old man.'

'You tried to do the honourable thing. Take comfort in that. You engaged Mr Wilson to find the child and you were ready to provide for her.'

'Honourable?' Grenville shook his head. 'The *honourable* thing would have been to provide for Aurnia months ago, instead of handing her a pretty necklace and walking away.' He looked up, torment in his eyes. 'I swear to you, I didn't know she was carrying my child. Not until the day I saw her laid open on the dissection table. When Dr Sewall pointed out that she'd recently given birth, that's when I realised I had a child.'

'But you never told Eliza?'

'No one but Mr Wilson. I fully intended to see to the child's welfare, but I knew Eliza would feel threatened. Her late husband was unlucky with his finances. She has been living here on my charity.'

And this new child could claim it all, thought Wendell. That her own darling son would now have his future threatened by the spawn of a chambermaid would be the ultimate outrage for Eliza.

'I am sorry, Aldous, that I did not take control of the investigation sooner. By the time I stepped in, that idiot Pratt already had the public in a blood frenzy.' Lyons shook his head. 'I'm afraid young Mr Marshall was the unfortunate victim of that hysteria.'

'Pratt must be made to pay for that.'

'Oh, he will pay. I won't rest until he's hounded out of Boston.'

'Not that it matters now,' said Grenville softly. 'Norris is gone.'

'Which offers us a way to limit the damage. Mr Marshall is beyond further harm. We could allow this scandal to die quietly.'

'And not clear his name?'

'At the expense of your family's?'

Wendell was so appalled, he could not hold his tongue. 'You'd let Norris go to his grave as the West End Reaper? When you know he's innocent?'

Constable Lyons looked at him. 'There are other innocents to consider, Mr Holmes. Young Charles, for example. Would you also force him to live with the stigma of having a murderess as a mother?'

'It's the truth, isn't it? We owe it to Norris. To his memory.'

'He's not here to benefit from any such redemption. We'll lay no accusations at his feet. We'll remain silent and allow the public to draw its own conclusions.'

'Even if those conclusions are false?'

'Whom does it harm? No one who still breathes.' Lyons sighed. 'At any rate, there's still a trial to come. Mr Jack Burke will almost certainly hang for the murder of Billy Piggott, at the very least. The truth may well be revealed then and we can't suppress it. But we need not advertise it, either.'

Wendell looked at Dr Grenville, who had remained silent. 'Sir, you would allow such an injustice against Norris? He deserved better.'

'There is my nephew Charles to think of,' Grenville said softly.

A voice cut in suddenly, 'And what of your son, Dr Grenville?'

Startled, Wendell turned to stare at Rose, now standing in the doorway.

'Surely you knew he was your son,' she said.

Grenville gave an anguished groan and dropped his head in his hands.

'He never realised,' she said. 'But I saw it. And you must have, too, Doctor. The first time you laid eyes on him. How many other children have you fathered out of wedlock, children you don't even know about?'

'There are no others.'

'How could you know?'

'I *do* know.' He looked up. 'What happened between Sophia and me was a long time ago, and it was something we both regretted. We betrayed my dear wife. Never again did I do so, not while Abigail lived.'

'You turned your back on your own son.'

'Sophia never told me the boy was mine. Until the day he arrived at the college, and I . . . I realised . . .'

Wendell looked at Rose. 'You can't be speaking of *Norris*?'

Rose's gaze was still fixed on Grenville. 'While you lived in this grand house, Doctor, he was tilling fields and slopping pigs.'

'I tell you, I didn't know. Sophia never said a word to me.'

'And if she had, would you have acknowledged him? I don't think so. And poor Sophia had no choice but to marry the first man who'd have her.'

'I *would* have helped the boy. I *would* have seen to his needs,' said Grenville softly. 'If only Sophia had come to me years ago.'

'She tried to.'

'What do you mean?'

'Ask Charles. He heard what his mother said. Mrs Lackaway told him she didn't want *another* one of your bastards suddenly showing up in the family. She said that ten years ago, she was forced to clean up your mess.'

'Ten years ago?' said Wendell. 'Isn't that when—'

'When Norris's mother vanished,' said Rose. She drew in a shaky breath, the first hint of tears breaking her voice. 'If only Norris had known! It would have meant everything to him, to know that his mother loved him. That she didn't abandon him, but was instead murdered.'

'I have no words in my own defence,' said Grenville. 'I have a lifetime of sins to atone for, and I intend to.' He looked straight at Rose. 'Now it seems there is a little girl somewhere in need of a home. A girl whom I swear to you will be given every advantage. Will you take me to my daughter?'

Rose met his gaze. 'When the time is right.'

Constable Lyons rose from his chair. 'I'll leave you now, Aldous. As for Eliza, this is your family, and how much you choose to acknowledge is your decision. At the moment, the public's eyes are on Mr Jack Burke. He is their current monster. But soon, I'm sure, there'll be another one to catch their attention.' He nodded farewell and left the house.

After a moment, Wendell, too, rose to depart. He had spoken his mind too bluntly. So it was with a note of apology in his voice that he took his leave of Dr Grenville, who remained in his chair, staring at the fire.

Rose followed Wendell into the hall. 'You have been a true friend,' she said as they embraced. Norris Marshall had brought them together; now grief over his death would bind them for ever. Wendell was about to step out of the door when he paused and looked back at her.

'How did you know?' he said. 'When Norris himself did not?'

'That Dr Grenville is his father?' She took his hand. 'Come with me.'

She led him up the stairs to the first floor. In the dim hallway she paused to light a lamp and carry it towards one of the portraits hanging on the wall. 'Here,' she said. 'This is how I knew.'

He stared at the painting of a dark-haired young man who stood beside a desk, his hand resting atop a human skull. His brown eyes gazed straight at Wendell, as though in direct challenge.

'It's a portrait of Aldous Grenville when he was nineteen years old,' said Rose. 'That's what Mrs Furbush told me.'

Wendell gazed at the painting. 'I did not see it until now.'

'I saw it at once.' Rose stared at the young man's portrait, and her lips curved into a sad smile. 'You always recognise the one you love.'

FOURTEEN

Dr Grenville's carriage took them west on the Belmont road, past farmhouses and wintry fields that were now familiar to Rose. It was a beautiful afternoon, and the snow glittered beneath clear skies just as it had when she had walked this road only two weeks ago.

'Is it much farther?' asked Grenville.

'Only a bit, sir,' Rose said.

'This is where he grew up, isn't it?' said Grenville. 'On this road.'

She nodded, then peered ahead at the tidy farmhouse that had just come into view. 'I see the house now.'

'Who lives there?'

A man who was kinder and more generous to Norris than his own father.

As the carriage came to a stop, the farmhouse door opened and elderly Dr Hallowell emerged on the porch. He came forward to help both her and Dr Grenville from the carriage. As they climbed the steps, Rose was startled to see yet another man emerge from the house. It was Isaac Marshall, looking infinitely older than he had only weeks before.

The three men who stood on the porch had been brought together by grief over one young man. In silence they regarded one another, the two men who had watched Norris grow up, and the one man who should have.

Rose slipped past them into the house, where grey-haired Mrs Hallowell sat rocking Meggie.

'I've come back for her,' said Rose.

'I knew you would.' The woman looked up with hopeful eyes as she handed over the baby. 'Please tell me we can be part of her life.'

'Oh, you will, ma'am,' said Rose. 'And so will everyone who loves her.'

The three men all turned as Rose came out, carrying the baby. At the instant Aldous Grenville gazed for the first time into his daughter's eyes, Meggie smiled up at him, as though in recognition.

'Her name is Margaret,' said Rose.

'Margaret,' he said softly. And he took the child into his arms.

The Present

Julia carried her suitcase downstairs and left it by the front door. Then she went into the library, where Henry was sitting among the boxes, now ready to be transported to the Boston Athenaeum. The letters from Oliver Wendell Holmes, however, they had carefully set aside for safekeeping. Henry had laid them out on the table, and he sat reading them yet again.

'It pains me to give these up,' he said. 'Perhaps I should keep them.'

'Henry, they need to be properly preserved. And won't it be wonderful to share this story with the whole world?'

'These mean too much to me. This is personal.'

She went to the window and gazed at the sea. 'I know what you mean,' she said softly. 'It's become personal for me, too.'

'Are you still dreaming about her?'

'Every night. It's been weeks now. Sometimes I think she's alive again, and speaking to me. Which tells me I've spent entirely too much time thinking about her.' *And what her life could have been*. Julia looked at her watch and turned to him. 'I should probably head down to the ferry.'

'I'm sorry you have to leave. When will you come back to see me?'

'You can always come down to see me.'

'Maybe when Tom gets back? I'll visit you both on the same trip.' He paused. 'So tell me. What did you think of him? He's eligible, you know.'

She smiled. 'I know, Henry.'

'He's also very picky. I've watched him go through a succession of girlfriends, and not a single one lasted. You could be the exception. But you have to let him know you're interested. He thinks you're not.'

'Well, I do like him.'

'So what's the problem?'

'Maybe I like him too much. It scares me. I know how fast love can fall apart.' Julia turned to the window again and looked at the sea. It was as calm and flat as a mirror. 'One minute you're happy and in love, and you think nothing can go wrong. But then it does, the way it did for me and Richard. The way it did for Rose Connolly. Rose had that one short taste of happiness with Norris, and then she had to live all those years with the memory of what she'd lost. I don't know if it's worth it, Henry.'

'I think you're taking the wrong lesson from Rose's life.'

'What's the right lesson?'

'To grab it while you can. Love!' Henry gave a snort. 'You know all those dreams you've been having? There's a message there, Julia. *She* would have taken the chance.'

'I know that. But I'm not Rose Connolly.' She sighed. 'Goodbye, Henry.'

SHE HAD NEVER SEEN HENRY look so dapper. As they sat together in the director's office of the Boston Athenaeum, Julia kept stealing glances at him. She'd expected him to be wearing his usual baggy trousers and old flannel shirt when she'd picked him up at his Boston hotel that morning. But the man she'd found waiting for her in the lobby was wearing a black three-piece suit and carrying an ebony cane with a brass tip. And he was actually flirting with Mrs Zaccardi, the Athenaeum's director.

And Mrs Zaccardi, all of sixty years old, was flirting right back.

'It's not every day we receive a donation of such significance, Mr Page,' she said. 'There are few native sons so deeply revered in Boston as Oliver

Wendell Holmes. It's been quite some time since any new Holmes material has surfaced, so we're delighted you chose to donate it to us.'

'Oh, I had to think about it long and hard,' said Henry. 'I considered other institutions. But the Athenaeum has by far the prettiest director.'

Mrs Zaccardi laughed. 'And you, sir, need new glasses. Will you both join us tonight at the trustees' dinner? I know they'd love to meet you.'

'I wish we could,' said Henry. 'But my grand-nephew is flying home from Hong Kong tonight. Julia and I plan to spend the evening with him.'

As Henry and Julia walked out of the office and through the lobby, they passed a gallery room, and Henry stopped. He pointed to the sign outside: BOSTON AND THE TRANSCENDENTALISTS: PORTRAITS OF AN ERA.

'That would be Rose's era,' he said. 'Do you want to take a look?'

'We have all day. Why not?' They stepped into the gallery. At this early hour on a Thursday morning, the Athenaeum was almost empty, and they were alone in the room. They studied an 1832 view of Boston Harbor from Pemberton Hill, and Julia wondered, Is this a view that Rose glimpsed when she was alive? Did she see that same pretty fence in the foreground?

They circled the gallery and Henry came to an abrupt standstill. Julia bumped into him and could feel his body had gone rigid.

'What?' she said. Then her gaze lifted to the oil painting he was staring at, and she, too, went instantly still. In a room full of strangers' portraits, they both knew this face. The dark-haired young man gazing back at them from the painting stood beside a desk, with his hand laid upon a human skull. His face was startlingly familiar.

'My God,' said Henry. 'That's Tom!'

'But it was painted in 1792.'

'Look at the eyes, the mouth. It's definitely our Tom.'

Julia frowned at the label mounted beside the portrait. 'The artist is Christian Gullager. It doesn't say who the subject is.'

They heard footsteps in the lobby and spotted one of the librarians walking past the gallery.

'Excuse me!' Henry called. 'Do you know anything about this painting?'

The librarian came into the room and looked at the portrait. 'Gullager was one of the finest portrait painters of that era. We believe the subject was a prominent Boston physician named Aldous Grenville. This would have been painted when he was around nineteen or twenty, I think.'

Julia looked at Henry. 'Norris's father.'

As the librarian walked away, Julia remained transfixed by the portrait of

Aldous Grenville, the man who had been Sophia Marshall's lover. I now know what happened to Norris's mother, thought Julia. On a summer's evening, when her son lay feverish, Sophia had left his bedside and had ridden to Aldous Grenville's country house in Weston. There she planned to tell him that he had a son who was now desperately ill.

But Aldous was not at home. It was his sister, Eliza, who heard Sophia's confession, who entertained her plea for help. Was it merely scandal Eliza feared? Or was it the appearance of another heir in the Grenville line, a bastard who'd take what her own son should inherit?

That was the day Sophia Marshall vanished.

Nearly two centuries would pass before Julia, digging in the weed-choked garden that was once part of Aldous Grenville's summer estate, would unearth the skull of Sophia Marshall.

She stared at Grenville's portrait and thought, You never acknowledged Norris as your son. But you saw to the welfare of your daughter, Meggie. And through her, your blood has passed on, to all the generations since.

And now, in Tom, Aldous Grenville still lived.

HENRY WAS TOO EXHAUSTED to come with her to the airport.

Julia drove alone through the night, thinking of the conversation she had had with Henry a few weeks ago:

'I think you're taking the wrong lesson from Rose Connolly's life.'

'What's the right lesson?'

'To grab it while you can. Love!'

I don't know if I dare, she thought. *But Rose would. And Rose did.*

An accident in Newton had cars backed up two miles on the turnpike. As she inched forward through traffic, she thought about Tom's phone calls over the past weeks. They'd talked about Henry's health, about the Holmes letters, about the donation to the Athenaeum. Safe topics.

'You have to let him know you're interested,' Henry had told her. *'He thinks you're not.'*

I am. But I'm afraid.

At Brookline, the turnpike opened up suddenly, but by then she knew she would be late. When she ran into Logan Airport's Terminal E, Tom's flight had landed and she faced a crammed obstacle course of passengers and luggage.

As she reached the customs area, her heart was pounding. I've missed him, she thought. She saw only strangers' faces, an endless throng of people. Suddenly it seemed as if she'd always been searching for Tom and had always just missed him. Had always let him slip away, unrecognised.

'Julia?'

She whirled round to find him standing right behind her, looking rumpled and weary after his long flight. Without even stopping to think, she threw her arms round him, and he gave a laugh of surprise.

'What a welcome! I wasn't expecting this,' he said.

'I'm so glad I found you.'

'So am I,' he said softly.

'You were right. Oh, Tom, you were right.'

'About what?'

'You told me once that you recognised me. That we'd met before.'

'Have we?'

She looked into a face that she'd seen just that afternoon gazing back at her from a portrait. A face she'd always known, always loved. *Norrie's face*.

She smiled. 'We have.'

1888

And so, Margaret, you have now heard it all and I am at peace.

Though your aunt Rose never married or had children of her own, believe me, dear Margaret, you gave her enough joy for several lifetimes. Aldous Grenville lived only a brief time beyond these events, but he took such pleasure from the few years he had with you. I hope you will not hold it against him that he never publicly acknowledged you as his daughter. Remember instead how he provided for you and Rose, bequeathing to you his country estate in Weston, on which you have now built your home. How proud he would have been that his daughter was among the first to graduate from the new female medical college!

Now the future belongs to our grandchildren. You wrote that your grandson Samuel has already shown an aptitude for science. You must be delighted, as you, better than anyone, know that there is no nobler profession than that of a healer. I dearly hope young Samuel will pursue that calling, and continue the tradition of his most talented forebears. Those who save lives achieve a form of immortality of their own, in the generations they preserve.

And so, dear Margaret, I end this final letter with a blessing to your grandson. It is the highest blessing I could wish upon him, or upon anyone.

May he be a physician.

With fondest regards, O.W.H.

TESS GERRITSEN

Home: Maine, USA
Novels published to date: 20
Website: www.tessgerritsen.com

Tess Gerritsen began to write novels in the early 1980s, when she was on maternity leave from her work as a hospital doctor. 'Actually, I'd been writing stories since I was a child,' she says. 'I wrote little books for my mom and bound them myself with needle and thread. Mostly they were about my pets.' But neither of her parents considered writing to be a suitable profession for their daughter. Gerritsen's father, in particular, who was a hard-working, second-generation Chinese American, wanted his two offspring to have secure careers. 'My father said writing was a nice hobby,' Gerritsen says. 'He strongly encouraged my brother and me to become doctors.'

The children's mother, also from China, had a poor command of English when they were young, but she found she enjoyed and understood US horror films. So, while other children watched Disney movies, Tess and her brother were 'dragged along to some pretty frightening films, such as *Godzilla*, *Dracula*, *The Birds* and *The Mummy* . . . Horror films taught me always to consider the darkest possibilities, to peep under rocks and look around corners for monsters. To this day, that's what I do with my fiction.'

After school, Tess went to Stanford University before moving on to study medicine at the University of California, where she met and eventually married Jacob Gerritsen, a fellow medic. The couple went to live in Hawaii, close by Jacob's family, and both pursued medical careers. In her spare time Tess continued to write, but once she embarked upon bringing up her two boys, Adam and Josh, she wanted to move back to the mainland. 'It was very beautiful in Hawaii, but I wasn't used to being on an island and needed wide open spaces. So, in 1990, we decided to move to Maine in New England.'

It proved to be a turning point. Gerritsen decided to give up her medical career to focus on her writing, while her husband Jacob established a private medical practice. When Adam and Josh started taking Suzuki violin lessons, Tess, who had followed the Suzuki method herself when she was young, took up the instrument again and soon became involved in the strong, local Celtic music traditions, ultimately forming her own band and playing in local pubs.

Her big writing breakthrough came in 1996 with the publication of *Harvest*, the first of the medical thrillers for which she is now best known. Before that she had written mainly romantic suspense. 'Fans are always asking me where I get my ideas from. The answer is that I'm very curious and I get inspiration from everywhere. I read the newspapers voraciously, so I know what's going on in real crime. I pay attention to the strange stories people tell me and I also read a lot of scientific and forensic journals.'

It was while preparing a speech about Mary Shelley's novel, *Frankenstein*, that Gerritsen discovered that Shelley's mother had died of the agonising 'childbed fever', which takes the life of the heroine's sister at the start of *The Bone Garden*. The medical history surrounding the disease got the author's creative juices flowing: 'While *The Bone Garden* is a crime thriller,' Tess explains, 'it's also a journey into a time when doctors killed as many patients as they cured, and when brilliant men like Oliver Wendell Holmes were just beginning to understand contagion. I began to wonder how Holmes came to his conclusions. What inspired his theories? Then I imagined a twisted killer inhabiting that same grim world . . . It's different from anything I've written before.'

Gerritsen's writing day starts at 9 a.m. with a cup of coffee in her office. 'If I can't face writing, I do some gardening. We recently bought some farmland where we're planting a vineyard. I'm really looking forward to bottling my first wine.'

NOW WASH YOUR HANDS . . .

In 1843, at the age of 34, Boston poet, author and physician Oliver Wendell Holmes (right), who appears as a central character in *The Bone Garden*, published a paper on 'the black death of childbed', otherwise known as Puerperal Fever. In the main, the condition afflicted women who gave birth in hospital, and Holmes's theory was that it was spread on the unclean hands and implements of the very doctors and nurses who sought to cure it. He advocated hand-washing and other sanitary precautions, but it wasn't until 1879, when Louis Pasteur's experiments with bacteria proved how the disease was transmitted, that Holmes's research was accepted and his suggestions were put into practice.

COPYRIGHT AND ACKNOWLEDGMENTS

FINAL THEORY: © Mark Alpert 2008.
Published at £11.99 by Simon & Schuster UK Ltd, a CBS Company.
Condensed version © The Reader's Digest Association Inc, 2008.

THE VARIOUS FLAVOURS OF COFFEE: Copyright © Anthony Capella 2008.
Published at £6.99 by Sphere, an imprint of Little, Brown Book Group,
an Hachette Livre UK Company.
Condensed version © The Reader's Digest Association Limited, 2008.

STEVE & ME: Copyright © by Terri Irwin 2007.
Published at £16.99 by Simon & Schuster UK Ltd, a CBS Company.
Condensed version © The Reader's Digest (Australia) Pty Ltd, 2008

THE BONE GARDEN: Copyright © Tess Gerritsen 2007.
Published at £14.99 by Bantam Press, an imprint of Transworld Publishers,
a division of the Random House Group Limited.
Condensed version © The Reader's Digest Association Limited, 2008.

The right to be identified as authors has been asserted by the following in accordance with sections 77 and 78 of the Copyright, Designs and Patents Act, 1988: Mark Alpert, Anthony Capella, Terri Irwin, Tess Gerritsen.

Dustjacket spine: Stock Food Creative. • 6–8 Science Faction; illustrator: Curtis Cozier; 4 and 152 © Don Pollard Photography; 153 © Jorge Sanchez-Conejo/Alamy. 154–6 Stock Food Creative; illustrator: Curtis Cozier; 4 and 336 © Anthony Capella. 5, 338–9 and 424–5 all images courtesy of the author's personal collection, except 425 (6) Greg Barrett. 426–8 Amana Images, Stone; 5 and 574 © Jacob Gerritsen; 575 © Lebrecht Music and Arts Photo Library/Alamy.

Printed and bound by GGP Media GmbH, Pössneck, Germany

020-255 DJ0000-1